REVIEWS

For Book I of **The Triempery Revelations**

SORDANEON

"Two elements elevate this work above standard fare. First, it's a character study at its heart, driven by the growth and evolving relationships of complex people, vibrant and varied, without any reduced to stereotypes of good or bad. Second, the mysteries of the Rill and the Wall are compelling and drive readers to explore this world more deeply. Stephens serves up a terrific first entry to a fascinating new series."
—*Booklist*

"An incredible introduction to a new fantasy series… layered, flawed characters within a fascinating world with a rich history and intriguing magic system that you can't wait to learn more about."
—*Smyco*

THE KHELD KING

THE TRIEMPERY REVELATIONS
- BOOK II -

L. L. STEPHENS

Copyright Information
THE KHELD KING
Published by

Forest Path Books

THE KHELD KING Copyright © 2022 by L. L. Stephens.
All rights reserved.

This is a work of fiction. All characters in the publication are fictitious, or are historical figures whose words and actions are fictitious. Any other resemblance to names, incidents, or real persons, living or dead, is purely coincidental.

Forest Path Books supports writers and copyright. This book is licensed for your personal enjoyment only. Thank you for helping us to defend our authors' rights and livelihood by acquiring an authorized edition of this book, and by complying with copyright laws by not using, reproducing, transmitting, or distributing any part of this book without permission.

Forest Path Books publications may be purchased for educational, business, or sales/promotional use.
For information, please address the publishers at:
info@forestpathbooks.com
or Forest Path Books, LLC
P. O. Box 847, Stanwood, WA 98292 USA

Stay informed on our releases and news!
Join the reading group/newsletter at:
https://forestpathbooks.com/into-the-forest

Front cover art © 2022 by Larry Rostant
Cover content is for illustrative purposes only, and any person depicted on the cover is a model.
Map of Essera © 2022 Christina Wooden
Cover & interior design by Mahli (https://*bookdesignbymahli.com*)
PR Compass Rose font © Peter Rempel (licensed for use)

Library of Congress Control Number: 2022901241
ISBNs:
978-1-951293-51-2 (hardcover)
978-1-951293-50-5 (trade paper)
978-1-951293-52-9 (e-book)

This book is dedicated to the readers of *Sordaneon*.
You bought *Sordaneon*. You read it. You talked about the
characters and world—and by doing so you have given this
series life. My heartfelt thanks.

Map of Essera

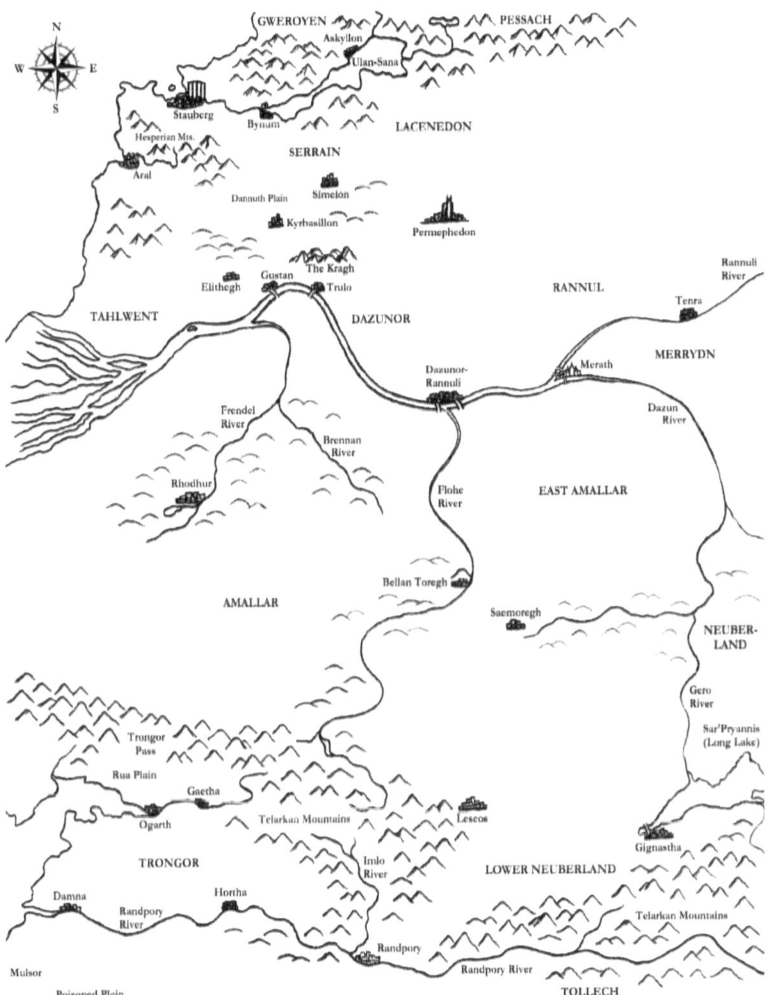

THE KHELD KING

1

A kiss on a dead father's hand. A final goodbye, the public act of a dutiful son and reverent subject. Dorilian had not been much of either. Now his lips pressed a hand of char and bone. A lingering stench of burnt fat and meat caused his stomach to rebel and he gagged. He might have managed to escape with dignity but for a faint taste, sweet and bright beneath the acrid residue of ash.

Blood.

Highborn blood, Leur-gifted and immortal, still alive within the ruin of Deben IV's corpse.

Taste ignited nightmare, and images exploded within Dorilian's skull. Sorcerous light. Ruptured defenses. Searing pain… his own maimed hand… a shattered king.

No. Dorilian must not think of that day… of *him*. Not now. Not *here*. The Vault of Incorruption beneath mighty Permephedon's foundations held a legion of ghosts. Dorilian had not wanted to be in this death-plagued City; he wanted to bury his memories, not visit them. Yet he had braved the Rill again and returned to the scene of all his pain. And for what? More useless sentiment?

He lurched away from his father's bier. His kinsmen, Rheger Dannutheon and that man's Heir, Elhanan, each grabbed an arm to steady him, but he pushed them off. Touch compounded dissonance. He needed to *stop* feeling, not feel *more*. Because they watched, he forced himself to cross the shining floor as though he were merely walking, not fleeing demons.

"Only your father, *fra'don*?" Elhanan's voice, then footsteps, followed Dorilian as he headed toward the central rotunda and the way out. "Are there no others here to whom you wish to pay respect? Not even—"

"No." It did not take Highborn gifts to know who Elhanan meant. "Especially not him."

Forty-seven of his kindred had died in the slaughter of the Highborn, an event people now called the Demise. Gifted. Godborn. Many of those men had been powerful. Now they were merely dead. Their corpses had been interred here weeks ago, along with the body of one singularly gifted king not of their race. Dorilian should pay respect to *all* of them. He had seen them die. He'd felt them die; still felt the voids they'd left behind. Two months had passed, and he could barely tolerate proximity to their remains. He considered it a mercy Marc Frederick's bier resided with the Malyrdeons, concealed by sepulchers. He had not felt that death and did not want to look upon proof.

Rheger had rejoined them, so Dorilian asked a simple question. "Did he receive my death gift?"

"Yes." Rheger stopped walking. Dorilian stopped also to hear the rest of the answer. "I placed it in his hand myself, as Emyli told us was your wish."

Dorilian nodded. That knowledge alone, about any of this, felt good and true. He should have guessed Rheger would not let him end with that.

"We did all you asked, *fra'don*. Now that we are alone and none but we can hear, will you tell us the fate of the Wall Stone?"

Dorilian closed his eyes in a futile attempt to seal off yet another memory. He had known they would ask about the blood-covered thing. Sacred. Death-burdened. The violence of the Wall Stone's taking had finished the job of decapitating the Prince of Stauberg. "I have it. I took it back from Nammuor. I carried it to Sordan when I fled."

"We know this. But, *fra'don*, the Wall Stone belongs with us."

An apt reminder. The Wall was a Malyrdeon entity. Elhanan, not Dorilian, was trained to use the artifact.

"And it will be returned to you when Stefan has convinced me he can be trusted to keep it safe—it *and* you."

Dorilian barricaded off further discussion of the matter. He opened his eyes again and walked away. Their voices followed, raised, asking questions to which Dorilian paid no heed. In the morning he would leave Essera to all its ugliness, abandon this cursed place along with his every memory of it. His left hand ached, and he glanced down at the arcane emerald gleam of the Rill Stone encircling his third finger. Rill-healed bones and flesh had restored his first two fingers. He remembered those fingers being cleaved from his body.

He curled his hand into a fist.

"All my son asks, in honoring his grandfather Marc Frederick's wish, is that his royal cousin, the Hierarch Dorilian, attend his coronation. He is already here in Permephedon, and—"

Emyli Stauberg-Randolph knew her request was outrageous, given the parties involved. For one thing, the family connection was flimsy to say the least: Stefan even claiming it was laughable. For another, Stefan had not officially recanted his accusation that Dorilian had murdered the grandfather in question. Her first surprise of this visit was that she had been allowed into the heavily fortified Sordaneon Tower at all.

Although Permephedon was a neutral City, one to which Dorilian had every legal right to enter and reside, his distrust of Essera in general and the Stauberg-Randolphs in particular ensured that the mighty tower bristled with enough swords to secure a domain. Emyli's second surprise was that she faced Tiflan Morevyen, Bas of Teremar and Dorilian's foremost advisor, in an antechamber furnished with only a spare desk and a handful of chairs. A brace of tall windows framed with jewel-hued tiles set in gold overlooked a breathtaking view of Permephedon's spires. The Rill structures shifted their shape above its buildings and platforms, moving with the pale grace of phantoms.

"He is here only to pay last respects to his dead." Tiflan rubbed a hand along his jaw. "It was very hard for him. The Malyrdeons delayed Deben's rites until he could face it. I don't think—"

"Stefan is being pressed on all sides to end this estrangement. His nobles wish for him to make peace. That, in conjunction with my father's letter—" Emyli reached into the deep pocket of her mourning gown to produce a document of folded, creamy vellum bound with blue and gold ribbon. "It was among Marc Frederick's papers at Gustan and was presented to Stefan only last week by Gareth, my father's most loyal serv—"

"Dorilian knows who Gareth is." Tiflan took the letter and gazed upon the late King's forceful script. He studied both pages closely and sighed. "So, your father seeks to extend his influence past the grave."

"Our families must surmount old hurts, not embellish new ones."

Both Emyli and Tiflan had at one time or another sought to end the rivalry between their respective young royals. Stefan Stauberg-Randolph and Dorilian Sordaneon had hated each other from the moment of their first meeting at Permephedon seven years before. They had been but teens then—and enemies ever since. Dorilian had even, on one occasion, sought to have Stefan killed.

Only eight weeks had passed since Marc Frederick had died, murdered by poison and sorcery, and eight weeks since Stefan had accused Dorilian of the deed. Had Emyli believed that accusation, she would not be here.

"Bas Morevyen." She didn't know this man well enough to be more familiar with him. Even so, she felt—as her father had—Tiflan was a man to be trusted. "You understand how important this is. The rulers of our two lands must not allow youthful mistakes to poison their current situations. They were children. Now they must be adults. Essera needs Sordan; we acknowledge it with every breath! And Sordan needs Essera."

Tiflan grimaced. "Dorilian might differ with that."

"He is all opposition of late. If he would but think about it—"

"He has thought about it for all twenty-one years of his life. He was born out of his family's opposition to yours, do not forget that. Your rejection of his father—"

"Yes. But surely we can put that behind us." Emyli did not regret running off with her young Kheld lover instead of fulfilling the marriage her father had planned. Stefan was himself a consequence of grand designs Emyli had single-handedly overthrown. She bowed her head and continued her entreaty. "Surely *they* can. Dorilian has succeeded in securing Sordan's autonomy. The military stage is over—won, at least for now. My son has agreed to negotiations—"

"As he must, because otherwise the Rill would travel nowhere and bring our economies to a standstill—and both our nations to ruin. Too many lives have been lost already fighting over who will control the Rill." Tiflan rose. His new regalia as Hierarchal Lord of First Rank accentuated his impressive figure. "Princess," he said, "I will present this petition to Dorilian, you know that. If I may include the letter—"

"Yes, of course. Just one favor more: Might I speak with him?"

"He's very busy."

"But not too busy for this letter."

Tiflan looked down at Emyli with compassion. "Dorilian is never too busy for any matter bearing your late father's name."

She lifted her chin. "Then he will not be too busy for *me*."

It was late night before Dorilian made the time to meet with Emyli. She did not doubt that the young Hierarch was indeed as busy as claimed. Dorilian's realm was vast and beset by problems. A hundred issues might be before him from any corner of it. In addition, he had enemies by the score, at least one of whom wanted his death. Nammuor the Mormantaloran made no secret of his hatred, and Sordan's armies even now were waging fierce battle against Nammuor in one of Dorilian's seven ancestral domains, Suddekar. The newly autonomous Hierarchate had political alliances to re-establish after decades of having been an Esseran subject state; there were trade relationships to foster, nobles seeking redress for seized lands, new constructions or policies to be approved and old hindrances to be dismantled. He was also engaged in delicate talks with the Brotherhood of Epoptes about allowing Esseran citizens to retain existing warehouse operations and mercantile charters on Rill properties in Sordan, Randpory and Hestya.

Emyli didn't know what manner of obligation Dorilian had just concluded. The lateness of the hour led her to hope he'd no other appointments and might spare her more than a few minutes of his time. That Dorilian could make her feel so uncertain disturbed her. He was young enough to be her son but self-possessed enough to make her feel like a child. *He is Highborn*, Emyli reminded herself, *born of a race bound to immortal Entities, worshipped in his own City as a god.* So many Highborn had died only a month past that simply to think of them brought her to tears. *That brilliant, gifted race all but annihilated. Only eight of them now remain... and, unfortunately, he is one of them.*

Dorilian made a point of meeting her in a soldier-lined corridor leading to the Tower's residential rotunda. It was an indirect insult of a sort at which he had always excelled, to meet her in public in a manner almost perfunctory. The dark garments he wore ill-served his complexion but accentuated his light silver eyes. His hair, which he had shaved off in the days following the terrible events that had put him on his father's throne, had grown to fingertip length and was a darker honey shade than she remembered.

Dorilian extended his left hand, upon which the emerald facets of the Rill Stone bracketed the third digit with amazing light. The Arch Epopte Quirin claimed to have seen the index and second finger shorn from that hand, a maiming Dorilian's detractors liked to claim had never happened. He had not extended his hand for her to look at, however, but to return her father's letter.

"Not exactly a subtle manipulation, even for him."

She took the folded document, welcoming the trace of heat that lingered on the smooth vellum. "Did you read it?"

"Yes. Did Stefan?"

Emyli did not like the look Dorilian gave, telling her he believed in her as little as he believed in her son. "He did. It was he who sent me to you. Along with this." She held out a second envelope.

Dorilian muttered a curse. "He made you his courier."

"He expresses his sincere wish that the two of you bridge this gulf between you."

With a look of sheer disgust, he took the note and opened it. His expression did not change upon reading its contents. "Even he must know this request is impossible."

"My father's wishes—"

"—have long since been flouted. Believe me, Princess, I know that better than anyone."

What could she say? He had done much of the flouting, and been the catalyst for the rest. Gathering her resolve, Emyli made another attempt to pry an answer from him. "I had hoped, now that some time has passed—"

"Two months," he said, "is not much time."

"I wish you would just—"

"Just what? Go away? Shut up? Die?"

She had, at one time or another, wished for all those things. He knew this. "No. I but wish you would listen."

He studied her intently. "Truly? And that is all?"

"Don't toy with me, much as that activity might entertain you. You know what I wish, what all of us wish. Our feelings bathe your synapses; you detect our naked wishes upon the very air you breathe, and refine our darkest fears through your skin. I am aware of your talents, Thrice Royal—and respectfully ask that you grant me the courtesy of treating me as neither ignorant, nor an enemy."

His gaze did not give way as she might have hoped. Something tangible retreated from her skin, a delicate weight that left behind only an icy, transient glaze. He had, all along, been assessing her trace responses the way another man might seek to discern a change in the color of the sky or a shift in the texture of the wind. Even she might wonder if he had found her as she presented herself to be. He looked away, toward the end of that long brilliant hall where courtiers and emissaries waited for him, then back again.

"Dine with me." As spoken, the invitation was both a command and a challenge.

"It will be my pleasure, Thrice Royal."

Emyli sat at one end of a table so long it could have served for a game of balls and pins. Dorilian sat at the other end, still robed in state attire. The beautiful room, its elegance so understated as to be piercing, announced that this meal was itself a performance. Waterglobes suspended above the black marble table cast gentle light upon plates of roasted fennel and confections, pungent cheeses, creamy flans, and fruits so exotic most inhabitants of Essera had never eaten of them. All Highborn princes ate richly and in great quantity, and Dorilian was no exception. Indeed, his affiliation with the Rill broadened the menu. He had access to the foods of a hundred lands.

"Why should I grace Stefan's coronation?" Dorilian's question landed gracelessly between them. They had not spoken the whole while. "He didn't come to mine." His silver gaze narrowed. "Neither did you."

"I told you at our last meeting that I regretted Stefan's decision and why I honored it. Things happened too quickly, too violently, for all of us."

He averted his gaze.

She decided to proceed. "Perpetuating a slight resolves nothing. Heals nothing."

"Healing." He shook his head.

"The Triempery cannot survive another amputation."

"You imagine I care."

"If you did not care, we would not be here."

Dorilian had not broken formally with the Triempery. He had threatened. He had raged and postured and had done everything except say the words or pen them in official ink. On the same day of the Demise, he had answered Stefan's order for his arrest with the corpses of Sordan's entire Esseran garrison. He had dismissed ambassadors, refused emissaries, and stationed what troops he could spare from his war with Nammuor along his northern border. He had commissioned and successfully recruited new armies. He had frozen assets, withheld payments dictated by the Archhalia, and was forcing unallied domains to choose between him and Stefan. He had become the single greatest obstacle to the free flow of Rill traffic. But he had not yet declared Sordan's historical bond to Essera null and void.

He also had not yet ordered her to leave.

"What does any of this have to do with me attending your wretched son's coronation?"

"My father's dream for Essera and Sordan. It's in the letter. A united Triempery blessed by the Rill and the Wall. Strong, visionary, and true to his ideals."

"I never believed in a united Triempery. I believed in *him*."

"And now you can't believe in Stefan?"

Dorilian scoffed, a harsh sound. "The only thing I believe about Stefan is that he's an ass. For me to attend his coronation would be a sideshow, a distraction—we'd probably just have another fight."

"It would be a statement. You swore to my father two years ago that you would not oppose Stefan as his successor. Would you now take that gift away?" If looks could kill, she would be dead already. She leaned forward, willing to match him glare for glare. "Do not make worthless the deaths of my father and yours, and all those others."

A hundred people, all dead in a single act of murder, sorcery and fire. The Highborn and human rulers of Sordan and Essera, and of several allied domains also, not least of them the new young Kheld nation there to be brought into the privileged circle of Rill users. The new Rill treaty would have opened frontiers and changed the political landscape of the world. Dorilian knew better than she what had been lost that day, and how much had been taken from them. He was the only soul to have survived the slaughter, the only one to know what promises had been made.

"They didn't die for *him*."

No. They died to advance the plans of a monster. "They died for a future. My father died for wanting something more than this."

His face hardened. "And now you want me to give Stefan legitimacy."

She had expected that insult. "Stefan's not asking for legitimacy. He has that already."

Dorilian shrugged. He knew better than anyone the shaky pillars upon which her son's kingship rested.

"Please, consider this opportunity." She was not yet ready to concede failure. "Stefan can be an ally. My father spent the last months of his life with him, imparting a greater vision and sharing all he knew. My son wants to cease these hostilities between our realms—"

"Hostilities *he* started—"

"Yes. He recognizes that he was unfair. That is why he is making this extraordinary move. He is asking that you put your hard feelings behind you, and he will do the same with his."

"He accused me—in the Archhalia—of *murdering* your father!"

Just as it had in Sordan two weeks ago, his pain at that accusation slammed against her nerves. "He will withdraw the charge—"

"—and my kindred! He is seeking my arrest. Maybe my execution." He stabbed at his food. Anger. So much anger. The world itself might not be vast enough to hold it.

"He wants neither! If you will meet with him—"

"Only if we meet with swords in hand."

Every encounter with Dorilian meant having to overcome his formidable hostility. Emyli steeled herself. Her father had shown that it was possible.

"You read the letter. Both letters. Stefan is willing. He wants peace and to keep his grandfather's vision. The accusation withdrawn and promises of cooperation given. Permephedon is the only city where such a meeting would be possible. He promises your safety and freedom. I will do the same."

His gaze bored into hers, asking if he could believe her. The gulf of distrust between their families was deep. Just because her father had bridged that gulf did not mean it had ceased to exist. Dorilian had reason to be wary. Betrayals had hardened him—but too many deaths had also left him in need of allies. Of peace. Emyli knew herself guilty of playing on those needs. She would have been ashamed had the stakes been less high.

I am contending for my son's survival.

"You hate me less than he does." Dorilian had finished eating.

"Stefan doesn't hate you, he—" *Fears you.* She squelched thought and words alike before either could fully form.

Dorilian rose and she closed her eyes, following the sharp reports of his boot heels on marble as he walked to her side. She placed her hands upon the edge of the table, where he could see them. His paranoia about assassins kept him from ever coming near people he did not know or trust. He was always armed, always dangerous. This was a youth who had, on the day of his father's death and while nursing grievous wounds of his own, drawn a sword and hewn off his wife's head. He had not yet, to Emyli's knowledge, expressed remorse for that act.

She inhaled sharply when he circled behind her and placed his hands on the arms of her chair. He leaned his face beside hers, his voice resonant in her ear. His breath delivered a familiar scent to her, costly and warm, all spice and resin. "I know the real reason you're here. You don't care about your father's legacy, or the wasted lives of dead men. I told you in Sordan that your father's Rill treaty has no chance in this hell or any other of being resurrected. You are here because in your maternal delusion you think you can persuade me to help your son, show support for him, do the very things I have refused to do for years." Her eyes flew open and she turned, looking at him eye to eye. Amusement tugged at one corner of his mouth, mocking her. "Don't deny it. My mother would do the same for me had our enemies not murdered her."

Emyli drew a ragged breath. He couched everything in violence and death. "Why, if you love my father's memory, can you not stay true to what he thought you to be?"

Dorilian stepped away. "I told you I would be the antithesis of that."

"How, when I remember? When other men will?"

He frowned. "What do you want of me? How can I be your son's savior? I cannot even be his friend!"

"Perhaps not. But you can be my father's."

She held his stare. Held it and would not let it go, because if she did, she would lose him. Lose the spark of naked emotion she glimpsed still burning beneath his cold facade, lose the battle in which she had engaged him, trapped between the desperate want of his need to remain true to her father and his desire to distance himself, as far as possible, from this city and her son.

He broke gaze first and walked to the door. The audience was over.

"Go back to your son, Princess. Tell Stefan he will have my answer in the morning."

2

"As far as I'm concerned, this City's only laudable use is as a repository for corpses." Dorilian had never liked Permephedon. A symbol of his oppression in youth, now the City reminded him only of pain, of death. Legon, his new Commander of the Eagle Guard, knew better than to challenge his opinion. Together they entered the massive, wide-open, bronze doors into the Redoubt, the heart of the City's many-towered Citadel. Just being in the soaring, unworldly building again made Dorilian's skin crawl.

The Redoubt split. The Arcana was destroyed. I was there, I saw it crumble and burn around me. But now the Citadel looks perfect, as if the Demise never happened.

"You honored your dead. I don't see why you are giving Stefan a chance to add you to their number." Legon disagreed with this venture and that he could not wear a sword. He strode beside Dorilian with the alert tension of a fighting hound. "Last time you and he were here together, he kicked in your face."

"I have not forgotten."

"What if he has soldiers?"

"There are no soldiers in the Redoubt. The City is neutral ground. Its Law forbids them."

Dorilian had specifically chosen Legon for this mission. Not only did his friend make an excellent bodyguard, with or without a sword, but Legon looked completely at home among throngs of similarly fair-haired, well-favored males of high Staubaun caste. Even when dressed in noble attire, Dorilian barely passed as Staubaun. Because

Permephedon was seat of the Triemperal Archhalia and hosted people from many lands, he attracted little notice.

A group of darker-haired visitors walked by, laughing and shoving. One man lurched off-balance and Dorilian flinched. The men in the Arcana that day—poisoned, dying—had staggered upon trying to stand. Stumbled and fallen. These men reminded him of Khelds... of...

Marc. Clinging to a broken floor, refusing to take his hand. Why hadn't Marc Frederick *tried?*

Dorilian blinked away the sting of memory. The haunting pangs of grief never stopped. Some days he barely kept it at bay. Nights... his nights were lost to horrors. And last night after seeing Emyli, he had broken out in a rage, throwing things and cursing and terrifying his staff.

Because he had made that promise.

Written in his blood, bathed with tears, and sealed within a finger bone threaded on a cord braided of his shorn hair. Dorilian's death gift to the man for whom he would gladly have traded his life. For whom he still would—if only that were possible.

That Dorilian was here, attempting the unthinkable in the very building where he had lost so much, was some manner of madness.

Several white-garbed Upholders of the Undying stood outside the entrance to the Hall of Harmonies, where on the morrow Stefan would be crowned as Essera's king. The Upholders, named for the one they served, were not undying themselves. When four stepped forward to bar his way, Dorilian summoned an *orbus* to fill his left hand with light and angled his fingers to show the green flash of the Rill Stone that marked him as Hierarch. To a man, they bowed deeply and let him pass. They could do nothing else. To so much as touch a Highborn prince without permission was a crime.

Being Sordaneon still meant something—everything—if only to a dwindling few. Permephedon had not yet fallen to Stefan's heresy.

From information gathered earlier, Dorilian knew he would find Stefan in one of the vaulted hall's side chambers, being fitted for his coronation robes. There was another entrance to the room, but Dorilian had preferred his chances of getting past the Upholders. He'd assigned Tutto to secure the other option, should Stefan prove false.

At his side, Legon assumed the aspect of a man ready to do battle.

I hope you are watching, Dorilian addressed Marc Frederick's memory. *Because I am honoring your thrice-cursed wishes.*

Immediately upon entering, he noted that Stefan was not alone. A dozen men, a mix of Staubaun and Kheld courtiers, gathered in attendance to Essera's king. Stefan stood on a platform at the far end of the room, his body draped in sumptuous velvet and heavy silk, half-finished garments aglitter with gold thread and stitched-on jewels, being fussed over by a tailor. He looked incongruous—ill at ease and quite unlike his regal grandfather.

The room's chatter fell silent upon Dorilian's entrance. Dorilian was used to that.

"Stefan." He used the familiar name to preclude any assumption he thought Stefan merited a title. "You said you wanted to talk."

Stefan blew out a sigh and pretended to listen as Robdan Aelfricson, secretary to his First Minister, recited a list of persons, noble and otherwise, who would be at the next day's ceremony. The Citadel's Harmonic Hall in which Stefan was to be crowned could hold a lot of people—half a nation it seemed, but not a whole one. None of the names meant a thing to him.

"Can you get a list to me tonight, with notes? I'll go over them then." Stefan didn't want to reveal in front of his courtiers that he was still largely unsure which noble families merited his personal attention. He would ask Erenor Tholeros, whom he had just elevated to be his Commander of the Guard, about any names on the list.

Robdan bobbed his head and closed the ledger, which he tucked into his waistband like a common street scribbler. Stefan saw a couple of his courtiers roll their eyes. His cheeks burned at the implied rebuke. His Staubaun subjects were forever judging any Kheld attached to his household, even Goff Horvadson, an influential clan chieftain and now First Minister. They judged Stefan too.

Because I look like a Kheld.

A stir at the room's entrance caught Stefan's eye and he turned toward it, twisting the cloth in the tailor's hands. Muttering about a pin, the man jammed an index finger into his mouth. *Sordaneon*, someone said. The name died on each tongue that spoke it.

Every head in the room, including the tailor's, whipped around like that of a deer surprised in a clearing.

"Stefan. You said you wanted to talk."

The bastard had actually come. Arrogant *and* an idiot. Stefan had never dreamed his ploy would succeed. He had written that note to Dorilian at his mother's urging. He'd even included a promise he didn't mean, because he had believed Dorilian would never set foot outside his armed camp of a tower. Yet here he was, to all appearances unarmed. Beside him stood another youth Stefan remembered from their brief schooling together.

"I expected you to send a response."

"Oh, I think this counts."

Of course it did. The impact of Dorilian's arrival showed in the nervous stares of Stefan's Staubaun courtiers. Uncertainty and hostile glances prevailed among Stefan's Kheld kinsmen. Though Goff looked eager to start a fight, Robdan's homely features displayed open alarm. Cullen, Stefan's best friend and someone else who knew Dorilian well, shot him a wild look of warning. Just having his rival in the same room—Highborn, Rill-bound, a murderer—power and portents didn't merely swirl about Dorilian, they clung to him like weapons.

Stefan needed to master this moment. Better yet would be if he could master his adversary.

But how? Dorilian stood before Stefan under protection of Permephedon's neutrality. No soldiers. No swords.

Several courtiers dropped to one knee, bowed their heads, and made the gesture of The Three: arms crossed over their breasts and hands on their shoulders. A posture that could only be called submissive. Stefan swore under his breath. Staubauns by and large still worshipped the Sordaneons as godborn. Well, he didn't—and neither did the Khelds. They and a handful of the Staubauns remained standing.

"How did you get past the guards?" A few of the kneeling men detected the tone of Stefan's challenge and, seeing how others had not followed suit, unfolded their arms and rose back to their feet.

Dorilian lifted his left hand. The ring that sheathed the lower portion of his third finger gleamed brilliant emerald. "I am Highborn and I wear the Rill Stone. I am bound to one of the Three. Triemperal Law dictates I may come and go as I please."

"Not anymore." Stefan frowned. "I'm going to change things."

"Why? Because you haven't done enough damage already?"

"Not as much as you."

Dorilian's eyes narrowed. "I see my coming here was a mistake. I thought you meant what you wrote."

"I did."

"But words fail you now?"

Dorilian always had this effect on Stefan. Disdain radiated from the Highborn prince as a kind of malignant energy. Marc Frederick, Emyli, and even the Malyrdeons had tried to teach Stefan that projective empathy was something he could mitigate, had

shown him strategies to keep himself from responding in kind—
but it wasn't working. Stefan didn't see why he should have to be
the one who made the effort.

"This isn't the place." The upper hand he needed was nowhere
to be seen. He had thought that, if anything, Dorilian would attend
the coronation itself. "We need to have a discussion about our
positions. I'm to be king, and—"

"And I'd like to see him try to stop you!" Goff stepped forward,
chest thrust out and fists cocked.

Dorilian simply stared, then directed a withering eye roll to
Stefan. "Are *all* your kinfolk this embarrassingly stupid?"

Goff's outburst might have irritated Stefan more had he not
welcomed the show of defiance. Dorilian's Hierarchate was
important—and the Rill was *vital*. Not a domain in Essera, save
Amallar, stood ready to abandon it. Much as Stefan hated to admit
it, Marc Frederick had been right about the dangers inherent in
the festering wounds between his and Dorilian's families. Though
Marc Frederick had found those dangers worth wading into, Stefan
simply wished Dorilian would go somewhere and rot.

"Like I've been trying to tell you, now isn't a good time for this."
Stefan walked toward the windows and more privacy. As he had
hoped, Dorilian followed, along with the Sordani youth—Legon,
he remembered—and Erenor.

"Make time. Or could it be you don't really want me at your
coronation?"

Stefan snapped a sharp look because it was true. He *didn't* want
Dorilian present at his moment of triumph. Marc Frederick had
wanted it. His letter had been emphatic on that point. As for talks—
did Stefan want to enter talks, of any kind, with this dangerous
Highborn prick? Even if they could manage it, if they danced around
the truth and never discussed what had happened on the day the
ruling princes in Essera had died, could they ever reach agreement?
On anything?

Stefan drew a deep breath and squared his shoulders. "If we talk,
I'm going to need some hard answers."

"I may not have them."

"Oh, I think you do."

Everyone in the room watched Stefan the way they used to watch
his grandfather. Expecting action, decision. Expecting him to make
something happen. Once he was crowned tomorrow, his power
would be secure—except for this man. This *one* man. An enemy
Stefan could remove from his path right now, right here, if he

handled this situation forcefully. Marc Frederick's letter had provided a golden, once-in-a-lifetime opportunity.

Instinct, however, warned him to be careful.

Dorilian too had grown cautious. "Before we talk about anything, I require you to withdraw your accusations about me."

"It might be best if we set a meeting place first."

Stefan forced his expression to remain calm. A few more of Goff's fellow clan heads had entered the room. Good. Stefan had more men. But his Staubaun nobles were looking alarmed, and Erenor ill at ease.

"Why not Stauberg?" Another Kheld chief, Lowen Toboldson, boldly put forth his choice.

"They don't learn very quickly, do they?" Dorilian snapped.

Stefan flushed. He shot a glare at Goff, entreating him to control the Khelds a bit longer. To Dorilian, he offered an explanation. "They loved my grandfather. And they're not the only ones who think you killed him—and all our kin who died in that slaughter—our best, our brightest—"

Stefan regretted the words as soon as they'd flown his tongue. He had said in his letter he would withdraw his accusation.

Dorilian turned on his heel. "I am done with this. Watching you get crowned would be pure torture."

"Don't turn and run, you damn coward!"

Cullen moved toward him. "Stefan, let this go!"

Legon maneuvered to Dorilian's shoulder and hissed one word. "Leave!"

But Dorilian stopped to resume the fight and faced Stefan with a wolf's snarl. "You are a preening, misbegotten excuse for his blood! I see what you are doing. You think to show this flock of capons you can stand up to me. Intimidate me. But you can't. None of you can! I am completely outside your experience. Any of you! And that just scares the stinking shit out of you!"

"Well, I don't think you're a god. And neither do they!"

"Has it ever occurred to you that's part of your problem? You don't know *what* the hells I am!"

No, Stefan thought. *I know exactly what you are.* A monster. A bully. Stefan would never rule in peace if he had Dorilian waiting in Sordan to take advantage of his every misstep. Dorilian, even if he was crazy, had allies… believers.…

Stefan had been pondering how to set up this opportunity for weeks. Lure Dorilian to the coronation just as Marc Frederick had lured Labran, and then seize him there. It would be a statement for the ages. But this room would do just as well. Better, even, with Dorilian alone except for Legon. The two of them couldn't possibly stand against a roomful of Khelds and loyal nobles. Stefan could seize Dorilian, hustle him out of the Redoubt in secret through the room's second door and into the hands of his guard.

Stefan had never thought he could feel bad about anything he might do against Dorilian Sordaneon. But then Dorilian had never trusted Stefan, not really. He had only trusted that Stefan would be fool enough to honor the terms of a letter written by a man who maybe, just maybe, had wanted Stefan to do this. After all, Marc Frederick had set it up so he could.

Stefan met Goff's fierce gaze, then lifted his chin. The chieftain nodded and the Khelds closed ranks to bar the door and prevent the Undying Guard from entering.

"I don't think you should leave just yet... *Cousin*." Stefan emphasized the word, knowing Dorilian would understand. Marc Frederick had used the same word, always, when addressing the Hierarch he'd taken captive. "You think I'm going to just let you walk away? You'd only go back to Sordan to make trouble."

Now it was Dorilian who said nothing. Who stared at him as if he'd gone mad.

"Marc Frederick's letter stated his wish that the Triempery stay in one piece. I intend to see that it does." Stefan gestured to Erenor, who, like the other Staubauns, was standing white-faced and stunned. Erenor understood. He opened his mouth to speak, but then didn't. He turned and left the room to alert the guards.

Among the Khelds, Robdan put his hand on Goff's arm. "Not this way."

"Quiet, scribbler!" the chieftain snarled.

"Stop this, you're doing it all wrong!" Cullen spoke up at Stefan's side, unexpectedly firm, and grabbed him by the shirt.

Stefan turned to look at him. Everyone did.

Everyone but Dorilian and Legon.

When Dorilian sprang, Legon sprang with him. Legon's well-aimed kick caught Cullen in the gut to send him sprawling to the ground. Just as quickly, Dorilian was behind Stefan, left arm locking left arm, and yanked upward to grab a fistful of silk collar. Stefan gasped at the touch of steel at his throat, cold against bare skin. Where the hells had the bastard hidden a blade? Legon, also with a short, thin knife in hand, stood beside them.

"I'll kill him!" Dorilian shouted. Everyone in the room stepped back, away from them.

Stefan stared. He wanted them to act, to save him… not just stand there. To a man, they'd all stopped cold.

"He'll do it!" Goff shouted.

"He won't!" Stefan screamed before Dorilian twisted the collar to choke off both air and words. *He can't! He promised Marc Frederick. Swore to treat Stauberg-Randolph blood as his own.* His mother had revealed how the Highborn never killed their own and they never broke their promises. Never. But no one in this room knew about that promise. No one but Stefan.

Erenor charged through the side door, men behind him with swords unsheathed. He pressed the door lock. "He has men outside the Redoubt! A full complement!"

"Fuck!" one of the Staubaun nobles yelled.

Dorilian's grip relented just enough for Stefan's starved lungs to gulp air. When Dorilian urged him to the right, Stefan obeyed as best he could with his locked arm and awkward stance. At the edge of his vision, he saw Cullen push back onto his feet before the knot of Khelds.

"Thrice Royal. Think. You don't have to do this!" Cullen clutched his middle as he forced out the words.

Dorilian shot a look at Erenor, who stood helpless at the head of Stefan's guards. "If you want this fool to live, unlock that door."

"Don't be cowards! Don't let him—" Another twist of his collar cut off Stefan's words. The knife edge bit into his skin to release a hot trickle down the column of his throat. Cullen, seeing blood, lurched to the wall to open the lock.

"You," Dorilian snapped at Erenor. "Don't interfere. If I die, your Rill stops running. If your king dies, you're out of a job."

"Go where you want, you bastard, just let him go!" Goff bellowed.

Legon led the way. The back of Stefan's head rested on Dorilian's shoulder, his arm bound behind him. Muscle, bone, and raw fury propelled them toward the chamber's side door. Half stumbling, half dragged, Stefan just wanted it to be over. His shoulder hurt like hell and he hadn't been this close to Dorilian since they were kids. Since the day Stefan's boot had bloodied Dorilian's smug Highborn face. It was too late now for Stefan to say he was sorry, but he was.

Sorry he'd left Dorilian alive.

Architecture blurred. Corridor flowed into corridor into antechamber. Sages and visitors to the Redoubt scattered at their approach. At last they reached an open place, an atrium. Sordani vowels filled the air along with the ringing of steel. The Hierarch's soldiers. Dorilian's shoulder remained tense against the back of Stefan's neck. At least the blade no longer bit into his exposed throat as they passed from that place into wider passages.

"*What* are you doing?" A rough voice, filled with gravel. By swiveling his eyes, Stefan saw the man. Short-necked with skin like tanned leather, clearly not Esseran. *Tutto.* The name came to Stefan from a lesson to which he wished he had paid more attention. Dorilian's old sword master, entrusted with the Hierarch's security.

"Preserving our freedom and our lives. Essera's next king here"— Dorilian gave Stefan a rough shake—"has decided he wants to set me up in my grandfather's old rooms at Stauberg. Give me your sword."

"Son of a—" But Tutto handed it over. He wore more than the one weapon and soon held another.

"You," Dorilian said to someone unseen, "Get the rest of my troops from the Tower. Legon, order my *charys.*"

Legon and the other person departed at a run. Dorilian urged Stefan along the short passageway, Tutto leading the way to the main corridor. He was headed for the Rill... of course he was. The Rill nexus sat at the City's heart and abutted its principal structures, including the High Citadel. Day and night, the mighty Entity spun and moved *charysi* of all sizes, from small as a barge to more massive than the largest seafaring ship. Stefan seldom traveled by Rill because he did not trust the thing.

Cullen's voice broke through from behind them. "Thrice Royal, I beg you. For the love of us all, for your sake and ours, release him and go in peace!" Stefan took heart that Cullen, at least, was still with him. Had anyone else followed?

"Stop him, Cullen!" Stefan twisted against the grip on his collar. "Whatever it takes!" He cried out in pain as his captor nearly wrenched his arm out of its socket.

"Are you trying to get him killed?" Dorilian growled. "His farts have more honor than all the words ever spoken by your lying lips." To someone else, he gave an order. "Make sure he doesn't interfere."

Surrounded by soldiers and with Tutto leading the way, they exited from the service passage into the flow of a corridor filled with stunned onlookers. Jerked along, Stefan noted how many people commented and yelled and shouted questions—but that no one tried to help. The space opened overhead and the crowd thinned, stood farther back. By floor pattern alone, Stefan knew he had entered the Aurora Atrium and was being hustled along the vaulted indoor passage leading to the Rill.

Dorilian's cheek touched Stefan's. Warm skin and cold promises.

"We are going to Sordan, Stefan. You've never been to Sordan, have you?"

"Fuck you!"

"You lost your chance at that."

Stefan was hurried up a flight of steps and along a soaring colonnade. He stumbled, recognizing the tall white columns and stark beautiful planes of the Rill complex as he and his captors emerged onto one of the passenger terraces. The platform sprawled to every side, naked to the sky and uncharacteristically empty, devoid of the usual bustle of travelers, couriers, merchants and diplomats.

Only a small delegation of Epoptes waited for them. Guarded by two full cohorts of soldiers now, Dorilian yanked Stefan to a halt. He placed his sword where the knife had rested. "Fight me, fool, and I will slice open your throat."

Stefan feared to even nod agreement. He breathed while he still could. He was to be crowned Essera's king tomorrow! Was no one going to stop this madman? Didn't he have troops in this city, too?

Where were they?

Dorilian sensed the Rill at his back—a monstrous thing that seethed of power and peril, a siren call to his flesh. Others did not experience the Entity this way. They *saw* it, structures vast beyond vast, elegant rings and soaring arches. To them the umbilici that tethered Dorilian to those structures were invisible, as was the frisson of energy that trickled over his skin. Since leaving the Hallowed Hall, he had been constructing his defenses. This near, he could not predict what the Rill might do—either to him or because of him. Between the humans besetting him and the monster at his back, he could not afford a single misstep.

"Psilant!" He shouted it to make certain the man heading the Epoptes would hear him. "Release my *charys*!" The Sordaneon *charys* was uniquely configured to protect the Rill-gifted from their Entity's incursions.

From the knot of Epoptes standing between them and the Rill run, Quirin, his cold eyes set in a face nearly as reptilian as his stare, strode toward them. His Brotherhood of highly trained mages was charged with the Rill's protection, and also the ordering of its manifold daily operations. If Quirin did not cooperate, Dorilian could be stranded at Permephedon, unable to reach Sordan except by an overland journey of several hundred leagues.

Or by naked use of an Entity that, this time, might succeed in consuming him.

"Don't do it, Rill man!" A Kheld voice. Ragged. Desperate.

Another Kheld yapped at the first one's heels. "If that bastard gets away with this, there'll be no end to his murder!"

Behind Quirin, Esseran troops were filing into the scene.

Stefan barked a laugh. "You're cooked. They won't let you leave."

"If I don't leave, you don't live." Dorilian twisted the blade he held to Stefan's skin, this time presenting the edge.

Tutto lifted his voice above the clamor. "You heard the Hierarch! Produce his *charys*! Do that—or break the Covenant that binds the Rill to the will of men!"

Doubt erased the smirk from Quirin's face. None knew what the effect on the Rill would be if the Covenant were broken. Generations had been unwilling to risk finding out. No one knew for certain to what degree the Sordaneons—blood, bones, and flesh passed down from Derlon the Rill-Giver—bound their Entity.

More people now crowded the colonnades that ringed the vast open platform. Shock and fear and the sight of soldiers kept them at a distance. Staubauns. Khelds. Foreigners with hidden faces. Essera's lords flanked by personal troops wearing heraldic colors. The immortal City of Permephedon overflowed with people come to witness the coronation.

To witness this.

A flurry of movement erupted at the edge of the crowd and pushed its way through onto the platform. Emyli, attired in a gown of rose and gold, layer upon layer with ribbons trailing from her sleeves, stopped when she reached Quirin's side.

"Do something!" When Quirin remained silent, unmoved, Emyli turned her back on him and ran toward her son. She halted when Dorilian's guards showed her bare steel.

"Thrice Royal! Oh, no, please… stop… *remember*."

Perfect. Dorilian had words for her, too. "Remember? Shall I tell you what I remember? Shall I tell *them*? Because I *remember* you saying this miserable creature"—he tightened his arm about his captive's neck, baring Stefan's throat—"wanted to talk! I *remember* being shown a letter that promised me safety. Written in *his* hand! I *remember* what *you* said and did!" Stefan tried to speak and Dorilian crushed enough of his collar to strangle the sound. "I took you at your word, Princess. And I took this sniveling waste of life at his!"

And he had promised Marc Frederick. *Take care of my family.* Did Emyli know Dorilian had *tried*?

"Please. He meant it. Just talk, that's all he wants… Stefan, tell him this is all a misunderstanding." Truth poured through her words like light itself, filling the lens of the Mind.

Dorilian hated Stefan even more for having tainted his mother with lies. "Don't bother. I won't believe anything this piece of shit says! Never again. And neither should you. His every word is devoid of truth." He looked past Emyli. "Psilant!"

Quirin folded his hands. "I think cooler heads…"

Idiots! Dorilian's blade moved on Stefan's throat, drawing a line of blood. Marc Frederick's blood. Dorilian damned the promise he had made. Held to it, as his body rebelled and his stomach turned. "Order my *charys*! Or I swear I will summon the Rill without it!"

He would do that, rather than allow Stefan or any of these enemies to seize him. And Quirin would remember. Quirin had witnessed the madness. The consequence. If Dorilian dragged Stefan into an active Rill stream with him…. Both of them might be lost, but only Stefan would die for certain.

Emyli turned to the Psilant. "Allow the Hierarch to leave."

"Princess Emyli, you have no authority—"

"Psilant, I beg you!" Regal and desperate, Emyli stood with fists clenched. Her gaze never left the blade pressed to Stefan's throat. "This man cut off his wife's head. I don't think he will hesitate to cut off my son's!"

Face clouded by fury, Quirin paused, then turned with a nod to another man, who raised a green banner in signal. Within moments, the channel bisecting the platform released a spindle-shaped mass of light that elongated and sheathed itself with webs of shimmering translucency that became within moments a solid, shining vessel: horned, crested, its surfaces scrolled with Sordaneon green and silver. An opening appeared in its side.

"The men first!" Dorilian barked. He backed with Stefan toward the *charys* as his soldiers rapidly filed into the conveyance.

Emyli moved toward him, hands outstretched. "I beg of you, Thrice Royal. Please don't harm him. I beseech you—consider the consequences. For all of us."

Consequences? All of… whom? About them Dorilian cared not at all. No more than the first time he had stood here in this way… but not *exactly* this way. No. He detected an alignment of events within this moment, a convergence between the Wall and the Rill. He stood at its nexus, upon the very spot where Austell Malyrdeon had crumpled to the platform and the Wall Stone unveiled the paired Entities' futures. Where Dorilian had taken the Wall Stone into his hand. Memory of Wall power seared his palm and flooded his mind... images burned upon his brain, a thousand fleeting moments, past... present... this very tableau. The Khelds. The Psilant. Emyli. Stefan in his stupid bright robes, and Dorilian himself holding a sword to the fool's bared neck. *This* moment....

And *another one* too—past hardened, not future soft... Marc Frederick and Labran.

Death. Imprisonment. A threat removed. Creation of futile regencies and a child heir reared to avenge. Fucking Stefan had sought to *recreate* their grandfathers' paradigm... *had recreated* it. He and Stefan both acted within the pull of predestination. Yet the paradigm in its first iteration had solved nothing, had led only to *this* recreation and continuation of... itself. Dorilian detected the shape of the thing. Wall-born, Wall-bound—a Malyrdeon construct.

Imprisonment would perpetuate the design, and so would striking a death blow. Either would suffice to spring the trap. Either would break Dorilian's promise to Marc Frederick.

Or he could do *neither*. Keep his promise. Rid himself of these chains.

The paradigm was not so constructed that it could not be broken.

"You're making a mistake."

A grip of iron held Stefan upright, displayed to the crowd. Thousands packed the colonnade. Soldiers—most of whom were Stefan's own, but standing back. The Psilant in helpless isolation. His mother, hands outstretched, continued to plead. And Dorilian simply stood with his sword to Stefan's neck, as though seized with... what? Indecision? Guilt? Though Stefan prayed for guilt, his gut froze with the sharp, terrible knowledge that Dorilian might just kill him anyway.

"Please," Stefan croaked. "I'm sorry. I didn't mean it."

Dorilian snorted, a puff of air and disdain. "Another lie. I don't think you will ever change. At this point I don't care. You have removed all doubt that you and I can never coexist." Dorilian tightened his grip again, causing Stefan to cry aloud as new pain tore through his arm and shoulder. "So listen to me, you lying sack of blood and piss. You know why your grandfather"—Stefan noticed that Dorilian did not say Marc Frederick's name, had not spoken it even once— "wanted me to attend your coronation, don't you?"

"To show unity... save the Triempery."

"No. To save *you*, because he knew I would remind the Epoptes and the Seven Houses and all your thousand little enemies why they *need* you. Sadly, the nobles you hope to rule fear me far more than they do you."

Sordan's soldiers had all boarded. Tutto stood just outside the *charys* door with Legon. With a grin that more resembled a wolf's than a man's, Dorilian turned Stefan to face Emyli and the Psilant. He raised his voice so all in the crowd could hear him. "Princess! Because of your son's lies, these people believe I murdered your family. Now, because of today, they will never stop believing that."

Emyli faced him in horror. "Please. Don't kill him. Take him with you if you must, but don't kill my son."

"See? You actually think I would."

Stefan's eyes teared as his mother, despair overtaking hope, began to sob. Why was this villain torturing her? But when he looked at Dorilian and saw that murderous look, piss trickled down his leg.

"Even if I let you live—you are dead to me. Hear that, you putrid little worm?" Dorilian's fury drove each word deep into the crowd's ears and Stefan's soul, freezing nerves so his legs gave way. Dorilian's yank on his arm to keep him upright brought a scream to Stefan's lips. Dorilian yelled over it. "Dead! I do not need to stain my hands or nation with your blood. Your enemies have my full blessing to kill you, or you can die old and sick and lying in your own filth. Your fate no longer concerns me. I will never see you again. I will never hear another word from your lying lips, because you have my promise, my most solemn vow, that I will *never* set foot in Essera *so long as you live*. I am rid of you, and you of me, just like you always wanted."

In some inexplicable way Stefan felt those words take shape in the world and lock about him.

Dorilian must have signaled, because Tutto and Legon came forward. Abruptly Dorilian wrenched his arm free from Stefan's and shoved him hard so that he rolled onto the floor of the Rill platform. He landed in a sprawl, the coronation robes twisting about his body as handfuls of gemstones, still only loosely stitched, broke off and tumbled like sparks across the pale platform surface. As Emyli ran forward, Dorilian and his two men stepped backward into the *charys*. Stefan stared as the *charys* surfaces became seamless, and he heard the high trill, then whine, then hollow thrum of the vessel being propelled out of the slip and into the rings to the south, toward Sordan.

Bile rose in his throat and he crumpled, hiding his face with a handful of robe as he vomited.

3

For many days, the volcano above Mormantalorus spewed ash that colored skies gray, painted sunsets red, and turned forests to landscapes of ghostly gallows. Shores of black sand acquired the same hue as the gray and sluggish sea. Only the white towers of Mormantalorus itself, its central spires nearly as tall as the violent mountain upon the side of which it was built, shone through the murk. When the ground rumbled, and the volcano erupted with sprays of molten rock that rained boulders upon the harbor town and incandescent rivers piled radiant heat about its foundations, the City lifted aloft spires of glittering green and white hope.

Mormantalorus had been built on that great wound in the world for a reason, and it had been built to withstand the mountain's torment. Deep tubes drew sea water for cooling the structure; the entire city sat upon adamantine cores that counteracted any vibrations they encountered. A bubble of film separated the poisoned air outside from the clean atmosphere within, cool and sweet. Adepts through the ages had studied the Leur city and marveled, but hundreds of generations had passed since any had fully understood its construction.

Nammuor just wished the volcano would stop vomiting its guts. The mountain had been throwing out plumes of ruby rock for weeks.

"I cannot see it," his sister's head complained.

After pushing up the sleeves of his peacock blue surcoat, Nammuor carefully gripped the blue-green metal handles of the frame holding Daimonaeris's head upright. Long arm muscles tensed as Nammuor lifted the shining brass contraption from the table and turned so Daimonaeris could look upon the fire-crowned mountain and its surrounding lava field.

"Dzalarad." Her flawless lips caressed the word. "So beautiful. I want a room overlooking it, so I can see it always."

"This room is yours. I knew you would enjoy the show."

"And a body?"

"That, my little Hierarchessa, requires a bit more work."

It pained Nammuor to see his baby sister as she was now: her beautiful face intact, her slender throat ending just where it should have merged into perfect shoulders, resting instead upon a framework of brass and *lr* crystals. It had taken enormous expenditures of mage blood to create the elaborate, energy-draining crystal arrays that sustained her life. Seven mages and twenty-three of Nammuor's most promising young acolytes had died solely so their life energy could be transferred into the crimson lattices supporting an array of pumps and diaphragms. These gave Daimonaeris's complexion its rosy glow and her lovely lips a voice. It was not, sadly, the same mellifluous voice he had once loved.

"My baby." The diaphragm's vibrations managed to communicate anguish. "Where is my baby? My breasts hurt! I need my baby—"

Nammuor's jaw clenched. Though Daimonaeris had no breasts, her pain was real. Dorilian's sword had cleaved her head from her body, but not her mind from its belief that she still had a body. Or from knowing that she had been pregnant.

"Oh gods, oh gods—what happened to my baby?" she cried.

At least, now, Nammuor could reassure her. "Your son lives. A Merceden corsair made it into the harbor last week. Dorilian cut the baby from your dying womb."

"I tried to flee, to bring him with me."

"I know." Nammuor remembered only too well the aftermath of his imperfect victory. He had slain the Highborn rulers of Sordan and Essera—but had failed to acquire the Wall Stone and the Rill Stone. Dorilian, despite generously contributing two fingers to the body count, had managed to snatch away the priceless artifacts. And then Marc Frederick had created confusion, attacked Nammuor with the Leur's Ring. Yes, *that* had been a surprise. Since when had the Stauberg-Randolphs been capable of wielding enhancers? Even so, Nammuor had thought his final blast of sorcery and fire— volcanic power bound into crystals by the life blood of five powerful mages—had killed the Sordaneon prince and Essera's king.

Back in his heavily curtained room in Mormantalorus—safe, exultant, exhausted—Nammuor had felt the prickle of an activated transport array keyed to his own blood. Daimonaeris's diadem of blood crystals, designed to bring her home to Mormantalorus if ever she were in danger. Alarmed, Nammuor had held out his hands, thinking to link his fingers with hers—only to find them holding Daimonaeris's head, her eyes blinking, mouth an open scream as blood streamed onto the floor.

"My son is born." Her tone was low and thankful. "He did not kill him."

"No. I never thought he would." Separating Daimonaeris's head from her body had been the only way to prevent her from bringing the child with her.

The irony of Dorilian ushering Nammuor's heir into the world would have prompted a smile—if Nammuor were not holding what was left of his sister. The weight tired his arms, so he walked to one of the room's several window-height pedestals of polished black obsidian and set Daimonaeris's container upon the wide round surface.

Although not the same as having her whole, Nammuor took pride in his achievement. Decades of experimentation in his dungeons and workshops, creating new and superior beasts, had given him the tools and the skill. He had—out of a desire to preserve his sister's beauty, and because he knew she would want it that way—managed to save both Daimonaeris's life and her shining gold hair, the remaining tresses of which a specially trained slave had arranged into an elegant coil.

Nammuor's experiments had not, however, saved the third finger on his left hand. His attempt to emulate the flesh-bound magic Endurin had worked on Marc Frederick, and graft Dorilian's finger to his body so he too might someday wield the Leur's Ring or Rill Stone, had failed. Either his flesh had rejected the graft or, more likely, Dorilian's had rejected *him*. Illusion concealed the amputation, for now, along with the scar Dorilian had laid across Nammuor's nose and cheek.

A gentle touch to Daimonaeris's face regained her attention. Her golden eyes, limpid and lovely, enhanced by the slave's application of dark powders and crushed amber, closed, then opened again to consider his.

"Don't you think it rich, Hierarchessa, that Dorilian and I should have the same heir?"

"I did it for you. I slept with that wretched old man."

She meant Deben, of course. Their plan all along had been for her to give birth to a child of Highborn gifts. A child who would be heir to Sordan, Mormantalorus—and the Rill. Deben, they knew for certain, could provide that. Dorilian's ability to perpetuate his race remained uncertain.

"You did all I asked, my precious sister. Now I will do all you ask. You just have to be patient."

"How can I be, when he is still alive? You swore you would kill him! I was to rule Sordan, with you in Mormantalorus—"

"Oh, we will. Until then, you are here with me. I will keep you alive. I will keep you safe."

"But you didn't kill him! Dorilian is Hierarch now. And I have no body! I will never eat again, or dance, or hold my child!"

"Yes, little Hierarchessa, he did that to you. And for that, I'll make him pay." Nammuor bent so he could kiss her temple. Her silken hair, perfumed with oils and costly floral essences, and the faint summery scent of her skin, gladdened his heart by reminding him how much of her he still had. "I will find a way. Your monster of a husband is going to die."

"Make it slow, and painful."

"I promise you."

Daimonaeris's lips and eyelids quivered, and tears rolled down her perfect cheeks.

4

Dorilian arrived in Sordan to the stares and shouted greetings of the curious. If Tutto had sent ahead to have the platform cleared, the Epoptes had ignored the request. It was all Dorilian could do to block out the swirl of noise and motion, to keep calm within himself. Simply riding the Rill had drained him to the point of collapse.

The Entity that inhabited the system had claimed too much of him—become too much a part of him—that day he had fled the murder of his race. Now every contact with it was a battle for his very flesh. For him, the Rill was not a benign servant.

It was a nemesis.

Shielded by guards and his companions, he left the Rill platform and rounded a corner past guards to enter a domed vestibule. Dorilian stopped before an unbroken wall at the far end, where he placed his hand. An iris in the wall opened to reveal a portal leading to the deep passage under the city. His soldiers fell back to secure the location while a few ran ahead to ready horses from the underground stable at the base of the ramp. Sunlight streamed through the jewel-toned ceiling to strew a meadow of shining flecks on the golden floor at his feet.

With the masses and the Epoptes out of sight, Tutto reached into the thick belt at his waist and pulled out a flask encrusted with emeralds. He flipped the cap from the neck and pressed the bottle into Dorilian's hand.

"Drink."

Tutto hounded Dorilian to drink restorative ambrosia after every Rill contact. Putting the rim to his lips, Dorilian tipped back his head and let the warm liquid fill his mouth. It was beyond sweet. A honeybee might gag on it, but he drank.

"Bastards." Tutto had a mutter for every occasion. "Damned fur-faces and ass-lappers, and that king of theirs the worst of the lot! What insanity moved them against you?"

Legon's jaw clamped tighter, but he held his tongue.

Dorilian thrust the flask back into Tutto's hands. "There, I drank some."

"How bad is it?" Tutto wanted to know. He didn't mean the drink.

"Nothing I cannot manage." Not a lie, but not quite truth. Dorilian closed his eyes against a memory of Marc Frederick saying he could handle or do anything. He had a nation to lead, and statements to make. An Entity and lives to protect. Dorilian drew a lungful of cool dry air, then turned to Legon. "There is no ambassador to kick out, and I have long since closed the borders. Travel is difficult already. Let us now make it impossible."

Legon nodded, lips taut. The Epoptes might control who used the Rill, and how and when, but Sordan's soldiers controlled who or what could enter and leave the City. Without Sordan's harbor, its docks and warehouses, Essera's mighty Rill economy—flush with metals, corn, wool and lumber—would have diminished access to the sea. Merchants would be forced to use shallow water barges at Randpory or transport their goods overland by beast and wagon to seaports at Stauberg and Aral, all at substantial hardship and cost. Essera's great highway, the broad, deep Dazun River, ended in an unnavigable morass of shifting, shallow channels and spongy fens, while any approach from the sea encountered only an incongruous egress of march upon march of fissured cliffs and roaring falls.

Without Sordan, Stefan's damned country lost access to nearly every market but itself.

"Perhaps a strike at their ports?" Tutto suggested. "We could reassign part of the fleet—"

"No. Nammuor is the main enemy. Essera guards our backside."

"And you don't think your little gambit with the Rill, cutting them off at the knees, will provoke retaliation?"

It would. Dorilian could count on it. But the retaliation would not include war. There would be words and threats first, and he would let cooler heads know he was open to negotiation with third parties— just not their king. That alone would drive Stefan insane with fury.

"Go. Do it."

Legon ran back the way they had come. Within the hour, virtually no travelers or goods would be allowed to enter or leave the vast Rill complex. Essera's warehouses and ships would be similarly hampered in the harbor below.

Tutto followed Dorilian down the ramp into the soaring underground passage known as the Va Haira. Connecting the Rill mount to the Upper City, the road served only the Sordaneons. Arches of milky green lined a cavernous corridor replete with watery light. Though air filled the tunnel, it seemed they moved underwater. Sinuous pillars upheld a high ceiling, shadowy and undulating with strange shapes and forms. Figures, some human in aspect and some fantastic, appeared to be trying to emerge from the walls. They were stone, milky and hued like the walls to which they adhered, but as a child Dorilian had eyed them warily.

"Wait a moment, if you value my knees," Tutto said.

Dorilian stopped before a doorway framed by ornate scrolls of gold. Tutto had spent his life protecting his Highborn charges and bore the scars of his service. Even his best walk qualified as a limp.

"And while I have you alone—did you see any of *them* while you were north? Were you able to arrange anything?"

"I told Rheger and Elhanan I was keeping the Wall Stone." It was answer enough. "I shouldn't have gone. I wouldn't have, except—"

"Except you sent your royal father from this world in dignity and honor, as a son should. You paid respects to your kin. That was well done."

"I didn't go to the Malyrdeon vault. I didn't... visit *his* crypt. I wanted to, but then—I could not bring myself to do it. I couldn't bear to see him broken." Dorilian tilted his head to keep back the sting in his eyes. Better that tears should fill his throat. "And now I cannot go there, which is just as well. I vowed to Stefan I would not set foot in Essera while he lived."

Tutto shrugged. "Not a problem. You can always have him killed."

Dorilian shook his head. "That, I will not do."

"Whyever not? He's an oath breaker, a Kheld and, worse yet, a fool. And most likely a fool who wants to kill *you*."

"Then see to it he does not succeed."

The air was cooler underground. They passed beneath a smooth archway distorted as though shaped by running water. Filigrees of waterlight glowed from the walls, captive in golden patterns as the main passage opened before them, its ceiling dotted with waterglobes like moons. Beyond the archway waited three horses who stamped with impatience, their hoofs creating echoes as their escort moved into position.

Home, Dorilian thought as he and Tutto mounted two of the horses. They set out for the Serat. Now that Dorilian was safe in Sordan, maybe he could banish his ghosts. With any luck, his domain's incessant demands would grind him down, consume his hours and his energy, leave his mind too fettered to remember a time when his passions had been pure like white fire, clear of doubt or shadows, and he had thought himself strong enough to dethrone a king.

Or control a god.

Tutto was right about one thing: Stefan probably wanted Dorilian dead. It was no longer prudent to rely on others to prevent it; Stefan was not alone in his wish. Fueled by greed, envisioning new ports, new lands and new riches, merchants and believers might bide their time, but the day would come when they would try to force Dorilian to meld with the Rill out of some futile hope he could awaken it again. And men who did not want that god to be revived, or their lands to be opened, would seek to kill him to prevent such an awakening.

Save for a dying old man in Tollech, Dorilian was the only adult Sordaneon. He would need more than wits and a few loyal followers if he wanted to stay alive and free—and human.

"Oh, no, not babies again," Tutto protested when Dorilian took a turn he recognized. "You have more important things on your hands. Ambassadors, generals, a war barking at your knees."

"Nothing is more important than my son."

They walked side by side along a high-ceilinged corridor within the secluded, utterly private confines of the Sordaneon Serat. Their sandaled footsteps pressed cool gray floors lined with potted palms and statues of Dorilian's royal ancestors. That Levyathan was not, in fact, Dorilian's son was something Tutto might suspect but would never speak. He couldn't possibly know the rest.

They rounded a corner and entered the nursery. A peaceful corner of the Serat, the suite occupied a wing far removed from the official state galleries where said ambassadors and generals would be hosted. Dorilian was earlier than usual, and the nursery was in disarray—toys of different sizes and colors littered the floor, one curtain was askew, and the doors were thrown open to a portico overlooking a walled, grassy courtyard. The main playroom was covered by a single carpet woven on Rebir's fabled looms, a pattern busy with animals of every kind known and loved, and images of brilliantly plumed birds taking flight. The wet-nurse—a plump woman wearing a white snood—lounged on a chaise laden with cushions. Raxa smiled on seeing him. So did the babe in her arms.

Dor! Dor! Levyathan's familiar touch tapped at Dorilian's mind, accompanied by a squeal of welcome. That cry was immediately seconded by another, coming from the portico.

"Da!"

Dorilian knelt and a young girl, dark curls bouncing above a bright blue shift that danced around her tiny body, propelled her chubby little legs across the room to launch into his arms. The nurse's young assistant dashed into view from the portico, a stick puppet with yellow frogs in her hand, and stopped when she saw where her charge had gone.

"Princess!" Dorilian swept the toddler up. Fahme laughed, round cheeks flushed and mouth open wide. She wasn't a princess by birth. She was the common-born daughter of Levyathan's former nurse and a man Dorilian had yet to find and kill, but he would never let the world stop him from treating this child as his own. He owed Noemi that.

"*Dor!*" The high squeal sounded more like "Dar!" Dorilian kissed Fahme's neck until she giggled, then handed her to Tutto. Doing so left Dorilian free to go the ample-bosomed woman holding Levyathan.

"He's getting loud."

"If he weren't such a bit of a thing, Thrice Royal, I'd swear the lad calls you by name." Raxa's agile fingers tucked an edge of swaddling under the babe's torso and held out the bundle so Dorilian could take him. "He's never so happy as when you come by."

"No happier than I am." He cocked the baby into his arms.

Rising, Raxa bowed her head and signaled her helper. Both women left the room. Tutto had Fahme seated upon his shoulders and was doing something that resembled a dance, leaving Dorilian free to spend time with his infant heir.

Levyathan's fat right arm batted a tiny hand against Dorilian's cheek. The boy's golden irises, fiercely focused, communicated excitement. *See colors! Hear sounds!*

"What sounds?"

"Burs!"

Dorilian understood the word better for hearing it also in his mind, spun out as both thought and sound, along with the rest of what Levyathan's infant vocal apparatus struggled to say. *Birds! Laughs. Doors. Raxa sings!* Dorilian wondered what Raxa's singing voice sounded like. He had not asked her to sing when he had auditioned nurses.

"What songs does she sing?"

Levyathan had never heard singing before, at least not *as* singing. He had only *heard* colors before. *Boats. Rabbits. Spiders.*

"When you look at me… what do you see?" Dorilian prompted. He had not asked before. Levyathan had been so new, so tiny. Only in the last several days had he begun to communicate with any structure.

"You!"

"I'm serious. What do you see? Do you see anything of the Rill?" One time and one time only, Dorilian had glimpsed himself through his brother's eyes. His *first* brother's eyes. He had seen someone young, human, but attached to a monstrous creation by milliform cords of invisible power.

Had the Rill power that clung to him changed since then? It felt vaster now, more oppressive.

Levyathan's little mouth, far too knowing for its tender age, quivered. *Not like before. Colors stay inside shapes. Different.*

Dorilian cloaked his response with a weak smile. In a way, he was glad. Levyathan was adapting well to having a full set of memories and remnants of another personality thrust upon his infant mind and body. He was neither Levyathan as first Dorilian had known him, nor was he solely the child created by Daimonaeris and Deben. His blended mind and new body were, however, experiencing a life unlike his first. A normal life with normal senses. Their relationship this time was bound to be different. Did Levyathan even remember that his original body had died a year before?

Dorilian knew he had forgotten to shield his thought when Levyathan quipped, "Yeh!"

He hugged Levyathan close and pressed his cheek to the tiny head covered by golden fuzz. For the second time that day, tears rose to his eyes, and this time he let them spill, wetting the sweet-smelling skin. Levyathan's mind slid alongside Dorilian's like fur across his skin, warm, buffering as he released his grief.

A mess, such a mess. Essera. Nammuor. It's not getting better. It's getting worse. My enemies increase by the hour.

Levyathan's calm soothed him. *Better. Soon. Bigger every day.*

Not big enough. Not yet.

I grow. You grow too!

He nodded. Levyathan might be different now, trapped in the body and mind of an infant, but he had always been wise. Like now, reminding Dorilian that his body too was still immature. He was but twenty-one years, undergoing the final stages of Highborn adolescence. He closed his eyes and hugged the boy tighter. His one victory. He had kept his dead brother's life coiled within his spine and pooled in his gut, until the day Daimonaeris, wanting to deceive him into thinking his father's child in her womb was his, had seduced him. Even knowing the truth, he had allowed it. Her beauty was the only thing about her that had not been a lie and the opportunity to have sex had pulled at him like a drug. He had never dreamed doing so would give Levyathan another chance at life.

At least, in killing her, Dorilian had saved Levyathan from Nammuor's plan, whatever that had been—or still was. Who knew what a man who twisted the forces of nature could do with a babe of Sordaneon blood? He lifted his head again and met Levyathan's baby gaze. Trust and joy looked back at him. "I love you," Dorilian whispered. "You are my brother twice over. I will protect you, no matter what."

Levyathan smiled toothlessly and jerked his arms and legs.

Raxa walked back into the room, a fresh towel over her shoulder. She waited until Dorilian placed the baby again into her soft rounded arms, then she settled back on the chaise to nurse, baring a breast swollen with milk, onto which Levyathan's mouth hungrily latched.

New shouts broke the nursery's peace as Fahme saw her opportunity. She squirmed until Tutto swung her off his neck. At once she ran over to a lopsided lump of bright blue cloth on the floor.

"Ball!" She picked it up and turned, tossing it in the general direction of Dorilian's boots. Stamping her feet, she held out both hands.

"Seems to me you might as well get some practice." Tutto looked resigned. He picked up the blue lump and tossed it.

Dorilian caught it and squatted facing the girl. He extended the ball out in his right palm. He focused. "Catch," he said.

The ball vanished and reappeared instantly in Fahme's tiny palms. She squealed in delight, then tossed the ball back. It fell halfway. While Tutto stomped to fetch it, Fahme toddled over to one of the room's three large crewelwork horses and plopped down behind it. "Ball!" she demanded.

Tutto retrieved the ball, handed it over, and Dorilian focused again. "Catch!" Again, the ball vanished from his hand to appear in Fahme's

They played the game several more times. Fahme never lacked in places to hide, her favorite being behind the curtain. Dorilian enjoyed the game, for the most part, because she did. Her laughter reminded him of his own childhood when he had played this game with his grandfather. Games had provided his first lessons in utilizing his innate Highborn gifts. Fahme would never learn the second part of the game, how to send the ball back. But someday Levyathan would, so Dorilian figured he might as well keep in practice.

He should be sending more important things than soft lumps of cloth from his hand, and farther than across a room. This morning aside, the remaining Malyrdeons were lying low in Dannuth, not communicating. Several times he'd tried to send message cylinders their way, only to get no response. He'd stopped sending them.

After a dozen rounds of ball, Dorilian rose and stopped the game. Protesting loudly, Fahme ran to the ball and grabbed it, then stood in front of him, throwing it as hard as she could to get his attention. It bounced off his knee. "More!"

"None of that!" Tutto swooped in and pulled her away, back up into his arms. "Attacking the Highborn! Can't let these little ones get ideas!" The girl arched her back and her little fists pummeled Tutto's scarred arms until the nurse's helper appeared to whisk her away, saying the child was just tired. Tutto scowled and rubbed his forearm. "You should wait twenty years and marry that one. She has plenty of fight."

Dorilian laughed, not just at the idea of ever marrying Fahme, as common a child as ever graced a Sordaneon nursery. No, another marriage was just about the last thing on his mind. More than that he didn't think he would ever want another wife—siring a child at this juncture would be a mistake. Additional Sordaneon heirs would remove one of the few reasons his Rill-greedy enemies still had for keeping him alive.

He had been thinking about other things while tossing the ball. All his best lessons had centered on games. After leaving the nursery, he turned to Tutto. "Find the emissary who came last week from the Lords of Gobba and Annech. He said he would stay in the city."

"I remember. Those Lords fear Stefan will open new lands to Kheld settlers in Neuberland."

"Meet him in secret, find out what they want, then use Philemon Leander to broker the deal. No one is better at concealing the movement of Esseran Rill shipments."

"Didn't you just stop those?"

"They will resume once we have the means to funnel arms through Leseos without any the wiser."

Tutto grinned approval, making chasms of the scars seaming his cheeks. "You're going to start a war, ignite a fire right in Stefan's own hearth."

Dorilian nodded. "Nammuor could not create a better scenario for my destruction than to engage Essera against me. Might as well give Stefan something better to occupy his time."

5

"You want to *what*?" Cullen bumped the stone he'd been setting into the wall he was building, causing the block to topple and nearly land on his foot.

"I want to give you an estate, make you a lord. The first Kheld lord ever." Stefan had been king for a few months and felt it time to put his own stamp on his reign. He tied his horse to a post Cullen had sunk into the ground near the stone pile. Not just for tying horses, the post likely was the start of a future fence. "If you had an estate, you wouldn't have to build a house for Asphalladra. It would come with one, even several."

"No, Stefan, I would still have to build her a house." Cullen squatted to pick up the stone again. "That's what a Kheld man does for a woman he wants as his wife."

At the moment, that house was just a set of stone steps leading down into a muddy hole in the ground, some timber framing, and four walls not as high as Cullen's hip. It would be a good house of three rooms and a cellar when finished, though that might take several months. Cullen grunted as he set another stone in place, rocking it back and forth until he liked how it fit. Deciding he might as well help, Stefan walked back to where Cullen had hefted the square gray stone into place and was tapping it with mortar made of lime and sand, bags of which lay near a trough. Stefan picked up the battered bucket and a trowel so he could scoop mortar around the stone.

"So, she's set to marry you?"

"If I can get her father to agree to it. You know how Staubauns are. But he's got two other daughters he can marry off, and…"

Stefan frowned. Staubauns held most, if not all, of the wealth in his kingdom, tied up in estates, ships, warehouses and Rill slot contracts. None of it was available to Khelds. Asphalladra's father, the Enlad of Chennor, would never marry his daughter to Cullen, a man without a lofty lineage and who owned nothing but a decent plot of land overlooking the Dazun River. Even a stone house of several rooms would not be fine enough for the daughter of a nobleman who owned four Rill slots.

"The Enlad'll never agree. And he won't say it's because you're Kheld, or that she's too good for you and he doesn't want little mongrel grandchildren." Stefan kept on even though Cullen grimaced. "He'll say you're too poor to provide for her, that he can marry her to a man with better prospects."

Cullen slammed another rock down on the wall. Sweat plastered curling strands of dark brown hair to his forehead. "Phalla doesn't want a man with better prospects. She wants me."

"And well she should, because you're ten times better than any lord. But she's not a Kheld woman free to choose her own man. What's needed is for her father to see some value in picking you."

"I made enough coin from our mines to buy this land, didn't I? Those shares still bring in a profit. And I'm your friend, Stefan. Being the king's friend counts for something already."

They were out of stones for setting, so Stefan went over to the pile with Cullen to pick up more. The work felt good, stretching muscles he was letting go soft with royal living, and giving space to a mind he'd let become cluttered with the demands of nobles and generals. Several trips back and forth from the pile soon had him sweating, too. Rough rock scraped marks across the leather gussets of his fitted sleeves and left smudges of dirt on the silk, but he didn't care. He had servants now who needed work.

Cullen dumped the barrow they'd filled onto the trampled grass. "There now, I can add a bit more by sunset."

Stefan had more to add, too. He hadn't come by just to help Cullen build his wall. "You never did give me your answer about being my trade minister."

"Stefan, I told you—"

"How can you tell me no? You filled that office last year, when I was Prince of Dazunor."

The sun settled low enough to drop behind a line of trees. Stefan watched Cullen's blue gaze flick across the land he had cleared, toward the bluff line and the dark gray expanse of the river. Here at Trulo the Dazun was so wide a man could barely see across it, a deep channel traveled by barges and ships.

"Things have changed," Cullen said.

"What's changed?"

"You have."

Stefan had hoped Cullen would be over that. They had argued fiercely at the time of his coronation three months before, because he hadn't listened to Cullen and all hells had broken loose. Angry Dorilian had imposed onerous restrictions on merchants and goods—even ordinary travelers—moving through Sordan, including kicking a bunch of Esseran merchant princes out of lucrative warehouse property. The unhappy nobles had been hounding Stefan for weeks, wanting him to restore their losses. Every time he looked upon their sly aristocratic faces, he was almost happy there was nothing he *could* do. He had no military forces in Sordan to command, and Dorilian, for all his faults, was staying true to his word and pretending Stefan didn't exist.

"Then help me change things back. We're friends, aren't we? You just said so yourself. You're my cousin, my blood. Nothing can change that."

"I reckon not. But Stefan, it was you who told me to go away, to get out, in front of everyone."

"I had to. You were telling me, in front of everyone, what an idiot you thought I was. Marc Frederick wouldn't have put up with it, you know that—and neither will I. But in private, like now, just the two of us, you can tell me anything."

"Then I'll tell you again." Cullen locked gazes with Stefan. "You were an idiot, putting Dorilian on the spot the way you did. I think he meant to come to your coronation. I think he would have done it and given your nobles something to think about besides whether they should get rid of you. Instead, you didn't have any Highborn in attendance, not one, because once the Malyrdeons heard about what happened, they stayed away too."

A flush of anger and embarrassment nearly loosened Stefan's tongue, but he held it. "All right, it didn't work the way I planned, but it was worth trying."

"Sure it was. Now you have Dorilian sitting pissed off in Sordan, plotting ways to make you suffer"—Cullen ticked off his mortar-crusted fingers one by one— "the Seven Houses and their Rill pals all pissed off in their palaces up here because they're not getting their way, Essera's remaining Highborn princes wondering what you intend for *them*, and me pissed off because I couldn't stop it. Even your own mother is mad that you made her look like her word was no good. And you want me to be your trade minister." Cullen expelled a lungful of air. A sharp wind off the water ruffled his coarse linen shirt. "Dorilian did you a favor, Stefan. I can't imagine a more dangerous prisoner. You would have had a war on your hands if you'd succeeded—and not just his folk, but Mormantalorus, too, because they make no secret they want Sordan for themselves. There's blood involved, with the Sordaneon Heir being their ruler's nephew and all."

Hearing his friend say these things was hard. Worse, Cullen had it right. Stefan pushed down the urge to defend himself, stewed for a moment, then finally said, "I know." Seeing Cullen's angry expression soften meant more to Stefan than all the flattery of his courtiers. "I wasn't thinking about those things. All I could think about was neutralizing the enemy in front of me. I wanted to gain the upper hand on the Rill."

"Well that was clear enough, seeing as you went for the exact way old Marc Fred did it."

Stefan sighed. "I tried it because the Highborn are going to be trouble. The Malyrdeons backed my grandfather, but they haven't said they're backing me. Rheger's correspondence is polite, but noncommittal—and when I was at Stauberg two weeks back, Elhanan's lackeys said he was in seclusion and wouldn't let me see him. Me! The king! Maybe there are only four Malyrdeons left, but all of them are possible rivals for my throne, especially those two boys of Enreddon's. I didn't want them to have Dorilian to rally around, or giving them help, and now—" He kicked at the pile of stones in frustration, causing one to shift and several others to tumble down. "People are saying it's because the Wall must have shown something, or foretold that I won't be king for long, or that one of *them* will be."

"The Wall? Really? It's communing with them again? Foretelling the future?"

"How would I know? It's all rumors, and they're not telling me anything. But one rumor says Dorilian has the Wall Stone, that he got it from whatever happened at Permephedon."

Cullen's eyes widened further. "That—and the Rill ring, too? But the Sordaneons aren't Wall Lords. He can't use it, can he?"

"It doesn't matter if he can use it—it matters that the Malyrdeons can, and they want it back. Who knows how he might barter it, what he might want." For weeks, Stefan had been imagining what Dorilian might want. He still woke up in cold sweats at night, recalling the touch of cold steel at his throat.

Staying king—and alive—would be impossible should the

Malyrdeons, guided by their time-spanning Wall and supported by Dorilian's Rill influence, find someone else they preferred to place upon their ancient throne.

"I need you, Cullen." Stefan faced his friend, as sober as he had ever been about anything. "I need men around me I can trust."

"I want to be a man you'll listen to."

"You're already that. I'm here, aren't I?"

Cullen's measuring gaze was followed by a frown. "If I say I'll be your minister, you're going to push that lordship on me, aren't you?"

Before he was crowned, they'd talked about Stefan doing that sort of thing. Staubauns might fight him every step of the way, but Khelds craved a greater role in Stefan's government. There was no better way to make a statement. "It will be to your advantage. Usually the king's ministers are aristocrats, or the sons of aristocrats, or high-ranking people from the Seven Houses or guilds. I have to make you an Enlad at least."

Cullen sighed, but nodded, his eyes again sweeping toward the river. "Then I guess I'm in. If we're making changes, might as well go full gallop."

Stefan and Cullen left Trulo the next day, headed by river to Gustan, where Stefan planned to visit his mother and young brother before sailing to Dazunor-Rannuli. Stefan had promised to be on hand for Hans's birthday. Travel overnight would get them there by morning. The last red glimmers of sunset rolled across the water and reflected off the wings of the schooner's gilded prow. On the deck, a fine ivory gelding stamped restlessly in one of several makeshift stalls. In the flanking stalls, Stefan's and Cullen's horses appeared more interested in their hay.

"His name is Felladoros. He's one of those blood horses with a fancier name and lineage than mine." Stefan snorted, then took a deep, sharp bite of ripe peach.

"You care too much about Staubaun ways," Cullen said. "Hans won't care. All he'll see is a horse and that his brother gives better gifts than his cousins."

"I hope he sees something. I hope he *says* something. It's been weeks, and Mother is at wits' end. The nightmares should have stopped by now, but he has them all the time."

Cullen frowned and looked out over the gunwale. "I only had it the one time, but Phalla suffered terrors for a week."

"Well, I never had any." Stefan pulled his arm back and threw his peach pit out into the stream. As it broadened toward the Fens, the Dazun was wide and slow, a ruddy slug of a river.

"It was bad, Stefan." Cullen's blue gaze looked troubled. "I was awake, and it hit me hard, same hour everyone else's did—screams and blood and folk on fire, folk I knew. Worst of it was not being able to move or even breathe, though my sister slapped me out of it, but she said my lips went blue. I heard tell fire's how the Highborn princes died, how all of them died... you know, that day."

It had been, according to everything Stefan had heard. He frowned. "I had it explained to me. So many empaths dying in the same way, the same time, the same place—it pushed into people's minds, those that are open to it, which I guess I'm not. And you only a little. But why is Hans so bad it's taking this long to get over it? Tell me that. He's just a kid."

"Maybe it hit him worse, *being* a kid. And his grandfather one of the dying."

Stefan shook his head. "He was my grandfather, too. And Marc Frederick wasn't Highborn; he was nothing like them."

"Maybe not. But he wore one of their rings, the one they won't let you wear."

Much as Stefan valued candor, he wished Cullen hadn't mentioned that omission. He felt slighted every time he remembered how Marenthro had refused to bestow the Leur's Ring as part of Stefan's coronation ritual. *You cannot wear it, Stefan. You would die the moment it slipped over your finger. Endurin Malyrdeon gifted Marc Frederick with something powerful that allowed him to wear it; you do not have that gift.*

It wasn't like his Staubaun subjects hadn't noticed the missing part of the ceremony. He probably should have been more careful about offending the Malyrdeons. Maybe one of them would have done for him what old Endurin had done for Marc Frederick. Stefan had known Dorilian wasn't the Malyrdeons' favorite person, but he hadn't thought it through.

"Fire on the water!"

Stefan jumped to his feet and ran to the rail. Cullen crowded at his side. Not far downstream, hanging on the dark span of the Dazun, orange light glowed and danced.

The river didn't stop when the sun went down, and neither did the boats that supplied the cities and towns along its banks. A Dazun River boatman might make half of his deliveries at night, in the dark. River men liked to say how on dark nights you could put your hand right up in front of your face and not see it. For that reason, most boats at night hung a light.

Only a handful of boats, mostly schooners like Stefan's or the pleasure barges of princes, used costly waterglobes to illuminate their vessels. The most portable kind of cheap light was a big metal lantern, and lanterns, of course, meant flames. All it took was a spark leaping out of that lantern onto the deck of a boat. Wooden vessels, made of dry timber and with planks tarred to keep out water, burned more easily than they sank. The number two rule of safety on the river was to have a light on your boat at night. The number one rule was to never leave your light untended.

The vessel ahead of them, flames ever more visible as they neared, was not a heavy cargo barge but a shallow-draft schooner of a build often used to convey merchant goods or passengers between towns. Smoke poured from the tilted boat's hatches. Wind off the river bore the acrid stink of burning wood.

Erenor dashed up. "Permission to send help, sire!"

He meant the escort ship, a swift one-masted *fetan* with a small crew of oarsmen and additional soldiers, outfitted to dock with and board other vessels.

"Do it," Stefan said.

Erenor opened a brass case and held aloft a lighted crystal, signaling the escort, which peeled off toward the burning vessel. The schooner continued to move past it at a distance. Stefan directed Cullen to follow up the steps to the upper deck for a better view.

"What do you think happened?" Cullen asked. "Knocked over a stove, or a lantern maybe?"

"Whatever it was, it got into the holds to judge by that smoke." Stefan leaned forward on the rail to peer more closely at the schooner. The boat he'd sent to the ship's help yelled for the crew, but he heard no corresponding shouts in answer. Flames had spread into listless, askew sails.

The aft mast fell forward as the schooner's deck collapsed and sent a fountain of sparks into the air. Smoke hung about the vessel in billows of dark orange and red. The further downstream they were from the burning derelict, the less they could see of it.

Stefan had just turned his back on the river when, without warning, the deck under his feet lurched violently once, then again, throwing him down. He landed hard on his left elbow and tumbled against the opposite railing. As he grabbed his arm and gasped with pain, he heard a sickening gurgle of water into some hollow place below. A deafening snap of breaking wood and roar of water followed a third shudder through the planks. His ship... they'd moved out into the main channel to get around the other schooner. Had they hit something? From the main deck, horses screamed and men cried in alarm. Still cradling his arm, Stefan got to his feet and looked for Cullen, only to feel Cullen already at his side.

"Are you hurt?"

"What the hells—"

The ship heeled hard to port. Erenor and two soldiers ran to Stefan's side. "We've been attacked, sire! The fire ship was a decoy to move us into this channel, where they triggered their trap. Compression bolts, anchored to the river bottom and released with enough force to break through the hull."

"We're sinking?" Stefan noted Cullen's round-eyed stare. He couldn't swim.

"Maybe not, sire," Erenor judged. His face looked tense and stretched, shadows exaggerated by night. "This ship is better built than any other on the river. But we are taking water, and—"

Shouts alerted them to movement off the starboard side. Shouldering Erenor aside, Stefan staggered over to see two small *fetans*, naked masts visible across the broad expanse of moonlit water. Smoke from the fire ship had hidden them until now.

"Gsch! Pirates!" Erenor darted down the steps to the main deck, shouting to muster his men.

Damn, I need a weapon! Stefan ran after Erenor, Cullen at his heels as he leapt down the last steps and his feet hit the planks. His cabin was below and, in it, his sword.

He would never reach it. One *fetan* violently bumped against the side, sending a shudder through the ship. Something clattered over the side and several men, mere shadows but for the glint of weapons they carried, climbed over the starboard rail. Though Stefan's guards cut down four of the attackers, two guards also fell, shafts protruding from their chests. The second *fetan* stayed back, its deck lined with archers.

Grasping Cullen by the shirt, Stefan dragged him over to the horse stalls and pulled him down. Unsettled by the fighting and crazed by the smell of smoke and blood, the horses reared and plunged inside their enclosures. Swords rang on the other side. A bale of hay for the horses concealed them somewhat, but not for long. Stefan reached up and fumbled with the latch to the nearest stall, within which Felladoros stamped and lunged.

"What the hells are you doing?" Cullen looked at Stefan in alarm.

"Saving our lives!" Damn the latch! Stefan didn't usually open one from down low like this. A soldier crashed over a barrel and onto the deck not far away, cut through the neck and shoulder, eyes glazing as his blood spilled across the planks with a gruesome sheen. Stefan saw Cullen dive for the fallen man's sword, which he wrenched from dying fingers.

"Who are these brigands?" Clutching the sword by its bloody hilt, Cullen crouched back behind the hay bale. The boat tilted worse now.

"We'll figure that out later. Right now, help me with this!"

"What? And not fight? We're trained in arms!"

Stefan grabbed Cullen by the collar. "I'm not a cadet anymore. I'm king. Saving me is what this fighting's all about, so I'm going to make my men's job easier."

Within the stall, Felladoros kicked at the boards and reared. Stefan worked the latch again. This time the bolt released. Eyeing the agitated horse, he edged into the stall and groped for the ring to which the lead rope was tied.

"When I tell you, open the gate!" Stefan shouted. He undid the knot, freeing the lead rope into his hand.

"What the hells good will a horse do? We're on a boat!" Looking over his shoulder, Cullen clung to the gate with the hand not holding the sword.

Using the hay bale and grabbing a handful of mane, Stefan swung astride Felladoros' back. The boat was a death trap. He needed to find a way off and make it to shore, and the horse was his best chance. "Open the gate! And climb up behind me!"

"How?"

The gate swung open. Felladoros charged onto the deck. Stefan pulled hard on the lead rope to turn the beast, reaching down to Cullen only for the horse to shy away.

The fighting had reached them. Cullen turned to swing at a brigand who ran at them. A hood concealed the man's face and hair, but the mask showed the eyes clearly, Staubaun-dark, before Cullen's well-placed blow dropped him. Cullen kicked the body off his sword.

"Get up behind me!' Stefan ordered. He tried to control Felladoros, but the confused beast reared in protest. Another groan shook the schooner and the deck tilted crazily. Men, swords and unsecured objects tumbled and slid. The movement threw Stefan forward, too, onto the horse's neck as he danced for footing. Cullen leaped toward Stefan, but had barely latched onto Stefan's shirt as

Felladoros jumped, carrying them both over the railing and into the dark, rolling water.

Stefan kept his head down, fingers gripping mane and knees clamped to the horse's ribs. He welcomed the sudden crush of Cullen's hands around his arm, digging into his skin as they plunged under the river's surface. Cool water enveloped Stefan, tugged at clothes and hair as the horse's muscles bunched beneath him. His shirt ballooned in the current. Water filled his boots. A long moment later, his head broke surface and he gulped air just above the water sloshing at the horse's outstretched neck. The animal's legs churned in the deep water and Cullen splashed in panic beside him, grappling and flailing. Stefan wrestled Cullen's grip to the horse's mane.

"Hold on."

Stefan didn't let go until he saw his wild-eyed friend look at him and nod. Then he slid off the horse's back also, lead rope in one hand, to let his body stretch alongside that of the swimming animal where he would be less of a target. The sounds of fighting receded, no more ringing swords, though plenty of shouting.

As Felladoros made for the north bank, Stefan looked back. The schooner lay on its side, dark but for the aggressive point of its gilded prow reflecting shards of moonlight. Sails drifted ghostly on the black water. Other men bobbed in the water, some striking for shore same as he was, and at least one other of the horses, swimming strongly. Stefan couldn't tell which men in the water were his. Neither could he see the brigand boats. He hoped they couldn't see him, that none of them could. Once he reached shore, he'd be better able to sort out friend from foe.

At least he had Cullen with him.

"I don't suppose you held onto that sword?" he asked.

Cullen shot him a wide-eyed look of disbelief. He was clinging with both hands to the horse's neck, gulping and spluttering, barely keeping his head above water.

Stefan looked over at the kneeling semicircle of captives being guarded by members of the local shore patrol. Alerted by the fire and fighting, the patrol had rounded up survivors as they reached the north bank. If Erenor hadn't known the patrol's leader from a youthful stint in Tahlwent's home guard and then come along to identify Stefan, he and Cullen would be among the prisoners.

Unfortunately, Stefan couldn't say for certain if any of the prisoners were part of his crew. He felt a pang, because Marc Frederick would have known.

"—but the attack appears to have been well-orchestrated," the officer finished.

"Pirates?" Erenor asked.

The man pondered. "I doubt it, sir. I've lived on the river all my life. Pirates don't usually sink vessels. They want the cargoes, or the vessel itself, and the passengers on occasion. But this—"

Erenor finished the thought. "They wanted to kill someone."

Stefan grew chill, and not just because he was wet to the skin. They had wanted to kill *him*.

"I would say so, sir. Yes. And they used our own weaponry. This battery of bolts you describe, well, they must be part of Trulo's river defense. Were but a rumor to the lot of us until this night. No mere pirate would know of it."

Maybe not. But Stefan knew someone who would.

Dorilian. The Highborn bastard had tried to kill him once before and not gotten it done, and now he'd tried again.

Except Dorilian wasn't working alone this time. There was a chance his Highborn kin, the Malyrdeons, were working with him. They'd been cool enough. They had also been privy for centuries to the highest levels of Essera's government and probably knew all about Dazun river defenses, things like bottom bolts.

Stefan shivered hard and glanced at Cullen, who looked like he wanted to start asking questions. To silence his friend, Stefan shook his head. They'd talk later, in private.

If the Malyrdeons really did foresee the future, they already knew he'd be coming after them.

6

G ustan Manor nestled behind a hill, hidden by woods from the road and the nearby town. Local folk said Marc Frederick had built his house by magic, and there certainly was none other in the world like it. He had crafted the walls of stone quarried in his native land, upon foundations set into a hill fashioned by arcane means from the otherworld soil of his birth. Every beam of wood in the house came from the forests of that other world; every bit of metal had been forged beyond the Rift that was the World's unhealed wound. He had surrounded the house with useful buildings and plantings of trees and flowers to remind him of his home. According to legend, the house—with its deceptively modest façade and courtyards, many floors, and three hundred rooms—had appeared in a night, though a few local folks still lived who could remember it being built. The Manor's architecture looked peculiar to most visitors, but very at home where it sat, tucked among exuberant plantings of shrubs and groves of towering oaks, overlooking the broad expanse of the Dazun River.

Emyli gazed out over that river now. Its broad shape curved into view at the bottom of Sonnen Hill and flowed past a moon-silvered meadow as a ribbon of ghostly water. Stefan had not come to Gustan last night as promised and now another night was near, increasing Emyli's worry.

"He will be here," Marenthro said.

Emyli sighed and let the curtain fall, then turned her attention to the one man who knew all her secrets.

"Something has happened, and you won't tell me what it is."

Berating him would not provoke clearer answers, but she did it anyway before asking the questions that would. "Is Stefan alive? Uninjured?"

"Yes. He's safe—and he will be here soon."

The world knew Marenthro as the Wizard of Permephedon, the Undying, and he was… maddening, no less now than when Emyli had first met him at her sixth-year birthday party. Quite simply, the man was beautiful. Hair bright as spun gold framed a youthful face warmed by eyes the color of polished copper—a face in which she had never, in all the years she had known him, found an imperfection and not a single trace of age. He looked as handsome and vital as a man in the first prime years of adulthood should, though Marc Frederick had told her Marenthro looked no different than when *he* had met him fifty years before. Marenthro also never gave satisfactory answers to questions about himself. The Malyrdeons believed he could commune with the Wall, though none had ever seen him do so. Marenthro's ability to contact the Rill was more certain, though he denied he had any ability to alter or revivify that Entity, saying only Sordaneons could do that and he was not Sordaneon. Never, in the time Emyli had known him, had Marenthro fully satisfied her curiosity about anything.

"Is that why Hans is worse tonight? Because of Stefan?" Emyli eased down onto the bed where her youngest lay propped on pillows. The wooden bed with horsehead corner posts seemed immense for its occupant. Hans looked so small and fragile, not the healthy nine-year-old she knew him to be. Tawny hair feathered above his forehead to cast shadows on pale skin. Dark hollows ringed his closed eyes.

Marenthro frowned. "Yes. The empathic surge of the Demise laid his mind open more than most. He loved his grandfather; he knew some of the other men. And now, Stefan's anger… Keeping Hans locked in sleep is not a path to healing, Emy. His body needs exercise, and his mind needs to engage the world around him. Let me remove his troubled memories for now and take him someplace where he does not need them. Let Hans experience childhood's lessons as any other child would."

"He's not any other child. He is mine. He's—" She closed her eyes. "He is Stefan's heir, a Stauberg-Randolph. If Hans goes away, no matter the reason, people will question his fitness to be that heir. Then Stefan will have even more problems than he has already."

"And if Hans is to help his brother at all, he has to grow and learn. And he can't do that if you keep him here in this bed, quieted by drugs and walled away from even his dreams."

She was going to cry again. How many times must she feel guilty about failing her son? Both sons. Not just Hans, but Stefan, too.

"He said his brother was burning," she whispered. "All of them, burning. I thought, after several days without those horrible dreams, maybe he was over them. But last night he wouldn't stop screaming."

Marenthro reached across the bed and laid his hand over hers. His touch was warm, human. He had always been able to find a path through her darkness. "Emy, I can help him. You know that. But not if he stays here. What he's feeling, it's still happening. All things happen in the same moment. So many empaths died at once, and—" He paused and averted his gaze. "Their deaths should have been the end of it... but Nammuor captured some, and he is destroying them, ripping those lifeforces apart one by one. He is creating something—"

She wondered if Marenthro felt everything Hans felt. In truth, Marenthro possibly felt a great deal more.

"Why didn't you prevent it?" Emyli had not asked the question before—because she feared the answer. "If you knew what was going to happen, how horrible their deaths would be... why didn't you stop it?"

"Because I am more of a monster than Nammuor is."

A rap at the door prompted her to wipe at her tears and compose herself. "Come in."

Gareth entered. The elderly man had spent most of his life as Marc Frederick's steward, and currently ran her household. The sight of his lined, familiar face was always welcome.

"His Majesty has arrived by horse, Ma'am. He should be entering the house soon."

Stefan was here!

"I have to go," she said to Marenthro. "Will you be here when I return?"

She saw him hesitate, a rarity. He had never been a frequent visitor—Marenthro so avoided people, Emyli often wondered what he did with his time—and for the most part he came and went from the Manor without being noticed at all. She, like every other person who knew him, craved more of his guidance and advice than he was willing to give. Whether he wanted to encounter Stefan was the issue. He glanced down at the sleeping boy.

"He should not be disturbed. Direct Stefan to your father's study and I will see him there."

Emyli smiled and wished she could thank him, but it would be unseemly to do so in front of Gareth.

Her skirt swirled against the fluted newel posts as she hurried down three flights of stairs. The heavy oak banisters, dark and polished to gleaming, flowed under her hand. No matter how grown up her firstborn became, her desire to see Stefan never diminished. She couldn't wait to see his sunny smile or the way his head turned to follow the progress of a pretty girl. Though she regretted some of his recent actions, she had watched these first months of Stefan's reign with pride.

He would be a good king, her father's equal—if only he would be more prudent about the enemies he made!

Stefan already waited on the compass star floor in front of the entry hall's double hearths. Cullen Brodheson stood beside him, and when the young Kheldman flashed a tired but happy smile in greeting, Emyli smiled back.

"Stefan!" She pulled him into a hug. "And Cullen, too! I'll tell the kitchen to cook up more pudding."

She expected Stefan to smile, but he didn't. He looked tired and tense, his jaw shadowed by dark stubble.

"We were almost killed last night. Someone attacked my ship—bottom bolts. And then assassins boarded. I was lucky to make it to shore. I don't know how many of my guards died, seven at least."

"But who—"

"Dorilian, who else? He wants me dead—or don't you remember the threats he made in front of witnesses?"

A quick look at Cullen showed he was not about to argue the point. Emyli decided to follow that wisdom. "Was there fire?"

Stefan gave her a sharp look. "A smaller ship was on fire in the main channel, forcing us to sail out toward the bolt line. Why do you ask?"

"Hans. He... he was seized again by terrors last night. He said he saw you burning."

Dismay flooded Stefan's face. "It happened again? Is he all right?"

"He's sleeping."

"Does he know I missed his party?"

"There was no party."

Stefan's face darkened.

"He was doing so well," she hastened to explain. "I would not have planned the party otherwise. Marenthro says—"

"Marenthro? *He* was here?"

"He's still here. Talk with him, Stefan—about Hans, and other things."

Why the hooded look across the room to Cullen? "Has he said

he'll talk to me? Marenthro isn't much for talking, you know. All he ever has to say to me is how I should make nice with Dorilian or—what was it last time?—oh, I remember—that I couldn't wear the Leur's Ring. Does he want to tell me this time that I can't wear the Stauberg Crown?"

"He only said it might give you headaches."

"But it didn't! I can wear it without any pain at all. Not even a twinge! I'm not Staubaun enough, I suppose, for it to be anything more than a stupid crown!"

His sharp tone silenced her. When he was angry, Stefan closed his ears to reason. Emyli had departed immediately following his coronation, in the aftermath of which she had lost her battle to bite her tongue. Leaving court had been the right thing to do. She had Hans to think of, her afflicted child, and believed Stefan protected enough. The men closest to him had good heads, surely. Men like Cullen and the young Staubaun lord Lucien Illarion, who was Heir to Serrain, would keep him from making mistakes. But what if he would not listen to them, either?

"Talk with Marenthro." Emyli addressed Stefan as firmly as she ever had before the crown had settled on his head. "He is in your grandfather's study. He's willing to help you. Let him."

Stefan turned away from her, headed toward the stairs. "I'm going to see Hans. Maybe, if I feel like it after, I'll speak to dear Uncle Marty. Come on, Cullen, I'll make sure Gareth finds you a room."

The young men trudged up the stairs, soft footfalls on carpet and the murmur of hushed voices once they had passed the landing. Maybe Cullen could talk sense to Stefan, but Emyli seemed to have lost all ability to do so. She no longer had her son's ear, and now wondered if she had made the right choice as to which child needed her more.

Marenthro's decision to speak with Stefan now chilled her to the bone.

Stefan almost didn't go to see Marenthro. He would much rather have gone down to the kitchen and joined Cullen at digging spoons into a pot of pudding. Or maybe bedded one of the maids he'd been letting under his coverlet for nearly two years and whose warm round body promised delights just as toothsome. Marenthro, on the other hand, still made Stefan feel like a schoolboy standing before his tutor, afraid of giving a wrong answer.

His grandfather's study—even after all these months, Stefan could not think of it as his—was part of the royal suite of rooms, reached through a door from the bedchamber. Sometimes it was there, and sometimes not. Immediately after Marc Frederick's death, servants said, the door had opened not to the study but to the room beyond the study, the king's private library. In his own youth, Stefan remembered the door sometimes led to the Queen's bed chamber, which was generally unoccupied. The study had reappeared following Stefan's coronation, servants claimed. Stefan put his hand on the doorknob, curious about what room he would find. It almost disappointed him to see the study, with its tables and collections, walls papered with maps and odd works of art. And Marenthro, wearing gray trousers and a burgundy tunic so plain it simply highlighted his bright good looks, was seated at a worktable and holding a strange-looking, pale green blade.

"Take a seat." The wizard of Permephedon pointed to a brocade chair.

Did kings obey orders to sit? Stefan doubted it, but Marenthro had been outside the sovereignty of kings for generations. He had also been a kind of uncle to Stefan and Hans for far too long to make an issue of it now. Marenthro's visits had generally been pleasant enough, until Stefan got older. Not that many years ago, Marenthro would give him gifts and perform tricks, like turning walnuts into butterflies. That might mean Marenthro could work real magic but Stefan didn't know—not for sure. Only recently had he begun to think magic a bad thing. Stefan took the seat.

"Your mother's happy. She was worried for you."

"You kept her calm, I suppose. Let her know I was all right?" Stefan had learned long ago that Marenthro seemed to know everything.

"I tried."

Despite himself, Stefan smiled. He might be irritated with his mother for her criticism of how he had handled the whole thing with Dorilian, but he didn't doubt for a heartbeat how much she loved him or that she'd worried herself sick.

"Do you know who did it?" Stefan scoured Marenthro's face for any clue at all, but saw only an infuriating, placid refusal to impart information. "Oh, that's right," he continued. "You don't ever tell us anything we really need to know."

"You don't need to *know*. You need to find out."

"You mean who?"

"No. Why. Why will lead you to who."

"And who might lead me to why. You know, you're not as helpful as you pretend to be."

Now it was Marenthro who smiled. "My help is greatly overrated. What I am, however, is knowledgeable. There are few doors in this world I have not opened. Some of them are doors I hope you never do."

"Which ones would those be?"

Marenthro turned the knife over, displaying it. It was long and thin, a green flicker. "Do you know what this is?"

"A knife."

"More than that. It's a *tullun* blade."

Stefan had heard of those. He had learned about them during his schooling at Permephedon, but he'd never seen one. When Marenthro held it out, Stefan took it. To his surprise, for something that looked so light, like it was made of glass, it had good balance. And the edge… "Ow!" He'd hardly touched his left thumb pad to it, but it had cut deep, nearly to bone. He slammed the knife down on the desk and wrapped his bleeding thumb in the bottom hem of his shirt. "Damn you!" When he looked at the knife again, the blade was clean, no trace of blood at all.

"The wound is deep, but the cut is so thin, so fine that if you bind it well it will heal quickly and without any scar. You should have remembered what you learned about *tullun* blades."

"I know, I know. They can cut anything. And the only thing that can sheathe them is a scabbard made of the same stupid skeleton." Stefan had remembered that bit too late.

"A skeleton of which there was only one. Both blades and scabbards are very rare. This one"—Marenthro gestured at the blade again— "killed Dorilian Sordaneon's grandfather."

Stefan's head shot up. "The Rill Lord? *This* blade?" He had been in Merath the day of that death, five years ago. He picked up the blade again, examining the edge.

"This very one. You know who wielded it, don't you?"

Only now did Stefan see where this was going. "A Kheld man. Trahoc Caddenson," he answered. Except it wasn't Khelds who had planned the deed—or who had provided a rare and priceless weapon for the job. Marc Frederick had always believed it was the Seven Houses, the cartel of noble families that controlled most of Essera's Rill traffic.

But Dorilian had been there when Sebbord was slain, had been just feet away, and had seen the knife wielding Kheld slash his grandfather's neck clean through. Dorilian had attempted to kill

Stefan after the Seven Houses presented evidence about Trahoc Caddenson's meeting with Stefan.

"Dorilian believed the who," Marenthro said.

"And not the why," Stefan acknowledged grimly. The cartel had wanted Sebbord dead for reasons of their own.

"Don't do the same thing he did."

Stefan nodded that he understood. He weighed the blade in his hand, marveling that he held the weapon that had killed a Highborn prince, a Sordaneon. That act had outraged Staubauns and led to the deaths of hundreds of Khelds. Stefan had never forgotten, but what he remembered most was the result… same as Dorilian. They were alike, in that at least—or it could be that history was trying to repeat itself.

But when he looked up, he was alone in the room with only a *tullun* blade in his hand and more questions than when he had entered.

"Did you see him?" Emyli sat in a chair at Hans's bedside. She looked tired and deeply troubled, but hope showed through as she studied Stefan's face. "What did he have to say?"

"Nothing much. He never does." Stefan looked around the small room—a third floor bedroom, part of the spacious nursery reached by a stair from Emyli's apartment. It was a child's room cluttered with toys and colorful diversions—books open on the floor, mock weapons in the corner. Stefan took a seat on the bed and touched Hans's hand. Such a small hand. Stefan wished it would squeeze his back.

Emyli sighed. "Marenthro wants to send him away."

"Away?" Stefan looked at her sharply. "Why?"

"To get better. You heard, I'm sure, how many children his age still suffer the terrors."

"I know. I heard." Very young children didn't get waking dreams and adults had only suffered for a short time, but children his brother's age—Stefan had also heard that mostly Staubaun children suffered them. He refused to think about rumors that Hans might not be his father's son. A Staubaun man's child would be brown-eyed, and Hans's eyes were blue like his.

"Marenthro said he could block Hans's memory. Just for a short time." Emyli spoke quickly, to cut off the word already on Stefan's lips.

"No!"

"Only so he can grow up without those horrors, without seeing those things. Terrible things. I heard what he saw. He would get his memories back later, when he's older, when he can deal with them."

"No."

"Stefan, the terrors keep happening."

"It's sorcery, the worst kind. Attacking the mind. Stealing what someone is. I won't have it!"

"Marenthro would never do anything that would harm Hans."

"Are you sure of that? Are you really sure?" How could she even contemplate letting someone send Hans away? Take away all memory of who he was? Of this place.... Stefan's heart tightened. *Of me.* "What is he up to? Not just helping Hans, you can be certain."

Marenthro had sounded so reasonable only an hour before, showing the knife, talking about distinguishing between who and why. Now Stefan was in just that situation, trying to separate the two—except Marenthro could not be separated that way.

"He only wants to help. Don't you see? It just so happens he can help in extraordinary ways!" How could she look so beautiful and trusting, sitting there, pleading with him to understand? Just like she had when he was a child and believed every word from her lips. When she had taken him from his cousins in Amallar and sent him to Permephedon because she thought he needed to learn Staubaun ways. "And I agree with what he wants," Emyli said. "I want Hans to grow up healthy. I want him to grow up whole and in peace, without his mind torn apart by memories that aren't even his, that no child should ever have to see."

"Cullen told me about them. They're like bad dreams."

"Except Cullen has stopped having them, hasn't he? And Hans hasn't."

"But he will. He just needs to be away from here." He didn't say the rest, that maybe Hans needed to be away from an overwrought mother who clearly wasn't thinking straight. And Hans especially needed to be kept away from people like Marenthro. Hans was important now. Important to *Stefan*—and to Essera, also. Questions leapfrogged in Stefan's thoughts. Where was Marenthro planning to send his brother to live? With whom?

"It'll be somewhere safe," Emyli promised.

"Where?"

"I don't know. Marenthro said it may be better if we don't know. We have enemies."

Stefan jumped back onto his feet. "Even more reason *to* know! Even more reason to keep him someplace where we can *protect* him! Hans is my brother—he's my *heir*! I need to know where he is at every moment. I need to oversee everything about him now. Where he lives, his education, even his friends. Marenthro is interfering! You actually *trust* that Staubaun sorcerer to do anything that's in Hans's best interest? Or mine?"

"He's the best friend our family has! Has ever had."

"I can't believe you'd even consider something like this. I forbid you." He hated the way she looked at him now, the slight tinge of fear. She had nothing to fear from him. So why did she look like that? "Don't you see? Hans isn't just *your* son anymore. He's my brother, and this kingdom's heir. I need to keep him close, make sure he's safe. You're right about that. I can send him to Amallar. Goff and his lads will make sure no harm comes to him. He'll ride horses and catch fish and then he can go to school, at Permephedon maybe, like I did, and Marenthro can have some say over that. But Hans likes being with his Kheld cousins, he's spent summers there. I don't want him to lose that."

"He will never lose that, Stefan. He'll always be a Kheld. But that's not all he is, and not all you are. There must be more. There should be *peace*! And it has to start by giving him a chance to be at peace within himself, not have a childhood filled with terror and uncertainty!"

The way she looked at him—hurt, betrayed—made Stefan want to cry. They were so much alike. They had the same deep blue eyes, the same dark hair, even the same enemies. She had to understand the pressure that was on him. He didn't want Hans growing up in some other household, maybe even among Staubauns—or worse yet, the Malyrdeons. Marenthro was rumored to be close with them. The Highborn were masters of these kinds of games, all politics and intrigue. They'd enticed Marc Frederick from his home world, seen Labran Sordaneon imprisoned for thirty-five years, and all for what?

"Listen to me." Stefan took her hands and pulled them between his. They were ice cold. "I don't think Marenthro wants to hurt Hans. But he's always been a strange one. Even you can see that. He says he's not a Malyrdeon, but what thing has he ever done that wasn't their work? Bringing grandfather here served *their* designs! Making sure he won and held the throne served their designs, too. What they did incited the Sordaneons, let the Malyrdeons *beat* them and Essera take control of the Rill! And it was all so noble, like they had no hand in it at all. Their Wall shows them something and they think they have to make it happen. They controlled Marc Frederick's life, and maybe yours, too. Marenthro has an agenda, you can be sure of it. Just like he had one when he wanted to talk to me tonight, trying to put me off their scent. But until I know what he's after, I can't let him decide what happens to my little brother."

Emyli's gaze raked his face, pleading and maybe something more. Something disbelieving. For what felt like the first time in his life, he couldn't read her.

"You'll see," he said softly, pulling her close, if only to break that uncomfortable gaze. Whatever she wanted from him, they'd sort it out. He would keep his family together, whatever else he did. How could he lead a kingdom if he couldn't even do that? "I'll take good care of Hans. I'll take good care of both of you. I'm king now, aren't I?"

Her arms clasped his ribs as tightly as tree roots clasped the earth.

Stefan was in bed with the pretty housemaid, tangled in soft limbs and silk covers, his lips grazing the warm paradise of her thighs, when Erenor rapped on the door to tell him Emyli had chased the nurse from Hans's bedroom and then locked the door. Stefan could guess why. He had forbidden Emyli from allowing Marenthro to visit again.

Cursing, he pushed the girl aside and grabbed for his trousers. Not bothering with a shirt, he stormed down the hall to his mother's room, where the nurse held the door open, and charged up the stairs. When he tried the knob, the door opened.

Emyli sat alone on the empty bed.

Hans was gone.

"What have you done?" Enraged, Stefan slammed the door behind him. The wood frame rattled. Books crashed over, a cup at the edge of the night table toppled to the floor and rolled under the bed.

"I did what I had to. I'm saving my son."

"From *me*?"

Tears streaked her cheeks as she shook her head. "No, not from you! It's not always about you! I need to save him from Nammuor, from what that creature is doing and what he's yet to do. I'm trying to save you, too! But you won't let me, you won't listen."

"To what? Tall tales about imaginary enemies? Just because Marenthro told you Nammuor killed Grandfather at Permephedon doesn't make it true! Where's the *proof*?"

"There *is* no proof. All the men who witnessed the travesty are dead!"

All but one. But what would Dorilian ever say, except to deny his own part? "That's right, no proof. Yet there *are* witnesses, credible ones, who saw Nammuor in Mormantalorus that very day, and it takes weeks from Stauberg by ship to get there—and weeks even by Rill and then overland. Not to mention Nammuor hasn't made a hostile move against anyone except the crazy man who beheaded his sister!"

"Your facts have explanations, if you would but listen. There are powers in this world, abilities, so many dangers you need to learn about." She rose to face him. "My father is dead. His allies—gifted, powerful men—are dead also. Ask who stands to gain from that."

"Dorilian."

"If that's what you think, you have not asked the right questions."

"Right now, I'm asking where my brother is!"

"Hans needs his own life. His own friends, his own enemies—not yours! But you'll always be his brother. That will never change."

"What do you mean it won't change? You changed it! You sent him away!"

Emyli lifted her chin and her wet eyes met his. "Yes, I did."

Only Marenthro could have gotten into this guarded house, into this room. Marenthro, who would not have done anything without Emyli's consent. Furious as he was, Stefan knew that.

"And he never told you where." He went ice-cold, remembering their earlier conversation.

She shook her head.

Of course, he hadn't. What Emyli did not know, she could never tell. That she could trust the wizard so much, and Stefan so little, made Stefan want to hit her. Instead, he hit the nearest inanimate object: the horse head on the end of the bedpost. When his fist slammed into it, the wooden carving broke off and flew across the room to clatter on the floor. He felt something snap, a bone for sure, and pain flooded his hand. He welcomed it. He welcomed even more Erenor and two soldiers, answering sounds of violence, stepping into the room.

Emyli reached out a hand, but he turned away.

"Take her," he told the soldiers.

"Your *mother*, sire?" Erenor looked uncomfortable, even apologetic, when his men took hold of Emyli's arms.

"Yes, my mother. Lock her in a room, I don't care which one. I'll decide what to do with her later."

She peered back like her heart was breaking, but not like she was scared. The soldiers forced her through the door. Stefan didn't call them back.

Damn, his hand hurt. His heart hurt. His whole damned world was cracked and falling to pieces and all his mother wanted to talk about was Nammuor, when Mormantalorus wasn't even a problem right now. In fact, Stefan was glad Nammuor was fighting Dorilian. For all he cared, those two could kill each other.

There was no way he could come out of this not looking weakened. His brother was nowhere to be found. And he could do nothing to make Marenthro reveal where he had taken him. For all practical purposes, Stefan had no heir. One thing was clear: he had to make a statement of some kind. A strong one, like send his mother into exile. Maybe at Maskos, the icy island where he had been exiled to harvest vent slugs for a year—yes, that would do. She hadn't talked Marc Frederick out of it then and she wouldn't talk Stefan out of it now. There was nothing he could do to keep Marenthro from seeing her anyway, but it need not be easy for anyone else.

He slumped down on his brother's bed and stared at the walls, pondering Marenthro's advice. He needed to learn why. Why had his mother done this? Why were people trying to kill him? He had too many questions... and no way of telling which *why* would give him the answers he sought.

7

Dorilian regarded the octagonal cylinder resting sideways on the desktop. It glinted gold in a patch of sunlight, and sparks gleamed from tiny jewels set into the metal. With a flick of his fingertip, he sent the empty device into a ponderous spin. The message it had conveyed was penned on a square of white in front of him. He frowned at Tiflan, who had brought it.

"They could have just *sent* the message."

"Rheger claims you're too well shielded."

"What? I block him just by *existing*?"

Tiflan pondered that for a moment before he continued. "He asks that you not send to him until you are ready to discuss the Wall Stone."

"The Wall Stone remains in Sordan. I am not changing my mind. They might as well stop asking."

"Stefan has presented an order to the Archhalia, demanding you return the Wall Stone to Essera. Rheger and Elhanan are cosignatories. The approval is overwhelming. It comes to vote this week."

Dorilian snorted. "A problem for you, I suppose."

Tiflan shrugged. "I am a monolith they cannot crush. No action against you will ever have my vote." He extended another paper, this one from a different cylinder. "There is also a petition to remove me as Bas of Teremar."

"We can add that to the stack calling for me to be removed as Hierarch of Sordan." Dorilian refolded the message and inserted it back into the cylinder, spinning the base to lock it before he placed it in his desk. The keyed seal on the drawer would keep it secure.

"How many more months will it take before they move on to more useful work?"

Unless the Archhalia changed the very laws upon which the Triempery was founded, Dorilian's descent from Derlon kept him secure on Sordan's throne, and his rank as Hierarch gave him veto power over any matter in which he or his Hierarchate possessed a direct interest. Enough ruling lords from Staubaun domains—including many in Essera—adhered to the Triempery's Highborn foundations for Dorilian's situation to remain intact.

Tiflan cleared his throat. "There's another matter."

There always was. Being a ruler could be annoying at times.

"Your Malyrdeon kindred have expressed concern about the safety and well-being of the Princes of Stauberg and the Eleutheron."

"What now? Is Stefan spreading word that I kill babies?"

"Not that I know of. No, their fear is more that the heirs are vulnerable to other threats."

"Palaistea's a capable woman." What little Dorilian knew about the mother of Enreddon's sons impressed him.

"She is also a woman whose infant sons are heir to almost all the Royal North. Stefan is going to want to secure that inheritance, if only to keep it out of the hands of possible rivals."

That presented an interesting angle. Stefan had recently survived an attack on his life. He must be feeling... vulnerable. "Is he proposing to marry her?"

"No, though that is what he should do."

Dorilian leaned back in his chair. He should have foreseen this. Stefan would not want to wed a woman so powerful in her own right, but neither could he leave her... available.

"Very well. Draft a proposal of marriage. On my behalf."

"Are you mad? No one's asking for that! Not her and not the Malyrdeons."

"What are they asking?"

"For the Wall Stone, so they can protect her."

Back to that again. The request was reasonable—if the Malyrdeons could demonstrate any ability to use the thrice-cursed thing. Dorilian hardly blamed them for trying. If they really wanted it back, they would have to do better. "Then let them petition the Archhalia. Again." He shrugged. "As for the other thing... though I am under no delusion about whether Princess Palaistea would be allowed to wed me, there might be an angle. If we became betrothed, it could solve both of our problems."

"How so?" Tiflan's brows drew together.

"She doesn't want a husband—and I don't want a wife. We could engage in the world's longest betrothal."

Tiflan shook his head. "I see what this is. You aim to provoke Stefan, and to what end? He already sees everything you do as hostile."

Because it is.

Dorilian had not cared about any actions Stefan, the Archhalia, or any person in Essera had taken against him in several months. Stefan's seizures of his Esseran estates and palaces had been an ugly move that enriched a handful of newly elevated nobles and awakened panic in hundreds more—but the losses had not seriously hurt Dorilian's wealth. It helped his finances, in fact, that he no longer needed to pay Esseran taxes, or the exorbitant costs of maintaining and staffing properties he never used. Now that Essera's bloated bureaucracy no longer leeched off Sordan's economy, he was richer than ever—and more influential. His calendar overflowed with Esseran petitioners groveling for him to renew their mercantile licenses. Some few he granted and slapped with burdensome administrative fees; most he denied and took joy in the denying.

Another thought came to him and he sighed. "Don't draft that proposal of marriage. The Princess's position is precarious enough. You are right about Stefan's hostility. I don't want any of it directed at her because of me."

"Finally," said Tiflan. "You have arrived at good sense."

"A pity. I was enjoying the prospect of Stefan frothing at the mouth."

"Only because you like distracting him."

Dorilian laughed. "Always. I learned—" *From Marc Frederick.* Before the fist of pain could tighten further, he rose and walked to the window looking over Sordan's harbor. The harbor construction he had funded five years ago was complete and ships from all lands filled the immense basin. Dozens more waited outside the harbor wall.

"Stefan needs to hate me. While he hates me, I am his excuse for all things that go wrong." Like the reluctance of powerful Esseran lords to fully commit to Stefan's proposal to elevate several Kheld family members to the nobility. They pointed to Kheld unrest in Neuberland—which Dorilian happily fostered.

"Is that wise? Maybe he should be looking at enemies closer to home."

Maybe. Dorilian frowned. "I have made known to the Seven Houses that if they move to depose Stefan, I will seize Essera's throne and make their lives hell."

"Can you?"

"Probably." In truth, he wanted all of them—Essera, the Epoptes, even his own people—to regard him as a political force and forget he had any power over the Rill. His affinity had never been established to the public. Other than Quirin and a few eyewitnesses to Dorilian's mysterious translocation the terrible day of the Demise—most of whom were not sure *what* they had seen— his exploit was largely rumor. The only thing everyone agreed on was that he had been wearing the Rill Stone.

The main door to the chamber opened and Legon gestured with hand signals, to which Dorilian nodded. "I have a meeting with Pandaros and some of his staff." Nammuor was making another push into Suddekar. But this talk of marriage proposals had given him an idea. "Before you leave, I am quite curious about what kind of marriage proposal you would have drafted. I want to see one. Do your best to make marriage to me sound appealing."

"Shall I laud more praise on your exceptional personal qualities, or your wealth?"

"Whichever would annoy Stefan most."

Tiflan laughed and grabbed up his leather travel bag. "I shall do my best."

Dorilian watched him leave and smiled. *Kampe archos.*

Royal gambit.

The city of Aral raised glinting towers against a curve of blue sky. Stefan and his party rode into the broad plaza in front of the Halasseon Serat. Above the palace gate floated the heraldic banner of the Halasseons—a golden crown above white-capped blue waves and a recumbent snow tiger. Beneath it Erenor Tholeros, sent in advance of Stefan's arrival, met him.

"The Gracious Queen did as you requested, sire. She arranged a ship. It is being outfitted in the harbor."

Stefan wished he felt more pleased. Nothing about what he was doing felt right. Even having his mother with him. Emyli had been silent the whole journey, not even looking at him with reproach.

"My thanks to the Gracious Queen. Thank you for speaking to her."

Erenor smiled. "She was great friends with my grandmother, who was one of her ladies. It was she who procured my appointment to the Royal Cadets. She still calls me Norrie."

"Ha! Why do old women do that?" Stefan's aunts in Amallar called him by a pet name.

"They think it endearing. I doubt they intentionally set up their sons and grandsons for ridicule."

No, probably not. And Apollonia, if anything, was rigidly decorous. Aral had been one of the most majestic of Highborn holdings until the death of its prince, Apollonia's father. She ruled it now, from a seat of greater power than Stefan yet commanded.

"Let the Gracious Queen know I'm here."

Erenor rode off immediately to arrange the reception.

Stefan dreaded meeting with Marc Frederick's widowed queen. 'Gracious' referred to a noble or royal consort whose partner was deceased. Otherwise, there was nothing gracious about Apollonia. Their relationship since Marc Frederick's death had been cordial, though never friendly. Nonetheless, Apollonia had been a perfect accompaniment to Stefan's coronation: regal, propriety itself, introducing ambassadors and rulers of distant minor lands as if all were old friends. She effortlessly moved within a world Stefan had yet to command.

After seeing to his mother's accommodations and posting guards, Stefan went to his apartment and changed into a fresh tunic of wine-dark silk with black borders and tawny hunting cats embroidered across his chest. He chose to don a short mourning cape fastened by crown insignia before he went in search of his royal in-law. He found her in the Sordaneon manse. Like many of Essera's Highborn Serats, this one had another grand residence located on its grounds reserved for their southern kindred, a visit from whom was considered a state occasion. This manse had not seen use in forty years. Stefan had ordered the property opened and its contents inventoried. Apollonia, when he found her, was assessing a table laden with a collection of statuettes, many of solid gold or silver.

She placed a horse figure back onto the table. "Must you pillage them? It's unseemly."

"So is Dorilian seizing all my property in his domains. I'm just returning the favor."

"He froze assets. You confiscated. I do understand the difference. When did you make the leap? When you noticed that his wealth here was greater than yours down there?"

Stefan's jaw tightened. Every time he talked with his step-grandmother, he risked cracking a molar. "I'm not a thief! He's a murderer and I refuse to let him profit by it!"

"I am sure the Archhalia will put their stamp of approval on the appropriation if you reward enough of them with the proceeds." Apollonia shot him a narrow look. "I don't care about that. At least it demonstrates a plan for funding and managing this kingdom. Your Khelds are good for nothing. They barely own a plot of land between them."

He bit his tongue to head off a retort. It wouldn't have landed anyway. Apollonia had polished her icy armor through decades of adversaries. And she had never made a secret of her dislike of his lowly relations. She disdained Emyli for being Marc Frederick's child by his first wife, a Kheld woman who had died before Marc Frederick ever became king—or who maybe had died so Apollonia could become Marc Frederick's wife when he *did* become king. Stefan more than half believed that part.

"I didn't intend to surprise you with a visit."

"You almost missed me. I only returned from Stauberg two days ago."

Had she? One more thing Stefan needed was better spies. The ones he had couldn't keep track of one old woman.

"I trust you gave my regards to Rheger and Elhanan—and Princess Palaistea. I missed them at my coronation." None of those Malyrdeons had been on hand to see him accept the crown. Stefan made his way to a bench framed by a grand half-circle of tall windows. Decades ago, before the Sordaneons had ceased to visit Aral, pots of flowering trees had probably shared the space.

Apollonia crossed slender hands that seemed amazingly youthful for a woman of seventy years, and rested them serenely in front of her gown's delicately embroidered neckline.

"They explained their absence. Rheger had a duty to perform on behalf of a deceased kinsman. And Palaistea," she arched an eyebrow, "was in labor."

Stefan flushed. He hadn't meant to imply he'd thought the woman remiss, just Rheger and his Heir. Palaistea missing his coronation to give birth to her dead husband's child was sad enough, and no insult to Stefan. He had sent a gift on the baby's birth, acknowledging its importance.

"Palaistea needed Rheger to be with her," Apollonia continued, "because no other Highborn were to be had, what with Elhanan and Margarid being needed in Kyrbasillon. What was she to do? Entrust herself and Enreddon's children to that madman in Sordan?"

Of course not, but Stefan wasn't about to let her get away with an obvious redirection. "Palaistea didn't need Rheger with her.

Other women deliver Highborn babes without men standing at hand."

"Very well, these are dangerous times, and she wanted him with her should the worst happen—which it did not. There was also need to establish the child's legitimacy." Apollonia shrugged imperiously as the apricot light of late afternoon spilled onto the gilt floor at her feet. "What is important is that Palaistea now take up residence in either the Danae Palace or the Asae Eranos to raise her sons in peace. The people need to see her, and most especially her children, safe and happy, and realize that they have continuity of rule."

Stefan frowned. Apollonia spoke as if he wasn't providing that continuity. The tiny Princes of Stauberg and the Eleutheron were subjects of the King; the people of those domains were *Stefan's* people. He'd be damned if he would let himself be pushed aside, first there, then everywhere, by a pair of Highborn heirs. *But they're just boys*, he reminded himself. *They haven't done anything yet, and neither has their mother.*

"If you had any sense at all, you would marry her," Apollonia said.

Stefan's head jerked up again at that. He expected her disdain, and could do little about it… but her suggestion? That rankled. "*Marry* her? Her husband has only been dead for six months!" Did any of this woman's thoughts not overflow with schemes?

Apollonia's face hardened. "As has mine. This land has been robbed of a generation of princes. Do not neglect your duty in providing replacements." The way she eyed Stefan reminded him he was small, in every way, among those he ruled. "I talked with Rheger and he agrees Palaistea would be an ideal royal bride. Oh, don't stand there with your mouth hanging open like a stunned carp. You are king now. You cannot marry just any woman. Reassure your subjects that you will secure their future and align yourself with a woman of lineage and substance, who will carry forward the very best of our traditions."

Stefan doubted she was concerned for the danger inherent in having a king who was unwed and childless. This was more likely a plot to tie him to the Malyrdeons. Either way, he didn't like it. No one, not Marc Frederick before he died, nor this widowed harridan of a queen, was going to tell him who to take to wife. If it killed him, he was going to retain a Kheld man's right to choose the woman at his side.

"I will consider her." Perhaps conciliatory words and a pleasant smile would be enough to mask his insincerity. "Palaistea is the most beautiful woman in the land, after all. She's now also its greatest heiress. It would be prudent of me to secure the heart of the kingdom."

No way in all eight hells would he do it. He would be slitting his own throat to bring Palaistea's two sons so near to his throne.

"You should consider other things also, such as building alliances that will help you far more than what you've been doing, handing out Sordaneon properties and palaces in exchange for dubious gains."

It didn't surprise him she knew about that. "Maybe if I can't win over allies with words, I can buy them with gifts."

"Oh, a few lordships, I suppose, in hope they will vote as you desire. You might do better to purchase mine."

Aral's vote, along with those of Apollonia's subject lords—who held votes in Essera's Halia and seats on every advisory council. "You mean to say that if I marry Palaistea—"

Apollonia waved her hand in dismissal. "No. For one thing, I cannot deliver her. She is a woman of property and standing, and she alone will decide who she will take as a husband. I still think you should make the effort. Perhaps we can bring Malyrdeon pressure to bear, but... no, I was speaking of something more—personal."

"Personal."

"Something I want done, that only you can do."

This was a new wrinkle. All the more reason to be cautious. "I'm listening."

"There is a woman. A creature of minor nobility whom your grandfather took as a mistress. I have been told she possesses a letter of bequest that will come before you for final disposition. It means to give her property that, by all right, should have gone to you."

Stefan had known about his grandfather's mistress. He felt no sympathy for her. Nobles of both sexes pandered themselves for gold. Just this week he had bought off a dozen of them.

"What do you want me to do?"

"Deny her the property. She will be impoverished... then she will disappear and cease to be a reminder of my husband's misplaced affections."

So one less nose-in-the-air Staubaun cow for Stefan to deal with. He sharpened his expression, telling Apollonia he wanted to hear the rest.

She complied. "Do this for me, and I will vote for that Kheld you wish to ennoble."

"I wish to grant Cullen lands as well. A former Sordaneon estate, Heddros. Near Trulo." He watched her eyes widen. The estate was one of Dazunor's richest.

"I will not oppose it—if she is gone."

Stefan nodded. He would hold her to it. Get her vote in writing, with witnesses, to be exchanged at the hearing. If he wished to rule this land, he must occasionally make bargains such as this one. No real harm would be done except to disappoint a woman who hoped to make a comfortable living off a dead man. And he could always put another property to good use.

"You will have what you want, Gracious Grandmother," he promised, "so long as I get what I want—and that includes ceasing your efforts to foist a bride upon me."

"You are overdue. Your grandfather wanted you wed two years ago."

"I don't think—"

"That much is clear." Apollonia fixed her critical glare upon him. "If Palaistea Malyrdeonis does not marry *you*, she might entertain a royal match you would like far less."

A *royal* match? Maybe a Highborn one? Stefan's stomach sank. "Dorilian."

"You see," she arched an eyebrow, "our goals in this are very much in line. Palaistea would make your crown more legitimate than even your grandfather's name can make it."

"I won't approach a woman who has just given birth." Stefan seized the best excuse. On that point, at least, most of his Staubaun subjects and all his Kheld ones would agree. "She will have time to mourn her husband and father, and she will have time with her new babe." *And I will have time to find a wife of my liking.*

He left more determined than ever to settle the matter. In the eyes of many of his subjects Palaistea was already as good as a queen. The last thing he wanted was a wife so wellborn she would be viewed as his better.

"You oughtn't send her away."

Stefan noted how Cullen eyed the ship waiting at the quay below the palace with grim disapproval. Nor was his friend done voicing his mind.

"That woman gave you birth. She's Faetha Argoellin and sworn to the Mother. She's fought for us! Given us her heart and blood.

She was there when we took Gignastha and no one was stronger to come out of that the way she did."

"She crossed me."

"So did I, and you didn't exile me."

No, he'd only wanted to. Stefan sighed and plopped onto a chair. It was a damned fancy piece of furniture, just like everything else in this over-decorated treasure chest of a palace. "She sent Hans away. My brother. My heir! Don't you see how that's going to look?"

"It'll look worse if you run around roaring about it." Cullen shook his head. "And maybe it's a good thing. Hear me out"—he cut off Stefan's protest— "because there're things you can do. Say Marenthro did it. It's true, for one thing, and she will help put around you agreed to it."

"I didn't!"

"You say you did. It won't go down easy, but it will go. Marenthro brought Marc Frederick to this world, and people—most people—like how that turned out. If Marenthro is protecting your brother, hiding him, who's to say he isn't doing what's right? Say it's temporary. Just until things settle down."

Which they weren't, and Stefan didn't see things getting settled for quite some time. He watched Cullen pace and reminded himself he had promised he would listen to his friend.

"You make all this your idea and that takes it off your mother," Cullen insisted. "As far as the world knows, she never crossed you. You keep her at your side."

"I don't want her at my side."

Cullen took the seat across from Stefan and gazed at him resolutely. "You need her at your side. She's a good advisor. Tell me the truth, has she ever lied to you? Has she ever not fought for you with all that's in her?"

How was he to answer? Stefan's every memory of his mother involved her doing battle on his behalf. She'd stood up to Marc Frederick. To Dorilian. To everyone except… "She didn't fight for me when she let Marenthro take Hans."

"Reckon then she was fighting for Hans."

Stefan dropped his head against the gilded back of the chair. Cullen was damned good at carving out truth. "Now that he's gone, she'll fight for me again? Is that what you're saying?"

"I'm saying your mother is a strong Kheld woman who won't ever tell you lies. And she'll never side with anyone against you. And I'll be honest, Stefan, you need someone else besides me who will tell you their mind. I don't want to be the only one."

And that was why he kept Cullen with him. He did need that. All kings did. He wondered who Marc Frederick had relied on—and didn't like the names that came to mind. Stefan's certainly hadn't been among them.

"Maybe you're right. People might get the wrong idea if I send her away." Stefan pushed to his feet and walked across the room to a large desk set before yet more harbor-facing windows. He picked up a pen with his bandaged hand and uncapped a jar of ink, then began opening drawers. "Where's the damn paper?"

Cullen lifted his head, his smile wide and hopeful.

A knock at the door preceded Erenor's arrival. "Your Majesty. The ship is ready."

Stefan closed the lid on the box of paper he'd found. Awkwardly, unable to press with his broken fourth finger, he scribbled a few lines on the smooth surface of the sheet in front of him. "It's no longer needed. I have decided my mother will remain in Essera."

Erenor diverted a glance toward Cullen. "Of course. That's... good news, sire."

"I think so too. We will spend a day or two here, then we will ride to Kyrbasillon." When the ink appeared dry enough, Stefan folded the note and sealed it with wax before handing it to his Commander of the Guard. "You will give my mother this note from her loving son." He smiled at Erenor's questioning look. "I do love her, you know."

"Naturally, Your Majesty."

"Go on. We will talk over more of our plans tomorrow."

When the door had closed behind the departing Commander, Stefan walked over and slumped into the chair again. "We're going to Kyrbasillon because I'm still working on getting votes for your lordship."

"Stefan—"

"This is important to me. I will talk with a few people on the way. And then I'll talk to more people as we make our way back to Dazunor-Rannuli."

"Good. Because that's where you need to be." Cullen ran a hand through his disordered dark mane. "I know Marc Frederick ruled from Stauberg. It was a good choice for him, but you need to be where you're most likely to find people working against you. The Seven Houses, for one. And the Purists for another. They're as likely to have attacked your barge as Dorilian was—more, I say. He had a fine chance to kill you, and he didn't do it."

Stefan resented the reminder and noticed he was grinding his teeth again. "No, he just made sure everyone and their brother who wants to get rid of me knows he won't stand in their way."

"And there's no taking it back, not for his kind. That's why here's what you do: you show everyone who wants to get rid of you that you aren't going anywhere. Be the best damn king any of them ever saw. Work on trade. Make alliances—good ones! You have Rill slots now, right?"

Stefan nodded. He had retained his grandfather's Keeper of the Purse, a crafty son of Gareth Morgen's, to manage them.

"I've some ideas on how you can use those slots to build Kheld trade on the Dazun." Cullen grinned at Stefan's surprised look. "Thought I wasn't taking my post seriously, did you? You want me to be your Minister of Trade, I'll be working up lots of ideas. For starters, how to handle the Seven Houses. We can't do anything about them controlling Rill trade in Dazunor-Rannuli, that's certain, but we can do something about trade flow on the Dazun River."

His river. Essera's golden highway.

Stefan leaned forward, lips stretched in a smile. "Tell me more."

8

A drop of sweat trickled onto the upper lashes at the corner of Nammuor's right eyelid, where it hung for a moment before sliding down into his eye. The resulting sharp sting pricked his awareness and he blinked. His focus wavered. On the verge of completion, the fine blue energy tube he had been creating between a pair of glowing blood crystals failed to stabilize; the thread of incandescence warped, expanded outward and disintegrated altogether.

"Imbecile!" Removing his hands from the crystals and the glittering, red-jeweled Diadem on which he had been working, Nammuor turned in rage to confront the quivering acolyte at his feet. A dozen cloud-wort wands tipped with spun cotton dropped from the youth's shaking hand to spread like accusing fingers on the obsidian floor. The youth had failed his only responsibility: keeping sweat out of the Master's eyes.

"Master, he is dismissed." Oarzas, Nammuor's Prime Crystallier, pulled the acolyte to his feet and propelled him toward the door. The white-faced youth did not even look back but fled the innermost sanctuary in a flurry of yellow robes. "He will be severely punished."

"I thought this one was your best."

"I will find you another."

Nammuor grimaced and stumbled over to a stone chair facing the horned altar, where the Diadem rested on a plinth of black deathstone, the sole material that dampened its malevolent energies. Only by doing so could Nammuor and the mages work in its presence while wearing enhancers. The one he was wearing, the Crown of Fire with its five red stones and tiers of golden wire, had been sending scythes of pain through his head and down his spine for half a night. Even before he was fully seated, he wrenched it from his head. He would have worn a band of cloth to catch his sweat, but his use of the device required uninterrupted contact between the enhancer's surfaces and his skin. He pulled off his *lr*-rings also, one by one, all nine blue gems glowing with power, and tossed them into a dish Oarzas had fetched from the table near the altar. Little by little, the agony inside his skull abated.

"Will you wish to try again?" Oarzas asked.

"Tomorrow."

He was being hopeful. Every contact with the Diadem of the Devaryati stole more of his strength than he could easily replenish. Even from here, Nammuor suffered the device's hunger—a hunger a hundred times fiercer than the day he had first discovered it in a coffin at the volcano's core. He had sacrificed a legion of his followers to free it. To feed it. Even so, the thing drained him of emotion and perception, so that the world around him, and everything in it, especially living things, turned gray. He had only to look at Oarzas to know this. The mage's gold hair looked silver, his fair skin like chalk, and even the red of his robe barely stood out against the pitch-dark wall at his back.

Oarzas walked to the altar. "Shall I sheathe it, Master?"

Nammuor nodded.

Still wearing his *lr*-rings, Oarzas touched the three triggers on the altar face, activating the deathstone to create an even more powerful null field around the Diadem. Not even light escaped, creating the appearance of a large black cylinder. The buzz in Nammuor's mind faded and he welcomed the void that followed. From the altar, Oarzas picked up a golden reliquary holding several glowing blood-red crystals and began closing the lid.

"I will return these to the vault."

"No. Bring them here."

When the coffer was held before him, Nammuor plucked one finger-long crystal from the midnight blue lining in which it nestled and held it to light. Beautiful. Even in this form, Highborn blood possessed such true red color it put every other shade to shame. Not muddled like human blood, it more resembled crimson honey. Of course, blood was just the binding principle. What gave each crystal its glow was the captured lifeforce. He could name each of his crystals, if he wished.

And each would vanish as a separate entity the moment he welded them into the Diadem. Two already were. Too bad it was such a painful process, or he would have incorporated these remaining crystals weeks ago.

Seven crystals remained. Nammuor had filled far more at Permephedon, but Dorilian had destroyed those and prevented the harvesting of more. Another of Nammuor's mages had been destroyed by sorcerous fire—along with the crystals he'd collected. Only one mage had carried crystals back to Mormantalorus.

Nine, all told—nine crystals laced with Highborn blood, the lifeforces within destined to feed the Diadem's infernal hunger. Nine—and the Diadem needed twelve to be made whole.

"Where am I to get three more, Oarzas?" There was, of course, only one answer. Nammuor needed more Highborn.

The sharp-faced mage ticked off the possibilities. "Four of the abominations cower in Essera. Tollech harbors an old man. And there's always the one in Sordan."

Nammuor's eyes narrowed. Was it insolence on Oarzas's part, the way he said it? A rebuke to remind Nammuor he had not yet moved against Dorilian?

"That one," he said, "I must get when he's away from the Rill." He carefully tucked the crystal back into the reliquary alongside its brothers.

Oarzas leaned nearer, showing sharp teeth. "Only Sordan's upper city and the Serat are fully dampened by that Entity. We can get agents on the island, mages even—"

"No." Others might understand Nammuor's hatred of Sordan's ruler, but they could not possibly grasp all the permutations of that hatred. The subtleties—or that hatred did not blind Nammuor to opportunity. "The Rill is a most interesting Entity, Oarzas. An *active* Entity. Its life is visible for all men to see. One hundred and fifty years ago, when Tarlon Sordaneon died, the Rill faltered. Just for a day, until Labran Sordaneon slipped the Rill Stone on his finger to activate the gift. Five years ago, when Labran died, the Rill didn't falter for even a moment. It didn't so much as stutter. It didn't even *notice*. Do you know why?"

Oarzas did not answer. Because the Rill did not run to Mormantalorus, it bred less fervent study—and worship—than in other lands. Why the Rill did anything held less fascination than the box in Nammuor's hands. The Highborn had been shown to have other uses, and men like Oarzas were more interested in discovering how to harness such power in crystals and create arcane arrays that made gods irrelevant. Even now Oarzas's gaze fixed upon the coffer and the power it promised.

Nammuor closed the golden lid, dousing the light from the blood crystals. He was feeling stronger again. Rising to his feet made him light-headed, and he handed over the reliquary for Oarzas to carry.

The dark, gleaming double doors separating the innermost sanctum from the mage cells and antechambers of the temple swung open. In the light of two bracketing waterglobes, Daimonaeris swept into the room, conveyed by Nammuor's most recent innovation—an apparatus-laden pavilion anchored upon a slave's broad shoulders, positioning Daimonaeris's head just above and behind that of her bearer. She had improved on the arrangement by having the slave wear a frame from which yards of silk, patterned in red and blue medallions, fell in vertical panels to conceal its head and upper arms, creating false shoulders. The contraption gave the impression of a stately dress, though it left the slave's eyes uncovered and peering outward from the chest piece like jewels. Those eyes, wide and lovely—surely the result of aristocratic bloodlines—were the reason Daimonaeris had chosen this slave over others Nammuor had offered. He had, to be sure, offered her only the best. A wide band of *lr*-jewels encircled his sister's forehead with gold points of fire.

"This slave is the best so far. It does everything I ask and protests only a little."

"It should not protest at all." Nammuor peered into the slave's eyes. Fear looked back at him, begging him not to implant more *lr*-triggered conditioning into its quivering brain. Already Daimonaeris's circlet gave her a high degree of control. She had only to order it to stop, or turn, or relieve itself, and it would.

"It picks things up, that I may smell them," she said. "I enjoy going to the gardens." She must have prodded the slave to go forward, because it did, moving around the silent Oarzas and his reliquary to stand beside the altar. "Hidden away again. I wanted to see it!"

"And you will, when my work is finished." Nammuor directed Oarzas to leave and was amused by how quickly the man placed the reliquary on its stand, then walked through the doors. Even the most skilled mages, those few who assisted in the work that kept his sister alive, found her present state disconcerting.

The slave turned so Daimonaeris might face Nammuor. She looked lovelier than she had in weeks, her lips tinted with deep plum rose and her eyes lined with lapis shadow. Her complexion looked healthy and pink, telling him the new pumps and filters were performing flawlessly. For now. Generating the life force needed to sustain her was taxing both the work hours of his mages and the supply of healthy young purebloods.

"I had hoped you would be done by now." Her smile was deliberately disarming. "Tomorrow is Bammon's birthday."

Nammuor forced a pleasant countenance. Daimonaeris failed to grasp the deliberation with which he plotted. She was fixated on regaining her son, who they had planned to name Bammon.

"It takes time to create blood crystals."

"Months?"

"If done properly. And then they must be mounted—in this case, perfectly, and very, very carefully." Walking to her, he reached up and tucked a stray tress of golden hair back into her elaborate crown of curls. "Allow me to do my work, sister. The Diadem of the Devaryati lives again. I feel the heat in its jeweled heart and taste its power. But it must be given more life still."

"Drain them all, if you must, so long as Dorilian is one of them."

"Oh, I look forward to that." Nammuor took the slave's elbow and guided Daimonaeris toward the sanctuary's great doors. Once Nammuor had passed through that portal, an oppression— corrugated, barbed—vacated his brain and released his spine. Exiting places of power was every bit as unpleasant as entering them. Acolytes stationed in the outer chamber closed the doors to secure the sanctuary. "But you must be patient, little Hierarchessa. Your husband is problematic. He lives in a fortress and is well protected. He is guarded by a god. I need him to be away from Sordan, or any active Rill installation. Only then can I be sure he will be without his Entity."

Mages of all ranks—acolytes in yellow tunics, black-robed probationaries, and even red-himation-wearing mages of the first order—stepped aside to let them pass. Other mages stood at their workbenches. Goldsmiths fashioned fittings for jewels to be worked into arrays. Crystalliers precisely cleaved newborn *lr* gems. Welders linked jewels far less dangerous than blood crystals and living diadems. Such work was the heart of Nammuor's enterprise.

Daimonaeris rolled her eyes. Scorn curved at the corners of her mouth. "Dorilian is afraid of the Rill. Deben instilled that fear in him, and the reports of our spies have been most thorough. He never calls upon it. It drove him mad that day he fled to Sordan to find me, everyone says so, and now he won't go near it. He even told that ridiculous Kheld ruler he would not set foot in Essera, just so he could forego using the Rill."

"His reluctance works to our advantage. However, until he grows complacent, or careless, killing him is going to be difficult. In the meantime, I have my Diadem to complete."

"Always your Diadem."

"Yes, my Diadem. *Our* Entity."

Now that they had passed the workbenches, they exited the Magistry by way of a dark vestibule and doors of the black, timeless metal for which Mormantalorus was famed. Tormented figures, images and shapes captive forever in the adamantine walls, twisted around them. Daimonaeris drank them with her eyes as Nammuor guided her, his hand still firmly on the slave, onto the nautilus corridor that ascended higher into the tower.

Nammuor did not live in the workshop. His private chambers were a floor above, an arrangement he preferred to the former Nuarch's Serat. Several years ago, soon after finding the Diadem, he had made the decision to reside in the same building as the heart of his obsession. The Ilgaon Tower, also known as the Tower of Fire, was a place of dangerous currents, perched upon a vein of wild energy that vibrated with the mysteries of crystal creation. Life and death were transmuted within its walls. In addition to the Magistry, where the most intensive crystal manipulation was done, the tower held a dozen halls where specialized work generated new kinds of beasts and distilled potent elixirs. Arts interdicted and forgotten after the Highborn defeat of the Aryati were now his nation's secret arsenal.

They reached a landing. A columned portico jutted out from the stairwell, overlooking a view of the city's elegant rings and the harbor beyond the ridge of hills, sculpted in the shapes of serpents, that guarded it from lava flows by shunting them toward the barren coast to the south.

"Stop," Daimonaeris said softly, and the slave obeyed. Nammuor's hand slipped from its elbow. He looked to Daimonaeris for an answer. Her golden gaze delved into his and he studied their depths, wondering that she and he could be siblings when his eyes were dark nearly to blackness. Of course, his own father, while noble, had been a mere Archmage, whereas hers... their mother had done well for herself after Nammuor's father had died. Daimonaeris's father had been Mormantalorus's Highborn ruler.

"Brother," and so began yet another complaint, "I am being so patient, but... I have no body still, after so many months."

At least she had learned not to complain about this in front of his mages. As it was, her constant reminders frayed his temper.

"I am doing all I can. I have tried dozens of times to attach a human head to another body, sacrificed dozens of slaves. None have survived more than a few days."

"But you won't use the Highborn crystals."

Immortal blood, holding a perpetual life force that could never be completely drained. Such power could well succeed where other blood crystals had failed. His mistake had been in letting her know their power.

"I have none to spare. I need twelve to reconstruct the Diadem. I have only nine."

"But you promised! When we killed them at Permephedon, you said you would harvest more than you needed."

Daimonaeris had helped him in that, but to what end? That she could be Hierarchessa, mother and regent of Sordan's Heir, and ruler over a nation. Nammuor's mage work interested her about as much as her poets and lute players interested him.

"I killed enough Highborn to fill forty-eight crystals with life!" Anger welled in Nammuor, black bile feeding his frustration. "If Dorilian had died as he was supposed to, and Marc Frederick with him, I would have had such a wealth of blood crystals I could then squander them on experiments. But I do not! I have *nine*!" He stalked along the portico, his red mage robe brushing the floor around his slippered feet. "Nine, Daimonaeris! And now I must find a way harvest the lives of men who are far away, are bound to Entities, and know that I am hunting them. Because I still need three crystals more. It's not like Highborn blood is found among the general population."

"I didn't mean to upset you!" Her voice filled with a throaty sob that surprised him. When he looked at Daimonaeris again, he saw tears flowing down her cheeks. His heart softened. She had always done whatever he needed of her. Had helped trap and kill her father, so that Nammuor might use Camas to free the Diadem. Had married one Sordaneon and conceived the child of another. Had poisoned the wine. But for her help...

"Ah, Hierarchessa." Nammuor touched his fingertips to Daimonaeris's wet cheek. "Don't you see? I made a grave error. I went for a grand victory and came up small. I wasted all those men and now I must scrounge for what I need. But I will be more careful this time. I will take them living. The Highborn are no different from other creatures, from the slaves we breed. They, too, can be bred."

Understanding lifted her eyelids and he saw fear behind her

tremulous smile. "But you will not use my son. Bammon's important!"

"Have no fear for little Bammon, Hierarchessa. My plans for him are much greater."

"Promise. Promise you will not harm him, even if you should wed and sire a child of your own."

"I promise." It was an easy promise to make. Women and men attracted Nammuor equally, which was to say not at all. He had always been more driven to pursue his work, and now the Diadem was the only consort he craved. Nammuor left the making of children to others. Politically, his sister's child was a far more interesting heir.

The slave's eyes blinked at him from the jeweled bodice of Daimonaeris's dress. Lovely eyes, very like agates with the gold color darkening toward the rims, but alert and intelligent. A sorry turn of events, really. Its ability to hear was a matter of his sister's comfort and safety—but in this case, perhaps it had heard too much. A pity. Daimonaeris liked this one. It hadn't been easy to find a pureblood slave of the height and beauty Daimonaeris favored. But there were always more slaves. If Nammuor couldn't find another similarly well-bred creature in the City's stock, he would commission one to be captured afield.

"Brother," Daimonaeris said again, to recapture his attention. "This Diadem, when it's finished, will you use it to kill him?"

He laughed. She meant Dorilian, of course. The young man had made quite an enemy for himself when he had robbed his sister of her body. He tugged at the slave's arm again, guiding it toward the stairs once more. Daimonaeris needed her rest. And Nammuor... he looked forward to being very creative indeed in silencing the slave.

"Oh, far better than that, little sister. I will kill him, of course. And then I will kill the Wall and the Rill."

9

"Nothing. After months of promises."

Emyli felt sorry for Palimia Kastryonis. Other than that the pretty widow had been her father's last mistress, Emyli barely knew her. "It's just the bequest letter that was revoked," she explained, "the house and the stipend attached to it. You may keep any other gifts he gave you, of course."

"But not my home." Palimia carefully folded the document again. She tucked it back into its vellum envelope and fingered the broken seal, before lifting her gaze to take in the quiet comfort of the canal-front villa with its faded appointments and broad doors open to a summer garden.

Marc Frederick had left her the property in a letter she had dutifully presented to his heir. Emyli felt heartsick knowing Stefan had revoked the small bequest in exchange for Apollonia's vote for Cullen Brodheson's recent lordship.

"Thank you, Princess, for telling me my fate in person." Palimia slid Stefan's letter into the pocket of her skirt. "I shall need to find another place to live. Might you persuade your son to give me a few days to pack my belongings?"

Emyli was relieved to be able to extend a kindness. "Of course," she promised. "I hope you know I tried."

Palimia made a show of rearranging the flowers in an alabaster vase on one of the tables. Yellow kite-tail lilies and blue asters. Late summer flowers. "It's just as well," she said. Her light voice sounded cheerful at this new adventure, but Emyli detected a thickness that prevented Palimia's words from being convincing. "I have family in Ilmar. My mother is getting on in years."

"Well, then, I suppose you must…"

Palimia turned and smiled brightly. "Yes."

Emyli studied her for a moment, then smiled in return. She also rose. "I'll tell Stefan you won't contest the decision."

"I won't."

"Thank you." As Emyli crossed the villa's simple foyer, she turned to say one thing more. "If you need a place to stay—"

"I'll be able to arrange something, I'm sure."

They stood in the open doorway overlooking a garden leading down to one of Dazunor-Rannuli's less-traveled canals. Steps led to a small landing where Emyli's gond awaited, its canopy as brightly colored as the flowers lining the banks.

"You have to travel through Sordan, surely. I know how impossible that's become."

"Thank you," Palimia said, "but I was born in Sordan. My family was well thought of there while my father lived. I think I'll be able to persuade Sordan's port authorities that my reasons for entering the City have nothing to do with Esseran trade."

No, save that one of Stefan's reasons for acceding to Apollonia's demands had been because of Palimia's land of birth, even though for all her adult life she had lived in Dazunor. Gazing into the woman's soft brown eyes, Emyli saw only deep sadness and none of the bitterness or anger she had feared. "Of course." She was only a little reassured, and angrier than ever at Stefan for breaking Marc Frederick's promise to this woman.

"I appreciate, I really do, that you came to me in person." Palimia remained gracious, even though doing so had to be painful.

"My father would have wanted that."

They parted, both leaving unsaid that Marc Frederick would have wanted much more.

Palimia walked onto the Rill platform, a leather travel bag on her arm and a transit voucher in her pocket. Signs of the tension between Essera and Sordan were everywhere. Soldiers crowded the platform lest Sordan should use the Rill to deliver troops, undesirables, or spies. More soldiers checked the papers of travelers, intent on stopping Stefan's targeted enemies from fleeing. Palimia had little worry they would stop her.

All she had ever been in Essera was now the stuff of memories. She had known two husbands: a forced marriage as a girl and a later marriage for companionship. Her first husband's family had divested her of her family's assets. Her second husband, though kindly, had left her with nothing but his good name. And now Marc Frederick, her most wonderful of companions, her robust lover of a thousand interests and surprises, was gone—and with him what little was left of her security. His assurances that she would not want for anything had been reduced to words others chose not to honor.

With a sigh, she looked out over the city where she had lived for so many years. Dazunor-Rannuli glittered, a lacework of small lakes and canals connected to the mighty river that tied it to an empire. Upon the highest ground sat the Rill Mount, linked to the rest of the city by five bridges. Barge docks crowded the Mount's base, dense with warehouses and holding yards. Higher still was the walled, secluded temple and school of the Order of Epoptes. Above all these things soared the Rill itself. White as bone, its monumental structures and surreal rings—twelve to the north and twelve to the south—dwarfed all else.

Given Palimia's changed circumstances, Sordan was at least a viable option. Her mother was indeed getting on in years and depended on her support. Now the means of that support were gone. She had only a modest amount of money—a pittance, really— though selling her horses, gond, and carriage had yielded enough to meet her expenses for relocation. She would soon need to add to her funds by selling more of the gifts Marc Frederick had bestowed during her time with him.

Clutching her voucher, Palimia walked with fellow passengers into the just-summoned *charys*, found an unoccupied cradle, and waited until the door simply vanished and the *charys* became a seamless shell. The interior glowed, a gossamer cocoon of light. Portions of the shell cleared, no longer opaque. Though people outside could not see into a *charys*, those within now had an unimpeded view: the next wave of passengers waiting for the Rill heading north to Permephedon; a flock of yellow-robed acolytes striding along the colonnade; the shining lace of the city's canals stretching to the broad, dawn-silvered ribbon of the Dazun River. A fine vibration, not quite a hum, alerted Palimia and she drew a breath. Having traveled by Rill before, she relaxed as the *charys* shell contracted, eliminating walking space around the seating area and securing each passenger. No one panicked, a welcome sign this trip would not be disturbed by the cries of the inexperienced.

She heard the first whine of Rill-shift as the platform outside faded. The initial low thrum registered in her ears and vibrated beneath her breastbone—then the terminal and everything in it appeared to burst apart. Many passengers preferred to experience the journey with eyes closed, but Palimia held hers open, exhilarated to see Essera vanish in a heartbeat, replaced by flowing streams of green, white, and turquoise. Between one heartbeat and the next, those streams broke into streaks of dark gray and rich emerald, then emerged into strands of bright golds and blues that gently coalesced as the *charys* thrummed and slowed. Her body felt only the slightest of tugs, and the light broke apart again into a lake, an island, trees and flowers—and a City soaring white and tall upon silver cliffs.

The passengers exited onto the platform. The *charys* dissolved, leaving the concave transport slip empty.

Palimia crossed the platform, then paused to breathe deeply of the orange-scented air. No matter how often she saw it, she marveled at the majestic planes and stepped terraces of the Sordaneon Serat. The Hierarch's palace, built on a level with the Rill port, rested just above the Upper City. Below, the tumult of the Lower City descended toward a harbor dotted with all manner of ships. That vision of prosperity fortified her. Holding tightly to her Letter of Repatriation, obtained only two days before from the Hierarchate, Palimia proceeded with the other passengers, queueing for approval to enter the City.

By evening, she had secured a modest apartment in a declining but still respectable quarter of the Lower City, on a tree-lined street overlooking the lake. The Rill loomed overhead with great sweeping branches, its glow painting the city silver.

When morning came, she would undertake the last of her promises to Marc Frederick.

It took two days of waiting in antechambers and answering crisp questions from one of the Hierarch's several secretaries before her petition was approved for inclusion on Dorilian's calendar. From having seen Marc Frederick's schedules, Palimia knew how her entry would appear: *G. Palimia Kastryonis. Consideration of S-R royal document. Personal.* She was to go to the Serat the next day, take a seat in the waiting area with other petitioners, and wait in hope the Hierarch would decide to receive her that day. If he did not, she was not to return.

Why am I doing this? I despise royal courts. But after this, she would have no more reason to frequent the halls of aristocracy.

While walking downhill from the Upper City, Palimia tarried. She stopped at a baker for bread and purchased white cheese and a pot of spicy orange preserves from one of the artisans who catered to Sordan's nobility. Although decimated a generation ago by Essera's hard-handed occupancy, that nobility now appeared robust and decidedly prosperous. Palimia had seen several grand residences being renovated on the way. Had things been different, her father might have lived in such a house. Now his daughter must attempt to find a position, perhaps as a governess or secretary, in the household of some aristocrat who should have been her peer.

The next day, following a plain breakfast, Palimia donned a long chiton of palest lavender silk, then tied a widow's cloak of thin, pewter-hued wool so it covered one shoulder. On her bared right arm, she wore one of Marc Frederick's gifts, a gold armband patterned with silver wire and a central medallion of amethyst glass. She did not go early to secure a more favorable seat, but appeared at the time directed and found a bench in a corner with good light. She had barely been seated when a tall, bright-haired man wearing Sordaneon colors of emerald and silver entered the room. Heads snapped up to follow his progress as he emerged from between gilded doors carved with the Sordaneon eagle crest and crossed the floor. Toward her.

Any doubt Palimia's name had caught the Hierarch's eye vanished. She remembered Legon Rebiran.

"Lady." Legon stopped before her and spoke softly. "Come with me."

Dorilian looked at his morning calendar and circled one name. This one. Gracious Palimia Kastryonis. Her old husband had died, and she had been, for over a year, Marc Frederick's mistress. As for what this was about…. Dorilian's informants in Stefan's court had mentioned a bequest denied by the king. Without her lover and now without property, she most likely needed funds.

Dorilian was neither in the mood nor position to rescue *all* of Stefan's victims.

This one, though… the note beside her name mentioned a document. He would not dismiss her until he knew what it was.

He looked up when Legon brought her in. Palimia was as Dorilian remembered: slim and graceful, artfully dressed in a way that was, in his court, slightly old-fashioned. But lovely. She had always been that.

"Your Thrice Royal Grace." Palimia knelt on both knees and bowed deeply, forearms on the floor with palms facing up. She understood how to present herself.

She kept her head lowered, eyes closed, waiting on him.

"A most unusual petition." Dorilian signaled to his chief secretary and ordered the man to leave the stone desk to one side of the dais. Best to have no one record this conversation. When the door closed, only Legon and Tiflan remained in the room with them. "I would like to help you, but my secretary did not specify what manner of Stauberg-Randolph document you are offering."

With head still lowered, Palimia reached into the large bag at her side and pulled out a hefty envelope.

"I'm not interested in love letters," he warned.

"You will be interested in this." From inside the envelope, she retrieved a book thick with pages. "The last two years of Marc Frederick's life."

He had braced himself to hear the name. Braced himself that he might be asked to confront intimacies. But this—

"His *journal*?"

Was it possible? The late king had been an energetic writer of diaries. Dorilian had thought all the volumes had been kept at Gustan and passed to Emyli or Stefan.

Palimia raised her head enough to meet his disbelieving gaze. "Marc left it with me, at our house in Dazunor-Rannuli, the morning he departed for Permephedon to meet with you." She ducked her head again, perhaps guessing it was best not to proceed further into what had happened that day. "I had to leave my house recently, and—"

"I know, Lady. I know, too, that you've been selling things off."

He saw her shoulders tense and heard her indrawn breath, and realized he had shamed her. She had not wanted to sell anything. She would have kept it all, if she could have, for memories and might-have-beens.

"Marc always told me never to turn away a gift, that I would find a use for every one of them someday." Palimia's voice slipped from tears toward laughter. "I never guessed he would be so right."

"He was always right."

Dorilian rose and walked down the silver steps from the dais. When he reached her, he extended his hand. If Marc Frederick was anywhere to be found in this miserable excuse of a world, perhaps it would be here… if the book was truly his journal and not some bit of malice concocted by Stefan.

Gaze downcast, Palimia held it out.

He took it and, distracted, walked away as he turned the pages. Yes, this was Marc Frederick's writing. Even paper and ink held enough of that man's unique signature for Dorilian to detect him on each page. The way the writing flowed as if crafted art. Marc Frederick had owned so fine a hand at letters, Dorilian had modeled his own script after it. And the words….

I have acquired a new guest….

Their Gustan year. All of it. Dorilian flipped to the back. Everything up until the morning the king had traveled—filled with hope, not suspecting he was doomed—to Permephedon for a treaty that should have been his crowning achievement.

These pages sang of everything that had ever existed between them.

A table ringed by wide chairs upholstered in emerald brocade stood before a wall of windows, and a view of city and harbor that made a perfect backdrop for diplomats. Dorilian seated himself in the carved chair at the table's head and kicked his feet up onto the polished surface. He went back to the beginning and turned another page.

"I could seize this collection of writings as vital to my state's interest, you know." He glanced over for a moment to measure Palimia's response. She looked remarkably serene. He resumed reading. "How much do you want for it?"

Opportunity dangled. Surely she knew he would pay a great deal, a king's ransom, for what this book contained. She would be justified. Marc Frederick might not disapprove, given that his heir had treated her shabbily. She might even suspect Dorilian, knowing her circumstances, would not hold it against her. He had resources to spare.

"One thing only, Your Thrice Royal Grace. Allow me to rise? And be seated?"

It was an incredibly bold request, one that caused Tiflan to lift one eyebrow.

Dorilian flicked a glance at her, deciding if he should be affronted. She did appear to be uncomfortable. He signaled for her to rise and join him at the table.

"Surely you want more for this heirloom than my indulgence, Lady." He waited while Tiflan showed her to a seat at the table. One at the far end of the table. Dorilian continued to keep his feet up, little caring for her opinion of his manners.

Palimia flashed Tiflan a smile of thanks. "Nothing, Thrice

Royal. My only goal was to see the book into your hands—as Marc would have wanted."

"Is that what he told you?"

"No. He said only that if something happened to him, I would know what to do. After I read for a bit… I did know. I knew it was meant for you."

What might her motives be? The intimate memoirs of a king could be either opportunity or peril, and she looked unafraid of either. Was it possible she felt only peace at having fulfilled the wishes of a man she had loved?

Dorilian released her from his gaze and turned to Tiflan. "I won't be seeing anyone else this morning. Handle any petitions you can and move the others to another day." He sank back in his chair, seeking comfort, and turned to the first page of the journal. To Palimia, he said, without looking up. "You may go. Legon will see you safely home."

Palimia's small apartment occupied the far corner of a rundown building that had formerly housed students attending a nearby academy. After the academy had closed, the dwelling converted to serving travelers who paid by the week and didn't mind having to carry water up three floors from the cistern. A vestige of gentility still clung to the walls. The pavement outside was swept, the house painted a hopeful shade of coral. Palimia liked the color and that the apartment's main room opened onto a tiny balcony from which, if she leaned over a railing and peered around a corner, she could see a sliver of lake. At the moment, however, she noted only the cracks in the walls, the flaking paint on the ceiling, and how the formerly fine carpet was too faded and worn to afford either padding or beauty. The few pieces of tired furniture offered scant comfort to guests, which she regretted.

Hearing the bell that announced someone at her door had been a shock, but opening it to find Dorilian Sordaneon standing at her doorstep had stolen her power of speech for several long moments. That he had come incognito she knew because her landlord's broom briskly and loudly swept the stairs, and the building's courtyard echoed with the happy cries of children at play. A formal visit would have silenced both.

"Your Thrice Royal Grace, I did not expect—"

Palimia's extensive experience as a hostess gave her the presence of mind to bid him enter. He had caught her half-dressed and her chiton was barely presentable, light and modest, though clean. Her hair fell about her shoulders in a tangle, held back from her face by a pair of hastily pinned jeweled combs.

"I thought this would be more private," he said.

Her mind raced around what those words might mean. He had come with only two men. Legon had entered with him and now leaned against a wall across the room, and a hulking retainer named Tutto stood outside the door, his attention fixed on the street.

She stood beside her barren sideboard, wondering what to do next as Sordan's ruler sat in the room's only chair, foregoing the couch she'd placed near the window for the breeze. His tunic of fine creamy linen and fawn cotton breeches had been chosen to downplay his station yet still managed to seem too elegant for his surroundings.

"I've delved into your situation," he said. "The journal clearly states your lover's wish that you receive property upon his death."

She bowed her head, looking at her folded hands. "It says a lot of things."

"You could have used it to support your case."

"It wouldn't have mattered. The letter was even clearer, and a legal document besides. It was authenticated by Marc's secretary and five Archhalial clerks."

Palimia glanced up again, aware of how bureaucratic it all sounded. Dorilian looked sympathetic, and very young. At least he was willing to listen. "I submitted the letter three times," she explained, "the last time to King Stefan personally. He kept the letter, that time, and sent me a response, handwritten, saying the bequest could not be granted because the property was entailed as a crown estate. He expressed his regrets."

Though she tried to sound dispassionate, her emotions burdened the words with bitterness. She had wished to keep that house and the trove of memories it held: Marc Frederick's laughter waiting around corners, his sensibility in furnishings and his smell still haunting the upholstery. The house and the small annual stipend attached to it would have been enough, with her frugal habits, to preserve her comfort.

"Stefan's an ass. I have not seen the letter, of course. Likely, it has been destroyed. However, the dead king's journal clearly states his wish that you should receive the villa in Dazunor-Rannuli. Had he known his heir would not honor his wishes, he would have done it differently, or given you a different house."

It was strange, she thought, how Dorilian avoided saying Marc

Frederick's name. The two had been close, antagonists at first but at the last fiercely united in defending some hard-won ground between them that few understood—and now he would not speak Marc Frederick's name, as if it were too hated to pass his lips, or too intimate. What Dorilian, the last man to see Marc Frederick alive, recalled of those final moments, no one knew.

"We were not lovers very long, Thrice Royal. A year only. Though Marc said he wished me to have the house, and gave me the letter, we never thought it would be needed so soon. After his death, to stay in the house we had shared—I wanted that. But aristocratic affairs are complicated, and Apollonia felt the need to make a statement."

"Which she did."

"Oh, royally," Palimia agreed.

He laughed, his amusement knife-edged. No one knew the workings of royalty better than he, who had been born into those acid coils.

"She cannot harass you here." Pride sharpened Dorilian's words. "I will make sure they leave you alone. She's afraid of me; they all are. Stefan most of all." He looked around the apartment, taking in the details: bare walls and broken slats shading the window. Palimia cringed at what he must think. She doubted this man had ever set foot in so shabby a dwelling. The Sordaneons slept on beds of gold, in rooms of pearl. "Are you bringing your mother to Sordan?" he asked. "You'll need a bigger place, with running water."

Where had he learned about her mother? No doubt he had set people to inquire into her family and marriages, her history, all the tiny details of her common little life. She drew herself straighter, to head him off. "I am looking—"

"Stop looking. I intend to make good on your lover's promise to you."

Palimia stared at him, not in hope, but with a sudden, new fear. There was real danger in getting caught up in this Highborn prince's battle with Stefan. Even more than others of his notably vindictive family, Dorilian could be terrifyingly single-minded.

Watching her with an unnerving, catlike intensity, he continued. "Your lover had a house in the Upper City, did you know that?"

"No. But Thrice Royal, I cannot—"

"The Songbird Palace. No one's living there now, of course."

Of course not. The idea that Stefan or any of the Stauberg-Randolphs would venture into Sordan, much less take up residence, was a political impossibility. But Dorilian's proposal veered along a road that ended at a cliff.

"Please, Thrice Royal, I didn't come here to seek anything for myself. I gave you the journal. I fulfilled a trust!"

"As will I, by appointing you administrator of your late lover's assets here in Sordan. There are other buildings—warehouses, for the most part, but also farms and mines, not to mention stocks of grain and ores that are currently stagnating—and he kept considerable deposits of precious metals in his own name here and in Hestya. I have, for months now, not allowed those monies or properties to be sold off or transferred."

His gaze terrified her. In it lurked something vengeful, but also incisive and calculating in a way she had never seen before. Even Marc Frederick, a man so crafty the Malyrdeons had deferred to his vision for their nation, had not shown her such a deliberative quality, fixed on far-flung consequences. What Dorilian proposed had very little to do with her, save that it allowed him to honor a ghost.

"Essera believes I will confiscate the Stauberg-Randolph's conveniently placed wealth the way Stefan confiscated my holdings in his domains. I am not going to do that. It pleases me more to hold the assets in trust. You can live in the residences, if you wish—or not, that will be up to you. I think doing so will allow you better to maintain them. In return for overseeing the estate, you will receive a fee of a tenth portion of any monies earned, beginning with what has been earned thus far. My treasurer will reconcile the books twice each year."

"I am not qualified!"

"I disagree."

How did one argue with a Sordaneon? Here, in his own city, Dorilian could do whatever he wanted. If only Marc Frederick were still alive, he could advise her how to proceed. He alone had known how to make this young godling see reason. All Palimia knew for certain was that everything Dorilian proposed had purposeful shape, like a javelin—sharp, deadly, and perfectly thrown at Stefan and Apollonia.

Dorilian accepted her stunned silence with a rare smile. Perhaps he saw that she recognized his maneuver. "There will be protests, naturally, but nothing that will require your attention. You are completely outside any authority but mine. Petitions filed with the Archhalia will not alter my decision, and any resolution to the contrary will be unenforceable unless Stefan should launch—and win—a war. I don't fear that possibility, and neither should you."

Palimia had few arguments left, but she deployed one of them. "Stefan hates you already; why provoke him further?"

"Because doing so amuses me." Dorilian rose and nodded to Legon, who left—no doubt to make ready their horses.

"Thrice Royal, out of loyalty to the memory of my late liege, I cannot accept any position that would embarrass or harm his family."

"They harmed—and humiliated—you."

"Humiliation, yes. But I was not harmed. I left Marc with no less than I came to him, and I kept my dignity throughout. I would not now impoverish his heirs."

"Nor would I, Lady." Dorilian appeared amused by her protests. "Your own words provide the reason why I can entrust you with his property. You will preserve the properties far better than some Esseran money counter who would rob Stefan blind, or some appointee of mine who might be tempted to divert funds. You have no loyalty to Stefan now, after what he did—you also are only moderately loyal to me. Your true loyalty belongs to a man who lies in a grave and to whom I owe a debt of promises I am sworn to keep. I respect your allegiance to him, so long as you honor my place as your Hierarch. This, I believe you will do. Your charge will be twofold: preserve the inheritance for the day I determine it can be returned to the Stauberg-Randolphs, and in the meantime, prevent them and others from using it against me."

"Thank you, Thrice Royal." The enormity of the implied trust rendered any further opposition silent.

Dorilian had just reached the door when he turned back to her and flashed another of his smiles. "A year from now, you are going to thank me for setting you free. It'll be fun. You'll see."

He left without waiting to hear if she had any opinion on the matter.

I pick my battles carefully. Marc Frederick had said those words to her on one of the many occasions when talk of Dorilian had crept into their conversation. *I can make him yield, but no man yields on every occasion.*

So what would Palimia gain by resisting this plan? Poverty? Hardship? An employer who might be kind, or odious, or take advantage?

Dorilian's offer did not demean her. On the contrary, by placing her in guardianship of Marc Frederick's assets, he had found a way to restore her lover to her. If Palimia were clever, she could both honor Marc Frederick and safeguard his legacy, all with the tacit approval of a man she knew to be dedicated to Marc Frederick's memory.

She leaned against the door, astonished, a smile on her lips.

10

"Is he insane?" In his rage, Stefan swept the inkwell from his desk to the floor, little caring that he stained a priceless rug.

"Not as insane as you are right now." Cullen glared at Erenor Tholeros, who had delivered the message, before he returned his attention to Stefan. "Dorilian sticks a thorn in your shoe and you go jumping around like a fool, just like he wants. Laugh him off."

"Don't you see what he's doing?" Stefan waved a sheaf of papers at both men. "First, he gives control over all my assets in Sordan to my grandfather's *mistress*, the woman I just promised Apollonia I'd give *nothing*—and, as if that's not bad enough, now he's trying to get at my throne through my *mother*!"

"Let him try. She'd never do it. Come on, it's not like he doesn't expect you to crush his proposal anyway."

Erenor said nothing, though his frown suggested he, at least, understood Stefan's right to be enraged. Stefan already had Apollonia haranguing him about Palimia being handed Marc Frederick's Sordan properties—the richness of which put that flowerpot-sized house in Dazunor-Rannuli to shame—but now *this*? Stefan threw the document on his desk.

The door opened and Emyli entered, wary. She held her shoulders rigid and back, her posture alert as she took note of the tension in the room.

Stefan could not have kept the growl from his voice had he tried. "Have you been communicating with Dorilian Sordaneon?"

"Dorilian?" She looked genuinely startled. "No! Why would I?"

"Because he sent this." He picked up the papers again. "A

petition proposing marriage! To you! Are you telling me you didn't know of it?"

"How could I have? You intercept all my communications."

Her reminder rubbed salt into the wound at the root of that necessity. Every time Stefan thought he might trust her again, something like this happened. He had caught her sending notes to people. Palaistea, for one, who had apparently chosen Emyli to whom to complain about being restricted from taking up residence at Stauberg. Stefan had reached the conclusion women complicated his life on purpose.

"So you knew nothing?"

"No. And I still know nothing."

He handed her the document and watched her expression as she scanned each page. Her eyes opened wide, and she caught her breath.

"This is a legitimate proposal!"

It was, as Stefan knew beyond certainty, far more than that. "Get past the part where he tells you how much he respects you and grandfather's memory. And the part where he says how rich he is and that he's a god among men and the prize bull of all the world in bed. Get to the part where he sets out in detail the treaty our domains would make. Rill allotments and lands to be entailed to you and any offspring—including succession rights to Sordan and *this* kingdom. *My* kingdom. That's what this whole damn thing is about. He's as transparent as air."

"But succession to *his* Hierarchate also?" Emyli looked skeptical.

"He's setting me up! He already has a son, doesn't he? Well, any child you give him would be a son also—a Highborn son! Every god-stupid, cock-sucking Staubaun in this land would choose a Highborn heir over a Kheld one—over *me*!"

"Stefan, don't you see? Dorilian is playing a game—pitting us against each other. I have no intention of entertaining this offer."

"That's for certain!" As if Stefan would let his mother marry his archenemy—

"I would never go against your wishes. I wish you would believe that."

"I want to."

Emyli handed back the papers. "I don't think this proposal needs to be taken as an insult. There is nothing in it that's offensive."

"Except the insult of even trying. After what he did at my coronation? After he pronounced me *dead* to him?" Why did she have to look at him that way? Always pleading for him to understand where he was wrong, when she was the one who never quite grasped the big picture. Stefan turned to Erenor. "You and I will draft a response. We'll be diplomatic"—he shot a look at his mother— "offer him another bride. Nobody Highborn, of course. Maybe one of the Red Quarter's more famous whores."

Erenor laughed, but Emyli looked dismayed. Cullen stepped forward.

"We're going to talk before you write anything," said Cullen. "You said I could interrupt you, any time I wanted—well this is one of those times."

Stefan knew what Cullen was doing, cooling him off. That he would do it in front of Erenor and Emyli showed how strongly he felt about stepping in. With a gesture for Erenor and Emyli to leave, Stefan relaxed only when the door had closed behind them.

"Hells, Stefan." Cullen slumped onto the bench in front of the window.

"That proposal's a slap at my face. He's making a play for my throne."

"Maybe not." Cullen cut Stefan off with a look. "Just listen. You said you would, and I'm calling you on it." He sighed and shook his head. "Dorilian's an ass sometimes, but he's not a liar. Either he would honor that agreement—or he is damn sure you'd do exactly what you're doing now and make a fool of yourself."

"And you don't want me to make a fool of myself. I understand. But I can't keep taking shots on the chin from that bastard."

"You don't take a shot if nothing comes of it. He says you're dead to him, so play dead. Let your mother handle this. Trust me, other people will laugh at that petition. A few might want her to do it, if you let out about it. But your lady mother has a say, a Kheld woman's say, and she sure as hells doesn't want *him* for a husband. All I'm saying is don't step up to take a shot at him. Don't give him the satisfaction of seeing he upset you. Either he *would* make your mother his Hierarchessa and he won't get her, which is a slap to *his* face—or he wants you to do something stupid and you don't, which is better."

Cullen was right. Again. Stefan slammed the papers in his hand onto the desk.

"It's not just him, Cullen. If the nobles hear about this, they'll start wanting Highborn heirs instead of Stauberg-Randolph. And when my mother refuses Dorilian as a husband, one thing I'm sure of is *my* highest nobles will start sending envoys in secret trying to arrange marriages with *their* daughters." Daughters they would rather marry off to stupid Dorilian instead of him—and he was their king.

"Come on, Stefan, you know they're doing it anyway, and you know why he'll refuse. He despises those lords! They would have stood by you and let him be imprisoned, you know, so there's no love lost between him and them. He would never wed one of their daughters. And besides, Sordan's Hierarch can't wed just anybody. He needs a princess—or a queen. That's why your mother makes real sense. That's why some folk will think it's a good idea. And that's why you have to treat this as something *other* than a joke."

Stefan nodded. "You write the response."

Cullen smiled. "I will. You'll have it by daybreak and can send it right back by Rill before he eats breakfast."

Stefan nodded. It felt good to know this matter would be done and gone before he traveled downriver to Trulo. "But this whole thing brings up another point." He met Cullen's gaze with hard purpose in his frown. "I need to see to the succession, *my* succession. It's time I take a wife."

"Thank you, Cullen, for making my son see reason."

Her son's friend, and now Enlad of Heddros, Minister of Trade, had sought Emyli out, hoping to put her mind to rest. She had long encouraged that friendship and was happy to see it enduring so well.

"Dorilian has just to breathe for Stefan to take offense. It's a wonder the two haven't caused a full-out war between them." Cullen had entered her apartment but declined to sit, saying he regretted he would not be staying more than a few minutes. He stood, minister's cap in hand. "Just thought you'd want to know you won't be asked to marry, and you shouldn't worry any trouble will come of it. I don't think Dorilian will take it too hard, being turned down. To be honest, I think he knows it will end this way. He does lots of things just to make Stefan angry. I wish he wouldn't, but"—he shrugged— "that's the two of them. I wonder, though, if Dorilian might do it, marry you." A mournful half-frown replaced the shrug. "I think he revered your father enough to do him the honor. And I know him well enough I don't think he makes offers he wouldn't follow through on."

"No, I'm sure you're right." Cullen's conjecture that Dorilian had opened the door to joining his bloodline with Marc Frederick's sent her thoughts racing. It was, Emyli thought, the sort of gesture someone who loved her father would make. To have Highborn grandchildren had been her father's greatest wish.

"I'll word it politely and make sure my name's on it, under yours, instead of Stefan's. Dorilian doesn't have it against me the way he does most Khelds."

"I would like that. Thank you." That the response would be private pleased her. "I hope Stefan realizes I am more surprised, even, than he. I haven't sought a husband at all."

"I think he'd be happiest if you didn't."

"That won't be a concern. I am very happy without one." Emyli lifted her face and smiled. "And what of you? I hear you're soon to wed Asphalladra?"

"In two weeks. I've near finished the house I'm building for her. The Thegnard said it's acceptable to have craftsmen do the final work, as long as I pay for it myself, so that's how I'm going. Her father, of course, says it's not good enough, but Stefan gave me one of the Sordaneon estates with a palace on it, so I figure I've got things covered."

Emyli laughed. If she had borne a daughter, she would have adored having this man court her. But Cullen looked sober again.

"It's not my choice that will present a problem," he said. "It's Stefan. All this got him to deciding he needs a wife, and he's right about that. He told me to set about finding one for him."

"But that's wonderful!" One of Emyli's great worries was that Stefan had no wife and, thus, no heir. There was a bastard daughter in Eastmeary, or so Stefan liked to claim, though the mother had admitted upon questioning that the child was as likely to be Cullen's or some other lad's.

"Might be. But his nobles are going to have a problem with it. Stefan doesn't want a noble wife. He wants a Kheld bride. I leave for Rhodhur right after my wedding, to confer with the clan chiefs."

"Kheld? But he needs an alliance."

Cullen shook his head. "The only alliance Stefan wants is with the Thegnkeld."

Palaistea would be the perfect match. The perfect queen for a land torn apart by differences Stefan would be wise to heal. Beautiful, heiress to two domains, with a bloodline none could question. Indeed, it would have made a great deal more sense for Dorilian to have sought to marry Palaistea himself. Why would that man propose instead to marry Emyli? Only as part of a silly game?

No. Dorilian understood a proposal from him would put Palaistea in danger.

Stefan had raged about that, too. About the danger posed by Palaistea and her two sons, Highborn and already heir to Essera's most ancient princedoms and richest domains, about how some of his high nobles wanted their king to marry her. And Stefan was just as angry thinking one or another high noble might cast a greedy eye Palaistea's way. Just three weeks past, Stefan had forbidden Palaistea and her sons from establishing residence at Stauberg, their hereditary seat—a city Stefan feared could be turned against him.

Dorilian had sidestepped that woman as he might sidestep an act of war. Sidestepped, and deflected. The thought tightened on Emyli's heart. Much as she wished to ignore him, Dorilian's instincts were Highborn-acute, sharpened on a whetstone of paranoia Stefan himself had provided.

Stefan, oh Stefan. Make an alliance with one of Essera's powerful families, please! Why not choose the Malyrdeons, as my father did?

Stefan's choice of bride would make a statement he loved more. He didn't want a Highborn kingdom, even with him as its ruler. He wanted to supplant one.

As she studied Cullen's tense face, Emyli knew she was not the only one afraid of what lay ahead.

11

"It's so… dazzling!"

Palimia stood on the wharf in Hestya and gazed at the gold-hued Lissam Palace. At her side, Dorilian looked pleased. He also looked relaxed, his body tall and easy, his gray gaze free of the cold reserve for which he was so famous. That he accompanied her on this tour of Marc Frederick's properties was nothing short of monumental. They had traveled by boat, first across the lake and then up the river. She had heard Dorilian had not traveled by Rill since Stefan's coronation a year earlier.

"I designed the outer wall," he said, pointing it out. She followed the strong line of his arm, marking how martial the movement was, how suited to a leader. He had an actor's instinct for movement.

"And I shall stay there?"

"You shall have your own apartment. I cannot imagine you staying anywhere else. After all, your properties here consist of warehouses and feed yards."

True, but Marc Frederick had owned *lots* of those. Over the past six months, Palimia had gained a firm grasp of the late king's holdings and found to her astonishment that she controlled a fortune. Her portion as administrator provided an annual income greater than the proceeds of a Rill slot portion. She was now, without a doubt, a rich woman. Her first act had been to move her mother and widowed sister into the jewel box of a palace Marc Frederick had owned in Sordan's Upper City. Her second was this accompanied trip to the thriving grain port of Hestya, where the bulk of Marc Frederick's Sordan assets were located.

Once within Lissam Palace, she found that the apartment Dorilian had promised consisted of several chambers for herself and her staff—she had hired a lady's maid to attend her and an old scribe to help her catalog the assets—as well as a spacious bath, kitchen, and garden. Dorilian provided her with a cook and gardener. Leaving her maid to unpack, Palimia visited two of the properties in town, then returned to the palace to rest for the remainder of the hot afternoon.

When she awakened, she found a summons to dinner. Dorilian did not issue invitations.

Legon escorted her to the royal residences dwelling, which occupied the highest floors of the main, heavily guarded building. Everything about the palace bore Dorilian's stamp. Magnificent rooms filled with light greeted her; floors of soft white stone yielded to carpets of rich earth hues beneath high ceilings supported by gold-veined pillars. To one side, a terrace rimmed with sandstone perched high above the city, looking out at the Rill mount and, beyond it, the copper ribbon of Hestya's sunset-gilded river.

Dorilian waited, looking as casual as she had ever seen him, clad in a plain white chiton with only sandals strapped upon his feet.

He guided her to a table set with a simple yet exquisite repast. Dishes of quail hearts in wine and delicate rolls of nearly translucent shellfish nestled among plates of dense, fresh bread and steaming pearls of Sordan's elegant native rice. If there were servants in this place, they stayed out of sight. Even Legon had melted away. She and the Hierarch were alone.

Palimia drew a deep breath, and spooned tiny hearts bathed in rich sauce onto her plate. "You completely defeated my intention in returning to my birthplace. I came only to give you the journal, then fade into the populace, a mere footnote. Now look at me, acting as a landlady! I enter a building; men turn over their account books... I ask where the real ones are—"

He laughed and so did she.

She related her adventures, not even attempting to conceal her excitement. There was still so much, really, for her to learn—barges and loads, contracts and leases. The old scribe, who had served as a Triemperal accountant during the occupation, was earning his salary by catching all manner of tricks.

"He's clever," Palimia praised the old man. "I have already given him a big bonus! I make him explain *everything* until it makes sense. That's the only way I will learn. I enjoy learning new things, visiting new places. So did Marc. That's why—" Palimia stopped herself, the name crashing between them. She could prattle terribly when excited. "I'm sorry, I—"

"You can say his name." Dorilian looked away, toward the Rill mount and its crown of surreal power. "I need to hear it. It keeps him from fading." After another awkward silence, he asked, "Did you read the whole journal?"

"Yes. I read it constantly those first weeks. I simply needed to have something of him still, to read his words. When I do, I hear his voice, even now. His letters, his books. Reading them helps me deal with the loss." That, at least, they shared. Pain… and yearning. "I thought—I hoped—maybe you would find healing, too."

"I was suspicious of you at first. I had my agents in Essera investigate whether their ruler had, by some chance stroke of brilliance, recruited you as a spy. But all they could find was that he had denied your bequest in order to placate the Gracious Queen. You could have attempted to change his mind by offering him the journal. But you didn't. And so you left, and nobody cared enough to try to stop you. They foolishly believed you could have nothing I would find useful." Dorilian set his silver fork upon his plate, indicating he had finished eating. Politely, Palimia followed suit. "Weren't you afraid I would try to silence you, because of what that journal says?"

"No," she said, though her confidence in that answer was false. The journal revealed in detail the promises to have been exchanged at Permephedon—world-changing promises, including Dorilian's agreement to attempt to awaken the god-machine that ruled their lives. Changing the Rill changed… everything. Essera's powerful merchant princes, and Stefan also, would have paid a great deal to obtain that information. That Palimia had delivered the journal to Dorilian instead had opened a different door.

"It includes numerous examples of my failings."

"But also Marc's own."

"I'm more concerned with mine. Do you agree with what he said about me?"

"That you have failings? Yes, and be glad. Else I would find you quite uninteresting." Palimia smiled to see how much his youth showed at such times as this. Dorilian could be uncompromising in his pursuit of self-discovery. In recent weeks she had even flirted with him as a way of pushing at his formidable boundaries. Yet there was something more tonight, a specifically masculine intensity in the way he baited her. Suddenly she felt it best to deflect. "Marc so wanted to earn your regard. Oh, how hard he tried! Reading his journal, I understood. At the end, he rejoiced at knowing you were his friend, however in secret."

"He never kept that secret from you."

"No. I knew."

"He trusted you. I'm glad you brought his journal to me. Reading his words… is like a final visit, a chance to have another talk with him. We—we didn't have time to say goodbye."

His grief pierced her. Whatever had happened at Permephedon that day had been so terrible Dorilian still was haunted.

A wall of fire. The cracks and mighty groans of a building being torn apart, filled by the howl of wind. Screams, silent screams, and the terrible crushing agony of a hundred hearts stopping one by one.

Run, damn you! someone cried. She recognized Marc Frederick's voice.

With a stifled gasp, Palimia realized the images that poured into her mind were not imaginings, but memories. Dorilian's memories… bleeding through, a consequence of unshielded Highborn emotion. A projective empath, Marc Frederick had called him. Powerful. Damaged. Hidden from terrible enemies, but maybe not hidden well enough.

Now at last her heart recognized the full extent of Marc Frederick's last request.

"I think I know why he wanted you to have his thoughts, his hopes," Palimia said. "I think Marc knew that if he died… he wanted you to know. To know he believed in you, to know he cared. He would have wanted to help you find ease."

For a long minute, Dorilian said nothing. His eyes dried as he gazed into places she had never seen and could not go. Places only he and Marc Frederick had ever gone. Sunset lent new heat to his striking, youthful looks, illuminating the high outline of his cheekbones and controlled sensual mouth. Almost always he looked cold, remote, so uncaring it was easy to accord him the distance his gifts demanded. Tonight, however, his gaze bore something new, glimmering on the other side of tears.

"I need ease… in other ways," he said at last. "Stay with me tonight."

The very air seemed to coalesce with meanings. Palimia stopped breathing. She recognized a sexual invitation, albeit an awkward one. From childhood Dorilian had been taught to command, not seduce, hence his abruptness. What Palimia needed was time to think through her response. The wine glass would serve. She lifted it and took a deep long sip before she answered.

"Were I to do as you ask, Thrice Royal, people would talk."

"People talk anyway."

"They will say I am your mistress."

"Will they be right or wrong?"

Did he watch her thoughts? Marc Frederick had said Dorilian could pluck emotion from the atoms of her breath and the heat of her skin, filter bright motes of truth from the slime of lies, even send his feelings into her with such force Palimia would think them her own. The godborn lived in isolation for good reason. Few humans ever learned how to fully manage their effects.

Truth was the one constant, the one immutable argument. Fear collected at the edges of Palimia's courage. "I don't have power of my own. I cannot afford to make mistakes."

"Neither can I." The ugly reality of his gilded life hung within those words. "My mistakes could kill me."

"So could mine."

Power hardened his gaze. "Do you mean *me*? You can tell me no. If you do, it will be as if this conversation never took place, as if this night had never happened. The esteem in which I hold you is such that I would never diminish you in any way. I would do nothing to offend *his* memory."

The thrust of that emotion pushed against Palimia's naked defenses. She remembered what Marc Frederick's journal had said about countering Highborn empathy and focused on Dorilian, not her fears. Dorilian's words carried the only truth that mattered.

"I am not asking you to love me, Lady. I don't expect that you will, nor can I say what it is I will feel toward you. Probably not love. But respect always, and—it's not true that I—" The blush that crossed his youthful face was genuine embarrassment at the nature of his request. Palimia doubted any other person had ever seen Dorilian look this vulnerable or desperate. "The fact is, I like women, but I meet very few and fewer still who are not thrust at me burdened with the intentions of men. You know what I mean. Every woman introduced to me has an ambitious father or brother. Every day I am offered women by men who seek my favor—and I don't intend to be in any man's debt, especially for that. Even tonight, when I said I was restless, the palace chamberlain offered to find me a virgin."

From Marc Frederick, Palimia knew how that offer would have stung. Dorilian's father had favored only virgins, and had even betrayed Dorilian by sleeping with his son's virgin wife.

"I don't want a virgin!" Dorilian sounded frustrated. "I don't want some helpless girl giving herself to me out of duty or fear. I want a woman who is beautiful and intelligent and knows how to please a man. Someone who doesn't feel false and wrong, veiled in lies. Someone who does not already despise me. Someone I can trust."

Her heart beat faster. Though he was attractive and powerfully alluring, particularly now with his desire infusing the air between them and igniting her blood, Dorilian was young enough to be her son.

"Thrice Royal," she said, and she knew she was floundering. He had said she could refuse him… so why couldn't she say those words? Maybe because the clamor of her body was already saying yes?

Marc, what do I do? However brief their time together, he had been the love of her life, though she had not been the love of his. That woman, a beautiful Kheld lady, had died in his arms. But he had loved Palimia and would want her to prosper and live the rest of her life fully. Even now she heard his voice telling her to follow her heart. Well, Palimia's heart told her she could trust this young Hierarch. He would be an honorable lover and his reasons for choosing her matched her needs. Though her heart would never belong to another, she could not imagine being celibate. She had only had much older lovers until now. Maybe she was ready for a younger man, especially one she might instruct in the arts of love.

He had risen from the table and now stood over her, extending his hand. She placed her fingers in his and felt his strength as he pulled her into his arms. Her body melted. They had never touched before this and something electric flowed from his flesh into hers, tingling of passion and sexual fire. She wondered how any woman could ever have called him cold.

But she must take control of the moment, and him, if she was to govern such ardor. She stepped back from the attempted embrace, noting the flicker of anger that crossed Dorilian's face as he thought she was about to refuse him. Just as quickly, he had mastered it and looked resigned. Holding his gaze, Palimia moved both hands to her left shoulder and unfastened the pin holding the panels of her lightweight chiton. When the fabric fell free, she moved her hands to the right shoulder, unfastening that pin also until it too fell and bared her breasts.

"You are beautiful." Dorilian stared for a long minute before raising his eyes again to hers.

Smiling, she took his right hand and placed it on her breast, where he immediately let it wander. His hand cupped the round shape of her flesh as his breathing quickened. The front of his chiton had tented instantly, pleasing her greatly. Her older lovers had needed more preparation.

"You are, too," she whispered. Dorilian *was* beautiful, so handsome her heart swelled. Palimia pressed her body against his, trapping his hand and lifting her lips to brush upon his. He was taller now than when she had first met him in Dazunor, and his manhood rested hard and thick against her belly. "Come," she said.

A long while later, Palimia felt Dorilian's chest lift with a deep sigh and she raised her weight upon her arms. She was not a tiny woman, and he certainly needed eventually to breathe again. Looking upon his face, she saw him smile.

"You are amazing." Dorilian's eyes opened and then narrowed at her grin. "Just so you know, for future engagements, I like to be on top."

Palimia laughed. Dorilian Sordaneon was going to be a most amusing pupil.

12

"The young lady in blue and orange plaid is the Rhodhur Cruichil's choice," Cullen said. "The other two are her friends. All are well-born lasses, high clan from good families. They attend the school at Aurddolen."

Educated, then. That had been one of Stefan's stipulations, along with being pretty and well connected. Stefan gazed down at the three girls in the courtyard below the window. He needed to make quick work of this trip to Rhodhur.

The young woman Cullen had pointed out first laughed and swung her raven hair as she used a stick to trace lines in the dirt at the other girls' feet. She struck Stefan as whimsical and he smiled. What was she drawing? Chickens pecked at the ground all around the tree beneath which the girls sat. Small sacks of grain sagged in the girls' laps, but the girls were more interested in their conversation than in feeding the birds.

"Her name is Nilla Lowenda." Cullen continued his presentation. "Goff Horvadson's niece. His sister's daughter. Her matriarchs hold large tracts of Frendel-Brennan bottomland and the family has amassed considerable wealth. Her father is Lowen Toboldson, so you got good kin there, and her uncles all sit on the council and are strong supporters of yours."

Nilla certainly seemed suitable. A little plain from what Stefan could see, but he could live with that for her family connections. Cullen had already confirmed that all three of the young women were fifteen years and were by Kheld law of age to wed. A wife schooled at the Sanctuary of Aurddolen would be literate in Khelda and possess skills devoted to at least one of the Mother's Three Faces: Knowing, Life, or Home. Stefan took a moment to consider the other girls.

"And that one?" He pointed to the prettiest.

"Aubrey Amundda. She's niece to Nalf Rhys here through his brother Amund, who was your grandfather's Forester." Cullen indicated Nalf, a stocky, bearded chieftain who straightened at the notice. "She holds Thegn clan right to lands in Ashmoss and Wydrike—and a king's grant to an even larger property in Saemoregh. Educated too. Speaks and writes Khelda, Stauba, and Esta and has studied economics and poetry. However"—Cullen paused to make another point—"her mother was half-Staubaun."

"Half?" Stefan frowned.

"Yes, though her grandmother never named the man. I know her history because Aubrey's grandmother was *my* grandfather's youngest sister." Cullen's wry smile acknowledged that admittance. "We're cousins."

What a shame. Though Stefan would welcome being even more related to Cullen, the girl was mixed-blood, a grandchild of rape. Under no circumstances could he have a queen his Staubaun nobles might snicker at behind his back. As for the third girl, the shortest of the three, topped with a mane of black hair...

"And that one?"

"Lark Rappeleye."

"Rappeleye? A Bog Witch?" Stefan had never seen one before. Rappeleyes were Old Kheld and the stuff of legend. Hard-drinking, hard-fighting men and powerful, odd women.

"They prefer to be called Rune Daughters. Shaped by the Mother, conceived under the Hill. Lark's matriarchy is rich, though, and near good as Wall Lords at prophecy. Her uncles and Mothers alike wield great influence. The bloodline is pure all the way back to One-Eyed Bess."

Pure, yes... but conceived under the Hill. A female whose father was unknown. Stefan was being steered toward the one the Cruihcil wanted. Stefan looked at the laughing girl again. Hadn't he asked them to find someone suitable? Nilla Lowenda looked pleasant. He could see her in his bed. Best of all, her matriarchy was one of Amallar's most respected, and her father and uncles were prominent. Petitions were already in place to make lords of both Goff and Lowen. If Stefan acted with any speed, he could be wedded by the Solstice.

Cullen squinted at him. "Would you like to talk with any of the ladies?"

Stefan nodded. "Nilla."

Stefan watched Goff lead Nilla into the Great Hall, where Rhodhur's foremost chieftains gathered in a display of finery. Still wearing her everyday plaid skirt and a loose flaxen tunic beneath a heavy wool cloak, Nilla dropped into an awkward curtsey. She'd probably learned the move moments before her uncle propelled her through the door. When her head bowed, a curtain of raven hair hid most of her face, though Stefan was charmed by the way her dark lashes fanned upon high pink cheeks.

"Stefan Stauberg-Randolph Erwanson," Goff intoned, "my sister's daughter, Nilla Lowenda."

"Sir." Her voice quavered, little more than a whisper.

"I wish you to call me Stefan. Has your uncle told you of my interest?"

"He says you wish to wed me, sir?" Nilla lifted her head and immediately looked to Goff. She appeared disbelieving and probably wanted to be certain she'd gotten it right.

Could she be more innocent? Stefan could not help but be pleased. He preferred a woman unschooled in wiles and cunning, who would not be critical of his efforts. He would undoubtedly need to woo her, if only to impress her family, but he had wooed girls like Nilla before. She would be flattered by his attention but shy, and he would win her over with chaste kisses and generous gifts. Before very long she would be happy to make a home for him and thrive within the circle of the many advantages he could provide to her and their children. Now that she was near, he saw Nilla's better points. Long glossy black hair served to show off her fair skin and rose-kissed cheeks, and her features, while ordinary, were in no way off-putting. Beneath the rise and fall of her tunic, her bosom promised a feast of temptations. When Stefan touched Nilla's smooth face her full, naturally inviting lips trembled. She looked like a girl waiting to be kissed.

But he would not do that here.

"We will wed at Solstice in Trulo," he told Goff. The hall full of chieftains roared approval and slapped each other's backs. They had begun to bring out drinking horns when the door crashed open.

"Oath breakers! Nilla, heed the Mother! *You* must choose—not these men!"

A small female wearing a cloak the hue of bruised mulberries stood in the doorway. Night-dark hair billowed around a sharp little face with eyes so blue and bright they matched the runestone clasp on her cloak. Stefan recognized her as one of the three girls he had spied on. Lark. The Rappeleye witch. The other girl from the threesome appeared at her side. Taller. A hot-eyed, watchful beauty.

Goff strode toward the girls. "Our Nilla *has* chosen! She's going to wed Stefan. She's going to be our queen! Begone, you little hag!"

"*You* chose him, not she." Lark's upper lip curled with defiance, and her body tensed with affront. "*You* put aside the Mother's Law. A woman should lie only with a man of *her* choosing. Who made this woman's choice?"

Stefan stared at the small intruder who dared to cast a shadow on his happy announcement. What the hells was this unwelcome shrew doing?

Dark-faced, Goff turned to the gathered men and the silent, terrified young woman with them. "Nilla!" he roared.

"Lark, please go!" Nilla pleaded.

"Get rid of her." Stefan counted on Cullen and Goff to salvage this occasion. Already two of Nilla's uncles advanced on the little witch. He had a roomful of men to defend Nilla's honor. He put his arm around Nilla's shaking shoulders and tugged her close to his side so he might look down into her uplifted eyes. "I'll keep you safe."

Lark moved around one of the advancing men to thrust a shaking finger toward Stefan. "You are Motherless! Motherless!" Both burly brothers seized Lark and she continued to shriek as they dragged her toward the door. "Nilla! Don't set the Mother's curse upon this man! On all of them! You did not choose him, they chose you *for* him!"

Before any man laid hand on it, the great oaken door swung open once more, this time for two crones to enter the Hall. Hoods of orange cloth covered the gray crowns of hair upon their heads, and cloaks heavily embroidered with intertwined symbols of moon and sun, oak leaves and roots, hung from their shoulders. The tallest of the old women clutched a walking staff which she pointed at the men holding Lark.

"Unhand the girl, lest I pronounce you dead to all women!"

Nilla's uncles released Lark at once. "Yes, Mother Aegdnis. Look here. Already done." Each bobbed his head and backed away, hands displayed to indicate their compliance.

It was Stefan's turn to curse, though he did so under his breath. This damned bog witch of a girl and her Staubaun-blooded friend had gone and involved the Old Mothers just to make things uglier. The clan chieftains had made their choice, and so had he. He could not go back on this marriage without offending the very chieftains whose alliance he needed. If that happened, the tale would get out. Why did nothing in his life go smoothly?

Green eyes within the Old Mother's deep sockets fixed upon Stefan and he held that stare. No other man in that hall would. It took the old woman longer than it should have to recognize what was happening, lower her gaze, and bow her head. "King," she acknowledged.

"Mother Aegdnis."

"Why is this child crying?"

Mother Aegdnis's words, and those of the crazy Rappeleye girl, stabbed at something harsh and cold. Belief in the Mother formed the foundation of Kheld society, yet Stefan had not honored Her hallowed ways. He had barely acknowledged usual Kheld practice. The young woman he embraced so protectively was sobbing, her tears wetting his sleeve. What if Nilla truly did not want him? Stefan had only just met her. He had not wooed her or asked to be her choice. In that, at least, Lark's condemnation rang true. Men had decided for Nilla.

Mother Aegdnis needed to hear something other than that.

"That girl"—Stefan indicated Lark, standing tense but silent beside the old woman—"has upset her. Nilla and I were happy and making plans to wed until *that* creature came in here and started shrieking." He took Nilla by the shoulders and turned her to face him. "Do you choose me, Nilla Lowenda? Do you choose your king, who would make you his wife? I will be kind to you. Our children will be princes. You will want for nothing."

He prayed she would speak the words he wanted. The words Mother Aegdnis needed to hear.

Nilla's tear-filled gaze searched his, then she closed her eyes and opened trembling lips. "I choose you, our king."

Stefan breathed easier then. He didn't want an unwilling bride. Such was anathema to the Mother. Though he, like most men, more closely followed Lud, no Kheld ever dismissed the goddess of Life itself, the Giver of Blessings and Door to the Grave. Best to invite Her to be part of the pairing, like now with Mother Aegdnis.

After exchanging a few words with Nilla, and then with Goff and some of the other chieftains, including more of Nilla's uncles, Mother Aegdnis kissed Nilla on the forehead and invoked the Mother's Bounty upon her. Both Old Mothers then had Stefan and Nilla clasp hands and bade them choose a rune. Their joined hands tumbled stones in the depths of the soft leather bag until they worked one stone—just one—between them. This runestone

Mother Aegdnis took from them, and wrapped unseen in a bit of rabbit fur tied with red thread. Only then did she tuck it into the leather pouch Nilla wore at her belt.

"The rune of your union. Hold it fast, and never lose it."

Nilla's tentative smile of thanks to Aegdnis warmed Stefan's heart. It would be all right. Everything. But when he looked up, just before the Old Mothers ushered Lark from the room, he caught her dark stare and a cold stave of fear plunged into his soul to stay.

"See it now?" Dorilian pointed to specks taking shape as buildings on the shore. He knelt on the deck of the ship that was taking him and his entourage on a state visit across the lake. "The Pillared Cliffs? Topped by the Palace of Dawn? That is Suddekar."

Levyathan clutched the railing and pressed against Dorilian's restraining arm. "Pink! Like roses. Cliffs from the First Age. Fossil sea lilies!"

The boy spoke exceedingly well for not yet being two. "We will look for some. Probably none so fine as the ones in the floors of the Serat."

"Like Deleus showed me. Will he be here?"

"No. Now that he is the Basarchessa's ambassador to the Triempery, he's at the Archhalia with Tiflan, defending our domains against preposterous claims."

"Our cohort is strong."

"Yes, always."

A shadow fell across them. "What a pretty palace!"

Palimia held young Fahme on her hip and was the very vision of a happy woman, shading her eyes with one hand while breeze-stolen tendrils of blonde hair danced around her smiling face. Dorilian had chosen well in taking her as his lover. Their hours together were sensual, passionate, and satisfying in every way. He had found a woman deserving of his trust and in doing so had unlocked an entire realm to master.

She had also brought him a measure of peace. In Palimia he could reconcile his promises to Marc Frederick in ways he had not been able after things with Stefan had shattered so badly. Since meeting her again, Dorilian had done nothing to provoke the Stauberg-Randolphs. It was possible again to think of Marc Frederick without feeling slapped in the face by knowing who people thought to be his murderer.

Sad. Levyathan's chubby hand patted Dorilian's cheek.

Stop it. With that warning, Dorilian rose and pulled the lad up into his arms. Levyathan reached for Fahme, who squealed in delight. Dorilian laughed and walked Palimia and the children to the middle of the ship, from which they would disembark upon reaching the dock.

His makeshift family. His son, his daughter, and a woman with whom he could share himself in ways the outside world need never see.

"A fine year behind you." Ermenthalia, Basarchessa of Suddekar and Dorilian's paternal grandmother, could make any observation sound critical. She and Dorilian enjoyed last daylight from a portico overlooking the broad origin of the Sorand'ruil and Suddekar's capital city of Batraz. It was here, between ranks of low hills terraced with fine estates and rich silty floodplains, that the waters collected by Lake Sarkuan sought exit to the sea and gave birth to the great river. "It appears you set the Stauberg-Randolph boy in his place. We hear very little of him anymore."

"Good. I want to hear nothing about him at all." Dorilian saw no reason to mention that his latest provocation—the proposal to wed Emyli—had elicited only a polite refusal and not the tantrum he had hoped for. Perhaps Stefan was, finally, listening to cooler heads among his advisors. It might be time to move on to more interesting diversions.

"One should keep close tabs on enemies."

"Of those I have more than enough."

"Most of your own making."

Even more than other of Dorilian's near kin, Ermenthalia was fiercely political. He had seen her father Mezentius, the last Highborn Prince of Suddekar, die at Permephedon. Dorilian's father Deben, Ermenthalia's son, had died there also. Consequently, Ermenthalia was Dorilian's oldest remaining relation. He had met her on five occasions: his birth and naming days, which he did not remember; his wedding to Daimonaeris, which he remembered only too well; his father's ascension to the throne; and his own coronation as Hierarch. On the latter occasion, Ermenthalia had expressed hope that trouble with Mormantalorus was all a misunderstanding and extended an invitation for Dorilian to visit her famous—and very pink—palace.

He had surprised her by giving short notice.

White-haired and regal, Ermenthalia wore robes of elegant native Ki silk produced in her domain. It was Suddekar's most lucrative export, seconded by dyes, grains, and cattle.

"The little one," Ermenthalia acknowledged, "has grown a great deal. He certainly is healthier than the weakling for whom you named him. I approve giving the boy some air. You must get him out from under your overprotective wing, let people see him."

Though Dorilian recognized her veiled rebuke of his own upbringing at the hands of Sebbord, he kept his expression neutral. He'd had plenty of air in Teremar and plenty of people had seen him during those years—just no one who was not in Teremar. Still, the idea nestled. It might be a good thing for him and Levyathan both to be more visible to their subjects. Sordan's people might like to see their Hierarch with his family. Doing so might even inspire stronger feelings of devotion. Wasn't that Tutto's refrain? That Dorilian's fate might someday depend on common men?

He recalled Endelarin Nemenor mocking Deben as being tiny in people's minds because they had only ever seen him from a distance.

"I will visit more places, now that Levyathan's getting older. He enjoys seeing new things and new places especially."

"He is a strange child. Very bright, of course, as is the way of our bloodline. And he speaks ever so well, far above the other child."

"I think you mean my daughter." Dorilian had officially adopted Fahme and given her Sordaneon status. If ever he caught up with her father, she would be an orphan anyway.

Ermenthalia waved a pale hand to show what she thought of that decision, but wisely said no more. "You for certain should be more visible. Take a tour of the river. A progress. Do it during the heat of summer. At such times cool breezes off the river can be very pleasant."

She leaned to pour honeyed wine into her cup. Dorilian signaled Legon, who stepped from a position in the doorway. His friend poured a cup and took one swallow first before passing it to him. Dorilian no longer drank wine that had not been tasted.

"The boy is still very young, of course," Ermenthalia continued. "It might be best if you would leave him with me."

That was not happening. "If he stayed with you, he would see nothing but courtiers and cliffs. I think it best we stay together."

"As you will. But I would advise a barge over a ship. Slower, but greater comfort. A floating palace, elegance on display. The majesty. The power. Your ancestor, Tarlon, used a barge for his progress."

Dorilian had heard tales of that barge. Immense. Gilded. A floating palace indeed. He would set his steward to find it.

The timing was right. His borders were stable and the fighting to the south was contained. Nammuor had been beaten back and was licking his wounds. In the past year, Dorilian had succeeded in bemiring Stefan with spates of unrest in Neuberland. Commerce between their two realms had achieved strategic equilibrium, while trade with other partners continued to expand. Dorilian could afford to take a month or so to visit a few of his far-flung domains.

"I need to talk with you." Stefan had waited as long as he could before taking Cullen away from his guests. Erenor stood guard at the cottage's rear doorway to make certain they would not be disturbed. Fence posts stood in stark relief against snow-dusted ground. Horses filled two enclosures hastily erected near a line of tents in the nearby field. Stefan frowned in annoyance. "This place is too small. You should have welcomed your king to your title estate."

"Another day's hard ride away and that much farther from the King's Road," Cullen pointed out. Heddros was tucked into the Glainoi, a lush hilly region north and west of Trulo, which was where they were headed. Wyre, on the other hand, was within a half day's ride of their destination. "You wanted to be at the Golden Palace for the Solstice, right? This is in the right direction. Besides, the chieftains think my house is fine. They like that I built it myself and my bride is happy here."

"Is she?" Stefan didn't truly believe an aristocrat like Asphalladra could be happy in so modest a house.

"We spend more time here than in that fancy palace you gave us." Cullen's sigh filled the air between them with a billow of frost. "That place… it's too much. Heddros has got so many rooms an army could get lost in it. I can't afford enough servants to keep the floors clean! Or enough fuel to heat it. It gets damn cold this time of year. Here everyone is comfortable."

At least the house had four bedchambers now, though only the one big room for socializing. The rest of Stefan's entourage had to camp in a tent village. Stefan shook his head. "I want Nilla to see the kind of life I will give her. Fine houses, rich furnishings, servants and all. What do you have here? A cook and one maid?"

"And a man to tend the place."

"She's going to be a queen."

"And you're a king, and I'm an Enlad thanks to you, but that doesn't mean we should put on airs, does it? Not among our own folk."

Except sometimes it did mean that. There were Staubauns riding with them. Erenor, himself newly made an Enlad with a former Sordaneon estate to support him, and several nobles like Lucien Illarion and Aureon Varney, who served in the King's Guard. Tomorrow at Trulo they would rub elbows with all manner of nobles invited for the wedding. Highborn princes, even. Stefan needed to present himself as a king *always*.

"I suppose she'll be impressed enough by the palace in Trulo." His uncle Jonthan, during his time as Prince of Dazunor, had redecorated the ancient residence. It was still less fine than the palace at Heddros, which Dorilian, prick that he was, had never even visited.

"Anyone would be. The Golden Palace is the prettiest in Dazunor. At least, Phalla tells me it is."

Maybe Nilla would like it then. She was inside the cottage, tired and happy to have stopped for the day. Stefan could impress her tomorrow. He looked out across the rolling hills at the winter-bare trees. Cullen walked to stand at his side.

"What's got you now? It's more than that you don't like my choice of house for the night."

"Dorilian."

"Damn it, Stefan—"

"He's done it again. Making a mockery of me. He made her *his* mistress!"

"Her? Who?"

"That woman!" Stefan clenched his teeth from anger, not cold. "The whore he put in charge of all my Sordan assets, my *grandfather's* fucking mistress who Apollonia told me to get rid of for her. She was supposed to just disappear." Stefan waved his hand in disgust. "The Archhalia sent a delegation down, demanding an accounting, and they wrote up a report that says it's all still there. The money. The properties. But do we know for sure? A stupid report on paper? Do we know *anything*? What we know is that Dorilian's flaunting his new woman in public! He took her along with his Heir and half his court two weeks ago on a trip to Suddekar. Him being with her doesn't even make sense. She's old enough to be his mother!"

"Settle down. On your current scale of problems to be solved, this isn't one of the big ones."

"You don't think so? Apollonia is demanding I do something."

Stefan pulled a paper from inside his heavy jacket. Blue markings from a broken seal stained the paper. "Erenor gave me the Gracious Queen's letter when we crossed the bridge. She's promising to stand in the way of every lordship or proposal I put forth unless I 'fix' this problem. Do you hear me? She wants me to *fix* it! So tell me, how am I supposed to do that?" Stefan crumpled the letter in his fist.

Cullen didn't say anything—because he knew there was no way to do it short of killing the woman. Stefan couldn't even *talk* to Dorilian. Any envoy from the Archhalia, even their ambassador whose job it was to talk to the Hierarch, was forbidden to speak Stefan's name. Simply to begin a conversation with 'Essera's king' got them booted from the Highborn ruler's presence.

"Fucking Dorilian!" Stefan kicked at a snow-covered stone and sent it scooting toward the nearest fence.

"He's not the problem. Think about it. Apollonia is. She's being unreasonable. You got the woman to leave, didn't you? Just like Apollonia asked. You had no control over what happened after that."

"You're right, but—"

"So tell *her* to go down to Sordan and tell Dorilian where to put his cock."

Stefan cut his friend a look. Cullen wore a grin as big as the Dazun. The idea he proposed was so ludicrous that Stefan laughed. Ludicrous... and brilliant. He would tell Apollonia exactly that. She might even do it.

"If I'm lucky, Dorilian'll get rid of Apollonia for me." The laughter eased Stefan, and he shook his head at the problems that roosted on his shoulders. "Damn it, Cullen, I just want things to settle down. Get married, start a family. I need an heir to make people realize I'm not going anywhere, that I'm going to stick around and get things done. Then they can stop talking about the old days with the Highborn kings."

"They stopped talking about that a long time ago."

"They've started up again." What Marc Frederick had silenced with his long, prosperous reign had never completely died.

Whispers were emerging from forgotten corners of Stefan's realm, longing for princes of power. Highborn power... and the Wall... and the Rill.

"This is the only room I like."

Emyli smiled at Nilla's words. They sat on opposite ends of a long window seat in probably the prettiest room in Trulo's Golden Palace. They had met for the first time two days before, upon Emyli's arrival in the city, but this was their first opportunity to speak alone.

"It is a lovely room." Emyli had stayed in it many times herself while her brother Jonthan had lived here. "Did Stefan choose it for you?"

"He asked which room I would like. I said this one, because it has such fine windows and a view of the river." And Amallar on the other side, to which Stefan's young queen no doubt wished to return.

"I suppose it has been a bit much, all of this. The ceremony, the people."

"The clothes!" Nilla sagged with exhaustion. She'd divested herself of the borrowed, bejeweled gown she had worn. The circlet Stefan had placed upon her raven head the day before still sat firmly in place. *You are royal now*, he had said upon doing so. "I don't think I can ever get used to wearing such heavy clothes."

"You won't have to. Only ceremonial garments are so heavy."

"And this crown… I keep thinking if I move my head it will fall off! I have so much to learn." Nilla gazed longingly out the tall windows toward the river beyond the terrace. "And I don't know anyone. Oh, my uncles and father… and Stefan, of course, and now you." The smile she directed to Emyli was hopeful. "They wouldn't let me have my friends with me."

No, Emyli had heard what had transpired with those two friends. Stefan had forbidden either young woman to accompany the wedding party to Trulo. He had also said Nilla could not have them as her companions at court. He had instead sent for Nilla's married sister and asked Asphalladra to serve as one of her ladies.

"You and your friends were at Aurddolen together." Such friendships endured. Emyli, too, had undertaken schooling at the Sanctuary of the Mother. That had been so many years ago.

"I was to go back. I'm not yet accomplished with books or runes, not like Aubrey, or Lark. Lark has a gift for runes, of course."

A Rappeleye daughter would. Emyli's rune set had been shaped by a Rappeleye Rune Mother and blessed by Amallar's most gifted wise woman. A Kheld woman armed with true runes and schooled in the reading of them could unravel secrets, cast light upon shadow, and pull forth truth from any manner of lie. Emyli had herself laid the Wheel the night she had met Stefan's bride, and what she had learned had both lightened her heart and introduced fresh worry. The girl was good and kind and presented no threat to

Stefan at all—but a taint from the core of Lark Rappeleye's warning hung like a pall over the reading.

More shadow lay ahead than brightness.

How could Stefan have let this happen? He had wanted a Kheld bride, but he had obtained her using Staubaun methods—he had chosen a woman by design, not desire, to make alliances with other men. And Nilla... had only claimed to have chosen him *after*. Her choice was muddled. Sincere, but its basis conflicted. Emyli could see for herself that Nilla was trying to make her choice fit what others had chosen for her.

"Have you embraced a Calling?" Those who studied at the knees of the Mother chose one of Her Faces at the end of seven years, though a student might stay longer to finish training—or even complete a second or third Calling.

"Home." Another soft smile. "I am one of the best spinners and weavers. I promised Stefan a shirt once I get my wheel and loom set up. It's not a great skill for a queen, I suppose."

"The best skill for any woman in a new situation is to be a quick study of other people."

"Yes, I can see that would be useful." Nilla took her lower lip between small, even teeth. "You would know these things, Princess. I... hope maybe we have something in common. You too married young."

Yes, Emyli had. A few of her memories remained joyful. "Erwan was my first love. So handsome! We should have waited, of course— I was only fourteen—but I was quite sure of myself. I was a student at Aurddolen and convinced of my choice of him. Naturally, we wed by exchanging our vows beneath my mother's oak and declared ourselves so. I was with child before two moons were done and... my father had our union declared legal here in Essera." Her choice had compelled that decision also.

"I hope the Mother blesses us." Nilla blushed. "Stefan wants an heir so very much."

"Have you—"

Nilla correctly deduced her question. "Shared a bed? Of course! Before we ever left Rhodhur. He wished to know we were a good pairing—as did I, because he was my first man. I've been too shy, and... the Mother does say a woman should not bed a man for any purpose other than that he pleases her greatly."

"Am I safe to assume he did?"

"Oh yes. Stefan is fashioned in every way to please a woman. And I think it pleased him to be my first." Nilla laughed brightly. "My friends told me to expect more haste and less pleasure." Then she looked sad again. "I wish they could be here, so I could tell them."

Ah. Stefan had done his part well enough, at least. Perhaps he and this sweet young woman would indeed be blessed by the Mother, and quickly. A child would bring joy and hope.

Essera needed both.

"It's a potential rebellion, that's what it is."

As he said the words, Erenor moved his finger across the map's detailed topography and minutely penned inscriptions. Stefan's gaze followed the damning arc. Bynum... Lacenedon... from which it dipped sharply south into Rannul, a crescent of trouble that threatened to cut his kingdom in two. Only Permephedon, guarded by the Rill and centuries of vaunted neutrality, stood untouched by the Royal North's growing discontent.

Outside the room's windows, Dazunor-Rannuli spread its prosperous skirts and did not at all notice the problems besetting its king.

"I don't like Hebron. I never have." Stefan had met Lacenedon's regent only once, on his coronation day. Hebron Ursenos, grandnephew of the domain's slaughtered Highborn prince, was cousin to Palaistea, whose young sons were the current heirs—not just to Lacenedon but also to Stefan's crown.

Goff hulked, arms crossed, at the table's corner. He shared a nod with Lowen Toboldson, who was new to Stefan's inner council. Lowen had little experience but was eager to acquire it. "We know the man," Goff affirmed. "Hebron Ursenos is a damned Purist who thinks his blood is higher than ours and should never be diminished by mingling." Goff turned to Stefan. "He's speaking out strong against you since your marriage. Says you're enriching Khelds and lowborn nobles at the expense of old families like his. If he's not plotting to throw you over, it's only a matter of time."

To someone like Hebron, Stefan would always be a commoner— and a pretender. He frowned. "We know who he'd want to see in my place."

"Highborn kind. Those brat cousins of his." Goff snorted his derision. "He's said as much. And by doing it, he'd put his own blood on the throne. Secure all lands as Staubaun lands and put us back to Highborn rule."

Erenor caught Stefan's gaze. He shifted his finger to tap the blue towers that marked Merath. "Your aunt, the Gracious Princess Ionais, appears to be steadfast. Her votes at the Archhalia align with yours more often than not. She is no friend of Hebron's."

"Good." Ionais was being smart. Her domain's prosperity depended on a Rill port a mere half a day downriver from her capital. Stefan pointed to the center of his kingdom. "I trust the domain of Serrain. I'm less sure of Dannuth."

"None can be sure of that Highborn lot," said Goff. He had complained to Stefan earlier about how Rheger and Elhanan, while they had attended Stefan's wedding, witnessed the ceremony, and even partaken of the feast afterward, had ridden out the next morning rather than join the two days of festivities Stefan had planned. "Think Khelds too low. They prefer Staubauns at every turn."

Lowen ventured an opinion. "Because Highborn *are* Staubaun. Royal ones."

A trace of a frown accompanied Erenor's answer. "The Highborn always stand apart from other kind. They did so even when your grandfather was king."

What they were doing was withholding support and making Stefan's life difficult. But at least they had shown up at the wedding, as had Ionais, herself a Highborn daughter. The same could not be said of the Bas of Rannul.

Burelan Phaeros. Handsome. Rich. A man in his prime. His mother was the daughter of the late Prince, who had died at Permephedon, but his father was a scion of the House of Phaer—the most troublesome of the Seven Houses. Burelan therefore presented a host of treacherous entanglements.

Stefan leaned his elbows on the table, the better to talk quietly with Erenor. "Tell me more about Burelan Phaeros."

"Popular in his own domain. Views more aligned with the Royal North than with yours."

"Is Burelan in contact with Dorilian?"

Erenor's brow furrowed before he continued speaking. "With Sordan? I think that unlikely. Burelan moves as the Seven Houses move, and the Seven Houses prefer not to engage with the Sordaneons. Dorilian complicates their desire for Rill control and welcomes none of them at his court. When it comes to Sordan, all seven of the Seven Houses remain your political allies. Sordan has been arming Neuberland's lords, as we know—primarily through Annech and Gobba—and though the cartel has undoubtedly helped facilitate these transactions, the Hierarchate has done no discernable maneuvering north of the Dazun. Sordan appears content to hamper trade through restriction of its Rill ports and obstructing you in the Archhalia."

Like Stefan's most recent proposal to annex the crown protectorate of Gignastha. The proposal had not been put before the Archhalia for discussion because Dorilian's ambassador had pronounced the Hierarch's veto, killing the measure. By that one action, Dorilian had spared Stefan's domains from revealing where their loyalties fell. How many of Stefan's enemies had that veto kept hidden?

He would never get any reforms through while the Highborn held this much political power. Unfortunately, the Archhalia preferred to maintain the illusion of a functional Triempery and refused to expel Sordan or its domains.

"So Burelan isn't talking to Dorilian?"

"Not openly, no, and probably not even in secret. That's not to say Burelan isn't plotting against you, it just means his rebellion will take other forms and will come from another direction." Erenor moved a marker and placed it on Stauberg. "There is your weakness."

Stauberg was second only to Dazunor-Rannuli in wealth and surpassed the latter in prominence. No location in Essera loomed more significant. By its immortal Wall and foundations, and its history as a Malyrdeon capital, Stauberg tied Essera to its ancestral legends—to gods and prophecies.

Prophecies that Stefan, unlike the kings who had come before him, could not use to advantage.

"I stopped Palaistea from resuming her sons' court there. I denied them residence in the city."

"Best move you made so far," Goff broke in. He'd counseled Stefan to do it, and was apparently keen to take credit. "Keep the Highborn out of Stauberg and you keep them from their god. Weakens their hold."

"Elhanan presents a problem." Erenor touched the silver embossment that encircled the city. "As an invested Wall mage, he cannot legally be prevented from returning to the city. Our soldiers would not dare deter him the way they did the princess and her boys."

"Do you believe that old story, that the Wall protects the Highborn?"

"To the extent it cannot be broken and so would shelter any person within its perimeter. That is well-proven." All knew the history. The Aryati had attacked the Wall soon after Ergeiron's transformation, and the new Entity had absorbed all weapons used against it, becoming even taller and stronger. The weapon that could bring down the Wall did not exist.

"Yes," said Stefan, "and the legend states the Wall will endure as long as Highborn blood lives within the city. But none live there now. Not one." He had just made sure of that.

Goff laughed. "Yet another lie they've forged to keep us in fear of them."

Stefan noticed Erenor's grimace. Like most Staubauns, Erenor probably believed yet another tale: that the Highborn did not, and could not, lie. That Erenor was close to such beliefs made him valuable in ways Goff was not. More of Stefan's subjects were Staubaun than Kheld. Knowing what they thought mattered to how Stefan framed and implemented his plans. Because of Erenor, Stefan knew most of his subjects were also dissatisfied with the Highborn, who they saw as aloof and disinterested—and increasingly irrelevant.

"I can keep Palaistea out of Stauberg by force, but she is still legal ruler of that domain and wields its Archhalia vote. As long as she presents herself as a loyal subject, I can't very well go to war against her."

"Attacking a woman never ends well," Lowen concurred. "The Mother lays curses on men who do such."

Goff, however, snorted. "And what curse does the Mother lay on women who seek to overthrow their king? Who seek to subjugate men through threats of unnatural power?"

When it came to the Mother, fear was a boon companion to awe. Many Khelds, however, were falling away from those roots. Stefan looked to see what Erenor thought.

"Princess Palaistea is popular with the people." Erenor dismissed Goff's eye roll and focused his attention on Stefan, where it belonged. "Prince Enreddon was much loved in Stauberg, and his subjects still revere the Princess as mother of his sons. They are Wall princes, and we would do well to remember that. As Regent of Stauberg and the Eleutheron, Palaistea commands a significant army, though it is promised by ancient treaty to Essera's defense. You're Essera's rightful ruler, so..."

"And if Staubauns say he's not?" Goff challenged.

"They're not saying that."

"But they could. They might. The Staubaun bitch might turn those men against Stefan, as could Hebron with his. If Palaistea and Hebron should decide to join their forces against Stefan, they could tear the kingdom in two."

Stefan saw that as only too possible. "You're keeping an eye on this situation?" he asked Goff.

"Yes. Burelan isn't the only man who has the intention of courting Stauberg's Princess. So too has the Bas of Gweroyen, which makes him another man to watch like a hawk. Women who feel endangered often warm to the prospect of taking a husband. One with a Highborn kin line might obtain the blessing of the Dannuth Princes and the Gracious Queen. She was unhappy you didn't woo Palaistea for yourself."

Perhaps, but Stefan preferred to think Apollonia's most recent pique was due to his letter telling her to go to Sordan herself with any complaints about Dorilian's love life. Stefan eyed the map again and reached a decision.

"I will send someone to talk to Princess Palaistea. Now that I'm married, neither of us need fear the other will seek to make a union. I want Stauberg to be stable and a trusted friend—and she wants to raise her children in peace. Our goals are not so different."

Erenor nodded. "Do you wish me to ride to Bynum?"

"Yes, but not alone." Stefan touched the castle within the silver ring that marked Stauberg. "Send for my mother."

13

The Eleutheron's pink-purple hills softened a landscape of sharp-crowned mountains and knife-bright lakes. Emyli had always loved the flowering stands of cherry and plum that lined the Royal Highway near Bynum. The ancient plantings harked back to the eldest days, when the last of the Aryati and their Staubaun minions brought to this land the fruits of their exile. The Sons of Amynas and Leur had founded Stauberg and revived the lost cities of Permephedon and Sordan, but the Aryati had founded their own kingdom in mountain-bounded Gweroyen beyond the glittering waters of Ulan Sana. Bynum hugged that splendid shore, upon silver sandstone cliffs whereon the bright red blood of Telarion, the martyred Highborn king, could still be seen.

A palace blue and white as crocuses presided above the outskirts of the city, a queenly crown upon a stately hill. Emyli had always thought the Danae Palace the most beautiful Highborn Serat, and it lifted her heart to see it. A dwelling built for the godborn. Protected. Hallowed.

As things should be.

Emyli had not seen Palaistea since before Stefan's coronation. Emyli was elder by enough years for it to matter, though they had become almost friendly after Palaistea wed Enreddon. Marc Frederick had considered Enreddon his close friend. It pleased Emyli to think her father would approve of this mission.

"Will she let us see her precious sons?"

Emyli stiffened at her companion's inquiry. She detected scorn of a mother's protective instincts and composed her reaction. She would not put it past Erenor to misconstrue her sympathy. Stefan had communicated his wishes clearly: Emyli was to explain his position and persuade Palaistea to formally renounce Eldon's and Enreddon's rights of succession to Essera's throne. Emyli could not imagine why Palaistea would do that. Stefan had a lot to learn about pushing people too far.

Erenor insisted on riding beside her, though she preferred he remain with the guard. Erenor claimed Stefan had impressed on him a need to stay with Emyli at all times, a claim she could neither verify on the road nor doubt was possible. The soldiers of her escort were under Erenor's command.

"I think Palaistea will keep her sons out of sight. The Highborn are protective of their young."

"I have never seen one of that kindred who was not already a youth, though I saw Highborn enough when I served as a captain in your father's Cadet Dragoons." Erenor lifted his chin with pride. "That was the first time I sought to protect my prince, *your* son, from a Highborn cub."

Ah, there lay the open wound. Erenor craved greater reward for his loyalty than Stefan had so far given him. What Emyli could not tell was if she dealt with a patient and cunning man—or an impatient and greedy one.

Palaistea's steward met them at the gate and accompanied their party into the compound. They ascended to the palace by way of silver-veined steps traced with ancient script that laid out the lineage of Emrysen I, who had built it.

Palaistea awaited them in an audience chamber. She stood before the unassuming chair that Malyrdeon princes used as a throne. A simple chiton of fine creamy cotton clothed her from shoulder to ankles, and she had draped a mantle of brilliant blue silk over her arms for warmth. Her smooth oval face and warm topaz eyes had not changed at all from those of the young wife and new mother Emyli remembered.

Only the remaining Highborn princes and Stefan ranked higher than this woman, so Erenor dropped to one knee and stayed there. Emyli bowed her head. Though she was only nominally Palaistea's peer, she held out both hands and hoped to receive a peer's reception. Relief flowed through her when Palaistea descended the single step and extended pale arms to her, taking her hands.

"I am so glad you came to see me." Palaistea's voice conveyed only sincerity. "It has been too long, and our families were so close."

"I would like us to be close again," Emyli affirmed. She was here to bridge a crack in that alliance before it could become a chasm. "My son, the king, sends his regards."

"And I hope you will convey mine to him."

Emyli noted how Palaistea bestowed upon Erenor only the briefest of glances. It bordered on dismissal, though she welcomed Emyli's entourage with a wide smile and offered the hospitality of her home. All things considered, a gracious greeting, as befitted a personage of high standing.

They found time to speak freely later, when Emyli accepted Palaistea's invitation to visit privately. Erenor had pushed to accompany her, but the invitation had not included him and the palace guards would not allow him to pass the doors of their lady's wing of the palace. Emyli had merely returned Erenor's glare of displeasure and said not a word to indicate she wished him with her; she didn't, and she cared not at all about what he might say to Stefan. She resented having a chaperone.

An older woman, her position in the household unclear, guided Emyli through several elegant rooms to one with doors flung open onto a terrace. Just past the marble paving and grassy skirt of the hill, where shadowy night took over, Emyli spied Palaistea seated before a large instrument pointed at the sky. Apparently, Palaistea shared her late husband's passion for observing the stars. Hair and skin silvered with starlight, Palaistea waved that Emyli should join her.

"Tonight I can see the moons of distant Mahjan. A string of little lights, so far away. Redd said the star farers once visited those moons, and plundered them, and even dwelt upon two of them in great cities built upon clouds. Clouds! Can you imagine that? I can barely do so, but the Wall showed that very thing—a Wall Lord claimed to have seen it." She lifted her eye from the lenspiece and gave Emyli a smile, bidding her sit on a chair placed nearby.

"The Wall Lords saw so many things." Emyli peered at stars strewn across the night sky above Bynum. A curtain of celestial jewels, so distant they appeared cold. She could not have said which one might be Mahjan.

"Yes. What a great loss. We hope Elhanan—" Palaistea did not complete the thought, so Emyli did.

"I hope also that he walks the Wall someday soon."

"Do you?"

"With all my heart." Of all the gifts to which the Highborn were heir, Emyli wished most for this one.

"And your son? The king? What does he wish?"

"To be allowed to rule according to his own mind, as my father did."

"Your father," said Palaistea, "kept counsel with his friends—and his enemies also. He listened to all voices. Redd liked to say Marc Frederick was one of us in spirit. He listened. And he believed. He made possible the impossible." She sighed. "And now people say Dorilian killed him and my husband, and all the kindred who died at Permephedon that day. Even his own father."

"No. Not all people believe that. I reject those accusations."

"As do I… and yet I remain uncertain." Another doubt turned Palaistea's perfect lips. "What of the rumor that he killed his wife? That he beheaded her?"

"I believe that one."

Palaistea looked out across the starlit hills. "Have you noticed people are forgetting about her? About Daimonaeris? As if she never existed, as if Dorilian never had a wife, as if she never died in that horrible way? Just yesterday I had trouble recalling her name."

The chill that trickled down Emyli's spine recalled the last words she—or anyone in Essera—had heard Dorilian speak. *You are dead to me, Stefan!*

"Do you think he is erasing her from the Mind?"

"I doubt it's intentional. Redd hoped Dorilian might someday be able to command the Rill, and the kindred has long known he's a projective empath. Such can affect the Mind simply by the strength of their beliefs—or their denials. You know this too, unless your father kept his thoughts secret."

"No, he shared his thoughts on that." How not, when Dorilian being a projective empath explained almost everything about his and Stefan's malignant relationship?

"So, knowing what you know, who would you blame for your son's enmity toward our kindred? Does he cast us alongside Dorilian? Or have we ourselves done something to earn his disfavor?"

"I don't know." Emyli resisted her urge to point to Dorilian. Though Stefan's fear of that Highborn menace was certainly at the root of this dangerous breach, other failings also contributed. "I lay the blame on one thing: Stefan has not had the advantage of my father's teachers. You know what I mean. The familiarity of your kindred. Endurin, Enreddon, Regelon—so many Malyrdeons taught my father what the Highborn are and what they can be. Even Sebbord and Labran taught him how to withstand and weather Highborn hostility! Who taught Stefan? No one."

"Then I would say that's where Marc Frederick failed, not we. He didn't prepare his grandson."

"No. He did not."

Palaistea glanced at her instrument. "Would you like to see the string of moons? It is really quite lovely."

"I would rather we talk about our sons."

"Is that wise? I very much fear what you might tell yours."

"The truth?" Emyli forced herself to meet the other woman's doubtful gaze. "Is it so difficult to believe I am your advocate?"

"Your advocacy in the past led to great harm for such as my sons."

Emyli hung her head. Even to turn aside her face could not distance her from painful memories. Had she not witnessed the deaths of the Highborn princes at Gignastha? Had she not *caused* those deaths? She had set terrible events into motion. "I was so young. I knew so little. And yes, I made choices that led to suffering and catastrophe. Just know I did not wish harm upon the Highborn then—not ever! Enreddon himself absolved me of those murders."

"He told me."

So there was that. Tears misted Emyli's eyes for the loss of that gifted man. Him, and so many like him. She would do whatever was in her power to save those that remained.

Palaistea continued softly. "I wonder if you can understand the great responsibility that lies upon me. To be mother to Highborn sons, to know the future of the race rests in my hands. Not all of it, of course, only these two small lives, but"—she sighed and looked out across the land—"so very much depends on them. Redd told me we must prepare for terrible things."

"Did he ever say what?"

"No. Only that preserving our kindred was paramount if the Creation is to survive this event. Can you imagine that? The Creation *itself*. This fragile world. And then the horror at Permephedon happened, the Demise. And because of that, all this followed."

Permephedon, yes. That collision resounded through everything after, even this moment. Echoes within echoes. Emyli twisted her hands in her skirt. "I tried to prevent what happened between Stefan and Dorilian. I wanted to repair the fragile alliance my father had constructed, the single thread of it that remained. I thought I could help."

Palaistea's gaze lifted, curved glimmers in soft starlight.

Emyli continued. "Dorilian will never refuse to see me. Because of my father... because of"—How much to say?—"because of a promise he made. You ask if I believe Dorilian killed my father, and I say again 'No.' For all the reasons I have to detest that man, he loved my father and I do not think him capable of that degree of betrayal. He even tried.... When Stefan proposed to meet with him, it was I who went to see Dorilian and begged him to do so. I promised he would be safe. I hoped he and Stefan might mend their quarrel. I didn't know... It all went terribly wrong."

"Nothing happened."

Emyli shook her head. "Everything happened, they went for the throat. I—"

"Nothing. Happened." Palaistea rose, slim and tall, clothed in starlight and cloth of silver. "Let's walk to the night garden—the moonflowers are in bloom."

Many minutes later, beneath a pergola draped with clusters of tiny blossoms and a spicy sweet scent that recalled childhoods spent in gardens such as this one, they found a place to talk. Here they could see neither the palace nor the stars, only each other. From the stony ground at their feet spilled a stepped fountain above which luminous fairy bugs performed bright dances.

"I do not suppose you, or anyone else, sees these things the way the Highborn do." Palaistea sounded regretful as well as uneasy. "All things happen in the same moment. Dorilian and Stefan, for example, carry their history with them and add to it at every turn. These things are concurrent. They hated each other before, but from a distance. They hate each other still—from a distance. Given that Stefan wishes to kill him, we count that as fortunate."

"Kill him? No, that's not true." But Emyli couldn't say so with the certainty she wished.

"You are blind to your own son. Stefan wishes to destroy us."

How could Palaistea think that? Because the Highborn had reached this conclusion? Emyli felt even her own faith shifting. Highborn connection with Leur was such that if one of their princes could say such a thing, he must believe it—and if that was the case... then his belief would take on the force of truth. Knowing the history between Stefan and Dorilian, it seemed only too possible Dorilian had somehow fashioned hatred and fear into a prison Stefan might never escape. Or was it possible someone else had built it?

Emyli had not considered the possibility of others who might attempt to imprison them both.

"Is that what you believe? Why, when Stefan has never said

such a thing? Look at his actions, not at rumors whispered by fools. Yes, he has good reason to be wary of Malyrdeon power in his kingdom. Imagine yourself in his seat. You, Rheger, and even Elhanan with whom he's been friendly, every one of you avoids him and moves in shadows at the edge of his reign, never taking him into your confidence." As Palaistea averted her gaze, Emyli pressed her point. "Is it a wonder Stefan feels slighted? Tell me my son has nothing to fear from you and your kindred and I will convey your reassurance to him. Better still, seek him out. Speak with him in person and see for yourselves that he can be the ally you need."

"And what of him? What does he need?"

"Assurances, only that. As my father did. He needs to know you, the godborn, will stand with him, at his side."

"That is something *you* need to know, a dream but not a truth. The truth is Stefan doesn't want us at his side. He wants us out of his way." No longer was Palaistea being careful. "Five months ago, I rode to Stauberg with my sons. I hoped to pass the winter in the mild weather of their rightful princedom, their hereditary home and birthright, but when I neared the gate, the king's soldiers turned us away. King Stefan, they said, forbade me and my sons from taking up residence in *his* capital." Palaistea's eyes were bright with tears. "As Essera's highest seat, of course Stauberg is Stefan's city, to rule from and to count among his loyal domains and subjects—my sons among them—even as Enreddon and his brothers served your father. But Stauberg is also *my* sons' birthright—a Malyrdeon principality, founded by Ergeiron, who presides over it still. The Wall is a Malyrdeon Entity. The Principality of Stauberg was Enreddon's holding and passed by law and sacred inception to his sons. So why is Stefan keeping us from it?"

Genuine hurt underlined every word. While Highborn daughters such as Palaistea did not inherit the Leur gifts of males born of that kindred, they were steeped in empathy and perceivers of truth. They discerned and felt and projected keenly. Not Dorilian-coercive keen, a blade of pure emotion hurled unerringly into the heart or gut, but a skill no less useful for being subtler.

That Palaistea wanted to raise her sons in Stauberg, close to their father's memory and in proximity to the Wall to which they might someday speak, was no presumption. Emyli would have been equally distraught if denied entry to Gustan Manor.

"I agree. Stauberg is your home. I will speak with Stefan."

"My boys are too young to present any danger to him, or to anyone. They aren't powerful. They are *children*."

"I know. We protect our children, don't we?"

"Yes," Palaistea agreed, fiercely. "We do. Maybe he will understand us better when he has children of his own."

"I think that would be a very good thing. Right now, who are his heirs?" Emyli had little recourse but to repeat Stefan's concern. "A brother Marenthro has hidden from him—and your sons."

"Yes, my sons, who are far too close to his throne." Palaistea hung her head. "You know I have been besieged by offers of marriage. Of all the reasons I might wed, the most compelling is that I might ally with someone powerful enough to protect me— and my boys."

A cold fist gripped Emyli's bowels. "Of all the men you might marry, there is one—"

"Dorilian Sordaneon?"

"Well, he is the most—" What word could possibly describe that man?

"Obvious?"

"I was going to say Highborn."

Palaistea laughed. "That, too."

"Have you communicated with him? At all?"

"Only once." Palaistea's smile faded. "The very day after Permephedon, after Redd died. A sheet of paper, hand-delivered by courier. He said my husband's death was quick and final, and expressed his sorrow. He called Redd noble and a great loss. The note was very short."

Emyli thought of the note she had received and looked away to conceal her emotion. *I want you to know I tried to save him.* "Dorilian hasn't ever been what anyone would call warm."

"No. Just know that was our only communication. He has not approached me since, or for the reason you fear. I honestly do not think he wants a wife. And I honestly do not want him as a husband. Could you imagine? Besides, Stefan… he would never let that happen, would he? He doesn't want Dorilian any closer to his throne. You see, I do understand your son's fears. I understand so very well. And maybe Dorilian does also. Beyond condolences, he has not made contact with any of us."

Palaistea might not know if he had. The Highborn princes had secret ways to reach out to each other, which made Rheger and Elhanan the greater threats. This woman and her sons were merely caught in a larger, vastly dangerous, game.

"Yet you mention you might consider marriage. If not him, whom?"

"Please understand, I would prefer to not take a husband. I can manage the domains of Stauberg and the Eleutheron very well on my own. My cousin in Lacenedon is an able regent there. My upbringing prepared me for this. My father and husband were wonderful teachers. Even if I were to wed, I would give no man control over my sons or their lands. The king should not fear that."

Emyli wished Stefan were here so he could witness how much better it was to talk openly of such things as concerned him, with a person who could lay his fears to rest.

Unless, of course, he believed he heard only lies.

Palaistea held out her hand to a swarm of fairy bugs. One lit upon her finger, then another, bejeweling her with light. "Did you know Stefan has proposed a husband for me?"

Emyli had not heard. Her son, clearly, was himself keeping secrets. Upon seeing Emyli's surprise, Palaistea lifted an eyebrow. "He sent a missive, not quite an order, and told me it was his wish I wed that man you brought with you. Erenor Tholeros. The king recently landed him, with Averrn."

Averrn was part of Tahlwent's royal grant. "But Apollonia surely—"

"I cannot speak for her, only for myself. It may be this is some plan between them. Her domain will accrue to the crown. But Erenor—is not to my liking. Perhaps you noticed."

That explained her cool reception. Erenor, even if given an impressive domain and title—and could claim a Highborn ancestor three generations past—could not be made suitable for the Gracious Princess Palaistea. Palaistea's kindred could have accepted a love match, perhaps. Such happened. But that was not the case here. Stefan's attempt bordered on insult.

"Talk to your son," Palaistea advised. She flicked her fingers and the fairy bugs flitted away. "Let him know I, and my sons, are his loyal subjects, and that I am willing to be ruled... but not played with. We Malyrdeons"—she included herself with her sons and the remaining kindred— "serve the Creation and what the Sons of Amynas built: this Triempery, with its Wall and its Rill. We acknowledge Stefan as Essera's legitimate king."

"So why will you not go and say that to him?"

"We saw what he tried with Dorilian." Palaistea rose and indicated they should return to the palace. "Let him know. What we say after depends on what we hear from him."

The next morning brought rain clouds and a return of early spring chill. Emyli wore her fox fur cloak fastened up to her chin and was glad to have brought gloves lined with *seshi* wool. Erenor rode at her side, his expression as stormy as the tempest roaring down from the Ulnossi.

"The Gracious Princess refused to see me." His complaint found little sympathy with Emyli and perhaps he sensed that. "Did she tell you why?"

"Only that she has no desire to take a husband at this time."

"The Princess is lying. She is entertaining suitors in secret." Erenor's upper lip curled unpleasantly. "Did you think Stefan has no ears on her? No eyes? I spoke with one of his informants while you were listening to her tales of a mother's woe and purchasing half-truths from her lips." He reached over to grasp the reins of Emyli's horse. She tried to wrench them away, but he held tight. "Maybe it's true she wants no husband, but she will take one to make greater her strength, and clearly she does not wish her strength to reside with any man loyal to the king. She has been receiving Burelan, Bas of Rannul, whom Stefan suspects of plotting against him. She said nothing of him, did she?"

"We talked of other things." Important things, Emyli might have said. Highborn things. But she held her tongue.

"You were supposed to persuade her to talk with me. You were to get her to agree to accept Stefan's restrictions on her and her sons and make a gesture that will put her at his side."

"I will have a great deal to say to my son when we return. But we are riding to Kyrbasillon, are we not?"

Visiting Palaistea was but the first stop on her assignment to bring the Malyrdeons back into the fold where their king wished them to be. Emyli intended to build a bridge—a bridge between the kingdom Marc Frederick had striven so hard to preserve, and the one Stefan was so determined to put in its place. She refused to envision a kingdom in which the Highborn had no place.

How strange was that? And how impossible. Decimated by Permephedon's horror and driven by Stefan's fear of them, the remaining Malyrdeons had retreated from the world and were more and more invisible.

Only in Sordan, far to the south and hostile to everything Stefan represented, was a Highborn ruler still open and proud and seen.

14

"Your husband is at last growing careless. He is treating his subjects to the spectacle of a progress down the Sorand'ruil, after which he intends to sail his newest warship up the Sansordan coast."

Nammuor wished Daimonaeris would cover her body slave. Seeing his sister's face atop the head of the blindfolded slave was… disconcerting. Glowing *lr* crystals pulsed at the slave's temples, linking its brain to Daimonaeris's eyes and commands. The crystal interfaces, devised by Nammuor's most cunning mages, were crude but allowed her to move at will.

She ran the slave's hands down its sturdy body. "You act as if I care what Dorilian does." She frowned, studying her image in the full-length mirror.

"You should care. He will be taking the boy with him. They will both be vulnerable. Will you stop looking at yourself?"

"I do not like this one. It is sure-footed but not shapely enough."

"Cover it, then, with one of your thousand costly robes. Beauty is not always paired with the strength needed to support my… embellishments." This slave was one of the prettier ones, possessed of a strong back, wide hips, and muscular thighs to balance the metal framework it must carry.

"I am growing tired of waiting for a body of my own. It would take but one of your Highborn crystals."

That idea, once in her head, refused to be uprooted. Nammuor didn't know how many crystals it would take. Keeping Daimonaeris's head alive and ambulatory required twelve mortal crystals every week. Twelve fresh crystals. Twelve healthy young slaves of high Aryati breeding slain for their lifeblood, just to keep her alive to torment him.

"Patience." Saying it had become habit. "You know my plans."

"For that *thing*." Having looked in the mirror long enough, she moved toward her closet, from which she grabbed a long robe of turquoise silk embroidered with flame flowers. "Yet you have no plans for me, for the rightful ruler of this land. You are my regent, after all."

Nammuor fought the growing tightness in his jaw. *Her* regent. That much was true. To be sure, the rumor that Daimonaeris was still alive was… only that. A rumor. He had not trotted her out in public. Neither did he deny she had returned by way of mage work or that the effort had left her much weakened. Most of the City believed she was dead, a confusion he continued to exploit in hope of someday turning her miraculous reappearance to advantage.

His power at this point rested on other bases.

"Try to enjoy your life, little Hierarchessa. Someday—"

"Someday. Someday. Someday! I am tired of waiting. I am your throne wife, brother, and my people need to see me. But not like this! You promised me a beautiful young body. A young woman of rank."

"Making beautiful noblewomen disappear without anyone noticing is not easy."

"What do you care about that?" She held out an unlidded jar from her dressing table. "I can barely smell anything. What of this one? Is it almond? Or floral?"

"Something else. But it's very nice. Use it. I must go." Nammuor left her holding the jar and looking confused. The corridor outside opened before him, mercifully silent and attended only by his own thoughts.

What fragrance his sister wore hardly mattered. That Daimonaeris could not detect the fragrance notes on her own was a problem.

It had been three years since Emyli had been in Kyrbasillon. The city commanded a strategic river valley presided over by palaces and prosperous estates. Generations of benevolent Highborn rule and riches had bestowed on the population a wealth of splendid architecture: libraries, theaters, galleries, schools, and spring-fed public baths. It was for good reason Dannuth's capital was considered the Jewel of the Glainoi.

As Emyli rode beneath the Arch of Mercy that spanned the north road into the city, she wished she could embody its teaching. Nearly four years had passed since her brother Jonthan's last birthday celebration here. Four years since her family's troubles had begun with, of all things, a horse race and Jonthan being gifted the winning horse. Four fateful years and Emyli had yet to forgive Dorilian for any of the harm he had done. It was fitting, then, that she rode beneath symbols of absolution on a day gray with rain.

At her side, Erenor looked nervous, and Emyli realized he mistrusted the Highborn as much as Stefan did. Her son increasingly surrounded himself with men who amplified his failings.

Rheger Dannutheon, Prince of Dannuth, greeted Emyli less formally than Palaistea had. The glass walled room in the Serat known as the Palace of Virtues overlooked the river and Kyrbasillon's most beautiful gardens. The Prince extended to her the offer of a chair but required Erenor to remain standing. The square-jawed man at Rheger's side remained on his feet also and was introduced as Grenant Aigelleros. Emyli greeted Grenant warmly. The stalwart nobleman was the husband of Rheger's niece, Reva. She and Reva had been dear friends many years ago and Emyli looked forward to seeing her again on this visit.

"I hope you do not find my visit presumptuous, Thrice Royal."

Rheger took a seat facing her across a low table laid with tea and sweets. "That would depend on its purpose. I cannot imagine you would overstep."

"Ah, but I come with a direct request. A request from the heart. I ask that you appear at the court of my son, Stefan. Pay him a visit." There, she had said it. In front of witnesses, no less. There could be no doubt now that Emyli had done as Stefan asked.

A bare trace of shadow passed over Rheger's handsome face. He had in full measure the breathtaking looks that so graced Essera's Highborn princes. Neat, finger-length white-blond hair touched his ears and his clear eyes, intelligent and wary, were a cooler shade of topaz than Palaistea's. Those eyes flicked for a moment to take in Erenor.

"I hope you, and the king, understand why I have been standing aside, Princess." Careful words, as the answer merited. "My absence from court has silenced many who might have felt nostalgia for the days when my brethren were their kings."

"Yes, but Stefan still would have your kindred *grace* his court— as you did my father's."

"Your father came to the throne in very different circumstances. Kindred against kindred. We stood at Marc Frederick's side to affirm him. To let all know he was our choice for Highborn rule. Through him, yes, but—make no mistake—it was Highborn rule. We had the Wall to guide us then. The Wall is silent now, however, so we must tread carefully. My absence sends a message that I and my family do not wish to unseat your son. We do not covet Stefan's throne. We want only to live in peace and allow him to rule without having us around to distract or interfere."

"Or advise." *Or blame.*

Rheger winced. "Stefan has made quite clear he does not want my advice."

Emyli could well imagine. She must be diplomatic here. "Any advice on how to handle Dorilian will always fall on deaf ears. But advise Stefan on how he might better steer the ship of state that is Essera, he will listen."

"You realize, I hope—and I hope Stefan does too—that the kindred is crippled by our inability to communicate with the Wall. We appreciate the king's efforts to recover the Wall Stone, but the fact remains it is not in our possession. Any insight I might give, any advice, would be drawn from experience, not foresight."

"The king understands that, Thrice Royal." Erenor spoke out boldly. "I dare say he prefers it so."

Emyli regretted two things: that Erenor had spoken up at all, and the subtle, quickly masked pain that passed over Rheger's face. What was Erenor doing, casting Stefan as an obstacle to the Malyrdeons regaining their Entity? He must know—as all people did—that the Malyrdeons were bound to their Wall by more than tradition. They were bound to it bodily as well. Their current estrangement cut deep. Emyli was not surprised to see Rheger's face adopt an expression far less diplomatic.

"Then accept that my experience extends only so far. I was not supposed to rule Dannuth. Ostemun should have ruled another sixty years and chosen an heir from his grandsons or nephews. I am a scholar, a huntsman, a man of leisure. I aspire only to a quiet life."

"A life filled nonetheless with influence."

There was no mistaking Erenor's point. Rheger grimaced. "Some. Though not where our king most needs it." He turned to Emyli. "Please inform the king that I will, of course, pay him a visit. Give me two weeks and I will meet with Stefan in Dazunor-Rannuli. I welcome the opportunity to talk with him and put to rest our differences."

Emyli rose and bowed her head, then left with Erenor at her side. She had made no progress. None at all.

They had not even talked about Palaistea, or the vital Highborn grievances surrounding the Malyrdeon heirs. Erenor had cut all talk of Stauberg, and the Wall, off at the knees.

"I am meeting them in the throne room, Mother, and that is my final say on the matter." Stefan stabbed a third jewel-heavy brooch into his velvet vestment. It took an arsenal of regalia, and the Emrysen Palace's throne room also, for him to outroyal a Malyrdeon.

"It's not necessary. Your grandfather counted Rheger among his friends."

"As if that matters. Rheger doesn't count me among *his*. He needs to be reminded he's my subject. They both do."

Two weeks had passed since Emyli's return. Rheger had come to Dazunor-Rannuli, and not alone. He had brought his son, Elhanan, with him. Stefan actually liked Elhanan—or had liked him, before events had placed them on opposite sides. Stefan wished his mother would cease her efforts to dictate the tone of his relationships with his nobles. He wasn't Marc Frederick—and never would be.

"They could be such wonderful assets for you."

He could only shake his head sometimes at the way Emyli looked at the world. "Is that how you see people? As a kind of economy?"

"No. But in politics certain people bestow more value than others."

"Well, the Malyrdeons don't bestow nearly the value they used to. They can't talk to their Wall anymore. Rheger outright told you that."

"Yes, but if they could recover the Wall Stone—"

Stefan snorted. "Fat chance of that. Dorilian isn't going to give it back anytime soon. He'll hold onto it just to spite me." He looked over his shoulder to see if she would challenge his remark and was gratified when she didn't. "I just want the damn Dannutheons to promise to not plot behind my back. You know they would rather see Palaistea's brat—"

"Eldon is a baby!"

"He's five! And lots of people would rather see him sitting on the throne than me." Let her argue that if she could. All of Stefan's advisers knew it to be true, even Cullen, who was just like Emyli in the way he counselled restraint. Stefan gave her a look of disgust.

"I'm not going to attack a toddler. I just want to make sure there won't be coalitions growing up around him."

Emyli appeared chastened. "Of course, you need to be sure of that."

He decided to cheer her up. "It would help, of course, if I had an heir of my own." He grinned. "Nilla is pregnant."

"Stefan! How wonderful!" His mother's smile had never looked more beautiful or joyful. "When?"

"She's still early. The baby will be born this winter. We'll make an announcement in another month or two." That would give people something to talk about besides damn Dorilian and his procession of golden barges. "For now, I will just have a pleasant talk with Dannuth's princes."

Stefan walked into the throne room with Emyli at his side. Rheger and Elhanan were already in the room, standing casually side by side, and looking completely at home amidst the elegance. How not? Their kind had built nearly every palace in Essera, including this one. Both men bowed their circlet-bright heads to Stefan but did not kneel. It irked Stefan that they did not have to. Being king merely made him *their* peer. That they would kneel to Dorilian just because he was Hierarch of Sordan and wore a Highborn crown brought on a surge of resentment.

These Highborn princes expected Stefan to thank them for coming. They should be glad he gave them the chance to explain themselves. He decided to lay it out plainly.

"I want to hear why you are embarrassing me by not appearing at my court."

He could almost hear his mother's held breath and saw the way her eyelids lowered, then opened again. Although Elhanan looked taken aback, Rheger appeared to have expected Stefan's bluntness and answered smoothly.

"As I have said before, at least for myself, I wished to give Your Majesty's new reign a period free of speculation. If I were at court—"

"People could have come to you and asked your intentions. You could have answered them. Instead you were far away, and people have been *wondering* about your motives."

"Many have asked, Your Majesty, and I have answered."

"But many more don't ask." Stefan paced toward the canopied throne but did not mount the dais to seat himself upon it. It gleamed with power, and he liked having it on display. "Especially Khelds. They don't even know how to *begin* to seek out or talk to a man of your rank. If they did somehow get up the nerve to approach, your guards would turn them away. You haven't answered any of *their* questions."

"We do not often speak with Khelds."

Stefan glowered. "It's time you do."

Rheger met Stefan's gaze and held it. Unspoken things hung between them. Marc Frederick had hinted to Stefan, many times and especially right before going to Permephedon that last time, that the Wall visions guarded by the Malyrdeons had included Khelds in important ways. It was time to get to that point.

"Do Khelds have a part to play in the future the Wall revealed to your kindred?" Stefan had studied up on how to frame such a question.

Rheger cast his gaze downward for a moment, though he looked up again. "We do not know all that the Wall showed our predecessors."

Stefan turned to Elhanan. "But you do."

Elhanan's expression, halting and evasive, was not what Stefan had hoped to see. "I do not, Majesty. The Archive is inaccessible without the Wall Stone. Anything I know, I learned before the artifact went missing."

"Was stolen, you mean."

More hesitation. Elhanan drew a breath. "It has been... displaced. Until then, we rely on second- and thirdhand sources or historical traces. Wall gleanings are dense, scattered, and difficult to interpret. The Archive itself is Time-warded and focus only becomes possible as an event draws near. Khelds are a known component of these hidden futures, yes. Perhaps even very important, but we do not know for whom or in what way they will prove important. We do not wish to... influence the course of any matter to do with Khelds."

"Even if that influence produces a favorable future?"

"We cannot, without the Wall Stone, discern *any* futures—favorable or otherwise. We have only bits of possible."

"What about Dorilian? What does the Wall have to say about him? What's... possible?"

The men wanted to share a glance. Stefan saw them hold back from doing so. There was something there. Feeling Emyli's light touch on the arm made him frown. As always, he was left wondering what *she* knew.

"Perhaps Endurin, the Last Wall Lord, knew Dorilian's... possibilities... or even probabilities, but *we* do not. He is a tangle of unknowns. Austell Malyrdeon's mind broke trying to use the Wall Stone to see into Dorilian's futures." Elhanan shook his head.

"Dorilian survived the Demise—the event that decimated our race, an event the Wall foretold. Any glimpses or gleanings beyond that are locked in the Wall's Archives—if gleanings exist at all."

"The Wall *foretold* everyone would die at Permephedon?" Stefan gaped at his mother, who met his gaze with terrible affirmation, then back to them. He stalked toward the two men. "They went there even though they *knew*?"

"The *Wall* knew." Elhanan stood straighter now. He had, before those events, been a Wall Lord in training. "Maybe Endurin knew. We... were not told. We... I... believe there was another future, maybe other *futures*, the Demise prevented."

"Or created. Maybe *this one*?"

"Perhaps. We don't fully.... Please understand, Stefan—"

"I am your king, not your friend, *Prince Elhanan*."

Elhanan swallowed. Hard. "Your Majesty, we are blind. As blind as you are, as Essera's nobles are, or the Khelds. Dorilian is blind, too. Now, in this time, all of us are blind when it comes to the Wall and what the Entity sees or does not see."

Maybe they did need their damned artifact after all.

"Could you use the Wall Stone to help me, if you had it?"

Rheger's posture slumped as though the weight of every possible future had just fallen upon him. Elhanan, though, lifted his head with hope. "We could help you, if the Wall showed anything useful. I am far from a skilled Wall walker—I have never done it, in fact—and I would require assistance, someone skilled at clearing courses. As of now—" He dropped that point, to continue with another. "We have to consider, too, that the Wall's vision may have altered *since* the Demise, or because of it. We have no way of knowing until we contact the Entity again."

With a smirk to Emyli, Stefan walked toward the wall of windows overlooking the golden city of Dazunor-Rannuli. He gazed upon a vista of shining domes crowned by a mighty Entity. The Rill, at least, never altered.

"You want to talk with Dorilian?"

"He is the one currently in possession of the Wall Stone." Rheger had resumed being the spokesman.

"And I'm the one who needs to trust you before I allow that." Stefan turned back to them. "Help me guide Essera and unite my domains. Some of my nobles need to be convinced your kindred supports me. Apollonia is being a bitch, for one thing. Can you do anything about her? Your support might also quell some of the Staubaun aggression against Khelds in Neuberland."

"These things we can assist with as needed, Your Majesty."

"Good." Stefan nodded. A glance at his mother showed her discreet approval. As if he needed it. He knew when he'd done well. "Thank you both. I appreciate your meeting with me."

They bowed, and he watched them leave. Emyli soon followed. Now at least he knew why he could never find a way around the damned Malyrdeons.

The fucking Wall.

15

Dorilian rode toward the sun on a river of gold. His gilded barge, longer than some of the towns they passed, conveyed him in palatial splendor. An emerald and gold striped awning shaded even the palm trees adorning his outdoor seating area. A palace of viridian marble figured with gold and silver rose in ornate stories behind him and, if he wished, Dorilian could dine at a full table, host a party for hundreds, or sleep in a chamber hung with silk and perfumed by incense. Water hot and cold flowed to every room of the structure, warming or cooling floors as needed and filling pools for bathing. Stones precious and rare formed the palace's mosaic floors. Deck terraces displayed gardens of flowers and fruiting trees.

Too ponderous for speed, the barge traveled at a stately pace. Small boats streamed out from towns along the way, crowded with onlookers gawping at the magnificent vessel and hoping to see their Hierarch. The sole time Dorilian had previously traveled this river—to Ilmar on his way to Stauberg—he had done so as a youth and in secret, completely uninterested in the small lives and concerns he bypassed on his mission. His interest then had been pursuit of a great destiny. He had found it and more, only to have that world shatter.

But he still had this. Sordan and its mighty river. A land and a nation Dorilian had made strong again and could make even stronger. Strong enough—perhaps—to keep his enemies at bay. Strong enough to keep him safe: him and his family and the Rill.

"Town! Town!"

From her vantage at the barge's eagle-headed prow, Fahme ran toward him. Her sandaled feet slapped the wooden deck. Dorilian rose from his chaise and swept her up into his arms. A squawk announced Levyathan had awakened from his nap. Dorilian gathered him up also and allowed Legon to fuss at the boy's tousled hair. Tiflan took Fahme in arms, an elevation which pleased the child. Levyathan nuzzled Dorilian's shoulder as they took a place at the north-facing railing. There Dorilian stood, flanked by his shining, armored commanders, to be seen by the crowd.

The Rillborn Sordaneons. Sordan's Hierarch and his Heir. Even from here Dorilian heard the roar of their approval.

"Our people," he said to Levyathan, who yawned.

Towns prosperous and painted with color crowded the river in jumbles of low buildings and throngs of cheering well-wishers. Dorilian had chosen to make a regal statement by wearing Derlon's Armor, the engraving of which dazzled upon his torso and spread its famous wings across his chest and shoulders. Derlon's gauntlets, too, gleamed on Dorilian's forearms, talons ablaze with sunlight when he lifted his left hand to wave. Anyone in the boats that approached might also see the Rill Stone's green fire on his hand.

For all of these people, the Rill created and maintained every part of their lives. The god-machine generated their economy, made possible their markets, and sustained their prosperity. Because of it, Sordan beat like a heart at the core of their nation. Knowing what the Rill had made possible for Dorilian to do, his people worshipped it and him in the same breath.

Between towns, Dorilian lounged on a platform piled high with cushions and shaded by a gauzy awning. Palimia curled beside him and together they watched the rolling, rich lands of his patrimony slide past as in a dream.

"All of this," she said. Palimia sat up to reach for a goblet misted by condensation.

"Sansordan. It goes on forever, or nearly so. It was never divided into smaller domains because, well, you are looking at the best part, the lands along the river, this one and the Randpory. Estates. Vineyards. Olive groves. Fruits and flowers and fish. Everything grows where the climate is moderate and there's plenty of water. The interior is desert. Nobody wants it. I could carve a domain out of that and give it away, I suppose."

"What a cruel joke that would be."

"Yes. Except there is a treasure buried under those poisoned sands. Iridonos, the richest Aryati city of all, glowing beneath the dunes. Legend has it, Iridonos sits atop a melted core. To find it would be death."

"That's even crueler."

Dorilian put the idea away for possible future use. "I am deciding a few things. Apollonia sent a message. She said if I did not put you aside, she would bar Sordan's ships from Aral." Stefan had barred his ships from Stauberg immediately after being crowned king, which left Aral and Ennsa, in Gweroyen, for sea trade with Essera. Dorilian shrugged. "I will divert the ships to Ennsa."

"That's a far less desirable commercial port."

"Alas, she is a far less desirable woman."

Hearing Palimia's laugh was all the reward he needed. What they shared might not be love, but it was something he had not even known he needed.

Jooar Zetharnna met the Sordaneon barge on the Lahgael side of the river at the dock of the Governor's Palace at Ben-Aranath. Dorilian noted Palimia's wide smile upon seeing the brilliantly garbed prince and his entourage of dignitaries. One of a dozen sons of the country's ruler, Jooar had been begotten on a royal consort, not a wife, and was therefore not in line of succession to Lahgael's throne. Through talent and military skill, Jooar had nonetheless secured and held fast the reins of his country's richest province.

"Your Thrice Royal Grace." Jooar greeted Dorilian with a deep bow, hands pressed together in a gesture of respect. The personages with him followed his example. "I am deeply happy you have chosen to honor us with this visit."

"And I am pleased you have opened your house to me."

"Not just my house. My city. My country. Sordan has been our greatest friend."

"And Lahgael ours, especially lately." Along an avenue of smooth stone strewn with a snow of tiny petals, they walked toward the governor's palace. Colonnades of tiled blue pillars faced the river and cooled an interior that promised both luxury and security. Tutto and Legon had come ahead with troops to see to the latter.

"Your need is our fortune. You are running out of friends."

Ah, Jooar. Always a diplomat. One thing the past few years had taught Dorilian was that nations, like people, were ultimately self-interested. The troubles he had heaped on Stefan were only possible because Stefan threatened the interests of Essera's nobles.

Lahgael, too, had fears and considerations—as did Sordan. These could have created conflict. However, Lahgael was historically pragmatic about its possibilities, and Sordan preferred to cultivate strong unions with its neighbors, and so their two nations had fashioned a mutual alliance.

Friends, then, while the flow of riches continued.

Dorilian made introductions to his companions. Jooar's gaze warmed on Palimia and the two children, and he greeted several others as he might old friends.

"Spend the night in comfort. Let us regale you. We rejoice that one of the Rillblood has come among us."

"Two!" crowed Levyathan.

In the shade of the riverfront colonnade, cushioned seating awaited, along with tables laden with refreshment. Silent boys lithe as cats and bearing platters of breads and sweets moved between guests with their offerings. Jooar's royal consort, a recent addition with a lilting name and even lovelier body, placed a circlet of vibrant orange flowers upon Fahme's head before guiding the women to a crescent of cushions.

Aware that Jooar would wish to converse with him, Dorilian sent Tiflan and Tutto to join Palimia and the children for food and drink. With Legon trailing at a distance, Dorilian and Jooar strolled toward a fountain that bubbled up from the marble floor.

Jooar spoke in a low voice. "As you warned they would, Esseran merchants, including some of the Seven House barons, have pressured my father the king for increased access to our river ports." Lahgael shared the river up to the very line where water met earth. "You understand, of course, that we consider the structures of our ports to also be our country. The wharfs. The docks and piers."

Dorilian nodded, though he wondered where Jooar was going with this. He hoped it would not be necessary for their countries to negotiate a more precise definition of their border. Lahgael's king, Bargasar, was almost certainly under siege from more than one front.

"We have so far said no." Jooar stopped beside the fountain rim. "You make this easier by having your ships patrol the river mouth. They have stopped many vessels trying to enter under false flags."

"I anticipated this development." Dorilian's restrictions on the river were a recent development. For eighteen hundred years, the Sorand'ruil had been a neutral channel, open to all ships save during wars.

"Yes, yes, but now the king has received a new ambassador from Essera. This man challenges our claim of neutrality. He says we are not neutral if we let you do this. If we are neutral, he says, we will give Essera's ships access to our river ports."

Of which there were several. Ben-Aranath was simply the largest and the last port before entering that part of the river where Sordan controlled both banks. Essera sought to break Dorilian's chokehold on Rill-transported grain. Merchants would simply divert those purchases to Ben-Aranath, where they could be loaded on seagoing vessels to Essera.

Very well, then.

"Bargasar wishes to avoid conflict with Essera. I understand this. And the access they seek is within his sovereign right to give. But if he wishes to avoid conflict with *me*"—Dorilian stressed that last—"he will not interfere in any way should my ships stop any Esseran vessel in any part of the river. If a ship of any flag successfully reaches your docks, I will consider that ship to be in your territory and my vessels will not harass or harm them while in port. Those ships may, however, be prevented from *leaving*."

"You have enough vessels to accomplish this strategy?"

Dorilian grinned. "My shipyards have been busy."

Jooar's deep chuckle rose above the sound of splashing water. "You did indeed foresee this turn."

"This river is vital to my country. You can be sure I would defend it. I appreciate that you also do so. But it does not fall on Lahgael to stop Esseran ships on Sordan's behalf. I will take on that task in whole."

With a gesture that made clear Jooar was happy to have settled that point, the conversation continued. "We will continue to be alert to incursions by Mormantaloran ships," Jooar said. "The Fire Lords have caused trouble in the south of our country, where they steal glowing sand for their mage work. They slaughter our people but for those they take as slaves. They too are building ships."

Building ships *again*. Only three years ago, Dorilian had helped Essera destroy a generation of Mormantaloran ships. Now he engaged in destroying ships of both countries, though only the Mormantaloran threat really mattered.

Jooar lowered his voice. "There is more you should know. My brothers in the south have detected unusual movement across our border with Orm. Men on horseback, usually solitary, no more than three at a time. They never leave the mountains, but cross over into Suddekar."

"Nammuor has found a new route for his spies." Dorilian had expected Ermenthalia would increase patrols in that area.

"We do not interfere. If you wish us to stop them—"

"Not just yet. I will find out what is going on, but for now I would rather they think I know nothing and keep doing it, rather than start doing something else."

Jooar chuckled. "My brothers will thank you."

"He wants to kill me, you know. Nammuor." When Dorilian looked to Jooar, he caught an affirmative grimace. "The monster wants to destroy my race. All my race. He has made a good start."

Better than the world knew. The death of the aged Prince of Tollech just a month ago had not been natural. The old man's throat had been slashed and his servants claimed to have seen a robed figure stand over the corpse with a crystal in hand. One more for Nammuor's trove. Dorilian wished he knew how many Highborn lifeforces Nammuor had captured... and how many he needed.

Dorilian steeled himself for touch and clasped Jooar's arm. An ally in this case was as good as a friend.

16

"**A**t least one of us should *try* to talk with Dorilian."

Rheger sighed. His son's frustration was leading to dangerous suggestions. It was unlike Elhanan to ignore the obvious.

"The king would consider it treason were we to contact Dorilian. As I recall, he specifically said we were not to do so."

Elhanan turned from the vista beyond the portico of the Illystri palace. The snow-white balustrade presented a view of the brilliant blue lagoon at Dazunor-Rannuli's heart, the Lago, above which the Rill's graceful limbs overarched the city's palaces. After their audience with Stefan, he and his father had stayed in Dazunor-Rannuli as the king had asked, their support on display for all to see.

"I had hoped Dorilian might show up at Taddeus's interment." The old Prince of Tollech had met his end the month before.

"And break his vow? That wasn't going to happen. He held a state funeral in Sordan." Rheger set aside the message cylinder he had opened. At least so far, his correspondence was not being intercepted. "I fear the day that young man returns to Essera. He will have changed a great deal from what people remember."

"What Stefan remembers?"

"What everyone remembers."

Elhanan stared at the Rill with something close to fear. "Then let us pray Essera changes more. The way things stand now—"

"The Wall Archives you accessed before the Demise showed nothing of this time?"

"Not that I could discern. I wasn't looking for notations about

Stefan, of course. Austell almost certainly looked upon forward events when he used the Wall Stone, but his recounting of those impressions—if he even saw any—is beyond fragmentary, not to mention unreliable. What Dorilian saw, though…"

They shared a glance. Elhanan's mouth pressed grimly before he continued. "Stefan's coronation… Dorilian saw at least *some* of that. I am sure of it."

They might never learn the full truth of what Dorilian had glimpsed the day he had touched Austell and the Wall Stone. The men to whom he had revealed his knowledge had all died at Permephedon. "A Sordaneon has no business communing with the Wall. If contact can be made at all, it would be pure instinct, unfiltered."

"Dorilian knows that. He cut his teeth on the dangers of pairing Entities. We are fortunate he grew up with men who taught him to respect his gifts. Do you think he might be tempted to link bodily?"

Elhanan was not asking about the Wall. Dorilian's impetuous vow to Stefan kept him at a safe distance from that Entity. The Rill, on the other hand, was near. And according to Quirin, on the day of the Demise Dorilian had at the very least employed the Rill in a way no one had ever seen. It was tantalizing to think the Rill Entity might already be partially manifest.

"Quite the contrary. I think he already has. The question is more of degree." Rheger walked to join his son. The grand portico of the Illystri Palace was private enough for such conversations as this. "We have a problem."

Acknowledgment tugged at one corner of Elhanan's mouth. A breeze lifted strands of white blond hair. "Dorilian? Or Stefan?"

"Both. Stefan is the closer one, however. His distrust of our kind runs deep. The best we can do for ourselves is to lie low. We must downplay our influence and wealth. Better yet, we will distribute both in ways that create goodwill where such can still sway hearts and minds. Stefan will seek to ensure we have no friends." As beautiful as this city was away from the squalor of its teeming canals, it was also filled with vipers. The sooner they returned to Dannuth, the better.

"And Essera?"

"May well be out of our hands. Palaistea and her sons are even more embattled than we."

After running a hand through his hair, Elhanan shook his head. "Surely there is something we can do."

"Other than stay alive? It doesn't matter what we do. Stefan is intent on reshaping the kingdom. He seeks to impose a new order to which we are, quite simply, unnecessary." Not to mention anathema.

"Not all of Stefan's ideas are bad."

"No, just enough of them to poison whatever it is he thinks he is building." Rheger watched two women play turrets on the lawn below. His Sapphia was enjoying her time here with Margarid, Elhanan's wife. "I miss Marc Frederick. He brought to his projects a deep well of patience; he might as well have been Malyrdeon. Stefan, on the other hand, brings an axe. He confuses obedience with consent."

"Maybe time will make him more patient. Maybe children will. I heard the queen might be pregnant."

Rheger knew very little about the woman Stefan had married. A Kheld, young and proclaimed to be of good breeding, timid and unremarkable. Rheger had seen her only once, on the day of the wedding. Since then, Stefan had surrounded his queen with the wives of his new nobles, almost all of them Kheld also. Sapphia and Margarid had never been considered as advisers and helpmates.

"Yes, maybe children." Rheger laid an arm over Elhanan's shoulders. Together they turned their backs on the golden domes of Dazunor-Rannuli's thousand palaces. "What this kingdom needs most is a future. It's what we all need. Something ahead of us, something to reach toward—not a past to which to retreat. We all need a future."

The lute player was very good, if a little heavy on swooning for his lady love. As the song ended, the musician's fingers left the strings and the music stopped, closely followed by Kheld roars of approval. Hands slammed on tables and set dishes to clatter. Stefan clapped hands to show favor. The player was famous, though Stefan could not understand why. Still, his Staubaun nobles also appeared happy with the entertainment.

Summer at the Emrysen Palace on the outskirts of Dazunor-Rannuli could be steamy. The palace dominated a knoll abutting one of the outer canals and was surrounded by formal gardens that perfumed the area. Among his many palaces, Stefan favored this one above all save the Golden Palace at Trulo, which was—like Dazunor-Rannuli—just across the river from Amallar. Because being near the Rill made travel to Permephedon for the Archhalia easier, he spent more of his time in Dazunor-Rannuli.

Entertaining his court with feasts was the pastime Stefan most favored. He preferred to gather his nobles where he could observe them. Like the Malyrdeon princes seated at the farthest end of Stefan's table, where he had relegated them to diminish their importance. That they were being ignored only proved he had succeeded. He also savored the attendance of emissaries and visiting dignitaries who would see for themselves that his kingdom was thriving. They would carry back reports that his rule was secure, his nobles loyal, and his queen pregnant.

Keeping Nilla at his court accomplished several ends. She was safest where Stefan was, of course, and her youth and attentiveness was guaranteed to make men envious. Draped in finest silk embroidered with gold and pearls, with a circlet of precious stones on her dark hair, Nilla was the center of attention at her table. She presided over her ladies with laughing good humor. Stefan watched lively Asphalladra, her long hair the color of ripe wheat and pulled back by combs, lean near and whisper something with an open grin.

He was close to liking Cullen's wife, who was pregnant also. Asphalladra's father, the Enlad of Chennor, might disapprove of having a Kheld son-in-law, but he surely approved of Cullen's estates and position. Even so, Stefan had needed to pressure the Enlad to make a Rill portion part of Asphalladra's dowry.

"I don't like that look one bit. What are you thinking?" Cullen sat to Stefan's left, goblet in hand.

"Only that you should not be the only Kheld, besides me, to own a Rill portion." The wine was good and still it managed somehow to taste sour.

"Ah. But it's my wife who owns the Rill portion. I merely get to manage it and enjoy the income it produces."

"Men shouldn't have to marry Staubaun noblewomen to get Rill portions."

Cullen reached with his knife toward a platter a servant had set before them and stabbed a slice of pork. "That's how it's done. I had that talk years ago, with your grandfather and someone else, who gave me that advice."

The remark rankled. Stefan knew exactly who that someone had been. Fucking Dorilian. The bastard probably shit Rill portions.

From his seat at Stefan's right hand, Goff leaned in. The golden chain of the office of First Minister gleamed just beneath his bush of gray-streaked beard. "Trouble is, men rich enough to own Rill portions don't pass 'em to daughters except to buy their girls into a better situation." He poked a leg of fowl toward Cullen. "If our Stefan hadn't twisted that man's arm, you'd have got nothing."

"Wouldn't have mattered," said Cullen. "Phalla was all I wanted out of it."

That might be true, but Stefan wasn't fooled. Even before becoming trade minister, Cullen had been intrigued by Rill commerce. Getting that slot portion included in Asphalladra's dowry had been the best gift Stefan, as King, could have given—and he was happy he'd done it. He hoped Dorilian choked every time he thought about a Kheld controlling one of his precious Rill slots. Stefan had heard from reliable sources that the Seven Houses *were* choking on it. He resumed listening to Cullen spar with Goff.

"It's not unfair. Think about it. Getting hold of a Rill portion is not very different from one of our men needing to wed a woman to get onto a bit of land in Amallar."

"That's different." Goff was having none of it. "All women—all clan-right women—in Amallar can and do hold land. Our Nilla brought a fine holding to her husband, land her daughters will hold after her, not any Staubaun husbands they might wed. We keep the land where it belongs."

"And Staubauns who hold Rill portions see it that way too, as keeping the wealth where it belongs. Just think of Rill portions as land and it makes sense."

"That's fucking ridiculous." Goff cut Stefan a glare and a shake of his head. "Being Minister of Trade is twisting his mind. He's getting too Staubaunish for my liking."

But not for mine. Truth be told, Cullen's analogy was a good one. Staubauns treated Rill portions exactly like land, laden with rules about how it could be owned or taxed, and by whom, all designed to exclude anyone not of the right social caste. Stefan had seen it in action, again and again, when the marriage offers of Kheld men were snubbed by Staubaun fathers who held Rill portions. They passed wealth and bloodlines only to their own.

And the damned Rill was the one thing even a king could not change. Both Stefan's subjects and his enemies wanted the Rill to stay just as it was. Forever. Just so an entitled ass like Dorilian could show off his wealth and power by sailing down his slow-moving river on a floating palace more elegant than *this one.*

"You're glowering again." Cullen extended a wine jug. Stefan offered his cup and admired the ruby ripple that danced into its depths.

He was sure his Staubaun nobles watched. But for them, he

would be drinking beer at his table and having more fun, instead of putting on airs. They resented his Kheld relations and the men he had raised to the nobility. Probably he should seat Erenor beside him at the next banquet, or maybe Lucien Illarion. Yes, Lucien. Lucien was the son of a Highborn princess and in line to inherit a domain. If Stefan did that, he would show he did not favor only Kheld nobles.

His grandfather had warned him rightly that ruling a kingdom would require sacrifices.

A new beer had been brought, some mild brew touted by Neddig Darronson's wife, and the ladies took turns bringing the jug to their noses. Stefan and Neddig had been friends since going to school together at Permephedon and just two months past Stefan had made Neddig Lord of Pelles. Stefan smiled at how happy Nilla and her friends appeared to be. Women had fewer cares than men and he envied them for that. Just the sight of their laughing, youthful faces, lips rosy and smiling, was enough to lighten hearts. He shared a grin with Cullen, whose Asphalladra had just taken the jug in hand and put it to her nose. Nilla had already poured a cup and her lips glistened from having enjoyed a drink.

"It's good, right?" Fredda, Neddig's wife, insisted on a verdict. She waved her cup, then downed another swallow herself as Asphalladra put the jug aside instead of passing it down the table.

"Don't drink it!" Asphalladra knocked the cup from Nilla's hand.

"Hey!" Nilla protested as beer splashed across the table and onto the floor. All other conversation in the room halted.

Stefan jumped to his feet and strode toward the shouting women. Some of his Kheld kinsmen joined him.

"Why did you do that? It's good!" Nilla reached for the jug. Asphalladra swatted that over, too, spilling the rest of its contents.

"What is going on?" Stefan caught Asphalladra's wrist before she could swat anything else. His action earned a white-faced stare.

"Th—the beer's bad. I think."

Fredda nearly leaped onto the table to get at her and blows would have landed if Neddig hadn't thrown his arms around Fredda's waist to hold her back. "It's from my holding! My own brother made it!" Fredda looked ready to claw out Asphalladra's eyes.

"He did," said Neddig in his wife's defense. He grunted when one of her kicks almost took out his leg. "Fredda! Stop now and let me tell it!" He shot Stefan an exasperated glower. "Edd brought it here himself. I saw him give it to her. It's damn good beer, made with honey malt, just what the Old Mothers say a woman with child should favor."

"Phalla," Cullen began.

"No... I think...." Now Nilla's face, too, was white and strained. "She's right." She clutched at her lap, then stood with a wobble. "Oh Stefan, I—oh no —"

"Nilla?" Stefan dashed around the table.

"Help me. I think I'm—" Nilla gave a cry and bent over, hands to her belly.

Stefan caught her up into his arms. She curled against him as he ran with her from the hall. Behind Stefan, taking charge, Erenor began barking commands.

"The bleeding has stopped, and she will live. That's a blessing. Not all women survive."

Words. More words. Stefan found comfort in none of them. Not even the ones his mother was saying.

Emyli had been with Nilla for hours. She'd come from Permephedon as soon as she learned, which thanks to Rill communication had been within minutes. Stefan had been at the bedside, supporting his weeping and inconsolable queen as best he could. Emyli giving Nilla a draught of sleeping potion had been a relief. Now Stefan sat with Emyli beneath a stately oak Marc Frederick had planted on the palace grounds to honor his half-Kheld mother. Tears stung his eyes. The bloody child he had held in his hand, too small to even draw a breath, had been a boy.

"Why?"

"You know why." Emyli laid her hand atop his.

"Nilla never hurt a soul. She's the sweetest, kindest—"

"And you will survive this. Both of you will."

Stefan hated platitudes. It better suited his current frame of mind to focus on facts. A chemist had been brought to the palace and tested the beer still in the jug. "What poison did they say it was?"

"*Merethe.*"

A Highborn poison, he'd heard it whispered. It caused women to abort their babies.

"And Asphalladra—"

"Detected its signature. A licorice scent, very faint. Staubaun noblewomen are taught to recognize it. The trace was very well disguised by the strong aroma of the beer."

"But she didn't do it? Add the poison?"

"No. Oh, Stefan, how could you think so?" Emyli removed her hand from his and touched her fingers to his cheek instead. "No, she saved Nilla from drinking more. More probably would have killed her, too."

It might have happened that way, even from what he'd seen. Asphalladra had looked desperate to help. But if that was true, Stefan had no one at hand to blame. "It's just... she's Staubaun. Nilla's other ladies are Kheld, and—Khelds *want* me to have children. It's Staubauns that don't." He tried to keep focus. "I can't believe it was Fredda. She bled too. Neddig wouldn't have wanted that. Or that stupid brother of hers that made the beer."

"It could have been kitchen staff. It could have been anyone."

"Rheger's wife? Elhanan's?" The wives of attending nobles had sat at another table.

"Oh, Stefan. Will you suspect everyone?"

"I suspect Dorilian."

Emyli looked stunned, though she was composed enough to take a deep breath. "I really don't think—"

"He wants me *dead!*" Stefan closely attended the struggle apparent in her reaction.

"You, maybe... yes. But not her. Not this. His own mother... *merethe* killed her."

"All that tells me is he knows it works."

"But he would never—he can't—break his promise to your grandfather. His death gift—"

"A secret promise? One even grandfather never saw or heard? The only evidence it exists is that you made *me* promise not to tell anyone about it." Stefan had kept *his* promise, merely because the very notion of it was laughable. He would be ridiculed for believing it. It was bad enough his mother believed it. "But you're right. I need to find out how this was done. That's even more important than finding out who."

The more Stefan thought about it, the more possible poisoners he added to the list. Dorilian and his Malyrdeon kin weren't the only ones who might be tempted to cut off his future. The Seven Houses barely tolerated Stefan, and for months he had been convinced they secretly backed the ambitions of the Bas of Rannul.

Many of Essera's nobles openly yearned for a return to Staubaun rule. And Palaistea, while distant, had supporters even in his own court who might seek to ensure her sons—and not any son of his—succeeded him.

If Stefan died without heirs, Essera would return to Highborn rule. He needed to find some way to force Marenthro to bring back Hans. Having an heir at his side would strengthen his position.

Cullen and Goff walked into view along the path, both still clothed in banquet finery and looking grim. After a quick bow to Emyli, they relayed their news.

"Both kitchen scull maids didn't show this morning," Goff reported. He ground his teeth before he spoke the rest. "Haven't found them, but they may be dead. Thing is, staff had to get two new girls. The damn wenches were all over the kitchen doing their work. One of those girls vanished right after and all bets are on her. She might have had a chance to put something in the beer, if she were sneaky and quick."

Which an enemy agent would be. "And the other girl? The new one?"

"Peeing herself such it's a wonder she's got a drop left in her."

"Don't let her go just yet." Stefan turned to Cullen, who looked even more burdened with worry than Goff. "Tell your wife I don't blame her. She saved Nilla, at least. I appreciate her care for her."

"Phalla would like to be with her, if that would be all right."

Stefan shook his head. "No. I know she means well, but I don't think it would comfort Nilla to see her right now." Asphalladra hadn't lost *her* baby. "Maybe after your child is born."

Cullen stiffened, but nodded. "Do you want me to send her from court?"

"No. Or rather"—Stefan needed to clarify this request—"I wish you, and her, to stay here in Dazunor-Rannuli. It's where your work is and, well, I need you, and Goff too, here to handle things. I'll send Nilla to Amallar and her mother."

Right now, all Stefan wished in the world was to be far away from this Staubaun-infested sewer of a city. Far away from the Seven Houses and their plots against him. Far away from chemists and poisons. And far away from the Rill, which he half-suspected Dorilian might have just used to attack him.

17

The Hierarchal progress concluded with docking the Eagle Triumphant Barge at the Nereid Palace in Ivernesse, Ilmar's capital city. Throngs celebrated the completion of the voyage and the arrival of their Hierarch. Dorilian planned to stay only long enough to give Palimia a visit with her mother, who was summering here, while he spent a day at sea on his new warship. He had drawn the plans for the ship himself and was eager to see the result.

"Mia is spending the day with her mother. Lev and Fahme will be safe here with you." Trusting Tiflan to take care of the younger Sordaneons was easy. Tiflan had taken care of Dorilian and the first Levyathan when they were children.

"They will be safer than you will be, at sea in an untested ship." For a man of mature years, Tiflan managed to look younger.

"The ship was tested upon launch. It floats. This is not the vessel's maiden voyage. It is *my* inaugural voyage on the ocean as Hierarch and Admiral Paramount." Dorilian adjusted the fit of his left gauntlet, situating the wings to wrap around his forearm. After a night of pleasant relaxation, he was wearing Derlon's Armor again, this time to impress his sailors. He held out his hand to receive the sword Tutto handed him, and belted it about his waist.

"You remember how to use them?" Tutto asked. He meant the armor. Both breast shield and gauntlets were enhancers with differing attributes.

"Yes."

"You are more likely to be attacked out there than on the river."

"Will you ever stop worrying about me?"

"Worrying about you is my job."

Wearing full dress gear and the winged helmet of Commander of the Eagle Guard, Legon appeared at the door. "We have established the whereabouts of both Mormantaloran ships seen yesterday. Our warships cleared them out, pushed them to the south and are keeping them in sight. They will be no trouble. Possibly an Ardaenan ship in the area."

"Endelarin isn't going to attack me." Ardaen's king was an embarrassment of a relation but actively embraced the many benefits of having Sordan as an ally and Dorilian as his blood relation.

Dorilian signaled to Tutto. "Let us see what one year's revenue from a Rill slot has bought me."

The ship was named *Raudra*, which meant "storm." The name was apt. Dorilian wanted his reign to be a storm—for Nammuor, for Stefan, and for the whole damned world. The ship's prow was plated with indestructible Sordaneon silver, its hull painted with his colors, and he had gifted the vessel with sails bearing the Hierarch's personal ensigns. Dorilian nodded approval as he walked onto the military dock.

"Impressive," he said to Haeskos Periskleron, the ship's commander and the fleet's admiral.

"As a Sordaneon flagship should be, Thrice Royal. You bring to mind the glory of your forefathers."

Dorilian's very intention.

For good or ill, they faced a day heavy with clouds and portents of storms, such as frequently plagued the Kolpos, the broad deep gulf separating Sansordan from Ardaen. The Rift, an unstable wound left by the Devastation, ever threatened to make an appearance in these waters, which gave the Kolpos its treacherous reputation. Today, however, the sail out from the harbor was smooth and even the rougher waves of the Kolpos barely rocked the *Raudra's* hull. Two escort vessels preceded the *Raudra* to the west and north, ready to intercept and divert any approaching ship. Dorilian braced at the rail and gazed upon the distant approach of Sansordan's shattered cliffs. His ancestral domain at this point was naught *but* desert and fissured rock. A broken land.

Dark sheets of rain curtained the north, between Sansordan and Trongor. A menacing line of gray sea awaited. The *Raudra* would turn before entering that zone.

"She's fast." Legon shared the rail at Dorilian's elbow. Together they watched the cliffs pass.

"Fast enough to make Damna by morning."

"And Ogarth by midday after. Don't you dare decide on a state visit to Trongor. I barely brought enough men for you to present yourself as a minor lord."

"No one will ever make that mistake while I wear this." Derlon's Armor could never be thought other than an artifact of a vanished time. Generations of learned debate had not established whether the armor was an arcane device or a product of forgotten technology.

Appreciation teased Legon's mouth and warmed his dark eyes. Sharp-faced as a youth, his features had balanced enough as an adult to render him handsome. Blond hair escaped from his helmet and just covered the tops of his ears. "I keep thinking about the Mormantaloran ships south of here."

"With any luck, our ships have sunk them."

The ship rocked and afternoon light danced along blue waves. To judge by the sun, it was nearly time to reverse course if they were to return to Ivernesse by nightfall. The escort ships had sailed past the headland of Sansordan's Horn and now the *Raudra* did also. Dorilian watched the cliffs change hue. Sandy gold to dusky purple. The Devastation had ignited near here and seared the surrounding land, turning it to a flaky crust called *skellai*. *Skellai* this glassy, streaked with veins of color, told him what they were near. They had begun to turn about when he saw what others had not. Legon saw it too.

"A blasted ship!" Legon turned and shouted. "Alert the Admiral!"

Dorilian stared at the approaching vessel. How had his escort missed it? The vessel stood out clearly against shore and sky. Not a warship. Built for maneuverability the ship had neatly slipped behind the *Raudra*. It now sailed between her and the open sea.

Knifing through waves, the narrow vessel drew parallel to the *Raudra*. Only the nature of its intent was unclear. Dorilian half-expected a coil-sprung bolt to rip into the bow or cripple the rudder. Tutto, who had just run to Dorilian's side, grabbed him by the arm.

"Stop being a target! Derlon's fucking armor doesn't make you immortal. This way!"

The *Raudra* had picked up speed, water surging up along her boards. She was going to outrace the surprise vessel.

On the raised command deck behind the main mast, Haeskos conferred with his officers. He disengaged on Dorilian's arrival.

"This is unexpected, Thrice Royal. The escorts did not see—"

"Illusion." Tutto identified the reason.

Haeskos's brows drew together. "A way of cloaking?"

Tutto jerked his chin at the offending vessel. "A falsehood that looks real. The Highborn are Leur and banish false realities by their presence. That is why all of us on this ship can see the thrice-cursed thing, while your other ships did not."

"But who—"

"Mormantalorus." Dorilian knew damned well who to hang this on.

Stefan and any person associated with him were utterly incapable of high-level mage arts. Nammuor, on the other hand, had employed illusion at least once to Dorilian's knowledge—to gain access to the aged Bas of Tollech. Servants claimed to have seen Taddeus's grandson, who at the time had been one thousand leagues away.

The admiral's lips pursed. "A ship of that size cannot possibly have weapons of sufficient military force."

"Don't be fooled!" Dorilian snapped.

Nammuor didn't need weapons of military force. What was being attempted here?

The answer came quickly. A brief glitter arched toward them. It barely missed the foredeck, then landed in the water. Lightning crackled. Virulent energy climbed the *Raudra*'s hull and snapped through the surrounding air in a percussive wave that threw men to the deck and caused clouds overhead to roil.

"Gsch!" Haeskos shouted. "That's a *Ir* attack! Those weapons are forbidden!"

Forbidden, yes… by a race no longer positioned to enforce the restriction. An entire world had forgotten why those weapons were forbidden: physical laws for the new Creation differed from those of the First. There were thresholds. Impossibilities and prohibitions. In the Second Creation, only Leur gifts—or arcane weapons—could generate vast energies. Already the sea had turned choppy and the sky from horizon to headland burned with amber streaks that had not been there before.

"Turn to sea!" The Admiral harangued his helmsman. "We're in the Slough, too near the Rift for this!"

"We do that, she might ram us!" yelled the helmsman.

Another ball glittered and this time struck one of the *Raudra*'s sails. The giant billow of fabric caught fire as lightning danced along the masts and spars and into the clouds. A scent of ionized gases filled the air. Lightning crackled across the water.

"What are they trying to do?" Legon's question was the first useful one Dorilian had heard.

Tutto answered. "Immobilize ship and crew, and us with it. Look at how many men are down because that stuff touched them. If one of those things hits our deck…"

Capture, then. The attackers had already gotten one sail. Incapacitate enough of the crew and passengers…

"Admiral, run her to ground."

Haeskos snapped his head at Dorilian's order. "Are you mad… Thrice Royal?" He added the latter belatedly.

"No. I want us to survive. We outnumber them, and we have the faster ship, but only if we are conscious and the ship intact can we put either to our advantage. If we turn to land, we present a smaller target and maybe we can stay in one piece. If we reach land, we can survive this—but we cannot survive it at sea!"

"We can fight back. We are armed with long bolts."

"And they are firing on us from out of range. They are trying to disable us and they are succeeding. Sacrifice this ship! Run her aground and get the men to shore!"

Overhead, storm clouds previously gray roiled black and crackled with lightning. Darkness plunged over the sea. Despite the wind, the water to every side stilled as if oppressed from above. This wasn't good. Even an ordinary storm could trigger a Rift sheer.

Doubt played across Haeskos's broad, weathered face. He was master of this ship—but a Highborn prince was never to be disobeyed. Even less so one wearing the armor of a god.

"Ashore. So be it, Thrice Royal. But do not think it will be easy. Between switch winds and squalls… and even if we reach it, that coast is hell. Our keel may hole too soon." Haeskos signaled the men hauling on the sails and yelled to his helmsman. "Take her in!"

Another glittering ball dropped just past the starboard rail. It missed because the *Raudra* had trimmed her sails and turned. The sky cracked with answering sheets of blue. Energy webbed the sea and spilled over the prow. Several sailors collapsed onto the deck as tendrils of blue cascaded to the midmast. All crew still standing ran to abandoned stations, hauling at halyards and line to set the remaining sails to their new course.

Haeskos and his men knew the Kolpos, its currents and winds and the coves of its shoreline. Sansordan's poisoned, crusted seacoast presented high cliffs with few points of ingress.

"There!" One of the officers, jacket scorched from having fought the burning sail when it fell to deck, pointed through the gloom and over the churning waves. "Crook of the headland. Gravel and sand shelf beach—deep enough, I think. If we can get past the rocks, the wind's at our stern and will drive us in. Especially if a Rift storm breaks."

"Good man, Tidus. Do it." The admiral turned to Dorilian. "You would be safer below deck, Thrice Royal."

Safer—or trapped. "No. I stay with my men." The Eagle Guard had joined the crew, pulling at halyards, following orders in ways that freed the sailors to perform more skilled work.

The enemy ship had fallen behind, but didn't relent. Another projectile hit, setting afire the Hierarch's emblem at the aft. The *Raudra* shuddered and a sailor on the mizzenmast screamed and fell, arm burning, to the deck, where another sailor smothered the limb in a jacket. Rain and wind pelted Dorilian's face. As *Raudra* cut through wild, storm-churned waves, water surged over her lower deck.

The sky overhead blossomed with purple lightning and sheers of red. Haeskos descended to the main deck to bark orders about speed and tides, dropping sail and shifting ballast. Vertical rock walls loomed before them, a towering horizon. The beach the officer had spoken of showed itself as a crescent of glassy pink in the broken elbow of the cliff.

"Thrice Royal." Tidus, the officer with the scorched jacket, turned his hopeful gaze upon Dorilian. "Dare we hope you possess the gift of your line for turning the wind and taming the waves?"

Tutto crowded the man aside and down the steps to the main deck. "You'll be damned lucky if he forgives your insolence! To bespeak the Highborn without permission!"

Removing the man for protocol did not remove the question of why a Highborn prince was just standing on deck, doing nothing. Dorilian felt the rare, ice-cold bite of impotence. Just like at Permephedon, he was helpless against an arcane peril. Why? He had access to power. His bond to the Rill was manifest. He had seen it himself. He *felt* it, and not only when near. He felt it now, coiling up his arm like a viper.

But how to use it… that he did not know. Though surrounded by all the power in the world, he was functionally paralyzed.

"Brace!"

The cliff face yawned with fissures above a coastline of tooth-sharp rocks. Only the cove ahead of them showed sand. Though the *Raudra* had scraped her port hull on the rocks, Haeskos had by skill with ballast and sail worked her free. Driven by currents and wind, the deep-keeled ship found shore, where she bit into the bottom and listed to port, her hull gouging. Cries rose from those who were thrown or fell. Haeskos had ordered his sailors to drop all sails and slow the vessel, and they had done so. Now they scrambled to heave anchors over the side and, below decks, shouted as they tossed bags of ballast to stabilize the vessel. The stern swung toward shore, pushed by wind and waves, and the list worsened as the port side hull came to rest on the bottom.

Dorilian clung to the command deck rail and gazed back over his shoulder toward the sea, where the pursuing vessel angled near a reef of sharp rocks. The enemy ship might yet avoid those rocks just as the *Raudra* had. He must get himself and the men on shore, where land would absorb the greater part of the energy. More ordinary means of fighting favored his forces. The *lr* weapons were still the danger, if any remained.

The Eagle Guard led the way. Dorilian jumped into the surf and half swam, half splashed his way onto the sandy swale, followed by scattered crewmembers. A hiss burst overhead, another projectile, and he turned to look. This one hit the listing *Raudra* square on deck. The ship crackled, fully enveloped in blue fire, boards splintering and catching flame. Men who had not yet made it into the water screamed and fell. On the sand, Dorilian got his feet under him and checked for his weapon, though there was nothing yet to fight. At his side, Legon propelled him toward the cliffs.

"Go with Tutto! I will bring up the rear."

An Eagle officer swung his arm, directing them to an inlet, upon the fissured sides of which a footpath led up to the headland.

"Run! Run!" the officer cried. "Gain high ground. Any who come at us now we will have to fight!"

Long hours of training for combat gave Dorilian the stamina to keep pace with his guard on the steep, crumbling path. The headland, when they reached it, was naked. Dorilian looked to every side and saw only flat stony ground. *Skellai* crunched and caked to his boots with every footfall. The only defensible position he could see consisted of a modest outcropping. They looked to be rock but were probably the brittle ruin of some pre-Exile structure. He gave Tutto the job of organizing a defense.

The last sailors made their way up the footpath, coming to stand with them atop the cliffs. A few carried or half carried dead and wounded comrades. Legon ran up to Dorilian, breathing hard. "Fighting broke out. Brigands spilled down onto the beach from the other side."

Tidus, who had helped Legon at the rear, also spoke with short breath. "Wreckers. They descend upon any unfortunates who founder on this coast. They are vultures. Some worse than others."

"The enemy ship?"

"Not as good sailors as we are. Storm's driving them onto the rocks."

Maybe the wreckers would take care of them. Dorilian drew a deep breath. The land on which they stood was barren, without shelter or defenses. The air tasted oppressive. Sulphureous. He peered through the lashing rain that cut across the crusted headland in glistening rivulets, into the heart of the storm. Black, slashed by veils of fiery opalescence, opened and revealed a heart of madness, a vision at once ethereal and terrible. Above and to every side of them soared a city, shining, sky-reaching and vastly beautiful.

Only one of the Five Cities gifted to men by Leur had ever stood in this ill-fated place—or looked like that.

Mulsor.

"Oh hells," Tidus whispered. He saw it too. "Gods forbid. Our dooms are sealed, all of us."

Dorilian was not about to let superstition interfere with survival. "Old tales. That city is not even real, not anymore."

Few people ever saw Mulsor—the ghostly vision appeared only during Rift events on the Kolpos, and ships avoided those. Destroyed by a calamity that had ignited the Devastation, the city didn't manifest with every event and most sailors or land dwellers who glimpsed it would never admit to what they had seen. All souls who saw Mulsor were branded as doomed either to greatness or disaster, and often both.

"Well, there it is. The fucking end of the First Creation." Tutto grunted. "As if we don't have enough trouble on our hands."

Even as they watched, violence shattered the phantom city. Riven towers, still beautiful, fell apart like sand as they collapsed into the sea. Broken. Crashing. Dying as the raging storm screamed. The image of Mulsor wavered before it blew away on the wind and was swallowed by the waves, its imprint on the Creation's shattered memory too insubstantial to endure.

Tutto's reminder that they faced more immediate problems was apt. Dorilian wasn't Nammuor's only prey here on the edge of Sordan's domains.

"Tell me how we fare with things that are real."

Tutto complied. "We have forty-seven men and eleven of Haeskos's sailors, all armed. Seven wounded, two unarmed. No water. No supplies. The ship is aflame. The enemy vessel is caught on the rocks and any men who reach shore are beset by what I can only assume are savages."

"We are in Sansordan, Tutto. Those savages are my subjects."

"I wouldn't count on that. If they were, they would have recognized your flag and emblems. Instead of attacking and trying to kill Legon and his men, they would have bowed down before them. Something tells me they aren't going to bow down to you either."

"They are going to attack us, then?"

"They saw our men run up the path and only stayed back for easier pickings. I say we hide our numbers and lure them in. Permission to set a deception."

The storm still hammered the windswept headland with nails of rain as Tutto set men to act as wounded, gathered in the scant shelter of the outcropping. He also positioned the corpses of their dead to heighten the impression their band of survivors was composed of sailors and hapless travelers. Legon's soldiers turned their cloaks inside out to conceal their insignia. This enemy would not be expecting a Hierarch's elite guard.

When the attack came, it was from men who whooped and hollered and wore little more than rags. They wielded as many clubs as swords. Tutto's decoys leaped to their feet and established battle formations. The attackers encountered three times as many fighting men as they had assumed.

"Get back!" Legon yelled as Dorilian joined him.

Dorilian saw no reason to retreat. Another sword would make quicker work of this rabble. He swung his blade, nearly decapitating the man who charged him. Twitching, the corpse dropped to the ground as Tutto made his way to Dorilian's other side. Together, the three men fought as a unit, years of sparring and practice put to work. At one point a man made it through their screen of flashing steel to swing a club against Dorilian's ribs. The armor absorbed the energy of the attack so completely he did not even feel the blow. He saw the club hit, and the look of surprise on the brute's face. With a single movement, Dorilian laid open his attacker's ribcage.

It took only minutes for the soldiers—better-armed and better equipped—to decimate their foes. Dorilian stepped back from the fight so Legon and Tutto could turn their attention to finishing the job. He returned to the outcropping and Haeskos, whose left leg had been badly burned in the final assault on the ship. The man had his sword in hand, though, and looked prepared to use it.

"Damn scavengers," Haeskos said. "They wait for Rift storms and hope for ships to fare ill. They pick off the survivors and steal all they can. Look!" He pointed to a few shadowy shapes fleeing the field of combat. "Cowards. They're running away."

Back to their den. Dorilian ran back toward the intact line of his Eagles, and Legon, who he interrupted from saying anything. "We're going after them! I want those vermin run down."

"But sire—"

"Do as I say." Dorilian wanted those wretches. He was their damned Hierarch, and would chase them to the ends of this World.

Dorilian gave Tutto twenty of his guards. If any Mormantalorans had survived the wreckers, Haeskos and others who needed to stay behind might need a defense. With Tidus and a few sailors to bolster his Eagle Guards' numbers, Dorilian led the pursuit. His daily runs in the Va Haira or along Rhondda's beaches now proved their worth. They encountered and slew fleeing wreckers who had neither the speed nor stamina to outrun them.

A scant handful of the scavengers made it back to their hovels. Deep violet twilight did not conceal them running toward a collection of huts built from scavenged ship wood in a tarp-strewn hollow. The primitive system might collect enough water to sustain their poor numbers, but clearly they lived on the edge of desperation. Upon seeing him and his men advancing upon their dwellings, the remaining wreckers threw down their battered swords and clubs. Following this, they fell to their knees. To a man, they faced Dorilian. He understood why. Derlon's armor clothed him with a glimmer of moonlight and power.

Legon's men gathered the miserable creatures at sword point. Then they went hut by hut and dragged out everyone else. Ragged, filthy figures tumbled out into a ring of firelight set so their Hierarch might examine them.

No old men or women. A few younger of the latter, barely clothed and obviously ill-used, cowered and kept their wild-haired heads lowered, eyes averted. One had a babe, a mewling, sickly thing. A handful of rag-wearing children huddled near two women clad in crude aprons. There were also two men, naked and unkempt, both wearing chains, one of whom wept and clutched at his right leg, which had been amputated below his knee. A stinking, blood-soaked bandage had been knotted about the stump. Something, maybe pain, made this man braver than the others and he looked up defiantly. At once his face transformed.

"*Mekan dantha, Nemenori! Adantefarren!*"

One of the *Raudra's* sailors stepped forward. "He speaks Ardaenan, Thrice Royal. He asks you to help him. He thinks you are a Nemenor noble."

Legon tilted his head to cover a laugh.

Dorilian had understood the plea. "*Nen. Nen Nemenori. Dorilian Sordaneon esh, Hierarch Sordanos. Vosno Sordano. Handu yedhetos?*"

The Ardaenan's black hair fell across his face as he ducked his head. His fellow captive looked equally amazed, and three of the huddled women at last raised their bruised faces to look upon him. They whispered and clasped at each other as the first man gave an emotion-wrought, halting answer. Dorilian's stomach turned at what he heard.

"Their ship foundered two months ago." He translated for the benefit of his men who did not speak the language. "These... animals took them. Now we know what these wreckers eat. When the provisions from these people's ship ran out, they ate fresh meat. Their last meal was this man's leg."

"Fucking hell!" Tidus swallowed hard and looked ready to vomit. He was not the only one.

Legon sent a narrow glare at the kneeling wretches his men held at the edge of the firelight. They did not appear to realize what was being said about them.

Cannibals. Predators and murderers, and probably rapists as well.

"We kill the unholy, Sordan man." One of the five men they'd just beaten in battle and followed to the camp spoke up loudly. "We kill the cursed ones. The Doomed. Those who see Mulsor we kill to spare the World."

Why did they want to tell him that? Dorilian merely turned his head to address the claim. "I saw Mulsor. So did you. Do you kill yourselves?"

"Already cursed. Doomed to suffer. Doomed to kill. Holy work."

Holy. What in Three Worlds was holy about slaughtering unfortunates? Mulsor was a specter, a curse writ on the World—an indelible memory of Aryati madness—not a command for the world to corrupt itself all over again.

"Well, you are not going to kill me." Dorilian turned to Legon. "Execute them. All of them, for attacking their Hierarch. Spare the women and children, and these two men. We will sort out their stories."

By the time Tidus and several other men accompanied him back to the cliffs, clouds obscured the moon and blanketed their way in darkness. Dorilian generated an *orbus* by which to see their path. Only Legon among the men had ever seen him do so and the resulting whispers punctuated his success with dire warning.

Sorcerer. Godborn.

Pooling ambient energy to create light was the least of Highborn gifts. Levyathan could already summon a flicker, albeit by using knowledge beyond his years. But the whispers proved too that any act Dorilian performed would be subject to comment and rumor. And rumor could mutate into weapons.

Secrets sheathed swords... but were difficult to keep.

When they reached the cliffs, they found a makeshift camp. Haeskos and Tutto communed by a fire. No other attacks had befallen them. The sailors had salvaged wood from the ship, along with some food and two barrels of water. At least one thing was certain: Dorilian's men would not be eating each other.

"She was a good ship," Haeskos lamented. Though the storm had passed, and the rain with it, gray hair was still plastered in curls to his head. "Shame to have beached her, but it was the right thing to do."

Dorilian hunkered beside the two men. "We had to give ourselves our best chance. I will rebuild the ship."

"New name," Haeskos suggested. "Better luck."

"Yes. Better luck."

"I trust you know the way to get the better of Mulsor's curse?"

Dorilian eyed Haeskos across the fire's steady flames. If anyone knew such a secret, it would be this man.

"Don't believe in it." Haeskos tipped his cup to add weight to his point. "And don't tell anyone who does believe."

Good advice, considering what they all had just witnessed. Dorilian glanced at Tutto, who he could see was in agreement. Probably the two old veterans had talked about it. He would have to surround himself with more people like them.

"I do not believe in Mulsor's curse," he assured them. "And I am not about to tell anyone. My life is difficult enough without people thinking I am cursed." Too many people already thought him an abomination. To Haeskos he said, "We have too few supplies to attempt an overland journey. Please tell me our escort ships will come back for us, and soon."

Concern shadowed the admiral's face. "*Raudra* serves as a beacon and my lads have set watchfires. Someone will come."

A glance to Tutto showed a grim frown. "We cannot know for sure if the escorts survived the storm. They may also have been blown off course. My fear is that those Mormantaloran ships we chased off anticipated the attack and circled around."

Which they might have.

"My money's on we sank them." Haeskos saluted some god or other with his cup. "I gave that order."

"Let us pray your men made good on it." Another, and darker fear clawed at Dorilian as he gazed upon the watchfires ablaze upon the cliff. Rescue, if it happened at all, might not come soon enough. "And let us pray those escort ships arrive soon. I am not the only target of this attack. My Heir is in Ilmar—and Nammuor wants Levyathan even more than he wants me."

18

Raxa grabbed Palimia's wrist and all but dragged her into the room that served the palace as a temporary nursery. Night had just fallen upon Ilmar. Far to the west, the sky no longer painted itself or the sea in fiery hues. The nurse pointed to a low bed, upon which two small figures curled.

"He's been like this for hours, Lady."

Fahme lifted her head when Palimia sat upon the edge of the bed. Honey-dark hair spilled over the girl's shoulders onto the mattress and around her distressed little face. "Lev won't eat."

It was more than that. Raxa wrung her hands. "The lad just stares and stares. If I touch him, he screams and all that does is bring in the guards. Fahme is the only one he'll let touch him. Lady, what do I do?"

Levyathan lay on his side, eyes open but not moving. Staring. Fahme patted his cheek.

Palimia's heart ached at what she saw. "When did this happen?"

"Just a few hours ago, after the meal. It was nothing he ate, I'm sure of it. Fahme ate the same thing. So did I!" Raxa was awash in fright and tears.

"Did he say anything?"

"Nothing I understood. He ran to look at the ocean"—Raxa gestured to the tall columns at one end of the room, beyond which was an open loggia; darkness currently cloaked the view of the sea—"and babbled about fire. But there was no fire, not anywhere to be seen."

This was starting to make sense. Palimia looked into Fahme's grave, pinched face. "Fire?"

"Blue fire," said Fahme.

Ordinary fire was never blue, and Levyathan would not invent such a thing.

Dorilian. This could be nothing else. The Highborn felt each other's deaths—but possibly much more. Possibly danger as well. Palimia had learned much in the year since Dorilian had taken her to be his intimate companion, especially about how sensitive the godborn could be to others of their kind.

"Lev?" She hoped her voice would reach him. Based on what Raxa had said, Palimia did not dare risk touching him. "It's Mia. I am here. I want to help. Tell me about the fire."

Tell me about Dorilian.

Levyathan's jaw sagged and for a moment Palimia hoped he would speak, but he didn't. He looked so small, so helpless—lips pale and eyes wide from things unknown.

Fahme's plump little hand gave Levyathan's shoulder a push. "Mia," she said, to make sure he heard.

When that received no response, Palimia turned to Raxa. "He's not ill. He is in contact with his father, I think."

Raxa blew out a sigh, part relief and part continued anxiety. "These Highborn—"

"Yes." Palimia felt much the same.

"Noemi would have known what to do. She used to tend the young Lord and she knew ever so much." Noemi had trained a younger Raxa. That, even more than Raxa's abundant milk supply after the loss of a stillborn daughter, had convinced Dorilian to retain her as his son's nurse.

Palimia had never met the first Levyathan, Dorilian's younger brother—a boy of whom she had heard a great deal. Gifted. Strange. His namesake was hardly less so.

"Please tell me you have alerted Bas Tiflan."

Puffy-eyed, Raxa nodded. "I told him first. He calmed the lad somehow, and then he went to ready the ship."

"The ship?"

"To take us back in the morning."

Tomorrow they were to start their journey back to Sordan. Dorilian had sent a schooner ahead for that purpose because the barge would have to be hauled upstream. "We will just have to keep him comfortable then. I think his state will resolve when his father returns."

None knew when that might be. Dorilian should have returned already from his sailing of the new ship. There were a hundred reasons a ship might be late in coming to port. He might even be at the dock, delayed by his admiral or by Tiflan reporting on the readiness of the schooner. Though if Dorilian had heard even a word about this turn with Levyathan, nothing would have kept him from the boy's side.

Palimia took a soft light blanket, woven of the gauziest *seshi* wool, and laid it over both children. Fahme did not want to leave Levyathan but continued to peer into his staring eyes. That he was odd, the girl accepted as ordinary. That Fahme would feel so much distress pointed to something gone wrong.

"Fire. Fire, fire, blue," Fahme whispered. She knew fire was dangerous.

Palimia had just resolved to offer a distraction, perhaps to play with Fahme for a bit, when Levyathan drew a shuddering breath.

"No fire," he said. His gaze focused on Fahme's wide stare. "No fire. No more. Rain. The ones who attacked him are dead." Levyathan's gaze sought Palimia next. "Dor is safe... we are not."

"Not safe?" Though Dorilian had taken a cohort of his best troops to sail with him on the new ship, he had left three hundred men of the Eagle Guard to protect his family.

The boy sat up in the bed, the blanket puddled over his legs. "He cannot help us." Though he spoke with a childish lisp, Levyathan communicated better than any two-year-old she had ever known. "Dor's ship was attacked. Mage fire. He is safe now but he is afraid. Afraid for us. He fears Nammuor will seize me."

If Dorilian feared this, Palimia must believe that danger was real. She turned to Raxa. "Find Tiflan. Search every corner. He needs to hear this."

While Raxa fetched the man charged with their safety, Palimia went to the loggia and looked out at the ink-dark sea. Light towers marked the many channels and shallows of the delta and its breakwaters. Inhaling a breeze redolent of salt and storms, she walked the colonnade's white length to the corner at the south end, from which she could look out upon the river proper. Below the palace was the pier, busy with activity as men readied the berthed schooner. She had no idea what to do. How would Nammuor or his agents approach this place? By sea? By land? What if they were here already?

Oh, why had she spent so much of the day with her mother? Yes, Palimia's mother was frail and enjoyed their time together, but for most of the year they saw each other every day. Had it really been that important to set in place every detail of the small estate Palimia had purchased as a summer home? It was not truly vital that the bed be just so or to determine how many *ucaja* trees must be moved to provide a better view. She could have left such details to the competent staff.

A light touch on Palimia's fingers alerted her and she glanced down. Wearing only a thin tunic, Levyathan stood at her side. She lifted him into her arms. The toddler laid his head on her shoulder.

"He is afraid for me," he said. "I am afraid for him."

She fought her voice for control. She was not built for danger. "So am I."

"Nammuor knew his plan. Found him."

"About the warship? I don't think that was a secret," Palimia pointed out. "Your father told me, and also you."

"He did not tell Nammuor," Levyathan whispered.

A shadow fell across them, cast by light in the room at their back. Tiflan joined them in looking out over the river.

"Raxa said something about Dor being attacked?" Tiflan asked.

"By *lr* fire." Levyathan met Tiflan's shocked expression. "He sailed his ship onto a beach. He is on shore, but his ship is broken and burned, and he cannot reach here soon. He is afraid Nammuor will try to get me here in Ilmar."

"You can communicate with him? Like that?"

"Sights. Sounds. Fears."

Tiflan's face creased with thought.

"Is it possible?" Palimia asked.

"Dor is a projective empath, we know that. He communicates without speech all the time, using emotion. Until a few years ago he often communicated mind-to-mind with his brother Lev... the Lev before this one." Tiflan turned an appraising eye on the child in Palimia's arms. "As unlikely as it sounds, it is possible."

Levyathan smiled, showing tiny baby teeth. "You championed him to Sebbord. Said because he could channel me, he could channel the Rill."

"So I did. I will champion you, too, once I know what you are."

"He fears Nammuor will find us here."

Tiflan clamped his jaw. "In that event, it might be safest to be sure we are *not* here."

"Can we make that decision?" Palimia clung tighter to Levyathan. Her heart hammered at how quickly things had changed... were changing.

Tiflan nodded. "It is our duty to protect them. I have ordered Raxa to gather Fahme and some things for the young ones. The ship is ready to sail, and we're getting on it. The only safe place for you, young man, is Sordan. Dor is unhurt, you say?"

The boy nodded. "Yes. Legon is with him, and Tutto too. He has many soldiers. They killed the men who eat people. A ship is coming to help him. He fears for us, not himself."

Palimia stared at them both. Dorilian was dealing with *cannibals*? Where in Leur's Creation was he?

"Then he will fend for himself. That, I know he can do." Tiflan reached for Levyathan with a big grin. Levyathan climbed easily into that brawny embrace. Tiflan carried him as easily as he might a book. Palimia followed and found herself walking so fast it was nearly a run.

As she hurried through pillared corridors and down back stairs, Palimia mouthed to Levyathan, whose wide eyes met hers over Tiflan's shoulder. *Can we trust him?*

At this moment, she trusted no one but the child.

Palimia found sleep impossible. Who could sleep with the world in upheaval? All her life she had searched for islands of tranquility, only to be swept up by changes over which she had no control. Now, as she sat ensconced on cushions outside the cabin where the two children slept with Raxa, it occurred to Palimia that Dorilian might well feel the same. Murders. Assassinations. Permephedon... and now this. The little perils of her life paled by comparison.

The Sordaneon children and their guardians left Ilmar aboard a schooner that slid from the palace's mooring into the night. Other ships dotted the entrance to the river, of course. Ships from all over the world used the Sorand'ruil. Few vessels entered the estuary under the cloak of night, however. Sordani patrols crisscrossed the main and navigable channels to prevent incursions by enemies or smugglers. There had been no sign, Tiflan said, of any patrols having been attacked—but that did not rule out patrols having been compromised in other ways. Palimia had seen only a few ships in motion as they departed Ilmar—an Ardaenan merchant ship heavy with sail, two Lahgaelan trawlers hauling net, and a Suddekan trader.

Determined she would not let the children out of her care, Palimia had planted her body at the door to their sleeping quarters. The chamber itself was small and Raxa was better at easing little ones to sleep. As time passed and night deepened, Palimia wrapped around her shoulders the only item at hand, the pretty shawl she had worn to visit her mother. Its gauzy weave and embroidered flowers had never been intended for warmth, but it was enough for a summer night. Dawn silvered the river while she listened to the steady beat of oars. Tiflan had rotated crews all through the night, and even picked up new crews of oarsmen at a military outpost. Travel upriver often required the use of oars, and swift travel almost always did.

She heard Tiflan's footfalls on the deck before she saw him appear around a corner. He slumped down the wall to sit at her side.

"This river is too damned long," he said.

"I don't suppose you have a way of changing that."

"None. But I think we have outrun any chance of a surprise attack by Mormantaloran ships."

Palimia had always found Tiflan interesting, both to talk with and look upon. She thought him handsome in the way of heroic sculpture, a man who existed to be admired and served to intimidate. He had a strong face to go with his imposing body, as well as a winning smile. That he was fearsome in battle, she well believed.

"Will he be upset?" She could not interpret the steady gaze that answered her, so added, "Because we took the children and left Ilmar without him."

"Not if there was reason. Do you think there wasn't?"

"I don't know what to think. We are doing this on the word of a two-year-old."

Palimia caught a glint of teeth as Tiflan chuckled. "Because of a Sordaneon two-year-old. One capable of articulating the sort of argument that leads to actions of this nature."

"Was Dorilian like that? As a child?"

"Not until he was six."

Tiflan sounded fond. Would a man who was fond of his royal kinsman betray him? She did not want to think so.

"How many more days must we be on this ship?" She rearranged her shawl and folded the ends in her lap.

"The fastest journey ever made up the Sorand'ruil by ship is four days."

Four. Palimia sighed.

Tiflan laughed at her dismay. "We may break that. This ship is very light, and the winds right now are very good. Today we will pass Ben-Aranath."

"Already!" It seemed too soon to be halfway home. Not long

past Ben-Aranath they would be in Sordan-controlled territory completely.

"We left at first dark."

How unruffled he seemed, as if all of this was but a bump in the road. Tiflan should have had a calming effect on her, the way he always had at Dorilian's court, but even after he departed, striding off to attend some matter to which the shipmaster directed him, Palimia's unease remained.

Without Dorilian near, she must depend on men she did not know well at all.

The sun settled behind their vessel and bathed the river with gold. *Silver at dawn and gold before night*, went the saying Palimia had learned in the lost days of her childhood, when she had played in the rushes along the banks of the Sorand'ruil. Her father had owned fine estates and rich land, as well as two Rill slots. Sordan to Dazunor-Rannuli. She had never inherited his portions, his land, or any other part of his wealth. All that had gone to the Esseran lord who had ruined Palimia's father and then wed Palimia to make things legal.

How much her life had changed, because of Marc Frederick and what he had allowed to be done to Sordan so that he might become king.

She sat near the prow of the Sordaneon royal schooner, with the domain's godborn Heir in her lap, as wind and oars propelled them toward safety in Sordan. They rode the center of the river and the banks to either side were but smudges of gold and green. Raxa sat beside Palimia and Fahme played with a toy boat on the deck, bouncing it over planks. Levyathan was happiest identifying ships and boats by type and flag. He had been doing so for an hour.

"Ardaen!" Even from a distance, the massive ship at which he pointed announced its land of origin by red sails blazoned with black. "Cargo hauler. Oceangoing." He pointed at another with red and blue striped sails. "Trongor! Bulk carrier."

Probably a grain ship.

"And that one?" Palimia indicated a lower-slung vessel.

Levyathan's small face scrunched as he squinted. "Suddekan flag. River hauler. High in the water."

Fahme sailed her toy boat up the folds of gown on Palimia's leg, using the folds for waves.

"Do you have to do that?" Palimia smoothed the fabric back down her thigh. The game was fraying her already thin nerves.

"High in the water," Levyathan said again. He squirmed to be set down, so Palimia did, watching as he went to the side and braced himself, his little body straining. Though he moved amazingly well for his age, he still barely could see over the bulwark beneath the rail. Shouts issued from the deck behind them, followed by the sounds of boots running over planks. The ships were drawing closer.

"Two," Levyathan called to her. "There are two. Flying the same flag."

Palimia lifted her head. Something about what Levyathan said pricked at her own childhood memories. Almost never did river barges travel without cargo. Upriver to Sordan and the Rill or downriver to seaports, they traveled *laden* to maximize profit. Low in the water. The only ships that traveled high carried passengers, like this schooner... or military transports.

An officer of the Eagle Guard ran toward them. "Lady, get to the other side!"

Palimia leapt to her feet and swept the boy up. "We have a problem?" The ships, while still upstream, were now angling toward them.

"Tell Tiflan!" Levyathan's face was close to hers and he stared at the officer. "Tiflan! Tiflan!"

A flurry of skirt and a cry of rage from Fahme announced that Raxa had followed Palimia in picking up a child.

Tiflan thundered into view. "Suddekan ships," he explained. "We've been watching them. I don't think they're friendly."

Fear turned Palimia cold and she gripped Levathan tighter. Suddekar? Not friendly? It did not seem possible.

As Tiflan looked toward the ships, which had gotten nearer, his face took on a warrior's scowl. "They are going to sheer the oars. Get to this side. Now!" He steered Palimia and Raxa around running crew and units of Eagle Guards taking position. Once Tiflan had guided them to the other side of the schooner, in the shadow of the streamlined shelter, he gestured to shore. "If they hit us, swim for it. The ship will be between you and our foes. Can you make it?"

Palimia nodded. The river was deep but the Sorand'ruil was so wide its surface current ran slow and smooth, even in the center. Nearer the bank would be even slower. More to the point, she was a strong swimmer. She looked to Raxa, who nodded also, though she looked too frightened to even move.

"Into the river? With the babies?" Raxa could barely cope with that prospect.

"It's the babies they want. Especially this one." Tiflan addressed Levyathan. "Stay with Mia. She is adult and strong and will cover more distance. You have the body of a two-year-old. Don't forget that."

Tiflan left them. Palimia tore her elegant shawl into strips and handed one to Raxa. "Undress. Then tie her to you."

"Take off my gown?" Raxa's eyes could not open any wider.

"And your shoes. You will swim better without them."

More people ran past them, toward the other side. Shouts of alarm and the ringing of steel being drawn preceded the clunk of what were probably bolts being loaded. *Hurry!* Palimia stripped down, leaving only her loin wrap. Usually when she dropped her clothing, men stopped to look—not one did so now. Levyathan raised his arms so she could tie her strip about his waist and knot it. Her childhood on the river had included learning to knot line. She wound another strip about her waist and then secured the other end of Levyathan's tether to that. "Now if we get separated, I can pull you back."

"I will stay with you so enemies cannot get me."

"I will die before I let that happen. To either of you." Any enemy daring enough to attack a Sordaneon vessel might spare the Heir, but would think nothing of harming her. Or Raxa. She could do nothing for anyone else. Working faster, she ripped another strip from her now-shredded shawl and helped Raxa tie Fahme similarly. Fahme was crying and trying to hold on to Levyathan, who reassured her.

"Stay with Raxa. It's just water. Remember how we swim."

A violent jolt shuddered through the schooner and threw Palimia and Raxa toward the rail. A great noise sounded on the other side of the ship. They clutched at the railing as the vessel tilted. Below them, men screamed. The oars. Palimia watched as the oars on their side retracted, pulled back inside, though the vessel had already begun to turn from the collision.

Now.

Levyathan hugged in one arm, she grabbed Raxa by her other hand and pulled her and Fahme over the side.

Water closed over Palimia's head. Her hair almost instantly worked free of its combs. She held tight to Levyathan and kicked toward what she hoped would be open water. The worst thing would be to come back up under the ship if it had turned. But she emerged with Levyathan holding a handful of her hair in his small fist. A spluttering Raxa and screaming Fahme appeared only an arm's length away. A quick look over her shoulder showed Palimia that the schooner had been boarded, and she heard cries accompanied by the ring of swords. She thought she saw Tiflan fighting on deck.

No one had yet noticed them in the water. The near bank was not too far, and she struck out for it, swimming on her side the better to help Levyathan keep his head above water. Raxa was pushing Fahme before her, the little girl doing her best to swim also. Faster, Palimia thought. She was glad to have freed herself of her garments. The river and her movements soon rid her of her loin wrap as well.

She thought she heard shouts. Orders to stop. The accents were mixed, Suddekan and Sordani, but she did not look back. Men might have jumped into the river to pursue them.

An arrow sliced the air above her head. No. Why would they shoot? Surely, they wanted the Heir alive. More arrows. She realized then they came from the shore. Not *at* them... shooting past them, at their pursuers. Maybe at the ships. With renewed purpose, Palimia pulled with harder strokes and did her best to keep Levyathan's head high.

Before they reached the reeds at the water's edge, men from the shore dashed into the water, dragging both her and Raxa, and the children, onto the bank and into cover. Men garbed in orange and red surrounded the women and ushered them away from the bank, toward another group of men, some on horseback and some armored.

Shivering and dripping wet, not to mention naked and with her hair tangled in a toddler's hand, Palimia clutched at Levyathan and looked up to see who had taken them. A man wearing a gold-rimmed helmet and holding a sword, with dark brows and darker eyes.

Levyathan coughed a bit of water from his lungs. "Jooar," he said.

The Lahgaelan governor dismounted to stand before them, his face perplexed. He gazed at dripping, naked Palimia and the bedraggled boy. "This is a surprise. Where is Dorilian?"

19

E myli looked upon the anxious young woman standing on the dock, and all she wanted to do was wrap the poor thing in her arms. It surprised her greatly to find Asphalladra awaiting her at the foot of the Rill Mount in Dazunor-Rannuli. Emyli gestured to the master of her barge that she would be a few more minutes.

She extended her hands and waited until Asphalladra tentatively accepted the clasp. "Has something happened? You look upset." Emyli hoped nothing was wrong with the young woman's pregnancy, visible beneath her light summer gown.

"Your Royal Highness, I—" Asphalladra's lips trembled along with her voice. "Please ask your son, the king. I have not heard at all from Nilla. She's not good at correspondence, and neither are the ladies she has with her."

Yes, Emyli knew that only too well. Asphalladra was the sole correspondent of Nilla's small circle of ladies-in-waiting. Several times Asphalladra had written to Emyli to prompt small kindnesses for the inexperienced queen. Emyli had always seen to it those efforts were rewarded.

"I—I wish only to visit her." Asphalladra made her modest request.

Emyli hated to dash her hopes. "I'm not going to be seeing Stefan this trip. I am on my way to Gustan."

"Oh. I'm sorry. I thought… I heard you were to be here today, that your barge was ready, and I just assumed."

Of course she had. Who would not assume the king's mother might visit her son? And Stefan was currently in Trulo, which was on the way. "You are more likely to see him before I do. He will need to return to Dazunor-Rannuli to plan for this year's Archhalia seating. Many seat holders are there already." Only another month of summer remained and this city, as well as Permephedon, had been humming with meetings for weeks.

Asphalladra lifted her pretty chin. "Of course. It's just that... I have heard not a word. If you have, please tell me. Is Nilla all right? Last I saw her, she was so quiet and pale, and no one will tell me anything."

It seemed Asphalladra truly cared about Nilla, though her determination to fish for information raised suspicions. Spies abounded at royal courts. Emyli hated that she had become cynical. Stefan's enemies were many, but surely did not include this young woman. Asphalladra had sacrificed her high position in Staubaun society the day she married Cullen.

Rampant suspicion was a poison Emyli's father would have cautioned her to avoid.

"Let's walk," she said. Her guard followed, far behind so she might converse with her visitor. This secluded wharf, set on the other side of the Mount from the huge mercantile piers nearer the Rill's massive elevators, was uncrowded and restricted to royal vessels. Directly facing them across the waterway was the Rillhome Palace, the former Sordaneon seat that Stefan had given over as offices and apartments for his ministers. Cullen and Asphalladra kept a sumptuous residence there.

"Nilla is doing well. Losing the baby was a great shock, of course, but she is young and strong and will recover fully. She is in seclusion, as she wishes, and is being tended by her mother and sisters."

Understanding took root in Asphalladra's gaze. "Oh, that makes such sense. I should have guessed."

"She and Stefan wish privacy for now."

"Yes, of course. I will stop asking. I have been wearing Cullen thin with questions."

Emyli could imagine that scenario. "Spare your poor husband. Write Nilla a letter."

"I have! And I have passed several personally to her other ladies in hope they would see them into Amallar. I don't know if Nilla gets them and even if she does... she is not much of a reader, I know that. I used to read correspondence to her and books, as part of teaching her Stauba. She liked that. It's just—" Asphalladra sighed. "I hope she knows I wish her well."

Asphalladra's frustration was clear. Emyli frowned. It was entirely possible Nilla had never received those letters. The notion that the queen's Kheld-born ladies would not play the same manipulative political palace games as Staubaun women was ludicrous. Probably every one of Nilla's ladies hoped to advance their husbands by making Cullen's Staubaun wife look bad.

The air vibrated with mighty thrums to herald the Rill's arrival. Such events happened constantly in Dazunor-Rannuli. Asphalladra's eyes shone as she looked up at the arriving *charys*. The young woman's Staubaun birth meant she could ride simply by paying the fee, but Stefan had warned Asphalladra that to do it too often, even to visit her sister currently in Simelon, would be taken as flaunting. Emyli had been at hand for that conversation.

It was time to depart, but Emyli wanted to leave on good terms. Asphalladra had impressed her.

"Write a letter to Nilla but disguise it as being to me. First line to me and every second line to her. If you send me a letter like that, I can see that she gets it."

"I can do that. But how can you get it to her?"

Emyli smiled. "I know her mother. You'll understand soon." She turned so they might walk back toward the boarding point of her barge. "We mothers have our ways."

Dorilian felt a brief flash of Levyathan's distress, though no danger… and then nothing.

Midnight had passed by the time the escorts had found the *Raudra*'s stranded survivors—entirely too long in Dorilian's estimation. He had boarded the ship Haeskos said was fastest, taking his men and Haeskos with him, leaving Tidus to bring the rest of the shipwrecked survivors to safety on the second ship. Undeterred by night, Dorilian had ordered the ship to sail hard.

In the cold gray of dawn, he found Ivernesse in a state of high alert and the Nereid Palace swarming with soldiers from the local garrison. Ilmar's Bas met him at the pier to relate what had happened. The once serene dwelling resembled the aftermath of an invasion—or a conquest.

Dorilian walked marble floors splashed with blood from a skirmish none understood at all. The Bas and two ranking officers claimed at least three score of soldiers without identifiable uniforms had invaded the palace, slain any who resisted—armed or unarmed, household or guards—and searched the residence. Upon determining that the Heir and his guardians had fled, the invaders had vanished into the night. The port's military commander and the man in charge of the palace's dock had scant news to give.

"The vessel that brought the soldiers was Suddekan. That we know, Thrice Royal. Painted with the Basarchate's colors. Flying the Suddekeon flag. We damaged the ship and drove it onto a bank not far upstream. Captured a few, but many escaped. We're hunting them."

"*Suddekeon?*" The Suddekeons were Dorilian's own extended family. Deleus was his trusted cousin. Ermenthalia was Dorilian's grandmother.

"Yes, sire. That's how they slipped past. It was late, night and all; it looked to the guard here at the palace like they had been cleared. Turns out they slew every man on the patrol boat, then used it to escort them in."

"But Prince Levyathan… and Tiflan Morevyen—"

"Were not here when the invasion happened, Thrice Royal. They had left on your ship two hours earlier, along with the women and the little girl. Took guards with them. Even took on extra crew."

The schooner. How had they known to leave? And were they doing what Dorilian hoped—or something too terrible to contemplate? The Suddekeon vessel presented a treacherous turn.

"They sailed for Sordan?" Dorilian presented the conclusion he most wanted to believe.

"That's what I think, Thrice Royal."

Not learning what he most needed to find out, Dorilian clung to what he did know. Levyathan was not dead. He would have felt *that*. As for Tiflan… if Dorilian could not trust Tiflan, he could trust no one in this world. He had Legon with him. And Tutto. And Haeskos could be left in charge of the naval force. Ilmar's Bas would hunt down the men who had invaded the palace.

Last night Dorilian had driven himself sick with fear—fear that the attack might extend beyond him, fear that he had failed to protect Levyathan and his family. This morning had revealed that the situation in Ilmar had moved beyond those fears. By whatever means they had known to do so, his loved ones had fled, leaving him with a new set of terrible possibilities. Nammuor was not the only monster in the world. Dorilian had experienced enough betrayals to know even people close to him could prove deadly.

Be wary, but beware. It is possible to see enemies for no reason other than fear has planted them. Marc Frederick had offered those words early in their relationship. Then, Dorilian had scorned the advice, though he had known it to be apt. His enemies worked in fear—planting it in fertile soil and harvesting results. To defeat fear, he must work from facts and pursue truth.

Sordan, then. Palimia and Raxa would not let the children come to harm. Tiflan would get them safely to Sordan. Dorilian needed to believe these things.

He exchanged crews, commandeered extra oarsmen and left Ivernesse within the hour. The port master conveyed news, gathered by way of watch towers and mirrors, of sightings of the Sordaneon schooner headed upriver. To Sordan, then—or Suddekar if not.

Unheralded, aboard a ship that displayed no sign it carried Sordan's Hierarch, Dorilian set sail into the heart of a plot he had not anticipated.

"This was Nammuor's work." He spoke of his conviction to Legon and Tutto. Both men stood with Dorilian at the front of the ship, from which he stared at the dawn-gilded river. On board the ship were the remaining Eagle Guards from the palace. Two hundred men. Right now, he didn't care if the damned gold-crusted barge he left behind made it back upriver unpillaged—or at all.

"I can think of no other who would or *could* attack you with *lr* weapons," Tutto concurred. "The arcane arts are all but lost. Permephedon's Sages and the Order of Epoptes restrict that knowledge too well. No one in Suddekar would know how to make these weapons. If they have such, Nammuor provided them. That and the cloaking illusion that allowed the mage vessel to get behind your escort ships."

"Yet the attackers at the palace used swords at every turn," said Legon. "Brute force, not arcane weapons."

"On land, a warrior can discriminate." Tutto spat into the river. "The *lr* weapons we faced were meant to cripple the ship, as well as every man on it. Especially *him*."

"Because Nammuor knows I cannot fight sorcery." Admitting it seared Dorilian's pride like a burn. He fixed Tutto with an unhappy frown. "I should have powers by now, don't you think?"

"You *do* have powers. I don't see anyone else on this ship able to make light pool in his hand."

"I am twenty-three years old. I wear the most powerful enhancers ever to be wielded by mortals and I do not even flinch. The almighty Rill has sunk its teeth into my god-cursed flesh. I should be able to do more than generate a damned *orbus*."

Legon looked on with grim agreement.

"Twenty-three years?" Tutto scoffed. "That's nothing for your kind."

"I am not going to wait until I am fifty."

"And now is not the time to try!" The scars scoring Tutto's face furrowed into a scowl. "I have no malt to give you. The last thing we need is for you to be weak as a babe. You drank the whole damned flask back at camp."

"I did that to leave more water for the men. They needed something actually drinkable."

The first light of day glimmered across the eagle-feather details of the divine armor Dorilian still wore. He would not take it off until he got Levyathan back.

Tutto glared up at him. "Heed a wiser man's wisdom for once: Do not rush into these powers of yours. Remember your uncle and how he died."

Delos Sordaneon, Deben's twin, had burned from the inside out by the very power he had unleashed against the Vermillion Aqueduct. Too much a man and too little a god. Dorilian shook his head. "Nammuor is not going to stop attacking me. You understand that, don't you? Nammuor. Stefan. The Seven Houses. I have too many enemies. I will never be safe—and neither will Lev or anyone I love—until I master the gifts other people are working damned hard to make sure I do not learn."

"Because those gifts are dangerous!" Tutto wrapped his mailed fist around the hilt of his sword. The weapon didn't flinch, but neither did he. "You think I would not teach you, if I knew how to do it? *Any* of it? I know a lot, but no one knows how to do what *you* want to learn. None but others of your kind!"

Dorilian sagged against the mast. He commanded armies, economies. Ruled half the remaining Triempery. Had driven Essera back on its heels and made millions of his people prosperous and secure. He had opened a thrice-cursed Rill node. He had even—somehow—traveled from Permephedon to Sordan in an instant and carried the Rill within him like a parasite. But he had no way to release or command the power under his skin.

That he did not opened the door to Permephedon's darkness and overwhelmed his efforts to wall off the Demise. Death and more death. A room filled with poisoned princes who could not fight back. Only Marc—

Stop. Stop. Stop and go no further. He used an arcane defense. Wall power...

Dorilian shook his head to drive back those thoughts.

He opened his eyes again to see Tutto's dark sympathetic gaze.

"I taught you how to read men, boy, and read them well," Tutto said. "I taught you how to use steel and wits to stay alive. I taught you how to defend and attack and to understand a few things about the devices to which you are heir. I have taught you observation and strategy and how to anticipate what men will do. I will keep teaching you these things. But in matters of the Entities, or those gifts native to your Leur flesh and being, you need your own kind. Maybe they won't come to you, and if you cannot go to them—"

"I do not regret what I said."

"To never set foot in Essera again while that fool Stefan lives? You forged your own chains with that one!"

Bitterly, Dorilian acknowledged both that fact, and another. "I bought us time. All of us. Stefan is… part of something I must avoid. Something that happened and wants to keep happening, only I won't let it. Except I think it keeps trying. That's why I have to put my time to good use. If my kindred will not come to me or teach me, I will just have to give them a better reason to do it."

The aura hit him without warning. His next breath tasted of water and distress, Levyathan's cold skin and the clashing of swords. But he could not unravel the confusion or pull it into focus. Was Levyathan safe? Or in danger?

No matter how long Dorilian stared at and into it, the river gave no answer.

Her hair lifted and dried by hot breezes and her body covered by bright lengths of fine Lahgaelan cotton, Palimia sat astride a horse at the side of Jooar Zetharnna to watch the end of the river battle. She kept an arm firmly around Levyathan, who sat in front of her on a pillow. Raxa and Fahme were mounted nearby. The Lahgaelan governor had thus far treated them as guests. The schooner drifted farther downriver, its masts pointing south and creating trails as spars dragged along the surface. The vessel listed so heavily its hull threatened to slide beneath the water. Both Suddekan vessels crowded near, and one had taken enough damage that it too began to sink. The other ship, beset by Lahgaelan rivercraft, was being subdued. Corpses dotted the river. There were swimmers, also. Jooar had given orders that any who reached his shore were to be captured and held.

"One of your poets would describe this scene in shades of red." Levyathan spoke to Jooar, whose careful face betrayed little of what he was thinking.

"You have read our poets?"

"Issahan. Dorilian read to me his 'Seven Springs in Agalor.'"

"Truly?"

Levyathan nodded. Sun-blond strands of hair were whipped across his face by the wind.

> *"In Agalor the sun breaks black rock*
> *Upon salt-moon heights and reaches not*
> *Into dark valleys where secrets remain hidden.*
> *There I came upon a town blessed by prophets*
> *And ruled by seven sisters*
> *Whose stone lips speak from wells of truth.*
> *There are seven springs in Agalor."*

Jooar slid his dark gaze to meet Palimia's. "You are aware this is not normal for one of his age?"

She laughed. "Yes. But you get used to it."

Shouts and greetings came from the direction of the river, so she turned to look. A group of maybe seven men guarded by Jooar's soldiers strode toward their party. At their head was a gold-haired man who commanded all eyes. Tiflan beamed to see Jooar's companions.

The governor also smiled. "I am pleased to see you again, and alive, Bas of Teremar."

"And I you, my good friend. Are you well, lad?" Water-soaked but whole, Tiflan spoke to Levyathan directly.

"You were right. Mia is the better swimmer. I breathed in only a little of the river."

Tiflan turned his gaze to her. Palimia had seldom been happier to see a man. "We are all well. And so very happy to see you. Do we know what happened?"

"Suddekan flags. We need to learn more." To Jooar, Tiflan said, "Finding you here is a welcome turn."

"We are within sight of my city's defense towers. Let us retreat to the palace. My men can finish this work, and we will continue this conversation in more comfort."

Palimia had never seen a more elegant map. Centerpiece of an open room bordered by pillars, the tabletop was a work of art. Its mosaic

of marble, precious stones and metals brilliantly represented the lands from Sordan's gold-laced crystal towers set within Sarkuan's turquoise lake to the lapis expanse of the ocean. The colors of the land ranged from white desert to golden plain to green lushness along the azure line of the broad river that bisected its surface—and from the mighty Telarkans to the emerald-rimmed southern sea. Jooar pointed to the wide deep blue of the Sorand'ruil, for the map portrayed its course.

"We have detected over the last week more ship movement by Suddekar. Ordinarily I would not think much of this. The Sorand'ruil sees many ships, from many domains, and Suddekar is on the river, as are we."

"And yet something drew your attention?" Tiflan prompted.

Though she was not part of the conversation, Palimia listened. She stood near the map and was glad Tiflan, not she, held Levyathan, who had insisted on being part of this discussion. What she was right now was *exhausted.*

Jooar nodded. "The vessels did not pull into any town or dock. They were not carrying cargo or passengers to a port, neither up nor downstream. They would turn around and return to where they started. They remained on the river for some purpose. This activity began after the Hierarch's barge left here to continue its journey."

"But they did not go to Ilmar." Levyathan looked curious.

"Not these. We now know they were waiting for someone to come back this way. Maybe another Suddekan ship, maybe yours." Jooar tapped an area of smoky quartz mountains to the south. "There is also this. Herdsmen in the high pastures have reported more movement of men on horseback passing through this area, near our border with Orm."

"Mormantalorus!"

"You know your geography, little prince. Yes, and the horsemen were seen to travel to here." Jooar tapped another part of the map. "To Suddekar. My father the king has been watching this activity. We believe it is because the border between Suddekar and Othgol has become more difficult to infiltrate."

"You would be right," said Tiflan. He frowned. "You did not think to tell Dorilian about these movements?"

"I did tell him, when he was here a week ago. Now, however—" Jooar picked up a pyramidal marker and placed it on Ilmar, near Ivernesse. He placed another on the point where the schooner had been attacked west of Ben-Aranath and a third on the mountains between Lahgael and Suddekar. "Prince Levyathan tells me his father is alive. Much as I wish to believe this—"

"Believe it," said Tiflan. "He would know. The Highborn feel each other's deaths."

Palimia noticed the way Jooar paused, then nodded. The only approach that allowed for Highborn ways was to accept them on faith.

Movement at the entry to this open room, bordered by pillars of glazed, turquoise tiles, paused their conversation. Jooar went to speak with one of his soldiers. Behind that soldier were three men, two more soldiers and what appeared to be a prisoner. From where Palimia stood, the captive looked to be Staubaun. The governor gestured for Tiflan to approach. After putting Levyathan on the floor, Tiflan did so. Levyathan, shorter than the big man's knee, refused to be left behind and trotted after.

Palimia stepped forward, thinking to stop the child, but then halted. *He is Sordaneon... and he only looks like a toddler. He can make his own decision about where to be.*

She trailed her fingertips along the edge of the table and its Lahgaelan script inlaid with gold: *Upon a River of Blood, promised We... to hold this River... to hold this Sea... His city crowned... our People free.*

She recognized the wording of a Highborn treaty, sealed by holy blood, as enduring as the Creation. Marc Frederick had told her Highborn treaties, because they were fixed in the Mind, shaped both sides to uphold them. She could see how that might be the case with Lahgael, bound to Sordan by a river and a promise.

"They were Suddekan." Tiflan's voice pulled Palimia from her thoughts.

Tiflan returned to the map, frowning at the domain that crowded Sarkuan's southern shore. Jooar still stood at the entry, attending yet another of his men who had just arrived on the scene. The soldiers with the prisoner were gone.

Palimia withdrew her hand from the table. "You have proof?"

"One of the sailors who attacked us. An officer, Suddekan navy. He says the order to take the Sordaneons into custody, presumably only the Heir, came from the Gracious Hierarchessa."

Palimia's chest tightened at realizing what that meant. "She knew Dorilian would be attacked?"

"She knew *something.*"

A tug on a pleat of her Lahgaelan gown caused Palimia to look down into Levyathan's urgent young gaze.

"I can tell you something, too."

"Can you, little man?" Tiflan lifted and perched the lad on the edge of the map table.

Levyathan was happier with his new elevation. "Grandmother gave Dor the idea to use the river."

Palimia remembered that visit. "That's true," she confirmed. "He only spoke of a progress after their visit. But I cannot believe his own grandmother would..."

Tiflan sighed. "I will see what I can arrange for ships and protection. To stay here puts our host in too great a danger. We will leave at once for Sordan."

"Don't," said Jooar, who had just joined them. He extended his hand to reveal a folded paper. "My watchtower has received an interesting set of flashes from towns downriver: A Sordani warship is moving up the Sorand'ruil at great speed. It will be here before dawn."

20

"Why did you change the bedcurtains? I liked the ones I had before. The afternoon light turned them the color of flame, just like the coral walls of our grotto." Daimonaeris's lips parted slightly as she smiled at the memory. "The new purple ones look gloomy and do not please me at all."

Nammuor clenched his jaw as he guided her down the last steps to the Magistry. The work area of the Sanctuary at the base of the Ilgaon Tower was empty, as he had instructed. Within sight of the Horns of Fire, a waterglobe cast clear light upon a stark, waist-high plinth. Oarzas, who was to assist him with replacing the lifeforce crystals that ringed Daimonaeris's collar, waited at the side table with its tray of glowing, finger-sized spinels. Twelve healthy *gifted* youths had been harvested to procure them.

At this point, Nammuor simply wished Daimonaeris would cease complaining about bed linens. He had not changed them. No one had. No one would have *dared*. The damned things were coral, just as they had ever been. She merely could not see that color anymore.

Maybe the last set of crystals had been less pristine than those he had used previously. The Diadem's need for arcane energy was such that he must set aside the very best, most potent lifeforce crystals to feed its demands. He bid his sister's slave body to stand very still and removed the cloaking illusion that concealed the mounting apparatus and gave Daimonaeris the appearance of being whole. One by one, he unlatched the attachments until he at last could lift his sister's head and supporting devices free of the slave that bore her.

"I think these new crystals will serve you better."

"The one is Highborn, isn't it?" Her excitement was palpable. As he set her head on the pedestal, her limpid gaze lifted to his. "Oh, say it is! You promised."

No, he had not. "These are excellent quality."

A wail warbled from her throat, followed by a dainty sob. "It is taking so long, too long. Why must I wait when you have what I need? I want a body of my own. You promised!"

"You have a body. I have completely enthralled this one to you; it performs your every command. And thanks to the illusion I have put upon you—"

"It's just an animal. It has to be fed and watered like a dog, or a baby! And if I don't remember to take it to the toilet, it makes a mess. All it can do is obey commands. In the meantime, I am isolated. Joyless! I see and hear and taste, but I don't *feel* anything."

The slave, standing *Ir*-collared with its head and shoulders crowned by a bejeweled apparatus, met Nammuor's dismissive glance with a terrified stare. It didn't know he was not in the mood at the moment to undertake the monumental task of finding another vehicle to meet his sister's exacting standards.

"I am not going to attempt another graft. Remember what happened last time."

"It almost worked."

It had. Nammuor's advancements in *Ir* magery had enabled him to fashion a means by which to bond one person's head to another's body. A collar of devices and arcane lattices, it had given Daimonaeris complete control of her new body. The collar drained lifeforce so rapidly, however, as to be useful for only a fraction of a day. He had told her he would work on extending that time. At that point, she had expressed more gratitude for his efforts.

Daimonaeris sighed. "I don't understand why you cannot take just one of your Highborn crystals and use its lifeforce to make me whole. You have more of them. Didn't you say you would turn Dorilian into one? He's young, and people say he's powerful. It would be such delicious irony to give me that one."

The only irony in this room was that she was making it impossible for Nammuor to do anything except listen to her. The complexity of the *Ir*-devices needed to filter and oxygenate her blood were difficult enough to calibrate without her constant nattering. Maybe next time he should leave this entire process to Oarzas. But he could not do that... not to her, or to himself. He confided in Daimonaeris, told her his plans. It would be careless to leave her in a position to be exploited and turned against him.

As for Dorilian...

Nammuor drew a breath. "My plan to snare your husband encountered a little problem called a shipwreck." A communication device mounted on the ship had conveyed its final moments, splintered onto a rocky shore. He had already executed the mage who had promised low-level *lr* attacks would not trigger the Rift. Not only had Nammuor failed to harvest the targeted lifeforce, but he did not yet know if Dorilian had survived.

Daimonaeris's lips trembled. "Oh no, my poor Bammon!"

"Not the boy. He was not on the ship. He was in Ilmar. You really need to give him another name."

"But I like that one."

He pressed the proper keystone to the device holding the oxygenation membrane, resetting the saturation. Through a web of tubing, Nammuor watched the mage replace the life crystal that powered the blood pump.

"You will give me the next one, won't you? The next Highborn crystal?"

"How about if it is bound by Bammon?" Oddly enough, Nammuor could see doing that.

"Not my baby! You promised. You promised you would not need him!"

"Then stop asking."

Fat tears rolled down her puffy cheeks. Nammuor hoped these new crystals would take care of the latter. As marvelous as his creation was, keeping his sister's tissues vital and healthy was... no longer working as well as before. Her color was off. Her skin appeared mottled and waxy, her eyes glazed and hair dull. Some minute element or essence was missing. He had tried various infusions, created crystals from unborn children, girls experiencing first menstruation, and even rare animals. None had reversed her deficits. He was no longer confident a crystal imbued with Highborn lifeforce would deliver the result she craved.

To use one on her would be to throw it away.

Nammuor held aloft a glowing crimson spinel and frowned. This faceted crystal, too, burned with precious power, a lifeforce captured to be amplified, its impermanent energies released... and used. His mages employed such crystals as this one to create powerful *lr* matrices and the arrays needed to communicate with Nammuor's far-flung agents. *Lr* weapons. Translocators. Slave collars...

He gazed once more into the eyes of the slave standing near at hand, controlled and incapable of independent action. It too was a waste. A slave of such sublime beauty was precisely the sort of gift needed for a certain prince of Lahgael Nammuor wished to turn.

Across the dark-pillared chamber, the deathstone box beckoned. Power unimaginable lurked within. When it came to the Diadem, he had to be patient. If he struck too soon, revealed himself too soon, his enemies might panic and join forces. Better to pick them off one by one. His plan to seize Sordan through Daimonaeris and her child had suffered a setback, but that battle had not yet been lost. The little Sordaneon bastard was still Nammuor's heir—and while the child lived, Nammuor's claim was intact.

"—you don't care that I am suffering. My baby is gone. You promised I would see him, be with him."

"All in good time." He had become quite accomplished at speaking through clenched teeth.

"Now that you can do illusion so perfectly and no one can tell, I want to go out among the people again. Let them see me." Daimonaeris's eyes turned up to look into his. "Do they know I am alive? Are they happy for me?"

"Yes," he lied. He had never revealed her existence to anyone outside the Magistry.

She smiled. "Good! I can be their princess again. Their Nuarchessa! Though of course I would let you decide everything."

Could her prattle get any more insipid? His beautiful sister had been reduced to a gabbling *thing*. All the hours devoted to her were hours stolen from his Diadem. The handful of crystals he had so painstakingly affixed to the device had already made it powerful beyond his original hopes. He should not be tarrying like this, spending life crystals on *her* while letting his masterwork languish.

Nammuor placed the crystal he had been holding back onto the tray. He reached into the apparatus and removed the lifeforce crystal the mage had installed but moments before: the crystal that powered the diaphragm which allowed his sister to speak. Such an elegant design. Her mouth continued to move, but without air to vibrate her vocal cords, no sound came from her throat. Daimonaeris's gaze swiveled wildly from Nammuor to the mage. The oxygenation coils and pump still kept her alive, so Nammuor pulled that crystal too.

"I love you, sister." He angled his face to hers, their lips almost touching. "I have done everything in my power. But I think you will be happier this way. I know *I* will be."

Voiceless, bloodless, features contorted in terror, Daimonaeris's face drained of life. It took a moment more for the light to leave her eyes. Only the jagged gasps of the slave accompanied her leaving. Nammuor laid the last crystal, fulgent with power, onto the tray and gestured for Oarzas to take them away. As for the head... he would embalm it and keep it to remind him of Dorilian's atrocity. One day he would place his sister's head alongside that of her husband.

Poor little Bammon was destined to be an orphan. Nammuor hoped to make it soon.

Slashed bloody by rays of rose and dawn, the warship towered over Ben-Aranath's wharves. Dorilian thought it made a suitably menacing statement. He and all his crew had seen the remains of the schooner and at least one other vessel not far downriver. The wreck's cause demanded an explanation. Jooar had permitted a Sordani vessel of war obviously armed to the last boards to approach Ben-Aranath without any display of defenses, and moreover allowed it to berth at the Governor's Palace. Seeing this prompted Dorilian to adopt a less martial tone. He ordered his troops on the deck to lower arms and the crew to attend to mooring the ship.

A line of Lahgaelan soldiers barricaded the end of the pier. After the ship was secured, Jooar strode onto the pier, accompanied by only two men, one his captain of the guard and the other his foreign minister. None of them appeared armed. When Dorilian disembarked with a precautionary guard of twenty men, in addition to Tutto and Legon at his side, Jooar approached to within a dozen paces away and bowed.

"You are welcome again, Hierarch. I hope you have noticed that I have stayed your friend. When my sentinels sent word of a Sordani warship not flying your flag, I still prayed you would be on it."

"There was an attack. My Heir and family—"

"Are here." Jooar gestured to the line of soldiers, from behind which another group emerged. Tiflan, looking out of place in bright Lahgaelan robes, and two women also in native gowns, carrying two squirming children. Behind them were a dozen or so men, some bearing bundles of what appeared to be belongings, all of whom looked happy to see Dorilian

Alive. The tension of two days fled. Alive! Not just Levyathan, whose existence in this world Dorilian would always feel, but Fahme too. And Palimia and Raxa, and Tiflan, who Dorilian could no more replace than his own right arm. His people. The feelings that washed over him could have filled an ocean of goodwill.

Levyathan took off running the moment Palimia set him on his feet.

"Dor!"

Kneeling on the wooden planks, Dorilian embraced Levyathan. Fahme screamed and was also given her freedom. Between Levyathan's kisses and Fahme pushing to do the same, Dorilian glanced up at a smiling Jooar.

"Thank you."

"I needed the soldiers to keep them safe," Jooar said. "They would not wait at the palace. But after what you surely saw downstream, I did not know in what manner you would choose to approach."

"I feared the worst." Dorilian granted Fahme the kisses she demanded and squeezed both her and Levyathan hard enough that they begged him to stop. Both children were clearly unharmed and smelled freshly bathed.

Fahme spoke urgently. "We fell in the river. Raxa and Mia were naked!"

Levyathan pushed at Dorilian's collarbone, earning his attention. "We had to swim. Did you have to swim in the ocean?"

"Some. I had to beach my ship."

Dorilian met Palimia's concerned gaze. The Lahgaelan robe she wore, azure striped with gold, moved lightly in the breeze.

"Praise Leur you're here. Is that your blood?" She had noticed stains on his armor and garments.

"No. I killed a few men. I lost my ship, but I got another one." Dorilian ruffled Levyathan's hair. "What do you say? Are you ready to go home?"

"Yes. But I think Grandmother is looking for us. Will we be safe?"

Dorilian nodded. "Yes. We are going to Sordan. I have this ship and two more not far behind me. Go with Tutto now." He gestured to his well-armed sword master, and also to Palimia and Raxa, who understood that time was key. They could not linger in Ben-Aranath. Dorilian stood and waited until his family and the Sordani survivors from the schooner boarded the warship before he turned to Jooar.

"Tell me what happened."

Item by item, Jooar filled in missing details of the plot. Dorilian connected each piece. Nammuor. Suddekar. Ermenthalia. *Nammuor found an ally.*

"I was never approached about any of this. Neither do I think my king and father knew."

Dorilian would find out if that was true. For now, it was enough to know Jooar remained his ally. Though weakened, the Mind still bound Lahgael's rulers to the treaty their dynasty had made with the Sordaneons. Until Lahgael did something to break that treaty, Dorilian was also bound. It would be a mistake, however, to rest all his faith in the work of ancestors. There were steps he could take to strengthen his hand here—and recognize a debt he could never repay.

"Today I must leave you with only my thanks. However, when I reach Sordan, I will stipulate that any ship bearing your flag, Jooar Zetharnna, will pay the same harbor fee in Sordan that my own ships pay."

Jooar's dark eyes widened. "Your own ships pay no fee!"

Dorilian wished that were so. "Ships belonging to the Hierarchate pay no fee. I personally own a number of commercial vessels, however, and those vessels pay a nominal fee. Only my personal Rill transport is free. I give you that also. I will issue Rill passes to you that you may bequeath to your descendants—all fees to be paid out of Sordaneon coffers. In perpetuity. This in gratitude for your help to my family and me."

"A thousand thanks."

"And not nearly enough." Dorilian looked at the serene beauty of Jooar's azure palace and wondered when, if ever, he would see it again. "In the meantime, I have another request."

The river shimmered like beaten gold, a tranquil highway. Though dozens of barges and masted merchant vessels shared the water, no Suddekan ships troubled their journey. Any that appeared kept the same respectful distance as every other boat and ship on the river.

Dorilian rested on deck but stayed alert. He had slept only in fits, mind and body too keyed by his ongoing crisis to fully put his greatest fear to rest. The women and children slept in the commander's cabin, watched over by Legon. Overhead, sailors hung in the rigging and worked on the sails. More mariners swarmed over the ship's railings and woodwork, painting those. As the ship raced under the full power of a stiff west wind in the sails and teams of seasoned oarsmen being paid top coin for speed, Tutto and Tiflan remained with their Hierarch. Together, they consolidated their next moves.

"Ermenthalia planned this. The procession down the river. The barge. That I take Lev with me. I told her myself that I would sail on the new warship in Ilmar. Next thing I know I have lost my ship in a Rift storm and my family is on the run for their lives. The only good to come of this excursion is that I rid Sansordan of a tribe of cannibals." Dorilian left out the part about seeing Mulsor.

Tiflan regarded him gravely. "I think you are right about Nammuor being involved in this plan."

"Yes, but I expect *him* to try to kill me. Why would she? She deliberately put me in his path, lured me out of Sordan. It was a two-pronged attack. Nammuor would capture or kill me, leaving Sordan without a ruler. The other prong was for her agents to bring Lev to her, my successor, the key to the Hierarchate."

Tiflan nodded. "A regency. As his grandmother, she would be legal guardian."

"Did she not know Nammuor would kill me? Or does she not care?" Had Dorilian's world gotten so small the only people who didn't want him dead were on this ship?

Tutto leaned forward with his own brand of comfort. "You might not be the one she cares about. Her mother was Mormantaloran, from one of its great families. I heard she did not wed your grandsire by choice. Called him a half man."

Dorilian had never seen Ermenthalia and Labran together but could imagine it. Thinking about it, Dorilian frowned. Daimonaeris had used the same word—for him. "Ermenthalia had a hand in choosing my wife."

And she had chosen a woman just like her. He discerned another repeating pattern; the temporal refraction pulsed just beyond his senses. A recurrence, uncorrected, like Marc Frederick and Labran, Dorilian and Stefan… the Dazun and the Sorand'ruil…

Tiflan was agreeing with something Tutto had just said. "Nammuor first came to Sordan with his sister at Ermenthalia's invitation."

As a possible bride for Deben, not Dorilian. Deben had made the decision to marry Daimonaeris to his son instead. Did Ermenthalia know Levyathan too was Deben's son? Dorilian tried to place that set of facts into the pattern he sensed but could not make them fit. Maybe none of it fit. He was beyond tired.

"I cannot uncover the truth of any of this until I pin her down. I will secure Suddekar even if I have to go in there and do it myself. Maybe Deleus is involved in this plot."

Tiflan frowned. "We cannot ignore that possibility."

No. He had ignored too many possibilities already. Dorilian looked upward at the sails, the sky. Crew he had picked up in Ben-Aranath to augment his exhausted force with more sailors moved among the masts and full-bellied sails. One caught his eye. Was that a... woman in the rigging? At this point only one thing mattered. He directed that question to Tutto. "Can we make Sordan by morning?"

Tutto squinted up at the sails. Once fields of white trimmed with green, the canvas was now stained with blue and red stripes. With a frown, he turned to look behind them, to the west. "Brisk wind like this... full oars... two days. There's a storm coming at our backs might drive us off course."

"Don't let it... and make Sordan in one," Dorilian said.

21

"She is my wife. She belongs with *me*, not her mother!"

Stefan flung message and envelope to the ground and hauled on the reins, causing his mount to rear in protest. He managed to keep it under control. Making a scene served no purpose. His nobles, returning with him from a successful hunt, filled the courtyard of the stables. Sun glinted off the windows of the Emrysen Palace where it rose above a display of flowering shrubs. After Stefan had calmed his horse, he swung down from the saddle. Goff had picked up the message and tucked it into his shirt.

Good.

Cullen trotted over. Stefan sent his other nobles away by saying he would meet them later in the banquet hall. Boar would grace tonight's table.

"Nilla wants to stay with her mother through the harvest," Stefan complained. "Summer's not even over yet!" He watched Cullen's expression pass from realization of what the problem was to concern over Stefan's response. Goff's grimace was even more telling. "Don't tell me I'm being unreasonable to want my wife to return to my bed."

Cullen and Goff exchanged glances before Goff gestured for Cullen to do the honors. "I'll tell you, then. You're being unreasonable. She went through a hard time, and so did you."

"Losing my heir didn't stop me from being king. I didn't use it as an excuse to run away. People need to see me moving on and getting things done. And they need to see *her*!"

"People understand, Stefan. They know a woman needs time to heal." Cullen didn't flinch away from Stefan's narrow glare. "If they think anything about it meaning something else, it's only because you're moping around like a man desperate to prove something."

"Like what?"

"That you've nailed the throne to your headboard? Put it out of other people's reach?"

As usual, Cullen was right. Partly, anyway. Even Goff looked relieved that Cullen had provided Stefan with an opening. "I want her here, all right? I want to show people—" What did he want to show them? How should he even say it? "I want to show them a royal couple. A symbol of unity. They need to see that I have not just a queen, but a wife—one that isn't running away from me. Because that's what it looks like."

Stefan led them away from the other courtiers and stable hands, toward the overlook at the high point of the garden, with its view of the Upper Canal and the golden façade of the Emrysen Palace's stately south wing. "Day after day I have to deal with problems and demands. Half my nobles think the Highborn should be in my place. Maybe they don't say it to my face, but I know they think it, and you know it too."

"Aw, Stefan—"

"He's right," Goff put in from his seat on the nearby wall. "The damn Highborn princes petitioned him to let them go home. Prince Rheger back to Dannuth, and Stauberg for his son that thinks he needs to walk on the Wall. Good riddance, except I had a man say to me just the other day he likes that they're here, the Highborn princes! And you know why? What was his reason?" Goff's beard jutted as he scoffed. "Said it makes him feel better with the world to know there's Highborn at hand."

"That's their religion," said Cullen. "They think about Leur same way as our faith in the Mother and Lud."

Stefan was tired of hearing it. "Well, there aren't enough Highborn to go around, are there? I've found I don't like having Rheger Dannutheon or his son too close at hand, showing me up. People compare me to them! And I sure as Mother's Milk don't like people talking about how important they are."

A faint thrum drew their eyes to the soaring Rill structures that crowned Dazunor-Rannuli, a *charys* gliding to roost high upon the Mount. Bare moments later, a bolt of brilliant light accompanied by an ascending whine split the day as a second *charys* shot north, high over the canal beside which they stood.

"They are important." Cullen pointed at the Rill. "They're especially important if people believe they give them *that*."

Wealth. Power. The ability to move with the swiftness of gods. Stefan distrusted the Rill more than the Highborn themselves.

"Burelan Phaeros gets to flaunt his riches because of *that*." Let Cullen chew on the full cause of Stefan's discontent. "He fields an army as large as mine. He's courting Palaistea, who has an even bigger army herself and more estates than I do, and he's been busy making friends. Or maybe buying them."

Cullen could not dispute the possibility. "His holdings generate enough trade that he fills his own book—but so do all the other great lords."

"Those great lords are barely loyal to me. Every tax I levy, they oppose and make me step back. They're all in arrears on the taxes they do owe. Nothing makes them happier than to make me poor!" Stefan had his own income, to be sure—Rill revenues and the proceeds of his properties—but he needed monies to fund the costs of running the damned kingdom. "Aren't you angry they won't support Kheld trade in any form? We grant Kheld merchants licenses, and still people go out of their way to sell their goods to someone else! Anyone else! No one will trade with Khelds. But my lords find ways to trade with Sordan. I know they do, even though I told people not to."

"You can't enforce it. Stefan, I warned you about that." Cullen's frustration was clear. "Rill trade is… like water. You stop it at one point, it just leaks out somewhere else."

"Dorilian cut it off at his end, didn't he? He doesn't allow Esseran goods to be unloaded in Sordan or Hestya. He made it so Esseran ships, from *any* of our domains, can't dock in Sordan. He stops them in his lake and impounds them! He stops them in his *river*. I have the Seven Houses chewing off my ears."

"Sure, but they're getting their goods through anyway. They use Trongorian merchants as go-betweens. Or they ship to Randpory."

"But they have to use Trongorian ships! Or Ardaenan or Mercedan. Because of that, our ships go wanting and our goods cost too much. Our merchants make less profit. We're being cut out by everyone!"

"Sordan is suffering, too." Goff spoke up surely. "They need our lumber, our metals."

"Not enough. Dorilian's been developing new sources, and new markets too."

"So are we." Cullen's jaw firmed. "In Amallar, which won't trade with him. And Trongor, which isn't playing sides, just wants the best deals. Kyredon, too. That domain is growing, Stefan. And didn't the Lahgaelan ambassador just tell you their king said our ships can dock in Ben-Aranath and they won't let Sordan stop them?"

"And what does that mean? Now we can get *close* to Sordan—just not get *to* Sordan except on Lahgaelan ships."

"There's Mormantalorus, too." Goff said what Cullen wouldn't.

"We shouldn't overlook them. They're big." Stefan had told Cullen to look into this option a year ago.

"And rich!" added Goff. "Just far away."

"Far away," Cullen agreed. "But more than that, they... they have no use for Khelds. None. Your grandfather—"

"Didn't trust them. I know that." Stefan more than knew it—he had argued that Marc Frederick was missing a bigger picture, that Sordan was the more dangerous foe. Sordan, which had stabbed them all in the back. As far as Stefan was concerned, Mormantalorus presented an opportunity. Not so long ago, that land had been part of the Triempery—a vital, trusted part. Maybe it could be lured back. "Are we trading with them at all?"

Cullen gazed at the canal and its display of recreational gonds preferred by the wealthy inhabitants of this quarter of the city. He exhaled in frustration. "We do have some trade with Mormantalorus. Pearls. Dyes. Gems. Those crystals used by mage-artisans in Permephedon to make waterglobes and all that. No traffic by Rill, of course, with the nearest node being at Hestya and Sordan being at war with them. Their goods arrive mostly on ships from Merced, Trongor and Lahgael. When I was in Maskos last year to confer about trade, I tried to meet the Mormantaloran ambassador. He... wouldn't." Cullen's face tightened. "I was told they don't conduct business with 'lesser men.'"

"Lesser men?"

"Us."

Which ruled out Khelds—but not the greater part of Stefan's kingdom. If Stefan sent the right man to negotiate, maybe a deal could be arranged that would bring Essera great advantages. He had heard Erenor mention Mormantalorus as a possible trade and political ally. It would be rich to not only align with Dorilian's enemy but also profit by it. If he could also establish strong ties with Lahgael, Stefan could actually flank his annoying nemesis.

"Let's go back to the palace," he told his companions. "Time for a celebration."

They had just stepped onto the paving stones leading to the imposing entrance to the West Hall, Goff bending Stefan's ear with a proposal for placing two promising young clansmen as tax collectors—a position Stefan felt had been dominated for too long by Staubauns—when Erenor dashed down the steps, breathless, his face animated and alert. At his side was Lucien Illarion, who looked more alarmed.

"I do not know how much to believe of this, sire, but"—Erenor drew air before he could continue—"something is not right in Sordan."

"I know *that*." Nothing had been right with Sordan since the day Marc Frederick had given back the Hierarchate's autonomy.

"No. I mean really not right. Dorilian Sordaneon isn't in the city."

Stefan rolled his eyes. "I know that, too. He's parading his wealth on some golden barge down his private river."

"Sire, it is something else. Our agent in the city has sent word that the Gracious Hierarchessa, Ermenthalia, is in Sordan—while the Hierarch is not, which isn't usual at all. What's more, she has called for Sordan's Halia to convene. They are not in session."

A development completely out of the ordinary, because it was something only the ruling Hierarch could do. Unless....

"Has something happened to Dorilian?" Stefan could only hope. His heart beat faster at the rush of excitement.

Lucien shook his head of gold-bright hair. "We do not know. *No one* knows. All we know is this is highly unusual."

Dorilian was on a progress into a far-flung corner of his Hierarchate. If anything had happened, it would take a longer time than this for news to travel as far as Stefan's ear. But not, perhaps, to the ear of the Hierarch's family. Or his grandmother.

"He might be dead." The possibility dangled so close that Stefan did not hesitate to take a bite from it. Retribution, juicy-sweet because it was perfect justice, too. It would be fitting for Dorilian to die on account of excessive wealth and pride.

"Now that would be a thing to celebrate!" Goff clapped Stefan's shoulder and seemed even more joyful. Cullen, however, looked thoughtful and sober.

Erenor, too, counseled caution. "We do not know anything yet. It is barely more than a whisper. The Seven Houses have the best information; they have placed spies so deep in Sordaneon business they know everything—and they would not tell me a thing. They are sitting tight, watching, just like we are."

Stefan smiled and resumed walking. There would be a banquet tonight to celebrate his hunt, and maybe something more.

Whatever was going on, and whatever happened because of it, Dorilian's troubles were clearly serious.

By the time Dorilian sailed into Sordan's harbor, his ship had changed allegiances—at least in appearance. Their wind-filled sails of blue with red diagonal striping proclaimed a Trongorian ship. So did the blue railings and trim, and the boldness of a red prow leading the way. Gone was the Hierarch's flag, replaced by that of the maritime Electorate. Only when the ship turned toward the military basin did he order that flag struck and Sordan's flag to be raised, along with the banner of the Hierarchate.

A ship intercepted them. The armed men who boarded were led by an officer Tutto knew for having commanded him in Sebbord's service. Upon observing the ranks of soldiers wearing Eagle armor and gear and seeing Tiflan in his Teremari regalia, with Dorilian standing at their head, wearing Derlon's Armor while displaying a fiery *orbus* in his right hand and the Rill Stone on his left, the man quickly pieced together the situation.

"Your Thrice Royal Grace," he stammered. "Why this—?"

"Who controls the City?" Dorilian doused the *orbus* to show his empty, unburnt hand. He had washed during the voyage and seen his armor cleaned and polished. No longer was he stained with blood.

"The Gracious Hierarchessa has convened the Halia. We feared—"

"So do I. Signal that my ship may dock and that I require horses and additional men."

"Yes, Thrice Royal!"

Dorilian's military would always stay with him. To them, he would forever be the prince who had freed Sordan from Essera's occupation. He was also sacred—Highborn and Rillborn and the last of a line descended from their god. Under his command Sordan's military had been elevated to greater prestige than in the last forty years. They would follow him in a heartbeat against an old woman whose only claim was that of having given birth to Deben the Conquered.

To Tutto and Legon, and two hundred Eagle Guards who had accompanied him from Ilmar, Dorilian said, "Protect my Heir and my family. I will send for you once I have settled matters in the Upper City."

The Gracious Hierarchessa was going to regret having summoned Sordan's Halia.

Dorilian reached the Upper City leading a force of several thousand. Word of his return spread quickly. Commanders who had tacitly stayed on the sideline of the Gracious Hierarchessa's political maneuvers instead threw the full weight of their allegiance to their Hierarch. Upon reaching the Dekkora, Dorilian sent a force of three thousand to seize control of the Serat from Ermenthalia's troops and another few thousand to secure the Rill. He doubted they would encounter much resistance.

Dorilian led his thousand upwards to the splendid Citadel itself, where the Halia held court in chambers wherein Aryati star farers had once walked and lived and perhaps ruled. With towers that soared to heights unparalleled by all but Permephedon's spires, the Citadel belonged to another time.

Hierarchal banners in profusion, flanked by Tiflan and Legon, Dorilian rode his horse down the inclined arcade, past the open arches and into the open, sunken courtyard. His troops encountered only brief resistance from a regiment of Suddekan soldiers. All but a few, upon seeing they were opposing Sordan's Hierarch, knelt and laid down their arms. Tiflan and Legon stayed at Dorilian's side as he spurred past a line of stunned Citadel guards and a smaller cohort of Suddekan soldiers, his mount leaping into the first level of the tower. The splendid rotunda within gave way to vaulted, wondrous corridors and ramps to other levels. Only when he reached the tree-shaded and beautiful Courtyard of Judgment and the grand doorway leading to the Halia Chamber did he draw rein and dismount. He ordered the soldiers still with him to secure the courtyard. With Tiflan and twenty men chosen by Legon, Dorilian advanced on the Halia Chamber.

The Halls of Government occupied a ground floor above the guardhouse and prison. City offices, courts, institutions of learning and healing, and a few public spaces filled several floors above that, all connected by walkways, courts and bridges. The remainder of the Citadel was sealed and restricted. The Hierarchate had, in setting up Sordan's charter, negotiated control and occupancy of the greater part of the Citadel's uppermost levels in exchange for a perpetual percentage of Sordaneon Rill revenues that kept Sordan's city treasury filled beyond those of most domains.

The squadron of Citadel Guards protecting the Halia Chamber knew Dorilian and his Guard on sight, and knew Tiflan also.

"Your Thrice Royal Grace—"

They could not stop him. Sordan and its domains put to death anyone who laid hand on a Highborn prince without permission. To a man, the guards knelt and put down their swords as Dorilian walked past. Two of the men nigh clambered over each other to open the tall bronze doors, crafted post-Exile and cast in panels that showed the Halia's establishment and history.

From his very first day as Hierarch, Dorilian had included the Halia, as the organ of the populace, at the center of his rule of the City. One man could not reasonably attend to *all* the business of governing. To that end, Dorilian had cultivated men and women willing to provide the needed level of administration. He took pride in knowing Sordan and its people were as ably led as they were prosperous.

He also understood completely why Ermenthalia wished to enlist Sordan's popular leaders to her side. The clever bitch needed them if she was to feed his people lies that would shift their loyalties to her.

He found Ermenthalia within, on her feet before the seated assembly, the chamber's ring of clerestories casting light to create a halo around her regal figure. She might have been a classic orator, tall and straight in a stola as elegant as it was archaic. The gathered Haliasts saw Dorilian first and immediately scrambled to their feet, whereupon they dropped to their knees and bowed to the floor. They looked confused.

Ermenthalia looked… dismayed, but only for a moment.

Dorilian strode to her side, though he kept a defensive distance between them. Tiflan and Legon assumed positions at the door along with their twenty men, as Dorilian addressed the Halia.

"What has Grandmother been telling you?"

Larissa Norsa, the Halia's recently elected Speaker, stood to answer. "The Gracious Hierarchessa expressed concern for your well-being, Thrice Royal, and asked our assistance in keeping the city calm and at peace until your fate could be determined."

He gave Ermenthalia a smile. "Peace?"

Lined, aged eyes as unfaded and clear as topaz glass rose to meet his. "I only ever hope for that… with you."

"Me? Good people died in Ivernesse because of you. I walked in their blood. More died in the attack on my schooner because of you. I lost a warship that cost a year of Rill revenue and, yes, more good men—because of you. I nearly lost my family! But I did not lose my life, or my Heir, or Sordan. You will not be the one who delivers me to my end." To the soldiers of his guard standing just inside the open door to the chamber, he said, "Arrest her. Remove her to the Serat."

"Thrice Royal," Larissa Norsa entreated, her voice sure and faintly challenging. "If the Gracious Hierarchessa has committed a crime…"

Dorilian's soldiers had already ushered Ermenthalia from the Hall.

"What crimes my grandmother has committed will be determined and summarily prosecuted," he assured Norsa, and the Halia. "I can attest, those crimes were against *me*, as Sordaneon and Hierarch, and not against this City. Her plea to you was not a crime, just… premature. I regret she called you here for nothing."

"Can you tell us what this is about, Thrice Royal? Are you under threat?" The Speaker's concern was genuine.

To that, Dorilian had only one answer. "Yes. Always."

The Serat teemed with activity when he arrived later, escorted by elite troops. His Eagle Guard had taken control of the complex and Dorilian's appearance before the Suddekan troops prompted their final surrender. They had believed him dead or captured when they had followed their Basarchessa's orders. Now they embraced his offer of amnesty.

Once he ascended the steps and he and Legon walked the cerulean floor of the Indigo Corridor, Dorilian broached the next important matter. "My family?"

"Safe. Both your son and the Lady Palimia are asking to see you. Fahme seems happy just to be home. Same with Raxa."

"You secured the Serat?"

"I and Tutto also, floor by floor, room by room, before you arrived. I spoke with the household staff and have detained all persons they did not recognize or who was attached to the Gracious Hierarchessa."

Good. "Do another sweep. Tiflan will spend the night with the children. You will guard me while I sleep. Tutto will head the night guard."

Legon nodded sharply. He had spent more nights with Dorilian than any other person; they had established their friendship as boys, first at Askorras and later at Permephedon. If Dorilian must tighten his circle of trust, Legon stood firmly within.

"Where is Ermenthalia?" He would not rest until he had delved into that nest of hornets.

"The Void. Bas Tiflan is with her. No one will get to her except through him."

Neither would she get to Tiflan. A secure situation for now. Let her stew. Dorilian could afford a short diversion. First to his chamber to finally remove the thrice-cursed armor, then to see his loved ones.

By the time he arrived, the light of late afternoon, warm and golden, bathed the nursery. The children were quiet. Fahme had fallen asleep on Raxa's soft bosom. The nurse put a finger to her lips. Palimia looked up from the book Levyathan had been reading to her. Dorilian walked over to the long divan near the open doors to the terrace and joined them on it. Levyathan spoke in a whisper.

"Did you stop Grandmother?"

Dorilian nodded. Now that he had removed the armor and returned it to the Trove, he felt more like himself. Less under attack, even though in so many ways he still was.

"Was she doing something awful?"

"No." Dorilian caught Palimia's questioning look. If not something awful, then what? "She informed them I might be lost and was seeking their help." While Levyathan cocked his head, pondering that answer, he clarified. "She did something awful before she went to them. I still have to find out exactly what."

Levyathan pushed the book off his lap and stood to hug Dorilian's neck, crushing the cutwork neckline of the otherwise austere tunic. "She's dangerous. She lies to us."

"I know that." Dorilian hugged Levyathan, then freed himself. To Palimia, he said, "I will not need company tonight. If you wish an escort—"

She gently shook her head. "I am too exhausted. We are all exhausted, aren't we? I will use my own apartment here this night." The Songbird Palace, her residence in the city, was not far away, but Dorilian understood her desire to stay. He had gifted her with an apartment in the same wing used by Tiflan and other family and she could just as easily fall into a bed there.

At least the world was returning to a semblance of order.

Dorilian stood and touched Levyathan's fine corn-silk yellow hair. "Do not fight Raxa when she sends you to bed. And wish me well. I am off to fight a monster."

The Void Chamber beneath the Serat was where secrets died. Sometimes secrets were born there. Almost never did they leave the room.

No memory remained, no history had been written, of how the chamber had come into being. Its walls, floor and ceiling appeared impenetrable and seamless, yet the room could not be flooded, and it was never airless. Its surfaces were so dark they seemingly drank light, yet light there was. The room's glow came from its sole adornments: waterglobes set in perfect balance atop featureless obelisks which stood behind an equally featureless—and black— stone throne. Though sound was possible within the chamber, no sound ever escaped to outside of it.

For generations, the Sordaneons had used the Void to hold, interrogate, and punish those who opposed them.

Dorilian entered the chamber to find Ermenthalia seated with regal defiance on the throne. She lifted her chin but granted him no other acknowledgment. He gestured for Tiflan, who stood frowning beside the door with arms crossed over his chest, to leave the room. Dorilian waited until the seamless seal of the closed door ensured privacy.

"Is this how you want to do this?"

"I am an old woman, Grandson. Perhaps some consideration...."

He tamed his annoyance into something more subtle. "Leur forbid that I deny you consideration... when I have enjoyed so little of it."

Ermenthalia blanched beneath the layer of powder that tinted her cheeks. She still wore her elegant garments from earlier, including a pearl-encrusted tiara of rank and ornate arm rings of silver displaying the Sordaneon kinship ensigns she had gained the right to wear upon her marriage to his grandfather.

"You were never to be harmed."

He tasted truth beneath her words, at least as far as she believed. "Who promised you that? Nammuor?"

"Do you think I would—"

"I know what you did. I also know with whom. I would like to know *why*."

Aged lips stretched in a false smile. "And you need me to tell you. You are that ungifted."

Perhaps he had cultivated that rumor too well. Only those closest to him knew he could attune other minds to his. The prospect of communing in that way with Ermenthalia nauseated him. Unlike the shared-fate bonds of Highborn kinship, purely human relationships were emotion-bounded, conditional. Visceral. He had never truly been able to count on Ermenthalia—for anything.

Except this: her smirk of superiority.

"Ha!" Her flinty gaze stabbed down at him. "The Sordaneons are doomed. Your father was wrong to hope you might evolve. You have no talent at all, save that of flinging far and wide your ill temper. An aptitude that in some other man might foster friends and peace, for you gains only enemies and war."

When he did not rise to her provocation, she snorted. "I was present at your birth. So little celebration. There should have been more. A Sordaneon heir! The world should have rejoiced, but it did not. Essera hated your father. Hated him and his brother. *My* sons! They only spent the one because they needed the other. To hold Sordan in chains."

"I know what they did." Dorilian had broken those chains.

"You should. You *are* what they did." She leaned back in the throne and lifted her head to regard him coldly. "Your father was gifted, and his brother too. Oh yes! The pure race flowed in *their* veins. Delos commanded lightning, but your father could hear Rill song; Derlon knew Deben by name. Deben could have done so much had those fiends in Essera not crippled his mind, rendered him weak. They wished to weaken the godblood and make themselves its masters. They conspired with Deben's nobles to force him to wed Sebbord's base-blooded daughter. They saw to it he got *you* for a son. You and a cretin he never acknowledged."

Now was the time to hold his tongue and allow her hate to spill truth. Dorilian did not have to approve, or agree, or let it move him. All he had to do was listen.

"You tried to fix it."

She nodded, though her attention on him sharpened. "Daimonaeris was perfect. The purest bloodlines. Highborn and Staubaun back to the Founding, with not one trace of lesser blood. Intelligent. Beautiful."

Treacherous. Hateful. Dead.

Ermenthalia's poisonous gaze seized his. "I am glad you never sired anything on her. I hope you never sire anything at all." Her upper lip curled. "No woman of any breeding would agree to you anyway."

Which might well be true. Dorilian had not exactly tested those waters. But at least she had answered the question of how much she knew about who had fathered Levyathan.

"So whether Nammuor slaughtered me or not didn't matter to you at all."

"He said he would not kill you."

"Did he tell you this in person?"

She dismissed that question with a wave of her hand. "No. Of course not. Do not be a fool. He cannot translocate and neither can I. I have it in writing."

It did not matter where the incriminating document might be. Dorilian's agents would find it... or not. Her words locked into the Mind solidly enough to seal its existence.

Probably because he looked thoughtful, she continued to speak. "I would have raised the boy to be a true Sordaneon. It seemed like a fair trade."

"And Deleus?"

Her head snapped up. "That fool? He is as base-blooded as you are. He would have run to warn you if he had known."

Truth filled that proclamation enough to remove Deleus from suspicion. More and more, Dorilian saw being despised by Ermenthalia as a point of favor.

She scowled at his lack of response. "Sordan deserves better than you. This City deserves pure blood. *Rill* blood such as might awaken a god."

"You know nothing about me at all, do you?"

Her fingers gripped the smooth arms of the throne, stark white against ebon. "Oh, I know you well enough, Dorilian Sordaneon. You are intelligent but you obey brutish instincts. You bully and threaten. You get what you want because your gift allows you to bludgeon people's emotions in ways that compel them to fear you. You seek out low men who will not challenge your perception of yourself, and turn away your betters. Anyone strong enough to stand up to you, you avoid or remove. Sebbord insinuated you might have opened Hestya. Might be Rill-Chosen. Leur-gifted. Ha! That barbarian in Essera believed it. Deben told me. We laughed about that."

They probably had laughed. "Did Father tell you why he went to Permephedon? Why *we* went?"

"We had no opportunity to talk before he left."

Good. He preferred the truth of that treaty remain secret. Dorilian knelt on one knee with elbow propped, chin on his left hand. Let her look upon the Rill Stone as he pondered what to do with her. His posture provoked a smile.

"What a puzzle you are," Ermenthalia said. "I almost think you are playing with me."

It did no harm to humor her. "I am starting to like you... a little."

"No, I don't think so. You find me cold, and I find you

unfortunate. Poor Deben never had a chance, once you were born. He had too many enemies and never quite found a way out from under them. Rather like you, except your enemies are of your own creation. I would have made a better Regent than you do a Hierarch."

There it was, the other part of Nammuor's offer. How neatly she fit into the monster's ambitions.

"After all, little Bassom—"

"What?" Had Dorilian heard that correctly?

"Bassom. The boy's name, the one his mother would have given him." Ermenthalia began a new tangent. "Bassom the Fire Lord, a great hero of Mormantalorus. I abhor the name you gave that child. Levyathan." She nearly spat the name. "The cretin had only been dead for a year. Unseemly!"

"At least I spared my heir from being named Bassom."

Her narrowed gaze would have speared him if possible. "Do not celebrate too soon. You have enemies ten deep to every side. You only barely escaped the fate of your grandfather, incarcerated so Essera might seize control of your Entity. Your father sought to arm Sordan with a powerful alliance—an alliance I brokered. We could have joined with Mormantalorus, recreated the Triempery, but you spurned that chance from the very first day! It is still there to be had, but for you."

Ermenthalia rose to her feet, voice louder and finger shaking to berate him. "At every turn, you cast aspersion on Nammuor. You accuse him of murder. You! You beheaded your wife, who was his sister!" Tears spilled down her wrinkled cheeks, choked every word gathered in her throat as her emotions at last opened the gates to her motives. "No one saw Nammuor at Permephedon that day. Not one soul saw him! But they *all saw you*. Nammuor was in Mormantalorus, hundreds will attest to that. And you wonder why people pronounce him innocent and instead heed those who say *you* killed your father? You wear the Rill Stone on your hand. You were seen wearing it that very hour! How did you get it if not off the hand of my son? You—"

The truth of why she had done it, all of it, cut like glass shards. This was what hate felt like, a person's rage launched straight into his senses. A thousand cuts. A thousand deaths. A thousand falsehoods held as truth. Ermenthalia was just like the rest. No different from Stefan or any of the multitude of others who condemned Dorilian without knowing the truth. Dorilian stood from his crouch.

"But you never asked what happened, Grandmother. You never asked *me*."

Ermenthalia blinked fever-bright eyes. "I was afraid."

Of the truth. Because he was Highborn, truth was what she would have gotten. Better to think him a monster, without proof, than know it for certain in his own words. Better to cling to her grief and hate, so she could think herself justified, than have to face what he might say.

He noticed how Ermenthalia stiffened when he walked behind her. He wanted her to focus on his voice, his words. "Sit down. I am going to give you a gift."

"So that is what you will call it." But she sank down again.

"Death?" He had considered it. "No, not that, Grandmother. I intend to punish you far worse. I am going to tell you what happened at Permephedon."

Her head turned so her gaze could follow him. Hunger warred with trepidation in her tense features. What she saw in his face made her look away again.

"Father and I went to the Leur Arcana to sign a treaty with Essera. We were to bind the Triempery's wounds. Recreate it. Marc Frederick signed the treaty. Khelds signed it. Deben signed it. Soon every prince would sign. But then Nammuor appeared in the room, inside the locked door. He and some of his mages." Her gasp was all the response Dorilian needed to hear. She had not believed it before. The world believed translocation was a Highborn gift, impossible for humans.

"So many details you don't need to hear. The hows. The whys. But I am going to tell you *what* Nammuor did." Dorilian dropped his voice to lower tones. "Daimonaeris poisoned the wine. The entire room drank it—except me, by purest chance, thanks to my father. Deben was paralyzed but conscious when Nammuor carved a knife through his throat. Deep. So deep I felt it. The monster made me watch." Ermenthalia's shoulders shook and she released a sob. So she did feel something, if only for herself. For better or worse, emotion opened doors. Dorilian touched the back of his grandmother's neck, cupping the base of her skull in his fingers.

"Do you want to *see*, Grandmother? I looked into my father's still living eyes while Nammuor collected his blood. Some foul crystal of that creature's invention drank it, filled itself. Immortal blood. Nammuor needed his Highborn sacrifices to live just long enough for him to trap the lifeforce of Leur before they died. All of us. He wanted *all* of us. He filled that room with blood."

Dorilian showed her. Her son. Her father. Princes decapitated and fingers cleaved upon a table. The blood and violence and sorcery, until she wailed for him to stop.

He broke the touch and three steps brought him to the front of the throne again.

"And you were willing to give me to him."

She sobbed into her hands and would not meet his gaze.

"He wants Lev too. Daimonaeris tried to flee to him with Sordan's heir in her belly. I prevented that."

Ermenthalia drew a deep breath and sniffed a few times. "What you did, what you showed… true, all true… it must be."

"Yes."

"So this is how you reveal you are gifted—and also that you are cruel."

"Cruel enough to do what I must do next. After how you betrayed me, and given what you know, I cannot let you be free. I will, however, honor that you gave birth to my father. You will be held under house arrest in the Citadel. You will have one servant who will also never leave. You will get news of the outside world, but never again will you communicate with it. As your nearest kin, I will take control of your assets. When you die, those assets will go to Levyathan, as you intended. Suddekar will, of course, get a new ruler. You are relieved of all concerns. From time to time I will visit to let you know how your beloved grandsons are doing."

Tear-bright pride sought his gaze. "I actually do want to see how this all ends."

"I expect you will enjoy a long life and a natural death."

"I suppose you expect me to thank you for that."

"No. But maybe for this: When people say I killed my father, they speak truly. I set his lifeforce free when I shattered the crystal that imprisoned it."

Her eyes closed and her aged lips slightly parted with new understanding.

"I shattered seven in all. I know which lives I sent from this world, my father's among them. Forty-seven of my kindred died that day, and I felt every one of those deaths. I still feel them. Dying. How they died. *Every day*. But worst of all is that Nammuor holds some in enslaved undeath, and I feel them too. And I know why he hunts those of us who remain. He is feeding the Undying Crown. And he is doing so in a world filled with people like you who would like nothing more than to help him destroy us."

Ermenthalia huddled, weeping, as Dorilian turned to leave.

"Goodbye, Grandmother. Finally, we know each other."

It was deep night when Dorilian sought the refuge of his own chambers. Rill glow spilled through the loggia's open portals to paint his floors with silver. He went at once to his private library and work space, which he had begun to use as he had seen Marc Frederick use a room at Gustan: a place of letters and study, where Dorilian might collect knowledge useful to his many interests and endeavors. A rare writing of Cibulitus, never published, lay unrolled on the table atop a drawing of third century Stauberg. An Epoptean text about Wall mechanics sat alongside an array of implements used for voice training. At this pace he would soon need another room.

For the past two hours Dorilian had done the work of saving his Hierarchate and his life. He had recalled Deleus from Permephedon and would have a great deal to talk about with his cousin in the morning. He had ordered his military to secure the domain of Suddekar until it could be purged of Ermenthalia's pro-Mormantaloran officials, officers, and troops. He had drawn up a requisition for a new warship, faster than its predecessor, to be named *Vata*, plans to follow. He had sent the order waiving foreign port fees for Jooar Zetharnna's ships and initiated paperwork and asset transferences that would grant lifetime Rill passes.

He had spoken with Sordan's ambassador to the Archhalia about matters to be raised at the forthcoming Archhalia session. He had considered sending condolences to Emyli Stauberg-Randolph on the loss of her grandchild, about which he had just learned, and then decided against it.

Only one piece of business remained.

On the writing table in front of him was a small square of paper and a pot of ink that nearly every creature in the world would see as clear. The pen tip in his fingers was poised to write. He thought the wording might be important, then realized it was not.

Dorilian scrawled on the fine vellum.

I am through with waiting. If you want your Wall Stone—
Teach me!

22

"*Teach me*." Elhanan looked up from the paper in his fingers. "He offers the Wall Stone in return."

"He is forcing my hand. It's just that—" Rheger shook his head. He leaned against the stone fence near which they had dismounted and on which Elhanan now sat. After witnessing the predictable behavior of Essera's nobles, Stefan had tired of displaying them, and released both Highborn princes to return to their own estates and their previous habits of seclusion. Elhanan was to depart in a week for Stauberg.

And then, two days ago... this. Details had filtered to Kyrbasillon since: Attack by *Ir* weapons. A Rift storm. The Gracious Hierarchessa's treason.

That Dorilian was under assault on all sides was clear.

"He's powerful." Their horses grazed nearby, bridles clacking. Here in the park at Dannuth, with only late summer grasses to witness or overhear their conversation, Rheger felt free at last to speak. "What can I teach him that will not introduce more danger? Not just to the world, but to him? I am not trained in how to teach a Sordaneon, someone whose gifts are keyed to *that* Entity. Enreddon was supposed to be the one to take on that challenge."

"Tell Dorilian your situation. Put the risk in front of him and teach him only what you do know." Elhanan lifted a loose rock from the wall and placed Dorilian's message on the stone beneath it. He then ground the first rock atop it, crushing and rending until the paper was shredded to bits, the writing destroyed.

Rheger could only sigh. "What I know? That would be next to nothing. I can translocate, if I use a powerful enough device. Dorilian... has the Rill. There *is* no more powerful device."

"But can he use it?"

How much to say? Rheger nodded. "Yes. He can. I am very certain the Rill is how he translocated on the day of the Demise. Quirin believes he used the Rill Stone and maybe the Wall Stone, but—"

"You don't think he used those?"

"No." Rheger gazed around the meadow, with its blanket of cornflower blues punctuated by vivid yellow daisies. "A talent like his... he's impulsive, intuitive, quick to anger. He is as likely to harm himself as gain an advantage."

"I think you are forgetting something. Someone. *Two* someones."

The reminder pulled Rheger's head up and gave him something more to consider. Sebbord and Marc Frederick. Yes, those affiliations... mattered. Marc Frederick had taught Dorilian a thing or two about consequences. Sebbord, however, had been among the most skilled of their kindred. He had to have taught his young grandson the fundamentals of their native abilities, especially if...

"Dorilian is covalent with the Rill."

Elhanan ceased grinding the rock and snapped a look of surprise. "Are you telling me he and the Rill *share* a tangible connection?"

"I detected it years ago, when I did a favor for Marc Frederick. The connection I detected was beyond merely tangible. It might even be the first stages of integration."

"Leur."

Rheger smiled at the ironic expletive. "The point being I cannot address such a bond or the kind of power it can, potentially, tap into. But maybe Sebbord"—he sighed—"maybe Sebbord anticipated his grandson's ability and instilled some tools, the kinds of mental and neural constructs Dorilian would need to develop and contain his powers. I cannot believe Sebbord would leave a Sordaneon heir unequipped to wield his own abilities."

"If Dorilian opened the Rill at Hestya—"

"There it is. Sebbord had to have trained him for that." Rheger clapped his hands together. "Enough to work with, I suppose. We certainly have no choice. Dorilian said it clearly enough: he is through with waiting. Wall Stone or no Wall Stone, if we do nothing to teach him, he is going to attempt to teach himself."

"I'd be happier if Dorilian was dead."

With Cullen helping, Stefan slipped into a royal blue surcoat embroidered in gold thread with the Stauberg-Randolph emblem. He then belted it with gilded leather. The buckle in the shape of a sunburst was one of his finest. His mood didn't match it, however. He hadn't been able to enjoy Dorilian's possible demise for nearly long enough. Not even three days had passed.

"What if he thinks you did it?"

"I hope he does think I did it. I want him looking over his shoulder every day, wondering when I'm going to kill him." With so little news to go on, no one knew for sure what had happened in Sordan—but so far it didn't sound like something that could be blamed on Stefan. "I'll do it, too, someday. I'm not through with him."

"And I say you have bigger problems closer to home. Like this woman you're meeting in a few minutes. She's got more power in this city than you do."

"She's certainly convinced everyone of that."

"Most folk don't need convincing." Cullen had dressed for the meeting with as much care as Stefan had ever seen him use. A vest of maroon velvet cut with gilded leather, with a cream silk shirt underneath it and breeches of tan leather tucked into a pair of new, beautifully made boots. It had taken three years, but Cullen Brodheson was finally dressing like a man with wealth and a title.

"Look, I know Chyralane is head of House Phaer, and she runs the Seven Houses like her own domain. So I treat the Seven Houses like a domain, which is what Marc Frederick did, right?" Stefan preferred to take a pragmatic view of his strategy so far.

"I studied the history of that, and they gave him lots of problems."

Which they were also doing with Stefan. "I can handle the Denizen of Phaer. Her agenda is always the same: she wants me to assign my Crown Rill slots to be administered by her cartel. Erenor thinks I should. He says if I do my revenues will increase."

"Sure they will, because the first thing the Seven Houses would do would be to jettison the Kheld merchants using those slots. Without your slots, Amallar would have no Rill trade at all. No one else is leasing to us. As it is, we have a fair trade in wool and lumber, and thanks to the mines in Orqho, we're building a market in metals."

They walked the vaulted corridor toward the throne room. Stefan wouldn't think of meeting Chyralane anywhere else. She required every possible show of power.

The Denizen of Phaer and her two companions made subtle bows when the king entered. They held these postures until Stefan had taken the throne and Cullen positioned himself to his right hand. Draped with silk so lustrous it shimmered like Rill glow itself, Chyralane could easily have been mistaken for royalty. By lineage, she was. Her headdress of velvet angles sewn with rubies and pearls suited a woman whose grandfather had been Highborn and whose dowry had given the House of Phaer a windfall of Rill slots. Marc Frederick's entries about her had been extensive, though his journals had ended shortly after a final few pages detailing how she had orchestrated placing the blame for the assassination of Sebbord Teremareon on Stefan.

As if Dorilian hadn't hated him enough already, this woman had provided both the kindling and the spark that had sent the crazed Sordaneon youth on a murderous rampage. At least now, for *that* who, Stefan knew the why.

"Your Majesty." Upon straightening, Chyralane was taller than either man with her.

"Denizen. It is a rare pleasure to speak with you one-on-one."

The lines around her eyelids creased, a sort of smile. "We could do so more truly if we send these seconds from the room."

"I will never meet you without a witness to any words we exchange."

"A pity, this level of distrust. I admired your grandfather and regret that we became adversaries. It was not always so."

"And need not be so with us. Perhaps this visit will be the first on which we can reach some point of agreement." Half of being king, Stefan had discovered, consisted of sounding reasonable. In fact, he didn't give a fig if he ever agreed with the Seven Houses. All he truly wanted of them was that they not work against him.

Chyralane bowed her head and folded her hands at her waist. Her rings bore gems the size of quail eggs. "This concerns a matter we plan to introduce to the Archhalia at its opening session, at which, according to tradition, Your Majesty will be present. If so, you will hold a significant vote. And a veto."

Stefan fought a smile. Did she want his veto—or fear it? "We intend to open the Archhalia as is our right and duty."

"Then, as you will personally hear this petition, I will reveal it in advance. We charge that the Hierarch of Sordan has illegally appropriated the Rill slots of his grandmother, the Gracious Hierarchessa. Furthermore, he has imprisoned her without trial."

"We heard she was his guest."

"Your grandfather taught him how to use that term." A withering look instructed Stefan to not play word games. He would have said that very thing had he pulled off Dorilian's arrest. "Oh please, our information is so much better than yours. No one has seen Ermenthalia—no one—since Dorilian had her arrested in the very chamber of Sordan's Halia. The Halia made a formal request to see her but he has not allowed it. He claims she is fine. Are we to believe it, or that his seizure of her Rill slots is anything but theft?"

Stefan eased against the padded velvet throne back. If he looked at Cullen, he would probably see his friend's head cocked with disbelief. Essera wielded no influence in Sordan—none at all, since Dorilian had pronounced Stefan dead to him.

"You talk as though I care about what happens to Dorilian or his grandmother. So let me make something clear: I don't care if they steal each other's thrones or lock each other away. I don't care if they kill each other. Nothing would make me happier."

The look that crossed Chyralane's face ceased to be dismissive. Cold calculation tempered the lift of her lip. "I think you misunderstand our interest, Majesty. Perhaps your trade minister will better grasp the nature of our petition. For many years, Ermenthalia's Rill slots have been deployed in ways that have benefitted Essera, and us, by way of trade, through Suddekar, from Mormantalorus. Her mother was from there and she has—or had— excellent ties to those lands. Very extensive, and her marriage to Labran bestowed upon her a collection of prime Rill slots. Two days ago, those slots were reallocated."

Cullen swore under breath. To Stefan's look of inquiry, he said, "Dorilian is at war with Mormantalorus. If there was trade with Mormantalorus, he would put a stop to it. I'm guessing he already has."

"He cancelled the contracts! All of them, using the pretense of being contrary to the interests of the Hierarchate." Chyralane indicated the man to her right hand. "I have brought along our Master of Revenues. The amounts involved are substantial. Mormantalorus buys significant quantities of Esseran and Sordani grain, metals, livestock, silk, and sweet oil, shipped to Suddekar to be forwarded to terminal destinations. On return voyages, Essera, through Suddekar, receives gold, pearls, sugar and rare spices and teas. For our contracts to be honored, those goods now must be diverted to other slots. If these goods cannot be rerouted, we risk losing that trade altogether."

"Mormantalorus is welcome to establish other contracts for transport of the goods." Stefan received Cullen's nod that he had spoken rightly. "Our markets remain open to them."

"Phaw! Unless you divert some of your Crown slots, or other of your subjects do so with theirs, there is not enough excess capacity to accommodate the contracts." The old woman scorned Stefan's grasp of the matter. "We are petitioning that this theft of the slots is a matter of Triemperal concern, and a violation of the Covenant."

Cullen looked thoughtful, though he was out of his element. The Covenant that governed Rill practices was something Cullen knew a lot about—more than any other Kheld, for sure—but true expertise on that matter resided with the Brotherhood of Epoptes and the Seven Houses—and also with the Sordaneons. Stefan saw no need to stick his neck into any of it.

"Then so petition. We oppose anything that makes the Hierarch of Sordan richer."

"This appropriation, in addition to being illegal, most definitely does that. Worse, he has gained additional influence."

"So call him on the illegality," said Cullen. "Challenge the appropriation as being political mischief, not specifically to benefit the Hierarchate. Maybe the Archhalia votes the way you want. Which is what, exactly? He gives them back?"

Chyralane sniffed and delivered a wave of her hand. "We will ask for that, but of course he will refuse to do it even if ordered. No, we need the Archhalial judgment—which we have enough votes to procure—to serve as groundwork to request a writ from the Brotherhood of Epoptes. The writ will demand that the Hierarch return the slots and restore the contracts. He will of course challenge the writ, but we will ask that the Order manage the slots and honor their original contracts until ownership is decided."

Which could take months, if not years. Until then, the Mormantaloran contracts would continue to be in force. Dorilian would be unable to use them himself. Essera, and the Seven Houses, would continue to prosper.

Stefan shared a grin with Cullen. This was just too perfect. "Dorilian will be stymied. And furious."

"Hardly our concern." Chyralane looked smug enough. "We simply wish the contracts to continue, to maintain the flow of goods."

"And what is it you seek from me? That I not use my veto?"

"We did not think you would, but yes, that would be our desire. More to the point, we seek your vote. Your vote, alone, cannot be vetoed by the Hierarchate."

As King of Essera, Stefan was the Hierarch of Sordan's political peer. They would cancel each other out, allowing the votes of the body of the Archhalia to go forward. Stefan had used this maneuver a few times already, most recently to demand restoration of Stauberg-Randolph assets still held in Sordan. Dorilian had rendered the victory toothless when he refused to turn over those assets. This turn with the Epoptes, however, had the kind of teeth Stefan wished to see more of.

"Your petition will have our vote, Denizen. And thank you for bringing this matter before us."

After a deep bow, Chyralane and the men with her walked away at a stately pace. Stefan admired the way the woman glided, her long robe seeming to float precisely to the floor but never touching. He could feel Cullen bridling like a muzzled thing at his side, waiting only on opportunity to speak.

"What?" Stefan asked as soon as the throne room door had closed and they were alone.

"We should've talked about this."

"There's no disadvantage for me. Those slots are his or not his, or… it doesn't even matter whose they are. They will be removed from his control by a legal process over which I have no control at all."

"Except for letting it happen. Maybe you should let him veto it."

Had Stefan heard that correctly? "Are you mad?"

"This isn't about Essera or you—not for him. It's not about getting richer, either. He doesn't need to get richer by impoverishing his granny. It's about Mormantalorus. You know, the people who probably just tried to kill him. It's about that and now you're going to go make it about *us*."

"Yes, I am."

"Why? Just so you can hammer a thorn into a nail?"

"I'll hammer it into a damn spear point if it will draw blood."

"Aw, hells."

"You're way too soft on him."

Cullen yanked at his elegant collar laces, loosening them. "Soft? It's not like I have any way to take him on other than to put words in your ear. He's not someone I concern myself with except for trying to keep *you* out of problems that you just don't need. Problems Essera doesn't need, and neither do Kheld folk, because anything you do that causes a problem, there's a good chance it will get turned back on us."

A fair reminder. Stefan rose from the throne and descended the steps to the floor with its inlaid pattern of stars and symbols of constellations. So much Staubaun architecture and decoration harked up to the heavens, as if they had done anything with heavens or stars in thousands of years.

"This will annoy Dorilian, and yes, I want that, but it won't come back at Khelds. This thing won't." Stefan walked Cullen toward the side entrance that would take them to the palace's private chambers. He didn't speak again until they'd passed the guards and were in seclusion on the other side of heavy bronze doors. A long atrium opened before them, a relaxing space with a pretty pool and greenery and flowers. Statues lurked among plantings of box and roses. "You know what annoys me? That the Seven Houses only come to me if they need me to do some kind of dirty work."

"That's how they get and maintain power: dirty work."

Stefan chose a bench beside the pool. Ruby-bright fishes swam in clear water the color of beryl. "Let's sit here and talk. I leave for the Archhalia in a few hours. I should've sent you ahead, so I could have you with me." Because he could not ride the Rill, Cullen would have had to leave Dazunor-Rannuli a week ago to get there.

"Just as well. Phalla will be happy to have me around."

Which was more than Stefan could say for Nilla. It still irked that she would rather be with her mother than with him. He had been as gentle and caring a husband as he knew how to be. He envied Cullen, whose wife enjoyed having him around and was also getting round with child.

"What would happen with the Seven Houses if Dorilian died?"

Cullen's gaze moved up from admiring fishes. "We almost found out. They were nervous that first day before we knew. Stefan, they don't want that. Nobody does! The Rill is too important to them."

"That old tale." Stefan picked a white bloom off a nearby rose tree and lobbed it into the pool, where it floated like a tiny lily.

"Bets are there's truth to it. More than makes me comfortable, to be honest, because of how much we depend on it. I know you have your reasons, but being at odds with Sordan isn't good for us. Essera needs more markets, not fewer, and that's double for Kheld folk. Amallar doesn't have a seaport and we never will. If we can't sell to the Staubaun markets that dominate in Essera, why not see if we can sell to markets in the south? Sordan is ringed by domains that could buy what we produce... some already do."

"They're Staubaun-pocked too."

"Not as much as Essera. Not even close."

As if it mattered. Those markets were closed to Essera, and

Amallar, as long as Dorilian lived. "I asked about the Seven Houses, though. What would happen with them? To me?"

Cullen squinted at him. "Nothing good. Why are you asking about this?"

His closest friend. His best friend. A friend he could count on to the end. But not a friend to whom he could tell everything. Stefan shrugged. "Like you said, Mormantalorus just tried to kill him. Sounds like maybe his grandmother tried it too. I figure one of these days, someone will succeed."

23

"You've reviewed the petitions being presented today?" Stefan noticed how the Jewel Tower reflected off nearby structures in such a way its thousand hues created iridescent patterns akin to insect wings. Spires ablaze in rainbows. Permephedon's mysterious Citadel rose higher still, its forked shape challenging the sky. The view added grandeur to the room, a backdrop of power. He turned his back to it.

Sinon Kouranos, Stefan's Ambassador to the Archhalia, stood nearby, robed in a particularly dignified shade of dark blue. A diplomat's hood of ivory velvet, hemmed in silk with Essera's colors and embroidered with the insignia of his office, graced his chest and shoulders. "I understand Your Majesty will be casting your own votes this session."

"Only for the petition the Seven Houses has filed regarding the Basarchessa of Suddekar's Rill slots."

Sinon flicked a glance to Erenor, the other man at this meeting. "The petition also demands that the Basarchessa be returned to her domain and resume her seat there. Given recent events, that will not happen. Indeed, the Archhalia will vote on investment of her successor, her great-nephew Deleus Pardakkos. On either count, the Seven Houses petition is a dead end, a needless provocation."

Stefan was not in the mood for reasonable arguments. "It's a legal maneuver to tie up the Rill slots and contracts so we can prolong the original contractual assignments. We need the Mormantaloran trade."

"Do we? Dealings with Mormantalorus are... problematic.

Why not use this opportunity to leverage trade concessions from Sordan?"

Did the man really think he had not thought this through? "Leave this one to me." Stefan extended his hand. "Do you have the agenda? There are other petitions that actually need your attention." When he had the document in hand, he shuffled all three pages until he found what he sought. "This one." He created folds at the items. "And this one."

"Ah," said Sinon. He scanned the creases and the items. "More dead ends."

"They are *my* proposals."

"Yes, sire. I realize that. I also realize no domain—other than Amallar—will vote with you on either. Sordan will certainly veto your attempt to install Lowen Toboldson as Bas of Gignastha; Sordan counts Gignastha to be an ancestral domain and your petition runs contrary to the Watergilt Agreement. As for the other matter, the Princess Regent of Stauberg will oppose her sons being made wards of the crown, particularly with the provision that they cede all claim to Essera's throne. Seeing as you do not yet have an Heir—"

"I have a brother!" Stefan damned Marenthro for having burdened his kingship with questions of succession. Neither the wizard nor Stefan's mother had yet revealed just *where* Hans was being kept. They also refused Stefan's every demand to bring his brother back. "Hans is thirteen years old. As soon as he returns, I will declare him my provisional heir and give him a domain and title of his own."

Sinon folded the agenda and placed it inside his diplomat's vestment. "A kingdom can have too many heirs—and also too few. All await your brother's return to this land. Until then, however, you do not have an heir at hand. It gives your subjects, me included, a feeling of security to know Essera has princes in reserve."

"I'm not dying!"

"May your life be a long one. I am merely suggesting it might be more prudent to make peace, not war, with your current heirs."

Erenor snorted. "Does that mean Dorilian, too? He has not given up *his* claim to Stefan's throne."

"A claim he is not currently pressing." Sinon's gaze drifted to the window, through which another structure loomed in sight: sinuous and beautiful, sheathed with smooth blue-green highlights and deep emerald valleys. The Sordaneon Tower cast its shadow across the verdant park below like the gnomon of a sundial. "Your

Majesty's grandfather used to have a saying for situations like this one. He would tell me to let sleeping dogs lie."

Stefan scowled. "If by dogs, you mean Highborn, then I don't see how letting them lie removes the threat. Dorilian should have renounced his claim when I became Heir—and the Malyrdeon princes should do it now. Go do your job, Ambassador, and leave this kingdom's policies and alliances to its king."

Sinon bowed and backed away until he could turn to leave with swift, hurried steps.

"He has done good work." Erenor squinted at the window, which displayed the hour within a shimmering circle. It was nearly time to leave for the Archhalia Chamber. "Sinon is a skillful diplomat. We averted a conflict between Leseos and Lower Neuberland last year because of his efforts, and his cautious approach to reforms has done much to ensure acceptance of your policies among the Purist domains. But have you noticed he is starting to balk? He was born in Sordan, even if he has lived here almost all his life."

Though Stefan had never trusted Sinon to the same degree his grandfather had, he didn't distrust him either.

"He's the best man I have for working around Sordan's wall of silence. Sinon has served loyally for three Esseran kings. He trained under old Endurin, you know, back when Mormantalorus was still part of the Triempery. That's one reason everyone will give him a hearing. He has a reputation for fairness, too. He governed Neuberland for a while, under my grandfather, and he did it from Gignastha, so he's got standing there. Khelds have nothing bad to say about him."

"He adheres to the Highborn, though. As you say, he trained under Endurin, and then he spent his entire career until now serving your grandfather. Marc Frederick was loyal to the Highborn, too."

Because the Malyrdeons had openly supported him instead of staying hidden away on secluded estates. Was Erenor issuing a reminder, or a warning?

"I'm dealing with the Highborn."

"Yes, sire. As they deserve. They wield too much power for being uninvolved in the difficulties of government."

A point of view Stefan shared. "Yet my petition will probably be voted down. I don't see why Sinon or anyone else would object to my making those boys wards of the crown."

"Misunderstanding of your intentions, sire. Or deliberate ill will. Those who oppose your petition might yet hope to place Eldon Malyrdeon on your throne."

Palaistea's eldest. A seven-year-old. A fucking *Highborn* seven-year-old.

Stefan was surrounded by a past that refused to die. All he wanted was to have his kingship unchallenged so that he might rule a kingdom that was united and whole. A kingdom at peace. The canker that was the Royal North swelled like an abscess on Essera's flank.

"Find out more about that, and if there's an actual plot going on." Stefan picked up his regalia, laid out on the table that stood in the center of the room. Essera's Staff of Office. The Belt of Ergeiron that looked more like a shield. Just before entering the Archhalia Chamber, he would don a crown. Then he would enter the Archhalia Chamber and face the Thrones of Light. Those three empty chairs would remind him—and everyone—that he was not, and would never be, a Highborn King. Unlike for Marc Frederick, who had worn the Leur's Ring, every damned time Stefan sat on Essera's Throne, it remained dark.

"Let's go and get this over with so I can get back to Dazunor-Rannuli. I don't like this place."

Dorilian sat at the table in his audience chamber and watched the two applicants depart. A man and a woman, one dressed in somber scholar's clothes, whereas the other appeared to be wearing a closet's worth of colorful scarves. Neither person was acquainted with the other as far as Dorilian knew or could tell, but they had no sooner left his presence than he heard them chattering brightly to each other. Had he been either of them, that would not have happened. People did not ever chatter—had never chattered, brightly or otherwise—in his presence. He saw Legon enter the room and resolved to ask the question. But first an explanation for the odd visitors.

"Tutors for the children. Lev is curious about sea creatures and Fahme wants to sing." Dorilian paused, then asked. "Am I unlikable?"

Legon made a full stop and blinked. "Sometimes. You are, without a doubt, intimidating."

That was good to know. Dorilian had worked all his life to be so. "I sense it is more than that."

"People find you uncomfortable to be around. You are someone who can ruin lives and has ruined them, often on purpose."

One of Dorilian's more unpleasant truths. "I have rescued lives also."

"Yes, though not as many—and you generally go about it in secret."

Which merited another observation. "You're not afraid of me."

"I would be, save I have known you since my seventh year, when my father dragged me by the ear to Askorras, threw me at your feet, and said you could use me for sword practice. I figure if you did not see fit to kill me when you were eight, you will not kill me now." Legon walked forward to set a cylinder on end in the center of the desk.

"What is this?" Dorilian picked up the object. Legon would not have put something before him without having checked it thoroughly for arcane or ordinary threats.

"What it looks like: a message cylinder. Brought by street messenger from—you are going to like this—the King's House." The object deserved the skeptical look Legon bestowed upon it. The King's House was uninhabited. No one had resided there in three years, since Dorilian had ordered even the skeleton household and maintenance staff to leave.

"Someone gave it to him?"

Legon nodded. "So he said. The outer cylinder was unremarkable. This is the one that was inside."

Indeed. Not mere common brass in the way of an ordinary courier tube, this cylinder was beautifully configured, its heraldic Malyrdeon pattern smooth from generations of handling, and its hexagonal base adorned with genuine gemstones, as was the lock mechanism. Dorilian settled back into his chair to sort out how he might open it. A message sent to him would be coded in a way he could unravel.

There was only one Malyrdeon capable of making his way to Sordan without using the Rill.

Rheger.

Dorilian detected the film of bestowed energy that empowered the lock and wondered at it. Was he being tested? Simple enough. He matched resonance and shifted the ring of energy once, twice... then twice again. Dannutheon was the *fourth* House of the Malyrdeons... Success. The lock nicked and the endpiece slid to one side, releasing the message into his hand. Dorilian read the writing it held and then picked up a stylus to scratch a quick response. After he placed the message into the chamber, he closed the cylinder and spun the lock, then keyed a gemstone sequence of the same number.

With a grin to Legon, who watched him intently, Dorilian held out his hand with the cylinder on his palm and focused. Years had passed since he had felt Rheger's touch, but he would always be able to locate that man's vibration in the firmament.

The cylinder vanished. If the message he had read was true, it was not going far.

Dorilian stood and wasted no time. "Come with me," he said to Legon. "You and Tutto. I have gained the attention of my relations."

Rheger met them in the shadowy rotunda on the lowermost level of the King's House, where the Va Haira provided discreet entrance by way of a hidden passage. A shining circlet of gold ringed with lambent blue stones crowned his blond head. When Dorilian and his companions stepped onto the mosaic floor, Rheger waved his hand to light the twelve small waterglobes ringing the ceiling. Tutto and Legon each dropped to one knee, heads bowed. Dorilian noticed Tutto managed to stifle a groan from his bad knees.

"*Fra'don*. Your Grace." Rheger granted the higher status. That was new.

"*Fra'don*," Dorilian acknowledged. *Sacred brother*. The kin word smacked of unexpected intimacy. He had all but walled off the word along with his memories of the men with whom he had once used it.

Rheger gestured for the kneeling men to rise. His gaze never wavered from Dorilian, even as he walked toward him. "I am committing an act of treason by being here. Stefan has expressly forbidden any of our kind, including Palaistea on behalf of her sons, from contacting you, in any manner."

"Is that why you never responded to my messages?"

"Because of Stefan? No. Because of *you*. You are a difficult man to send to." Rheger caught Tutto's look of surprise. "You think not, sword master? Have you ever tried? Or even thought about it?"

Tutto's rough face registered immediate affront. "Thrice Royal, I think too highly of your race to believe you are ignorant, and I resist that you disdain such as myself. Both of us know common flesh such as mine cannot send."

"Forgive me. You speak rightly. My question was unnecessary.

But your answer tells me you do not know everything about your prince. Perhaps it is time you do." Rheger fixed his gaze on Dorilian. "You feel like your Entity."

Truth, not simile, resided in that statement. Rill energy lurked within Dorilian's skin, and had been there the first time Rheger had touched him, in the lodge outside Gignastha, on the night Rheger had captured him for Marc Frederick. Since then, Dorilian's bond with the Rill had only become stronger. And here, in Sordan, the Rill surrounded him.

"I—" At the very least, he owed Rheger an apology. "I did not realize. I withdraw all ill thoughts I had for your lack of response."

"Imagine my end of this, if you will. I simply could not risk sending through *that*. Wall Lords have a similar dilemma, although it is not so much a matter of *where* a message ends up, because it will end up with the Wall Lord, but *when* it will appear."

"I am not a Rill Lord."

Rheger's look questioned that conclusion. "Aren't you? Because if you are not, you are very close to one." He drew, then expelled, a long sigh. "That is not what I am here to debate with you. I cannot inform that part of your being. All I can do is, perhaps, help you to preserve it."

Tension fled Dorilian's shoulders and he noticed how Tutto's eyes closed though he lifted his face to the ceiling. Perhaps guessing what was taking place, Legon looked from Dorilian to Rheger with renewed intensity.

"If you will teach me our ancestral ways," Dorilian said, "I will return your Wall Stone."

Elegant, framed by the rotunda's pale and ghostly statuary and displaying a cynic's smile, Rheger looked far from convinced. "Dare I hope you have it with you?"

Dorilian matched that smile and shook his head. "Teach me first."

"Someday you will realize that *not* doing something is also taking a risk." Another sigh, this one deeper. "You are about to discover I am not much of a teacher. But I will teach you what I know. All of it. For the rest, you must resort to other sources. Or books."

"*Books?*" Dorilian needed to learn physical things: command of his body, bones and blood and nerves capable of channeling arcane forces. Infants did not use books to learn how to walk.

After a moment, Rheger looked to Tutto for assistance. "Your late prince, Sebbord, was an Archmage, from a long line of Archmagi. He surely had a library."

"I am not seeking to become an Archmage!" Dorilian seethed.

Tutto ignored him to address Rheger. "Yes, Thrice Royal, a vast one," he confirmed. "After his death, it was moved here to Sordan. It is intact"—he glanced at Dorilian before adding—"last I heard."

Rheger met Dorilian's hard stare. "You need to learn control of your Entity. I have nothing to teach you that will help with that, except to point you to Marenthro—or those books."

"All Marenthro ever does is watch people die."

"Then do not give him another death to watch. Learn to your strengths, which I suspect are greater than you want me to know. I am going to start your training with spatial mechanics. You already know how to send, so I am surmising Sebbord taught you those basics. We can build on his lessons."

"Now?"

Rheger walked toward a statue of a woman twined with a two-headed serpent. He picked up a golden cylinder slightly bigger than the one he had used earlier for sending. "Sending is a form of translocation. You realize that, of course."

"Yes." Dorilian could see already where Rheger was going with this. "Do I learn to go to people first?"

"Do not leap ahead of your lessons. No. *Sending* transfers matter to another person, a lifeforce you can detect in the firmament. It is easy compared to what I am going to try to teach you, which is how to send to a physical *place*." Rheger held out his hand, cylinder in his grasp. It was there, and then it was not. "Let's walk to the gallery, shall we?"

They exited the rotunda into a long corridor, ill-lit and filmed with dust, illuminated by the *orbi* both Rheger and Dorilian created. The corridor ended with tall blue doors which opened onto a long loggia that faced a glass-roofed inner courtyard. The courtyard's long pool with its three musical fountains had gone dry and silent several years ago, but the roof, though darkened by dirt, still allowed fitful light. Something golden flashed on the floor at the base of a statue of Ergeiron. While Dorilian hung back, Rheger walked up to the cylinder and took it in hand.

"I sent it... here. To a place. I could have sent any object of reasonable size—or myself. The key to translocation is creating contiguity. For sending to lifeforces, your mind performs the calculations without difficulty because it organically matches resonances with the target. The process is innate and intuitive. You anchor the translocation at your end. The other person is a target. Others of our kind are easy for us to find. Usually." Rheger smiled at Dorilian's look of censure. "Targeting places is more difficult.

Locating a place in the firmament is more complicated than finding a person who will feel the translocation and complete the action."

Dorilian had grasped enough cylinders to understand that part. "How do I do it, then?"

Rheger walked to Dorilian and handed him the cylinder. "You start with what you know. To increase your skill, increase what you know."

Dorilian looked at the statue. Firm-jawed, long-haired, hands clasping symbols of History and Mathematics and arms crossed to symbolize the joining of Past and Future, this Ergeiron was a copy of an original he had seen in Stauberg; other copies existed, including one in the Sordaneon Serat. In a garden, beside a wall covered with amethyst-leaved vines. He would have to study that one. This one, however...

"Send to where I can see."

Rheger smiled. "We will start with this because it is a size and shape your mind is familiar with sending. You first sent a pebble, did you not?"

Dorilian nodded. He had been ten the day Sebbord had pressed smooth white stones into his hand. He had been able to send cylinders by the first time he went to Permephedon. Sebbord's lessons remained bright, polished by use. Sordaneons instinctively mapped the interstitial spaces of the world. Dorilian could, while sending, often recognize where people *were*. Not down to the nearest piece of furniture or anything so fine, but... where. And he routinely sent to people he could not link in the Mind but who were in proximity—like little girls hidden behind curtains.

"Catch." Dorilian smiled.

"What?" Rheger did not appear to understand.

"Catch. The child's game. Sebbord taught me."

"This—"

"Fahme doesn't always catch the ball, of course. And Lev can't yet send back." Seeing Rheger's open-mouthed surprise was victory enough for the moment. Dorilian made a point of displaying the cylinder in his hand, then played the game. The plinth had a corner wide enough for even a much larger cylinder to rest upon. The cylinder vanished from his hand...

... and reappeared at the plinth, where it landed at the edge, teetered, and toppled from there to the dust-heavy floor, upon which it rolled several feet.

"Close enough," judged Legon. He, like Tutto and Dorilian, looked to Rheger for a verdict.

The man drew a deep breath. "We will work on accuracy."

"That's the lesson? Sending an object across a room? Something I can already do?"

"Maybe next time I will teach you what's needed to send yourself across a room. I think we should start small."

"I can clearly send—"

"Yes," snapped Rheger. "Better than expected. My first attempt landed half the distance—behind me. But can you be accurate every time? Can you be consistent? With much larger objects? I am not just teaching you; I am *training* you—body and mind. Accept the lessons if you wish me to continue. I will return here in three days at the midday hour to see if you have progressed. So read the thrice-cursed books and be careful; this talent can kill people, including yourself." With a touch of his right fingers to the rim of his crown, he was gone.

Silence reigned for a long moment.

Legon pointed at the space where Rheger had stood. "You are learning *that*?"

Dorilian nodded. "That and more. I intend to arm myself with every gift my forefathers ever poured into mortal flesh."

Tutto grunted. Together they walked back to the rotunda. "If that is to be the case, I will show you where your father stored your grandsire's library. He had a trove of tomes back to antiquity—and if you are to develop even half the gifts he possessed, you will need them all."

24

Nilla arrived in Dazunor-Rannuli aboard a grand wagon drawn by ivory horses, beasts and conveyance alike adorned with tassels and banners that proclaimed her royalty. Stefan greeted her at the Arch of Dominion that formed the official city gate where the King's Bridge across the Dazun entered the city. An imposing monument of deep purple porphyry, the Arch proclaimed in gold letters that prosperity was the root of mighty empires.

Stefan guided his horse alongside the wagon where Nilla rested, and kept pace as they proceeded toward the New Wharf.

"I have plans for tonight," he announced. He counted on his grin being enough to convey that his plans would be fun. "I've missed my queen."

Nilla granted him a tentative smile. Though draped with bright finery, she conveyed little joy. Whether uncertainty at being with him again, or just unhappiness at having left behind Amallar and the comforts of being with her mother, he could not tell. A glance to Goff, who had led the escort from Amallar, revealed only that the man Stefan had sent to bring his wife back looked determined and dutiful, not happy.

He returned his attention to Nilla. "You heard, I hope, that I'm going to title your father Bas of Gignastha. There's some opposition in the Archhalia, but I'm leveraging votes. It would be best for you to have a noble father."

"Him not having a title hasn't mattered before now."

Her naiveté was as strong as ever. "It matters to me," Stefan said.

"It will matter to our son, too. He will be glad to have influential relations."

Leaving her side, he rode with his attendant lords across the Unwelcome Bridge. Unless raised, the bridge blocked masted ships from entering the Lower Canal or reaching the Rill Mount. Once everyone had crossed the bridge, Stefan rejoined his wife.

"I'm moving my court to Trulo." As he had hoped, that bit of news brightened Nilla's face. She had told him more than a few times that she preferred the Golden Palace to Dazunor-Rannuli. "I've had the east wing redecorated for you. It's all yours, so you and your ladies can have all the privacy you could possibly want."

"Please tell me I can choose my own ladies?"

Excitement at that possibility teased a smile. Stefan would have given his eyeteeth to tell her yes, but he had heard already from Goff about how Nilla yearned to share company with the wretched girls from her maiden years. Though Goff had spoken in favor of the other girl, the pretty one, she was unwed and might cause talk—and the last thing Stefan wanted to have at his court was a curse-spouting rune hag.

"We'll talk about it," he promised. They would have time for such conversations during the journey downriver.

Nilla firmed her jaw and turned her face away. "If you won't let me have Aubrey or Lark, I want Phalla to come back. I know she's pregnant and it might only be for a few weeks, but she's the best at teaching Stauba and she's the most patient with helping me get the words right."

"Seeing her give birth to a child won't bother you?"

Her blue eyes flashed to his again. "No! Does it bother you, seeing Cullen become a father? Or Phalla a mother, and not me?"

Yes. Seeing Cullen's Staubaun wife so far along with child ate at Stefan's soul. That Cullen's child lived and Stefan's had been murdered was something he struggled with every day. But he could hardly say this to his more forgiving wife.

"No, of course not. I'm thinking of you. If you want Phalla as one of your ladies—"

Nilla's jaw remained set. "I do."

"Then you shall have her. But not that crazy friend of yours." Stefan sighed. He had wanted Cullen to leave his wife behind because Stefan liked having his friend's full attention.

Women placed a great many demands on a man's patience.

At the King's Wharf, the royal barge waited, fully supplied and crewed. With luxurious common areas and private quarters for household and guests, the giant vessel easily accommodated a king's needs. Stefan sent Goff with Nilla to get her settled in her stateroom. He also sent a man to the Rillhome Palace to let Asphalladra know she would be coming as well. They would leave Dazunor-Rannuli within the hour.

Erenor Tholeros met Stefan on the foredeck nearly an hour later. A full company of the King's Guard had boarded along with Erenor. He, at least, looked happy to see Stefan.

"It will be a good change, going to Trulo," was Erenor's opinion. "Farther from enemies and closer to friends."

That much was true, mostly. At Trulo, Stefan would be closer to the Kheld's Thegn strongholds in Amallar and also his mother, who had taken to living at Gustan, a day's sail downriver. But Trulo also put him closer to Kyrbasillon and the Dannutheon princes. Not to mention his unreliable ally, Apollonia, who ruled in neighboring Tahlwent.

Stefan leaned on the rail. The stink of fetid water rose from the canal on which the barge floated. "Don't make any plans for your time in Trulo."

Erenor lifted his head, for all the world like an eager sighthound. "Will I at long last get to recruit those reinforcements I requested?"

"No." In fact, he would be relieving Erenor of his post. "I have a diplomatic mission for the Archon of Avernn."

After a moment of surprise, Erenor bowed his head. Avernn was a holding with royal proyenance and being its Enlad already gave him a seat on the Principate of Tahlwent's Advisory Council. As an Archon, Erenor would sit on Essera's Halia. "Thank you, Sire. You are of all men the most generous. What do you wish of me?"

"We'll talk more when we reach Trulo." That conversation would take place without Cullen around to question Stefan's plans.

"You're making quite a few men new lords."

Stefan grinned. He rewarded those men loyal to him. "You already were a lord when I met you."

"True. Third son of an impoverished Enlad. I chose well to make my career in the king's service."

"More like you chose your friends well."

"I have known men who chose badly, to their detriment. Most put their hopes on hoary old warhorses that served well for their fathers. Better to bet on a fresh horse than one long ridden."

A fresh horse. Stefan felt like such—never shod, never saddled, racing across open ground because he refused the road others would have him run. He needed men like Erenor who were willing to abandon old ways and not seek to harness him or themselves with the past. New horses for new times. The day had arrived to create such men and surround his kingship with them.

Activity on the wharf drew his eye. People moved forward to welcome an arriving gond. One man threw ropes to the low-slung vessel's pilot, who moved quickly to tie them. Before long, Stefan saw Cullen's dark head bob as his friend stepped from the gond onto the stone wharf. Once there, Cullen's fur-trimmed cloak swept the stones as he turned to reach behind him. Asphalladra appeared, a vision in rose, clasped in her husband's arms and smiling at him, as round and happy as a woman could be.

No man alive could compete with a woman's smile. A distant thrum reached Stefan's ears and he frowned. Nor with *that*—

A silver *charys* materialized overhead within its containment rings and glided to the Rill-crowned Mount that dominated the city. All canals led to that mount. All purposes. All plans. Even Stefan's. It would be a blessed pleasure to leave this Rill-worshipping city behind. He would set up his court at Trulo with its human pace and human pleasures and stay there through the winter. Trulo was prominent and storied and had an array for easy communication with the other parts of his kingdom. It was also closer to loyal chieftains in Amallar and two of Nilla's sisters, which would please her to no end.

Finally, after four years, Stefan could put his own stamp on this damned kingdom.

"Mormantalorus, you say. From what I've heard, they're a snotty lot. Worse than the Sordani!" Goff's bulky frame looked even more so in the soft light that illuminated the Golden Palace's ornate frescos. He saluted Stefan with his fourth crock of ale.

Stefan snorted. "Sure of that?"

Cullen knocked cups with Goff's. "Way worse."

"No one's worse than Sordan." Stefan took a good swallow from his mug. "The bastard Sordani won't even let Khelds set foot in their city. Not that there's any way to get there except by ship or Rill."

"And yet more Khelds have been to Sordan than have been to Mormantalorus." Robdan Aelfricson, Stefan's granduncle and Goff's chief secretary, had joined the court in Trulo. A slight man with many gray hairs, Robdan had a way of simply being in a room without anyone ever fully realizing he was there until he spoke up.

Stefan wished the man would stop scribbling or speaking and just drink like everyone else. Robdan probably would, except Goff liked having notes to consult the next day when he'd sobered.

"Mormantalorus is farther away." Stefan favored distance as a reason. Distance was difficult to argue. "I'm pretty sure *no* Kheld has ever been there."

Goff coughed out a laugh. He nudged Cullen and lifted an eyebrow of warning to Stefan before taking another deep drink.

Robdan cleared his throat. "Not so! It so happens Aebner Gethedson traveled there some sixty years ago. It was quite an adventure. He sailed from Trongor to Lahgael, and from the Lahgaelan king's court he trekked the Moonsick Desert's many-colored sands and crossed the Irup Mountains into Orm. He even saw Mormantalorus, the City of Fire, surrounded by glowing rock bled from a mountain, but only from a distance and he did not set foot in the City itself. It's treacherous to approach. He did, however, set foot in Sordan on his way back. He was gone from home three years. He wrote about his adventure in a book, a very rare volume written in Khelda, *To the Mountain of Fire*."

Stefan stared hard at Robdan. Why had Goff not warned him that any observation at all would cause this fool of an uncle to think him interested?

Silence had no effect, because Robdan kept talking.

"Your grandfather had a copy, Sire, in which the author handwrote notes. Perhaps you can find it. Or I could lend you mine, which has no notes and is more battered, though it is back home at Rhodhur."

"I don't need a book to tell me how to get anywhere in three years." Stefan stretched out his legs. He too had drunk a good amount of ale. Probably best not to drink more. He wanted to be of some use when he joined his wife this night. "We're not going to trade by land; I want to do it by sea. I sent Erenor to open talks." Damn the ale. He hadn't meant to let that slip. To address the look of affront and surprise on Cullen's face, Stefan added, "Cullen warned me Mormantalorans are Staubaunish and might not receive a Kheld ambassador."

"Yes, I did." Cullen slammed his cup hard enough for ale to slosh out. "I also warned you how hostile that land is to ours."

"I've heard that too. Heard they're Purists," offered Goff. "Worse than Hebron that sits in Lacenedon. They're bad enough already."

Robdan, again, piped in. "Purists for sure. Mormantalorus broke from the Triempery when Marc Frederick became king. Mormantalorus's ruler, the Nuarch Camas, said he could not—would not—accept Marc Frederick as an equal. According to Aebner, they nearly broke with Sordan, too, for the same reason, decades earlier, when the Sordaneons allowed Nemenor blood to marry one of their bloodline."

"But Mormantalorus *didn't* break with Sordan, did they?" Maybe that would shut up this oblivious kinsman.

"No, Sire. I think maybe because the Sordaneons are Highborn still, whereas your grandsire was not."

And neither was Stefan. He was only surrounded by them. His stomach turned sour. Too much ale. Too much talk. His plan with Mormantalorus was a good one. He didn't need people assailing him with reasons not to attempt it.

"Time has passed. Times have changed. My family has ruled Essera for forty years. And seeing how Nammuor is at war with Sordan, I'm betting he's receptive to allies." Stefan saw Robdan's mouth open to speak, then watched it shut and his gaze turn aside. "What? If you have an opinion, you can tell me. I won't bite your head off."

"Of course not, sire."

Cullen leaned forward. "Stefan—"

"Just say it." He wasn't in the mood to be placated either.

Robdan hunched and looked uncomfortable. "As secretary to Cedrec, I overheard many conversations between him and your late grandfather about this Nammuor. He's not Highborn, true—but he might be something worse, something else at least as ancient. He's said to be calculating and dangerous, filled with ambition. And he has access to sorcerous devices. I would advise caution."

"Would you?" Stefan narrowed his gaze. "As I recall, you are not one of my advisors."

Cullen looked ready to push to his feet, but Goff placed a hand on his arm and coughed, this time without the laugh. "We're all in our cups. Rob here answered your question, and that's the end of it."

Yes, it was. Stefan forced a smile and put aside his cup, prompting the other two men to do the same. Cullen would not look up from his. "Talk enough. It's been a good evening, but time to end it. Lots to be done in the morning."

Stefan held back Goff after Cullen and Robdan had left the room. "Send my uncle back to Amallar and get yourself another secretary. I'm sure there's something useful he can do. Hoary advice in my ear is the last thing I want."

Palimia extended her hand, palm up. She lifted her voice so it might carry through the walls between them. "If you say you are ready to do this, I trust you."

She stood two rooms and a portico away, at the far end of a garden. Dorilian envisioned her brightly draped figure framed by centuries-old mosaic images and sprays of dangling bellflowers. At his side, Legon shook his head violently.

"This could go badly. That thing could end up impaling her hand or buried under her ribcage."

"And I tell you that will not happen."

Dorilian weighed the cylinder in his hand. He had been practicing accuracy for weeks. Much to his surprise, his grandfather's books had proven useful. The firmament of Leur's Second Creation functioned on strict laws. Dorilian had needed to learn those laws before he could engineer basic manipulations. This principle, for instance, involved the mathematics of extending extra-human Leur perception to accurately calculate destination densities. It was important to distinguish flesh and bone from air or stone or greenery.

"Let me be your target." Legon moved toward the door.

"No. You stay here. I need your hands intact for my protection."

Even at this distance and through intervening structures, Palimia felt... distinct. Warm, liquid, female and unflinching. Dorilian appreciated her bravery. He focused on her hand, also flesh and extended, its water-thick heat discernable from both her somewhat amorphous main body and the air around it. He focused and simultaneously performed the calculations. By concentrating deeply, he pulled the edges of that space until it met this one. A nudge, only that, was needed... and the canister vanished.

"Yes!"

Palimia. Her voice penetrated the distance.

"You're not hurt?" he called.

"Not even a little!"

Dorilian and Legon jogged to join her. She beamed to see them emerge at the far end of the long garden where she waited, cylinder in hand. A light breeze teased her hair. Dorilian took back the cylinder.

"I should say my accuracy is good enough."

Palimia shook out her skirt as they walked back toward the loggia that would lead them to the residences. "How far can you send something?"

"About what I just did." Dorilian bridled at lessons that, so far, struck him as unimpressive.

"Rheger travels a lot farther." Legon's contribution earned him a glare.

"He uses a device. I have a few of those, you know." He passed the cylinder to Legon. "I think this time I will bring one with me."

Dorilian and Legon made one stop before they went to the King's House. Tutto already waited and stood in conversation with Rheger, who looked impatient. Though translocation cost no time at all, the Dannutheon prince's absence, if discovered, could lead to questions.

"What have you there?" Rheger gestured to the velvet pouch Dorilian bore.

Dorilian plunked it on the central table, the rotunda's sole piece of furniture. From the bag he lifted a crown of light and emeralds.

"Leur," Rheger swore. "You brought it. The Sordan Coronal."

"Go to the next room and hold out your hand, and I'll show you how accurate I am *without* wearing this."

"A device will not make you more accurate. It allows you to—"

"Send further, maybe bigger. I suspect it will let me do more." As Rheger did not dispute that conclusion, Dorilian brandished the cylinder. "I will prove my accuracy. Tell me where to send this."

Rheger held up a platen of silver. "On this. I'll go place it."

A few minutes later, a shout came from deep within the King's House. "Now!"

Weeks earlier, Dorilian had not known how to deploy his senses in ways that would simultaneously discern the architecture of this palace, the densities of its labyrinthine walls and floors and ceilings, the open spaces and, within these, objects of differing materials. He had not yet conceived of mapping the world in relation to... itself. Or that the Creation was infinitely foldable, such that he could crease space to form exploitable, if temporary, proximities. Sensing was the first part of the lesson. Sending was the second. Folding was... more complicated. He could not extend this ability beyond the Serat just yet and had folded only within its confines, but he had practiced so intensely that his dreams were filled not with images but vivid streams of calculations.

Silver. A platen the size of a child's face. Neither the element nor the shape was hard to find. It's location... was interesting. On a floor. Not a silver floor, but one nearly as soft. He differentiated the edge of the platen, calculated its center... and sent. Through senses he kept fixed on his target, he detected the cylinder's reemergence. Upright. Stable.

He nodded at Tutto and Legon when they looked to him for confirmation.

It took several minutes, but Rheger reappeared, his walk quick and his expression a concession. "Accurate. But you should never have used people as test targets."

Dorilian frowned at Tutto. "Volunteers."

"I suggest you read more texts on ethics, in particular the ethics of projective empathy and matters of consent."

"Consent isn't usually the issue that trips me up."

"No. That issue would be hostility." Rheger slid the canister into his hip pouch. On the table before them, drawing all eyes, Sordan's state crown glittered with dangerous power. "Are you sure this is the device you want to train through? A *greater diadem*?"

Dorilian looked pointedly at Rheger's gem-encircled head. "You wore a crown the night you translocated to take me by surprise. You started the night in Dazunor. I checked."

"I suppose I should resign myself; you will never let that go. But yes, I have trained my gift of translocation through diadems. Lesser ones for the most part. Other devices probably would serve, but... I have always used diadems. Usually this one." Rheger looked Dorilian in the eye. "That night it was the Dazunor Crown. But *that*"—he indicated the crown on the table—"is many times more powerful."

"I need to learn how to use it."

"Then use it, but don't start with translocation. Start with augmentation—of your senses, or your natural abilities. An *orbus*, in gifted hands, can become a fireball... or lightning."

"Reconfiguration—of generated energy," said Tutto. A correction.

Rheger grimaced but nodded. "Generated energy. I cannot teach you about using or controlling such. I do not generate sufficient energy to create fields, active or passive."

"Passive?"

"Defense. Fields that absorb arcane or natural energies. I—" Rheger shook his head. "Such gifts are native in your bloodline but less so in mine. Enreddon could generate energy fields of both kinds. I can barely summon an *orbus*. Translocation is even rarer, though, and yet for some reason I can do that. It involves spatial manipulation, not energy generation. So... can you fold space such as to translocate something as large as yourself?"

"Start small. Inanimate object first?"

"Always. The price of failure is horrific."

"Then I shall make a dummy of myself and start moving that around."

Joyful sound penetrated the walls of the King's House. Cheering in the street. Some person favored by the people was passing. Rheger listened, then smiled. "You still live in a semblance of how we once did. Our lives in Essera are terribly changed. You have no idea. You cannot, not from here, where you are surrounded by believers. In Essera, for our kind at least, belief is fading. So is safety. There is a sense of peril waiting around every corner, every conversation. You are incredibly free, Dorilian. Stay that way for as long as you can."

25

"**Y**ou sent Erenor to Mormantalorus and didn't tell me?" Stefan watched Cullen's jaw go slack. Clearly stunned, Cullen slowly sank down onto the stone bench. It had been a good idea to deliver this news in the garden.

"I sent him because I couldn't send *you*. We discussed this last night. They don't talk to Khelds. I had to send a Staubaun, one I can trust."

"Him? A man who has yet to sit well with anyone but you?"

"I like that about Erenor. He's loyal, the same way you are."

"At least you give me that."

The way Cullen said it turned the words bitter, but Stefan told himself it didn't matter. He had too many irons in the fire.

"I'll give you a lot more, if you let me. There's hard work to be done, but I have to step on toes to do it. I have to follow my own head, my own way—even if people don't like it. Even if you don't."

Cullen looked up with a pained grimace. "A king's mind must be his own."

Finally. "Yes. And the first thing I want to do is free us from Sordan's glove on our throat. That means doing whatever's needed to gain new markets, new allies."

"Not allies like Mormantalorus." Cullen got to his feet and began to pace, looking exactly like the stressed soon-to-be-father he was. He was probably sex-starved as well, given how enormous Asphalladra's belly had gotten.

Though Stefan was happy for Cullen's impending fatherhood, he ached to the core for his own little babe, who had drawn not a single breath. He remained convinced Dorilian had played some role, even if only in wishing tragedy upon him. Stefan decided he and Cullen both needed to blow off steam and rose to his feet. "Let's go down to the pond," he said.

The Golden Palace was too formal a seat for the kind of proper pond Stefan preferred, but it did have a nice pool in the long garden. Rimmed and floored with marble, and filled in summer with pretty fish, each more amazing in color than the next, the rectangle of serene water at this season showed only a few sparse pads from hardy water lilies. Stefan was pleased to see a basket of smooth slim stones waiting at the broad white edge. He reached down to pick up a stone, which he threw flat, so it skipped along the water's surface.

Cullen shook his head then grinned and did the same. His stone skipped farther, and he whooped. "It's true. You never forget how."

Stefan skipped a few more stones along the water. He took hard aim and hopped the next one over a pod of tattered lily pads. "Did you see that?"

"Impressive." Cullen focused intently with his next stone. It skipped atop a broad, leathery pad and landed on another nearby, a wet, glistening fail. Jaw set, he gamely tried again. "Hah!"

Clouds gathered overhead, heavy and gray. Stefan decided he might as well get to it.

"I'm sending you to Gignastha." He braced for Cullen's displeasure and was not disappointed. He knew Cullen had counted on being in Trulo for the remainder of his wife's pregnancy. Just last night, he had spoken of how happy he was he could be at hand for the birth. Before Cullen could mount a protest, Stefan explained. "I need you to smooth things over for Lowen in advance of the vote. Settle the local lords. Let them know we have big plans to expand their region's influence and trade."

"It isn't trade they're unhappy about."

No. Gignastha's petty nobles didn't want a Kheld, even one related to their king, to hold lordship over a domain. Especially not theirs. Apollonia had spoken for the aristocracy when she had sneered at Stefan's plan to bestow Gignastha on Nilla's father. *Elevating a hog to a palace won't make its daughter any less of a sow.'* What Stefan needed more than anything was to rid himself of snakes like Apollonia.

"Do what you can. I'll have the votes soon."

"But you don't have them now." Cullen sucked for a moment on his lower lip. "Just give me 'til the baby comes. It won't be long. You see how things are."

"I see Nilla fussing over your wife as much as you do."

"She's like a sister to her. But I'm the father! I want to stay with my wife and be with her when her time comes, the way the Old Mothers teach, not be one of those men who just plants his seed and says his part's done. You can find someone else."

Why did Cullen always make Stefan do this? "There is no one else! And the matter can't wait. Days turn into weeks. Don't you see? I need Lowen in position, and I need you to go now. Not in two weeks. Not in a month."

Cullen's face changed from desperate hope to frustration. "You told me you wanted me to stay for the baby. Isn't that what you said last night? That's why you didn't have me be part of the delegation to Mormantalorus? Well, I believed you. I told myself you were being a friend, not just a king. Now you're sending me away anyway!"

Stefan had wanted to soften the slight of sending along delegates Erenor had suggested instead. But Cullen would always be his first choice for matters closer to home.

"I need your skills, Cullen. I need your good sense. People are already sharpening knives over the way Sordan is sending arms through Annech and Gobba."

"And that's not even the first of ten good reasons why you shouldn't raise up a Kheld as Bas of Gignastha. You want Lowen there? Fine. Maybe make him governor first."

"I have a fucking governor, someone who wanted the job, but he turned into just another useless noble with too high an opinion of himself. He's pocketing taxes and begging more money every damn time I turn around. I'm sick of it. I need to work Gignastha to my advantage—a loyal domain with a loyal Bas, loyal to me! It's been nothing but a damned thorn in this kingdom's side since my grandfather was king. Lowen wants a high title with good revenue, and that's what he'll get. Gignastha's rich!"

"And I'm telling you it's not going to sit well. Not here and *definitely* not there. Think about it. People remember foul deeds nearly forever."

"Then I will make them forget. Forget the past and forget Sordan's threadbare old claims. Give them something new they can remember and count on, something good." Stefan snatched another stone, hard and flat and cold, and skimmed it across the pool. "Lowen's a good choice to be Bas. Gignastha just needs to see. He's high clan with a rich and influential wife, and his grandsons—*my* sons—will be princes. Just like the damn Highborn. How can they be unhappy about that?"

He waited, but Cullen said nothing, so Stefan added another enticement. "I'm elevating you to a higher rank and greater holding. You deserve it after all your hard work securing this kingdom. You'll be an Archon. Archon of Heddros and Enlad of Wyre. I've already decided, so I'll do it now, before you go."

Cullen blew out a sigh. He picked up a new stone but didn't throw it, just turned it over and over in his hand. "Do you think giving me some nose-in-the-air title is going to matter? Or that I can convince the lords and people of Gignastha that Lowen will be good for them? I can't promise them that any more than I can promise them the Lords of Gobba and Annech will stop attacking Kheld settlements— or that Lowen won't levy taxes to defend those settlements."

Stefan ground his teeth at the mention of taxes but held his tongue and let Cullen continue.

"They need a strong hand—and I'm not even close to being that, no matter what lofty holdings or titles you give me. Hard truth is, most of Gignastha's trade goes through the Seven Houses. That's who holds sway there." Cullen turned away and dropped the stone he'd been holding back into the basket. His sigh seethed with resentment. "Listen to me for once. Don't force anything, not right now. Go to the Archhalia, then stay in Dazunor-Rannuli a while to line things up, and I'll stay too to help you take this thing by the horns."

"What thing? The thing you're going to handle for me?" Stefan threw another stone and admired its string of leaps. "I can't stand Dazunor-Rannuli, and Nilla hates it even more than I do. She's happy here in Trulo, and that matters. I want a son, and I'm not going to get one on her from Dazunor-Rannuli."

"So you don't get one on her now, you get one on her later. Important thing is, your subjects will see you being where you need to be."

"Oh? Is that where I need to be?" If Cullen wanted an argument, Stefan was ready to give him one. He threw another stone, but it only gave him two hops. "How about Stauberg? It's high time I visited there again, don't you think? Three-quarters of my fucking domains, including the Seven Houses, voted against my petition to secure wardship of Stauberg's princes, a wardship I should have by right because they're *my* fucking heirs." That vote had prompted Rheger Dannutheon and Palaistea to openly oppose him. The damned Highborn always protected each other. "And being at Dazunor-Rannuli just puts me closer to Burelan Phaeros, who we both know would like nothing better than to put a sword through my neck. So unless you think I need *that*—"

Cullen shook his head.

It was time to head back to the palace, to shelter and other people. Dark clouds lowered in a gray veil beyond a line of pollarded elderberry trees. Cullen fell into step beside Stefan and together they ascended the worn stone steps to the terrace.

"Essera's changed, Cullen. The kingdom we grew up in is gone. It blew away the day Grandfather died along with the Highborn princes. He's dead and they're dead and so is the smoke dream that peace with Sordan could hold the fucking Triempery together. It died along with them."

"Did it, Stefan? Did it have to? Maybe we should have tried harder."

"How? Nobody wanted it anymore."

Cullen lifted his head and his mouth pressed in a tight pale line. Stefan could see he wasn't convinced. "Seems to me that's the problem. People don't know what they want. Except you—you do, and if you really think it will help, I'll go to Gignastha. Not that anyone there will have anything to do with me, because they won't. I'll go because you need somebody there you can trust to tell things back to you straight. And not just about them accepting Lowen, or the Seven Houses' take on trade. Maybe I can learn a bit about how to make things better again between Essera and Sordan—because I still think your grandfather understood a thing or two that maybe we don't."

Stefan didn't think that. Sleet stung his cheek and his clothes were getting wet. He was glad they were near the steps leading back up to the terrace and the warm comforts of the palace.

"Old tales and wishful thinking. We're past all that."

"And I'm telling you, as your friend and someone who wants you to come out on top—we're not past it, not one bit, and we won't ever be. Not as long as the Rill is the backbone of Essera's trade and commerce, the thing your people count on to feed them and protect them and make them rich."

"The thing Dorilian holds over all our heads like a sword!"

"That too." Water and bits of sleet dripped from Cullen's hair, tracing the lines of his frown. "Because the Rill is as good a reason as I can think of for putting things right."

"Jon would have voted for Lowen."

"Don't talk to me about what my son would have wanted."

Two weeks had passed since Cullen had left Trulo and Stefan had traveled to Gustan just to attempt to sway one old woman. He placed a hand on the stone foreleg of one of the equine statues standing guard at the door of the Stauberg-Randolph mausoleum. The iron gate, painted black, was well oiled and did not creak when Apollonia swung it open. The mausoleum's interior was gray, sparsely lit through openings in the stone ceiling. The sepulchre of Jonthan, Stefan's uncle, stood within.

Because Marc Frederick had built the mausoleum thinking he and future generations would join his son, there was plenty of extra room. The regal structure stood on Gustan Manor's grounds, on a knoll overlooking the river and Sonnen Hill. Stefan had traveled to the Manor to meet up with the Gracious Queen on her journey to Permephedon for the Archhalia.

Apollonia placed a branch of laurel at the foot of the tomb as she had done every winter for the past five years. Stefan knew this from the groundskeeper. She cast a disdainful look about the empty vault. "His father should be in this dismal place too."

"Why? So you could visit him?"

"So people could be reminded of his utter failure."

Stefan clenched his teeth and wished he did not need this old crone's vote in the Archhalia. She never ceased to lament that he, not her son, sat on Essera's throne. To Apollonia, Marc Frederick's greatest failure was that he had left the kingdom to Stefan instead of someone more worthy.

"Even you know what needs to be done. It's time we bind Gignastha to the crown."

"Your crown?" She brushed a bit of debris from Jon's effigy. "It was a Highborn crown, founded so and always so. A Principate. Bound to its own prince."

"A Sordaneon prince. I'm not going to let them have it."

"Dorilian? I suppose not. So you wish to keep him at bay? Marc Frederick knew the way to do that." She turned her aged gaze upon Stefan. "Do nothing."

"Nothing doesn't accomplish anything."

"Nothing accomplishes a great deal. Nothing is a way of keeping what you have so as to prevent something else."

"That's not how things work."

Apollonia pressed her hand to the face of Jon's stone effigy. "It's how Gignastha works. My poor son. He would have known that."

Strangling her right here, with no one at hand to see, occurred to Stefan. The Gracious Queen was old, he could say. Her heart failed from grief and she died at the foot of her son's stone likeness. No one would believe it, though. Apollonia was too bitter and tough to die of sorrow.

"Gignastha's status as a crown protectorate means I have to defend it but get no advantage. Its nobles do nothing but complain about taxes."

"As do all nobles. As do you. Only the Sordaneons command the riches to run a city-state without taxes. Though they do have fees. A great many fees. My Sordan contracts are eaten up by fees."

Which was yet another problem Stefan yearned to finish off. Right now, however, he needed to settle this matter of votes.

"You voted for Cullen to be made a lord. And Goff."

"Yes, for favors you delivered. One of them turned out well. Brodheson actually manages the land and estates you gave him and married better than you did. As for that other Kheld, Goff, he came to plead his case to me in person. His courage impressed me. He, however, is a spendthrift who is driving his properties to ruin. All he does is buy horses."

"Lowen is better with money. Just meet with him. Give him a chance to impress."

Apollonia had finished paying her respects. Hand trailing from the stone face of Jon's effigy, she shook out her skirt and walked past the sculpted horses into the sun again. "I have met him already. An unimpressive man who brings so little to the table he must call upon you to advance him. Ask yourself why."

Stefan knew why. None of his damned nobles gave Lowen the respect he deserved. Just because Lowen didn't come from a lofty gold-haired family that had been landed for a thousand years and built palaces instead of homesteads, that covered itself in jewels and lived off wealth regurgitated by the damned Rill year after year. There was no way for a man to break into that kind of privilege except by being shoehorned into it.

"Lowen is good and decent. He will hold just courts and levy fair taxes."

"Hold courts? The man barely speaks Stauba and has no background in law. Your grandfather saw to it you had that, at least, before he died." Apollonia sighed, and turned so Stefan could see her face with its faint lines of age. White strands brightened her already pale hair. Her years were beginning to show. "Make your wife's father an Enlad with some small estates, and I will vote for that so as not to embarrass you. If you wish to advance these Khelds you will give them the means to *become* what you wish them to be. Landed. Educated. To be respected at all, they will need to be better than their titles—and that man isn't. If you need an example of how it is done, look to your own grandfather. He came to this world with nothing but a Wall Lord's recommendation."

"At least he had that. It appears my recommendation carries less weight."

"You are a petulant boy."

"What I'm not is Endurin Malyrdeon. I don't get to snap my fingers and name a man a prince, the way he did Marc Frederick."

"You are right. He did do that. But do you think people simply accepted it? Hah! Marc fought hard for recognition of his qualities. He earned his place. He proved what he was, again and again and again. He won battle after battle, with steel and with wits, until no one could say he did not deserve his throne."

Stefan recognized good myth-building when he saw it. He also saw the lie. "The Sordaneons said he didn't deserve his throne. They said that a lot."

Apollonia brushed aside the widow's veil a gust had thrown across her face. "Yes, but they stopped saying it, didn't they? Dorilian does not say that."

No. Not anymore. These days he said nothing about Essera's former or ruling kings. *As if Grandfather never existed. As if I don't exist at all.* Dorilian fashioned even silence into insults.

"So you're suggesting I test those Khelds I wish to advance?"

"Tests are for fools. Give them ways to demonstrate their quality." She waved her mother-of-pearl walking stick as if it were a royal scepter. "This Lowen lacks quality. Give him something important to do other than stand beside his daughter looking proud while he waits for people to bribe him. Give him some lands and some books and have him assist a magistrate somewhere. Maybe he will learn law."

She wasn't budging. She probably would never budge. Damned Highborn-fathered bitch. Stefan stifled a curse and looked up at the comforting angles and windows of Gustan Manor above the naked winter hedges. How had his grandfather ever won over these thorn-pocked aristocrats? They were immovable, their hierarchy designed to be impervious to penetration. Marc Frederick was no kind of example. He was and had always been an exception. Stefan was the example, and he was failing miserably.

"You're just waiting until Palaistea's sons get old enough, aren't you?" Stefan noted how Apollonia's shoulders stiffened, the tense lift of her chin and refusal to match his gaze.

"Rule well and you won't have to worry about those children."

"You voted against my petition to make them wards of the crown."

"Their mother is perfectly competent."

"Their mother openly plots for them."

Apollonia turned to him then, eyes narrowed to slits of gold. "Leave her alone. Mark my advice, Stefan. This kingdom cannot afford your obsession with removing threats that exist only in your imagination. The Malyrdeons made their bargain years ago. Hold to the bargain your grandfather made. Rule them. They will allow it."

"Why?"

She huffed. "The Wall, of course. It showed them something— a path, a way, an end they wish either to achieve or avoid. They knew the Demise would happen. Maybe not that very day or hour, but my father said goodbye just as would a warrior going to battle. His death was part of whatever lay on the other side of that terrible event. Maybe even this"—she spread her hands to include Stefan, the tomb overlooking the river, and the chimneyed Manor at his back—"maybe even you. Whatever your rule may amount to, they didn't try to avoid it. You can take some heart from that at least."

"So it *could* be my rule is what they hoped to achieve."

She bent her head. "We do not know."

Mouth dry, Stefan wondered what else might be on the other side of whatever the Wall had foretold and the Malyrdeons embraced. So many had died—so that *what* might happen? Dorilian, too, had survived. And Rheger and his son. And those two boys...

Or maybe, just maybe, as Stefan had said all along, it really was him, so he could usher in an age of change, change Essera needed to make if the Triempery were to survive. If so, he really could depend on the Highborn not to oppose him.

"I think you should hedge your bets, Grandmother." He deployed the term she had always hated for him or Hans to use with her. "Vote for my choice when I name Lowen to be Bas of Gignastha. You don't know what the Wall was pointing to. I am pointing to this."

Apollonia sighed and resumed walking up the path. She lifted her gaze to the Manor. "How I despise this house."

"Well, I don't know if I should be scared of that thing, or sad for it."

Ranwulf Forbasson craned his neck and rocked back in the saddle.

Cullen watched questions rise and fail to be answered as Ranwulf gazed upon the otherworldly shapes crowning Bellan Toregh's prominent hill. In Dazunor-Rannuli, the Rill burned bright as the moon and the structures atop the mount moved in ways that wove stories in the mind. Here they shone less brightly and did not move at all.

"I told you, it's sleeping." Cullen couldn't look upon the dormant mount without recalling rumors about the never-signed Permephedon Treaty. The thought that the station slept tantalized him. Things that were asleep could be awakened. What lifted above Bellan Toregh mocked those dreams.

Ranwulf, whose grandfather Tobold had been Thegnard and died at Permephedon, and whose cousin was now queen, had campaigned unsuccessfully to be raised to noble status. Though he had resisted an administrative position at first, he was proving an able assistant. Cullen had sent two other men of his staff ahead to Gignastha to prepare for his visit. Arton Metagoras, Cullen's chief purser for Neuberland, and Kyros Eulodes, curator of the region's taxes and fees, had both traveled by Rill to Leseos and should have reached their destination a week ago.

Because Cullen and Ranwulf could not use the Rill, they were making the journey by horse. Bellan Toregh at least was a big enough town to have quality inns wherein two travelers could enjoy a hot meal and sleep in warm beds for the night. There would also be a fine breakfast in the morning, with hotcakes and eggs and sausages as well as proper bran to brighten their way.

The following day dawned cloudy and cold, prompting Ranwulf to sleep in. After starting late, they crossed into Neuberland but failed to reach the good inn Cullen had planned for and ended up spending the night in a farmhouse. An early start the next day brought them by late evening to the town of Saemoregh and the large house of Amundhal, the holding of Cullen's cousin, Aubrey.

Ranwulf assessed the property's stone buildings, cultivated fields, and prosperous village with unfeigned admiration. "This cousin of yours—has she a husband?"

"Stay away."

Ranwulf laughed. "I'm a good Thegn lad. She could do worse." He gazed around and blew out another breath. "All this from the old king?"

"A king's grant. Her father, Amund Rhys, was Marc Frederick's forester. He tended the oak groves at the king's estate in Gustan. Guess he did a good job. When Amund married—and he married *my* father's cousin, mind you—Marc Frederick gave the couple this land, along with some coin and a few of his cows, and established a garrison in Saemoregh to keep the peace."

At the bottom of a wooded hill, the road crossed a run of marsh grass and curved toward a stone bridge over a small river leading to a mill pond. Beyond it lay a lane toward the main house. Movement along the road alerted them to a chestnut horse with a russet-cloaked rider who crossed the bridge at a gallop. Cullen grinned.

Aubrey reined her horse to a prance alongside his. "I got your message two days ago and made the house ready. You picked a cold time of year to travel."

Cullen noted how Rannulf's jaw dropped. Even in fading winter light that drained all things of color, with her hair tucked under a wool knit cap and her face shadowed by a hood lined with rabbit fur, Aubrey was pretty.

"I thought you'd have baggage." She looked behind them as if some might still arrive.

"No. No baggage." Cullen had sent all that ahead by Rill with Arton and Kyros.

"And no protection either? Shouldn't a lord with a fancy title have men?"

Ranwulf's expression hinted he felt slighted, so Cullen spoke up first. "Nothing about me suggests I have a fancy title. We've stayed on main roads. I'll pick up an escort in town. A meal and a bed would be welcome, though."

Constructed as a fortified house like those of wealthy families north of the Dazun, Amundhal commanded a rise above a pond surrounded by meadows and backed by deep woods. The main house, larger than the one at Wyre, lifted in three stories of timber and stone, with fine glass windows and several chimneys. When the party reached the courtyard, Aubrey jumped down from her horse and greeted a waiting group of staff and holders. Cullen recognized the sturdy man standing at the foot of the steps as Wodd, a former soldier who had served under Marc Frederick before retiring to the settlements with Amund. The ample woman speaking to Aubrey was probably Wodd's wife.

Cullen dismounted and claimed his heavy saddle bags before turning his horse over to a brace of lads who seemed excited to have visitors. While the horses were led to the stable, Aubrey formally introduced Cullen and Ranwulf to Amundhal's staff. Upon completing that duty she gave Cullen a quick embrace and soft press of her cheek so she could whisper to his ear. The rabbit fur of her hood tickled his nose.

"You have to tell me everything."

She pushed back the hood and yanked off her knit cap to release thick hair the deep warm brown of old cherry wood. It tumbled over her shoulders like that of the girl she still was. Beneath a russet cloak, her budding figure didn't quite fill out determined layers of gray matronly wool. A ring of keys upon a beautiful knotted belt marked her as the property holder. It was a necessary statement. Even Kheld men raised to revere the Mother often failed to grant younger women the respect they were due.

Cullen turned to Wodd. "It's good to see you again, Wodd. Would you kindly help my companion find his room for the night? We leave early on the morrow."

"That we will, Cullen Thegn."

Handing his bags to Ranwulf, Cullen turned again to Aubrey. "Let's pay respect to your Oak."

There was still light enough and they could put the privacy to good use.

An oak tree held court at every Kheld holding, planted in a place of honor. This one's acorn had come from the venerable Thegn Oak that shaded the Barrowgrave, Rhodhur's Motherhome. Though young and not yet stout, Amundhal's oak promised a mighty crown in years to come and presided over a fine plot of ground at the edge of a formal garden, where it overlooked a vista of forest and fields. Wildflowers almost certainly grew around its feet come spring.

"I should have my mother send an acorn from our Oak and have Phalla plant it at Wyre." Cullen and Asphalladra planned to raise their family at the house he had built for her. The estate was the least grand of his holdings, but he could not imagine raising children in Heddros.

Aubrey snorted. "No Staubaun lady would ever dirty her hands in honest ground."

"You give her too little credit. You have yet to meet her." From the inside pocket of his jacket, Cullen pulled out a folded, sealed letter, which he passed to Aubrey. "Nilla wrote. Phalla asked me to forward it. I thought I'd bring it in person."

"Nilla wrote? We weren't permitted to see her when she was at her mother's. Lark and I tried. Can you believe her sister said Stefan wouldn't allow it?" Aubrey grabbed the letter and opened it. Because the light was failing, she held it close to her face to read the writing. "Look! She wrote in Stauba!" She eagerly read the short paragraph and laughed. "She wants me to tell her, in brutal honesty, if she got the words right."

"She's trying so very hard."

Aubrey looked up in surprise. "If she got the words right, you're going to be a father."

Cullen grinned and nodded. "We're hoping for a boy, to secure my newfound title and properties."

"Just as well, because your daughters will be landless." Her grimace made him laugh. "I'm happy for you both. Phalla will be a good mother, I hope." Aubrey folded the letter carefully and slid it into the pocket of her skirt. "I'll write a response tonight and send it by courier. You're headed the wrong way."

"King's business."

"It must be important for him to send you to Gignastha in winter."

"To Stefan, it is."

For a long moment, she studied him, clearly waiting to hear more. He drew a breath of crisp late winter air laced with scents of witch hazel and buckrod. The garden's plantings harked back to its founder's work at Gustan, including specimens that lived nowhere else. Cullen often thought Stefan didn't give Marc Frederick enough credit for having included Khelds in a new vision of the Triempery, as allies with power of their own, independent of Essera.

Aubrey heaved a sigh. Her features assumed a harder set, keen and self-assured. "If you know something important is going to happen, you'd best tell me. What happens in Gignastha affects things here, usually in ugly ways. I have a seat on the Neuberland Cruihcil now."

"Do you?" It jarred Cullen to realize that, by Kheld law, his young cousin held full holder rights.

"They would rather I was a gray-haired matron, but I'm a strong voice for our settlements in this region and speak for us at Rhodhur when they let me." Aubrey looked quite proud of that. "We need to be taken seriously. Neuberland is—"

"In dispute. Stefan is working to resolve that dispute."

Dusk had deepened, rendering Aubrey little more than a ghostly suggestion. "I was going to say rich and growing. We're not a *dispute*. We're people, we live here, we have homes and families to protect. And we don't like being pushed around by Staubaun landowners who give us fields to work and improve and build on, then take those lands and everything we built away from us."

"Stefan is trying to stop that." Cullen looked toward the house. Aubrey took his hint and began to walk back to Amundhal with him at her side. "Saemoregh is lucky to have you," he said, meaning it. She was in no danger of losing *her* land, which as a king's grant was guaranteed by the same laws as gave Staubaun landholders their rights. "At court we hold this town as an example of a successful Kheld settlement, the kind we'd like to see more of." More and more he was convinced that was what Marc Frederick had intended Amundhal and Saemoregh to be.

"Towns don't thrive when dishonest landholders take people's hard work. They *take* it, and whatever they can't take, they destroy so no one prospers."

"And *they* say we take land to which we have no right."

"Only to live on. We don't destroy it!"

He had gone around and around with Stefan on this. Stefan favored seizing and reassigning land rights from absent Staubaun holders in Neuberland and giving those rights to Kheld settlers. Many holdings were contested anyway since the death of the Highborn Prince of Gignastha and, most recently, the confiscation of former Sordaneon holdings. The trouble was, too many Kheld chieftains salivated to get those lands into Kheld—not Staubaun— hands, and were pressuring Stefan to declare them forfeit. Existing landholders opposed doing so as destruction of their very laws.

"Is that what you're going to Gignastha to do, put a stop to it?"

Cullen nodded. A sliver of the truth would satisfy her and make his short time here more peaceful. "More like a start. I'm going to argue for good sense, settle some fears, and try to change a few minds. Maybe I can build a foundation for something else, something better."

They had reached the house. Light from uncovered windows striped the steps. At the top landing, Aubrey put a hand on his arm.

"Don't trust them." From inside came sounds of merriment and laughter. A Kheld house always had those things. Aubrey's warning hooked on his fears. "Staubauns, you know, they're made of lies. Stefan's name won't protect you there. Neither will words. Keep a sword on your belt—and a hand on your sword."

"There it is. Other side of the lake. Because it's winter and low water, we can travel by causeway."

Cullen patted the neck of his horse and squinted across the blinding reflections off Sar Pryannis, the Long Lake. Encroaching sunset painted the tall walls and steep roofs of Gignastha with rose. Kyros Eulodes proudly beamed at the sight.

"If you look hard enough, you can see it." Kyros pointed. "Over that way, those red arches. The Vermillion Aqueduct."

A blood-bright line of narrow, symmetric arches marched above the blue-purple angles and towers of Gignastha before vanishing toward distant mountains. Beautiful and massive, one of the Second Creation's great wonders, the aqueduct supplied vast amounts of fresh water from the mountains and also served to lock the impregnable gates of the Watergilt Palace. It had been raised up by Highborn magic fifteen hundred years ago and shattered by sorcery in Cullen's lifetime.

"It looks... whole. I thought it was broken."

He and Ranwulf nudged their mounts to follow Kyros's lead down the paved road past houses and other buildings of wood and stone. The small village called Lagurn served as a stop for traders and other travelers not headed to the city.

"Patched it, we did, with new arches and channels of regular stone, then painted it over to match. It's a marvel, the original parts. The patch leaks."

Cullen thought it strange to see a lake without boats, though he had heard all his life how cliff-ringed Sar Pryannis was as deadly as it was pretty. Creatures that lived in its waters grew extra limbs, even heads, or teeth outside their mouths. Locals forbade the eating of them. The water, too, was bad, sour as lemons and poison to drink. Only the lake itself was deadly, though. Water from the surrounding mountains and mist-drenched hills was sweet and pure, good to drink at any point before it reached the poisoned shore. The towns that ringed Sar Pryannis thrived on industries powered by fast streams from the region's rugged hills. Lumber from Gignastha's many mills found its way to Leseos, as did ores from its basin and, most importantly, rare metals and powders distilled directly from the red crusts that formed atop the lake's poisoned waters.

Wealthy was what Gignastha was. Prosperous. A city-state as important in its way as Randpory, Leseos or Dazunor-Rannuli, but without the Rill.

The Bitter Causeway cut across a narrow end of the lake to the other shore, where the road joined other highways from Randpory and the towns of Lower Neuberland until it reached Gignastha, which was built on high cliffs above the lake, a city connected to its various neighborhoods by bridges and aqueduct-filled waterways. Even from afar the city was gorgeous to look upon. And the Vermillion Aqueduct, from this side of the lake, presided over the city with graceful, storied magnificence.

"Lud's Breath!" Ranwulf nearly fell backward off his horse, so intent was he on gazing up at Gignastha's window-lit towers and, above them, the beautiful arches still aglow with the last reds of sunset. "To think we almost had this."

A shadow of anger flitted across Kyros's face. Cullen saw that expression before it vanished, replaced by forbearance. Before they'd even set foot in the city, Ranwulf had managed to awaken deep-seated resentment. For a son of a Gignasthan noble house like Kyros, the domain's brutal history lingered—and not just in the haunting reminder posed by a forever-scarred and broken aqueduct. The remainder of the ride to the Watergilt Palace, through a wonderwork of massive, presumably repaired, metal gates, was silent.

Within a cold and shadowed courtyard, Cullen greeted the men who would host his visit. Gignastha's governor, Verteus Cordegos, an appointee of Stefan's, had a pleasant face, full and well fed. He introduced his various assistants, whose names Cullen would endeavor to learn in the coming days. This was a part of being noble he hated: meeting and getting to know people who without a doubt despised him. Ranwulf aside, not one of these men believed Cullen merited his title. It was lunacy to think they would believe Lowen Toboldson worthy of being elevated to town gravedigger, far less Bas of their exalted city-state.

Cullen hoped to all hells Stefan didn't try to make Lowen more than that.

Kyros, as one of Cullen's entourage, accompanied him to his rooms and assured him of their quality. "The Governor has seen to your station. You will have good light in the morning and quiet for the night."

His window did not overlook a guard station, then. In the morning he would discover if he had a view. For tonight there was yet a dinner to attend and conversation to endure. Cullen would rather be almost anywhere else. He was so far from the Rill that letters to Phalla were unlikely to reach her and get back to him with news outside of a week.

"Everyone's wondering why we're here." Kyros was fishing for that reason himself. Cullen had only told his staff he needed to go to Gignastha on the king's business.

"Rumors afoot, as always?"

Kyros opened the last of Cullen's wardrobe chests. Ever careful about such things, he hadn't allowed servants to handle the garments. "A few. Most of all about how the king wishes to install a Kheld as Bas here. Word gets out. He petitioned the Archhalia to revise the domain's charter."

No need to mention Stefan thought he would soon have the votes. Cullen was here to relieve tensions and ascertain what concessions would work best to ease the installation of a newly created noble at the head of Gignastha's government. While he was doing that, he might as well snug up trade agreements and lay groundwork for stronger commercial ties with Amallar.

"We're here to talk trade and fees." Cullen sorted through garments in the first chest before turning to the second. Soon he found the suit of clothes he was looking for. They needed a press. He held the items up for display and Kyros grinned.

"I will give these to the matron of chambers to get ready. There's a banquet tonight."

"A chance to meet the natives?"

"Gignasthans are good folk, sir. My father, you'll meet him tonight, is fond of saying a Gignasthan man would rather spend his days knee-deep in a stream catching fish." Kyros laughed. "And the women would rather marry men from Leseos."

"And who again did you say you are?"

"Erenor Tholeros, Archon of Averrn, and emissary of His Royal Majesty, Stefan Stauberg-Randolph, King of Essera."

Nammuor settled into the hard embrace of the Incandescent Throne and gazed down at the man who knelt on the carnelian floor. To every side of the Nuarch's Throne Hall, arches of flame soared overhead and lava flow glowed through the walls. Only an immortal Leur city could keep a volcano at bay.

So, Essera's fool of a king had finally wandered near. Nammuor found Stefan interesting only in that Essera continued to tolerate him. As for this emissary, this Erenor... he might have potential. Staubaun lineage, almost certainly pure. Gold-bright hair. Brown eyes clear with intelligence and good health. Straight of posture. Handsome. Such things mattered for purposes of flattery. Not to mention the man had proven bold enough—or ambitious enough— to test hostile waters.

"I am intrigued. Our nations have been at odds for decades."

Erenor did not disagree. "A stance of the previous king. Stefan wishes to improve relations between our empires."

"He seeks my help against Sordan, you mean." Nammuor saw

nothing to be gained by diplomatic posturing. "Or perhaps he wishes to ascertain the extent of my interest in the Sordaneon Hierarchate."

A film of perspiration glistened in tiny beads on Erenor's fair face. "He does seek cooperation as regards the Hierarchate. Know, though, that he acknowledges your interest, and has pronounced it legitimate."

How interesting. "That's more than Sordan has done for him."

"Sordan has very different views of things like legitimacy."

"The Hierarch and I are at war. Dorilian would call that legitimate."

Erenor nodded. "Then we share a common enemy. Sordan's commercial policies constitute a warfare that threatens Essera's well-being."

"All economies are at war."

A bold look. "Not yours and Essera's."

"Well, we don't have the Rill, do we? But, when it comes to Mormantalorus, neither does Dorilian—or your king." Nammuor found Esseran arguments facile.

"Your nephew is Dorilian's Heir. You wish to place the boy on that throne. Stefan has… ideas about how to make that happen. If we were allies, we could set up a joint regency."

Nammuor resisted a frown. This fool and his king actually thought Nammuor would be happy if *they* killed Dorilian—a misconception he could let stand while it advanced his ends, but one to watch carefully. "Your king would do best to leave Sordan to me. My investment surpasses yours. I have no interest in a joint regency. With anyone."

Erenor bowed his head. "Understood, Powerful One."

How accommodating might Essera's ruler be? This emissary appeared eager. A man who yearned to bring his monarch a success. What Nammuor craved, Essera might yet deliver. Stefan presented a host of opportunities. Nammuor had kept abreast of Marc Frederick's successor and noted a weakness: Stefan distrusted and feared the Highborn. He stood *against*—not with—the few remaining scions of the Wall. And here Nammuor sat, with his Diadem in need of two crystals of immortal blood.

"An alliance would not be… impossible."

It was too easy. The Esseran fool wore a smile when he lifted his head. "Trade? Cooperation? Together, we could rule the seas."

"Oh, I think we will."

"And we could help you in your war against Dorilian too."

How transparent. Trade, of course—so Stefan might sell this joining of interests to his people and convince them of his effectiveness as a monarch—when his real intent was to best a man he had never needed to fight. The Stauberg-Randolph threat had effectively crumbled.

It would be amusing to watch Stefan destroy what was left.

26

"I am making dummies of myself and embedding them in walls all over the King's House, where they won't cause much comment—at least for now."

Palimia watched Dorilian devour the last two honey-laced sweets, his decimation of which he had just explained. Even when not using Leur gifts, he consumed more food than the hungriest of regular humans. The spread she had prepared, enough for three men, was now bare.

"Will you be able to translocate soon?"

"Once I better grasp and command my own proportions. I am… much larger than a cylinder. I have also learned that structures are tricky."

She saw for herself how focused he was. Over the last few months, Dorilian had turned over more of his administrative responsibilities to retainers and cut back on hearings and audiences. Rumors spread that recent events had triggered in him the same paralyzing paranoia which had claimed his father. Only she and a trusted few knew that Dorilian Sordaneon spent his freed-up time memorizing antique math from archaic books or in training at the King's House, attempting to master gifts for which he had no teachers.

"You haven't killed yourself, or anyone else, yet. That's promising." Palimia laughed at his glare. "I'm teasing you. But everything I've ever heard about these powers of your kind tells me they are dangerous. I am glad you are taking time to learn about them first."

He exhaled audibly and sank back against the cushions lining the stone seat. The shaded terrace they occupied overlooked a stunning vista of lake and city. Insect sounds rose from the garden along with the click of shears being used to trim the jasmine arbor on the path below. "I cannot afford mistakes. We talked about that once, remember? My mistakes can kill me, and not me alone. My life is... connected to an Entity. That Entity is one that protects and nurtures a great many people. Entire nations, Sordan in particular. This Creation, even, in ways I have yet to fully ascertain. I have seen my enemy too clearly not to fear what lies ahead if I cannot fight it."

"You have often said you are buying time. For whom, I wonder."

"For myself, mostly. If I am to command any gifts at all, I need to grow stronger—and older." He shot her a grin. "I believe I may soon achieve an adult body. It has been a full year since I have grown more than a finger width, though according to Sebbord's books, final maturity might need more time. Tutto never tires of reminding me I am still an adolescent."

She laughed. "You certainly have an adolescent's energy."

"All the more reason to learn everything I can, while I can. I will need to teach Lev someday. Maybe sons or grandsons if I ever have them. I don't want to go down in history as the endpoint of Leur's grand experiment."

"I really cannot see you as the endpoint of anything."

His shake of the head offset a dismissive smile. He thought her placating. And yet how very far they had come. Even after three years as his mistress, she did not fully understand Dorilian, but she enjoyed his company and it pleased her that he sought hers. Though she had been his lover for longer than she had been Marc Frederick's, it never felt that way.

Palimia had at last fully renovated the Songbird Palace, which Marc Frederick had owned for decades but never lived in. His nearly forty-year kingship, marked as it had been by hostility with the Sordaneons, had seen the residence fall into disrepair. Old-fashioned and beautiful, it presided over the Upper City's grandest neighborhood, classic bones graced with hints of gentility. Songbird bore nothing of the stamp of Marc Frederick, so she imbued its rooms with the colors he had loved and filled private spaces with memorabilia gathered from every corner of the world. A portrait of the king on horseback, painted by a lesser prince of Lahgael. A clock Marc Frederick had gifted Eldonus and which she had purchased from her former husband's legal heir. With Emyli's discreet help, she had restored the gardens with plantings similar to those at Gustan and the villa in Dazunor-Rannuli, and took pleasure in the views they offered. Like this one, from the arched portico outside her private rooms. Ranks of fragrant lilies glowed like alabaster candles just beyond the balustrades, though the lake and the sky above it had turned silver-pale.

Her crowning achievement, however, was a collection of letters. She had kept those Marc Frederick had written to Eldonus and any written to herself. To this trove she had painstakingly added purchases made through brokers: letters to some of the Denizens of the Seven Houses, two to an Elector of Trongor, seven he had exchanged with a Cibulitan scholar, one with a Mormantaloran noble and sometime emissary, and one from the man through whom Marc Frederick had purchased properties in Hestya.

… do not purchase many properties at once, or in any other way drive up prices. We have no wish to draw either attention or speculation to our activity.

Dorilian had found that last interesting. She shared all her findings with him.

"I knew it. We were doing the same thing, my friends and I. When all was done, he owned too many properties not to have guessed what we were up to. The Rill rained gold on every holding, including his." No bitterness lurked in Dorilian's assessment, no remnant of former enmity. Marc Frederick had mended that breach so well only Stefan remained an open wound.

"He liked having his own money."

"Which is why his heirs now have so much."

She supposed they did, if what she controlled was any indication. Palimia surveyed the beautiful grounds and smiled to think of what Marc Frederick might think of her hard work. Gardens, even more than nations or people, rewarded the effort put into them. She turned to Dorilian, who had just eaten the last candied plum.

"I want to show you something." She walked to the serpentine balustrade of polished marble and stopped to point to a near corner of the garden below. A column of sticks and twine stood at the center of a circle of soil ringed by a paved area. "It is not much to look at just yet, but I planted an oak."

He would know she had done more than that. "An oak? Let me guess."

She laughed. "You would be right. Come this way." A stair of weathered stone framed by cypresses led to the open garden she had painstakingly planned to look natural. Sordan gardens, such as those of the Serat or elsewhere in the Upper City, tended to be formal and symmetric, and generally built around fountains. After crossing a grassy yard, they arrived at the oak. When he knelt to get a better look at the sapling, she did the same.

"Two years ago, I procured an acorn from a special oak that grows at Gustan."

"His mother's Oak." Dorilian reached past the twine of the tiny tree's cage to touch a green, lobed leaf.

"You know about that?"

"He told me, part of his effort to introduce me to Khelds and their culture. Which is how I know Kheld women plant oaks from the trees of their *mothers*—not their lovers."

A gentle remonstrance. "It's a remembrance. I think he meant the tree in Gustan for his daughter."

Dorilian's expression changed. Like all the surviving Stauberg-Randolphs, Emyli remained a sore point. Palimia stood and moved her hands to brush debris off her skirt, then staggered. Pain shattered her back and ribs, causing her to cry out as she fell. Dorilian caught her and clasped her body, hard arms and protection and pain. She wanted to draw another breath, but the agony was too blinding.

She tried to move her legs but could not feel them. Shouts broke out on every side. Palimia tightened her arms around the man holding her.

He had been watching Palimia, as ever appreciating her grace and wistfulness about her former lover. Nearly as soon as she toppled into his grasp, Dorilian noted the blade in her back. Curved. Deadly. He dragged Palimia's unresisting shape with him behind the tree and its flimsy protection just as a second blade sliced through the space where his head and shoulders had been. "Legon!" he shouted.

"Thrice Royal! Stay down!" Four Eagle Guards who had discreetly secured the terrace surrounded Dorilian now, their bodies forming a wall of armor and bone. Any new attack would strike them first. Legon was not with them. Shouts broke from another part of the garden. One of the guards looked around before he issued a command. "This way. Come with us."

"Her too." Palimia's shuddering body filled Dorilian's arms, her face and ragged breath pressed to his chest.

"Thrice Royal, your safety—"

"Her. Too."

Two of the men gathered Palimia between them and, flanked and propelled by the first man and a burly guard easily as big as two men himself, Dorilian hurried across the open area and up the stair into the palace. Once within, more guards secured the location. The men carrying Palimia laid her gently on a carpet patterned with lilies, face down. The blade protruded from her back, a sickening, bloody statement.

A guard reached for the thing. "Perhaps we should—"

"No." Dorilian stopped him. "Leave it. Fetch a surgeon." He got down onto the floor to do what he could, though his mind reeled. Attacked in a garden, a situation secured by her guards and his. But who had been the target? Surely not her. Palimia had never offended a soul to his knowledge, except…

Now was not the time for leaping to conclusions. She—everyone, this entire household—needed calm, not panic. He must control the situation, provide the environment needed to sort out what had happened. Action, he reminded himself, not reaction. Calculation, not guesswork.

"We're safe," he assured her. Palimia's hand clutched for his and he gave it. He heard his guards exchange information. The attacker had been caught. Legon had witnessed the attack and gone after the source. All Legon's years of deep training had provided the means. A split-second to make a decision, and he had made the right one.

Dorilian wanted whoever had done this.

Blood coated his hands, warm and thick with life. Palimia's breathing was getting slower, less ragged, her mind less frantic. He gazed down into her eyes. The trust he saw there broke his heart. He had not warned her strongly enough that to be with him could be dangerous. "I am sorry," he whispered. "Because of me you came to harm."

Her lips formed the word "No." Gods, the woman still found ways to amaze him.

Activity across the room alerted him to the arrival of several more Eagle Guards and Legon. A man struggled in their custody, half dragged and carried into the room. Two other men dressed like the first in plain garments of the type worn by workers, filed in and looked nervous. They would wait until Dorilian had time to deal with them.

Legon walked over. Leaves and twigs clung to his boots and light armor. He waited a moment before he spoke. "How fares the Lady?"

"Strong." Dorilian continued to hold Palimia's hand in his.

"I've… felt better." She answered for herself, even offering Legon a weak smile. "Do you know… who?"

Legon's dark gaze sought Dorilian's, who nodded. Legon's mouth set in a firm line. "We have the man. Not sure who he is. He's not talking yet."

Yet. Rage stacked within Dorilian like a storm building. Forced calm was merely a stopper. It no longer mattered who had been the target, all that mattered was the attack. A new stir at the door announced another arrival. The surgeon. Dorilian recognized her as Thuraya Lares, his household physician.

"Thrice Royal, I was sent by Raxa. Prince Levyathan told her—" Thuraya's eyes widened at seeing blood on his hands and clothing.

He rose to his feet. "I'm not hurt. Lady Mia is. Tend to her."

Brusquely, he gestured to Legon for the guards to usher the prisoners into the next room. A bedchamber, smaller and more private. Less light. Good. Someone, another of the Eagle Guard, shut the door behind them.

Legon separated out the man wearing bonds and being held by the guards. "Time for you to answer some questions."

Dorilian indicated the other two detainees. "These men?"

Both had already dropped to press their faces to the floor. The older of the two spoke. "Elno and me saw him do it, Thrice Royal. That's all. Looked like a set of hedge trimmers, but then we saw him take 'em apart and he threw 'em."

"Take them to another room and hold them. Talk to them again, and again, until you are satisfied there is nothing more to their story."

Legon nodded and gestured to two of his men to follow that order. If there was more to this plot, they would soon learn it. Dorilian turned his full attention to the remaining prisoner.

The man was short and stocky. Narrow nostrils flared beneath flat hazel eyes half-hidden by rough-cut dark hair. Resistance marked his defiant mouth and clenched jaw. By far more interesting were his arms and hands, which were unusually muscular, with callouses prominent on the right hand. Dorilian knew the reason as soon as Legon handed over a blade akin to the one he had seen buried in Palimia's back. Without a doubt it was the one that had narrowly missed Dorilian's head. He took the object in hand. A blade, but neither a sword nor a dagger. Lightweight, curved, short and polished smooth with purposeful balance and wickedly sharp curved edges.

"Nasty things, *skifrs*." He shared a frown with Legon. They had both seen weapons like this before.

The man tilted his chin. "It was supposed to be you, not the woman. She chose the wrong time to stand up."

Pure chance, then, Dorilian recognized. Palimia's back had saved his neck. The explanation did not improve his temper. *Skifrs* were Kheld weapons and the attacker's characteristics, even without scrutiny, made him likely a Kheld half-breed. Only one other question remained.

He handed the weapon back to Legon. "Keep this, and the other too."

"Yes, Thrice Royal."

The prisoner's knees visibly shook, but he did not look away. His emotions were rank, palpable. Fear, yes—but nothing of concealment. Dorilian paused before relieving the man of more waiting. "Stefan sent you."

A short bark of a laugh. "He wanted you to know. He said you'd live long enough after, even if it took off your head. That your fucking grandfather lived long enough…"

Screw Stefan! "Silence him!" Stefan had been there at Merath. Had heard somehow. *Damn him!*

Dorilian turned away from the would-be killer. Legon had but one question. "Orders?"

"Throw this creature in the Citadel. Give the Halia permission to be creative."

With a crisp nod, Legon ordered his men and they left. In their wake, silence filled the room. Now that he was alone, Dorilian relaxed until his senses resumed their proper realms. The bedchamber teased his nose with notes of Palimia's perfume and flowering branches in a nearby vase. She had used light colors for the walls and also the fabrics. A brief flick of his tongue across his lips shocked him with a trace of salt. Tears? Or blood? Neither would be his.

The physician, Thuraya, waited in the other room. Palimia lay on a stretcher, which two sturdy men were in the process of lifting. One of the guards held the blood-stained *skifr.* "Give that to your commander." Dorilian went to Palimia's side. Quiet, eyes closed, but breathing. Her hand when he took it in his was relaxed but warm. She did not stir when he brushed strands of sun-bright hair from her cheek. He turned to Thuraya. "Tell me."

Thuraya dismissed a servant holding a bowl of red-stained water and finished drying her hands with a square of cloth. "I gave the Lady a potion to kill pain. I will accompany her litter to the Physician's College. Perhaps they can help her. The wound is serious and deep, but she will have a chance to survive it if no infection sets in. I am more concerned"—Thuraya's face tightened at having to give ill news—"the weapon cut into her spine. She cannot move her legs and I was unable to arouse any sensation. I am hoping, but…"

"Not much hope." Any relief he had felt plummeted.

"It is too soon to know. What a terrible thing. The attacker was Kheld, I hear?"

"Yes."

"What violent, horrible people."

"I plan to deal with them."

"I wish I could offer more, Thrice Royal. Lady Palimia is healthy, but she does not heal like..." The physician's voice softened.

Like he would. Like Levyathan or others of their kind. Palimia was common flesh. A sweet, generous woman as ordinary and wonderful as all the other common flesh people who willingly placed themselves between him and his enemies. His mother. Noemi.

Marc Frederick.

This time, however, the damned fool who had destroyed Palimia was within Dorilian's power to punish.

"We had higher hopes for you. We should have listened when Dorilian Sordaneon called you an idiot and a bungler."

Stefan glared at Chyralane's words. She and the gathered members of his advisory council had descended on him like rabid weasels. Quirin from the Brotherhood of Epoptes wore a dark, forbidding frown. Ionais of Merrydn shot Stefan a stormy stare and Estevan of Gweroyen simply looked sick. Goff, on the other hand, was tense with worry, not only about the failed assassination but because, with Cullen gone to Gignastha and Lowen stranded at Permephedon, Goff was the only other Kheld in the room. Sinon Kouranos sat with chin on hand, clearly unhappy. Like most of the others, Essera's Archhalial ambassador had just arrived from Permephedon, where word of the attempted assassination had led to an uproar that had resulted in delegates walking out of the Chamber. Some had called for swords. Most considered it fortunate the delegates from Sordan and its domains had followed Tiflan of Teremar to the Rill node and departed from Essera altogether.

Lack of violence hadn't gotten Stefan off the hook, though.

"He's not dead. He's not even hurt." His reminder earned only looks of incredulity.

"No, though you may have succeeded in killing the woman," said Ionais. The news brought by Rill had come from multiple sources and were conflicted on that point.

Stefan took what comfort he could in noting no one cheered that

Dorilian lived. The Hierarch was a thorn in everyone's ass. At least Chyralane had ceased glaring—probably because she had turned to Quirin. "Can that Sordaneon do anything, take *any* action, that might alter the Rill?"

"None." The Psilant sounded confident. "The Entity is unperturbed. Dorilian is forbidden from entering sanctums. He has no access to Rill operations."

"But he *can* use it?"

"To travel and communicate within restrictions. To conduct commerce. To move his military within and administer his domains, according to Covenant."

"Watch him. Closely." Chyralane clicked the jeweled nails of her aged fingertips on the deep midnight stone of the table. "We do not yet know how this event might move him."

"If it makes any of you happier," Stefan said, "he will probably try to kill *me*. He's fond of murder, you know. Or have you forgotten how central he's been to the murders of my family? My grandfather. My *uncle*." At the last, Stefan cast a look at Ionais and was satisfied to see her blanch. "All Dorilian has to do is get rid of me and then who's going to stop him from seating himself on Essera's throne? Is that what you want?"

"No!" snapped Ionais. "We want *you* to stop trying to kill *him*."

"The Sordaneon bloodline is precarious, even more so than the Malyrdeons." Quirin leaned forward in his seat and cast his gaze around the room. "Do we really want to risk finding out if our own myths are true? What would it mean to us if we lose the Rill? This Triempery would not survive."

Maybe not, but Stefan was pretty sure Essera would. His kingdom had more people and better land. It was also more insulated from attack. Sordan, on the other hand, was ringed by covetous rivals poised to strip it of domains.

"Then tell him to step back." Stefan rose. He had Dorilian where he wanted him: reminded of his mortality and knocked off his game. He saw no advantage in sitting on his ass while his advisors twisted their hands like old women. "You still talk to him, don't you? Some of you must. Well, I don't. So you can tell Dorilian to stop being an ass using your way, or I will tell him using mine: if he doesn't stop pushing me, if he doesn't cut off sending weapons to Neuberland to be used against settlements I've chartered, if he doesn't stop raising grain prices or strangling shipping routes just to deplete my treasury, I'll come after him again."

Sinon lifted his head and placed both hands on the table,

indicating he wished to claim the speaker's spot. "If what these communications said is true and you sent that assassin, you have broken our law. You do realize that?"

"I never said I sent the assassin."

"Sordan will prove it before long." Ionais looked almost gleeful. "I assure you, they're torturing the man already."

Chyralane held out her hands in an eloquent shrug. "So yet another Kheld attempts to slay a member of that family. Any of that degenerate breed could have conceived it, and that will be your story."

Stefan caught Goff's look of censure. Though Goff had known of Stefan's plan, and had helped in finding the man to do it, he had been nervous about this very outcome. Having Khelds blamed for yet another attack on the Highborn was risky. But only while people still gave a damn about holy blood.

Chyralane, however, was far from done. "Your lack of outrage betrays you. Heed my words: your attack on the Sordaneon is not benign. Through him you have attacked the Rill and all of us. You threaten the foundations of your own rule. Of our power. Of our way of life!"

Estevan of Gweroyen moved to speak. "That the attack failed may prove a mercy. While Dorilian is aware of the offense, the Rill most likely is not."

Nods all around the table. Stefan didn't bother to count them.

"True," said Quirin. "We are still, at this point, dealing with a man."

It was a relief to see the council adopt a position that diminished his action. Stefan smiled. Dorilian might be Highborn, but he wasn't a god. It was time people realized that.

Sinon did not wait to be recognized before speaking again. "Open a communication with Sordan. Find a way to throw calm on this. We cannot afford more strife."

Stefan tightened his jaw until his teeth ached. "Screw Dorilian. He says I'm dead to him. Well, he is just as dead to me. I am not going to do a damn thing. He will have to come to me first."

Which Dorilian never would. The bastard preferred to play games. Well, Stefan could play games too. To protect his kingdom and his family, he would get down in the dirt with this living god and prove to the world what they both were.

27

"Pain. Too much pain." Levyathan's small body curled into shadow where the square column at his back met a wall. The colonnade faced the Well of Birds and its mossy, starlight-kissed paving. "Her pain. Yours. The world screams."

Seated on the paving, cool stone at his back and arms on his knees, Dorilian felt made of stone as well. "Pain will pass. It always does."

"Yours does not."

Dorilian closed his eyes and swallowed hard. Damn the boy. Levyathan felt all of it. His torment. His memories. The agony he had tried to bury along with his dead, awakened now, of Sebbord's slaughter and Marc Frederick's tragic end and Stefan's betrayal, all rolled into this rage against Essera and its king.

"I will handle it. I can close my mind to yours."

"No. Never that."

He would do it anyway. Levyathan's distress just added to Dorilian's anguish. Fahme's was easily shunted aside. Legon and Tutto provided better buttresses. And Tiflan was back in the city after what Dorilian could only assume had been a disastrous Archhalia.

Levyathan's tears glistened in bright trails. "Alone, then. Your pain cuts. Your anger is too thick, I cannot breathe."

Dorilian tried to recall himself at Lev's age. Few memories came to mind. The remembrances that flooded his brain were those of an older child, razor-edged images of his mother on her deathbed, blood and fear and pain mingled with Levyathan's tortured, original birth. It was cruel to inflict himself upon anyone right now.

"All right. Alone. You will visit Mia alone, with neither me nor Fahme in the room."

Levyathan lifted his head to give a weak smile. His features looked disturbingly adult for a four-year-old. "For her."

"She needs to know how much we care about her."

"Mia is family."

Yes. That was it, of course. The essential matter at the core of all this pain and Dorilian's anger. "Family. She has no one else. Her mother is in Ilmar, so Mia will live with us now, here in the Serat. We will help her."

Help her. Avenge her. Sink steel into Stefan's heart. Light pressure on Dorilian's arm prompted him to look down at his brother's small hand.

"Dor, no more. Too much anger."

Dorilian winced. Not so many years ago, Levyathan had warned how a darkness inside Dorilian would kill something bright. But he felt no brightness at all, not now. "Remember what I said about pain? Anger is the same."

"Anger destroys. Burns reason."

Or enhanced it. Dorilian's reasons for sending hurt Stefan's way burned white-hot. Even though reborn and holding memories of his original fourteen years, Levyathan was not even close to understanding the scope of the threats against them. This dangerous turn could not go unanswered.

Levyathan breathed in gasps. "The pain needs to stop."

I cannot stop it, Dorilian wanted to tell him. *I have put things in motion.* But Levyathan had been and still was a child—while Dorilian was not. It fell on him to be both parent and brother and tell a different kind of truth. "My anger will stop. Someday. I promise."

"When?"

When else? "When I no longer need it."

He walked the boy back to his bedchamber and saw him put to bed, then retreated. Levyathan would not sleep while Dorilian was near and in this mood. No one within the Serat would. Dorilian needed to be elsewhere. Propelled by ghosts, he summoned Legon and left in secret for the King's House. Anger might be destructive, but it was vastly useful. Dorilian had learned his emotions were generative; he could cast enormous power through the Coronal when angry. Doing so was perilous, to be sure—his body was a fragile conduit for gifts best suited to immortals—but tonight he did not care.

Tonight, he wanted to destroy something.

"Changes? People don't like changes. Change is incompatible with happiness." Alban, Lord Eskeros, poured a stream of ruby-bright liquid from a flagon into Cullen's glass. "Here, taste of this wine. It's from my own vineyard. I have an estate in the foothills near here. A treasured little pocket climate exposed to southern sun and protected from harsh winds. It produces just enough grapes to make all my friends happy."

"You should send some to the king." Eskeros's wine was very good, complex and sweet. There would be a market for it. Cullen had encountered a number of such products over the last few days.

Silver-haired Eskeros set down the flagon with slow precision. "Oh, the king does not much like wine, I've heard."

"True, from what I have seen he favors ale," Verteus Cordegos agreed, having spent a year at Stefan's court before being appointed governor. "Quite to my amazement, I have developed a taste for the brew myself."

"And so he has." Arton, third and landless—but very well educated—son of the Archon of Eddethel, was Cullen's right hand. He had traveled with Kyros from Dazunor-Rannuli. "Verteus orders barrels of the stuff brought in from Leseos, where quite a number of Khelds have established breweries."

Cullen regarded Verteus with interest. "Perhaps we should encourage such enterprise here in Gignastha."

The table fell silent. Men exchanged glances with their female companions and each other. Arton's interest turned to the buttons on his sleeve.

"You might have noticed we have few Khelds in Gignastha." Verteus admonished Cullen from beneath a furrowed brow. "I think you understand why."

"A bit of murder called the Bloodletting." A local lord whose name Cullen had yet to learn provided that reason in case it was needed.

Cullen respected the chill that settled over the room. He had known he would run into this. "That was fourteen years ago."

"A hundred generations will not erase holy blood, neither from Kheld hands nor from this land." The man who spoke those words fell silent as his companion placed her beringed hand on his arm.

At Cullen's side, Eskeros muttered something undoubtably meant to be useful. "Land where Highborn blood is spilled is Highborn land thereafter."

The angry local lord continued. "Your king—"

"*Our king*, Periskes. Our king." Verteus signaled his head servant for the meal to be brought in. "I think Stefan's predecessor, Marc Frederick, settled that matter here and in Leseos once and for all."

"A forceful man." Alkron Eulodes, Enlad of Rhiarren, was Kyros's father and one of the region's most prominent lords. The family's lands nestled profitably between Gignastha and Leseos. "Marc Frederick settled that we should be administered by crown appointment, rather than a hereditary prince."

An utterly sensible resolution, given that Gignastha's hereditary princes had been a side branch of the Sordaneons and the murders had left no other heirs. By designating the domain as a crown protectorate, the king had sidestepped a morass of insults to inheritance rights and Triemperal laws. Cullen knew himself inadequate to the task of putting those insults to rest.

"Stefan merely seeks to strengthen ties between this domain and the rest of the kingdom. Stronger ties would increase this domain's prosperity along with giving Gignastha an independent voice in the Archhalia. He is also pressing for treaties with the Lords of Annech and Gobba that would raise them formally to Enlad status."

"Enlads, yes. But Gignastha was founded as a *royal* domain, a princely domain, and deserves to be counted as one still," Verteus pointed out. A youth in the governor's livery placed a platter before him.

"And we deserve to be governed by a bloodline fit to rule a royal seat." Periskes, the angry local lord, again.

As he acknowledged the meal being put before him, Cullen resolved to listen more and talk less. He could present his points another time, with each of these people in person.

"Yes, Periskes, true." Eskeros adjusted his fur-trimmed sleeves before addressing his plate. He picked up gleaming utensils. "To that end, our king might best choose his own brother. That is, if he has not forgotten where he put him."

Periskes smirked and cut into his meat. Cullen watched the slab of ruby-red flesh part to spill pink juices onto the plate. He had not heard Hans's name mentioned, save by Stefan, in years.

"He knows where Handurin is." It was the best Cullen could offer, even if not strictly true.

"Questionable legitimacy, though." This time it was a venerable older woman who offered her opinion with faintly curled upper lip. "We all know what happened *there*."

It was all Cullen could do to bite his tongue. Allegations that

Emyli had given birth to a child sired by Ral of Leseos, rather than her husband Erwan Cedrecson, had run rampant ever since Hans had been born—a blue-eyed, blond-haired child who looked to be as much Staubaun as Kheld. The rumor ran hottest here in Gignastha. It was here that Emyli had led a failed attempt to change the region's balance of power, and here that she had been captured by Ral and held captive for several weeks in this very palace. Cullen had been thirteen years old when it all happened. He and Stefan, had been safely at school in Permephedon without a care in the world. They had barely known Gignastha existed.

Now here Cullen was, seated in the midst of Staubauns sniggering about a woman's misfortune and thinking their domain deserved better than a Kheldman to rule them. In that moment, the full force of Stefan's miscalculation came home to roost. This palace. This room, these floors and walls... the bed Cullen slept in each night. Gignastha had been a Highborn domain. The Watergilt Palace had been built by and housed generations of Sordaneon princes. It was no different than the Rillhome in Dazunor-Rannuli where Cullen conducted his work. Or Heddros, for possession of which he was so roundly resented.

A stolen domain, tainted by murder. In this land, no Kheld would ever be clean of that deed.

As he stabbed at whatever hunk of game lay on his plate, Cullen conceded that fourteen years had changed nothing in Gignastha. Or anywhere. New grievances simply piled on top of old. The further the Highborn retreated, the more affliction they left behind.

Why in the world had Stefan sent him to this wretched place?

The next morning, Cullen joined Arton for a stroll along a path that overlooked the city. The Watergilt Palace possessed over fifteen hundred years of architectural marvels and splendid water features, including waterfalls and deep, wondrous wells. As with other Sordaneon palaces, this one had beautiful, illuminating views. Cullen paused with Arton on an overlook high above sudden, thundering falls and gazed upon the lifted and broken remnants of an island just offshore, white-crowned by ruins and ringed by ghostly reflections. Sar Pryannis spread around the broken island with a soft sheen like that of a silk gown.

"The Rill." Cullen had seen Rill ruins before, most spectacularly at Simelon, though none quite so broken as this. "Even here."

"I suppose there was hope in the beginning that one of the Sordaneons could fix it."

"I don't think anyone could raise the Rill from as little as that."

"Maybe not." Arton braced his elegant boot on the low wall of their lookout. A stiff morning breeze ruffled his tousled blond hair. "But the second Deben did build this palace here, as well as the Aqueduct." He turned and pointed past Cullen's shoulder toward the palace's breathtaking spiral turrets and a line of red, dawn-brushed arches challenging a gray sky.

From this vantage Cullen could detect the places where the Vermillion Aqueduct had been broken. The repaired channel and portions of two arches did not quite match the original structure. Not as smooth, its surface texture was devoid of a translucence that allowed inner color to show through the original structure. Color like blood. But no one had ever said the aqueduct was a living thing. Not like the Rill.

"Do you think—"

Loud gongs of alarm sounded from different parts of the Watergilt Palace. The clamor soon multiplied a hundredfold. Arton sprang to his feet and stared up at the towers from which the alarm sounded.

"We are under *attack*? Leur's blood!"

"Attack? Is that what those mean?" Cullen joined Arton in racing toward the main keep, leaving their open location for the deep safety of stone. "Who? Why?"

"If I knew, I would tell you. This way!"

One of the Governor's staff saw them and waved them over. "Go to your rooms. You will be safe there."

Cullen followed that advice. As soon as he entered the room, Ranwulf leaped from where he'd been sitting on his bed along the inside wall. White-faced, the young man clutched a naked short sword in his hand. Cullen quickly located his weapon hung from a hook beside the bed. Whatever the fuck was happening, he preferred to face it while armed. He had just secured the belt around his waist when the door banged open.

Four soldiers rushed in with blades bared. Green and gold tabards blazoned with sword ensigns announced them as members of the Governor's Guards. Two men grabbed Cullen by the forearms before he could draw his weapon. Ranwulf, his sword already in hand, charged the men. One man bellowed as Ranwulf's blade bounded off his left pauldron. The remaining man bowled Ranwulf to the floor, and the first soldier took advantage of it to strike directly at the Kheld youth's bared head. The blade bit deep with a sickening thunk.

"No!" Cullen's scream was futile. Ranwulf ceased thrashing almost instantly, his skull laid open. At the sword's violent removal, gore spilled onto the elegant carpet.

"Fucking Kheld." The bastard who had slain Ranwulf kicked his body for good measure.

The men holding Cullen wrenched his right arm behind his back and twisted until blinding pain brought on a cry for mercy. The third soldier removed Cullen's sword and belt. "Don't be stupid like your friend. Don't give us reason to kill you too."

The klaxons had ceased. Shouts sounded from other floors, other spaces. While the soldiers hurried him along corridors and down flights of stairs, past confusion and soldiers, Cullen sought to make sense of it. What had happened? The Governor's Guard was treating him like an enemy. His captors dragged him around a corner, then into a room, where they immediately threw his face against a wall and pulled both arms behind his back to be clapped in metal cuffs. Only then did they release him. Through a curtain of pain and confusion, he heard men speak in low asides. Sharp orders to be silent reduced those voices to whispers and urgent hisses of warning. It took a few minutes to grasp he would be permitted to move. By the time he turned around, Cullen saw just how much his situation had changed.

He shared the room with a dozen or more other men who appeared to be captive just as he was. Cullen recognized some of them. Elderly Eskeros, his neighbor from dinner the night before, looked uncomfortable, huddled on the floor beside someone Cullen did not know. A handful of men wearing the Governor's colors stood guard. One jerked his head in Cullen's direction.

"Fuck it. Look what they brought us. A damn murdering Kheld."

"Keep him apart. He's the King's Man."

That again? The only person Cullen wanted to murder right now *was* the king, for sending him into this. *But he wouldn't have done it. Not to this place. Not if Stefan had known Gignastha was about to revolt.* Cullen rocked back against the stone wall and tried to think. The room had been emptied of all furnishings and had nothing to distinguish it; even the windows were high and bare, mere sources of light. The people around him appeared to know more than he did. They murmured to each other, and several cast unhappy looks in his direction. Though both Arton and Kyros were also in the room, they were too far away to contact. Cullen caught the gaze of the man nearest him.

"What's happened?"

The man studied him for a few seconds, undecided, then provided an answer. "We have been taken over. Sordan. The Governor surrendered the city, including the Watergilt Palace, this morning."

The door swung open. Two men entered the room. One was a high-ranking officer, to judge by the silver insignia on his emerald-green clothing and polished armor emblazoned with Sordan's heraldic eagle; the other man carried a portable desk which he set up at the door and from which he immediately took out paper and a writing implement. Cullen got to his feet along with the other men when their guards began bringing them forward, one by one, starting with silver-haired Lord Eskeros. One by one each of the detained men was asked his name, followed by a few other questions heard only as low murmurs. When done, each man was hustled out of the room. When a guard indicated it was his turn, Cullen walked forward.

"Name?"

"Cullen Thegn Brodheson."

The man doing the writing tilted his face, asking either for how to spell the name or for the rest of it. Staubauns invariably included their titles. Cullen noticed how the officer's gaze, already hard, sharpened.

"Kheld, then." The man wrote something on his paper. From behind came Arton's voice.

"He's the King's Man, Cullen Brodheson, Archon of Heddros, cousin to the king and Minister of Trade."

Cullen hung his head. Arton was pouring honey on the biscuit. But why? Trying to save Cullen's life—or end it?

He met the scribe's glance and nodded. "I am."

"Speaks Stauba." Another note on the page.

"If I may ask—"

A jab of the pen toward the other man. "Direct any questions to him. Bersyas Garheleon, Commander of Sordan's First Viper. He is in charge of everything now."

Hard-eyed and strong-jawed, with skin browned and toughened by the sun, Bersyas wore the golden good looks of Staubaun birth as proudly as he wore his rank. Cullen lifted his chin, not from belligerence, but because it was necessary to do so in order to meet the taller man's eyes.

"Why break the peace? Marc Frederick's peace. We never invaded your land."

The scribe's eyebrows arched higher and he, too, gazed at the Sordani commander.

Bersyas's mouth tightened. "Oh, but you did. When your king sent an assassin to kill our Hierarch."

Cullen's heart felt like ice, filled with cold blood. Every breath hurt. Was Dorilian dead? Murdered? What the hells had Stefan done?

Stefan wrapped his night robe tighter to his body and sank into a chair. His valet had awakened him with claim of a visitor insisting on seeing him about some urgent matter. Now he faced Sinon Kouranos across a blue pattern of celestial spheres on the floor of the King's Study.

"Sordan did *what*?"

"Invaded Gignastha. Seized the city and control over much of Lower Neuberland, everything between Sar Pryannis and Randpory Crossing. This happened more than a day ago. Because the city lacks a functioning array, it took that long for news to reach Leseos."

"My garrisons?"

"Captured or slain. Both Horcrod and Gignastha."

"How far have they penetrated?" Gignastha's border abutted Kheld settlements in Neuberland.

Sinon spread his hands. "Uncertain. Intelligence from the region is scant. Do you want me to travel to Sordan? I believe I could learn more. Perhaps negotiate—"

"No!" Negotiation would just show weakness. What Stefan needed to do was strike back. Get rid of this smooth-tongued diplomat and summon his generals.

"This move is almost certainly in response to the attack on the Hierarch."

"I fucking know that!" Would the man just stop talking? Stefan needed to think.

A quiet knock on the door preceded the valet's announcement of another visitor. "The Archon of Kelmene, sire."

Goff. Good. He preferred to talk with someone who knew his mind. He signaled to allow his First Minister to enter, then turned to Sinon.

"Leave me. But stay near. I—I might need you for something." He watched Sinon depart and noted the subtle bow which the man acknowledged Goff. At least that much of Stefan's reordering of the kingdom was working. With a start he realized the full extent of this catastrophe.

Cullen. Cullen was in Gignastha. What the hells would happen to him, might have happened already, now that Sordan had invaded?

"Trouble?"

"Sordan captured Gignastha."

"Mother's Tits!"

"We don't know everything yet. We don't know how, but—Madrock's Hells! I sent Cullen to Gignastha ahead of the Archhalia vote. He's fucking *there*. I got his letter this afternoon, he said things were 'difficult' but he hadn't given up trying. Hells, Goff—I need to find out if he's all right."

Goff tugged at his beard. "If any of us can handle being in Sordan's clutches, it's him. Good head, speaks Stauba, and he isn't alone, is he? Got Ranwulf, for one thing, and that son of the Archon of Eddethel with him. And that other fellow on his staff, he's son of a Gignasthan lord. They ought to help matters."

Except Dorilian was being wrathful. Except Sordan's soldiers were probably looking for Khelds to kill on account of a Kheld attempting to kill their Hierarch. Word had reached Essera just the day before about the brutality with which Sordan's Halia had executed the assassin. The man had been impaled alive in front of cheering thousands, his genitals sliced off, then eviscerated expertly so his entrails could be unspooled and burned while he still lived. Finally, the corpse had been fed to dogs, leaving nothing to recover or bury. Except shit. The Sordaneons reduced their enemies to what they considered their worth.

"Cullen may be dead already." Stefan lurched to his feet and paced across the blue floor to the elegant hearth, cold and swept clean. "Maybe I should hope for that."

"If they know who he is—"

"Do you think they'll care? That they care who any Kheld is? And if Dorilian finds he has Cullen, he'll torment him just to hurt me. He'll kill him for sure."

Goff stared in disbelief. "So you won't ask about him? Try to redeem him?"

"I am not going to tip off Dorilian that Cullen is in reach. Maybe Cullen can lie low. Maybe he can get away, make his way to one of our settlements in Neuberland." Except those might also be under attack. "I'm going to have to tell Nilla, as well as Asphalladra. Tell them and warn them to keep their mouths shut. Hells, the woman's in labor as we speak."

Goff shook his head. "What can that do but upset them? Fact is, we need news. The kind we can't get unless we have someone on the other side—or at least talking to them."

"Sinon offered, but I don't trust him, not all the way. He's from Sordan himself."

"Might be an advantage in this situation."

"Maybe."

Goff understood Stefan's concern. They'd talked about it often enough. "Well, you're not sending me!" he warned.

"I'm not sending anybody except a fucking army. Why did I have no intelligence of this? I have administrators in Gignastha. A governor. A garrison of soldiers. I have spies! What use are spies if they never spy anything useful?" Another thought pierced the tight clench of Stefan's gut: the Seven Houses and the Epoptes had better spies than he did. Had they gotten wind of this and not warned him?

The more he chewed on that, the worse it tasted.

Sordan's invasion had not happened out of thin air. It would have taken too long to send an army across the Telarkan Mountains in winter, while snow closed the passes.

Dorilian had to have used the Rill to move that many soldiers into Randpory.

28

At one end of the long gallery, Legon and Tutto stood with arms folded, tense and unhappy. Dorilian noted that only Tiflan, who looked very small at the other end, appeared at ease. "This will work," Dorilian said. That he wore the Sordan Coronal lent his words the weighty emphasis of a proclamation.

"If you don't end up inside a wall."

Legon was being pessimistic. None of the dummies Dorilian had used on his last two tries had ended up in a wall. He wasn't going to abandon these lessons just because he was again without teachers. Rheger had appeared at the King's House the day he had learned of the assassination attempt and stayed only long enough to see for himself that Dorilian was alive—and then warned him not to make contact again.

"Stefan has shown what he is willing to do. He is poisoned against all our kind."

So Rheger protected himself, and his kin, at Dorilian's cost. Fair enough. Dorilian would finish training himself. The long gallery of the nigh-abandoned King's House provided a perfect testing ground for translocation in sight. Dummy, after dummy, after dummy…

To translocate himself, however, required a critical shift in focus. He was not transferring an inanimate or secondary object, but a living, breathing primary one. *Myself. This vessel for Leur, this unique pattern.* At all times, he must keep his body intact. Inviolate. The rest was just… mechanics. Generate a fold of the Creation's seamless fabric. Keep things in the same moment, both origin and destination.

His destination was the opposite end of the gallery. In front of Tiflan, not behind him, not to either side, neither above nor below. Dorilian also must avoid the massive container against the far wall near the railing, holding plants long dead from neglect.

The Sordan Coronal—Derlon's Crown—amplified Dorilian's perceptions a thousandfold as he focused through it. Color striated into prisms. Dimensions assumed useful and avoidable shapes. He stood ... *here*. He reached for... *there*. Made tactile those coordinates and mentally took hold of them, calculated... then pulled together what was in-between until the spaces aligned. *Go*.

Go was different from send, more *step* than *toss*. A single step. He did not, ever, inhabit two spaces at the same time, but moved instantaneously from one into the other.

The world turned inside out, sideways then back again. Tutto was gone. So was the rotunda. Tiflan appeared at his side, beaming. Dorilian's breathing and heartbeat were still with him but amplified, too loud, too *here*; some sense beneath his skin rebelled at suddenly vacating one layer of air and being pushed into another. He gasped at that air as, without warning, bile rose violently in his stomach. Whoops sounded from behind him. Dorilian looked over his shoulder to see Legon running, and Tutto trotting, toward them.

"Well done!" Tiflan stepped forward and clapped Dorilian's shoulder hard enough to almost send him staggering. It also exacerbated the sudden, splitting headache that accompanied his nausea. He removed the Coronal and found that helped. Not soon enough.

Damn. His stomach won the war and he lunged for the nearby urn. Bending over, he vomited into the dead plants.

Tutto and Legon joined him. Tutto held out a jeweled flask. "Maybe this time you won't argue. Drink."

His sword master's vile malt, of course. By now, Dorilian knew it would help. He took a deep drink, followed by a second, before capping the flask. Foul-tasting as it was, it was moderately better than vomit.

"I did it." He gave Legon a triumphant grin.

Legon grinned too. "You did!"

Tutto snorted. "Your grandfather called you reckless and a fool. I agree. You tried this too soon."

"By your account, then, I have succeeded too soon. The day will come when this skill will prove useful."

"All skills are useful," Tiflan observed. "Even dangerous ones."

Tutto knew when he was outnumbered. When Dorilian passed

him the Coronal, Tutto took it with the care it merited. "Be cautious, my prince. I have seen too often how quick you are to act on impulse. This is one skill not to attempt on sheer intuition. Even The Leur would tell you as much."

Tiflan chuckled. "I am sure he would, if he were to pop up someday to offer his advice."

Together the four of them walked the length of the gallery toward the rotunda. Dorilian stepped carefully, his senses still too heightened for him to trust his balance. Despite the price his body was paying at the moment, he had been confident of putting his many months of learning into practice. *Fuck you, Stefan, and Rheger too. You can drag each other to ruin.*

Dorilian had not heard yet if the general he had dispatched to take Gignastha had succeeded in doing so. The man he had sent, Bersyas Garheleon, had received a promotion and orders to move against Neuberland's weak underbelly with lightning speed. Dorilian had supplied horses, weapons and troops by stealth—the horses marked as being for trade, the men, equipment, and weapons concealed in containers slotted into commercial lots conveyed by his personal Rill portions from Hestya. All destined for Randpory.

Let them guess how he had assembled his army. What he needed now was to hear that he had achieved his goal.

Dorilian and his companions had reached the end of the gallery. His nausea had subsided, so he took the Coronal back from Tutto's hands and placed it again on his head. Power surged into his nerves—arcane, amplified, drawn from inhuman blood and bones.

He didn't need the King's House anymore, either.

Raising the hand armed with the Rill Stone's verdant gleam, Dorilian cast a blade of power at the gallery ceiling. Blue energy slashed across the space between, struck the vault and webbed its surface. The heavy stone creaked, then cracked and caved with a roar of dust and ruin. His companions dragged him into the safety of the arched doorway as chunks of plaster and stone rained down.

"Gsch!" Legon gaped.

"Now that wasn't necessary," Tiflan chided. "You had proven your point."

"Not to anyone that matters."

Tutto jutted his chin at Tiflan. "See what I mean? He's intuitive. The powerful ones often are. It's what kills them in the end. Remember Delos? What he was like after he broke the Aqueduct? Sebbord worried the same might happen to this one."

"I am standing right here." Dorilian frowned through the dust-filled air.

Tiflan stepped in front of him. "Then let me be the one to point out your recklessness. Tutto is not wrong. You come from a line gifted with great power and purpose. It has not always been gifted with great restraint and even less so with wisdom. If your enemies seek to kill you, ask yourself why."

Dorilian nodded. He included Tutto in that gesture, and Legon also for having warned him. "You are right. Both of you. All of you."

The assault hit without warning. Dorilian suddenly clutched at his forehead and clenched his jaw against a shearing pain behind his eyes, inside his skull. A *new* pain. Legon steadied him, arm around his shoulders. Legon's voice asking what was wrong sounded like a mere rumble.

Lev. Agony. Sordan... blood crystals... a thousand images... too many... too wrong... people, places, events that sliced like blades through screams of terror.

"Lev," he gasped. Dorilian moved away from Legon's arm.

No one could stop him. The Sordan Coronal burned power into his brow.

"Don't!"

Someone screamed it. Maybe all three did. He did not care. Locating Levyathan was simple. Dorilian had done this all their lives. *Where* hardly mattered—now that he knew *how.* Aligning their two spaces took but an instant. All he had to do was move.

Go.

The moment Dorilian arrived in the dimly lit chamber, a sudden weight carried him to his knees. Darkness reigned but he recognized the Trove, the vault beneath the Serat that safeguarded Sordaneon artifacts and devices. On the floor Levyathan gasped and arched, a glowing white shape clutched in his small hands. Pain worse than that in his head sheared through Dorilian's left arm, which ended elbow-deep at the ribcage of a soldier also on his knees. Fallen, same as he. The man gaped at him, dark-eyed with surprise, and struggled for air as his heart squirmed against—within and around—Dorilian's hand. Dorilian tried to spread his fingers, to give the organ more room, but couldn't. Heat and flesh encased his fingers.

Relocate! Go! But it was too late. Even if he could do it, the man's heart was ruined. Dorilian's translocating flesh had pushed aside all that was not itself.

"I'm sorry."

The man spent his final breath on just one word, "Liege!" before he toppled, his weight pulling Dorilian on top of him. Arm trapped, Dorilian could not free himself. Pain blinded his single attempt to focus through the Coronal. If he were to try, and fail… Levyathan, open-eyed and mewling, lay within reach.

Footsteps broke the moment. Fahme, her young face as pale as her dress, darted into the treasure room through the open door. The second of the guards who should have secured the door to the chamber ran in on Fahme's heels.

"Thrice Royal." The man stared but dared not approach. "Yeved. What—?"

"Leave us!" Dorilian barked. With any luck, the man could not see everything.

The guard attempted to explain. "The girl, she—"

"Did you not hear me? Leave! Now! And take her with you!"

This time the guard obeyed and rushed Fahme from the Trove. Dorilian leaned over the dead man and reached out with his right hand to grasp the Wall Stone by its blood gold chain. Power, amplified by the Coronal, crackled through his body in the bare moment before he yanked the artifact from Levyathan's grip. He dropped it to the floor. Arcane light created patterns on the polished stone. Dorilian grasped the Coronal from his head and placed that beside it, green gems burning with inner fire alongside that of the moon-bright Wall Stone.

The pain in his head remained blinding. And that of his arm…

Lev? Dorilian sought for an answer but found only a madness akin to dreams.

He grabbed what he could reach, a handful of shirt, and tugged Levyathan, still gasping and no longer jerking with seizures, toward him.

Braced on the warm body of the dead man—Yeved, Dorilian recalled, the most intimate of strangers—he pulled Levyathan to his side and cradled him. Wracked with pain and crumpled at the base of the massive basalt plinth that had held the Malyrdeon artifact, Dorilian pressed his face to Levyathan's head, hair warm and silk-soft beneath his cheek.

"Lev? Help me find you." He pressed his thoughts deeper, the way he had so often done in Levyathan's first childhood. No longer familiar, the boy's mind was inchoate and unshielded, a realm for which Dorilian had no map. He found the terror, the tumult, and slid his consciousness alongside that. *It isn't real. None of what you saw. None of it has happened yet and maybe never will.*

Dorilian too had touched the Wall Stone, seen impossible things. *Why did you do it? Why?*

Why?

Levyathan's ribcage expanded with a ragged breath, his mind with a thought. *You.*

Me? Damn, Dorilian hurt. His trapped limb screamed with agony. He bottled the pain within, determined Levyathan would never feel it. Mental disciplines and constructs he had not used for years reasserted and became barricades.

Help you. Levyathan's eyes, open and aware, swiveled to meet Dorilian's. "I wanted to see the next attack. Who. Where. To warn you."

"Warn me."

"I could not see you. Only the Wall… and myself."

"I know. It takes a Wall Lord to see anything else."

"Death. Only death." Tears filled Levyathan's eyes. "They cannot save you and neither can I."

"I don't need saving." The pain in Dorilian's arm said otherwise. Even drawing breath had become harder.

"Nammuor. He isn't the Destroyer. He is a hunter. Promise me—"

"Anything."

Terror gleamed within Levyathan's tearful gaze. His pale lips moved. "Don't make me leave Sordan. Not ever. If I leave, Nammuor takes me. Over and over, so many places and ways I saw where and how. But never in Sordan. Do not let him take me, not ever. I saw the Creation broken, Permephedon broken. Sordan too. I saw the face of the Destroyer, a monster clothed in sorcery among the ruins."

"Don't."

"I saw myself, Dor. *I* wear the bloody crown. You will break the Wall, but I will break the Rill. I will kill everything." Choked by sobs, Levyathan curled against him, a trembling creature, water and bones. So small. Too small and too young to be chided about the unreliability of Wall visions. Dorilian clasped Levyathan tight and kissed his head.

"You have my promise, my most solemn vow, that I will never take you from Sordan or require you to leave." He felt the promise lock about them both, armor and chains. If even the smallest portion of what Levyathan believed he had seen was true— "The Rill protects us from the Undying Crown. It protects you. Protects me. The Entities do not abide the Diadem."

Dorilian no longer felt his left arm at all, only an icy cold. Too much flesh in too little space choked off his blood. On the floor beside him, the Wall Stone's chill light gleamed upon the Sordan Coronal's silver points and kissed the green glints of its perilous power. He stared at his arm buried inside Yeved's chest.

You're right. Both of you. All of you.

"Dor!"

Someone had found them. Maybe the guard he had sent from the room had gotten help. Dorilian looked up at Legon's horrified face and was gratified to see him avert his gaze to assess Levyathan's sniffling form.

Tutto grunted as he got down on one knee. Tiflan, too, did so.

"Vllyr's Cock. He got himself entrapped." The sword master heaved a sigh.

Tiflan frowned. "To this man's misfortune."

"Seeing as I cannot bring him back to life, can we at least pull my arm out?" Dorilian asked.

Tutto snapped a look up at Tiflan. "We could just leave His Thrice Royal Grace like this. Have him explain to this man's widow and children, and the rest of the world, the manner of his death."

Dorilian held Levyathan tucked under his chin and blinked back tears. Failure stung like nothing else could… except this. He would never apologize for using the gifts at his disposal to reach Levyathan quickly. It might take days to know what damage Levyathan's brief contact with the Wall Stone had wrought. But Dorilian had erred, and badly. His hurried, entirely intuitive calculation, not pausing to account for the unexpected yet predictable—he had killed this unknown guard, this Yeved, as surely as if he had blindly thrown a javelin into the room. The man's destroyed heart enfolded his hand.

I've been reckless. Destructive. Truth tasted like ash. Dorilian knew his own history, in particular the parts his companions did not. For him, *because* of him, people had died, including innocents slaughtered by soldiers he had sent against them. Now, because of that history, enough people hated and feared him to fill an arena. A domain. Probably several. They might also think the world would be better off if he were not in it. To change their minds would take more work than he cared to invest. But he could take steps to not make matters worse. The last thing he needed was to give his enemies even more reason to hate or fear—or try to kill—him.

His first step would be to never let anyone outside this room know the extent of his powers—or that he had any at all.

His second step would be to make right those things he could. For that he must start by expressing his remorse to the only persons whose opinions he still valued.

"I—I tried. There was—" No room. No time. No way. "I acted without thought and he paid the price. Once it happened, I could not undo it. I watched him die. I felt it... I—I can help his family, ease their loss as I can never ease his, and I will. For what I have cost them, they will not suffer any further hardship that I can prevent. But I cannot give him back his life."

For a long moment, Tutto said nothing. He studied the tableau before him, then drew his short sword. "Amputation of your arm would be faster but would raise too many questions and we can't leave the Rill Stone in there. I will cut him open and get you out. Legon, take the boy, don't let him see this." To Tiflan, he said, "You—think of a good explanation. This poor bastard deserved a better death."

Rheger felt the sending through deep veils of sleep. Prodded from a pleasant dream of being on a hunt with his brothers, he yanked his hand from under covers just in time and tightened his fingers over the cylinder when it arrived. His movement awakened Sapphia, who stirred against his back and inquired what had happened.

"I don't know yet." He sighed. "I told him not to send to me again."

Her breath warmed his shoulder. "And you expected him to obey your wish? He thinks nothing of our danger here."

"I thought I had made clear the situation." He turned the rings and unlocked the message but needed a light to read it by. "There is a spark and a lamp in the night chamber. I will read it there."

Once that door was closed and he was certain his activity would not alert any watchers, Rheger lit the lamp and sat on the undignified fixture to read the message. Two words.

Come. Now.

The punctuation persuaded him. He tucked the message back into the cylinder and twirled the lock shut. After dousing the lamp, he retrieved the Kyr Coronal by moonlight from its hiding place in the headboard and kissed Sapphia, who shook her head and buried her face in her pillow, though she would undoubtedly not sleep until he returned.

Not more than a moment later, he stood in the rotunda of the King's House, its walls ringed by now familiar low waterglobe lights, his feet bare upon a floor littered with dust and grit. Though dim, the lighting revealed that the ceiling in the next room had met a violent end. Rheger was confident he could guess what had transpired. He was just as certain that his orange and white striped bed shirt looked ridiculous. Dorilian stood before him, showing every sign of having been in a battle, his left arm stained red as were his garments on that side. The Rill Stone glowed through a coating of blood.

"I did not take your training seriously enough and made a mistake." For once, Dorilian sounded chastened. "I thought you might appreciate knowing I am fallible."

He had translocated! Successfully. Rheger could imagine into what consequences. "I always knew you were fallible." Acknowledgment flitted across Dorilian's face, attesting to something newly prudent. Something... fundamental. Rheger's interest sharpened. "What happened?"

Dorilian walked toward him. He extended his unbloodied right arm to offer a black box the size of his hand. "Take it. Another mistake I wish to put to right."

The box surprised Rheger by how heavy it was. *Deathstone*, he realized. The material nullified arcane forces. When he lifted the box's fitted lid to look within, he understood. The Wall Stone glimmered, ethereal light spilling from it in streams of beauty. The pulse of its immortal connection to the Wall thrilled him. His very nerves sang with recognition of Ergeiron's being. Dorilian's voice pulled Rheger out of his immersion.

"In Sordan it serves no purpose but temptation. Maybe your son can use it. Maybe you can."

"I believe you are telling me you no longer need me." Rheger closed the lid on the box.

A faint smile. "I no longer need for you to endanger yourself on my behalf. I have much to learn still, this I know, but you have taught me enough for a foundation. For that, I am forever in your debt. Going forward, I will practice. I will be careful. I will not use my gifts in anger or fear—or for any to see. Those would be failures we can ill afford."

Enreddon had called this Sordaneon impetuous, rebellious, and warned Marc Frederick that the kindred must wait upon more maturity before undertaking to train him. Now Rheger worried they might have waited too long. He was not the teacher this man—no longer a headstrong boy—needed. However, if Dorilian was any kind of example, it might be possible to learn enough on one's own.

Rheger clasped the smooth black surface of the box holding the Wall Stone. A possibility occurred to him. "Did you use it again?"

A flash of annoyance. "I never *used* it."

"Achieved contact with the Wall, then."

"No." Truth, though Rheger sensed another answer behind Dorilian's wry expression. "Look to the future as only a Malyrdeon can, *fra'don*. You have regained the tool to enlist your Entity. It is time I undertake to secure a future for mine."

"Bloodbloodblood... blood and death and fire..."

The nursery felt dark and dismal. Raxa had retreated with Fahme to her own nearby chamber. Levyathan sobbed in Dorilian's arms. Dorilian tucked the boy's head under his chin and endeavored to instill calm. Hours had passed and still Levyathan would not sleep. His mind insisted on continually reliving what he had seen.

I have been with it. I did this too. Years ago, Dorilian had given Levyathan life when life was needed. Blood. Air. Sight. Language. Tonight, he would drain memories if memories could be drained. Wall them off. Find a way to ease this pain.

He had sealed his own pain behind walls. Aside. Away. He had done so with their mother's death. Sebbord's. With Permephedon. There were ways, he just had to show Levyathan how... maybe even do it for him. *Let me help. Let me.*

"I don't want to feel you."

Dorilian's pain. His rage. "It's gone. I let it go. I let it all go." Tears slicked his skin, all the hurt he had inflicted without ever meaning it.

"Mia?"

The boy knew him too well. "I will always ache for her."

"For me?" Levyathan's tear-choked voice and wet eyes stared, bright with accusation.

Dorilian could not lie. If he so much as tried, Levyathan would know. "For you. For myself. Pain for what I have done."

Sobs wracked the boy's thin body and Dorilian cradled him closer. "How do we live in this world?" Levyathan whispered. "I saw things..."

"You did not see everything. The Wall Stone... I saw other things."

Levyathan's bright eyes widened. Dorilian's words opened a path, curiosity alongside hope, leading to a place they both needed to go. He slid his mind into Levyathan's without disruption, a touch known across the child's two lifetimes that penetrated structures shared and deep and familiar. A storm filled those channels, so Dorilian calmed its currents, pushed aside swirls of terror. Into that place, he instilled himself, his name—the fact of him and those Wall visions he had seen: being cheered in Sordan, bowed down to in Dazunor-Rannuli, riding at the head of an army in snow; the Rill and a sword. Against a Wall.

There. You see?

Yes. With a deep sigh that lifted his ribs, Levyathan relaxed in Dorilian's arms. *Stay... stay...*

Not for this.

Dorilian withdrew. Every Wall image in Levyathan's mind now led to him. To the Rill. He and their Entity created a barrier. The memories behind it were there, still there, neither buried nor gone— Dorilian had suppressed them into a cache requiring conscious recollection. *I will protect you.*

Safe.

Dorilian nodded. Breathed deeply. Felt Levyathan slide into quiet in his arms. *Yes, safe.* As safe as Dorilian could make him. He would keep Levyathan in Sordan, within the stronghold Leur had built, that Amynas himself had claimed for their offspring and Derlon made invincible. And he would make Levyathan's life in this Serat as secure and tranquil and full as was in his power to do.

Foremost among Dorilian's projects must be to remake himself.

His flaws were deadly. Anger destroyed. Impulse weakened. Both traits put him in harm's way—and not him alone. Levyathan. Their people. The Rill. Too much stood at stake for Dorilian to risk fits of rage.

His embryonic gifts required prudence and cold logic. Secrecy.

Only one path would produce the results he needed. He must become *less*, not more. Less accessible and, because of that, less visible. Part of the background. Perceived but never known. Misperceptions and erroneous conclusions could create a guise all but a chosen handful would believe. He must be present only in the tightest circle of trust. Such would be his armor.

Now that he had become a weapon, it was he who must remain sheathed.

29

"Yeved Orgadnos had no wife. He is survived by his parents, two grandparents, and five siblings."

Tiflan had a magisterial way of imparting information. Dorilian wasn't sure he liked it, but his opinion of his cousin's way of speaking did not weigh on the matter at hand. The more Dorilian learned about Yeved Orgadnos—that he had been wounded in combat and decorated for bravery under Pandaros Vidyamemnon and served more recently as a twice-promoted officer of the Serat Guardians—the more he wished he had known the man. Yeved's death brought home everything Tutto had ever tried to teach Dorilian about the value of "common" men.

No person was "common" to those who knew them. To everyone who knew him, his family and comrades, his officers and lovers, Yeved was extraordinary. And so Yeved was to Dorilian.

"Full officer's pensions to the parents and grandparents."

The secretary, seated at a portable table nearby, scratched the terms onto a paper. Dorilian did not usually conduct Hierarchal business while at breakfast, but he had roused early to receive a dispatch announcing the capture of Gignastha and had decided he would just press forward with his day. He selected another sweet tart and bit into the flaky pastry while continuing his contemplation of Yeved's death gifts.

"Full pension to both parents—and the grandparents also?" The secretary was being thorough. Dorilian approved of the trait, however annoying it could be.

"Did they contribute equally to the making of him? Did they lose the surety of his support? Each suffers from his loss, so each gets a pension." Which brought him to the siblings. "Marriage portions of one-year salary to each brother and sister who comes of age." That too seemed fitting. He had made Yeved a generous man as well as a hero who had saved the Sordaneon Heir from calamity at the cost of his life. Dorilian had already ordered and would pay for a funeral with high honors and placement of a monument with Yeved's name and statue along the Avenue of Heroes. He would attend the ceremony. His meeting with the family was to be this afternoon.

"Thrice Royal?" The secretary's voice intruded on his thoughts. "Shall I prepare the writ of dispensation?"

"At once." Dorilian watched the secretary leave before he turned to Tiflan again. "Some things can never be put behind us."

"We measure ourselves by those things. Those people. Those places. Those acts. Some make us stronger; some weaker. Some increase us and some diminish."

"Whatever happened to you, that you became so colossal?"

Tiflan laughed and reached for the glass ewer at the center of the table. He refilled juice for them both. "Monumental things. It pleases me to see you handle your life responsibly."

"Not much of that lately."

His cousin did not argue with him. Even Tiflan could not deny the dismal events of the last few days. Dorilian had visited Palimia, who remained sedated in the Citadel, in the hands of Sordan's College of Healers. Only at Permephedon might better skill be found, but he could not bring himself to send her there. Essera, even Permephedon, could not be trusted with anyone he cared about right now. Speaking with her when she awoke would be a difficult conversation. As for Levyathan... Dorilian had done what he could to ease Levyathan's mind. He had left the boy asleep and trusted his efforts of the night before to provide respite from Wall visions. Going forward, however, what Dorilian most needed was to work on himself.

Retrain his quick temper. Shape it to something more useful. Purposeful.

"Da?" Fahme stood in the doorway, still wearing her nightdress and with little bare feet.

He gestured her over and she ran across the polished floor. When she was in his lap, she put her head on his chest and he combed his fingers through her hair. Abundant honey brown curls flowed over her shoulders and back. Her puffy eyes reminded him she too had cried herself to sleep and suffered from nightmares. Those, too, he must prevent from this day on.

He put his face nearer hers. "Are things better now, Princess?"
She nodded.

"Good. Can you do something to help me?" Dark eyes exactly like those of her mother looked up at him, suspicious, yet wondering what he might ask. Noemi would have had a few choice things to say to him about last night. "I want you to help Raxa take care of Lev. I cannot be with him all the time and you are his favorite person. He asked you to help him yesterday and you did what he wanted, you pretended to be hurt and tricked the guards to leave their posts to help you."

She nodded, her gaze firmly on his. He softened his expression and did his best to use words to shape the thrust of his message. What the girl had done had been... wrong, and yet not completely so. "You showed loyalty. Lev trusted you and you did not disappoint him."

"Did I disappoint you?"

Children, Dorilian had learned, could be incredibly astute. Another response needed to be framed. "Yes. But only because I wish you, and he, had talked to me first."

"One of the soldiers went back."

"I know."

"He was dead. I saw."

Regret flooded through Dorilian, sharp enough Fahme certainly felt it, saw it on his face. He did not look away. "Yes, he—"

"Scary."

She had felt that, too. His fear. To his relief, there was movement at the door. Raxa and Legon entered, along with an officer from military dispatch. Tiflan rose and scooped Fahme into his arms. "Yes. It *was* scary, little cousin. But it is not scary now, is it? Look, there's Raxa—is she scary?"

Fahme giggled. "Yes!"

"Your father has to talk to Legon and this man, so let's go find something fun to do." Chuckling, Tiflan ushered Raxa and Fahme out of the room.

And just like that another gear of Dorilian's life rotated, concealing and revealing him.

Dorilian turned to Legon and the officer, Bevan Kavar. Legon's second-in-command wrote concise reports and had been chosen to coordinate military communications through Randpory.

"Your Thrice Royal Grace, a list of captives taken at Gignastha." Kavar extended an envelope.

Back to the business of war. The report Dorilian had received before dawn had detailed the military aspect. Bersyas had defeated Stefan's main force at heavily fortified Horcrod by riding past the garrison and drawing them out, allowing troops Bersyas had hidden in a ravine to swarm the fortress. Horcrod's defeat eliminated any significant Esseran military presence in Lower Neuberland.

The main body of Bersyas's troops had driven straight through to Gignastha, which he caught by surprise. Stefan's garrison in the nearly impregnable Watergilt Palace had been captured and disarmed by the Gignasthan governor's forces. The city's subsequent surrender had neutralized elements loyal to Stefan. The arrangement with Verteus Cordegos had been straightforward: he and his followers would retain their ranks and positions, except they would do so under Sordan's banner. Verteus remained Governor of the occupied province.

The men on the list were persons Verteus knew to be loyal to Stefan or believed would otherwise prove troublesome—or useful.

Dorilian signaled for a writing implement, which Legon immediately provided. He crossed out one name. Alban Eskeros. A minor lord and a faithful old friend of Sebbord's. Eskeros was a man so well-concealed even Verteus did not suspect he supplied Dorilian with information. Most of the other captured persons were, like Eskeros, nobles or otherwise citizens of influence. Some might be ransomed to help pay the cost of this venture. Others could serve as hostages for the good behavior of parties still free in Gignastha.

A name near the bottom of the list caught Dorilian's eye. *Cullen Thegn Brodheson.*

He checked the name along with several others and handed it back to Legon. "I want everything you can learn about all of them, but especially these people."

The guard's fist slammed Cullen's jaw and he fell backward against the stone wall, his skull hitting hard enough for red pain and darkness to explode behind his eyes. The next fist pounded his gut and he crumpled to the floor, where he curled head down and knees to chest. That usually worked. They *wanted* him to be cowed. Broken would work even better.

"Stop being assholes! What the hells are you doing?" Arton, Cullen's cellmate, stood with fists cocked as he yelled at the guards. "He's an Archon!"

"Not in proper books!" The man who had struck Cullen delivered a hard kick. Cullen smothered a cry at sharp tearing in his ribs. "Damn murdering Khelds aren't noble. Never were and never will be. They're barely human. We should just kill the lot."

Both guards departed. They pulled the door shut and barred it, a rasp of wood and metal.

"Aw, hell, sir." Arton knelt and helped him sit. He turned Cullen's face to the light from the high narrow window. "They cannot keep doing this."

The other man in the room barked a laugh. "Who's going to stop them? Not me. Not on his account."

"That's because you're an ass. You can make yourself less of one by getting off the bed." Arton hooked an arm under Cullen's armpit and helped him stand. He assisted him to the room's only bed, which their companion had begrudgingly vacated, and helped Cullen seat himself.

"You're a fool, trying to stop it." The other man, named Konstan, sank sullenly onto a stool that was the room's only other seating. "They'll beat him anyway and will just injure you too for good measure."

Cullen hated that the man was right. He eased his body down flat upon the mattress and stared up at the ceiling. He had discovered the first day that the vault over their heads was beautiful, intricate, beamed by golden wood and painted with patterns of the hunt: horses and riders, foxes and pheasants, woodland and fences and fields.

Arton continued to protest. "Third day of it now. If they are going to kill him, they should just do it and get on with all our fates."

Cullen closed his eyes and sought to escape the bickering. He was still alive, a victory of sorts. And he'd learned that Arton had a good heart to go with his talent at numbers. About Konstan, Cullen had a lower opinion—though it was unlikely his opinion would ever matter again, in this or any other circumstance. Evidence of the extent to which Khelds were hated in Gignastha blossomed black and blue on every inch of his skin. His left hand had turned purple and ballooned to twice its size from being kicked the day before. And it wasn't even enemy troops doing it. Except for that first day, he hadn't seen Sordan's soldiers, not a one. The Governor's Guard held control of the captives.

Even that might be a blessing. The guards taunted him at every turn with the fate of Dorilian's would-be assassin. Impaled.

Castrated. Eviscerated. Dismembered alive on the stake and his body parts fed to dogs. They openly wished the same fate—one or all of those things—for Cullen. He'd just as soon be executed now than be handed over to the Sordani.

Though fear hollowed him at times, he knew better than to give in. To show fear or pain signaled weakness, which would just embolden the guards, and he was none too sure of Konstan either. Konstan's grandfather had been slain by Khelds during the Bloodletting. Only Arton's honorable nature offered a hint of respite. Loud sounds penetrated the walls from the corridor outside. Boot falls. Many men. Voices and drawn steel. Cullen's gut turned cold. Now what? Were they going to do it here and now? Send Stefan his head or some other part as the guards had threatened?

The door opened and several men poured in.

"All three!"

Cullen hardly cared when hard hands grabbed him and dragged him to standing. He didn't resist when rope bound his wrists in front of him, looped by more rope to those of the other men.

The hood, however, was a surprise.

Once hoisted onto a horse, Cullen's world consisted of trying to keep his feet in the stirrups and his hands on the pommel of the saddle. He remained hooded, though with his lower face mercifully exposed so he could breathe and drink. A large number of horses and men surrounded him; Cullen guessed he was one of many prisoners being transported. A few of the captives talked with each other, but he had been separated from Arton and no one else talked with him. Instead, his thoughts wandered to Phalla and his mother, and those he cared about in Essera. Did they think him dead?

Stefan surely knew by now. Knew about the capture of the city. Knew Sordan had invaded Essera. Stefan sure as damn hells knew why.

Cullen knew less. He was certain his captors wanted him alive for some reason, none of them good. He was no longer being held by the Governor's Guard, but the Sordani.

The slightly nasal vowels and sensual inflections of Sordan's version of Stauba accompanied all commands. He knew the accent. He'd heard it spoken by Dorilian: at Permephedon for sure, but more memorably at Gustan. It was amusing, almost, to hear these men—clearly common soldiers—crudely curse Cullen for being

Kheld, like the assassin they despised. They didn't know their Hierarch was the one who had taught him to speak proper Stauba and win at playing courses, or that he had exchanged more words with Dorilian than any of them ever would.

They handled him roughly onto and off from the horse. Yanked him about when he asked to relieve himself. Threw food onto his lap and showed him less respect than they did the dog that followed the leader's horse and ran down game for their dinner. They called Cullen a dead man, a waste of good dog meat. But they didn't beat him. The hood was hot, and his sweat soon made it stink, and he was always thirsty. But his bruises faded, except for the worst ones on his left hand and ribs, and the swelling in his jaw went down and by the time four days had passed it didn't hurt as much to breathe.

On the sixth day they reached some sort of town. New noises and smells rose to every side. Vendors called their wares. Women laughed. The language changed, then changed again, a rise and fall of foreign tongues, some of which Cullen understood. Even from under the covering of the hood, he smelled spices on the air: cardamom and peppers roasting, ripe fruit rotting in the sun, all mingled with the dung of cattle and goats and the tantalizing aromas of grilled meat.

Using the stirrups, he shifted in the saddle and hoped the soldier would come around with water soon. He was thirsty. Dust coated his lips.

He heard it then. A distant double thrum. Far away, and then, with a deeper note, not far at all. Another, nearer still, deep and upon him and vibrating his chest. Overhead. Only one thing made that sound.

Cullen's heart raced. He was at a Rill port. There were six Rill ports, only two of which could be reached from Gignastha in six days. Leseos and Randpory Crossing.

Randpory. The languages. The dust. Leseos of the Pines would be colder at this time of year. It would smell and taste of clear air and trees. His heart beat harder, this time with the start of panic. They could not be thinking to send him to Sordan by Rill. The others maybe, but not him. For Khelds, the Rill was deadly. A killer.

It would tear him to shreds.

The horses stopped and jostled; one by one, soldiers ordered the captives to dismount. Cullen heard military greetings followed in short order by strings of commands and a changing of custody.

"This one." A rustle of papers. Footsteps.

Hard hands dragged Cullen away from the others. Two men grabbed him, one to each arm. He knew better than to ask questions. He focused on not stumbling, on not giving them reason to get angry. Through the soles of his boots he felt uneven paving, probably stone, that before long became something smoother. Muffled voices. The creak of what might be a gate. Sunlight and shadow. Steps. More steps. The taste of the air changed and he no longer breathed dust. New scents penetrated, civilized and clean. A light trickle of falling water teased his ears and sharpened his thirst. Warm air touched his skin and enemy hands released him. The hood was lifted.

Cullen stood, blinking, in an open, airy room with walls the color of clouds on a sunny day. At his side towered two soldiers wearing light armor bearing an insignia Cullen did not recognize. In front of him waited the man for whom they stood at attention.

Neither tall nor fair, the man nonetheless had a Staubaun air, his posture straight and tight with military precision. He held his hands and arms behind his back with the effect that doing so pushed his chest forward to show its massive breadth and depth. The stance also displayed the intricate stitchery on his garments: the same ensign of crossed swords as worn by the soldiers, hemmed by deep borders with elaborate needlework and silk in a pattern of fighting eagles. Beneath close-cut steel gray hair, eyes of darkest brown commanded a scarred, weathered face and a nose flattened by many blows. Cullen had seen that face before but could not remember where.

"Are you Cullen Thegn Brodheson?" The man's rough voice had clearly survived many blows as well.

"Yes." It was strange to hear each of his names pronounced incorrectly.

"Hmm." The man strode up to him. He lightly pinched the skin under Cullen's right eye and tugged at his lower lip, then frowned. "This man is dehydrated. Water, not cold."

One of the soldiers ran to fulfill the order, but Cullen struggled to understand. Why care about that? His mind was too dull to ponder answers.

The man continued to examine him. When a light press at the base of Cullen's badly bruised left thumb evoked a wince, his captor frowned. "Did our men do this to you? Any of your injuries?"

What did that mean, *our men*? Sordan's?

"I don't... No." Cullen realized his answer was imprecise. "Gignastha. The Governor's Guards."

The man stepped back. "Tell me you will not cause trouble or attempt to harm yourself and I will order your bonds removed."

Another kindness? Perhaps a courtesy? A small part of him began to hope. His dry lips stuck to his teeth when he spoke. "I will not cause trouble or try to harm myself."

The bonds came off. Cullen did not feel any freer for it.

"Do you need to relieve yourself?"

Cullen shook his head.

The man signaled to the door and a woman entered. She was sturdy and well fed, with skin of a honeyed glow and dark hair half-covered by a blue veil that drifted over her right shoulder and arm. In her hands she carried a tray with a silver ewer and heavy cup of tourmaline glass, which she set on a ledge beside the room's main feature, a large stone tub. Condensation beaded on the ewer. Cullen fought the urge to lick his lips. He watched the man lift the ewer and fill the glass. For so many days now, soldiers had tormented him by doing exactly that, then drank the water themselves while he watched or poured it onto the dirt in front of him.

This man extended the vessel. "Drink."

The cup felt cool to Cullen's hand and the water tasted like the Mother's own, pure and bright. He drank it all. When asked if he wanted more, he nodded. Only when he'd finished the second cup did the man put the glass aside.

"You can have more later. You might give some thought to your appearance—and stench." He pointed to the tub of pale stone filled with water. The ledge around it held bathing supplies—brushes and soaps, bottles, sponges. A table beside the tub held a stack of towels. "Make yourself clean. Be thorough. I will stay to be sure of your safety. The matron will send in a barber."

When the woman left, Cullen did his best to ignore the most recent man to have gained control of him and stripped out of his filthy clothes. Fine as they had once been, the garments were torn and stained, unworthy even of the floor. That was crafted of smooth stone interspersed with beautiful tiles, each a work of art. Everything about the room was refreshing, even his treatment so far. The water was warm, perfectly so, and scattered with *ucaja* petals. Blissful. He sank into the tub and began to address his filth.

The woman came to the chamber again, this time with fresh clothing. The garments weren't of Esseran style, neither were they

Gignasthan. They were similar, though, and Cullen understood how to wear them. The ivory lightweight woolen breeches and shirt with ribbed upper sleeves fit well enough, and the sleeveless jacket of sable velvet that hung to the bottom of his hips was finely made. He hooked a woven belt, elegant with gold thread and a buckle in the shape of a horse, about his waist and put on fresh stockings and his own boots, which a youth had cleaned and conditioned while he bathed. When he looked in the chamber's tall mirror, he realized two things: he looked thin and tired… and two weeks of beard hid the worst of his remaining facial bruises.

Cullen had wanted to shave off the beard, but his custodian, as he now considered the man, had ordered the barber to merely trim it. Cullen hoped that was because of what he saw in the mirror and not because the powers at work wanted an obviously Kheld man to execute in public. Receiving fine clothes reassured him.

When he was led from the bathing chamber, Cullen saw it was located at the perimeter of a palatial residence. A corridor led to a tree-shaded garden of fountains at a juncture of other, half-hidden buildings, a courtyard of restful loveliness bordered by magnificent colonnades. The stone floor was interspersed with refined tiles much like those in the bathing room. They passed room after glorious room until they came to one that was bright and open to the elements. An expansive awning shaded cushioned benches around a blue stone table set with an assortment of ewers and plates. Though Cullen wanted to take hope from the food and drink, he felt uncertain. None of this felt right.

"Do you wish to eat?"

"Is that a question? Or an offer?"

"An offer."

The man gestured for Cullen to be seated. Two quiet youths attired in simple calf-length, belted tunics appeared, bearing plates of food. The woman from before directed them to the table and fussed with how the plates were positioned and ewers—one of water, one of golden juice—were poured.

"Will there be anything else, Most Noble?" she asked of the man.

"No."

The woman bowed and left the room on the heels of the servants.

Most Noble. That explained a lot. Cullen was in the presence of a Bas. If only he could identify the heraldry of the ensign, he might know which one.

"Eat." This was a man accustomed to giving orders. "Drink."

Permission granted. Cullen had been obeying orders for nearly two weeks and had gotten quite good at it. He picked up the glass of water.

"I see you can walk on your own. How is your hand?"

The barber had tended to that as well. "It's helping. Thank you." The inquiry added to his confidence. What reason would anyone have to treat the hurts of a man they wanted to torture or kill?

Cullen took a deep drink of water. A quick inventory of the table showed a variety of food. Cheeses. Fruit. A bowl of fat jellied eels glistened in purple broth. The eels were unexpected, but then so was everything else about this day. Half-afraid he had mistaken his luck, he pulled the bowl over and picked up a spoon. While the other man watched him intently, Cullen popped a bite of eel into his mouth.

"Those look disgusting."

A sentiment he'd heard before. Cullen sopped some of the eel broth with bread. "When prepared this well, they're really good."

"My man got them from a food stall in Dazunor-Rannuli. Satisfactory, then? The meal?"

Cullen nodded. For well over a week, he had barely eaten enough to keep alive.

With water to drink and food before him, his life no longer seemed in immediate danger. Reassured, he appraised his surroundings beyond the table. His hand stopped cold between plate and lips. His jaw dropped. Directly across from him, beyond this open sunlit terrace and low wall, loomed the Rill, its surreal structures so monumental he had not recognized it. He had never been this close or seen it straight on. Bracketed by massive rings, the platform cradled a lone *charys* at rest in front of the sanctum, a communication nexus that made all humans who walked near it look puny. The Rill though... even as he watched, a distinctive whine rose, small at first as the structures before his eyes fell away, rearranged and flowed. Like something from a dream—lightning fast—the *charys* departed, visible one moment and gone the next. In a single heartbeat the glitter of its passage had disappeared into the distance. North. To Essera.

As the Rill structures smoothly resumed their former stasis, Cullen caught his custodian's inquisitive stare and closed his mouth to swallow, then said the only thing he could: "It never ceases to amaze."

Despite deep scars, the man's face softened. "That it does. May it and the Sordaneons live forever."

Finally, Cullen had reached a kind of connection. There was still something he needed to find out. "I don't know how to ask... I'm unclear about a lot of things. Like what happened. After Gignastha was captured, I heard… there was an assassination, an attempt. But no one will tell me more than that. Is Dor—" Cullen caught himself and rephrased to correct the relationship. "Is the Hierarch all right?"

The Bas's sharp look, critical at first, turned curious. "He survived the attempt on his life and took no hurt from any weapon."

"Did *anyone* take hurt?"

"A woman close to him. Near to death."

Cullen released a breath. "I'm sorry. That someone got hurt. But I'm glad he's not. We're not friends or anything, but… I spent some time with him a few years ago. I never wished him harm."

He ate more food—fruit and cheese—and washed it down with the juice, unable to cease staring at the Rill. The god-machine inspired awe everywhere—here, so close, it awakened worship. Movement drew Cullen's gaze to a line of people being walked onto the platform, single file. Soldiers in Sordaneon colors guarded the string of hooded, shuffling men.

"Aw, hells."

The Bas turned to see what Cullen was looking at. One corner of his mouth twitched into a smirk. "They are going to Sordan."

"And me?"

"You're not."

Why not? Because he was Kheld and the Rill would not transport him? Was he going to be held captive here? By this man? Cullen firmed his jaw and wished he was not bearded, that he looked less like the savage breed Sordani nobles like this one believed his people to be. He'd overheard enough talk during the last many days to grasp why the other captives were being sent to Sordan. They were worth something. Hostages for good behavior. Ransoms to be gained. Vengeance to be had. Fear returned to strike Cullen full force in the stomach. Any value he might have, resided in his king.

"Am I being held for ransom?"

"No."

If not ransom, then what? Cullen leaned forward tensely. "I realize why you hate me. Just tell me why I'm here."

The man walked forward a few steps, probably so he could look down on Cullen even more sternly. "I'm not sure. But I think *you* might have just told *me*. Are you through eating?"

Cullen nodded and pushed aside his plate. "Yes." To the woman, who stood nearby with her two servants, he said, "Thank you for your kindness."

She bowed her head. "Our privilege, Archon."

The Bas nodded to her also, then indicated Cullen should

accompany him. "Let's go. We'll both stop at the privy and be on our way."

"Where?"

"Where else? You're going home."

At the gate of the palace complex, horses waited, saddled and stamping their hoofs. Fine horses as befitted high lords. All beasts and men wore emblems of the man who rode beneath royal banners, one of which was that of the Sordaneon Hierarch. Cullen was given the reins to his own steed.

He was being sent home. Why? Had Stefan purchased his freedom? Maybe he wasn't being held for ransom because the ransom had already been paid.

They rode along a sunlit path striped by shadows of tall trees shaped like foxtails, then passed between silver doors into an underground passage lit by sunlight through openings overhead. At one point, the Bas turned to Cullen and said, "I have met few Khelds. I expected a barbarian."

"I expected to be impaled, eviscerated, and fed to dogs."

"Did you?"

"They told me that, the whole way here. Is that really what happened to the—the man?"

"The Kheld assassin? It did indeed. In Sordan's Dekkora. Sentence passed by the City's Halia."

"Not the Hierarch?"

"A kindness. He might have done it differently."

They emerged from beneath a high archway of stone onto a bridge that connected to the white expanse of the Rill platform. Mounted Epoptean guards met them and provided an escort through a handful of bowing Rill patrons to where the platform waited. The line of men—no longer hooded—was boarding a waiting *charys*. A man who had been talking with the guards walked toward them. Cullen recognized Sinon Kouranos.

Before he dismounted, Cullen caught a glimpse of Arton Metagoras, who waved and shouted to him before being cuffed into line and onto the *charys*.

While his horse was led away with the other beasts, Cullen stared at the enormous free-standing rings through which the *charys* would pass. He barely had time to think of asking to say goodbye to his aides who were aboard. With a soft sweet vibration that lifted the hairs on his arms, the first whine of Rill sign filled the air. In the next moment, the Sordan-bound *charys* was gone.

"I can't go home this way." Panic dried his mouth and blunted his words. He noted the steady regard of the Bas and explained. "Everyone knows Khelds can't ride the Rill. I don't know why I'm even alive right now, standing here this close."

The Bas turned to Sinon, who had joined them. He jerked a thumb at Cullen. "He thinks the Rill will kill him."

Sinon considered the possibility. "Will it?"

A shrug. "Am I a Sordaneon? He said to do it this way."

Sinon frowned and flicked a glance of warning to Cullen. *Say nothing.* "Thank you, Bas Kolgya, for delivering our countryman."

The Bas nodded. "I was told to deliver him in good condition. This is the best I could do."

Cullen stood straighter. "You and your staff treated me well, Bas Kolgya. I have no complaints. Thank you."

"I am not the man you should thank." The Bas turned again to Sinon. "I trust our business here is completed. You saw the hostages, confirmed their identities, and ascertained they are alive?"

"Every one of them. I believe we have both comported ourselves to satisfaction."

Though now was not the time to upend good fortune, Cullen decided to say one thing more. "If you would... please tell the Hierarch I thank him for his mercy."

The Bas snorted. "Mercy? My guess is he doesn't want Khelds in Sordan any more than he wants them in Gignastha."

Taken aback, Cullen said, "He could have done that by killing me."

"Something to keep in mind when questioning what the Rill will do. I was also told to give you this message." The Bas pressed a green velvet bag into Cullen's hand.

Cullen teased the bag open and found something within, small and white. A tooth. Before either man with him could ask about it, he dumped it back into the bag. Leave it to Dorilian to make things this clear.

Small dark eyes locked on his and the Bas allowed a thin smile. "Now go home—and meet your son."

"My *son*?" Cullen stared after the departing Bas. "Phalla had the baby? We have a son?"

Sinon brightened and gave a congenial grin. "Indeed, you do. A fine healthy boy, born at the Emrysen Palace a week ago. Your wife is also well."

And Cullen was going home, home to meet that babe. Wrap his arms around his wife. Maybe. If the Rill didn't kill him. From here on the broad deserted platform, cleared of all but those needed to conduct the Hierarch's business, Cullen had only to look across the white expanse to see the impressive walls of the residence in which he had washed and eaten. It wasn't that of the Bas. Sordan's Silver Eagle floated above its ramparts. There was a Sordaneon palace in every Rill port.

"I owe Dorilian, then, for letting me go. And Stefan too for paying my ransom."

"No ransom was asked or paid. No concession. In fact, His Majesty explicitly told me not to ask about you. Apparently, the Hierarch simply wished you to be released."

What? "Stefan said not to ask about me?"

"After the invasion, information was hard to come by. He did not want to alert anyone you were there."

Maybe, though it didn't make sense. Cullen's mission to Gignastha had been common knowledge. Verteus had made certain of his capture in the very first hour of the invasion. Yet there had been no talk about him at all? If some negotiation had taken place behind the scenes, Sinon would have been in on it.

"So who is *that* man? The Bas, the one who delivered me. He clearly knew."

Sinon didn't look surprised. "He is not a diplomat. What he is, though... his name is Tutto Rhunnard. He was Sebbord Teremareon's sword master and has served Dorilian since. He was created Bas of Kolgya two years ago. Few are closer to the Hierarch or more trusted."

Now Cullen recalled where he had seen the Bas. Permephedon, ahead of Stefan's coronation. That day. Tutto had commanded the soldiers who had facilitated Dorilian's escape. Dorilian had given the task of getting Cullen's ass out of Sordan's territory to a man he trusted.

Stefan had not given that job to anyone at all.

"I find it interesting Bas Tutto said he was *told* to deliver you in good condition." Sinon's steady regard had turned curious. "Only one person can tell Tutto Rhunnard to do anything."

Cullen curled his fingers around the velvet bag.

Booms announced an arriving *charys*. Long and sleek, the vessel emerged above Randpory Crossing and glided onto the platform. Cullen swallowed his fear. He no longer needed it. Either the Rill would kill him using this *charys*, or he would find himself back in Essera, safe and home. His world had turned inside out so many times, faith reigned as strong as belief.

"How did it happen?" In the short time he might have left, Cullen wanted an answer to one question. "The attack that led to all this... the attempt on Dorilian. Did Stefan order it?"

A mask of caution slipped over Sinon's affability. He averted his gaze. "About that, I cannot discuss what I know."

But he would have, if Stefan *hadn't* done it. Sent the man. An opening appeared in the *charys*'s cloud-silvered skin. Sinon and Cullen were to be the only passengers. Cullen wondered how his return had been arranged. Forged letters of identity? A secret deal with the Epoptes? He wouldn't put it past the Epoptes or Seven Houses to hope the Rill would do him in, but he didn't think Dorilian would have gone to the trouble, or given that message about having a son, just to kill him using his family's Entity.

Cullen entered the *charys* prepared to encounter its *otherness*. He found that... and also familiarity, a refuge for humans. Cool. Muted colors and lighting. Soothing. Cullen seated himself, as Sinon did, onto a kind of cushioned bench, and a moment later he was gently cocooned. No emotion, not even his, attached to whatever it was that welcomed and supported his body with such intimate utility.

Sinon's long familiarity with the Rill and its *charysi* no doubt explained why he looked relaxed and completely at ease. Despite having made his peace with the Entity, Cullen tamped down a lingering sense of certain doom. It was almost a relief when he noticed Sinon gazing the velvet bag. Questions rippled behind the ambassador's conscientious expression.

Why not? Cullen poured the tooth into his palm and showed it. "It's his. A message."

Sinon said nothing, just lifted his gaze in astonishment.

"I had a chance once to kick him when he was down, you see—and I didn't." Cullen returned the message to its bag. "He's saying now we're even."

30

The platforms at Dazunor-Rannuli were as empty as those at Randpory. Dazunor-Rannuli's platforms were *never* empty. Cullen understood this aberration for what it was: an Epoptean maneuver to conceal that Khelds could, in fact, ride the Rill. Whether that had always been the case or something foundational about the Rill had changed, Cullen hardly cared.

Khelds could ride the Rill. Dorilian had almost certainly known this for years.

Well, Khelds can't ride the Rill, Cullen remembered saying during a breakfast at Gustan. And Dorilian had retorted, *Ask yourself why.*

The why obscured everything.

Now, more than ever, Cullen believed the rumors he'd heard about the Permephedon Treaty and what it would have delivered. Marc Frederick had not planned his achievement alone. Dorilian had been part of it. Those days and months preceding the Conclave... they had been laying the groundwork. Now Cullen's mind tumbled with what it might take to make the dream still happen.

Stefan did not meet him at the Rill Mount. Cullen and Sinon were met by Epoptes and quickly ushered away, and when they emerged by hidden passageways onto a terrace on the far side of the station and its grand platforms, they were well concealed from prying eyes. Clouds scuttered across a gray lifeless sky. The city's manses and warehouses looked empty, abandoned, despite heavy traffic on the Lower Canal. Across the river at the edge of the city, in forested Amallar, Ranwulf's mother went about her life, as yet unaware that her son was dead. No one yet knew. Sinon had not asked about Ranwulf either.

Cullen stood on that heretofore unknown vantage and looked out at a city wreathed in shadows and lies.

He drew a breath of cold heavy air. Winter gripped Essera more harshly than Randpory. He watched Sinon receive a message from their Epopte escort, who then returned to the complex by way of an iron door that loudly closed and locked behind them.

Sinon joined Cullen again and looked apologetic.

"I know you must be weary. However, the king wishes to see us. You primarily. I sent a message ahead relating the success of my mission and informing him of our arrival."

Cullen cursed under his breath. He was not in the mood for this. He wanted to see Asphalladra and hold her. Hold their baby. Change out of these clothes. He didn't want to see Stefan. But a temper stretched thin was poor excuse for pissing off a king. He had just been freed from two cruel weeks under the boots of men who held power over him, doing every possible humiliating thing to survive. He might as well add Stefan to the list.

He made a rueful plea to Sinon, who he had begun to like. "Can we make my part of the visit short?"

Sinon looked doubtful. "I will do what I can. His Majesty… can be difficult to escape."

"You have important information. Stefan will need to make decisions, critical ones, based on what *you* have to say."

"You understand these things." Something wistful touched Sinon's sigh. "Affairs between sovereign nations often become delicate. Situations can and do change without warning. When what is needed is a meeting of cool heads and open hearts, it can appear impossible to bring those minds and hearts together. Overcoming such barriers is what I am trained to do. I went to Randpory to establish communication with Sordan. You saw the extremely limited extent of my success."

"Is that what Stefan asked of you? To establish communication with Sordan?"

They resumed their walk downhill. "I believe he said that I should find out what that asshole in Sordan was up to and if there were any of our people he could account for."

That sounded more like Stefan.

Cullen was back. Stefan stood at the window overlooking the sluggish dark current of the canal and willed the gond he had sent to appear. The Rill loomed bright across the Lago, slashing the sky. Cullen would arrive soon, maybe had arrived already. He wasn't dead or languishing in some dank cell in Gignastha or Sordan. He wasn't being held for an exorbitant ransom designed to humiliate, neither had he been executed cruelly to deliver a message or been turned into a fucking *punishment.* As impossible as it seemed, someone along the way had mistaken Cullen for nobody, overlooked his importance. Or maybe Cullen had befriended someone of influence or, even better, had tricked them. That must be how this had happened, the only way it *could* have happened. Against every fear, every terrible prospect, Cullen had been handed over to Sinon Kouranos in Randpory and was coming home.

What didn't make sense, none at all, was that Cullen was making the journey by Rill. As far as Stefan knew, Cullen owned no Staubaun blood through either his father or mother. Not a drop. Stefan looked down at his palm and the thin scar of their blood bond. Maybe, unwittingly, all those years ago, *he* had made it possible.

When he saw the covered gond near the Kings Gate that would bring the vessel into a watery courtyard with access to the residence and state apartments, Stefan summoned his chamberlain. "Archon Heddros and Ambassador Kouranos will be here shortly. Have the kitchen send up food, bread, and meat—nothing too fancy. And ale, the best we have." The man left to do as bidden.

Stefan liked having people do his bidding. Life was far simpler that way. Stefan resumed staring out the window at the vastly rich, Rill-crowned city he ruled, its towers and cupolas bold against gray clouds. Corrupted to its core, Dazunor-Rannuli nonetheless beat at the center of his kingdom, a mighty engine of commerce, politics, and power.

He turned toward the door when it opened, the chamberlain announcing the ambassador and the Archon of Heddros. Cullen. He looked thinner and was clothed in garments clearly not his own. The beard was new. It had been years since Stefan had seen him with one, even though as king Stefan had urged men he raised to a title or high post to display Kheld pride by show of facial hair. He often did so himself. Seeing Cullen with a short, neat beard challenged Stefan's memory of his fresh-faced, boyish friend.

He walked forward, arms open for their usual embrace. "Lud's Spear, Cullen! It's true. You're here and whole!"

"Mostly."

Cullen didn't lean in to greet Stefan. His clasp felt perfunctory, not at all what Stefan expected. He stepped back, confused.

"Are you all right? Did those bastards hurt you?"

That earned him a sharp look. Sinon spoke up and probably prevented a sharp answer.

"I was pleased to see Archon Heddros returned in good condition. His name was not on the list included in documents I had been given by Sordan's representative." The ambassador held out an envelope thick with papers. Stefan took the lot without looking at them. Cullen was behaving strangely. Dulled. Subdued. Tense and silent. Stefan knew the signs... his friend was angry. About what?

It was probably best to discuss this other business first.

"How many?"

"Twenty-seven. For those hostages with lands or landed relations, or wealthy families in Essera proper, ransom terms are included. Persons tied to Gignastha or either iteration of Neuberland are noted as being held hostage as security for the conduct of their families going forward. Those people cannot be ransomed. I obtained a general promise that they will be well treated."

"A general promise?"

"I believe the statement was, 'the usual understanding.'"

Which meant not much of anything. "Did the 'representative' give you an explanation for why Dorilian broke the fucking Watergilt Agreement by invading *our* land and taking *our* city?"

"The documents lay out the official—"

Cullen snorted. "He did it because *you* sent a fucking assassin."

Stefan noted how Sinon inhaled sharply through clenched teeth, then bowed his head in resignation that the explanation had been laid out so bluntly. Had there been words exchanged beforehand? Because what the hells was Cullen doing?

"If this man told you—"

"Don't blame him." Cullen's blue eyes narrowed. "I heard *that* bit in Gignastha when I asked the Sordani commander why he invaded. He said straight to my face that Essera invaded Sordan *first* when my asshole king sent an assassin to kill their Hierarch."

"And you believe that tale? An enemy's lies?"

"Are you telling me you didn't do it?"

"I'm telling you I think you need to cool down." It wasn't like Cullen to challenge Stefan this way, like no one else was in the room. Something broken lurked at the edges of this.

Sinon lifted his head again to make a timely request. "If Your Majesty would allow it, I think I should retire."

Yes, that would be for the best. Stefan had the man's damned reports. "Leave us. We can talk later."

And they would, much later. Because he and Cullen were going to talk now. Stefan waited only until the door closed behind Sinon. "Listen, Cullen—"

"You made me a promise, Stefan. A promise I could talk plain to you. Well, I've got things to say."

"And so do I!"

"Then we'll have a fine time, won't we?" Cullen ignored the food-laden table and ale set in front of chairs facing a cheerful fire and instead paced to the windows so he might overlook the Upper Canal.

"None of that business with Gignastha was supposed to happen, Cullen." Stefan needed to set matters straight. "When I heard Gignastha got invaded, I was sick about it, knowing you were there."

"Because that's where you sent me!"

"It was safe. I had a garrison in place."

Cullen granted him the point. "Well, that's who they killed off first."

Six thousand men. Hundreds slain in the fighting. Scores of men, all Kheld, had been pushed into the bone-dissolving Sar Pryannis. Hundreds more had been slain at the fortress of Horcrod. So many men captured or lost, Stefan had needed to explain to the Thegnkeld and the Seven Houses, and his nobles too, how it had happened. It didn't seem right that a failed attempt to remove his rival had cost him a domain as well as precious support at home. That Gignastha's Governor had surrendered the city had been a major embarrassment. And the Malyrdeons weren't even speaking to Stefan anymore.

"Well, they didn't slaughter *you* and I'm glad. I was sick with worry what might happen if Sordan found you. Rumors were terrible about what was going on down there. They're killing Kheld folk every chance they get. So when I heard just a few hours ago, when Sinon sent that message that you were alive and coming home—"

"And you knew nothing before then? About me? About where I was?"

Was Cullen hurt because he thought Stefan had known him to be captive and not tried to help? He could put that to rest. "Nothing! Nothing at all, not until Sinon—"

"That's because you didn't fucking ask!"

"Think about why! I didn't want to put you in danger, in case you'd gotten away!"

"Put me in *danger?* By asking if I was even alive?" A tone entered Cullen's voice that Stefan hadn't heard in years. Not since they were boys, when anger could erupt into fists.

"Yes, danger. Danger from every side. Dorilian's an asshole. A complete bastard. You remember what he did at Orqho—sent his soldiers straight after me!" Stefan pointed to his ribs. "I still bear the scar. If he knew you were at Gignastha—"

"He *did* know! *Everybody* knew I was at Gignastha! The Governor knew. All the nobles. Half of fucking Essera! You could have found out they hadn't killed me. Let my wife know I was alive. My family. Sordan had my name the very first day. Put it on a list."

"I never saw the list! You think I knew he had one? All I could think of was what he would do with such a prize. He'd have hunted you down just so he could dangle you in front of me. Break me with a ransom so high it would bankrupt this kingdom. Maybe execute you the way he did the man they caught, torture and kill you for the world to see. To humiliate me! He'd do anything just to cause me pain!"

Cullen remained unmoved, a bearded angry man in foreign clothes, framed by the powerful city behind him. "You? What about *me*? Did you ever think about how fucked I was?"

"Every day."

"No, you didn't. Because if you'd been thinking at all about me, and not your smoke dream of giving a royal domain to Lowen, you would *never* have sent me into that box of kindling. Gignastha lives and breathes that Khelds need killing, and you knew that. But what's worse is that you knew when you sent me, you *fucking knew*, that you'd sent an assassin—a bloody Kheld—to kill Dorilian Sordaneon!" Cullen was screaming now. "Did it ever occur to you to tell me *about that*?"

"I couldn't tell you about that."

"Why not? It wouldn't have changed anything. I would just have told you not to do it. And you wouldn't have listened—the same way you never listen—and done it anyway."

Except then Cullen would not have gone to Gignastha. Point made and taken. Stefan ran a hand through his hair, wishing he could disagree with the way things had happened—or how that conversation would have gone.

Cullen gave a deep sigh and shook his head, accusation in his eyes. "You put me right in his path, Stefan. Your stupid stunt started a war—with me smack in the middle—and you put me and my people right where that crazy bastard would strike. And don't tell me you didn't know that. What did you think was going to happen?"

"I thought it was going to work." Stefan shook his head. "I thought he would be dead! He should have been. The woman got in the way."

Stefan could not decipher the silence that fell between them or the sorrowful look on Cullen's face. Right when he needed Cullen to understand and advocate for him, his friend refused to take his side.

"Stefan, I just—this is… it's too much. It's bigger than me. Every time you do something like this, you only see one outcome: the one you want. Sinon told me that woman will never walk again, not for the rest of her life."

As if that mattered. "I guess Dorilian will just have to find some other woman to jiggle his cock."

"Is that what you think this is about? That's not it, not for him." Cullen rolled his eyes. "I'm damn lucky to be alive. And I'm not alive because of you. I'm alive because of *Dorilian*!"

Stefan stared.

"Don't you understand? He knew he had me. All those things you were afraid he'd do? He could have done them. Done them for the world to see. Hells, maybe you *did* save me. Maybe Dorilian only let me go because he saw you didn't give a fuck!"

If Cullen thought that—

Stefan scoffed. "If he's that squirrel-head stupid, I'm glad! But he's not, is he? He's just showing off again. He's playing games! With me, with you… with everyone. The way he always does."

"Maybe so. And maybe I was just useless to him. I don't care! I want out. His damn games and yours too. Two loon-crazy idiots going around and around until one of you kills the other. Well, I don't want to be part of it. I'm done." Cullen's anger had deflated and the tension in his body had fled. "Mother's Milk, Stefan, I don't even know you. I don't know you anymore. I'm not the only one you didn't ask about. Do you know Ranwulf is dead? Lowen's nephew—remember him?—that I gave a post as my assistant? A soldier cut him down right in front of me and spilled his brains on the floor."

Oh shit. Stefan hadn't asked… he'd talked to Ranwulf's kin about how maybe he had escaped too. "Hells, Cullen."

"I have to visit his mother. Tell her what happened. Don't you see? People are going to *die* over this. People have died already! Khelds. Staubauns. The whole of Neuberland is going to go up in flames."

"I'll take Gignastha back." Stefan had sent two of his commanders and ten thousand men to the region using the Rill to Leseos. That domain's Bas had been unhappy about the troop movement but had honored the request because Leseos was Dorilian's likely next target.

"No. You won't. I can't even tell you why you won't because you've made clear you don't listen to a word I say, not like you used to. And I can't stand beside you with my tongue always between my teeth. I can't be your Minister of Trade anymore. I can't do it, knowing you were willing to throw me away."

"That wasn't what I was doing."

Cullen looked over his shoulder, past the room's fine furnishings to the twilight outside the window, where the Rill glowed above Dazunor-Rannuli like some creature out of dreams, spinning webs of power. With a shake of his head, he walked toward the door. "I need to get home. I need to see Phalla, and my son."

Another slap to the face of this reunion. Stefan had wanted to be the one to give Cullen this news too. Would have given it already but for this ridiculous argument. What other news had Sinon spilled? The man clearly could not hold a secret.

"Go," Stefan said. This day couldn't possibly get any worse, but he didn't see the point of keeping Cullen around to prove him wrong. "At least you'll be glad to see *them*."

Cullen stopped within a few feet of Stefan and faced him. He looked regretful and aware he'd gone too far. "I'll always be your friend, Stefan. Nothing can change that. And I'm your subject too... today and forever. Nothing can change that either."

"I'm your friend too. Blood bond." Stefan held up his left hand, showing the faint scar on his palm.

Cullen did the same. A bandage concealed the scar on his palm, but Stefan remembered what it looked like. Thick and knotted. On making the bond Cullen had cut too deeply and loosed enough blood to make a bond last forever.

Except it hadn't.

31

"Apollonia is dead?" Stefan's first thought was he had not heard correctly.

"The day after I arrived. She died in her sleep. But not before she gave permission for Mormantaloran ships to use Aral's harbor. She spoke with Nammuor's emissary, Coram Barzanes, who was most persuasive. Her minister of state transmitted her will by array and it is already here, awaiting your reading."

Erenor looked sea-tanned and fit. Stefan had received his initial communication from Aral and looked forward all week to hearing good news about his endeavor. A carpet of spring crocus and fragrant snowcaps greeted their boots as they walked past the Emrysen Palace's hedges to the Damselwing Marsh, where they could talk in complete privacy.

"It almost worked. I almost got that bastard." The path Stefan followed led from the lawn to a wooden walkway, and from there to a raised bit of ground at the spongy heart of the wetland, with naught but grassy weeds at the water's edge and a wooden bench to sit on. Marc Frederick had spent time there in all seasons, looking at birds.

Erenor turned his face away. He rubbed his hand over his mouth. "That was a bold maneuver, sire… and a dangerous one, especially had it succeeded. Imperiling the Rill—"

That old fear. "Do you really think the Rill will die if he does?"

"The mere possibility should terrify us all. The Entities"— Erenor shook his head —"are what makes this Triempery what it is. Our power resides in the Wall and the Rill, our economy, our influence. And now we must hope the attempt on Dorilian's life does not upset our agreement with Nammuor. He spoke against doing anything that might threaten the Sordaneons."

Fuck that. "I'm not going to let Nammuor dictate my actions."

"Of course not, but you said yourself when you sent me to Mormantalorus that I was to assure Nammuor that we recognize and respect that the Sordaneon boy is his Heir also."

"Which you did."

"Oh yes."

Stefan nodded and plopped onto the bench. The smooth wooden seat, polished by decades of weather and asses, welcomed his without splinters. Of late it seemed to Stefan that his kingship was plagued by other people's children. Erenor, thank the Mother, moved on from that.

"You will be pleased to know Nammuor has agreed to increase trade with our kingdom. Wool and wines and cheese. He is also willing to purchase lumber in large quantities, certain types, of course. He will sell us more waterglobes and other devices. Your trade minister can settle the specifics with Barzanes, who waits word in Aral."

"He understands, I trust, that he will be meeting a Kheld."

"Yes."

Not Cullen, of course. Cullen had left court entirely six weeks ago and withdrawn with his wife and son to Wyre. He had wealth enough to live comfortably, not least because Stefan had not taken away his titles or the extensive lands attached to same. Though Cullen had recommended the ransomed Arton Metagoras to be his successor as Minister of Trade, Stefan had wanted another Kheld in that role and appointed Neddig.

Stefan cocked his head to listen to the rest of Erenor's report.

"Nammuor's ships will also shadow and protect ours at sea. Dorilian's sea wolves will take some losses, I expect."

"Good. Maybe that will make him back off."

"Probably." Erenor's brows drew together. "I expected you to be happier about my news."

He was happy enough. Erenor's news so far had been everything Stefan had hoped for. More trade. Military cooperation. His foreign overtures were paying more dividends by far than his domestic ones. "Have Nammuor's man, Barzanes, come to Trulo. I would like to pursue this further."

"Yes, sire."

"You're the only person who hasn't failed me." Not only had

Cullen abandoned him, Lowen was complaining that his new lofty position as Bas of Ellys was merely nominal and lacked sufficient income. No one was happy with Stefan anymore. "This morning Palaistea petitioned the Archhalia to ennoble her sons with their titles. Prince of Stauberg and Prince of Lacenedon! She wants her brats to be invested with domains! The one boy is only four! I can see where that's leading."

"The Highborn are making their move, then."

"What else can it be?"

Erenor pressed his lips and gave no answer. There was none. The look on his face was grim but supportive.

"The only petition I granted was that of Elhanan Dannutheon. He asked to go to Stauberg to be there for the Festival of Seven Days. He does it every year." The festival celebrated Ergeiron's raising of the Wall, which had led to the defeat of the Aryati and, not long after, the founding of the Triempery.

Erenor appeared to approve the decision. "The Wall is too important. And the Malyrdeons don't have the Wall Stone, so it is all for show. You did the right thing."

"Maybe so." Stefan hadn't wanted to let any Malyrdeons go to Stauberg this year, none at all, and to hell with their stupid Wall—but his advisors had warned that the people might riot. "I'm tired of buying votes to get around them." A spent flowerhead from the year before drooped toward the bench, its sodden mass dripping condensation on his leg. Annoyed, Stefan broke it off and tossed it into the glistening, ice-glazed bog. "I can't afford it anymore. Buying votes. Owing favors. Having to confront opposition, then having to back down. I can't get enough people into titles high enough to support me. Fucking Gignastha! Now Neuberland is worse than it ever was. There are so many settlements under attack and needing defending, and so many Sordani troops marauding about, my generals can't even *reach* Gignastha to take it back."

"Maybe Nammuor can help with that too." Erenor leaned toward Stefan, fingers steepled before his face. "He impressed me, sire. He's clever and powerful, and he has the same goals we do. The Highborn cold-shouldered Mormantalorus for decades before he took charge. Before the Sordaneon ever tried to strangle us, the Malyrdeons were strangling Nammuor."

That was true. Upon becoming Heir to Essera, Stefan had spent endless hours with Marc Frederick and men assigned to elevate his education. Their message was always the same: that Mormantalorus—not Sordan—presented a mortal danger to his family and the Triempery, and must be ostracized to prevent them from gaining allies or making use of natural advantages.

The volcano on which Mormantalorus was built facilitated the production of arcane crystals. Scholars and physicians valued such crystals. The Brotherhood of Epoptes, which relied on *lr* devices to enhance interaction with the Rill and, to a more limited extent, the Wall, distrusted Mormantalorus and would not use crystals forged there. Rumors existed of *lr* weaponry possessed with enormous destructive potential.

But Stefan had been told, too, that such weapons carried a price. Some kind of price.

Stefan regarded Erenor's hopeful visage. He probably should wonder more about what Erenor wanted out of this. Most likely a higher title and place. A lofty marriage. The usual prizes. Mormantalorus could give Erenor none of those things—but he might achieve them through greater usefulness to his king. Tahlwent had just become available.

"Let's go read Apollonia's will. With any luck, I can find a way to make *that* vote a friendly one."

Emyli laid the fine broadcloth on her lap and turned over the seam of the armhole for the sleeve she would attach. Shirt making was not something she did often, though she had learned how to wield loom, needle, and scissors years ago at Aurdollen. Her education as a proper Kheld woman had been thorough and included all Three Faces of the Mother.

Wisdom—the arts of poetry, letters, science, lore, and reading of runes.

Life—the arts of healing, agriculture, nature, and sex.

Home—the arts of textiles, preparing food, running a household, and childrearing.

Making shirts belonged to the home and, in her case, at least with this shirt, to children as well. Nilla, seated across from Emyli, nearer the fire and sewing intently, was determined to keep Stefan well stocked with fine shirts. After nearly four years as Stefan's queen, the young woman had become adept at embroidering with gold thread. The Kheldic pattern now being stitched—oak leaves and acorns twined with rune symbols—was deeply beautiful, fit for a king.

"You don't have to sew through the day. I am certain the shirt will be finished by Stefan's coronation anniversary." Emyli resumed attaching the sleeve on which she was working.

"I don't want to disappoint him." Nilla lifted a gaze heavy with regret. "He's had so much of that lately."

Yes. Stefan's falling-out with Cullen had disappointed a great many people. Nobles who had looked to Cullen's clear-headed influence either felt upended or hoped to take that place themselves. Emyli had counseled her son against some of them.

"I miss Phalla." Nilla sighed and laid aside the shirt front panel she had been embroidering. She looked to the windows and a view of the river. Fresh green dotted hosts of budding trees. The Golden Palace was enjoying a spell of warm weather. "She writes to me, you know. Keeping up my lessons in Stauba. I'm getting quite good. She and Cullen are adding to the house at Wyre and she says the baby's getting big. I think that's what I miss the most, having her and little Wulf around. They left court so suddenly."

Emyli wished she knew exactly what had led to that. Cullen's ordeal at Gignastha, to be certain. Asphalladra had revealed some of the awful details. Sadly, Emyli suspected Stefan's role in the precipitating event. She didn't know how to convince Stefan to just leave his enemy be. Though bound by his promise, Dorilian had proven he would, if provoked, retaliate.

Stefan might already have turned Dorilian so much against him that he could not be turned back.

"I'm sorry, Lady. I know you worry about him, too."

Nilla had noticed Emyli's preoccupation. "How can I not?" Emyli admitted her great weakness. "Mothers never stop worrying about their children, no matter how big they get, no matter how powerful. I read Stefan's runes every day, though I really shouldn't do that. They are quite confused right now." This morning her runes had promised good news, yet there were also, as always, portents of calamity from paths still hidden.

Like all prognostications, reading runes was fraught with pitfalls. Any attempt to force interpretation laid traps for the unwary.

Nilla picked up her needle again. "Wisdom is such a demanding Face, so much to remember! Mother Gifu tried to teach me to read runes, but I could make no sense of them at all. I haven't used my stones even once since Stefan and I wed."

"Not every Kheld woman possesses the gift."

"True, though only our women do." Nilla made three long stitches. "Is the Bog Crone Kheld?"

Now it was Emyli who put down her stitching. The Bog Crone

was a dark myth, a creature of folk tales designed to frighten children. "I don't suppose anyone knows for certain."

Nilla continued to stitch. "I think she must be, because she foretold my fate." She lifted a smile that hinted at secrets. "I never told Stefan, but years ago, when we were but thirteen, Lark and Aubrey and I spent the summer at the Rappeleye holding near the Bogs—and we saw her. The Bog Crone. We were in some high marsh grasses and we spied a hut or something in the mist, so we went to see. Her hut had roots like a tree, and she lived inside it. She was white-haired and old and had but one good eye, and the other was black and missing. People say she's One-Eyed Bess, you know."

"Yes, I have heard that." Rapt, Emyli waited for more.

"We asked if she was, but she didn't answer. She didn't ask our names. She just held out her bag, shook the runes within, and bid us each take a stone—and of course we did. When we were done, she laid our Wheel. Three of us on one Wheel, imagine that." Nilla stabbed her needle and its gold thread through the fine cloth she'd woven herself. "I can't tell you everything she told us. Old Mother Rappeleye made us promise never to tell. 'Alter one; alter all,' she said. But I will tell you my part because mine has happened already. 'For one girl, a king' is what the Crone said. And that reading came true when Stefan chose me."

Nilla's words laid bare something terrible. *Stefan chose me.* Words carried power within their arrangement. Runes were but one aspect of Wisdom. So were words and song and a Wheel's revelations about the Mother's Path. The summer Nilla had been thirteen, Stefan had just become king. Emyli felt her lips grow cold. What else had the Crone foreseen?

"I'm with child again."

Shocked out of her thoughts, Emyli looked back to Nilla, whose blue eyes shone with the secret.

"I told Stefan this morning, after the *faetha* confirmed it." A *faetha*, a Kheld woman who had mastered the Face of Healing, had taken the place of the Royal Physician. "It's still very early. The babe will be born after the harvest."

"What wonderful news. I—"

"I hope you'll stay with me, as part of my household. I asked Stefan and he said you could. I made a case for you, because I so miss Phalla and, well, you are a *faetha* in your own right. After the last time—"

"You'll be fine. Of course you will be. And of course I will stay. I will help you and him, and the baby too." Emyli wanted nothing more than to be near her son and do everything in her power to help him. Stefan's coldness and suspicion over the last few years had been miserable.

"I do hope he'll be happy with the new shirt." Nilla rose and walked to the mannequin of Stefan's form, which she liked to dress and accessorize. She pinned the front panel to the form and flattened the fabric to better assess her design. "He didn't like the last one. He said it was too plain."

"Men should have to stitch and adorn their own shirts, and they would be less critical."

"They probably should. But for women, men would have neither shirts nor babies. They would have only each other." Nilla laughed. "Stefan might not be so unhappy. He prefers men for all things other than in bed. I didn't mind so much when it was Cullen he needed always at his side. But he has taken to Erenor of late, and I don't like him so well."

Emyli turned the side panel in her hand so she could make the last few stitches. "They've known each other for years."

"Stefan has known Cullen too, since they were boys. Cullen would talk to me, though. Erenor pretends he doesn't notice me at all. Just two mornings ago he returned from a visit to Aral and walked into the room, talked to Stefan, and then they both walked out. Neither acted for a moment as if I were there."

Emyli hid her interest by looking closely at her work. Erenor was spending a great deal of time in Aral.

"The Gracious Queen's passing was so sudden. I didn't think she was that old."

"She wasn't. Women of high Staubaun birth can live well into their hundred years. You've met Kathanos's mother, Smaragda—she's a hundred and three."

"Truly?" Nilla's wide gaze and open smile celebrated such an accomplishment. "Imagine being such an age. Stefan said Smaragda was too old to be one of my ladies when I asked. Still, I think she has wonderful wisdom to share. The Mother works through us all, not Khelds alone."

"All women, all men." Sons, as well as daughters. Emyli held up her panel, sleeve attached. "Done."

"I used to wonder what work the Mother did through the Gracious Queen. But Phalla explained it, I think. She told me how the throne came to the old king, your father." Nilla took the panel from Emyli's hands and proceeded to pin it to the form. "The Mother worked things so Essera's throne would come to Stefan."

Emyli rose and went to stand beside Nilla. The golden embroidery would soon be finished.

"Yes," she said. But the Mother had seen to much more than that.

Rheger closed his eyes the better to open his senses. As he stood upon the cliffside wall of the Dannutheon manse perched above Stauberg's magnificent harbor, more than sunlight kissed his skin. Wall energy sang along his nerves and he wondered, with fresh appreciation, if Dorilian Sordaneon felt the Rill in the same way. Probably. A pure human would not have felt anything at all. Rheger opened his eyes again, this time to gaze upon the source of his experience.

The Wall. Mysterious, always in motion, cascading and contained. Time Binder. Protector. *Father.* Generations linked Rheger to his Entity, life by life and century by century. Those lives linked the Wall to Stauberg as well.

A footstep alerted him. A stone underfoot. He turned to greet Elhanan, who embraced him with a grin. "Father! I had heard you arrived!"

"A miserable journey. I avoided visiting anyone on the way." To do so might have subjected his hosts to scrutiny from Stefan, whose distrust of his kindred remained high.

"Then it's good Margarid and Mother came to join me ahead of you. They spent a few days in Bynum. Palaistea is doing well and the boys are thriving. It's a crime, if you ask me, that they cannot be here."

Rheger flashed his son a look of warning. For all that he agreed with Elhanan's sentiment, it was best not to speak such thoughts aloud. "That day will come." A quick glance to each side revealed how open their vantage was and how visible to many. "Let's go inside."

They entered a nearly circular room purposed for the viewing of Entities. The sea view showed the Wall and, out in the harbor, the ghostly shape of the Rill. The windows on the room's other side framed a fine view of the Wall's city aspect, in particular its monumental and largely ceremonial Gate of the Transformation. The original gate of the city, the structure had itself transformed. High and white and blue, carved with the story of the Entity's birth and crowned with arches of adamant topped by horns of sublime power, the Gate stood above the Aidion, the Eternal Shrine. From a mortal gate in a mortal wall, Ergeiron had undergone his immortal metamorphosis—a soaring protector above a sea of humanity.

Te'eros Vllyr. Ergeiron's pronouncement was carved into the Aidion's base.

Guardian Against Vllyr.

Rheger grimly acknowledged the mystery of his ancestor's ethereal, shifting structure. *You were supposed to warn us, Father. Did you?*

New movement at the Aesa Eranos caught Rheger's attention. The royal palace towered nearby, glimpsed past trees and the grand manses of nobles. The plaza in front of the palace swarmed with activity, the displacement of one crowd by arrival of another. The Festival of Seven Days meant the city was filled to overflowing. In years past, those celebrants would have believed the Highborn mythos. Believed in Wall and Rill, and that Leur still lived in the World of its Second Creation. Unfortunately, the Aesa Eranos no longer housed any descendants of Amynas or Leur, but feted guests of the king.

A king who sat upon the throne of Rheger's forefathers.

Elhanan noticed his father was being thoughtful. "What are you thinking?"

Rheger reached into his jacket. He pulled out the deathstone box and held it out. "About this."

Elhanan took the box in hand and examined it. He located and pressed the lock, which opened to his flesh's signature. Wonder widened his eyes. "The Wall Stone! He gave it to you?"

Rheger nodded. "I think something happened. He would not tell me what, but... as you can see, it is back in our hands."

"And with Stefan none the wiser." Elhanan looked for confirmation of that conclusion.

"I would say not, unless Dorilian told him."

"I don't suppose he would. This is amazing." Elhanan lifted the Wall Stone by its chain and put the box aside. The artifact glowed as brightly in this sunlit room as it had in the night-shadowed rotunda of the King's House. "I—I've never used it. I never walked the Wall. Enreddon only showed me how to use the Stone to access the Archive."

"Then that may be where to start."

Elhanan swallowed, then spoke in a lower, worried voice. "What am I looking for?"

To that, Rheger could only frown. Though he was Wall kindred, he possessed no affinity and had never been apprised of exactly *how* the Wall Lords went about their business. But he could surmise a few things. "I suggest you start by looking at Stefan. And Dorilian, too. The Demise... one survived it. And the other should have been there—but was told by our kindred to stay home."

Stefan thought his meeting with Coram Barzanes had gone well. He walked the west-facing terrace of the Golden Palace and watched the flow of barges on the Dazun. Though Gustan and Cobbe, both downstream, were the last navigable towns on the river and served as ports for Tahlwent, Trulo was larger and saw more traffic. It was also home seat for the Principate of Dazunor and, currently, for Stefan's court. It made a fair setting for meeting a dignitary from a land he wished to impress.

Fair. But not awe-inspiring. Coram had looked unimpressed. He had departed downstream an hour ago.

I should have met him at Stauberg. The Wall would have impressed him. Next time. They were to meet there later this year.

"We are getting what we want." Erenor was determined to cast the visit as successful.

"And what is that?"

"Markets. Money pouring in for our goods. Ships to harass Sordan's in our waters."

That was perhaps the best outcome. Essera's merchants still wanted to conduct trade with Sordan, but that didn't mean Stefan had to make things easy for them. Having Nammuor's ships using his ports would put a dent in that activity. Coram had promised Mormantaloran merchant ships to arrive at Aral and Stauberg within two months.

Erenor broached another matter. "It's important to settle disposition of Tahlwent. The Gracious Queen's death without an heir means—"

"I know what it means." Stefan had been advised by his legal counsel, Kathanos Niarchos, about Tahlwent's succession. Apollonia's marriage to Marc Frederick had brought the domain to the crown, the intent of the contract being that it would pass to her son. Her will had not challenged that intent. Though Kathanos had counselled Stefan to keep the title and add it to his crown holdings, Erenor had pointed out Stefan might gain more leverage to bestow Tahlwent on a loyal supporter. If Tahlwent remained one of Stefan's holdings, it would become as toothless as Dazunor or Gignastha, neither of which held an independent vote in the Archhalia.

The old bitch thought she'd live forever. Now, thanks to her, I'm richer. I have her Rill holdings, per that contract. I have whatever gold she amassed. He did not really need the title, or the lands.

But he did need every vote he could get.

A sound of footsteps and the soft rustle of fabric caused him to turn. Erenor followed Stefan's movement to discern who had joined them. To see Emyli was not a surprise. She looked relaxed for once, unhurried and smiling. Seeing her so made him happy, so Stefan moved to embrace her, wrapping his arm over her shoulders and presenting his face for her light kiss on the cheek. It was just as important for his subjects to see his mother at his side, lioness-fierce, as for them to see his wife.

Even Erenor, secure in Stefan's favor, bowed his respect.

"Your Majesty. Princess. Permission to withdraw until later?"

"Go." There were people to whom Stefan preferred to speak in total privacy. His plain-speaking mother was one.

"I spent the afternoon with Nilla. She told me your news."

Of course she had. Women couldn't keep secrets at all, especially not from each other. Stefan didn't really mind; his mother hoped for an heir as ardently as he did. "We're taking precautions this time. Nilla only trusts *faethas* to attend her. Her own cook, a Kheld, from her own kin. All her ladies are Kheld now. Tasters, too. Our enemies will find Khelds harder to recruit."

"I would do the same, I think."

He led the way to a bench between pots of blue hyacinths and mounded pinks, fragrant splashes of color on a sea of marble beneath of pale blue sky. He had noticed lately how he felt more at home when out of doors. Emyli clasped his hand in hers.

"The Gracious Queen will be interred at the Halasseon Palace mausoleum in another week or so." Emyli's voice suited quiet, solemn things. "Will you be there?"

"Hells no. We despised each other. She despised all of us, even grandfather. No, I gave that thankless mission to Erenor. His grandmother was Apollonia's sister. Did you know that?" Stefan laughed at her look of surprise, understanding where it came from. "Seems the Highborn aren't that different from other men—they sire bastards too. Maybe I should scout around the Royal North and see if old Enreddon left behind any by-blows to cause trouble for me."

Emyli sighed. Stefan immediately wished he hadn't said that.

His mother had dealt for years with accusations of Hans being a bastard. His fucking brother. Stefan had stopped asking her where Hans might be, and he couldn't even find Marenthro anymore.

When he looked up again, he saw that her gaze upon him had softened. "You really do take the cares of the world on your shoulders."

"Just the cares of this kingdom, which is fighting me every step of the way." Stefan looked at the river again. "You might as well know… I am giving the Principate of Aral to Erenor."

"No! Stefan, you can't."

He had expected that note of censure in her voice. "Actually, I can. I am king and Aral is legally a crown holding."

"You cannot make that man a prince."

"Maybe not. Kathanos explained it to me. But I *can* make him a Bas. I would have given it to Lowen except Tahlwent would never accept a Kheld." No more than Gignastha had.

"They would, had you given it to your brother."

"Really?" Stefan shot her a narrow glare and curled his lip. "Maybe they would accept him, but there's one big problem with that: he's not *here*. I need a vote in the Archhalia, Mother, not a domain with an absent prince."

She opened her mouth to speak, but he stopped her short.

"You made sure, didn't you, that I couldn't give Hans anything? Land. Titles. A brother's guidance that might benefit this kingdom."

"You can give him everything! He is your family, your own blood. When he returns, he will be your ally."

"Or my enemy. I don't know him at all anymore, do I?"

Shouts from the veranda penetrated the quiet, followed immediately by sounds of laughter. Emyli shook her head, disbelief etched on her distraught features. "He will be your brother. Your friend. Your *champion*… oh, Stefan! He will have your back and stand at your side to help fight your enemies. You two will be so strong together, so much stronger than anyone could ever know."

"Or he may not return at all and none of that will ever happen." He sighed and stood, looking down at his frantic mother. "I need to do things that will help me here and now. I'm making Erenor Bas of Tahlwent. Once that's in place, I will have the votes in the Archhalia to get a few things done in this kingdom."

Stefan could see that she wanted to say more—of course she did—but he left before she could speak.

32

"You should have seen me trying to turn a calf, up to my shoulder in a cow's pudding."

Stefan laughed at the image of Cullen standing behind a cow and performing that service. A year had passed since their hard words, and his friend looked healthy and tanned. Beardless again, as he had been in the early years of Stefan's reign. They walked the fence line along the bluff overlooking the Dazun and it felt like old times, natural and right, except too much had changed. Stefan had stopped by Wyre before heading north to settle matters in Bynum and Stauberg. It was high time he dealt with that part of his kingdom.

"I would have given Tahlwent to you, had you been available."

Cullen's expression hardened. "No, you wouldn't have—because people more powerful than me would have stopped you. Tahlwent is a crown Principate. You're daft if you think your nobles would let you put a Kheld over it. You wouldn't have gotten one vote, not even Phalla's father."

Maybe not, though the Enlad of Chennor had bartered his vote in return for being made an Archon and given overlordship of three prime Dazunor estates. Even with that vote, Stefan had barely managed to shove Erenor into position. He had succeeded only because Tahlwent had no legal heir besides the crown—and Emyli had refused to bring Hans back. The nobles, angry about the unavailable prince, had allowed Stefan to settle the domain on Erenor and declare him a Bas.

"I still would rather have made you a Bas than him."

They stopped to gaze out over the river. A Kheld town occupied the bank opposite Wyre and a ferry ran between the two settlements, a steady source of good Kheld trade and also a market for the produce from Cullen's estate. As ever, Stefan noted Cullen's good mind for commerce.

"Erenor does good work for me. The deal with Mormantalorus, it's bringing new trade. To Aral, as well as Stauberg. I'm headed there, to make sure it gets done right." Stefan shot Cullen a look. "You can come with me."

A shake of the head. "Not doing that work again—and especially not for that lot."

"You'd be doing it for me, for Essera. Stauberg's becoming as important as Dazunor-Rannuli. Trade below the Dazun is a mess. We lost a lot of contracts in Lower Neuberland. Stauberg, though, can handle more trade. It has the damn Wall."

"Trade isn't your biggest problem."

Stefan snorted at that. When it came to problems, Dorilian reigned supreme. A full year had passed and the Hierarch's army continued to occupy Gignastha and Lower Neuberland. Worse, Dorilian had brought in a second army to foray into Neuberland solely to attack Kheld settlements. Though the Archhalia had censured Dorilian and attempted to force him to relinquish the domain, the arrogant asshole ignored the ruling. Bitter as that drink was to swallow, Stefan now considered Gignastha a loss.

"Name a bigger problem than having two Sordani armies on my border."

"How about the next time you raise taxes, you will face a revolt."

That old care. "I won't have to raise taxes anytime soon. When I inherited, I took Tahlwent's treasury and paid off the crown's debts."

Cullen blinked and pondered Stefan anew. "The Gracious Queen must have been really rich."

"Halasseon gold. Generations's worth. That's where the money is, the Highborn and their Rill slots."

"And Erenor doesn't mind that you left him with an empty treasury?" Cullen waved to a passing wagon coming in from one of his fields. The house lay ahead, its sturdy walls of creamy local limestone rising above a fine lawn and well-tended shrubbery. Stefan had helped Cullen lay the foundation of that house. The walk to the main door was lined with banks of blue hyacinths and gold-throated narcissi. Sometime during the last year, a new wing had been added west of the main hall.

"I made him a Bas. He can tax his new subjects, and those

Mormantaloran ships too, to get the domain back in the gold. And when he marries Palaistea—"

"She agreed?" Cullen looked surprised.

"Not yet. But now that Erenor's a Bas, I can negotiate something."

"Aw hells."

Abruptly, Cullen veered from the path and walked toward the river again. Away from the house.

What in the world...

"I'm not going to force her!" Stefan ran after him. His boots sank into soft ground thick with tufts of grass and yellow-flowered cupmoss. Clumps of mud clung to his heels. He would need to clean the dirt off before he rejoined his escort.

Cullen stopped beside a low wall near a stand of flowering crabapple trees. "I know you won't force her, because you know better than to offend the Mother. A woman should only be with a man of her choice, or didn't Mother Aegdnis make that clear enough over how you got Nilla as your wife?"

"Nilla chose me too." Stefan said it from between clenched teeth.

"She did. But I was there, remember? Things didn't get off on the right foot. That's why I'm saying to leave this lady in peace. The Mother would frown just as much should you, as Palaistea's king, take that choice away from her, or any woman, as it would be for some man to force himself upon her."

"I'm giving her a choice: wed Erenor or stand in defiance of her king."

"That's a false choice, and you know it." Cullen blew out a sigh, as he always did when he knew argument would get him nowhere. "But why him? Why put that man so near your throne?"

"Because better him than someone else. I need someone besides *her* to do what I need done in Stauberg!"

Cullen simply stared. Even after everything, his eyes looked the same as ever, blue-gray rimmed with darker blue, thick-lashed and clear, and honest as daylight itself, straight out calling Stefan a fool. But no such words passed Cullen's lips as he looked past Stefan to the house front.

"Can you stay? Maybe for the midday meal? I have the same cook I did in Dazunor-Rannuli, though he's leaving in a few days to be innkeeper at Rhodhur's Great Hall."

Stefan should stay for the meal. Break bread with his friend. Cullen's cook, Gerd, was a wonder with meals. When he turned his head to see what Cullen was looking at, though, Stefan changed his mind. Asphalladra waited on the garden-lined path to the door. Cullen's young son, more than a year old now and probably walking, squirmed in her arms. Stefan would have to meet the child now that he had seen him—but he didn't think he could stand a whole meal of watching Cullen and his gold-haired wife cooing over the boy.

"I don't think so." Stefan swung his gaze back to Cullen. "I—what is that?" His friend's collar, unbuttoned for their walk, had fallen open. A thick gold chain and a medallion of some sort gleamed against Cullen's dark chest hairs. Stefan reached for it, to look at it, but Cullen tugged his shirt closed.

"Something I had made for myself."

"You sure your wife didn't give it to you? I know Rill glyphs when I see them."

Cullen flushed. "I commissioned it." Though his jaw tightened, he sighed at Stefan's unrelenting stare. "You want to know? Here." He hauled forth the chain so Stefan could see the pendant: a swirl of stars circled by a silver, three-loop Rill glyph. At the center of the star swirls was something lumpy and white.

"What the hells?" A fucking *tooth*?

"Dorilian gave it to me, or rather the man who released me gave it to me. Called it a message. And it was, Stefan—I understood it perfectly. This is *his* tooth, one of those you and Neddig and Machon kicked in that day. He must have kept it. He gave it to me so I would know that he let me go to make us even... because I *didn't* kick him." Cullen tucked the damned thing back into his shirt.

So that was why. Stefan had wondered, even thought this might be the case, but... fucking Dorilian had hammered the point. He always hammered the point. Always nailed Stefan to his mistakes—and now he was doing it again, hanging proof around Cullen's neck of something that happened when they were kids.

"You can't wear that in public. Nowhere, because you can never explain it. Not to anyone."

"I'm not an idiot. Neither is he—you'll notice he gave me a message without using a single word." Cullen grabbed Stefan by the shoulders and looked him in the eye. "I only told you because you already know. And because I promised you that when you ask me something, I will always tell you the truth. So there you have it." Gaze resolute, he stepped back. "The choices we make have consequences, and I wear this to remind me of that."

Stefan attempted a grin, though it hurt his pride. "Not to

mention that tooth is probably worth a small fortune. Genuine Sordaneon. A piece of a god, right?"

It felt good again to see and hear Cullen laugh. "I'm not quite ready to call him that."

Because Dorilian wasn't.

Together they walked toward the house, where Asphalladra, smiling and happy, waited with her crying, fussing child.

"There stands the palace of my future wife." Erenor sounded quite pleased with himself. "I cannot believe you never laid eye on it before now."

Stefan admitted the Highborn penchant for beautiful dwellings. The Danae Palace crowned the next hill and looked for all the world like a temple. "I was never invited."

No Highborn subject had ever invited him to visit. He needed to impose himself—every fucking time. To be sure, they never failed at being good hosts, but his visits had been frosty affairs. Even his staunch ally, his aunt by marriage Ionais, in Merath, tolerated him only for reasons of state. He did not understand the godborn, didn't want to understand them, and hoped he never would.

"Palaistea will receive you. She would not dare refuse." Erenor, at least, sounded confident as they urged their horses forward along the manicured avenue. Bynum's roads surpassed those of most domains in quality, being wide and paved, lined with trees and even wells along the way. "I look forward to the Princess's reception of my suit now that I am a Bas. I am the holder of a Principate even if you could not make me a prince."

Stefan had looked into it. Esseran—and Triemperal—law restricted the titles of Prince and Princess to men and women of Highborn birth and a single exception: the Stauberg-Randolphs, Marc Frederick and his heirs. Endurin, a Wall Lord, had forced *that* exception. Stefan didn't wield Endurin's clout.

"It's just as well. I should think a Bas of Tahlwent good enough for any woman."

"She is very proud. But if you can persuade her..."

Stefan was determined to try. He had not come to Bynum strictly as a visitor. At his back rode armed and mounted men.

Erenor had delivered on his promises. He had garnered more votes for Stefan in the Esseran Halia by retiring recalcitrant old holders, whom he had replaced with men more to his king's liking. One of those holdings, Elithegh, he had given to Lowen Toboldson. Now Stefan's father-in-law held both political influence and a rich estate, complete with an impressive fortress. Erenor's enhanced wealth and prestige, along with how he had acquired them, swayed many ambitious lesser nobles to Stefan's side.

No one, though, could budge the Highborn from their lofty perches.

Palaistea herself met them at the Indomitable Bridge across the Twice-Riven Gorge. Legend had it seven Highborn princes had combined their gifts to destroy the Aryati city of Saelthalor in a battle that had caused the very earth to split. The Highborn had defeated the Aryati, then founded a new city, Bynum, to celebrate their victory. They had also built bridges across the scar they had left behind, like this span, which was sound enough to have lasted a thousand years.

"Princess." Stefan gave her the slightest of nods. Palaistea looked lovely, willowy and serene, clothed all in white and astride her great horse.

"Majesty." Palaistea bowed her head also. She did not do so to his companions. She also eyed his soldiers with concern. "Welcome. I have prepared our home to receive you. Your troops, of course—"

"Will cross this bridge. I require as much protection as you do, Princess."

Her expression did not change, only her gaze shifted. In other times, Essera's kings had visited their subject princes and princesses without heavy guard, entrusting their security to their hosts. She glanced to the captain of her guard before she spoke again.

"His Majesty honors us by his visit. He may of course bring his army if to do so gives him peace of mind."

Stefan seethed at the woman's choice of words. His men numbered only two thousand. Had he wished he could have brought a proper army.

To present a message of unity, they rode side by side toward the palace, his men paired with hers until they reached the broad steps and columned entry. Together they ascended those stairs and walked into the great atrium, a rotunda beneath a dome painted like sky, ringed by dusky blue pillars and floored with gray-blue wood. The trees that produced such pillars and wood were rare, found only in one place: the distant and icy mountains of Cjta. Stefan had heard about this entrance hall from his mother and grandfather, and he took a moment to marvel.

He turned a smile on Palaistea. "This *is* the prettiest palace in all the Triempery."

She accepted that praise. "It has rivals. I do favor it, though. It has so much warmth."

As did she, now that they conversed in the tranquil beauty of her own home, away from halls of empire and politics. Always before, Stefan had met with Palaistea at the Archhalia where their purposes differed, or at some grand function where he must appear regal to the many personages around them. Here he had only to contend with Erenor and Lucien Illarion, whom she had known since childhood. When safe in chambers, with an entire wing of the palace given over to the king's entourage, Lucien seemed happy with their reception.

"I should call this a fine start to your business." Lucien gestured to the room's regal aspect and appointments. "If any man can find a hint of insult, I will myself stand and call him out."

"The Princess is most gracious." Stefan prayed she would continue to be so. "Dare I hope she sets a fine table?"

"The finest in the Royal North."

Yes, the Royal North. After years of avoiding the region, Stefan at long last faced his kingdom's cancer. The domains of Stauberg, Gweroyen, the Eleutheron, Pessach and Lacenedon were lands steeped in history and legend. Unlike the Dazun-centered domains of Essera's south, held in thrall to a Rill-dominated economy, the riches of the Royal North more resembled those of Amallar— deeply agrarian lands unified by identity with their rulers. Even landlocked Lacenedon considered Permephedon, not Dazunor-Rannuli, to be its main trading port.

In the Royal North, Khelds had no place at all. Not one Kheld held a position of importance. Khelds owned no farms here and not one inn. A few Khelds lived or worked in some of the cities, shopkeepers and cooks and the occasional bard. Stauberg, in particular, had a small but determined enclave. But Stefan would find few people in these lands who looked like him. He had brought not even one Kheld with him but had chosen his companions from noblemen of Staubaun birth.

A few hours later, as Stefan shared the evening meal with Palaistea and two lords from nearby estates, Stefan noted how little he fit in. The elegant pale beauty of the Princess and her nobles matched their surroundings, clothed in wealth and secure in their positions. Their smiles were a little too animated. Their conversation a little too merry. It worked to Stefan's advantage that his Kheldish looks and unconventional ways awakened consternation. Let them wonder about his intentions and his ability to alter their circumstances. Stefan made good use of Lucien, who in addition to tasting Stefan's food and drink also fielded much of the conversation. Talk flowed smoothly of upcoming festivals and weddings, of horses to be raced and children born and even mention of fortunes lost at sea.

At the meal's end, Palaistea turned and said, "Majesty, if you would be willing, I would show you the Crown of the Eleutheron. Our terrace has one of the best views."

Shadowed by guards, they exited the grand hall and trod a footpath fragrant with thyme to a terrace paved by dragon moss and outlined by marble. Sleek, sinuous statues dotted the darkness and glimmered in moonlight. Palaistea guided him to an outlook below which he saw the bright gleam of the Stariel River, and to the east of that a broad body of water against which flickered the spires of a city. Bynum. Above that sparkling landscape soared mountains white-sheathed and mighty, their peaks forming a perfect, symmetrical crown of seven points.

The Crown of the Eleutheron. Lauded in poetry and immortalized in art. Evoked in the state coronals of nearly every Triemperal domain.

"Mother's Tits."

Palaistea softly laughed. "The powers that be will take that as a compliment, I think."

"They should. There are no finer." Stefan pointed to the Crown. "A sight worth seeing. You are blessed to always look on such a view."

"Blessed, yes. In so many ways." Her gaze weighed him. "What is your purpose in coming here? If it is to force that man upon me, you and I are at cross purposes."

As if they were not already engaged in a game that could have only one end. "Now that he is Bas of Tahlwent, Erenor is a suitable husband for a woman of your stature."

She tilted her head. "You think so? A title does not by itself make a man worthy. Of anything."

"Consider it a suitable alliance, then. Tahlwent is a fine prize. My grandfather thought so when he married Apollonia."

"Ah, and by that marriage he secured the Malyrdeons as his allies. Blood kindred to his heirs." Her lovely gaze, bright with moonlight, latched onto his. Passion and confidence lent heat to her next words. "I have not Marc Frederick's need to secure allies. A husband will not improve my situation. Indeed, I fear the worsening of it."

"As a mother to princes. Yes, I can understand that. But don't you want a partner in your... life?" He could not bring himself to say she might wish a partner in her bed.

"If I wanted that, I would have one."

Not a point Stefan could dispute. Palaistea was so beautiful it was a god-granted privilege to gaze upon her. Now that they were this close, near enough to touch, Stefan grappled with knowing that, had he wished it, he could have had her for *his* wife. Fertile. Royal. Wealth beyond imagination. This woman inspired fever dreams. The only thing he knew for certain was that if she *had* wed him, it would have been to secure her kindred's interests—and place her sons closer to his throne.

She had also just told him she did *not* want Erenor Tholeros. Cullen had warned Stefan rightly about the danger of pressing the matter. As a Kheld, Stefan must respect Palaistea's stance—and would. From this point, it fell on Erenor to change her mind.

"While I am here, I would like to meet your sons. Eldon and Enreddon. You haven't brought them to court."

"I hope you understand my reasons."

Rheger had explained those. The same old convolution about not encouraging seditious thoughts. The Highborn trafficked in appearances, the creation of some and downplaying of others, forever managing perceptions. When it came to those children, Stefan understood why they were being cautious.

"And I hope you understand mine for wanting to meet them. I haven't commanded you to bring them to court, and I want you to know I won't put you in that position. You're protecting them, of course, and a royal court can be a dangerous place."

"Yes. Very."

Palaistea was being evasive. Clearly, Stefan was the one she thought dangerous. They had begun to walk along the terrace, following a path thick with night-blooming spires as ghostly as dream candles. The air he breathed was spiced with their perfume. He decided to try a new tack.

"Someone poisoned my queen—you heard about that?"

"Of course." Her expression was all sympathy and horror. "A vile attack. Is that why she has withdrawn?"

"From Dazunor-Rannuli, yes. She no longer trusts that city."

"Neither do you. It explains why you moved your court to Trulo."

"Trulo is less accessible. And far from the Rill. Like this place is." He approved how removed the Royal North, as a whole, was from the troublesome core of the kingdom.

He had earned back some of her warm regard. "We do not worship the Rill Entity the way southerners do. It is simply not part of our politics. And yet it is, it must be, because the Rill and the Wall are part of a whole."

"What whole?"

"Leur's Second Creation." When he looked to her to go on, she did so. "This world of ours, made new again. We destroyed it once before and"—her explanation faltered for a moment before she continued—"and they remade it, *are* remaking it. The Three. The Sons of Leur and Amynas, who are the Wall and the Rill, the architects of this new world. Leur gave its whole body to the Second Creation, and its children also, and this world manifests through them."

"So where is the third one? Amynas and Leur had three sons. I've often wondered about that. What became of the third son?"

She looked out into the night at the Crown. "The Wall has never answered that question. Some say it is Marenthro."

Stefan snorted. "If he's a god, he has yet to show it."

They walked along a pathway lit by glowing stones and waterglobe light, soft and low.

"Other immortal beings dwell among us, though they are even more mysterious and less seen. According to Jharbalan ascetics, the Third Son is with Amynas and Leur, perhaps on the other side of the Pillars of the Sky. Mystics in the Pitiless Isles suspect the Third Son rims the Fallen Sea. Like his brothers, he belongs to this World and yearns for its completion. The Second Creation is not finished, you see."

"Yet it is finished enough, because here we are."

She stopped walking and turned to face him. "Yes, here we are." The terrace had ended, and they stood on the threshold of a covered loggia. Two figures at the structure's far end leaned upon a wall and appeared intent on something below. They looked up when Palaistea moved toward them and Stefan saw that they were but boys. When she directed a beckoning look his way, Stefan walked to join them.

"Don. Redd. Come meet the king."

The boys straightened. Gold-haired like their mother and not dressed for royal presentation, they exchanged glances but bowed deeply when Stefan stood beside their mother. Stefan recalled that Eldon was only seven years and little Enreddon but five. Too young to have powers or be dangerous.

Someday, sooner than he would like, these Highborn heirs would think themselves important—and better suited to be king than he was. At the moment, though, they were but children, wide-eyed and impressed.

Both boys eyed Stefan with questions they were too polite or shy to speak. Stefan did his best to put them at ease. He had never been good with children, in part because he had so little practice at it. He was pleased when his efforts, saying he had known their father and hoped they would soon see Stauberg, prompted a smile from little Enreddon.

Redd, Palaistea had called him. It was the same nickname Marc Frederick had called the lad's father and namesake, though Stefan, being neither familiar enough nor of high enough rank, had never called the man other than Prince Enreddon. He should have addressed both boys as Thrice Royal but hadn't. He refused to elevate them.

The whole thing was awkward. The journey here. The reception. He had come to Bynum with every intention of taking the Malyrdeon boys into his custody. It was only proper they be made Wards of the Crown. Perhaps Palaistea discerned his purpose, if he was to read anything into this meeting.

His suspicion was answered as soon as the lads were escorted away by their respective governesses, ostensibly to bed. He and Palaistea remained on the loggia, standing in shadows cast by thick pillars as moonlight splashed upon the paving at their feet. High full-bellied urns planted with tall, thick grasses stood at intervals along the walls. Torches burned from brackets nearby and added golden light to their faces.

"Do not try to take them from me," she advised.

"Would it help if I told you I mean to house them at Stauberg where persons of rank and integrity would see to their education?"

Her previous lovely demeanor turned hard and cold. "No, because they would still be prisoners."

"I don't imprison children!"

"What else would you call it? What else would anyone call it? Would you call them 'guests' the way Marc Frederick did Labran? For how many years?"

Until Stefan's reign was secure. Until he had sons of his own, three or four of them, and of sufficient age to stand up to the damned Highborn. He wasn't going to mistreat the boys. He might even grow fond of them. If their mother behaved herself, he would let her visit.

"Don't make this difficult," he warned. "I have barricaded your guards in their barracks and your household staff in their rooms. My troops hold the bridge."

Palaistea stepped back, fists at her sides and teeth bared by stiff lips. "The bridge. My barracks. You actually think—" Her sigh morphed into a sad laugh. "We will need to negotiate a safe passage."

"For you? Where do you intend to go?"

"No. For you." Palaistea walked to the nearest torch, lifted it from the bracket and swung the fiery head into one of the grass-filled urns. The spiky foliage caught fire and within moments became a full, bright blaze. When she walked toward him again, her figure showed clearly through the pale thin fabric of her gown. Red lights gleamed on the gold and jewels in her hair.

To Stefan, she seemed a creature out of myth, some southern war queen from Mormantalorus, clothed in the fire of a volcano.

Bootsteps clattered near, drawn by the fire. Lucien looked from Stefan to the woman before he removed his cloak and moved to fling it on the flames. Palaistea stepped in front of him.

"No."

"You cannot just leave it burn!"

She *was* just letting it burn. Stefan noticed how her gaze never left his. How she waited... how she knew what would happen next. What had happened already.

More men, his men, joined them, at a run. Erenor stopped while still on the long terrace, his breath coming in gasps. "We are surrounded, sire! The palace. It is surrounded. Our troops at the bridge are cut off and, only a hundred soldiers are here in the residence. There are thousands of people, armed and unarmed, between us and relief. If we try to fight our way through—"

"You will not have to do that."

Palaistea's voice. Stefan ceased to look at the Princess when he noted the dozen men who had somehow joined her. Armed men. Every one of them looked well born. She stood before them, a vision of royalty.

"Eldon is Prince of Stauberg and the Eleutheron. Thrice Royal and Malyrdeon, Son of Essera and Heir to the Wall Lords. His people do not want him to be removed, not from his seat, not from their lives. You are free to leave, King Stefan. You and all your men—but you will not be taking my sons with you."

Did she really think she could do this? "What you're doing is treason! Rebellion!"

Her tiara of golden holly leaves and ruby berries flashed with fitful light as she shook her head from side to side. The fire behind her had died down to flickers. "Not yet. I defy your will, yes, but no lawful command. Your proposal was denied by Essera's Halia. It is I, not you, who follow the law. Eldon and Enreddon are not your wards to claim. I remain their sole guardian and regent. *My* sons. My sacred charge. And our people to enforce it." Palaistea indicated the men and women arrayed to every side. "We do not defy you in any unlawful way. You are unencumbered here, not to be harmed. Accost no one and you will not be touched. Partake of our food. Drink of our wine. You and your good soldiers, who are our countrymen. But then leave." She turned away, then cast a final look back.

"And do not return."

33

Dorilian handed the reins of his horse to a groom and watched Levyathan's easy dismount. At just turned six years, his Heir was an excellent rider, and morning rides had become part of their daily routine. Levyathan went to the gelding's head and stroked his smooth cheek, then nose, and spoke softly to him. Animals had been more accessible than other humans to Levyathan's first embodiment, and he retained his former affinity. After handing over his horse to the groom, Levyathan walked with Dorilian along the landscaped path to the Serat's royal residences.

"It worries him to hurdle obstacles with me on his back. I told him to trust me, but he isn't so sure. Jumping feels unnatural to him."

"Tell him it is only for emergencies."

The brightening light of early morning gilded an archway view of the Long Court, which was sunlit and serene, though a bit worse for wear from hooves. Gardeners already worked to repair the damage. Together Dorilian and Levyathan walked a shaded passageway of stone angles softened by century-old plantings of star clematis and roses.

Levyathan looked up. "Have you ever jumped a horse in an emergency?"

"Once or twice. Riders must be prepared to encounter such things."

Dorilian's whole life had been a series of such preparations. How to swim. How to fight. How to touch and contain and ward off the Rill.

Though he had gotten better at appearing ungifted, the more Dorilian developed his talents, the more difficult the concealment. Among its other attributes, the Rill was terrible at keeping secrets. Entities saw no need to hide themselves. But if Dorilian avoided the Rill, and any people who might ascertain his differentness, his enemies could perhaps be lulled into not looking too closely.

A woman in a wheeled chair awaited them in the courtyard surrounding the Well of Birds. They had just missed that morning's feathered eruption and brilliant plumes of the tiny, winged creatures flowed overhead like swirls of otherworldly ink, creating patterns against the dawn sky. As they stepped from the breezeway and drew near, Palimia turned to greet them, hand shading her eyes. She had only begun using the chair a month ago, having recovered enough strength to sit upright for longer periods. Though she remained thin and pale, her smile was as warm and open as ever.

"I saw you from my balcony. Lev rides so well!"

Levyathan perched on the broad stone rim of the Well. "Dor calls riding an essential skill."

She thought about that. "It is, where the Rill does not run."

"I may never leave this Serat—but if I do, I will know how to ride. And swim. And cook an egg. Nikos Obar insists the most essential skill of all is that of feeding oneself."

"I hired Nikos Obar to teach you philosophy, not cookery." Dorilian joined Levyathan on the rim of the Well. No one knew for certain how many thousands of years had polished the stone to its current smoothness. The Serat had been built around the Well and included numerous pre-Return structures.

"He is," Levyathan explained. "We are examining the nature of truth, whether truth lies in practice or theory. Which is truer: what we know about food, or our experience of the food itself? The wisdom of our bodies in digesting the food, or of our minds for knowing from whence it came? I have asked him if we might move on to the nature of divinity, and how it is related to truth—and whether godhood lies in practice or belief." To Palimia's tilt of the head, Levyathan winked and added, "Also why must a god *learn* how to cook an egg."

Dorilian met Palimia's broad grin. "At least I am getting half my money's worth."

"He may surpass all your cooks—and your scholars too."

Levyathan leaned forward, all elbows and knees. Now that he had gained a handspan in height over the last year, it mattered less that he talked more like an adult than a child. "I want to learn everything there is to know about what we are. About what I am and can be. I have experienced for myself the depth and pervasiveness of our connections to Leur. Cibulitus does not explain these very well, even in Aryati."

"He is better for history," Dorilian said. "I will send to Jharbala for a philosopher more suited to explore your questions."

"Good, because I have a great many."

How not? Levyathan's mere existence begged questions philosophers could argue for years. "Cibulitans consider questions imperfect. Questions manipulate truth and are flawed by simply existing."

"I should think you would want the answers anyway."

Dorilian shook his head. "I don't think answers matter, not to that question. What if we are gods? Or men? What does that change for us or the world? I will worry about the nature of godhood if I ever become one. For now—I am a man and have problems enough being that."

"You are still doing it, aren't you?" Levyathan's voice wavered. "Pushing your body. Testing yourself."

He was. Dorilian no longer shared the details of his explorations, however. Why feed the boy's fears? It was his job to help Levyathan grow and learn, not turn him into a fretful accessory. Terrors had always lurked just under the skin of their relationship.

"Go," Dorilian said. "Change your clothes. Meet your tutor for the morning."

He watched the way Palimia's gaze followed Levyathan's dash from the courtyard, happy, young limbs in motion. More than physical pain dulled the shine of her eyes. Memory, too, tormented her.

Dorilian stood and walked behind her chair to grasp its handles. "Let me wheel you."

"Thrice Royal—"

"I have a name. You are one of the five people who may use it."

"But the staff will hear."

Even now, she was scrupulous about appearances. A fine quality, and one Dorilian continued to find useful. "I do not care who hears," he said. "However, I do care who might hear what else I wish to say to you, so let's retire to somewhere more private."

Palimia had always admired the way Dorilian's private rooms combined his preference for open spaces with statements of precise and elevated elegance. Sun-filled. Open. Punctuated by striking artworks. His two rooms for study, in contrast, seemed given over entirely to clutter and books. It had been well over a year since she had been in these rooms and now found her gaze leaping from stack of tomes to stack of tomes, from open atlases to architectural models to easels with maps.

She pushed her hands against the frame of her chair to situate herself more comfortably as Dorilian positioned her beside his desk. The chair had been designed in Permephedon by physicians dedicated to assisting persons with afflictions like hers. As a result, it was light and maneuverable, crafted of amazing metal and beautiful polished woods. It more resembled a throne than a chair.

In the endless months that followed her injury, Palimia had recovered as much as was possible. Physicians both in Sordan and Permephedon agreed she would never regain use or even command of her lower body. For the remainder of her life, she would have need of servants to attend her most basic needs. The Hierarch had ensured she would always have that assistance. They might not be lovers in the same way they had been, but Dorilian made clear his continued interest.

She reached over to pick up a thick parchment.

"This is a very old map of Stauberg."

"It shows the original contours of the Wall." Dorilian glanced at another map on an easel opposite his worktable. "Quite a change over the years."

"Why are you studying Stauberg? Please tell me you're not going there."

"Not while my promise stays in force."

His refusal to say Stefan's name had hardened of late. Palimia was one of the few people allowed to reference the man at all.

"He miscalculated terribly, attempting to seize the Malyrdeon Princes the way he did." She put down the aged map, noting as she did so that it was one of several.

"He was fortunate he could return to friendlier lands by way of Serrain."

True. Even so, Stefan had not escaped unscathed. Many weeks had passed since the incident, and the Royal North verged on open rebellion. The Bas of Rannul, Burelan Phaeros, had raised an army and marched to defend the Princes. Stefan had narrowly defeated Burelan near Simelon and driven him back, but now found himself chasing down Burelan to prevent him from reaching, and holing up in, his domain of Rannul. Merrydn had petitioned the Archhalia to broker a truce before more damage could be done. Only Palimia and a few close advisors knew Dorilian had told Hebron of Lacenedon and Estevan of Gweroyen that Sordan would not support an insurrection to place a Malyrdeon—any Malyrdeon—on Essera's throne.

If you dethrone the Stauberg-Randolphs, you get neither them nor me.

Worse, a new player had emerged to complicate matters. Stefan's alliance with Nammuor now included Mormantaloran naval support and contingents of troops in Stauberg and Aral. Palimia sighed.

"Are you feeling well? Strong?"

Dorilian's question surprised her. He usually respected her wish not to dwell on, or talk about, her infirmity. She put aside thoughts of Essera and resumed her smile.

"Well enough. Surely Thuraya keeps you informed of my condition. What is this about? You did not bring me here to inquire about my health."

"No." Always when she was with him, she detected Dorilian's regret at having been the cause of her injury. "I am inquiring if you are in good enough condition to… help me with something."

How intriguing. That he knew her physical impediments—perhaps even better than she did—and had an offer to make was reason enough to listen. "I am willing to serve in whatever capacity you ask, within my limitations."

"Your limitations are part of what make you so suitable. No one will question why you take up residence in Permephedon."

"Permephedon?" She visited only to consult with the High Citadel's physician Sages.

"I wish to undertake projects that would benefit from having you there. You would live in the Sordaneon Tower, of course, in my own residence, which is impregnable. Everyone knows you are my mistress. I have never renounced you as such."

Maybe not, though people would hardly be fooled. She ducked her head. "So I sit in Permephedon and… what? Let people see me quietly set aside?"

"You are not being set aside." He extended his hand and she placed hers within it. "You remain as dear to me as ever. And as fully trusted. What people see and think can be manipulated. What matters is that you will be near the physicians who most help you and you can manage your guardianship of the Stauberg-Randolph assets just as you now do, through your staff. Your nephew does a good job with your personal properties."

As a reward for saving his life, Dorilian had raised her to the nobility. She now enjoyed the title of Basarchessa of Sandalya, which comprised a region rich in vineyards and groves, complete with several estates and many profitable businesses. Her nephew Lazaros, whom she had discovered years ago to be thoughtful and intelligent, she had brought to Sordan to manage her newly acquired estates.

"And these projects of yours?"

"I will put you in contact with people and they will put you in contact with other people." Dorilian passed her a sheaf of documents. "You are to facilitate charitable endeavors."

"Ah." A quick perusal of the documents showed proposals for a school, a public garden, and a library.

"You shall enjoy as busy and full a life as you wish. Resume relationships in Essera at your discretion. You already know my ambassador to the Archhalia, who has a residence in the Tower. He and his lady spend most of his year there, as do Tiflan and Deleus while the Archhalia is in session. You should know, however, that you will be approached by people who wish access to me, through you."

Palimia laughed. "Please. That happens already. And would you object if while I am in Essera I engage in projects of my own?"

"No, though I prefer you to present them to me first."

"In case you should find them useful for your own purposes?"

Dorilian smiled. "You understand me too well."

Yes, she did. Of the many gifts Marc Frederick had given her, this man had done the most to change her life. The loss she regretted above all was that she would never again know his lovemaking. The assassin's attack had done too much damage to her organs and spine—such that intercourse would lead her to feel nothing of pleasure, and Dorilian would feel only her pain. Not to mention the sheer inconvenience. Despite this, they were in many ways more intimate than ever.

He sank back into his chair and studied her. "I notice you haven't asked what I hope to accomplish."

No, she had not. "If you wish me to know that, you will tell me."

"I am not trying to ruin anyone in particular."

A small part of her, a new and bitter part, was disappointed. "I suppose you did enough toward that end with Gignastha."

"I made my point." He narrowed his storm-silver gaze upon her. "I will look the other way if you choose to make points of your own."

War could not be put behind a man, even one who was king. Stefan
had learned from his grandfather that kings were never far from taking
up arms. The stench of the battlefield assaulted his nostrils, voided
bowels and opened viscera, men and horses alike, but he needed to be
here, striding through the dead and maimed, stepping upon the fallen
banners of his enemy. He dismounted and walked the red ground,
needing to see for himself that fucking Burelan Phaeros was dead.

His Kheld mercenaries had done for him what Staubaun soldiers
would not. They had ridden down the fleeing army and hacked their
way through Burelan's defenders. Some of Stefan's Staubaun officers
had pleaded for him to spare Burelan and those of Rannul's nobles
who fought with him, and had offered to broker a peace, but the
Khelds had not cared about that. They had cloven Burelan's neck
and sent his head rolling down the hill. Someone had retrieved it
and brought it back, to set it in its proper place, features muddied
and distorted by agony and mortis, gold hair matted with blood.

"Good riddance, that one." Goff gripped a blood-stained axe,
though not the one that had finished the Bas.

Yes, very good riddance, and done in a way that removed Stefan
himself from the deed. No one could lay blame on him for a man
slain in the teeth of battle.

"Himself, and his brother too," Goff noted. "No heirs to run
down."

Erenor stood with them. "Only the sister. You were right to
think she would flee, sire. We captured her trying to make for
Permephedon."

Good. Permephedon might have provided sanctuary. Too many
people would be invested in the woman's fate for her to simply
disappear, but Stefan might still turn an heiress to his advantage. One
way or another, Rannul would cease to be a thorn in his side. If only
to make sure the domain did not fall under the influence of Purists
or the contentious and difficult Seven Houses, he would tie Rannul
closer to home. Euella Phaeros would be wed to one of Stefan's allies.

Stefan nudged Burelan's dead head with his boot. "I've seen what
I need to see. Keep his corpse. We can barter it for something
useful." A sound of hoof falls told him that one of the soldiers had
brought his horse. A minute later Stefan was mounted again and glad
to be above the muck. Goff and Erenor had their mounts brought
and did the same. By leaving the field, they put death behind them.

That night, Stefan celebrated victory in his well-secured tent, surrounded by an army and the few hundred Kheld sell-swords now in his employ. He was as safe as it was possible to be in Rannul. Wine flowed freely for his captains, along with boastful presentations of loot. It was a pleasant thing to hear his name shouted by joyful voices. One of the loudest belonged to Peric Goffson, who had recruited and led the mercenaries. Peric wore ill-fitting armor and bore a new sword, both courtesy of Burelan, whose corpse he had stripped. Fair reward for the warrior who had swung the killing blow.

Stefan pointed to Peric's right hand and held out his own. "Hand it over."

By his expression, it was plain the young man didn't know what Stefan asked. Goff jabbed his son with his elbow. "The ring. The one the Bas of Rannul wore."

With a sullen growl, Peric twisted the big golden ring from his finger. "But I like this one. It's damn heavy."

The men around him laughed. Most of them. Stefan noticed his Staubaun captains had fallen silent. Even Erenor, though at least his frown faded once Peric had dropped the signet ring into Stefan's palm, where it rested, warm and bright, blood black within its crevices.

"Full see, I do, why you want it." Harc—the burly, full-bearded leader of the mercenaries—chuckled. "Melt it down and that thing would pay half my lads!"

Though not strictly true, the jibe landed a painful point. The Khelds had been told six wagonloads of Stefan's gold waited for them back in Dazunor-Rannuli—except there weren't any wagons or gold, and Stefan hadn't found the right time to break to the lot that he couldn't pay them just yet. His treasury in Stauberg was substantial, but it required a writ from Essera's Halia to access. He had depleted the Crown's usual funds on deposit with bankers in Dazunor. As for his personal fortune, he had spent most of that buying off votes for lordships.

For the hundredth time of late, Stefan missed having Cullen at his side. Cullen would have advised him not to try to seize the Malyrdeon boys, to be sure—though Stefan would have tried it anyway. More importantly, he was confident Cullen could have found the coin needed to pay the damned mercenaries.

"Seems to me I should get some recompense."

Stefan snapped back to hear what Peric was saying. To judge by his flushed face and vapid grin, Peric was feeling the effects of victory ale, and wine too, of which he'd been drinking liberally. Dark hair matted by battle fell in front of his eyes as he pressed his case.

"The sister, I hear, needs a man—one what can keep the land and tax it for you."

Not now! Stefan saw that jaws had tightened on every Staubaun who had overheard those words. The Kheld men laughed like the Motherless drunken idiots they were. Stefan glared at Goff, who was deep in the cups himself but recognized the signal. Goff got onto unsteady feet and wrapped Peric in an embrace.

"Mother forbid and protect us. No need to win the battle and lose to drink. Let's get you to bed."

"—could do with a high wench like that, Da."

"Couldn't we all."

The tent flap closed behind them. Aureon Varney, one of the Staubaun captains, toasted the king again, to renewed and slightly forced cheers followed by more wine being poured. More food arrived on trenchers and one of the men produced a stringed instrument. Soon there was music, and conversation followed.

Erenor leaned in to claim Stefan's ear. "You cannot wed her to one of your Khelds. Not after that."

Not to Peric, for certain. Stefan shook his head. "I'll wed Euella to one of my lord allies," he confirmed. "I just have to think it through first."

He could and should make a deal similar to the one he had made for Tahlwent. Marry the woman and the title that came with her to someone who would not strengthen Rannul by marriage but would give over Rannul's treasury in exchange for elevation in rank. Lucien maybe... no. Lucien was betrothed. But he did have a brother in need of a title, and there was also Arton Metagoras. Cullen would approve of the latter and Euella could do worse than a man whose father was an Archon in Merrydn. The two domains were neighbors. For Stefan to elevate a Staubaun aristocrat, however, would sit ill with his Kheld chieftains, who expected bigger rewards than they'd been getting.

I can't just hand a woman over to a man she would not want.

Khelds, even disgruntled chieftains, would understand that much. The woman was not the prize. Rannul was. All Stefan wanted from it was a vote he could count on and the gold in Terna's coffers. The hard truth was, because of Neuberland and chasing down Burelan Phaeros, Stefan had spent too much coin of late on armies. He could not afford his own wars.

Dorilian, at least, was safe. Stefan didn't have the money to invade Sordan.

Upon reaching Simelon two weeks later, Stefan shared a cordial with his grandfather's old friend Phellan Illarion, Bas of Serrain. Stefan had chosen Simelon to be his stronghold for putting down the restive nobles of the Eleutheron. With Burelan's defeat, he'd put only one rebellion to ground. To her credit, Princess Palaistea had cooperated by declaring her situation to be secure and unthreatened, that the king had promised she would remain regent for her sons. Stefan had done so in large part on Phellan's urging.

"There are many kinds of power." Phellan studied the ruby nectar in his glass. "The best power is that which allows people to happily embrace you because you do not threaten them. Indeed, you make their lives easier, and so they cannot imagine embracing anyone else."

"That's the kind of power Marc Frederick had."

"You think so?" Phellan put down his glass. "In the end, perhaps, but not at the start. Mormantalorus broke from the Triempery and not one sliver of Marc's power could prevent that sundering. Sordan openly rebelled and only terrible deeds kept the Hierarchate in our sphere. Your grandfather's reign in the beginning was... difficult."

So had Stefan's been. "Are you telling me to just stay the course? Be patient? Look at Rannul. The Royal North. I have domains lining up to oppose me."

"Perhaps. But the Highborn are staying out of it. You are fortunate in that."

Stefan followed Phellan's gaze out the window, past thick diamond-shaped panes of glass. Simelon's dormant Rill mount filled that view, silver-white and broken atop a mound of autumn gold. Nearer the palace, copper leaves danced in swirls across the road.

"Dorilian isn't staying out of it. He attacked me in Gignastha."

"On the contrary, he attacked Gignastha *instead* of you." Phellan lifted the decanter to pour himself another glass. "Your grandfather left you, and all Essera, a mighty advantage in his alliances with the Highborn. Why are you finding so many ways to break with them?"

Stefan seldom talked this openly with his advisors. Too many of that lot wanted him to give them things—lands or positions or advancements for their relations—and to those ends told him what they thought would most advance their ambitions. Phellan, however, was already Bas of a princely domain, gainfully wed to a Highborn prince's daughter, and blessed with two grown sons whom Stefan counted as friends. Phellan's three young daughters were the joy of Serrain's court. Phellan wanted only to enjoy what he had and asked for nothing.

"Dorilian was never anyone's ally… and never will be. I think he's proven that. And the way I see it, the Malyrdeons are breaking with *me*. They counsel like women, always telling me to do nothing. And they're forever protecting those boys—" Stefan cut short the complaint. How best to frame this? "Are you going to pretend the noble houses of the Royal North prefer to have me as their king, even over Palaistea's sons?"

"No. Many do want a Highborn prince on the throne. But the Malyrdeons themselves do not. The Wall told them something, we know not what, but they bound Essera to your grandfather because of it. *To his bloodline*, whatever would befall it. They did not abandon Marc Frederick when Prince Jonthan died, remember that. To him they remained steadfast, and now to you."

"Because of the Wall? That thing stopped talking to them when Austell lost his wits."

"They had set their course by it long before that. A generation ago. Whatever outcome the Wall Lords hoped to achieve, your grandfather secured for us. All of us. And you are the continuation of that hope. So no," Phellan's gaze firmed on Stefan's, "the Malyrdeons do not wish you to fail."

"They don't help me, though, not the way they did him. They pretty much told me I'm on my own." Stefan rose and walked to the window. Chill penetrated the heavy glass and he felt it on his cheek. His gaze swept the Rill mount at the center of the city, its grassy slopes and pale broken crown. More than merely serene, it looked enigmatic, a mystery. For him, it was not even a remote possibility.

Another matter needed to be addressed. "Is Lady Euella situated? Secure?"

"Yes. Frightened and tired, naturally, after the long ride. I think she is uncertain about your plans for her."

Stefan frowned. "What I wish is to see her domain secured, and quickly, to a man I consider loyal. I won't force her into some man's bed, though." All that was still Kheld in him rebelled at the thought. Cullen's reminder rang true: the shadow of the Mother hung over Stefan from how he'd chosen Nilla before ever giving her the chance to choose him. He looked over to Phellan, still seated in one of the room's grand chairs. "All the ride here I listened to men suggest Lady Euella be wed to whatever man I choose for her, against her will. Like I would give her to one of them to rape just for a title and some land. I am trying to do something honorable, something that will stick, not get me pelted by rotten eggs next time I show my face in Amallar—or Rannul."

"There's also her mother to consider, the Gracious Princess Themacrysa."

Yes, yet another tatter of Highborn privilege with whom Stefan must deal. He had small chance of winning over the mother of his slain rivals. "I'm presenting Euella with a match I think she *and* her mother, and the people of Rannul too, will find acceptable."

"Who would that be?" Phellan rang a small bell for a servant to come for the empty decanter and used glasses.

"Arton Metagoras. He's noble, well educated, hails from Merrydn and is of pleasing appearance. I would have considered Lucien, of course, were he not already betrothed to the Archon of Chennor's daughter." Asphalladra's father had finally landed one of his daughters on a man who would someday rule a domain.

"And did you consider Raphelon?"

Lucien's brother had been a possibility. "I asked him. He said absolutely not. I won't force a man to marry against his will either."

Phellan pushed his rotund body from the chair and walked to join Stefan at the window. "Metagoras is a good choice. I know his father and… a good choice. Let's hope all involved agree to the match." He heaved a happy sigh. "How I love this view. See how the land is open all the way to the hill. We keep it that way. Don't want to block the sight of the Rill with some dumpy new wing or fortification."

"Even though it's just a ruin?"

"Ruins can be beautiful. This one happens to also be a promise."

Of wealth. Of power. Of things that, for Simelon, would never come to pass. Stefan turned his back on it.

"I hear the Queen is due to give birth soon. Any day now." Phellan had probably been hoping Stefan would bring up that news first.

Of course, everyone cared about that. It was *how* they cared that bothered Stefan. He heard what lurked unspoken beneath the words—fervent hope and just as fervent unease that the Kheld who ruled them might sire a dynasty. Even Phellan, most assuredly an ally, sounded more resigned than joyful. Stefan's enemies were almost certainly gnashing their teeth.

"Yes. Any day now."

Arton arrived at Simelon a day later. Upon receiving Stefan's summons, he had traveled by Rill from Dazunor-Rannuli to Permephedon, and from there had ridden without delay. Arton was damp but well-dressed and somewhat confused when Stefan greeted him in one of the palace libraries. As rain slashed the windows, Stefan detailed his expectations: Have the lady freely declare Arton her choice, and Rannul was his.

Though he answered with measured words, Arton appeared interested. "Euella is a fine lady, sire, accomplished and gentle. I know her already. Our families share bloodlines and move in the same circles. As a third son, of course, I have never aspired to—"

"Aspire. If you succeed in winning her hand, all I ask is that you use your new rank and position to support me and follow my wishes in terms of policy."

Still looking a bit like a stunned fish, Arton nodded his thanks and hurried off to meet with Euella, who was being held in the Basarchessa's suite of rooms, as protected as she was imprisoned. Stefan savored a rare moment of encouragement. Arton and Euella knew each other. Possibly even liked each other. If Stefan could pull off this match, Rannul might cease to be a problem altogether.

Things were looking up. He was still enjoying his impending triumph when Erenor entered the room, announced by the chamberlain. Eager to share his success in securing Rannul, Stefan summoned Erenor over. Only then did Stefan see that Erenor was not alone but was accompanied by another man, handsome and tall and robed in dark red with glints of gold within his hair.

Coram Barzanes. Stefan had known Nammuor's emissary was in Essera—but at Stauberg, not deep within the kingdom. Not here at Simelon.

"Sire," said Erenor. "Lord Barzanes has brought word from Stauberg." He lowered his voice to convey the importance of his next words. "They are *using* it."

"Who are *they* and what are they using?" Stefan resented having new problems thrust upon him. It seemed he had nothing but problems of late. He wondered how Coram had traveled and along what roads. Between Simelon and Stauberg stretched lands on the verge of open rebellion.

Erenor found a place to stand beside the marble fireplace, where he might listen in.

"The Malyrdeons." Coram looked from one man to the other. "They are using the Wall Stone."

Stefan snorted dismissal. "Last I heard, that artifact is still in Sordan."

"Clearly they have it again." Coram's hands, fingers pale within deep sleeves, flashed with rings. "I have just arrived from Stauberg, where the Wall has been quite… animated."

"I'm familiar with the Wall."

"Yes, but there is more to the Wall than its conspicuous exterior. Have you visited the Aidion? The shrine where Ergeiron transformed? The Aidion's foundation rings itself with light whenever the Wall Stone is active within it. Most particularly when an adept is walking the Wall."

Stefan knew of the Aidion—and that only Malyrdeons were allowed to enter it. He knew too that walking the Wall was how the Malyrdeons communed with their Entity. Was it possible they were doing it again? While he had been distracted by Burelan, had the Malyrdeons gone behind his back to retrieve their Wall Stone from Dorilian? Stefan seethed. The vengeance-eaten bastard had given it back—of course he had. And now the damned Malyrdeons were up to old tricks, peering into time. Yet another fine way to stab Stefan while he was already beset.

The light armor Stefan wore day and night wouldn't protect him against this latest treachery. No, all *this* news meant was that he would need to wear armor forever. Be forced to rule by sword. He had just spent two months putting down Burelan's rebellion in Rannul, riding at the head of an army, doing in person what needed to be done. He had made short work of Burelan's rabble, but the fighting had drained him, *and* his treasure, and he still had to deal with all the insurgents Burelan had inspired. And now this.

"If anyone is walking the Wall, it would be Elhanan," Erenor expounded on Coram's information. "He assumed the role of Enreddon's student after the last Wall Lord, Austell, became incapacitated."

Stefan knew the facts of that situation better than either man before him. Austell's shattered mind had been only the first disaster Dorilian had inflicted on the Malyrdeons.

"Just on the basis of an insinuation, I'm not going to try to remove a Wall prince from Stauberg. Elhanan hasn't fomented rebellion. I have to be careful here. Both he and Rheger explicitly denounced the Rannuli uprising and threw their support to me." Burelan had also appealed to Lacenedon and Merrydn for help and been rebuffed. "Do we have any *proof* that Elhanan is communing with the Wall?"

Erenor looked to Coram, who merely pressed his lips. "I have not personally seen these things. Adepts such as me are not allowed into the Wall sanctum."

An adept, yes. Someone who could, possibly, use ancient arts. Stefan looked to Erenor, who added, "We have a few reports from staff inside the Dannutheon palace. Some days Prince Elhanan sleeps late and later asks for restorative foods. Wall contact could explain his requests. The Highborn… consume more food when they use their gifts."

"I don't know a lot about Highborn food habits. As far as I care, they can all eat bear bait."

Erenor looked unconvinced. "If Elhanan does have the Wall Stone, however, and he *can* walk the Wall…"

Therein lay the rub.

Anyone able to walk the Wall could possibly look into the future… and if Elhanan was doing so, what was he seeing? And to whom might he reveal it? Stefan remembered he had been frosty at his last meeting with Elhanan and had rebuked him for being familiar. The damned crux of the matter was that Stefan could not travel to Stauberg just now. Doing so would require riding through the Eleutheron.

Something *Coram* had just done. Stefan kept his gaze on the Mormantaloran as he walked across the room. "I would like you to tell me how you traveled here. By what roads and what impediments you encountered, if any."

Coram made a soundless chuckle. "I traveled by other means."

Unlike Erenor, who still wore travel clothing and bore arms because of an errand he had run earlier that day, Coram was attired strictly for indoors. His floor-length robe, velvet patterned with silk, belted and trimmed with gold leather, was not that of a man intent on fitting in with his surroundings. Stefan found the answer provocative, laced with disdain. It hinted at something Coram wanted him to explore.

Magic, then—or rediscovered Aryati arts. While in Mormantalorus, Erenor had been shown several examples, though none quite as stunning as this might prove to be.

Stefan arched a brow. "Translocation?" From childhood he had heard the Aryati were fabled to have done so. The Highborn too. But not mere humans.

"Yes. Our Master has perfected the manufacture of *Ir* gems and the many applications to which they can be put." Coram lifted aside a lock of hair on the left side of his head to display an ornament adorned with golden gems that encircled his ear and pressed flat disks upon his temple. Two attached, finger-long red jewels dangled just in front of his ear. "The *lr* crystals in this device are cleaved; their other halves are in Stauberg. By activating it I can return to there this very moment." He let his hair fall again to conceal the powerful thing. "I wore a different one to get here, using crystals keyed remotely. Less accurate—and much more dangerous. Only an adept might attempt it."

The precise *how* of creating a translocation device—for certain it involved the production or acquisition of forbidden, altered *lr* crystals—was something Stefan burned to know. Just thinking about the possible uses of such an ability was intoxicating.

"Good, then. We can talk in private about how to handle this news about the Wall Stone. Maybe you have some wisdom on what I can do to keep my Malyrdeons in line." Stefan was not going to blindly follow Phellan's path of simply embracing Marc Frederick's stale alliance.

Purple light bruised the sky outside the window and painted the Rill mount with somber hues beneath a canopy of fire. Stefan took a moment to drink in the sight before turning away. Marc Frederick had been misguided in always chasing the Rill. That Entity was fallen. Dormant. A degenerate god become a machine.

Nammuor's discoveries interested Stefan more. In them he saw a future filled with freedom and power.

34

"And do you choose him for your husband? Knowing the Archhalia will make him Bas of Rannul by right of that marriage?" Stefan needed to hear Euella say the words.

Euella glanced at Arton, though she immediately dropped her gaze. "Yes, Majesty. Full knowing what your Archhalia will dictate. Arton is a good man and if my mother will bless this union, I will enter into it freely."

At least Stefan had what he wanted. At his side, Phellan stood witness and approved those words with a nod. Arton looked happy enough. Only Euella was not smiling; neither was she in tears. She simply looked doughy and sad, and probably accepted that marriage to Arton was better than some alternative her mind had invented while Stefan's prisoner.

"Good enough." Stefan turned to Phellan. "You will keep her in your care until I receive an answer from her mother." He felt a need to say something more to Euella also, so faced her again. "I regret the necessity for you to wed this way. My argument was never with you, but with your brother for raising arms against me. His death has removed that offense, and I bear you no ill will."

Euella met his gaze, her face so smooth of expression he could read nothing of her true feelings. "Then Your Majesty will not object if I retain my dowry assets when my domain's treasury is reallocated?"

Stefan slipped a side glance to Arton, who tilted his head and arched his brows. The clever woman had probably asked directly what was to happen with Rannul. Put on the spot, Stefan clenched his jaw. "By all means, you will have your dowry. Only the inheritance from your brother is subject to penalty."

Euella dropped into a curtsey and allowed Phellan to lead her from the room.

Arton backed away a few steps when Stefan turned on him. "Do you know how much gold I just gave that woman?"

"Yes, sire. And I know too that you would have had a fearsome battle on your hands if you attempted to deny it to her. Her mother, Princess Themacrysa, bestowed those properties, which she herself inherited, to the dowry."

"Rill slots—"

"Yes, and estates, and jewels. Euella is quite the heiress." As a man versed in finances, Arton had deep understanding of just how great an heiress. "The good news is you have secured that the Princess will likely approve the marriage—if her daughter keeps the dowry, and our children inherit the domain. I will honor whatever financial settlement Your Majesty requires. Borrow against her dowry. Whatever I need to do."

"I'm getting half the gold I thought I would." And also getting fewer Rill slots and only half the jewels to sell. Stefan lowered himself into a chair and stared at whatever Illarion ancestor's portrait hung in a place of honor on the chamber wall. Probably some yet-to-be-forgotten Highborn Prince of Serrain. He had the look of one. Bright-haired, richly dressed. Entitled as fuck.

"If Your Majesty is open to a suggestion…"

Stefan rolled his eyes. Arton was a junior trade minister… not Cullen, not even Neddig, for all that he did the actual work of Neddig's job. Arton didn't get to make suggestions. "Not today."

That earned a swallow of understanding. "Then let me merely *inform* Your Majesty that when I was at Permephedon I paid call on someone who has petitioned to buy a crown property. A noblewoman from Sordan, the Basarchessa of Sandalya."

"Who?"

"Palimia Kastryonis."

That got Stefan's attention. "Dorilian Sordaneon's *whore*?"

Arton blinked. "I believe she was his mistress for a time."

Until an assassin paralyzed her. *Stefan's* assassin.

Arton continued. "The Basarchessa resides in Permephedon now, apparently, and has for several months. The property in which she has expressed interest is a villa in Dazunor-Rannuli."

The fucking villa she'd shared with Marc Frederick? Stefan had given it to Nilla for her sister. He couldn't remember which Kheld relation was currently living in it.

"Why?" he asked.

"I believe she wants to turn it into a library and public garden."

The idea was ludicrous. Last Stefan had seen the place, the garden had gone to seed. But if this woman was buying things... whose money was she using? Her own? Dorilian's?

Or Stefan's?

The Stauberg-Randolph assets controlled by Sordan had finally wandered near enough for Stefan to reach.

"Your king has left Simelon? For what reason? I thought he was to attack the Eleutheron."

Coram lifted a miniature statue of a lion from one of the gallery tables to examine it. Erenor watched the way the Mormantaloran handled the object, the way those dark eyes wandered over smooth lines and assessed angles while his long elegant fingers caressed the metal. Gold and copper, the base etched with blue *illumina* to identify the artist.

"Stefan won't be attacking the Eleutheron," Erenor stated. "He never intended to. He has gone to Permephedon on personal business."

"He won't gain control of the Malyrdeon princes that way."

"No, but he also won't bankrupt his kingdom."

"Always a concern, I suppose. He doesn't have nearly the same wealth as Sordan's Hierarch or your Seven Houses. Either of those powers might be financing his enemies." With great respect, Coram placed the lion back on the table. "A beautiful piece. I have found the Royal North to be quite a trove of fine art."

"One benefit, I suppose, of a thousand years of affluence."

"Stability. Prosperity. History. Yet your king appears to be intent on dismantling it."

Erenor noticed how Coram never spoke this way to the King. Though often sly, Coram tempered the acidity of his observations when addressing the king in person. At those times he sounded almost removed, an observer. In truth, Coram seldom strayed from his master's stances. He disdained Stefan in the same way earlier generations had disdained Marc Frederick, as a creature of inferior birth elevated by crude politics instead of history or merit.

Erenor, on the other hand, he treated as someone worthy of investment.

This stroll along the palace's Heroic Gallery was one such indicator of that assessment. Erenor sensed camaraderie, an exchange of ideas and diplomacy. It did not take much to detect Nammuor at work within their conversations—as Coram immediately went on to prove.

"A pity your king failed to remove the young princes. He would be so much more secure if he had."

"Unfortunately, their mother anticipated his intent."

"His attempt was crude and obvious." Coram's gaze slid sidelong, perhaps weighing whether Erenor agreed. "He did not need to place himself at the scene. There were better ways."

"Perhaps, but no one offered one. Given how things turned out, I don't see him trying again."

"He need not do it himself."

The Heroic Galley ended at a cross-corridor to two wings of the palace. Coram had been assigned a room in the less prestigious wing and when he extended an invitation to his quarters, Erenor accompanied him. Though Stefan had instructed him to learn what he could, and influence where able, the full scope of Erenor's involvement required privacy.

As much shadow as man, Coram closed the door behind them and moved to a side table, where he poured two drinks from a glass vessel. Silver goblets glinted reddish in slashes of sunset through the glazed window. "Did you do as I asked and hide the *lr* stone in the Danae Palace at your last visit?"

"Before I was ignobly run out? I and the king? Yes." Strange as he had thought the request at the time, Erenor had learned the value of following Coram's plans. He had himself hidden a stone here in Simelon on the way to that fateful meeting. It had seemed small repayment for Coram's aid in disposing of Apollonia and elevating Erenor to his current holding of Tahlwent. Having enjoyed what had come of that small act, Erenor was even more intrigued.

Coram handed over one of the goblets before taking a sip from the other. "Good." He set aside the goblet to fish inside the sash he wore. His fingers emerged with a slice of golden gem. "I hold the other half of what you hid. It can be used to fashion what we need— if you are agreeable with my scheme."

"Which is?"

"To procure the Malyrdeon boys. I possess the means to bring them here."

"Here? To Simelon?"

"Yes, away from their mother. Stefan will have no more need for concern."

"And how would you do this?" Was the man suggesting—

"The way I traveled." Coram's dark gaze mocked Erenor. "Don't be obtuse. I am showing you the fruits of arcane power. I have two devices, small but each sufficient to transport a child. Several months ago I listened while your fool of a monarch ranted and railed about those boys and their mother. How the woman guards them like a lioness. How they complicate our accommodation in Stauberg. How the woman won't marry you." A smile slid icily across Coram's lips. "But maybe she would, if that meant she could see her darling sons again."

Yes, she almost certainly would. Palaistea would do anything—anything—for her children. Most mothers would. A bit of treachery might be worth it to gain a princess for a wife. Erenor might then sire sons who would be princes themselves, half brothers to the Highborn. And they would inherit portions of their mother's riches.

He would also have the gratitude of his king. More than anything, Stefan wanted those boys in *his* hands, not those of his enemies.

"You can do this? Bring them here?" Erenor's heart pounded as though caged by a fist. "Without putting them in danger?" While the boys might be problems in a political sense, they were godborn, sacred, and to harm them would be ruinous. He had known and liked Enreddon.

Coram indicated a curtained alcove, tucked into a wall and draped with dark velvet. A round stone plinth stood within. "Over there."

Erenor walked over and touched the flat stone surface, the deep cold of which kissed his fingertips. A statue of a hound that had formerly occupied the plinth now sat on the floor at the back of the alcove, enfolded by decorative draping. He looked back to watch Coram pull a heavy black case from beneath the bed and work open its intricate lock of jewels and dials. After opening the lid, he lifted the object within. Wide and sinister, fashioned with smoky globules and polished to mirror brightness, the thing glinted in the room's low light. When it was set upon the stone table, Erenor examined it more closely. A mirror, clearly, flat and silvered, though he could see nothing in it. Neither his face nor the room. The object drank of light.

He watched as Coram fixed a large golden gem to one of the device's murky orbs.

"What is it?"

"A mirror." Coram rimmed the gem with his finger. "A *lr* device. It will reveal to us what is happening at the other end of this crystal."

"The one I placed in Danae?"

"No. The one to be worn by my agent." Coram stepped away from the device. He looked thoughtful. "I could do much to help your king... and you. But I cannot do so openly. It would reflect badly on both my Master and your king if they appear to have joined forces."

"Are you suggesting we kidnap the princes in secret?"

"That would be best. The only way, really. Use of arcane devices tends to... alarm people. The Highborn especially, but I can see Khelds taking offense."

Something they would certainly do. A deep vein of suspicion prevented most Khelds from embracing anything that resembled witchery. But if kept secret enough... "Only we two will be in the room when you do it, right? No one else will know."

"No one. They will simply vanish there and appear here."

And Stefan would be blameless. He wouldn't even know until he returned to Simelon that the young princes were in his possession. Erenor could present them to him as hostages, as charges—a gift gained by cooperation with Stefan's new ally—and the king would probably reward him. In order to punish him, Stefan would have to accuse Mormantalorus and Erenor both. Alienating a sorcerer could be dangerous. Stefan could always claim the princes had fled to him somehow. He could then declare the boys under his protection and use them in ways both compassionate and political.

Risky.

Risky making a move like this against godborn blood, against a powerful enemy. Risky, without the approval of the king. But the rewards could be immense.

"Let's do it."

Erenor and Coram chose late evening, when the princes would be prepared for their beds and interruptions would be few. Horse masters, tutors, visiting family or dignitaries did not accompany princes into their bedchambers. Governesses, however, aroused no suspicions.

Silvery taupe hair showed beneath the woman's dark lace-trimmed cap. Coram had procured the woman, a former governess to the princes who had been dismissed from that position two years before. Born a generation ago to refugees from Othgol, she had been secretly in service to Mormantalorus all her life. Encountering proof of espionage in the kingdom would have alarmed Erenor, were it not so interesting to see it being set into play.

Secrets held power. He could use whatever knowledge he gained today later to help Stefan or, if necessary, create an advantage for himself.

The woman stood silent and still as Coram placed a velvet choker around her neck. A *lr* crystal the size of a small hen's egg glowed at the center of an arcane filigree of darkened wire. She accepted two small crowns from Coram, which she slipped into the deep pockets of her crisp pinafore. With a sweep of her hand, the woman then lifted a side panel of her cap so Coram could curl another bit of wire, also bearing a glint of lr gem, behind her left ear. When Coram stepped back, the woman delivered a quick nod, touched her left hand to her ear... then vanished.

Erenor followed as Coram walked across the room to where the mirror shimmered upon its plinth like heavy oil within a ring of metal and jewels. One jewel glowed a somber, malignant yellow. Upon the mirror's surface, shadowed but clear, moved images at once recognizable but impossible. Corridors. Rooms. People appearing as though they were encountering... Erenor. Speaking to him...

"Lady Ophenia! It has been too long."

"So good to see you, Evos."

Not him. It was the woman they were seeing, someone they knew... and the woman who answered, speaking with polite confidence.

The mirror and this Lady Ophenia had by some magic become one! The device heard what she heard and saw what she saw and so—through it—could any who watched her. Erenor's surprise earned one of Coram's knowing smirks.

"Our magery has its uses."

Upon the mirror's surface a new chamber came into view. Two children stood within, boys Erenor had seen but a few months before. The chamber appeared to be a wardrobe. The vantage showed another woman wearing a sober, crisply collared gown and a youthful man in plain garb as befitted a servant. Both appeared to notice Lady Ophenia.

The sober-dressed woman asked, "Has she rejoined the staff? Why were we not told?"

"So many new people lately."

Was it the young man who had answered? Erenor could not tell.

He licked dry lips but could not tear his gaze from the mirror. Coram too watched the progress of his plan.

The princes—prepared for bed—clearly waited for their mother to come say good night. The older boy smiled warmly as Lady Ophenia said she had a gift for him. He even told the other woman to stand aside so Ophenia could place the crown on his head. Golden metal and amber jewels, like his hair and eyes. Erenor's throat thickened. Eldon Malyrdeon looked in every way a godborn prince, certain of his right to wear such a thing.

However the younger boy, Enreddon, backed away from Ophenia's hands when she sought to place another crown on his head.

"Just place it on him, woman. Do it now." Coram's mutter held an impatient hiss. His hands cradled yet another device, prongs of dark metal embedded with yellowish tourmaline gems. At its base sat a burning *lr* crystal the size of a plum.

"—a special gift. See how fine the one worn by your brother looks." Lady Ophenia extended the crown again toward the child.

"No! No!" The boy batted the circlet from Ophenia's outstretched hands. It fell to the carpet. The child looked past her. "Mama!"

"What is this?"

Palaistea's voice, though herself unseen, caused Erenor to blanch and Coram to curse. The mirror showed a slim and elegant female hand, ringed with white stones set in silver, reach for the small crown on the floor. Lady Ophenia must have straightened, for next they saw the Princess in full, clothed in blue, framed by servants and holding the crown in her hands. She looked at it for a moment, then slid her right hand through it, so it hung on her wrist. Young Enreddon clutched the leg of the male servant, but Eldon stayed where he had been and appeared about to explain to his mother about the crown on his head, which he touched.

"We can get one, at least," muttered Coram. He pressed a dark jewel embedded in the base of the device he was holding. The *lr* crystal at its core blazed, dark power expanding within, and its cage of metal glowed fiery orange. The crystals on the prince's head blazed also.

Palaistea's eyes widened. "Oh! No. No. Take that off—"

"Ma, I like it!" Eldon held onto the crown with both hands, clamping it to his head.

Thwarted, Palaistea reached for the largest fiery stone and pried at it. Virulent green light seeped from its setting. Dazzling jewels encircled her fingers, her wrist.

"Fool!" Coram's mouth dropped open as he stared in horror. He tossed the device in his hands into the deathstone case at his feet and slammed it shut just as blinding gold light laced with crackling green energy burst through the seams of the lid.

A blaze bright as the sun flooded the mirror. So did screams.

A moment later imagery resumed, but just for a heartbeat. An angle much lower emerged, changed and darkened. A woman burned like a torch, her every garment aflame... screams, so many screams... the room in flames... draperies, carpet, furnishings all ablaze. Bodies burned like logs on the floor... and then that sight too was stolen as the mirror shrieked and went dark.

"What the fuck... what just happened?" Erenor heard himself cry aloud before Coram slapped him hard enough to knock him to the ground.

"Shut up! No one knows about this, you utter idiot, unless your hysterics alert people to our activity." Coram stared at the deathstone box. "Molten hell! The stupid bitch disrupted the translocation linkage."

"Prince Eldon isn't here!" Erenor looked around just in case he had somehow missed the arrival. He clambered to his feet. "You said we were getting one at least. He isn't here! What happened?"

"I don't know. He—" Coram hurriedly covered a gem on the mirror frame, darkening it, and removed the device from the plinth back into its heavy box. He slid that and the smaller box back under the bed. "He is gone, one way or another. The amount of energy bound by paired *lr* crystals in a translocation array is immense. That boy is dead, and probably so is everyone else in that room, or maybe the whole damned palace." He hauled forth a large carrying bag and began throwing in clothing from his wardrobe. "I am leaving."

The thrice-cursed thing on his ear. Another fucking translocation device. His baggage probably had them too. Coram was leaving Erenor to face Stefan on his own.

"I never knew anything about this." Erenor stepped close to Coram, close enough to see the unease in his darting eyes. He grabbed Coram' sleeve. The bastard was going to go nowhere until he had listened. "I have no knowledge that *anything* happened. Neither will you, until you return to your master to tell him how you just brought Gsch down upon us all."

"An accident!" Coram seethed under his breath.

"That you initiated!"

Footsteps sounded in the corridor outside and they both froze, gazes locked on the door until the steps had passed. Unnoticed, then... at least, so far. Erenor was far from done.

"Whatever the hells happened, this is going to be a *problem*. Stefan is going to be furious. He may be blamed! Was that the plan all along? Is Nammuor trying to get rid of him?"

Coram shook his head. With a sigh, he stepped back and sagged against the wooden frame of the wardrobe. "No. Nammuor maneuvers against the Highborn. He doesn't give a fuck about Stefan, except as someone he can use in his war against Dorilian."

"Well, *that* man is going to be *really* unhappy about this."

With a glare, Coram tugged his arm away. "*Nammuor* is going to be really unhappy about this." He licked his teeth. "He is nearly as good a truth-teller as the Highborn can be, and much more dangerous, so I will be telling him the truth. He will know you cooperated, but the attempt failed. Stefan may get blamed, yes, but only because people will be looking for someone to blame and finding *no one*. If he wants to, Stefan can blame Dorilian like he always does."

Stefan was nothing if not predictable. Erenor walked to the deathstone box and kicked it. "Take these with you. I cannot have them around."

Coram nodded. "Suspicion won't fall on you or your king, at least not directly. Neither of you could possibly have been there. Blame may fall on me, though. So I will be in Stauberg before that can happen and in Mormantalorus soon after. I may not return to Essera for quite some time."

Good riddance, Erenor thought the moment Coram was gone and the room emptied of his belongings. As he stood at the window and stared westward across the first edge of the Eleutheron's wide prairie, a blood-red sunset spilled along a purple horizon.

35

The Sordani woman had spurned Stefan's summons to the Jewel Tower. She had proposed instead to meet in Permephedon's Court of the Three. The location was open and public, the kind of place that stripped away rank and rendered advantages unimportant. An imposing pavilion at the park's center, a shrine of sorts, shared the breathtaking asymmetry of the buildings that surrounded it.

Palimia Kastryonis had arrived ahead of him and chosen an east-facing terrace that overlooked a mall of surreally perfect pointy trees and a view of the Rill. The might of the Sordaneon Tower, its deep aquamarine surfaces slashed with turquoise, dominated to one side and the Rill to the other... perfect. Stefan glowered at her for being obvious and directed his companions, Lucien and Goff, to stand away.

Palimia's people, a woman in gray robes and a scholarly looking man, already stood at a respectful distance.

"I suspect you know why I'm here." Stefan might as well get right to the point.

Palimia tilted a frank, unafraid gaze upon him. "An apology?"

Stefan's jaw clenched. Even had he wanted to—which he didn't—he could not apologize because he had never publicly owned the deed. "Essera sent official condolences. We are moved to pity by your situation." Though seeing her this way bothered him, there was nothing to be gained by revisiting how it had happened. "I am here, however, because you are withholding from me an inheritance."

"Ah."

He waited for Palimia to say more, but she appeared content to simply study him. Her expression was… unsettling. They were not strangers. They had met before, attended events at the Golden Palace and in Dazunor-Rannuli several years ago. At the time, she had been his grandfather's mistress and inconsequential. She looked different now. Thinner, weaker, with hollow cheeks and pain shadowing her fawn-brown eyes. Stefan recalled the bequest she had presented to him and how he had denied it, and ducked his head.

"The villa you requested in Dazunor-Rannuli—I cannot sell it to you. I gave it to my wife's sister."

"That's too bad. I had hoped to convert it into a public garden and library."

"Is that what you're doing? Using my money for gardens and libraries?"

She offered up a soft laugh. "Hardly. I am spending my own money. I hold none of yours."

"Don't play games with me. Do you know how many Archhalial petitions I have directed at recovering the Stauberg-Randolph assets you hold?"

Palimia turned her gaze away from him at last. "Seven, I think. You understand, I hope—indeed, Your Majesty, I am sure you do, because it has been explained seven times to your accountants—that I do not hold *any* of those assets. They are held in trust."

"By Dorilian."

"His Thrice Royal Grace has been explicit from the beginning. I but *manage* the assets. I collect rents and pay taxes and invest proceeds so the assets grow or are maintained in value. Legal possession resides with the trust, which will in due course revert to your family—though almost certainly not to you."

It shocked him to hear her say it openly. Always before, responses to the Archhalia had made vague references to eventual return of those assets without ever explicitly saying to whom. Now he knew for certain what he had guessed all along.

He's doing it to hurt me. Damn Dorilian knows I need that money.

"You still could give me some—or all—of that money. I've had people look into it. You could issue a loan, repayment to the trust. You don't even have to ask him."

Stefan knew he had hit the mark when the shadow of something bold entered her look, along with a hint of a smile. "You're right, of course. I have full discretion to give out loans and set repayment terms. You've made some attempts in that direction, through proxies."

He had. "You turned away those attempts."

"I uncovered who was behind them."

"You hate me that much?"

Palimia inhaled sharply and glanced past his shoulder. Not toward the Rill, or the Citadel and the two regnal Towers, but toward a pretty walkway between ranks of needle-shaped trees the color of blueberries. White spires of summer bells interspersed with azure lilies lined the path. "Not for the reasons you think. Others have caused me far more hurt over the years. But you... you are so reckless with the legacy that was left to you, so ready to throw away every bit of ground your grandfather won—and why? So you might stand here on your pride? You have no sense of irony, of history."

Neither did she, if she thought she could dictate terms simply because she had slept with Dorilian Sordaneon. Stefan placed himself between her and the view she preferred. "I bear you no ill will, Lady. I never have. We don't have to be adversaries. You talk of legacy but withhold it. There's no irony or history at stake in wanting to receive what is rightly mine!"

A sigh accompanied the tilt of her chin. How could she meet his gaze so serenely? She clearly had no intention of acknowledging him as wronged.

"But you already have what is rightly yours, Your Majesty. You have the throne. You have also taken things that were *not* yours by right and for which you have no intention of ever rendering compensation. You have borrowed against assets you do not even realize you own—so heavily and so often that you have bankrupted your chances at peace." Palimia folded her hands upon the blanket of silk and pearls that covered her legs. The gesture called attention to her bared forearms, which were still shapely beneath smooth skin pale as milk. Even her bracelets of gold and pearls were delicate and fine.

"You will not help me, then."

"No."

Stefan cursed and shook his head. This ridiculous visit had been pointless. "He told you not to, didn't he?"

Palimia lifted her head and shook back strands of blonde hair teased by a light breeze. "No, he didn't. How could he, when you never enter his conversation at all." She placed her hands upon the wheels of her chair, which moved and turned much more neatly than Stefan would have thought it could. "I simply wanted to see you for myself."

The Jewel Tower of the Malyrdeons floated above a vast multicolored pool ringed by silver. The pool was known as the Mirror of Songs because every disturbance of its surface created music. The tower hovered above its melodies on a shimmer of a thousand hues and its underside, reflected in the Mirror, looked like iridescent honeycomb, if such could have been made by giant bees. Where the Mirror adjoined the Court of the Three, a great stone ring stood on its edge. When Stefan, with Goff and Lucien accompanying him, approached the ring, it changed color from solemn gray to dusky blue. Onlookers saw nothing but water and air when the men walked through the ring into an entrance court concealed from outside eyes.

Unnatural though the Jewel Tower was, Stefan had gotten used to it. Mostly. The air had no smell. None, except when people were near. Also, all daytime light in the Tower was wholly natural, even in the deepest core of the building. And except for a few decorative changes of elevation in some parts, there were no stairways, even though the damned thing soared into the sky.

A line of attendants stood at the ready just past a portal white as clouds. Stefan greeted these servants, then entered a brilliant rotunda. The ceiling—so high over his head it seemed to spiral upward forever—was ribbed with golden honeycomb much like the underside of the tower.

"I want an order on the table at tomorrow's Halia meeting." Stefan turned to Goff. "I'm making a levy on the Crown treasury." His own coffers were beyond empty. Palimia had turned him down and approaching his bankers in Dazunor-Rannuli would be fruitless.

"You expect me to push that through? They don't listen to me."

Was Stefan really going to have to do this? Go to every damned sitting member and argue his case? "Make them listen."

Portals ringed the domed rotunda, dozens of them, framed with the same silvery metal that delineated the Mirror. Stefan knew which portal to use and stepped through it to emerge, followed by Goff and Lucien, in yet another circular room. That room too was ringed with portals, fewer in number but framed more ornately. At the center of this quiet and elegant rotunda, Stefan was met by Caddo, his chamberlain, and Goran, his valet.

"Majesty." Caddo bowed and extended a message cylinder. "Important. From your Lady Mother."

Stefan removed the crown he had worn thinking to impress a ridiculously unimpressible woman and handed it to Goran. He snatched the cylinder and keyed it open.

"This had better be good news." His fingers unrolled the paper within and he read it. "Nilla's had the baby!" The next words wiped away his smile. "It's a girl."

Goff appeared to understand. "Where there's one babe, there can be more."

Lucien, however, exclaimed enthusiasm. "Sire, this is great news! A new little princess! What will you name her?"

"I don't know."

Lucien's eyebrows pulled together quizzically. "Did you not pick out a girl's name?"

No, Stefan had not. He had been certain the child would be a boy. The *faetha's* runes had promised him a son.

"No. I was going to name him Marc. Marc Erwan Stefan. I don't know what to name a girl." Or what in the world to do with one. It would be years before he could even marry her off to his advantage.

Goff clapped him congenially on the shoulder. "You must go straightaway to Trulo. Be with your wife and name the child. Luc here is only the first of many who will ask you that question." Goff paused, then asked one of his own. "And Nilla, is she well also?"

Emyli had mentioned her as well. "Yes. Healthy and happy."

At least there was that. Childbirth presented all manner of peril to women. Stefan knew he should leave at once to go to his wife's side; he had done all he could here. Erenor would take care of things in the Eleutheron. He would send Lucien to join that effort and Goff could ride with Stefan to Trulo. Sinon Kouranos would push the levy through.

It was then that he witnessed Marenthro simply *appear* several feet behind Goran, the valet. The Undying One of Permephedon wore a look so grave and cold it hammered a stave of fear down Stefan's spine.

"Eminence!" Lucien's cry alerted Caddo and Goran, who immediately dropped to their knees. Goff gawped for a long moment, then decided to follow Lucien in doing the same.

"Marty?" Stefan could think of nothing else to say. Though Permephedon was Marenthro's City, he was seldom anywhere to be found. The most recent sighting had been at Stefan's coronation.

Marenthro waved his left arm in a half circle that rearranged the air around him to create a large sphere filled with an image of horror—of fire, smoke, and screams. Motes of flame streamed from a burning building and some appeared to be human, afire, running and writhing until they dropped to the ground. Other motes flew up into the sky on maelstroms of flame.

"What the fuck!" More than amazement at the proof of magic, they all recognized the location. Horror gripped all their faces. Lucien looked ready to vomit.

"The Danae Palace." Marenthro fixed the image in place somehow and walked behind it. "It will burn to the ground, all but the stone. A fire that hot destroys all it touches." He emerged on the other side and peered into the fiery ruins as if he could, indeed, see into the conflagration. More moments passed until he turned his gaze upon Stefan. "The bodies within will be but bones and ash. The Princess and her sons were known to be in residence."

"Are you sure? This isn't just one of your… predictions?" Wasn't that what the Malyrdeons said, what Marc Frederick had said on more than one occasion? That Marenthro foresaw futures even without the Wall—saw, but never, ever acted to prevent those futures?

Like what happened here at Permephedon six years ago. When the Arcana broke away and my grandfather and all the princes burned.

"What you are seeing is what is happening at this moment. I am showing it to you, so you have immediate knowledge. I do help out sometimes."

In this case, by giving Stefan a chance to prepare for the consequences of the horrific event.

"No one else needs to stay." Stefan didn't get many chances to speak with Marenthro at all, far less alone. "Goff and Lucien, meet me in the Red Room." They would know which portal that meant. He watched them leave, as well as his staff.

He half-expected Marenthro to vanish also, but the wizard remained along with his disturbing image-sphere. Stefan lifted his chin.

"That"—he indicated the burning within the sphere—"is real?"

"Yes."

The Princess… her sons. Stefan could hear already what people would say. "You'll testify I was here, I suppose." Something else came to mind. "Are you still helping out? Because I need to know other things too… like where my brother is. Those boys—I need you to bring him back."

A subtle sadness moved one corner of Marenthro's youthful mouth. "Someday. Today, however"—he indicated the burning palace—"I am showing you this. I am also telling you it matters. Find out how… and find out *why*."

The image evaporated as if it had never been there. So did Marenthro.

Stefan cursed and his shoulders drooped. He wouldn't be going to Trulo after all. He would be blamed for this. The Royal North would remember that he had tried to seize the young princes, had brought in mercenaries to crush Burelan Phaeros. Of course they would condemn him for the fire, for the deaths.

It was just like what had happened here at Permephedon, the day of the Demise. The day the Arcana had burned—the *way* it had burned. Whatever power had been used that day could have done the same thing at Danae. Sorcery, then, answered the how.

But not the why.

"How did they die?"

Dorilian stood with Tiflan upon the eagle wings of the stone barge. A mere spear's throw away, the Viridian River spilled down the Serat's white wall in a long, thundering fall into mist. Beyond and above the Serat walls, the Rill shifted to receive an incoming *charys*.

Tiflan had just come from Permephedon and brought with him a report from Bynum, sent by relay to Permephedon. The Danae Palace had burned to only charred stone. The few bodies found had been but cremains. Princess Palaistea and her sons, Eldon and Enreddon, were missing and presumed to have been consumed by the conflagration. Due to the crisis, the Archhalia had suspended session.

Children. Helpless children... two boys and their mother. And how many other people with them?

Dorilian struggled to contain the emotional residue. He had felt death in the Mind—muted, diffuse but no less sharp for not knowing who—and had spent two miserable days of waiting for the full truth of what had occurred.

"None know how it happened. Stefan"—Tiflan, ever impervious to Dorilian's whims, hesitated only slightly in saying the name and flinched not at all at the glare of warning—"was at Permephedon at the time. He left that same day with troops for the Eleutheron because he knows trouble will break out there."

"Is there a chance one of them is *not* dead?"

"If lack of proof constitutes a chance."

The boys were young, unmanifested, mere smudges in the Mind. Dorilian had never sought them there before—and could not find them now. Though hollowed, the Mind contained folds and shadows. Dead or merely missing, the loss of the Malyrdeon princes and their formidable mother was a calamity.

Why? To remove them from the succession?

That made sense only if Stefan had become a monster.

Turning his back on the City, Dorilian retreated to the shade of the pavilion atop the Eagle's back. He dropped onto cushions and indicated a vessel of wine. "Drink," he directed. If Tiflan did not drop dead before answering the next question, Dorilian would drink also.

Tiflan shrugged in rebuke but poured a goblet, from which he took a long drink. "One day you will get over your fear of being poisoned."

"You clearly have." Dorilian took Tiflan's cup for himself and splashed wine into the second cup, which he pushed toward him. "Essera is ruled by a fool, but I don't think he ordered this. Get whatever information you can."

"I will."

"Without Palaistea, and after that debacle in Rannul, the Eleutheron will be up in arms. And Stauberg—" Dorilian glanced at Tiflan and saw him unaffected, so put the cup to his lips. The wine was good, from his own vineyard at Rhondda, with a sweetness that other wines never quite achieved. "If we know of this news, Elhanan and Rheger know too. They must be taking precautions."

It was something new for Dorilian to be concerned about his Malyrdeon kindred. His stomach turned as he realized only *two* Malyrdeons remained.

The last four of our race. Lev and the two of them—and me.

"I should bring them here."

Tiflan considered the proposal. "Rheger and Elhanan? I don't think they would come. They are both at Stauberg for now, and the Wall will protect them."

Maybe. Dorilian had heard all his life how the Wall protected their race. Just as the Rill protected him—though that was less certain. His one shred of evidence that the Rill might do so had been the day so many of his kindred had died at Permephedon. If he had not been bleeding, or wearing the Rill Stone, would the Entity have allowed him within its shield? It certainly had done nothing to protect him since.

He had seen images of blood in his Wall visions... so many images of blood, many of which had come to pass. Some, though, remained unaccounted for.

Another of his Wall visions, however, had just happened.

… a woman in flames… a burning wall…

He inhaled through clenched teeth and closed his eyes.

"Are you all right?"

Dorilian saw no reason to turn away from Tiflan's inquiry. "It's just… the Wall showed me this. A fragment of it. Not in any way I could have warned anyone, of course. The Entities are heartless."

"You saw but a flash of the Wall's being, a mote only a Wall Lord could have deciphered. You did not exactly share what you saw. It's possible they never put it in the Archive."

Even Tiflan didn't believe that.

"They put everything in the Archive. Elhanan might at this very moment be taking my bit of prescience and moving it into the 'so that's what that meant' volume." Dorilian sighed and breathed the sweet scents of almond trees and the rare striped lilies that grew along the Viridian River's banks. The Serat provided beauty and peace—and safety, too—the very things Palaistea had surely thought the Danae Palace would provide. He had visited the palace during his year with Marc Frederick and spent two days there, enjoying its sublime comforts. It had not seemed like a place that would easily burn.

Dorilian picked up his wine again. "I will instruct my generals to hold their positions in Gignastha but cease provocations in Neuberland. Let someone focus on stabilizing the Royal North."

Tiflan nodded gravely. "A wise move."

More than that, it was necessary. He needed Essera to remain in one piece, not present a feast of easy pickings.

Tiflan was not through with questions. "What will you spend your time on now?"

"Add to my forces in Mokkasa and Suddekar. Recruit more spies. Build more ships. Increase my war chest. And send some fucking warnings to Rheger." Dorilian did not need the Wall to know what lay ahead. "I fear Nammuor has begun making moves in Essera."

And Dorilian was trapped in Sordan, manacled by his own words—with no way to stop him.

36

"I thought Aral would be prettier. It's really quite bland." Nammuor turned his back on the views of the city and a somber sea and returned to the even blander interior of the clifftop tower Coram had procured for him. Already it served as a base from which Nammuor could, either in person or through proxies, embark on his manifold goals. He had correctly assessed Erenor Tholeros's potential. Ambition saw only its own ends and little cared about anyone else's.

"Wait. Sunset makes things better." Eyes closed, Coram tilted his head against the chair back and held a cold compress behind his left ear.

Human flesh, being ridiculously rudimentary, responded poorly to spatial translocations. Even a single translocation could be disorienting. As for *this* halfwit....

"Translocating three times in one day was foolish," Nammuor observed. "We could have set our plans here in motion weeks sooner had you not panicked."

Coram opened one eye. "I wasn't going to wait around in Stauberg for the Dannutheon Princes to learn of what happened. They are using the Wall Stone again. Maybe even walking the Wall. How was I to be sure their damned Entity wouldn't smite me?"

"You greatly overestimate the Entities. They are weakened, inert." Nammuor paced to the dark mirror he had attuned to an array atop a nearby stone table, the only furniture in the room suitable for that purpose. Each crystal was linked to a matching *Ir* fragment, either placed in a location he wished to monitor or being worn by one of his agents.

He tapped one crystal and looked upon his workshop in the Ilgaon in Mormantalorus. His mages were hard at work.

Coram knew what Nammuor watched. "I had hoped.... The boy could have made it if not for his stupid mother."

"A shame." The devices in the crowns Coram's agent had given the young princes had been keyed to transport them, but not to Simelon. To Mormantalorus. "He was too damaged, of course. Burnt blood, even if immortal, loses its character and can neither flow into a crystal nor hold a lifeforce." Nammuor had wasted three precious caged crystals in futile attempts to harvest blood from the charred and dying ruin of Eldon Malyrdeon.

The Diadem was nearing completion—five caged immortal lifeforces attached, with five more to go. Nammuor was, however, still two Highborn lives short of his goal.

The child's blood, even if unburned, would have been less than ideal for his creation, but it would have sufficed until a replacement could be found. It certainly would have surpassed the slave blood currently feeding two of the Diadem's crystals. Every waking moment and even in dreams, Nammuor endured the Undying Crown's incessant demand to fulfill their conjoined destiny.

Until he did so, however, he was pressed to deal with the clumsy machinery of humans and their societies. Coram remained a useful weapon. Reason enough to keep the man alive. Nammuor turned back to his lieutenant.

"Let me know when your head stops hurting."

Coram turned his open eye upon Nammuor. "Where now?"

"You must return to Stauberg. But if you do not disappoint me in the next several hours, you may travel in the usual way, by ship."

"But is it safe for me to go there? The Wall may know me."

Nammuor scoffed. "The Wall most certainly knows you. It knew you, and what you would do, the moment it first touched you a year ago."

"It knew?" Coram's face blanched, eyes widened to a stare.

"It knew—but it had no one to tell. That may not be the case now, if your suspicions about the Wall Stone are true. So when you go back this time, you will need to move quickly." A reddish light spilled through the narrow windows. The color resembled that of the skies of Nammuor's homeland, the land of fire, and beckoned him back to take another look at the sea. Orange and vermilion lined the sky to the west.

How appropriate.

"You feel certain they have the Wall Stone?"

"Yes. The signs—"

"Find out, then do what you must to get it for me."

"You honestly believe they would give it up?" Coram slapped the ice back onto his head.

"No. But Stefan might. He craves power and the advantages that come from it—and he hates the Highborn. It has taken nearly a year of his life to pacify the Eleutheron and now he marches on Stauberg to make sure of his Malyrdeons. There is our opportunity. Stefan is suspicious, easily turned. Erenor is his trusted lieutenant, and Erenor is a man we can use. That will be your task. Turn Stefan against his Malyrdeons, so we might acquire them and their device. I cannot reach them while they are in Stauberg. The Wall blocks my powers."

"But you *can* go there."

"Yes, if I use ordinary devices. Ordinary arrays. The Highborn themselves use such. But the Diadem cannot be there, within the Wall's being. Their Entity does not protect the Malyrdeons from you, but from *it*." A greater danger would be if the Wall recognized crystals filled with the immortal blood of its descendants.

The Wall Stone would be as great a prize as Essera itself. The energy to be leached from lifeforces bound by immortal blood was nothing compared to what might be gained from an artifact that was an actual piece of an immortal. In addition, the Diadem might gain the powers of the Wall, of Ergeiron himself. A god.

But Nammuor needed to move carefully. The Wall might protect against this maneuver, and it might warn its princes. Coram would be a loss, if that was the case.

"The Dannutheon princes are not unsuspecting boys. They have studied me and would know me, even without input from the Wall. They already know you."

"And they know Stefan also."

"Yes, they know him and avoid him. They fear looking at him too closely, and that will be our trap. Whatever he does will catch them off guard."

Redder light spilled across the western sky as the sun sank into the sea. Nammuor contemplated the last of day and what he planned for those to come.

"Dorilian offers us refuge in Sordan." Rheger found the low light within the Aidion oppressive. A steady ruby glow emanated from walls that, if touched, would be soft, spongy, and warm.

"We would never make it. We are too well watched." Elhanan trod the intricate, interlaced pattern of the mosaic floor beneath the Aidion's cavernous ceiling, itself a convoluted marvel. One foot on white stone. One foot on blue. A game, nothing more. He glanced up at his father. "You can go, and probably should. But I won't flee and, well, Margarid is with child. How in the world could I leave her behind?"

No. Of course he would not do that. Neither would Rheger leave his family behind only for them to face… whatever was coming. The Royal North was too restless, too fraught with dangers still in motion and finding new shape. Just that morning in Ennsa, Rheger had dissuaded Estevan, Margarid's brother and Gweroyen's Bas, from formally declaring himself in opposition. An alignment of Gweroyen with the Royal North's other hostile domains, Pessach and Lacenedon, would present an impossible challenge to Stefan— and effectively break Endurin's hope to save them all.

"We stand with Stefan. We hold to the Wall's design and will follow only the true line of Marc Frederick." With those words, Rheger had reaffirmed the kindred's stance at every meeting, every opportunity.

Though Rheger had ridden to join Stefan at Bynum in a show of support, rebellion nonetheless rumbled beneath the Royal North's skin like a beast not yet killed and too soon buried. The catastrophe that had befallen Palaistea and her children continued to burn within the hearts and minds of leaders and populace alike. It resonated within the remaining time paths of Ergeiron's descendants. And not his alone… Derlon's, too, stood endangered. Rheger peered upward from this place deep inside his father Entity's heart, into soaring floor upon circular floor of golden, imprinted Wall corpus.

"And the Archive told you nothing?"

"Bits. Pieces. The Archive is not a History. It's a map, a cross-referential filing system that allows Wall Lords to visit Time and bring into focus events or persons proximal or attached to those points. So…" Elhanan resumed slowly walking the white and blue stones. "I cannot penetrate Endurin's Paradigm. That's the crux of the matter. The timeline curls inward, back on itself, again and again, almost a golden spiral but… not quite. It prevents Wall Walkers from seeing what lies on the other side, or seeing if there even *is* an 'other' side, the very blockage that lured Austell to attempt pairing the Entities."

Only to fail. Rheger sighed. He did not want Elhanan, a far less experienced Wall adept, to attempt that course.

"Dorilian, it turns out—now that I can use the Wall Stone to look into the Archive again—is a product of the Paradigm in some way. No wonder Enreddon and others, Austell included, approached him so cautiously. But he is not the only event unfolding." Elhanan had paced to the curved wall beside which Rheger stood and he slouched onto one of the benches placed there. "Endurin crafted something—not the Paradigm, something else— maybe in tandem with the Wall. It had to do with Marc Frederick, of course—but not Stefan."

"Not Stefan?" That made no sense.

"No. Stefan is consequential, but... he's a vector, a shadow."

"Of Dorilian?"

"No. Maybe Marc Frederick, but... misshaped. Stefan is merely adjacent."

If that was the case... "There might be someone else."

"Or something else. That's what no one has identified. Whoever or whatever is unfolding within the Paradigm is not on the map— we don't know how or why. Nothing points to it, and yet everything points to it. The Paradigm prevents us from seeing it, maybe even from reaching it." Elhanan tipped back his head, gold-bright hair spilling against the soft, dusky wall. He stared at the oculus high above, through which not even starlight shone—only Wall light. "I have looked, but... the Archive does not include Endurin's calculations. Without them, I cannot pinpoint or walk that time path. If I had a Tether, I could explore, maybe find something. That said, I am not deranged enough—or trained enough—to walk the Wall unanchored."

"Let me tether you. I play a good game of courses." Most Highborn did. They understood the basis for the game's mechanics.

"You're too close to me. Emotional attachment—"

"Can be problematic. I understand that. However, some of the best Tethers have been siblings—or lovers."

"And *not* Highborn. There are reasons we forbid our own kind to tether Wall walkers."

The danger of both parties being subsumed within the Entity was not worth the risk.

Until it was.

"You said it yourself," Rheger persisted. "Events are unfolding. Events about which we need knowledge. There's more danger to this World than just in walking the Wall."

Elhanan nodded, and even that nod was haunted. "Yes. That much is clear. The Archives.... We stand on a cliff edge. Not just of a Demise, but an Annihilation. Nammuor has found the Undying Crown and devised a way to power it. Dorilian told us what Nammuor did at the Demise. Lifeforces and blood, trapped in crystals. The monster is feeding it... with *us*, because he plans to use it again. This is certain. That is the event the Wall Lords saw and recorded generations ago. The Paradigm was to be a way out, except... the door is closed. We have not done what is needed to push it open. Maybe it ceased being a door and has turned into a trap."

"If that's the case, what have we to lose?"

"Our lives—and the Wall with them."

Rheger put his hand on his son's shoulder. "We are part of Endurin's Paradigm, too. We might as well engage it. Let me tether you."

"Stefan has put to rest that rebellion you started." Erenor frowned at the Mormantaloran merchant ship being loaded nearby. Stauberg's wharfs swarmed with activity, ships and men and machines. The movement and noise of loading this ship alone would make it difficult for anyone, even Coram, whom Erenor faced, to overhear what he said.

Irritation tightened Coram's perfect upper lip. "I started nothing. The stupid woman—"

"If I had known *lr* crystals could do *that*, even by accident, I would never have agreed—"

"I should think your king is pleased to be rid of those Highborn spawn."

Much as Erenor wanted to deny it, he knew otherwise. Stefan was not unhappy at all to be rid of the Malyrdeon princes; he had only been sorry they'd died so horribly. "At least people know he wasn't to blame. He was at Permephedon. There are a whole lot of people, though, who think I might have done it."

"If the truth ever got out..."

Erenor despised that smirk. Almost as much as he despised, and feared, Coram being able to hold over his head that he had approved the plot to abduct the young princes. If the damned devices had worked, if the princes had been translocated to Simelon, he might have gathered rich rewards. He would have risen even further in Stefan's favor and very likely, with the king's help, could have maneuvered Palaistea into marriage. Instead, he had just spent months in the saddle, shitting in chamber pots and sleeping in flea-ridden campaign tents, while riding at Stefan's side to put down an insurrection.

Now that Stefan had crushed the rebellion, Erenor had been sent ahead into Stauberg to arrange for how the city would welcome its king. He had just spent two hours with the city's Citizens' Council and Stauberg's new Prince, who had accompanied him from Bynum. Rheger Dannutheon had barely spoken to him on that journey, conversing only when necessary.

A crane groaned overhead, its boom and ropes straining to lift pallets of lumber onto the ship. Erenor eyed it in case the lines failed, but the mechanism succeeded in swinging over the deck. Mormantalorus had a massive appetite for tall, straight Eleutheron timber. Erenor focused on Coram again.

"I am not going to try to tell Stefan what he should do with his Highborn princes. He knows where I stand, and that is to let him handle them, the way people here in Essera always let the king do. I liked them better in Dannuth, to be sure, but now that *circumstances*," he glowered at Coram, "have elevated the Dannutheons to be Princes of Stauberg, Stefan's hands are tied. He cannot change the laws of succession. And they have done nothing to give him cause to think them disloyal."

"Not even that they are using the Wall?"

Erenor grabbed Coram by the arm and pulled him several steps toward the warehouse, getting them both out from under yet another load being lifted. He had visions of being crushed under a ton of lumber. "Stefan has only met with Rheger, who is not using the Wall. Stefan asked him directly when they were together at Bynum."

"And the son?"

"Elhanan?" Erenor shrugged. "He hasn't left the city. Stefan has not met with him yet."

"You are wrong if you think I would counsel Stefan to kill them. Far from it. The Highborn are quite vital to this kingdom, and my nation also—if only as a countermeasure." Coram's stare fixed on a point over Erenor's left shoulder. The Rill mount dominated the largest island in the harbor, connected to the mainland by a causeway.

"Dorilian? Fear of assassination has turned him into a recluse. But for what influence he has on the Rill, he is impotent."

"Hah! Gignastha says otherwise. My master says otherwise. We fight him in Suddekar and along the Teremar border. You should fear the day *that* prince turns his might against you."

Might? Perhaps. Dorilian had military and economic power to spare. What he appeared to lack was enough spine to push his might beyond Gignastha into Essera. Much to Stefan's satisfaction, Neuberland's scrappy Kheld settlers were proving troublesome for Sordan. In the last month Kheld rebels had pushed into Lower Neuberland and destroyed the invader's camps.

Erenor shrugged. "The only fear I still hold about Dorilian is that the Dannutheons might refuse to assist should the king need to move against him."

No Highborn prince in the history of Highborn princes had ever warred with another.

Coram acknowledged the point. "How disappointing. Stauberg might not declare for your king when that time comes. Hell, the Dannutheons could join forces with Dorilian and the Highborn rule again. Let's go to the wine merchant at the harbor gate. An urge for drink has come upon me."

A bottle and a table sounded good. Sharing wine with a representative of a foreign power appealed to Erenor far more than having to humor some Kheld chieftain over a jug of beer. Sour swill. As a nobleman of the host country, Erenor bought the wine—a very good vintage from Merced—and put down a coin for use of two goblets, then joined Coram at a table set beneath the shop's awning.

"You realize," Coram resumed their conversation, "that this city is woefully undefended against the Sordaneon."

"Stauberg cannot be attacked." Erenor pointed past the port to the curtain of light extending from the harbor islands and Rill mount to Stauberg itself. "Wall."

"I am not talking about a military attack. I am talking about how Stefan may be caught with his pants around his ankles if he thinks Stauberg will fight against that Highborn menace—only to learn it will not."

Before today the possibility had not occurred to Erenor—and probably not to Stefan either. By pleading neutrality, the Prince of Stauberg could wreak havoc by depriving the Royal Navy of its primary port. And if the Prince refused to engage...

"Do you have evidence Dorilian is planning to invade the Royal North?"

"Not at the moment," Coram admitted.

"Well, that's a good thing... right? All Stefan wants right now is peace. He has other things he wants to do, important things, none of which were getting done while he was on the battlefield."

"None of his grand plans and none of yours. I've been watching."

How not, with Mormantalorus so deeply entrenched? Erenor pushed his goblet and watched the water ring around the base create fat patterns on the tabletop. "Stefan finds statements easier to make with his Kheld chieftains now that I am a great noble. He gave my post as Commander of his King's Guard to Goff's son so he could elevate *him*. He bestowed some estates in the Eleutheron on a few of his more loyal lords. The prize for me was to be marriage to Palaistea, and control of the princes, but—" He circled his cup to make a new, bigger water ring. "Stefan knows I am loyal, but he has lost interest in helping me secure a lofty marriage."

"Finding marriage-worthy women is easy. It is far harder to make oneself indispensable." Coram lifted the ewer and poured more wine. "Decent wine. I commend your selection."

"I suppose you have ideas on how I might make myself indispensable?"

"A few. To start with, Stefan really should consider following in the footsteps of his famous grandfather."

When Stefan rode into Stauberg four days after defeating the last rebel army of the Eleutheron at the Battle of Stariel, he found the grand road into the city lined by kneeling soldiers, their weapons laid upon the ground. Inside the city, at the Gate of Transformation from which the Wall itself emanated, the immense and shining ceremonial portal lay open. He dismounted to face Stauberg's Prince, Rheger Dannutheon. Rheger knelt on pavement of gold in front of his Entity's most sacred shrine. The Prince's Heir Elhanan knelt at his side.

"King. Welcome and accept the genuine love of your capital and its people."

How genuine that love might be was something Stefan found suspect—but Stauberg's submission was real. Rheger's first act upon inheriting Stauberg from his deceased Malyrdeon cousins had been to send troops to Stefan's aid. He had accepted Stefan sending troops into Stauberg, acknowledging the city as rightly the king's, and then ridden forth to personally negotiate at Stefan's side in Bynum. Having a Highborn prince at his side had provided Stefan with both a weapon and armor—none could challenge Rheger's proclamation that Stefan was blameless for what had happened at the Danae Palace.

For the first time, Stefan felt the weight of having the Highborn on his side. For once, the godborn bastards had his back.

In welcoming his king into the city, Rheger put on a convincing display of fealty. A flawless performance, one that Stefan understood as having been designed to placate him.

He seeks to downplay how much of a threat he is.

To the cheers of the populace, Stefan accepted Rheger's welcome and together they rode side by side to the magnificent towers of the Aesa Eranos, the Malyrdeon Serat, that crowned the high point of the city. There Stefan greeted the wives of the princes and the staff that would serve him. Within the hour he had settled into the royal residence and begun the long process of putting his stamp upon his kingdom's most iconic city.

His first order of business would be to set up a government in his own capital.

"Strike the Prince's banners—and my grandfather's too." Now that he walked the bedecked corridors, the profusion of old banners reminded him of something that had annoyed him on the ride in. The Stauberg-Randolph flag was everywhere, as it should be, alongside the Prince of Stauberg's—but the flags showed Marc Frederick's ensign. Even the flag floating atop the highest tower— which should have been the King of Essera's flag—was that of Essera itself.

"Yes, Majesty." The silver-haired man at Stefan's side scribbled into a small book. "At once. As soon as we... should we copy the banner currently flying out Your Majesty's window in the Aesa Eranos? Or that of your military?"

"Don't I have someone for this?" Stefan snapped to Erenor, who walked on his other side, as did Goff and Lowen. The question echoed slightly in the vaulted corridor.

"That is usually the job of a minister of state."

Goff glared at Erenor but did not defend himself. "I never knew I was also a Minister of Flags."

Much as Stefan wanted to lay blame *somewhere*, he could understand Goff not knowing every detail of being a First Minister. To the palace clerk awaiting an answer, he said, "Yes, the one at my window. A stag with a large rack, golden antlers. Don't make the crown too subtle, or the stars. And use brilliant colors, the right ones."

"Yes, Majesty! At once. As quicky as scissors and needles can fly." The clerk hurried off, an unimportant man looking to make himself useful.

Goff grumbled. "Think they could have known to change the damn flags themselves."

Erenor wrinkled his nose. "A consequence of not having a Prince in residence. After Enreddon died, no one was ever really in charge of correct royal protocol. The palace administrator probably just followed orders but didn't pay much attention to banners."

And Goff—or whichever underling should have seen to such things—had not sent instructions. Stefan sighed.

They entered the grand rotunda from which seven famous corridors fanned out like spokes to seven just as famed towers, each a gilded wonder. The Aesa Eranos was a treasure house, an accumulation of centuries of art and riches, added to with every generation and never plundered.

Stefan remembered the location of the Throne Hall and led the way. In addition to his companions, soldiers trailed in his wake, an ever-present guard he had adopted since his attempt to kill Dorilian had failed. Only Kheld soldiers could be trusted completely with Stefan's life, though he made a point of elevating Staubauns as officers to other branches of his elite troops. He had rebels in his own kingdom to worry about, such that any outing, however spontaneous or minor, exposed him to risk. Now that he was in the Aesa Eranos again, surrounded by its strength and beauty and the majesty it represented, all his to command, Stefan questioned his decision to rule from the south, from his domains near the Dazun River.

Because being close to Amallar had made him feel safer.

Dorilian, though he lived in distant Sordan, had felt too close, too near, and Stefan had wanted to be ready for him. Dorilian would use the Rill to attack—and it had scared Stefan to think he might be unable to marshal his kingdom's resources if he were anywhere but in Trulo or Dazunor-Rannuli.

Dorilian still felt too close. But not to *this* seat.

Stefan walked the length of the Throne Hall, a way paved with gold-laced blue onyx as bright as the sky, laid between pillared galleries backed by tall windows and great sweeping views of the city and its immortal Wall. As he did so, a feeling of power settled upon him and he embraced it. Banners arrayed overhead in magnificent procession proclaimed mighty Essera's subject domains. *His* domains. He sensed Goff, Lowen, and Erenor fall into step behind him. He sensed too when those men stopped at the broad border of black onyx and gold script Stefan crossed to approach the cerulean steps up to the Star Throne.

Carved from the Timebinder's Rock, a single block of gray stone, the throne was plain and unadorned save by a high headrest that bore an immense and indescribable gem. Polished and aglow, the gem's light never dimmed. The High Throne of the Malyrdeons. Stefan touched one arm and found it smoothed by time, by generations, then took the last step and sat himself upon the hard seat. He knew from having seen his grandfather on this throne that the jewel in the headrest glowed in a halo around his head.

"King of Essera." Erenor knelt. Goff went to one knee also and Lowen followed suit.

"King Stefan!" The soldiers arrayed near the door, led by Peric, drew their swords and crossed blades with a joyous ring of steel on steel.

"It's done. I put Burelan's Purist rebellion to ground. And I tamed the damn Malyrdeons, too." Stefan sank back against the hard angles of the throne. He needed to order someone, maybe that palace clerk, to ferret out the throne's fine velvet cushions.

"Use caution, sire." Erenor had issued nothing but warnings all morning. "You have not settled matters with them. Are you sure you wish them to remain in this city? They are Wall Lords and have the Wall Stone again in their possession."

That Rheger and Elhanan had recovered the Wall Stone appeared certain. Numerous witnesses had placed both men at the Aidion and described how sorcerous lights had accompanied their entrance into the shrine.

"I'm no happier about that than you are, but I have seen no sign they are using it against me."

Lowen lifted his bowed head and scratched behind his neck. "If we're going to talk, could we sit at least?"

Though Erenor looked affronted, Stefan chuckled. One thing he liked best about Khelds was how little they thought of putting on airs. He rose from the throne and descended a step, this time planting his ass on the top step of the dais.

"Sit," he said. "All three of you."

Lowen sat the step nearest his king, as did Erenor.

Goff chose a lower step and stretched his legs in front of him. "This damn city is full of problems for you. For all of us. Kheld folk, anyway." He met Erenor's frown. "Too much magic and too much witchcraft. That Wall is not a natural thing."

Erenor chose to counter that view. "And the Highborn would argue that it is. Completely natural to the World the Entities themselves create. Scholars claim the World Itself is a magical construct, the Second Creation, remade by gods to replace a dead world."

"Do they?" Goff took up the argument. "Well, Kheld folk follow different gods. We think *our* gods created this world, and the world *they* made has walls of dirt and stone and sturdy trees, not… whatever that thing is."

Erenor was unimpressed. "That thing, as you call it, is an immortal being that buttresses the Rift, spans time, and talks to its descendants."

Stefan caught Goff's eye roll.

"Witchcraft."

Much as Goff had a point, Stefan had only one answer. "You know, it doesn't really matter which gods or world you care to believe in. The Wall clearly exists in whatever world this is. And it doesn't do anyone's bidding. Even if I could get my hands on the Wall Stone, it doesn't command the Wall or anything like that."

"It provides *access* to the Wall." Erenor made that point. "We don't really know what kind of access."

Lowen cocked a questioning look at Stefan. "Didn't kings use the stone in the old days?"

"Hmm," said Goff.

Was it possible? Stefan had never considered that he could use the Wall Stone himself. He had always been told only Malyrdeons could use it.

"I spoke with Coram Barzanes." Erenor opened a new direction for their talk. "He congratulates Your Majesty on waging a successful war and I acknowledged, on your behalf of course, the help his country provided."

Indeed, Mormantalorus had supplied Stefan's army in the Eleutheron with food and goods shipped to Stauberg's booming port. The rebels had not planned ahead for war, and though Stefan had not planned ahead either, his superior supply lines had positioned him to win one.

"They lent you coin, too," Erenor added.

"For which they will be repaid in full. Tomorrow. I have full access to my treasury now." Stefan's creditors could all rot atop the stacks of gold he was about to give them.

"He didn't mention payment, though he mentioned that Nammuor would of course lend you much more upon request. The exchange in trade between our nations has been quite lucrative and the Nuarch wishes it to continue. Coram's concern is that Mormantalorus might lose port privileges. They invested heavily here."

"Here? You mean in Stauberg?"

"Yes. Warehouses and new wharfs. Housing for their men."

"Quite a lot, it sounds like," offered Lowen.

"So everyone profits." Stefan heard only good news. "That's as should be."

"And is. Though with Rheger's succession as Prince, Mormantaloran presence in the city might become difficult. The Highborn Princes of Essera are historic adversaries."

That much was true. "I'm still king. Rheger will do what I tell him."

"Nammuor isn't convinced of that."

Goff shared a snicker with Lowen. Stefan glowered.

"I don't know what reassurances Coram—or his master—thinks I can give. Prince Rheger is rightful ruler of this domain."

Though he had briefly hoped to swing Stauberg's succession his way, Stefan had no chance at all of claiming the Highborn principality for himself—not as the law currently stood. The Archhalia had made clear that any male descendent of Ergeiron, the original Wall Lord, counted ahead of Stefan. As an act of deliberate humiliation—or maybe to deter him from removing the Dannutheon princes—they had additionally pointed out that Dorilian Sordaneon, as a direct descendent of Ergeiron's *brother*, currently stood to inherit the Principality after Elhanan.

In fact, Stefan had learned that Dorilian stood to inherit *every* Highborn domain except those that accrued to the Crown— Dazunor and Tahlwent—or had passed to lines founded on Highborn daughters. At least Kathanos had pointed out that things also went the other way: if Dorilian and his child Heir died, Rheger would inherit fucking *Sordan*.

Given the magnitude of his own problems, Stefan didn't give a flying rat's snout about Nammuor's concerns.

"Look," he said, "Coram can come to me if he encounters any problems. I don't think he will."

"Probably not. But he rightly warns these Highborn royals might want your throne." Erenor held Stefan's look of reprimand without flinching. "There's room for concern. They are popular, crowned in glory upon the seat of their forefathers. Stauberg. *Their* city. *Their* Wall."

Lowen looked worried and Goff nodded agreement before he, too, spoke. "The princes in Bynum were boys, years from becoming rivals and we saw how loyal people were to them... but these are men. One of them, folk say, is a Wall Lord. He could be working against you."

"The Highborn are impossibly dangerous enemies." Erenor kicked at the design on the floor. "They protect their own kind. They form a shield wall none can penetrate. We saw that with Palaistea and her sons. They were always placing their power behind her in the Archhalia and rejecting your offers of protection."

"Those boys are dead. I wish people would stop talking about them." How would Stefan ever put those dead princes behind him if people kept bringing them up?

"No, but do remember why they are dead, and not safe where you would have placed them. Here, in Stauberg, under the protection of their Wall."

Goff heaved a sigh. "That should have happened, but for the Dannutheons. Them and that bastard in Sordan, stirring up trouble."

"And killing *our* children too." Lowen believed as Stefan did, that Dorilian had played a role in Nilla losing her and Stefan's first child.

Hard warning looked up at them both from Erenor's dark eyes. "He could kill every child in Essera and they would never call for arms against him. Not ever. It's our law that no man may raise sword against them, but neither do they raise sword against each other. To have them in Essera at all is a problem, but to have them in this city... I'm not sure you can afford it." He glanced again to Stefan, then continued grimly. "Send them to Aral. I can be sure of their safety there and they will not have their Wall to use as a weapon against you. Hold them in house arrest until things settle."

"Put someone in charge here you can trust." Goff approved the plan. He probably envisioned Peric doing the job, or maybe Lowen, who had perked. "Be safer, and no harm to them."

Could be... but without proof, Stefan was not about to head down the path of heresy just yet. Too many in his kingdom still believed that the Highborn were godborn, that they were *necessary*. They would think so even more now that Stauberg's new Prince and his son had proven themselves loyal.

Stefan rose to his feet and descended the remaining steps back onto the room's pretty onyx floor. "I've just gotten to this city, and I've just begun putting its affairs in order. I will be talking with both Rheger and Elhanan later today about what I foresee their future role to be. While at it, I will make clear that our agreement with Mormantalorus is vital and not to change in any way. Still"—he had been thinking about what both men had said—"we will take precautions."

"Only those with Ergeiron's blessing can enter."

With Rheger's warning in his ear, Stefan pondered the silver sheen in front of him. The Aidion Portal. Carved blue basalt from deep beneath Ergeiron's shrine framed the Portal's soft glow. That same stone formed a sunken courtyard lined with ancestral statues, reached through the vaulted subterranean passage Stefan had just walked from the Aesa Eranos. Pillars of black stone cast shimmering reflections upon floors and walls so polished Stefan could imagine he stood and walked upon water. Unseen above, concealed by stone and mighty buttresses, Stauberg rose into the sky, a god's legacy and crown.

The Portal stood directly beneath the Gate of Transformation. Through the Portal in front of Stefan, hidden, lay proof of what Ergeiron had become.

So far, so good. Rheger and Elhanan waited at Stefan's back, along with the two men he had chosen to accompany this venture. Lucien and Erenor were both sufficiently well born to approach the Wall. Stefan's Kheld Guards remained at the bottom of the steps at the far end of the sunken courtyard.

"Where do I enter?" Stefan saw no door.

"As I told you before coming here," Rheger explained, "Ergeiron alone decides—"

"And I ordered you to show me the Wall. The guts of it. I've been inside the Rill at Permephedon."

Rheger glanced at a silent, unsmiling Elhanan. To Stefan he said only, "You stood within an antechamber then as well. And even in that, the Wall and the Rill... are not the same."

"But there is something beyond this... obstruction."

"Yes."

"Open it."

Rheger tipped his head back, then said, "It *is* open."

Magic, Goff would have said.

Stefan reached forward. His fingertips touched... nothing. Neither heat nor cold, nor anything at all of texture. Yet mere silver shadow somehow presented a barrier his flesh would not pass. He folded his fingers into his hand and used a fist to push harder. His fist pushed against an unfathomable resistance.

"Tell it to let me in."

"I cannot. Ergeiron cannot be commanded."

"I am king!"

"Ergeiron knows this."

"But kings do enter."

"Some have."

Highborn kings. Wall Lords. Highborn princes so exalted they barely walked the same earth. But not common, Kheld-blooded Stefan.

"But *you* could just walk in, is that right? Both of you?" Might as well challenge the smug bastard.

Rheger hesitated a long moment before answering. "I'm not sure."

"Try."

Jaw clenched, Rheger placed his hand, palm forward, to the barrier. His hand remained outside of it. Unconvinced, Stefan grasped Rheger's wrist and tried to force the hand through. Though Rheger winced, his hand did not penetrate.

"You don't have it with you."

Rheger swung his gaze to meet Stefan's. "What?"

"The Wall Stone. You need it to unlock the way." Stefan turned to the other possible artifact-bearer.

"I don't have it either," said Elhanan.

Had Stefan asked them about it directly, he would have known. Highborn princes did not lie. He had thought to lull them into bringing it, then seize it that way. Stefan seethed at the waste of his time. Not only had he not captured the Wall Stone, he had failed his attempt to gaze upon his kingdom's Entity and the sacred structures through which Wall Lords supposedly looked into Time. The damned Wall was making this personal. He turned to Erenor and Lucien.

"Back upstairs."

"Sire—" Erenor hesitated.

Stefan pulled him nearer and spoke quietly. "We talked about this. Find the Wall Stone if you can. And do the other things. Take Lucien with you." He patted Erenor's shoulder and rejoined Rheger and Elhanan. "I promised this conversation would be private, and it will be. The guards will remain at a distance."

Peric and twenty of Stefan's elite Kheld guards stood in the courtyard. Stefan watched them part to let Erenor and Lucien climb the steps to leave. Only Rheger and his sullen Heir stood with Stefan now. Elhanan had been uncommonly quiet all morning.

The Wall's silent, ghostly portal suited the topic at hand. Stefan faced Rheger again. "I know the Wall Stone is here in Stauberg. You've been using it. People have seen signs... strange lights, a ring on the dome."

Rheger's mouth pressed in a grim line. "Yes, Ergeiron reveals when we associate with him. That used to be a common enough occurrence that no one paid much notice."

"Well, I noticed. I've had people watching you this whole time. Did you think I wouldn't?"

"Hardly. We knew."

"I thought you couldn't commune with it." Stefan scowled at the uncooperative portal. Everything about it stood in his path. "But that changed, didn't it? When did Dorilian return the Wall Stone?"

Rheger met Stefan's angry gaze. "Months ago. I will not tell you how."

"I don't care the fuck how. I care about why."

"My guess is that he realized its danger."

Elhanan spoke up. "Artifacts can only be safely handled by those with the corresponding Entity's bloodline." Stefan thought Elhanan's voice sounded ragged, tight and strained. He fixed on the younger man.

"Handled—or used? He didn't return it as an act of goodwill. He doesn't even like you. He wanted to use it himself but couldn't, isn't that right?"

"No. He… I don't know."

"Do not badger him." Rheger dared this time to raise his voice.

"Then you tell me. What does Dorilian want? What did he ask you to do for him?"

Neither man answered. They were holding back. Protecting Dorilian… or protecting themselves… did it even matter? Stefan frowned at the Aidion Portal, half wishing the rebellious princes would run through the doorway, enter their damned Wall, and give him justification to seize control of the city. The people might oppose him doing so, but how could he trust these men?

Elhanan, especially, was behaving strangely. Nothing about him whispered of secrets or power or Time, yet he wore a faint suggestion of knowing about such things. Only a simple tunic of linen belted with a thin band of leather clothed the man's body, which Stefan thought looked too thin, wasted somehow or weakened by affliction. Faint hollows ringed Elhanan's amber eyes so that they appeared too bright in his gaunt face. He looked alert, but not in a good way.

"You don't look well."

Lips tight, Elhanan averted his gaze. "I'm as well as I need to be."

Stefan pondered how best to press for answers. When younger, he and Elhanan had verged on being friends. Elhanan had assisted Stefan's studies at Permephedon, and on a somber river journey together they had talked about weighty things and even agreed about injustices. Now, it seemed, an entire world stood between them. That Rheger was also present was not helping matters. "Elhanan, talk to me. I need to know. Are you walking the Wall?"

A movement, a hiccup of laughter, caught at Elhanan's shoulders. "What if I am? The Entity is fixed on an anomaly. I cannot walk past the discordance, or around it. I see only broken things—the past and answers from the past."

Maybe Rheger could explain what was going on. "Is he all right?"

Sadness clung to Rheger. "No. But he is not mad. Which is worse: to see too much, or not enough?"

"The future lies on the other side of a void in which I see nothing. The way you put your hand against the door just now— that was me against all of Time." Elhanan looked Stefan in the eye and managed a tight smile. "The Wall spans not just one time, one place; it spans all times and all places, a million puzzles each with a hundred million pieces. Some matter and some don't. Which puzzle? Which pieces? Wall Lords delve into the wells of Time for answers. We map what we find for those who come after. But I mapped *nothing*. I saw no wells. No vast mosaics from which timelines are woven. I saw only the now—a now so small, so imminent that it has only one piece, but no puzzle. Just a piece. One piece."

"What?" Stefan asked. "When?"

"El," Rheger warned.

"Shut up!" Stefan snarled at Rheger. Elhanan might be unraveling, but at least he was talking. "Who did you see? Dorilian?"

"No." Elhanan's smile hardened. "You."

37

Night had fallen. From his residence high in the Aesa Eranos, Stefan stared down at the glowing transcendence that was the Gate of Transformation with its gold-paved courtyard and night-shadowed shrine. The Aidion was empty tonight. Dark. He hadn't wanted it to be.

Elhanan had refused to retrieve the Wall Stone and use it to enter the sanctuary. Refused Stefan's order to walk the Wall again or seek to find more answers. Had refused to say anything more about what the damned Wall had revealed about *Stefan*. What had Elhanan seen?

Me. But what about me?

Stefan frowned at Erenor as he entered the room. The man looked grim, which said how little success he'd had in his mission.

"Was the Wall always this worthless?" It seemed to Stefan that the Wall glowed especially bright tonight, perhaps in acknowledgment a king was in residence. He could think of no other reason, so settled on that.

"For prognostication? Difficult to tell." Erenor crossed the room to join him. "It may be that the Wall Lords vary from very good to not good at all. They undertake decades of training and not all succeed. And then, of course, anything a talented Wall Lord might put into motion would look to the world like things happened just as the gods intended."

Stefan didn't appreciate the reminder that he waged war against gods. "Nothing like the Rill, then."

"Oh, the Rill is completely different. It doesn't require interpretation."

No. That Entity just did what it was designed to do. Gaining control over a god-machine should be vastly easier than gaining control of something as incomprehensible as the Wall. Stefan could always count on the Seven Houses to help him with that.

"So they won't yield their devices?"

"No. The women refused. I asked when I took them into custody. I think Sapphia knows the location of at least one device, but she would not reveal it. Short of torture, I don't think she can be made to. And the princes… well, they are of the highest rank. Our laws do not allow them to be tortured. Remember Gignastha? The Prince and his son are, however, being held in the Aerie."

A secure enough location, given that it had been locked up for a decade and before that had held Labran Sordaneon for thirty-five years. Stefan sighed. Although he saw no better way to handle the uncooperative princes, he didn't like at all where this path was taking him.

"I think there's someone you should speak to, sire, about these devices."

Stefan knew where this was going. "Coram Barzanes? He has already approached me about the Wall Stone and his master's interest in obtaining it. The answer was no. Though I'm intrigued by his suggestion that it might be possible to pair the Wall Stone with *lr* technology."

"He mentioned that to me also."

"If I could do that and use it, why would I hand over that kind of power? Or give Nammuor power over *my* kingdom's Entity? He must think I'm an idiot." Just because Nammuor was a useful ally didn't mean he could be trusted.

"He reminds us, correctly, that Mormantalorus, not we, possesses the needed technology."

"But we might be able to learn that technology or obtain it. Not all *lr* crystals are made in Mormantalorus." Just most of them and the best ones, though Stefan had heard there were storehouses of mage crystals in Permephedon and Sordan, secured in deep vaults to which only the Highborn had access. Which raised another point. "How sure are we that only Malyrdeons can use the Wall Stone?"

Erenor also gazed upon the glowing shapes of the Gate of Transformation and Aidion. "As sure as we can be, if we trust what wise old men have told us all these centuries. Do you think that's not true?"

"I'm not sure. I mean, has anyone else *but* a Malyrdeon ever *tried* to use it?"

"Not that I have ever heard. I'm no scholar of Highborn history, but I do not think the Wall Stone has ever been out of Highborn possession. Dorilian got it somehow after Enreddon was slain at Permephedon, but he's Highborn too."

"Yet he gave it back."

"Or they stole it back—if what you told me about Rheger being able to translocate is true."

"That's what I've heard. I've never seen him do it." Stefan wiped his hand down his face. Lud, he was tired. His fingers rasped across stubble, which could only mean his beard was visible. While in the Royal North he had taken to shaving his face twice a day or even more, all in hope of presenting an appearance his northern subjects would find less threatening.

The work of the last three months had been brutal. He had been iron-handed, even cruel, in doing what was needed to secure Essera's stability and future, and the peace of his kingdom lay within reach. He had put down rebellions in Bynum and settled the lands of the defeated on those lords who had stayed loyal. With the installation of a strong governor, he had finally restored order to the region. Rheger had secured the pledge of Bas Estevan of Gweroyen by allowing him equal say with the new governor over the regional council. Stefan had even gone against his own grain to bestow inheritance of Lacenedon on Hebron Ursenos and accept him as that domain's Bas. Though not exactly the loyal ally Stefan would have preferred, Hebron at least was not actively fighting him.

It didn't help matters that Rheger's wife was Hebron's aunt, and Elhanan's was Estevan's sister. If Stefan had ever wondered what glue held Essera in one piece, he now knew the answer. Sons were for holding power, but daughters were for binding it. His own little girl, who Nilla had named Moreen, might someday bind other kingdoms to his.

He might even wed her to Nammuor's nephew, the Sordaneon boy, if matters to the south worked out as planned. Maybe *that* was what the Wall had foreseen, and the Wall Lords would not share: how Stefan would, through his girl, rebind the Triempery.

"Let's go," he said to Erenor. "It's time to show my troublesome cousins who is king."

Rheger and Elhanan took note when Stefan entered. Though their prison was large and splendid, appointed with every comfort,

Rheger had not explored it but had stayed with his silent, nearly unresponsive son. They sat on a pair of plain chairs, facing each other at the center of the first, and sparest, antechamber. When Stefan entered, Rheger looked up but did not stand. Elhanan, for his part, chose not to acknowledge they had visitors.

Though Stefan had dismissed the guards, he was not alone. Rheger thought very little of Erenor, a man who never looked other than sly. Rheger chose to look at his hands instead. Stauberg's princely signet ring encircled his left forefinger.

"This isn't what I wanted to do," Stefan began.

"What a man *does* matters more than what he *wants* to do."

An exchange of glances between Stefan and Erenor confirmed the king's displeasure. Rheger regretted he had never quite worked out how to *be* when with Stefan.

"I hope you understand you owe me answers," Stefan said. "That's all I want. I don't want to hold you this way. You've demonstrated your loyalty, powerfully. That you stood at my side at Bynum secured the peace! So why are you doing this now?"

"Doing what?" Rheger replied wearily. "Not answering the unanswerable? Not attempting, yet again, acts that have proven fruitless? The Wall does not spout prophecy on command."

"Maybe I need proof of that. Where is the Wall Stone now?"

Elhanan made a broken sound between a sob and a whimper. "He took it away."

Stefan gazed down on Rheger. "You. Again. What are you trying to do?"

Rheger bowed his head. That he had come to this day—a silent Wall, a broken son, and an angry king—weighed on more than his mind. He did not know yet whether he had already misplayed his hand or had yet to carry out a design hidden by greater forces.

"I am fulfilling my obligations, as a Malyrdeon and a father. I helped El walk the Wall. I... I am not.... He kept trying and trying, kept going back in though he said there was nothing there. That is when I sent the Wall Stone away, to make him stop."

"Sent it away?"

Rheger grimaced at his king, who was no longer a youth but still a far cry from being a man. The time had come to cease pretenses. "It is something we Highborn can do. I sent it elsewhere. So he could not use it... and the Wall's enemies, including you, could not use it against us."

Stefan's face turned stormy. "*Where* did you send it? To Dorilian?"

Rheger swallowed a laugh. "You think it would be safe there? With what's breathing down *his* neck? No. I sent it to a place you can never go."

Let the fool think it had been sent to the Aidion, or beyond the Pillars of the Sky or to the bottom of the sea. Even if Stefan figured out or learned the truth, that Rheger had sent the Wall Stone to Permephedon to join the corpse of the last Wall Lord in the Vault of Incorruption, the king would have no recourse. None but a Son of Amynas and Leur could ever enter that necropolis.

Nammuor would have to destroy Permephedon to its foundations before the Wall Stone would fall into his hands.

Stefan exhaled and stomped toward the room's lone window. Erenor merely regarded Rheger coldly, his expression inscrutable.

Fool. You, we foresaw.

Only Stefan had never been fixed by the Wall into the design. Not fixed, not mapped, yet still a part. That Elhanan could not see how or why did not alter that the Paradigm continued to dictate events. Rheger saw Elhanan's head lift, lip curled with defiance. Too late, he clamped down on thoughts too near the source. *No, El! No... no...*

"You are the reason why." Elhanan's words brought Stefan's attention, anger-bright, to bear on him. "Why I can't see anything, why no one can."

Rheger attempted to put himself between the question and the answer. "Majesty—"

He earned a royal snarl. "For the love of all the gods! Elhanan," Stefan persevered. "Is there something I need to know?"

Elhanan snickered. "Knowing won't help you find answers. It won't help you find anything. There was a thread—a tiny thread— in the past, that might have opened the door... but you killed it."

"Killed... what?"

Rheger bowed his head. There was nothing to gain by shedding light on a promise that had never come to pass.

"What was born atop the Maw. That is where your grandfather planted the seed. Marc Frederick was the key—still is the key. He was a key all along. Endurin worked within the Paradigm to create him."

A fierce new expression took hold of Stefan's face and burned hungrily in his gaze. Rheger thought it looked like hope and his heart sank. "Am I a key?"

Elhanan seemed to become aware of himself and of the danger awaiting his answer. He took a moment to gather himself.

"No, Majesty." Elhanan looked past Stefan to the dark night outside the window. "You are a shadow. An inflection within a terminus trapped inside a Paradigm." He managed a weak grin. "So am I. So is my father. So are we all until we fix what is broken."

Rheger understood why Stefan turned to him, but he shook his head. "I have not studied the Archives. I have but bare knowledge of Endurin's masterwork."

"So *he* made it, my grandfather's great-grandfather. He made this thing, this Paradigm as you call it. For what purpose?"

"To save us, to save all of us from something we did not even know was coming." How could Rheger explain it when he knew so little? "If you will give me time, Majesty, and access to books, I might—"

"You're still hiding things from me. You always do. You Highborn, you hoard secrets the way the Seven Houses hoard gold. You carve off slivers as currency, but those slivers are useless because no one ever gets to see the rest of the coin… if there even *is* a coin. I'm tired of it." Stefan paced across the room's carpet of thick silk woven in patterns of stars and trees. Priceless, beneath leather boots.

Tired, yes. They all were tired. And they stood upon the Paradigm's threshold.

Rheger tried one last argument, more concrete than Wall speculation. "I will tell you what I know. Nammuor is the enemy. He has acquired a device."

Erenor smirked at Stefan, signaling an attack anticipated. Stefan merely looked disgusted.

"I was really hopeful you would not seek to weaken my alliances."

"This is not new information!"

"No, just regurgitated. Dorilian tried to blame Nammuor and some device for the Demise at Permephedon—but if Nammuor had such a device *then*, if he was that powerful, why has he done nothing since, not in eight years? You know who *has* attacked Essera? Attacked *me*?" Stefan stood over Rheger, hand on the hilt of his sword. Threat filled that gesture and the king's taut stance. "Dorilian. He never stops attacking me, and *he* has devices. An arsenal of them. So do you."

Rheger glanced at Erenor. He saw nothing of what he thought he might, no trace of complicity or knowledge, only tense interest in the conversation. The Undying Crown, then, might not be known to Erenor; maybe less, even, than it was to Stefan. That deadly Entity stirred in the shadows where ordinary men had yet to look. But the Wall had looked, known what approached, and had attempted to arm what was left of Leur.

What no one yet knew was whether the Wall had succeeded.

Stefan frowned at Rheger's silence. "I want you to hand over the Kyr Coronal. You can do that, can't you? Don't make me threaten your wives."

Seriously? Rheger found the thought of Stefan trying to intimidate Sapphia amusing. How often had she pronounced their king a bully and a coward? She would not believe Stefan's threat to harm any of them. But Rheger did.

"Of course. You will need me to open the touch-lock. I will give it over willingly." Rheger managed a wry grimace. "I doubt I will have any more opportunity to use it."

Stefan's gaze narrowed. "None. Maybe you will see a crown again someday, but not soon. I can't let you stay in Stauberg." Rheger glanced up in disbelief, only to encounter the king's grim affirmation. "You have too much support here and far too much power. I must have complete confidence in this city. It is my capital, after all, and the religious heart of my kingdom. I am sending you to Aral, in the custody of Bas Erenor, to be held securely in the Halasseon Serat under house arrest. You won't be living in a prison or anything like that, and your accommodations will be suited to your rank. You will have every privilege and comfort except, of course, your freedom."

Elhanan shot to his feet. "Margarid? She's with child."

Stefan turned to him. He shook his head and his tortured gaze, far from looking stern, begged understanding. "You have nothing to fear and neither does she. Your wife will stay here, in my custody, my personal custody, along with Sapphia. I regret this so much."

"You would keep me from my pregnant wife, the birth of my *daughter*."

"I don't *want* to do this! Don't you understand? I don't want to—I have to!"

Coldness settled over Elhanan, an aloof fury taken root from his narrowed gaze to the set of his shoulders. Rheger rose and inserted his body between that of his enraged son and the frustrated, distressed king.

"El, she is nearly due. Your mother will be with her. She knows the dangers."

"It won't matter, Father. I see the danger now. It's all quite clear. The Wall showed it all along."

Stefan stepped around Rheger. "What are you talking about? I think you'd better explain that remark."

"I was wrong. You are *not* a shadow. You are a void. A nothing where something should be. The Paradigm stops... at you. The great design cannot go forward. Yet. It is only waiting for the way out."

"The way out of what?" Stefan looked ready to roar—or explode.

Elhanan cocked his head as though the explanation was obvious. "The thing that's blocking the way. This. Same as before." He shrugged. "You."

38

Dorilian woke with his hand beneath his face. When he pulled his hand away, he felt something he had never felt before. He bolted up to sitting and stroked his fingers over his cheek and lower face. Hair. Not on his head but on his *chin...* and not just his chin and cheek, on his jaw as well.

Gsch!

He kicked away the sheet across his legs and went to a mirror he had positioned to show the loggia outside his room. No intruders approached but he would not have cared if there had been. A hard look in the mirror revealed what he feared. Fine blond hair stood in a golden fuzz on his face. Behind him, his bedchamber door cracked open and Legon peered in.

"Thrice Royal, if you are awake—"

"I'm awake!" Before Legon or the secretary who was certainly nearby could go into a recitation of his schedule, Dorilian issued a preemptive order. "I need to talk with Tutto. Find him now."

"But, sire—"

"Now!"

The door closed and would remain closed. Tutto would be the next man to enter. Until then, Dorilian needed to collect himself. There must be a way be rid of this hair, some trick, some... He could not appear this way, not in public. Not ever.

I am the blood of Amynas and Leur, not a fur-faced commoner.

He peered more closely at the offending growth, prodded it with a fingertip, gave it a swipe. Definitely hair. Scant and short and rooted in his skin. It was also mercifully fair and therefore not easy to see. Perhaps he could make it go away. His body possessed traits common-born bodies did not. He had kept Levyathan's lifeforce coiled as an interstitial part of his spinal column and muscles for a month. He had mastered his corporeal being so well, he could bar the Rill from penetrating beyond his skin.

Sebbord's books discussed Highborn corporeal abilities at length. Dorilian had attempted nearly every one of them. Already he could prevent his fingernails from growing.

Hopeful of his skill, he sat on the floor, naked, and focused on his face and the skin of his face. Pores finer than those of human skin linked to sebaceous glands and delicate follicles of… not vellus hair, so short and fine, as appeared elsewhere on his body, but hair with roots and shafts grown thicker through follicles bathed by blood and hormones. And not just on his face.

The face, to start. Within his physiology resided cellular keys, deep within glands and peripheral receptors, switches tiny yet powerful. He willed them to reset.

"What's happening?"

Dorilian lifted his gaze to see Tutto walk across his bedchamber floor. Even this early in the morning, the sword master wore his weapons and armor and had probably been up for hours. "Puberty's last throes."

"Hnh." Tutto grunted as he lowered to one knee. His dark gaze scoured Dorilian's face and folded limbs. "How old are you now? Twenty-seven? It's hardly a surprise that you have finally become a man."

"And what about this?" Dorilian pointed to his cheek.

"Ah. Facial hair is not unheard of in your kind."

"Do tell."

"Labran struggled with a beard as a youth, Sebbord claimed."

There was the reason. Dorilian's thrice-cursed grandfather. And his mother. Both had been born of Nemenor mothers—a race known to sprout beards. Only Staubaun men of pure blood, like their Aryati predecessors, were truly free of facial hair. Yet again, as with his eyes and coloration, Dorilian failed to meet the royal standard.

Tutto lowered his gaze. "I see puberty has arrived upon your chest also. And probably under your arms."

"Yes, but I can hide that." Dorilian sighed. "And I already know how to make sure it doesn't happen again, not on my face. My problem is that I need to get rid of this particular outbreak. I tried to get my skin to reabsorb it, but that didn't work."

"So I see."

"It's ugly, a sure sign of low birth. I need it off my face."

"Easily done." Tutto unsheathed the shorter of the two daggers he wore and displayed the edge. "I keep my blades sharp enough that I can do it with this. Or you can summon your barber—"

"No." The barber styled Dorilian's hair for the public to see and never shaved skin. "Not my barber. No one is to know about this." He narrowed his gaze. "Except you."

"You may remove my head if I fail you."

"I could be dead if you fail me. Do you want me to sit somewhere more convenient?"

"If you would, Thrice Royal." Tutto stiffly rose from the floor. "Over there where the light is good." Dorilian seated himself on the bench where his room opened to the loggia. Tutto applied a soothing soap he had found on the wash table and began carefully scraping Dorilian's face. "Let's relieve you of this burden of shame."

"You remove yours every morning."

"I don't do it because I'm ashamed." Another pass of the blade removed more beard. "It's best you not talk while I do this."

Tutto turned Dorilian's head and tipped up his chin. The rasp of the blade felt vaguely threatening.

"I scrape my face every morning because of attitudes like yours. If you think a few hairs on a man's face say anything about that man's quality, I have failed to teach you anything."

The criticism stung because it was apt. Was Jooar Zetharnna lowborn because of a few hairs? Dorilian had just named Tutto to be such, though he could think of no one more honorable. And Marc—Marc Frederick, too, had sought to avoid criticism from his subjects by shaving his face twice a day. Upon a time, Dorilian had despised him for it. If he should be ashamed of anything, it was that.

"I apologize," he said through clenched teeth. Tutto was doing him a favor, after all, and he wanted the job to be well done. Another swipe rasped along his jawbone.

"Accepted. And look at the positive," Tutto advised. "Your adolescence has been a long one. In your kind a long adolescence signals a life of longer years." Tutto denuded Dorilian's cheek. "There's not much beard here, because you are a young man. But that you have these hairs says your body is fully virile."

Was Tutto suggesting Dorilian start siring heirs? Sebbord's books had revealed a bodily manipulation even more useful to a man than blocking the growth of inconvenient facial hair—the prevention of unwanted offspring. Dorilian was certainly going to begin doing that should the opportunity arise. His enduring memory of his mother was of how she had died because their enemies wanted to kill or control her children. The fiery remnant of a Wall image burned in his mind, the Danae Palace in flames. All the powers that ruled in Essera had not kept Enreddon's sons safe from the forces against them.

Nammuor hunted Highborn kind for blood, and Stefan—he wasn't the only enemy who would kill any child that Dorilian sired.

Why bring children into the world only for them to be prey?

The Harbor House presided over Stauberg's port just as the Wall did over the city, a grand and stately building that commanded the view of all who approached by sea. From its broad, harbor-facing terrace observers could look upon two Entities, both Wall and Rill, though the latter was silent in all but majesty. The shining dome and painted columns of the Harbor House proclaimed Stauberg's stature as queen among the world's ports.

At the Harbor House's feet sprawled the Royal Wharf where only ships from Stefan's own fleet were authorized to berth. He had granted permission to Erenor, as Bas of Tahlwent, to dock his personal vessel there. The ship had arrived in Stauberg two days before. Erenor had made plans earlier to return to his domain—and now he would be taking the Dannutheon princes along with him.

Stefan drew a lungful of sea air and wished he felt, well... better about this day. What he was doing was right, reasonable. Only a madman or a fool would allow the Highborn to continue to run his capital or even dwell there. Marc Frederick himself would approve this move. Hadn't he kept Labran Sordaneon at Stauberg because the city had no Rill? Well, Stefan was sending his dissident Malyrdeons to a city that had no Wall. A good move, one that would secure his kingdom.

It was unfortunate, but Stefan had known nothing but trouble since Rheger had become Prince of Stauberg and the Eleutheron. Though outwardly loyal, Rheger commanded far too much reverence from other ruling lords. When deciding how to vote or what forces to commit, those lords looked to Stauberg before they looked to Stefan. No one was better positioned to challenge Stefan's kingship. Not only was Rheger popular, he had an Heir—a fucking Wall Lord. More than anything, the last two days had convinced Stefan that the Highborn princes could not be trusted. Even Coram Barzanes had counseled as much at their meeting the night before.

That they are honorable as reputed, I do not doubt. Consider, however, that honor among the Highborn extends first, always, to themselves.

As for Elhanan, who Stefan had originally hoped could be reasoned with and maybe help him by using the Wall…

Apparently when men walked the Wall, they slipped their minds. Either that or the Wall spoke in riddles only sages could decipher. Shadows and voids and… something the hells about a design. Nothing of threats to be thwarted or directions to go.

Why does Elhanan talk of voids, and then says he saw me?

Both Highborn princes stood with Stefan on the expansive terrace, tall men dressed in somber, plain clothes suited to travel. Rheger wore gray and Elhanan had chosen dark blue. Hands bound by gilded iron, they looked resigned. Neither had spoken, not even in greeting, so that it fell to Stefan to acknowledge the silence between them.

"It won't be a long voyage. A day only, maybe two."

Elhanan bit his lip and looked away. Stefan noted where.

"Too bad the Rill doesn't run from here to Aral." Stefan could taste the acid in his own response. He wouldn't have sent them by that means even if it were available.

"You see nothing real. All you see are ways to justify your worst impulses." Rheger wore no headgear and a breeze off the ocean lifted his silver-blond hair. "Perhaps we erred in trying to appease you."

"I didn't create this conflict and certainly not to justify anything. I'm not going to change my mind." Seeing Elhanan smirk and shake his head only made Stefan more certain. "You both are nothing but trouble. You have done nothing to help me from the day I became king. You went behind my back every chance you got. You would have helped Palaistea place her son upon my throne. That's what you wanted. You're lucky I don't have you executed for treason for using the Wall against me."

Rheger laughed. "The Wall is not a weapon. It is a way."

"A way to what?"

"Survive."

Stefan bit his tongue. What could prompt such insolence but that Rheger had lost all respect for his king? Stefan was glad he had chosen to do this with only his Kheld guard present along with a dozen Staubaun courtiers he knew he could trust. Having witnesses strengthened his hand. He would be called on later to demonstrate to the Archhalia that he had treated the princes with proper respect.

Two men walked along the wharf below, approaching the Harbor House. Erenor and Coram Barzanes. To avoid the appearance, or possibility, of foreign involvement, Stefan had ordered the Mormantaloran emissary be removed from the passenger list. That appeared to have been done. The ship, then, was probably ready. Soldiers gathered at the bottom of the steps to escort the prisoners.

To Rheger Stefan said, "I am being merciful."

"Are you? Then I will tell you your mercy is a trap. A mistake. We are a far greater danger to you alive than dead. Trust me when I tell you this. Our lives can be used against you, and will be, if you put us on that ship. You would do better to kill us."

Now this man, too, had lost his mind. "Do I look like an idiot? Killing you would be a crime, even for a king."

"Then free us. Here. Now. Or, if you will not, hold us here in Stauberg, where our enemy cannot reach us."

"I told you—"

"That you won't." Rheger's gaze followed Erenor's progress and Coram's. "Then you have killed us already. So *be* merciful and do it now."

Mercy? What the hells was he talking about? Had Rheger just appealed to Stefan's better nature? Stefan offered a half-hearted laugh. "Very well. Give me one good reason, and maybe I will kill you."

Rheger swallowed heavily. "I am not the best man for this."

"No, I am," said Elhanan. Though bound, he stepped forward and before anyone could move to interfere, he pushed Stefan full body against the nearest pillar and pressed his face beside his.

Smaller and caught by surprise, Stefan gasped. Pinned cheekbone-to-cheekbone and eye-to-eye, his vision opened but not to the sights of the Harbor House. Not to Stauberg at all. To every side of him were men fallen onto tables, onto a red-splashed floor, men he knew—Enreddon, Regelon, Ostemun—knives slicing, throats gaping open to scarlet-robed, hooded men who held glowing crystals into spouts of gore until the things turned crimson. Gathering blood. And a crown, blood-red and encrusted with those same crystals, towering upon the head of a man seen from afar, from behind, a man wielding lightning again and again...

"Blood. Your blood," Stefan whispered. *Highborn.*

"Yes," Elhanan spoke to his ear. "The Destroyer wants us."

A roar from behind him, and then Stefan was free, staggering against the pillar at his back. Peric pulled Elhanan off him and drove a sword into the Highborn prince's ribs. A howl more like triumph than pain broke from Elhanan's throat.

"Kill them!" Stefan bellowed.

Kheld voices rose along with the terrible ring of drawn steel.

"To the king!"

Chaos erupted. Stefan's Kheld guards, weapons in hand, swarmed his attackers and grasped both princes. Swords swung, and axes too. Men screamed. Red splattered the ground and pillars. Stefan stared, seeing a stain on his reign that he would never erase. All his life he had heard that Highborn blood was sacred. Royal. *Immortal.* He had just watched blood being gathered into crystals, destined for a crown of unimaginable power.

Someone—Dorilian or Nammuor or a monster yet to come— was building a terrible weapon.

"Don't!" Lucien, among the Staubaun witnesses, cried in protest. "You'll kill the Wall!" Others followed and ran toward the milling Khelds. Coram, his face a mask of horror, stood rooted at the bottom of the steps.

"Cut off their heads!" Peric shouted. "Only way to do it!"

Too many men, at too-close quarters, could deliver no swing that would sever a man's neck. Short strokes and stabs accomplished less. Rheger roared in agony, but only once. Horrible gurgles followed. Stefan watched as Elhanan twitched for a full minute before an axe finished him.

Overhead and to every side, a wholly unnatural moan broke over the Harbor House and rolled over the city. Low at first, the sound gathered force and volume until it wailed in pure anguish. Daylight darkened. The Wall's heights, no longer bright, towered over the city with monstrous, vaguely human shapes. Stefan clamped his hands over his ears, hoping to block out the howls, and watched in horror as men hacked at the now fallen Dannutheons until mercifully—finally—their heads rolled free. Blood painted the terrace, pillar, king, and the men with their swords and axes. Erenor, who had just run up the steps from the wharf, stood at the edge of the blood and stared at Stefan in disbelief.

"What have you done?"

"Not me. Them! They showed me... the Wall, something it saw, and those monsters would unleash it!"

"Oh, fuck. Fuck! Stefan... oh gods!"

With the force of a storm, the Wall continued to roar, its upper reaches curling inward, downward... toward them.

"What is the damn thing howling about?" Peric, eyes wide,

stood with bloody sword in hand. He pointed at the bodies. "Them?"

"Yes, them!" Erenor snapped. "They are—they *were*—its blood. You killed… Leur, what idiots! They were the last of them!" He spun on Stefan. "And you *ordered* it?"

Why was Erenor acting like Stefan was to blame? "They showed me. They showed me what the Highborn are, what would happen if—" If what? He could not even remember it clearly. "When! When it happens. The fucking thing that's going to destroy us is *made* of their blood."

The Wall's screams had thinned to ghostly moans, hollow and haunting. Maybe it *was* dying. Other sounds began to hold sway, horns braying alarm and the screams of people in the streets, wondering what was happening to their Entity. Soon, all of Stauberg would know.

One of the Khelds had picked up Rheger's head by the hair and held it aloft to the cheers of his fellows.

Stefan grasped Peric. "Stop him! Gather the bodies—with respect!"

But before any could act on that order, silence fell. The Wall ceased to howl. It no longer writhed but froze, massive and distorted where it loomed above the city. Voices stopped.

Marenthro stood in their midst, clothed in blue and silver such as Stefan had never seen him wear, boots planted on the white paved terrace where the fallen princes had lain. A giant swirling orb of what looked like blood floated in the air above his extended left hand, upon which blazed a ring bright as the sun. All knew where the blood had come from. The terrace was clean of it. So too those who stood there, all but a handful of Khelds who had taken cuts in the confusion and so wore their own blood. Even the bodies were gone. The Kheld who had held aloft a severed head looked at his empty unbloodied hand and gaped at the wizard.

Stefan opened his mouth but could not even think of words to say.

Marenthro cast his copper gaze upward toward the shimmering and darkly liquid shape of the Wall. "I have seen to the slain and that no part of them can be misused." Marenthro rotated his arm and the orb also vanished before he lowered his hand. He spoke to Stefan. "Ergeiron wants you gone. You and those who murdered his children. I suggest you respect his wishes."

"It wasn't supposed to happen this way."

Marenthro paused and drew a long breath, then met Stefan's

gaze without his usual forbearance. His expression warned Stefan that he was done with giving counsel. "You walk a path you created. Today happened as it did because of *you*. As will tomorrow. All things happen in the same moment—and you... are happening."

Then Marenthro vanished, too, and left behind a space where so much should have been that wasn't. No trace of two men; only the memory of them. No trace of two murders; only the murderers. No trace of a king's crime; only the king.

The Wall, however, remained, and it refused to either be silent or die. Like a terrible wind, the dark curtain above Stauberg began to moan.

Dorilian dropped to the ground. Tutto's latest invention swung over Dorilian's head and he leaped back onto his feet behind it. He sliced between planks to reach the weight's tether, cutting it and releasing the pendulum that controlled the mechanism. The automaton clattered to a halt. From the midst of timbers, leather, and steel, Dorilian shot Tutto an appreciative nod.

"Good training." Tutto was pleased. He had put hard work into this variation. "Would be better could I still take you on myself, but the contraption does a good job of approximating speed."

"The blows had weight." Dorilian had taken a few knocks. His body needed such work if he was to stay limber and strong. Muscles, bones, and sinew were his first and most accessible weapons.

Still breathing hard, he handed Tutto his sword and stripped off his padded armor. He had just lifted the upper body pads over his head when agony slammed into his brain. Inside his skull. Pain exploded, followed by disorientation. Dark chased dark.

Dorilian fell to his knees, head clasped between his hands as part of the Mind ruptured.

"Dor!" Tutto hunkered beside him. "Tell me!"

"Someone's dying. Lev—"

Tutto helped him to his feet. "He's too young."

"We're linked!" Dorilian set off at a run toward the main residence.

Tutto shouted after. "Then you would know it was him!"

No, not Lev, not Lev... Dorilian knew this now, but still he needed to find the boy. Levyathan might be feeling this too. A life gone, severed from the Highborn body... *two* lives...

Panting, Dorilian reached the wing where the children were tutored. Fahme's voice trilled from one room, declensions of Aryati verbs from another. He followed the verbs and found the tutor droning syllables.

Already standing beside the table, Levyathan stared at Dorilian with dread and bewilderment. "Who is it?"

"Elhanan, I think. Rheger too. I—" Dropping onto a bench near the window, Dorilian stared at the City beyond.

"Both of them," Levyathan whispered. The tutor had noted the interruption and stopped speaking.

Leur. They are both dead. Both. Dorilian could feel neither man, only vast emptiness where those lives had been. For a moment only, he had encountered his kinsmen's final, ephemeral thoughts. For such violent deaths—beheading, stabbing—their thoughts had been strangely... accepting. Welcoming. Triumphant, even. Dorilian lifted his gaze from the tranquil view of the Citadel gardens and the Terminal's Temple of the Inception to look upon the Rill.

The Entity stood stretched against the sky. Pale. Rings in stasis. Not moving.

"I need to go."

Levyathan's eyes filled with fear. "Where?"

"The Dekkora. When our people see *that*—" Dorilian gestured to the window. Tutto had just reached the doorway and leaned, breathing heavily, against the frame. "Stay here with the children," Dorilian directed. "People need to see me."

He left the room to find guards running toward him, with Legon at their head. "I am unharmed. Saddle Caillessar." The big ivory charger with his long mane, tail, and feathered fetlocks, was an impressive mount. The horse had been sired by Rheger's Caillepern, and Dorilian wanted that connection to the dead man. Today, he *needed* it.

Gone. Fear seized him then, that Nammuor had taken them. But no... Dorilian did not feel that.

A detour to his suite of rooms provided a rich tabard stitched with his Hierarchal emblems, which he hastily donned. When Dorilian reached the courtyard where his steed awaited, he vaulted astride. With a color guard leading the way and with a full phalanx of Eagle Guards to the rear, he rode out from the Gate of Wings.

Concerned citizens already thronged in front of the Gate. Even more people packed the Dekkora, though the City Guard and Epoptean Protectors had secured the landings leading to the Rill complex. The Eagle Guard rode past him and the color guard also, charging up the steps and occupying every landing to establish a defense. A clutch of yellow-robed Epoptes milled on the top landing but gave way as they were pushed behind the mounted soldiers. Once he was as safe as human lives could make him, Dorilian rode out onto the first landing in full view of the crowd. They shouted his name and that of the Rill, and a great cheer erupted when he lifted his left hand and showed them the green blaze of the Rill Stone.

"Sordaneon!" The name rolled like human thunder across the great square. "Sordaneon! Sordaneon!"

Dorilian spoke the only words he could: the truth. "The Rill grieves its brothers. The Malyrdeons of Essera are no more."

The cries became wails of disbelief and horror. "The Wall?" people shouted. "What of the Wall?"

To that he had no answer. The Rill might be behaving the way it was *because* of the Wall.

"The Wall stands!"

The crowd's stares focused behind him, so Dorilian turned his horse the better to see for himself the source of that booming pronouncement. The Psilant, Quirin, stood at the forefront of a line of Epoptes and Eagle Guards, his arms raised to command attention.

"We have received word from Stauberg. The Wall stands and continues to serve." As Quirin spoke, the Entity before which he stood resumed its elemental shapeshifting, structures monumental and in motion above the buildings and colonnades of the Terminal. "As does the Rill!"

Cheers rose again, celebrating the continuance. Celebrating their proof that the Sordaneons still lived and, with them, their god. But Dorilian continued to hold the Psilant's mocking glare, knowing he looked upon a heretic.

Quirin had told him—told them all—what mattered most. As long as the Rill, and the Wall, continued to serve, why mourn the deaths of princes?

Men were dead. Good men. Wall walkers and the continuation of an Entity. But did any of the people among whom they had lived care?

Two. Now we Highborn are but two and the Mind is nearly emptied. The only survivors of Leur are Lev and me. And this Psilant, this City, this World, would not care at all if we died—so long as the Rill continues to serve.

"You are our liege. We are of course yours to command."

The two women standing before Stefan, heads bent in submission and eyes red from weeping, wore gowns of mourning purple and black. Stefan regretted their pain. The widowed princesses had loved their husbands. By all he had heard, theirs had been happy marriages. Rheger's wife Sapphia, taller and older, retained a quiet, fine-boned beauty and thus far had done the speaking for the pair. She resembled her son Elhanan so much, it hurt Stefan to look at her. As for Margarid, the plump mother-to-be of Elhanan's child, she had yet to say a word or meet Stefan's gaze.

"I hope you understand my position." Stefan faced them in the reception room of the quarters in which he had been holding them. "I wish I could leave you here in Stauberg, but that's impossible now. You will board ship with me. We sail for Aral."

"You could just kill us now and be done with it."

He had good reason to recoil. The Gracious Princess Sapphia looked like she wanted to murder him. She didn't understand, neither woman did, that he suffered as much as they did. Stefan couldn't stop seeing their husbands, over and over, being hacked to death before his eyes. "I don't want you dead! Why would I want that? You've never done me any wrong. You will just stay with me until the baby is born."

Margarid turned her head away, an edge of purple veil angled across her face. Her rejection of his attempts at goodwill stung and raised the possibility that she had discerned his motive for keeping her with him. Stefan regretted the necessity, but he would have to kill a male child. Though Elhanan had said Margarid was to give birth to a girl, Stefan could not trust that.

"I don't want to be with Khelds. Not anywhere near them." Margarid spoke at last, her words sharp and clear.

"Do you mean me?"

Her cold gaze met his. "Especially you."

"Well, I can't trust any but Khelds to hold you, so you're coming with me." He turned to Lowen and Nalf, the Kheld captain who had replaced the already departed Peric. "Put them on the ship. And for the sake of all that's decent, treat them as if they were the Mother's own daughters." Stefan watched as the women left with their escort. Just Lucien and Erenor remained, both men as gloomy as if they'd watched their own kin die. "Damn, that was hard."

"We must now pray for a male child." Lucien interpreted the reason the Wall had *not* died as being because Margarid carried a boy. "That the Wall still lives is hopeful. But it is horrible now to listen to it. We had best leave quickly, sire, like Marenthro said. Once we are gone maybe it will stop howling like a sea monster."

For two hours since the deaths of the last Malyrdeons, the Wall had moaned and groaned like a dying thing. Every soul in the city was slowly going mad. But at least the Wall hadn't killed anything or anyone. Yet. "I won't be unhappy to see the last of it. That crazy thing never did me any good. And Elhanan just spouted gibberish."

Erenor studied Stefan. "You haven't said much about what he told you. What the Wall had to say."

"Say? It never said anything. Not one single glimmer of any future at all. Just that I was some sort of puzzle piece." Stefan swept up his travel cloak. "I will take the ship. I can't stay here, so I'll go to Aral with as many of my Kheld troops as can board." The main force of Khelds had already been run out of the city. Even the most battle-hardened were so spooked by the Wall, they had wanted only to leave. Worse, Khelds were pariahs, called murderers and heathens and attacked in the streets. "The rest of Peric's men will cross over the mountains and meet me in Tahlwent." To Lucien and Erenor Stefan gave different orders. "You two will ride to Permephedon immediately. Use courier and military relay posts. The Archhalia will be gathering. I need you there to help put this to rest. Tell them the truth."

Lucien shook his head. "What truth will put to rest that these Khelds of yours, who spilled Highborn blood, who killed two Wall Lords, are not being punished?"

"Defense of their king." Erenor spoke surely, carefully. "Elhanan attacked Stefan first. He was trying to kill him. And the Highborn wield powers, including over people's minds. Everyone knows that they do. We only need to say what people already know."

The Wall's howls were growing worse. Stefan reached for the cotton bolls one of the servants had put upon the table. He took two puffs and wadded them into his ears. "Just get to it. Convince them. I don't care how."

Lucien cast Erenor an unhappy glance before he spoke again. "The Archhalia won't be your only problem, Majesty. Sordan—"

"Dorilian can rot. No one tried to kill him; not this time. They tried to kill *me*, so he can just step aside. Erenor has the right of it. I want you to have the Dannutheons charged with trying to murder *me*. And conspiracy, too, because they walked the Wall and lied about it."

Lucien winced. "This will not be believed."

Stefan indicated the door. "Lucien, you have your mission." By a look, he showed that he wished Erenor to stay. Once Lucien had left the room, Stefan spoke what remained on his mind. "He's right about Dorilian. That bastard's going to come at me. Find out all you can about what he's up to. I need to get him before he gets me."

"He needs to be isolated and rendered powerless—not killed."

"Still worried about the Rill? You can reassure the Archhalia about that too."

Stefan would get both Sordaneons. Kill them before they could be part of whatever foul magic Elhanan had shown. Only by doing that could Stefan finish the work he had been put here to do. The Wall had revealed something after all. Stefan now understood that he wasn't here to rebind the Triempery—he was here to destroy monsters.

Later, Stefan stood at the prow of the ship when it entered Ergeiron's Eye. Here at sea, he embraced looking into the distance and rejoiced at how clear things looked ahead of him, how free of expectations he could never meet. He hated the city he left behind and never did he look back. Not even when the howling stopped. As soon as the ship's bow had cleared the Eye, putting him beyond it, the day brightened—and the Wall fell silent.

"It's quiet!" Lowen shouted. Other Khelds joyously picked up the cry. "It stopped! Great Mother's Blessing! Look! Look! It's back to what it was!"

Stefan didn't look back at that, either.

39

"My plan was that you bring the Dannutheon princes here. Alive. Preferably with their Wall Stone. Not that a horde of beasts with swords hack them to pieces." Nammuor stood over a cowering Coram Barzanes and wondered if carving *him* to pieces might satisfy his wrath.

While still in Mormantalorus, Nammuor had witnessed the debacle in his Great Mirror through the lens of Coram's brooch, which possessed one of the best and clearest mirrored *lr* gems. What Nammuor had seen had made him scream in a red-colored rage so violent that it had sent the mages assisting him scurrying for cover. Stefan's bearded savages had spilled precious blood with no thought for it at all, crudely, without elegance or any chance of harvesting life while life remained. They had danced in godborn power. Had *mocked* it.

"How could you have let *that* happen?"

"It happened because I succeeded, Master," Coram spoke up in his defense. "I went to Stauberg and handed Erenor the seeds, subtly as you suggested, and he *planted* them in fertile soil. Watered them. Stefan came to see as his solution the very thing you wished, to send the princes into exile. The ship was *there*. The princes were *there*. They were to be brought here, to this very palace, where you and your mages could reach them. It went exactly as planned!"

"Not *exactly* as planned."

"Stefan ordered them killed. No one knows why. And the Wall was so terrifying after." Coram peered up through wide, desperate eyes. "I begged to sail with him. He values your alliance enough that he allowed it. But the whole journey here he was wrapped in foul temper and would not speak to me, nor anyone else but his Khelds."

Yes, those Khelds. Brutish, violent creatures of an irksome king, a man neither clever enough to have ordered the deed by design nor to have avoided his own conclusions. A born puppet. Nammuor sensed Malyrdeon meddling in this. The Wall, ever a devious Entity, had to have worked through the now-dead princes. Yes, a Wall Lord, or several—past or present—could have divined his plan. And Coram's brooch had shown something else.

Marenthro had put in an appearance and done so in a manner very unlike his usual nonassuming self. Attired like a prince of old, with the Leur's Ring afire on his hand, holding aloft a ball of spilled blood and transporting the corpses as if they had never been there.

The Wall had paused its wailing to listen to what Marenthro had to say, had attended to what Marenthro did with its descendants. The Wall and the wizard were... interesting.

Coram clearly thought Nammuor's silence indicated permission to continue speaking. "Stefan is here in Aral at the palace as we speak, along with the Dannutheons' wives. I heard he is going to hold them there, and remain in residence himself, until the one gives birth."

Elhanan's cub. If the child proved Highborn, Nammuor would get his hands on it after birth. Though of little value in its newborn state, barely a lifeforce at all, the infant would *eventually* grow to useful size.

"Rise. I've decided not to kill you. I have other goals in mind. Essera is on the table in ways it was not before. What of the Wall Stone? Have you any news of that?" Nammuor watched Coram rise from his prostration and brush imagined dust from his robe with mage-ringed hands. A handsome man and an envoy suited to this work. Such were not easy to develop, even for a man of Nammuor's resources.

"Erenor told me Prince Rheger claimed he sent it away to a place Stefan could never go."

"Sordan?"

"Stefan accused him of that. But Rheger said no. Think about it—Stefan could conceivably go there."

True. Much as Nammuor disliked it, he could think of several *other* places only the Highborn could ever go. "So to put the thing beyond his reach, the prince put it beyond ours also. Stefan is... proving difficult, isn't he?"

Coram nodded. "He's impulsive. He acts out of fear. This

weakness allows him to be manipulated—but his reactions do not always lead to desired results."

"And Erenor? He did not return with you to Aral."

Morning sunlight edged past the tower window and spilled golden beams into the room. It touched Coram's fine robe with pink fingers. "He was to have, until the princes died. Stefan sent him to Permephedon. For politics and the keeping of his alliances, he trusts Erenor above all others. His Khelds have neither political skill nor silver tongues. But not all is as seems. Erenor confides in me, Master. He has spoken of being unhappy with his king's recent troubles. He would have handled Stauberg differently."

"Unhappy with his king? And willing to tell you?"

Coram's smile held a trace of smugness. "He knows you are the only other person I would tell."

And perhaps wanted that.

One window of the tower faced the Halasseon Serat, a palace reminiscent of the princes and powers that had once ruled from its storied heights. Wall Lords and Kings. As always, Essera's history undergirded all choices. Nammuor would eventually need to break the kingdom, grind down its legends, and destroy its myths. Only then could he kill its Entities.

"He is going to want to kill the Sordaneons." Nammuor noted how Coram lifted his head like a hound to the scent. "He has tried before and nearly succeeded. He's not Highborn and is quite capable of lying. To you. To me. My Heir is not safe from him."

Though Nammuor had told Daimonaeris he would spare her child, that assurance had been easier to contemplate before the supply of Highborn had become so grievously depleted.

His Diadem must be made whole. Nammuor's own body and life could not generate the power it needed. Mere mortal lives weren't enough, and were soon consumed. The Highborn lifeforces he had bound satisfied the Diadem, yes, but were still not enough for it to achieve full godhood. He had two still to attach and needed two more. Dorilian's life, Nammuor craved with a hatred too fierce to contain. Nothing would give him greater joy than to open that body, claim that life and bind it by its own blood forever to the Undying Crown. Let the Diadem use Dorilian. Rillblood was the strongest of all.

But now that all other Highborn were dead, how was Nammuor to create the *twelfth* crystal, if not by harvesting the boy also? Must he wait until Dorilian... what? Decided to perpetuate the Sordaneon lineage? Could be captured and bred? Each of those options required the hated enemy to remain *alive*. Nammuor detested Stefan as much for creating *that* dangerous complication as he did for having killed the two princes.

To Coram, Nammuor gave a new order. "I am returning to Mormantalorus. My device is nearly complete. Inform me as soon as Elhanan's child is born. If it is male, I will come for it. And keep close to Stefan—find out his plans. If he or any of his murdering Kheld kin hope to kill Dorilian or my Heir, I want to know."

"I interred them in the Vault of Incorruption. Corpses and blood. There was no one else to perform their rites."

"No one?" Emyli asked bitterly.

Marenthro's look chided her. "No one who could be there."

She heard pain within the wizard's words. Worse was seeing terrible resignation etched on his features as he looked past her, toward the palace that loomed at her back. The weather in Trulo had been unseasonably warm for days and lemon-bright pollen dusted the Winter Terrace of the Golden Palace. Even the wide bend of the Dazun below the bluffs wore a yellow sheen. Insects buzzed among the trees.

"Did they suffer?"

He nodded.

She blinked back tears. Rheger. That solemn, lovely man who had spoken to her so kindly the day she asked him to put Dorilian's death gift in her father's hand. And Elhanan too, so young and promising, excited for the birth of his first child. Reports from Stauberg claimed the Wall had screamed, and the Rill and Permephedon too, just as they had on the day of the Demise. Because of Stefan. But how? How had this happened? Marenthro would not tell her other than that he had recovered the bodies.

"Stefan hasn't written to me. I wish he would. He... he tells me very little anymore."

And you will tell me nothing.

"Sometimes to say nothing is a form of kindness."

But not in this case. Not when she needed to know what had happened. There had to be some explanation as to why Stefan had allowed the last of the Malyrdeon princes to be murdered. Why he had *ordered* it. That he would do so made no sense at all, but reports she had received all stated he had given that order.

"What's going to happen now?"

Marenthro didn't speak or move, though his mouth pressed more tightly.

Eyes closed, Emyli held back new fears.

"Bring Hans back." She made the plea for which she had asked Marenthro to come to her. "Remember why we did this. You can return him today, can't you? Or soon. Stefan sees only enemies now. He needs people around him who he can trust. Friends. Family. He needs his brother. He hasn't been the same, not for years, not since we sent Hans away."

"You blame yesterday on that?"

"I blame myself, because I broke his trust."

Marenthro's gaze weighed her indictment along with her guilt. "You would be wrong, even if you are thinking only of how your decision affected Stefan. We do not know how having his brother at hand would have influenced the course of his reign."

"*You* can. You do."

He ducked his head, then looked off into the distance. "The sole betrayal *that* day was of Stefan's expectation that you would do only as he wanted."

"Tell me what would have happened if Hans had stayed. Yesterday. Would he have been at Stefan's side? Would it even have happened?"

"That timeline never existed—it or a thousand others. We extinguished those."

But any of those timelines *could* have existed, had Emyli chosen otherwise that night eight years ago. "I understand why we can no longer know things that might have been, but surely enough time has passed to consider those things that still can be. Hans is no longer a child. No longer frightened of the world. He's grown enough. All these years you have been telling me he's safe and whole and strong. He's sixteen. Seventeen." She put her hand to her mouth. "I've lost count of the years!"

"Do you remember our agreement?"

"Yes. But I—"

"You promised to trust me." Marenthro took her face between his hands and bent his forehead until it touched hers. "Stefan does not need Handurin to return. Essera has a king, and the king has an heir."

"A daughter."

"An *heir*. Just as you are... Marc Frederick's daughter."

Emyli pulled back so she could gaze fully on his face, and his smile warmed her heart. He, more than anyone, knew who she was. Other people saw only whatever facet suited their need of her, but Marenthro knew her as surely as if he had cut every facet.

"What did Endurin design that my father was so much a part of? Will we ever know?"

"Watch. It will reveal itself."

"Did you design me somehow? When you brought Father to the World?"

"No. Though maybe Ergeiron did. He works that way." Marenthro peered more closely at her. "Maybe you sense him sometimes, your great-great and many-more-greats progenitor. He has sacrificed much, and he is so aware, so much more present in the World than people know. Endurin designed something, yes, but only in concept. The temporal components follow physical laws of Ergeiron's crafting. The human components have free will. The Wall foresaw what Stefan might do, but I do not think Stefan or any of the people who took part in yesterday's slaughter were designed to do those deeds. Ergeiron, and the Wall Lords also, worked on a vaster scale."

"Rheger and Elhanan did not have to die."

"No. Not by design."

Emyli sighed as she recalled conversations past. "Things are getting worse, just like we knew they would. Father and I talked so many times about this, about what was coming. That horrible crown and the disaster it would bring and the steps he was taking to help us survive it. I warned Stefan not to trust Mormantalorus, but he didn't listen. And now—"

"Nammuor is growing stronger again, yes."

"At least this time, he didn't get what he wanted."

Marenthro stepped away. "True. Stefan did accomplish that." He gazed to the west, where Gustan waited tucked among green hills and distant Aral loomed upon the silver cliffs of a bounded sea.

Her heart sank to see Marenthro resume his mask. Remote as a god. Implacable as an executioner. The decisions he faced every moment of his life required such distance. "I won't ask. I just wish—" She blinked away tears, though there were more to come.

"So do I."

"My life has been everything you said it would be, sweet and hard, gilded and beautiful, and terrible too. Filled with tears, I think you said." He met her gaze and its acceptance of her choices. Emyli wanted him to understand. "I don't know how to save my son, and I know now that you won't save him. Maybe you can't. I just think maybe Hans can. Someone Stefan will listen to and keep close. Someone who can reach him. Someone who can *teach* him."

Marenthro closed his eyes, but she knew she wasn't going to change his mind. She couldn't even change her own.

"Marty, I love both of my sons, and that means Stefan too. Even with what he's done, I have to believe… I *do* believe he didn't want to do it. Something terrible must have happened. Until I know what, I have to support him."

"I know. I've always known." He kissed her forehead and even that gesture made her want to scream. "Go see to your granddaughter, Emy. She and her mother have decided to take a walk through the fen."

"The letter states my position more eloquently, but I believe my statement is quite clear: I resign my office as Essera's Ambassador to the Triemperal Archhalia. I no longer serve or represent the King." Sinon Kouranos placed a long envelope with official seals onto the table.

Erenor steepled his fingers and grimaced. This development was one he had not seen coming. For two weeks he had been beset by the disturbed and the furious, the terrified and the rebellious. He had made a host of angry and rebellious lords back down by using threats of Stefan's obvious military superiority. It was too soon for any of them to have aligned or found allies willing to do what they were themselves unsure of being able to do. As for the disturbed and terrified, Erenor had assured them the Wall still stood guard over Stauberg just as it always had. Their Entities were intact, as was the Triempery—because aside from a letter of condemnation, Dorilian had done nothing by way of threats.

Sinon Kouranos was none of those types of men. Or maybe he was all of them. He would also be difficult for Stefan to replace.

Erenor studied Sinon above his precisely pointed fingers. He trusted that being seated at Stefan's desk in the Regnal Suite of the Archhalial Offices gave him the needed presence.

"This matter of the Dannutheons—"

"It is more than that," Sinon explained. "The letter explains to the king my differences and regrets."

"You should probably explain these to Stefan yourself before doing anything rash."

"And you should probably examine why you are making excuses for a man who has done inexcusable acts."

For the hundredth time, Erenor steeled himself. "Elhanan attacked him. I saw with my own eyes. I don't know why people refuse to believe me about that."

Sinon's smile tightened. "You might ask why they *would* believe you. I am not challenging your testimony, Most Noble. I am simply resigning my position and trust you to relay to King Stefan that it has been my privilege to serve him and this great kingdom." With a deep bow, the elder diplomat backed away a few steps, then turned and walked out the door. Lucien closed it behind him.

"What do we tell Stefan?" Lucien asked. There was no mistaking the reason for his consternation. Sinon was a far more serious loss to the kingdom than the Chief Royal Secretary or the Head of the King's Stables, both of whom had also quit.

"We will tell him he needs to name a new ambassador to the Archhalia. Preferably someone who can still get an audience with Sordan's Hierarch. I am assigning you the task of coming up with some names for him to consider."

"Maybe my father?"

"We need a diplomat, a real one, not a ruling Bas with conflicts of interest. Go. Recruit some names. I want to send a preliminary list along with the letter."

Once Lucien was gone, Erenor got up from the desk and walked to the cabinet holding a collection of spirits and drinking vessels. Kheldish brandy and a fine crystal goblet did nothing to soothe his mood but did provide him with some reassurance of wealth and position. Just not the power to actually do anything. Stefan, he thought, really should be here fielding these problems, not sitting in Aral keeping watch over the pregnant wife of a man he had ordered killed. He obsessed more over that child than his own. Did Stefan want a Wall heir so he might mollify and reassure his people of their Entity's continuance? Or did he want to make certain of a bloodline's extinction? Erenor could not say and feared to guess.

Stefan should be arguing for his positions, not me. Winning these battles for himself. He should be fighting for his own survival.

For all his bluster, the damned Kheld was a coward.

40

When Stefan saw Cullen waiting at Gustan, he had known in the core of his heart something terrible had happened. Since that morning in Stauberg weeks ago, nothing had gone right—but he had thought maybe it would if he could finally reach home.

Accompanied by the remainder of his Kheld troops, Stefan had traveled from Aral with the Dannutheon princesses, whom he was more than happy to send on their way. Margarid had given birth two weeks ago. A girl, just as Elhanan had said it would be. Even as Stefan stood right in front of them, relieved he need not kill the child, they had named her Elhana Palaistea. As soon as his party reached Gustan's outskirts, Stefan made his way to the Dazun and joined the envoy from Merrydn at the manor's private landing. There he put the women and the infant onto a schooner that would take them into exile. He had forbidden them to reside in either Stauberg or Dannuth but had accepted Ionais's offer of refuge.

At least they were out of his hair. Stefan hadn't slept at all those two weeks. Just fits and starts between nightmares. He would deal later with disinheriting the newborn Princess of Stauberg.

And now this. Stefan had just finished waving farewell to his problems, only to turn and see Cullen standing in the lane looking grim.

"It was a warm spring, and the fen flowers were blooming," Cullen explained as they neared the looming gray shape of the Stauberg-Randolph mausoleum. The bronze horses at the entrance arched their necks beneath a somber, clouded sky. "Nilla didn't think it would be dangerous. Bog fever doesn't usually take people this early in the year."

Bog fever. Who the hells caught bog fever?

Cullen had brought the key. Stefan took it from him and opened the heavy bronze door. The entry and two narrow windows provided good light.

He walked up to and put his hand on the small sarcophagus. It was plain, hastily fashioned, a holding place until something finer could be made. For now, Moreen's remains rested beside the sepulchre of her great-uncle, Jonthan.

"And no one else caught the illness? Nilla? Anyone?"

"Well, other people did, quite a lot of them. Not kin or anyone you know, though." The weather had turned chill again and Cullen wore a coat with a wolfskin collar. "And before you say it was poison, it wasn't. Your own mother said so, as did the *faetha* Caohme, who Nilla keeps near. Same with the surgeon they called in."

Not every death was an assassination.

"How did you hear before me?" Stefan hadn't been informed that Cullen lived anywhere but at Wyre.

"Your mother sent for us when the sickness first showed. Later, she knew you had already set out from Aral and reckoned the news wasn't going to change however long you took." Cullen looked regretful enough, though he had more to say. "It wasn't me she sent for. Truth is, Nilla wanted Phalla at hand."

Of course. His queen always craved friends near. Cold passed from the stone into Stefan's bare hand. Too many dead things occupied this space.

"I want to see her." He expected opposition, but Cullen merely met Stefan's gaze like he understood. "She was embalmed, right?"

Cullen nodded. "And given the Mother's Blessing and prayers. She was also given a death gift." He answered Stefan's questioning look. "Phalla put little jewels in her hair. It's her people's way, Stefan; please don't think bad of it."

He didn't. Staubauns put great store in death gifts. The items were often valuable and always personal. The crime was that Phalla's offering was almost certain to be the only one. Stefan would be surprised if any other of his Staubaun subjects would think to honor his child.

With Cullen's help, he lifted the lid of the stone box. Moreen was wrapped in fine cloth, cerise in color, cotton and silk and of marvelous weave, with only her head left bare. Eyes closed and lips unexpectedly still pink and perfect, her head crowned by dark curls, she was beautiful. Two dainty combs of gold and pearls shaped as swans and flowers glinted in the hair at her temples.

"Gods." Tears welled from nowhere. Ten months old and Stefan had never seen her. Or even touched her. He put his right fingers to her cheek. Cold as only death could make a body.

"She looks like you."

If he looked dead. Stefan pulled his hand away. "Help me put this back." Together, they wrestled the lid until it sat tightly over the sarcophagus once more. "I'll put stone masons to work right away. I want her effigy on top, like Jon has."

They left the mausoleum. A groundskeeper closed and locked the bronze doors behind them, and Stefan's guards kept a protective but discreet distance as he walked with Cullen toward the great house to be seen beyond the trees. Nilla would be there, filled with grief. With her would be his mother, who would fret and chide him, probably about killing the Highborn, and Asphalladra, who would probably avoid him. The staff, for the most part, would not know him. When Stefan thought of Gustan at all, he thought of it as his mother's house.

"Did you bring your children?" He might as well ask. Acorn tops crushed underfoot.

Cullen shook his head. "No. We left them well looked after at Wyre. My mother's there on a visit."

Just as well. "Too bad. I would have liked to see them." Cullen had added a daughter to the family, born the year before Moreen.

"And I wanted to see you. I think of you lots—too much really. These last months…"

What could Stefan say? "My life feels like a nightmare anymore. All of it, the last couple years. Every time I deal with something terrible, something even more terrible comes after. I think the damned Highborn put a curse on me."

"Aw, Stefan—"

"My babies miscarry or die. My nobles rebel. The Seven Houses all but rule Dazunor-Rannuli. I keep raising taxes even though I said I wouldn't. And Neuberland is being torn apart, just the way you said it would." Stefan stopped on the path. They were still among the oaks and had a chance at privacy. "Doesn't all of that seem cursed to you?"

Cullen kicked at dried leaves and debris. "If you want the truth, I don't believe in curses. Troubles tend to be things we bring on ourselves. And bad luck sometimes." He frowned at whatever other thoughts he harbored before he settled on what he wanted to speak. "I've known you my whole life, and I know you're not a killer. You told me once you'd never put a man to death unless he'd done something terrible. That's why the stories I hear curdle my blood. I can't stand to believe you killed Elhanan, or his dad either, so please tell me you didn't."

Stefan clenched his teeth. "I didn't kill them, not with my own hand. But Elhanan did attack me, and Peric stabbed him and... things got out of hand. I haven't told anyone else this but I'm going to tell you. Elhanan didn't attack me to hurt me. His hands were bound and he had no weapon."

"Hells, Stefan!"

He clutched Cullen's arm, the better to make him listen to the rest. "Other people know that part. What they don't know is that Elhanan got inside my head"—Stefan nodded at the look that earned him—"yes, that's right! Everyone knows they can do that. Well, he did it to me. He showed me things, things even he could never have seen, like how Enreddon Malyrdeon and all the princes died at Permephedon, and he even showed me who murdered them... an enemy I didn't know existed. Some man with a crown. A blood-red crown. And he showed me what that man took from the Highborn—he took their blood."

White-faced, Cullen stared. "For what? Just to kill them?"

"I don't know!" Stefan spread his arms helplessly. "But Elhanan and Rheger knew. And that's why they showed me, so I wouldn't send them away, because something bad was sure to happen."

"So you could have kept them at Stauberg, with the Wall and soldiers. You didn't have to kill them."

Stefan laughed, because Cullen was missing the point. "That's the other thing—I *did* have to kill them. Because as long as they lived, that thing was going to hunt them. And get them, eventually. I think it got those boys of Palaistea's. Elhanan knew it was coming after him and his father next and he showed me that, and I didn't know any other way to stop it." After the past couple weeks, he had figured it out. "Rheger and Elhanan wanted me to kill them, all but begged me to do it. To prevent it."

"You figure you did?"

"Not completely." Stefan looked into the naked depths of the oak woods with its carpet of low shrubs and white and pink masses of wildflowers. It amazed him how a world so beautiful could be so filled with unnatural menace. A crown of blood-filled crystals haunted his dreams. And the Wall considered him an enemy now. He would never again set foot in his own capital, and neither would most Kheld folk after what they'd seen.

Cullen still looked amazed and shook his head. "What you saw... what Elhanan showed you—all those deaths at Permephedon. Dorilian didn't do it!" His eyes widened further. "That thing's hunting him too."

Stefan had been thinking about that also. He'd been thinking about a lot of things. "I'll send him a warning. And condolences for his kinsmen." That lie would mollify Cullen.

Cullen shot him a look that hoped he meant it. "We may need his help, if this enemy turns on us next."

"Or maybe it will just go after him and leave us alone."

"Could be, but nothing you told me points to a curse." Cullen squinted down the hill toward the mill pond, where black and white cows gathered and lowed as the afternoon grew long. "The only Highborn curse I ever heard of was one they put on the Dog Men who hunted them a thousand or so years ago. Those folks they made live in the wild and never be welcome again among men. That why Dog Men live in the Kragh these days and get attacked on sight."

Stefan knew of the Kragh. A wilderness of jagged hills, steep ravines, and white water, the forbidden land lay north and just a little east of Trulo. Nilla probably would not want to return to that city, but...

"The Kragh is where the Maw is, right?"

Cullen's brow furrowed with thought. "I think so."

"I need to go there."

"Why?"

Because of something Elhanan said.

"Something happened there. Or was supposed to happen. I don't know really, but I think it might be important." Stefan had already sent someone to scout the land and find out more about ways to approach it. Lucien's brother, Raphelon, had spent much of his youth in the region.

They began the walk down the path toward the big house and its formal gardens.

"Marc Frederick talked about the Kragh once," Cullen said, "something about going to see it. It was that same year I broke my leg. I think he went there, after I left to join you back at Orqho."

That year. The year Dorilian had spent at Gustan. The year that had changed the whole damned world by putting Stefan on the path to being king.

"That seals it, then. I'm going too." Stefan offered Cullen a grim smile. "Want to come with me?"

"I would be so much happier if you went with him."

Emyli regretted the look that crossed Cullen's face at her words. Just that morning, he had put off Stefan about joining his expedition to the Kragh. They stood in the west-facing drawing room and warm afternoon sunlight gilded her skirt and Cullen's fine leather boots. Together they gazed through open doors into the library where Asphalladra sat with Nilla before a fire, reading to her.

"You know why I don't want to."

"You and Stefan were such good friends."

"We still are," Cullen corrected. "You know how we manage it? I don't attend Stefan's court or do any work for him or get sucked up into his politics. We can still be friends because I don't have to pretend to agree with how he does his business."

To that, Emyli could only sigh. She did much the same. "He has so few people who care about him. Why do you think he holds onto your friendship so tightly? It's because he knows you will always do the right thing by him. You could never be false. He's stronger with you by his side."

Cullen didn't say anything. His gaze stayed on his wife and Nilla. Emyli could not read what weighed on Cullen's mind, but doubted it had to do with either young woman. A moment later, he sighed and shook his head.

Emyli sensed that his resolve had weakened. "A ride into the countryside is not the same as being at court. It is an outing, only that, and then you can return to your family. My Commander of the Guard is going with him. Trevor was my father's Commander and accompanied him to the Kragh on more than one occasion."

"I know the man."

"You'll be safe."

"I reckon we would be," Cullen conceded. He frowned, then regarded her directly. "I'm not sure I can do it, be with Stefan like old times. I can't just pretend away the last few years, or how those men died—or that he ordered Khelds to do the killing."

"He explained it to me."

"He explained it to me too. He's convinced himself he's blameless, but he isn't, and you know it. And so do I, better than he does. Wounds like those he laid on this land stain our people in ways we can never be rid of! He can never go to Stauberg again, think about that. How far does the Wall's interdiction go? His sons? His daughters? Half the country is saying that with the Wall against him, Stefan's not fit to rule!"

The way Cullen's gaze stayed on hers pierced her wish to deflect. Emyli too had caused Highborn deaths. The trouble that had led to Cullen's ordeal in Gignastha had started with her. She was possibly the only person in Essera who fully understood what Stefan had done, how he had delivered both death and mercy. Their enemy's machinations remained hidden.

But Stefan had also crippled the Wall, possibly forever. He, not she or Nammuor, had purged Essera of Highborn blood.

Only Dorilian and his son, in distant Sordan, remained. Was this what the Wall had foreseen? If so, had the Wall sought to prevent the slaughter... or bring it to pass? Or had the Entity simply been helpless in the coils of a broken paradigm?

"Stefan knows what he's done," Emyli pleaded for Cullen to understand. "If he is to heal himself or this land, he needs his friends. His family and those who love him. He needs *you*."

Cullen hung his head. "Maybe he does, if he means to set things right."

"He does. And you can help him."

"I don't think me not being at court mattered much. Stefan is different than I remember, more scared, I think. Stauberg was bad enough, but losing Moreen hit him hard."

Emyli blinked back hot tears. Moreen had been all brightness and hope. Just learning to speak. Only two hours ago, she had held Stefan in her arms while he wept about never having seen his little daughter alive. "Oh Cullen." Emyli reached for his hand and clasped it between hers. "Don't you see? He can't lose you, too. Give him but a few days; remind him of who he is and can be. Be his friend. I will stop by Wyre on my way to Merrydn and see to your family."

Stefan wanted Emyli to smooth things over with Ionais and the Dannutheon princesses. He had yet to decide whether to hold Sapphia and Margarid captive, or set them and little Elhana free. Emyli was charged to reassure all three women that if they observed his restrictions and removed Elhana from the kingdom's succession, he would leave them in peace.

"It would be just my mother and the children at Wyre," Cullen said. "Nilla won't go back to Trulo because that's where Moreen took sick and died. She wants to stay here near the grave until that's all finished and proper. Phalla has said she wants to stay with her and Stefan gave his consent."

"Your mother and I are old friends." Ample and vivacious, Sunbridda Rhys was the embodiment of a high-clan Kheldwoman: skilled at all things domestic. "Thank you, Cullen."

He cocked her a grin. "I'll go give Stefan the news. He wants to go to the Kragh before heading to Dazunor-Rannuli for the Archhalia—and you can guess how little he's looking forward to *that*."

Stefan spent a few days at Gustan with his grieving wife, doing what he could to ease her sorrow and making the sweetest love to Nilla he'd ever made with any woman. After promising he would return to her in two months' time, he set off for Trulo with Cullen, followed by a full force of his Kheld Guards and Trevor Allen. A tall sturdy man with black hair nearly gone to gray, Trevor had been Marc Frederick's Commander of the King's Guard, and during that time he had ridden with the late king to the Kragh. He was also Gustan-born, descended from two generations of Morgans and Allens, families that lived only at Gustan and served the Stauberg-Randolphs exclusively. Even Peric, now wearing the gilded helm of a King's Guard Commander, deferred to Trevor's qualifications.

They left Gustan on a spring morning heavy with clouds and rode east. The next day, as afternoon crested, they left the King's Road and headed north. They made camp when twilight fell, on the far bank of a river they had crossed, and erected their tents on high ground.

"The Hyllorhose," Trevor named the fast-flowing river. He stood with Stefan on a rise above the camp and pointed to the cloud-wreathed hills in the distance. "The Kragh creates its own mists and mystery."

"You went into their land? You never spoke of it."

Trevor nodded. "Your grandfather swore secrecy on the mission."

"Well, he's dead, so I remove the secrecy."

Trevor's gray eyes weighed Stefan for a moment before he answered. "The king had funded an expedition of excavators. Historians. Geologists. He wanted to know what secrets the Maw held, and so did the Hen Kyon. The team went there to dig. And the king went there to see what they found."

"What did they find?"

"You would have to ask them. I was there only to guard my king and the Sordaneon prince. I didn't ask a lot of questions."

Stefan remembered how Marc Frederick had kept Dorilian in nearly constant company that year, even more so after Jonthan's death and with the succession in crisis. It seemed like everything pointed back to that time and the events it had spawned. Dorilian would of course tell Stefan nothing, and at this point neither could the Wall Lords.

"Are they people? The Dog Men? Of a kind that men can talk with?"

"Oh, yes, sire. Many are bestial, to be sure, but not all. Some are barely distinguishable from men and speak as we do. Your grandfather gave their leader a title, made him a lord. His name is Baran. He seemed a man very much."

"Good." This Baran had petitioned for an audience once, soon after Stefan had become Prince of Dazunor. As Stefan recalled, he had sent someone else to deal with him.

The night saw rain and the next day they rode into forested hills on a path that wound beneath a canopy of dripping boughs. Stefan's proud banners hung sodden and heavy from water-dark poles as his party advanced among the trees. His men hunkered down in their saddles. Even Cullen, riding beside him, looked more miserable than anything else. What had started as a fun jaunt to renew their friendship had become a slog.

"I didn't know the hills would be this steep, or this many," Stefan confided. At least the trail had broadened enough to allow their two horses to walk side by side. "I hope those maps were right and we don't end up in fucking Dannuth."

"That would be poor luck, seeing as Rheger ruled there. Good thing Grenant pledged himself."

The man Cullen referred to was father and regent to Dannuth's new Bas, a minor youth, and had sworn an oath of fealty to Stefan. Even so, Dannuth would most likely be a hostile place to go.

Cullen looked up into the trees. For whatever reason, the rain had slowed, though the trees still dripped. "I'm glad we're riding with fighting men. I've heard tales about these hills. Locals say folk who go in don't come back."

"Grandfather did. Went in *and* came back. And with Dorilian too."

"And so did Trevor here." Cullen jutted his chin at the soldier who rode just in front of them, alongside Peric.

"I'm certain we'll survive these beasts and their hills," Stefan judged. "The hard part may be finding them. It's all gorges and cliffs."

Up ahead, two massive thrusts of rock, smoothed by time and crowned by trees, pushed into the trail on each side and rendered it narrow. Symbols carved into the rocks were covered over by layers of lichens and mosses, but Stefan made out a wolf head and a spear. The banner-bearers passed under the rocks' shadow beneath a canopy of overhanging branches. The horses ahead slowed, then stopped. Trevor rode forward to scout and before long returned to signal that Stefan should ride forward.

"'Tis Lord Baran, sire. He and his folk bar our progress."

"Well, I guess you found them," Cullen said.

Stefan hesitated. A glance at the rocks to either side showed movement. Soldiers? Animals? Or maybe just the wind. No matter. He had brought enough men to handle this rabble. He urged his mount forward and was gratified as Cullen followed. Rounding the outcropping, Stefan saw what had halted his party.

One man. On horseback. The sturdy blue roan was draped with skins and adorned with strung claws or teeth. The older red-haired man astride the horse barred the way with barbaric splendor. An antique coat of russet velvet threaded with spirals of gold proclaimed his importance, as did the gold ornaments woven into his beard. A sash of tiny skulls and a heavy collar thick with medallions spanned his broad chest.

"Approach, if you are who your banner claims you to be." The deep voice actually rumbled.

Stefan guided his mount between the horses of his bannermen until he took position in front of them. "I am Stefan Marc Frederick Stauberg-Randolph, King of Essera and rightful sovereign of these lands you claim."

The big man sat straighter in the saddle. "Lands which my people hold by the promise of Emrysen Malyrdeon. Are you here to revoke that promise?"

Stefan wished he had done more study while at Gustan or consulted with his annoying but sometimes useful uncle Robdan before undertaking this expedition. He had been handed the impression that the Highborn had cursed these unfortunates, not given over land the same way they had granted Amallar to the Khelds.

"No." He wasn't here to give or take away anything. "I wish to speak with Baran, who I have been told is your leader. Would that be you?"

"I am Baran, Lord of Gloannech." Orange eyes narrowed with feral assessment. "If the king comes in peace, I welcome him and promise safe passage, but I will not welcome so many armed men into my stronghold. Either disarm your men or choose fewer to ride with you."

"That's hardly a welcome for your monarch," Stefan noted, looking to all sides. Baran appeared to be alone on the trail with the way on the other side of him clear and unguarded, but the woods were thick and Stefan had seen movement. No doubt the forest crawled with Dog Men. One word from Baran and those creatures would descend upon Stefan. He caught Cullen's attention, which only gained him a shrug that asked what he could do otherwise. "I believe I am in my authority to enter your lands."

"You are, but why should we trust you? We know what you have done."

"Sire." Trevor prevented Stefan's angry response. "This man has proven himself honorable on many occasions. Your family is revered here. If you will permit, I will choose ten men to safeguard you. That was the number allowed your grandfather."

Baran waited for an answer. Stefan delayed until things became uncomfortable before he nodded. "Do it."

Darkness had begun to fall by the time they reached a collection of low hovels, most made of timber and stone, scattered in a hollow between lofty hills. Even Baran's residence, adorned with the horns of great beasts and graced with peaked roofs, was as poor a dwelling as Stefan had seen lately. Of far more interest were the surrounding hills. One summit especially, stark with streaks of last light, etched itself against a rain-heavy sky. He reined in his horse to stare at it.

"Is that it? Is that the Maw?"

"It is," said Baran.

At last, the Dog Men came into the open. Town folk emerged from the dwellings. Male and female, young and old, they stood nearby, none bearing weapons, their gazes fixed upon Stefan. Though Trevor remained calm, the other soldiers were alert and on edge. Stefan had brought only Kheld guards with him, including Peric, who bridled at knowing Trevor held command. All were men Stefan could count on to see first and foremost to their king's well-being.

The Maw. It was just a hill—massive, naked, and ugly. Stefan had expected more. "I want to go to the top. I trust there's a road?"

"A path only. And none for you."

Was Baran telling him he could not go? To make his point clear, Stefan pointed at the Maw. "I came here for but one reason: to see the top of that hill."

The Dog Men appeared to have increased in number. Maybe they were just venturing nearer to better hear and assess their visitors. Now that he looked at them more closely, Stefan noted deep-set yellow eyes beneath bony brows and above protruding noses and jaws, a glimpse of longer teeth between parted lips, facial hair too extensive, and limbs too hairy and oddly bent to be called human. Though poorly clothed, the creatures he looked upon were lithe, clawed, and dangerous.

Baran shifted his seat astride his horse, the better to glance at the Maw. He grimly regarded those heights, though he spoke to the king. "You ask to tread upon sacred ground. From the days of Emrysen the Merciful, we have guarded this land." He turned his gaze upon Stefan. "That I have allowed you to enter this far into it is a courtesy to a king who is also the grandson of my friend. We have shown you that which you came to see."

"No, you haven't. I came to see the *top* of that hill. My grandfather planted something there."

"Then you have come here for nothing. The summit is bare. That which he planted never grew."

Elhanan had said as much. Yet there was something here in this place, either on top of the hill or because of it. Ancient and secret and guarded by creatures out of legend. Wind blew off the Maw and stirred the brass chimes that hung from Baran's horn-framed hut. Other chimes, deep and sonorous, sounded throughout the hollow. Rain began to fall.

"I need to know what he planted."

In Baran's gaze, Stefan saw knowledge deeper and more dangerous than he would ever penetrate. "You will never know that. Your grandfather is dead. You came here only to see what you have yourself created."

"That?" Stefan pointed at the Maw's forbidding hulk. "That's nothing!"

"As you have condemned it to be. Now you must go. An oath binds the Hen Kyon, Emrysen's Doom, and it does not fall on us alone. We must drive forth from our land all of your kind."

"What doom? And what do you mean by *my* kind?" Were Khelds despised by Dog Men, too? Stefan twisted around in the saddle to look at his men. They had been chosen from his elite guards. Every Kheld face was tense and pale beneath its helm. At his side, Cullen breathed hard and looked ill at ease. Peric and a few others appeared affronted and ready to bare steel.

Trevor guided his mount alongside Stefan's. "Sire, there is more to this. We should go. Lord Baran is exercising Highborn landright."

Stefan was having none of that. He urged his horse toward Baran, though the beast fought to turn back. "I don't care what right you think the Highborn gave you a thousand years ago. You better explain your damn insult. I'm fucking royal! What other kind do you think I am?"

"You are a Highborn killer, a slayer of holy blood… and not you only. Others of that kind ride with you."

The pronouncement ignited something in the Dog Men. Heated gazes burned brighter as they crowded nearer. Trevor's horse shied, tried to whirl and escape. Cullen also battled his horse. Nearly all the guardsmen's horses reared and fought the rein. There was no mistaking why. Snarls lifted lips among the Dog Men who circled them. Teeth glimmered. Words sounded more like growls.

"Highborn killers!"

"Spillers of god blood!"

"Forsakers!"

Baran lifted his right arm, his fist holding aloft a staff carved from bone and scrolled with gold. The feral voices faded. Only a glow of hostile eyes remained, tracking the visitors with bared teeth and tensed bodies.

"Leave, king. I promised you safe passage, but only that. We are sworn to defend the godborn, and on you and those with you we smell the blood of murdered princes. If you value your lives, leave our land at once. Emrysen's Doom they laid upon us—and now also on you. Ride," Baran said, "and ride fast."

The skies opened. Stefan could control his horse no longer. Maybe the beast saw ghosts. Definitely it saw Dog Men and witnessed lightning strike atop the Maw like a trident. Thunder clapped. The way to the road out of the town lay clear before them, darkened by twilight and populated only by fleeing guards. Stefan kicked his horse to take their lead. Howls, some from his men and some from the creatures he glimpsed in pursuit, joined with the wind until it sounded like a host was after him.

"Peric was stupid. So were the men that followed him when he charged back to kill the lot." Cullen tugged a blanket of wool and silk over his shoulders.

Though Stefan glowered at him, Cullen was right. The two

survivors of Peric's hot-headed decision to fight back against the Dog Men had seen their captain torn apart along with their less fortunate comrades. Teeth and claws had not been the Dog Men's only weapons. Six men had died. Fortunately, the creatures had stopped their pursuit at the symbol-covered rocks that marked the boundary of their territory. It was possible they had done so only because they had encountered the remainder of Stefan's King's Guard.

Now as dawn rose, Stefan and the survivors of his ill-fated mission huddled in the well-guarded camp they had left at the bank of the Hyllorhose. Rain fell in curtains. Both he and Cullen had changed out of wet clothes and sat near a brazier in Stefan's fully furnished campaign tent.

"All right. So Khelds aren't the best soldiers."

"We're terrible soldiers." Cullen, being Kheld himself, was allowed to say such a thing.

"At least Trevor survived."

"Because he stayed with you and me and kept riding."

Stefan hung his head. "All for nothing. This whole expedition, this trying to figure it out."

Using a discarded sock, Cullen lifted a mug he'd been heating on the iron grate. Though the brazier had yet to take the chill off the tent interior, it had done a fair job of warming some cider. "You never did tell me what you thought you were going to find."

"Answers."

Stefan couldn't talk about this with other people. Nilla didn't have any background at all by which to understand the forces that tore at his confidence. His mother, who knew his grandfather best of anybody, would just find a way to chide Stefan. As for Erenor... though Stefan trusted the man, he never shared any feelings with him. Nothing that might reveal weakness. Which was the crux of Stefan's dilemma: feelings were all he had to work with. Thank the Mother for Cullen. He needed to get this off his chest.

"Elhanan told me some things." Stefan kept his voice low, barely above the crackle of wood turning to coals. Cullen leaned nearer to hear him. "Wall things, at least I think they were Wall things. He spoke in riddles and—fuck," Stefan swore under his breath. "I did it all wrong. It took me a while to put it together—that's the way the Wall does things, it's all bits and pieces. And why the Malyrdeons were important, because they knew ways to turn riddles into sense. But Elhanan was just thrown into the job and he couldn't do it, not by himself, so that's all he could give me."

"Riddles."

Stefan nodded. "He said crazy things, like me being a void and how there's some sort of design that's not working right. I don't think the Wall can see me clearly. But Elhanan did say something I thought I could find a way to make sense. Not a future thing but something that already happened. He said I killed something."

"Some*thing*, not some*one*? And it had to do with the Maw, or the Dog Men?"

Stefan poured cider from the crock into another mug for himself and did a quick slip of that onto the grate. "He said it was something born atop the Maw. Because grandfather planted a seed there. He said I killed it."

Cullen drew a deep breath and rocked back on his heels. He put his cup of cider on the carpet near his feet. "I heard you ask about it. That Baran… he said it never grew."

"He also said I looked upon my own creation. A place where whatever it was never grew."

After a long moment, Cullen swallowed and looked Stefan in the eye. "We've seen hills like that one. Not usually surrounded by other tall hills, but… big. Symmetrical."

"Naked." Stefan recalled those other hills and frowned. "My grandfather was obsessed by the Rill. And he took Dorilian with him on that visit."

"Lud."

Together they stared at the glowing orange light within the brazier. As Cullen had earlier, Stefan wrapped his hand with a sock and retrieved his cider. Heat penetrated the damp cloth and felt pleasant on his palm. He took a sip of the hot beverage and savored its notes of apple and brandy as Cullen continued.

"People talked, you know, that it was him at Hestya. That maybe Dorilian did it. Maybe that's why—"

"Why what?"

"I could ride the Rill back from Randpory." Cullen picked up his mug again. "We never talked about that, did we?"

"No."

"There could be reasons, I suppose, and I never pressed my luck by trying it again."

"As if you could ever get close enough." Nothing had changed about who was granted access to the Rill. Khelds were forbidden from using it in any way, not just for riding but even getting on the platform where people waited or watched, as well as the structures for lading, with the same reasons given as ever: The Rill abominated Khelds and was certain to kill them.

Except that it didn't. Maybe it never had.

Damn the Epoptes… and the Seven Houses—and Dorilian too, for hating them but hating Khelds more.

Making it so Khelds might use the Rill was yet another battle Stefan could never win.

Now that his cider and brandy had cooled, Stefan took a deeper drink before he frowned. "None of it matters anyway, about the Rill. The Epoptes aren't going to budge. And Dorilian never woke another mount, did he? Not even in his own country. Looks like he amounted to nothing after all. Just another dead hope."

A pensive smile crossed Cullen's face. "Would be amazing if he could."

That was just like Cullen, to dream of such a thing. Stefan was satisfied with the Rill in its current state. The god-machine performed its functions flawlessly: it moved people, powered economies, cemented alliances, and created a sense of permanence. Why hope that new Rill nodes might be enabled that could move armies, enrich enemies old and new, create rivalries, or bring about change?

Baran had said something about hope. Was that what Stefan had killed? Hope of the Rill?

If so, he was glad.

"I want you to return to court," he told Cullen. The time had come to press the matter. "Nilla needs Phalla right now, and I need you. I won't put you to work or send you on missions. I won't put you on the spot to do anything except be at hand. You will be beholden to no one, not even me. And you will always have my ear."

"Stefan—"

Stefan held out his left hand. In the glow of the fire, the scar of their blood bond cut a thin white line across his palm. Cullen granted a smile and extended his left hand also to show a thicker, corded scar.

"You swore," Stefan reminded him. "We swore together to change the world."

The smile turned wistful. "We did, didn't we?"

"So let's make good on it."

41

"You're going back to Aral? Why not Gustan?"

Emyli caught Cullen's look of agreement. Though they were with Stefan in the Emrysen Palace, where the king had been conducting two weeks of meetings in advance of the new Archhalia session, Cullen too would prefer Stefan to hold court at Gustan, which was closer to Cullen's own estates. Stefan ignored them both to give instructions to a courier charged with carrying correspondence to Permephedon.

Several months had passed since the deaths of Rheger and Elhanan, and for the most part Essera was at peace. Stefan's actions at Stauberg had sparked rebellion—but quelled it also. If the king would kill the Highborn, no lord in the kingdom was safe from seizure or execution. Essera's nobility opted to watch and wait and pointed to the Wall, which stood guard over Stauberg just as surely as it always had.

While Cullen sat on the other side of the room and turned the pages of a book, Stefan joined Emyli at the broad window seat. Together they looked out at the Rill-traced night sky above Dazunor-Rannuli's glowing domes and cupolas. "I'm going to Aral because I need to keep Nilla happy and safe. I also need to rule from a seat of power. We both hate *this* city, and she's never going to be happy in Trulo again. I can't go to Stauberg, so…"

Emyli sighed. All of this was true. Even her father, who had so loved Gustan he would have happily lived there the year-round, had moved his court among the many cities of his kingdom. "Erenor is being generous, I know that. Hosting a king's court is terribly costly. But Ionais—"

"You're mad if you think I'm going to Merrydn while the Gracious Princesses are there," Stefan said.

"They are why you should go."

In the wake of the killings of Rheger and Elhanan, Emyli had spent a month in Merrydn with her sister-by-law Ionais and the men's grief-stricken wives. To this day she had not told Stefan the extent to which Ionais's loyalty had shifted. At this point, Ionais had been listening to the widowed women for months. A steadfast Stauberg-Randolph ally before, Merrydn's Princess was aligning more and more with Estevan of Gweroyen and Hebron in Lacenedon. And though Stefan had charged Erenor with living in and administering Stauberg, the surrounding domains only appeared to be calm. Emyli was hearing far too many whispers of discontent from the Royal North.

Be careful, my son. Please be careful. You have made too many enemies.
Worse, she thought Erenor might be one of them.

The problem was, Stefan heeded her counsel less than ever. At least there was still Cullen. As she had hoped when she'd called him to Gustan for Moreen's sad passing, Cullen had resumed his friendship with Stefan as if it had never been broken. Though Cullen refused to take a position in government, he attended Stefan's court and provided a counter to Erenor's powerful influence. It seemed no other voice could reach her son now.

Stefan took her left hand in his. "I want you to know something and, well, there's no easy way to tell you."

What could it be? Emyli gazed at his face, seeing in it everything she loved—the slight crook of his lips as he tried not to frown, the dark dignity of his beard, features so Kheldish and handsome that the sight of him called to mind her father and his. Erwan, dead now for so many years. Eighteen. Dear Mother, Stefan looked just like him.

"Tell me what?"

"Nilla's pregnant again, you know."

"Yes, I do." Emyli had known for some time. Nilla was seven months along.

"The Archhalia asked me to appoint a regent in the event anything should happen to me."

"Oh." How odd. She did not recall him being asked to name one before.

"I'm naming Erenor."

It seemed to her all the air had left the room, because Emyli could not fill her lungs. And then she could and did. "Not me? Not the *grandmother*?"

"Mother—"

"Why not your brother?"

Now he did frown… and sighed. "You mean the one who's not here? He's still young enough to need a regent himself. I'm not going to do something that daft."

"But he… Hans will be back soon. Very soon! We're at peace. We're…"

Stefan turned her fingers in his and covered them with his other hand. Warm and strong. "Hans has been gone for eight years. I've stopped believing he's coming back. Maybe he will, and I hope he does, but I'm certainly not going to plan the succession around him. I just wanted you to know. I'm not sick; I'm not dying. But I'm also not blind to the fact that I'm mortal. You should know why I couldn't choose you."

Because someone has been talking to you. Her stomach turned sour. Nilla disliked Erenor and would not have asked that he be placed in authority over her child or her. "I don't see that there are any reasons."

Stefan held her gaze, his calm confronting her confusion and anger. "I was given an Archhalial opinion paper. Your role in the Bloodletting at Gignastha hasn't been forgotten."

"Enreddon—"

"The Malyrdeons forgave you, yes. But no one else. Sordan certainly hasn't."

No, probably not, though it was not Dorilian who was putting forth this grievance. Since the deaths of Rheger and Elhanan, Dorilian had become more and more a recluse. This move was purely Esseran and political. A maneuver, as surely as getting Stefan to create such a document at all. "I don't think—"

"It doesn't matter what you think… not about this. I just want you to know, so you can find it in you somehow to support my queen and my son should that day come. I know you understand why Nilla can't serve as regent, and that's the same reason Lowen can't, or Cullen. They aren't of royal birth."

"Neither is Erenor!"

"He's a great-grandson of a Highborn prince."

A bitter laugh escaped Emyli. "By his own proclamation. Since when have you made that your opinion on what makes someone worthy?"

Stefan let go of her hand and rose, the better to look down on her. "I haven't! But I also can't change Triemperal Law. I've tried, and you damn well know it."

Yes, he had. Stefan had introduced changes to the laws of succession several times over the years. Sordan had vetoed every attempt to alter Triemperal Law on that matter. Even Stefan's proposal to change only Essera's succession laws to more Kheld-friendly versions had met stiff opposition from within the kingdom and been voted down.

Emyli nodded and folded her hands. They missed his touch and the strength that so conveyed his passion. "You're right, of course. Those laws bind your choices the same way they bind us all." The same way they still bound hers.

His gaze on her turned tender. "You were my first choice. No one ever fought harder for me than you have. You would stand up to Grandfather for me, to Apollonia. You even stood up to Dorilian on my coronation day, and not many did. Maybe you're even the reason why he didn't kill me or haul me off to Sordan. Maybe you didn't fight for me when you sent Hans away, but I know you'll fight tooth and claw for my heirs. I don't need to put your name on a piece of paper to be sure of that. You aren't enough, though, not by yourself. They will need people to fight *for* them, not fight them because of you." He leaned down and kissed her on the cheek, and she closed her eyes rather than show him her tears. Oh, how this betrayal stung. "I want you to come to Aral and spend some time at court. Get to know Erenor better. I think he'll surprise you. Nilla is there already with Lowen and Goff. She would also like you to be there for the Feast of Imenos."

Emyli watched Stefan walk away. Cullen put down his book and gave an apologetic bow before he followed Stefan from the room, leaving her alone. Only then did she let fall the tears she had been holding back.

Yes, she had fought for Stefan. She had fought all those he had mentioned and also herself. All these years she had battled to fit the king her son was into the king she believed with all her heart he could be. A Kheld king. Noble and just and strong. A bringer of change and progress. A king whom Essera would honor in generations to come.

Oh, yes. They would remember him.

She had fought for Stefan every step of the way—but now when she needed him to fight for her... he hadn't.

Why?

Because he—or Erenor—controlled the Archhalia too well? Just a few months ago, Essera's Halia had changed the law to allow the execution of Highborn princes for treason. At that session, a majority declaration of Rheger and Elhanan to be traitors had absolved Stefan and the Khelds who had committed the killings. Of what before had been a crime. A crime for which, in all the years before this one, Stefan and those men would have been put to death.

No wonder he felt protected and empowered.

But he wasn't. Her father's mighty allies, who might have afforded protection against horrors to come, were gone. Powers made possible by the greater enhancers were now beyond Stefan's reach because—in Essera at least—none remained to wield them. The Wall and the Rill could still help, perhaps, but with every day, it seemed, Stefan was making appeal to the Entities impossible.

And Marenthro had made clear he would not intervene. She had not seen him, not even once, since that day Moreen had taken ill.

Feeling bereft, Emyli retreated to her own suite of rooms, where a solitary message waited for her on a silver tray. The array-transported message cylinder, ring-locked and slender, was keyed as being from Aral. Concentric bands beaded with precious stones and filigrees of metal identified the sender as Asphalladra. Finally, a ray of sunshine. The young woman often passed along queries or bits of news from Nilla tucked within her chatty sentences and neatly penned letters. Occasionally more weighty information found its way into the missives, discreetly conveyed. Emyli smiled and immediately unlocked the rings to extract the message.

She read only a few lines. Her thoughts staggered.

Everything surrounding her seemed to become insubstantial, even her body for a moment. Deep breaths restored her equilibrium and the world resumed its usual state. She rolled the thin paper and slipped it back into the cylinder, then rekeyed the lock.

Dear Mother. She could not let Stefan do this.

When Stefan left by river schooner in the morning, headed for Gustan, from which he would ride for Aral, Emyli remained behind. She had assured her son that she'd already promised a meeting in Permephedon to assist a scholar with translation of original Kheld documents. Honoring that obligation might take her a few days, but she would afterward join him at court. From the quiet south edge of the Rill platform, Emyli watched the King's regal gond approach the riverfront quay where the massive schooner awaited. Heavy of heart, she turned away and boarded the *charys* that would take her north.

Though Stefan disliked Permephedon and spent no more time there than he must, Emyli loved the city. As soon as she set foot upon the paved plaza outside its Rill sanctuary, she felt at home, welcomed, and above all protected. Greatest of the Five Cities, Permephedon was also the most Leur. Created and sustained by magic, it lived and shared its joy in living with those who dwelt there. Its colors changed in tune with otherworldly seasons, as did its sounds and spaces and moods.

In every part of the City, she sensed Marenthro's presence. He lived here in ways she did not fully understand but which she grasped as innate.

On this occasion, however, Emyli had not come in search of him. She went to her manse in the Jewel Tower and, once her privacy was sure, sent a message. After taking several minutes to instruct her staff on a few matters, she made her way to the highest level of the Jewel Tower and a portal purposed only for secrecy. Most of those who knew this portal's secret and how to activate it were dead.

She stepped from the portal into a domed and gilded space at the pinnacle of the blue-green monolith of the Sordaneon Tower. She used the sole exit to enter a small rotunda, where she was greeted by a tall woman wearing a simple gown of exceptional cloth and beautiful purple color. Brown hair pinned by amethyst combs framed her round face and dark eyes.

The woman curtseyed. "Your Royal Highness. I am Minora Haska, Secretary to the Basarchessa."

"Will your mistress receive me?"

"Indeed, she will. If you will follow me."

Two portals later, Emyli walked into a sumptuous residence filled with light from floor to ceiling through seamless windows. They were high within the tower, nearly above the clouds. In Permephedon such addresses were usually royal. She thanked Minora and chose a chair, which she guided by hand to near a window from which she could gaze upon the High Citadel and its shifting angles and planes while she waited.

Emyli rose again when Palimia entered the room.

Her father's former mistress could no longer be called beautiful. Palimia's body was thin and frail, supported within a wheeled chair. Hair pale gold and lustrous only a few years ago was white and sparse. Her skin, once flawless and supple, had a sallow hue as it clung to the still fine bones of a face sunken and shadowed. Arms veiled by silken gauze propped upon armrests of polished wood chased with gold, while a soft blanket covered her visibly withered legs. From informants, Emyli knew that Dorilian still kept company with Palimia when she was in Sordan. He dined with her, sought her opinion, listened to her advice. He had not, to anyone's knowledge, taken another mistress.

"Princess!" Palimia greeted. Another lady attended her, one

who wore the soft gray gown of a Sister of Mercy. "Oh, how often I have thought of you."

"And I you. Oh, Mia—"

"Hush." Palimia spoke softly in a voice as lovely as ever. As Emyli followed, the Sister wheeled the chair and its occupant to a sitting area set for a visitor. The chairs' brocade upholstery, softly tufted, was very pretty. Palimia had always had good taste. "You of course should be seated first, however... please. I cannot tell you how surprised I am that you would pay me the honor of a visit."

Emyli lowered herself onto a chair. "You would not have come to me."

"I have certain... restrictions, among which is distrust of your son. But I would never turn you away. You have always been good to me." Palimia gestured to a table set with goblets and a selection of spirits. "Do you still like peach brandy and cream?"

Of course Emyli did. Moreover, she rather needed the brandy. She accepted the glass the Sister poured for her.

"Thank you. Though I fear I must prevail upon *your* kindness, Mia. Dare I do so?"

"Of course. I mean, I don't know what it might be, but I will help if I am able... though only for myself. You understand, I hope, that I cannot promise the help of any other."

She had expected Palimia to guard that relationship. People probably schemed incessantly to use Palimia's influence with Sordan's Hierarch for access or gain. But Emyli had no other choice. She paused, lowered her head, and made one more request. "May I speak with you alone?"

Palimia paused for a long moment, then turned to the Sister. "Xia, if you would—"

"Of course, Most Noble." Xia cast a warning glare at Emyli as she walked past. A glare undeserved but well earned.

Once the Sister was gone, Emyli felt free to speak.

"It's about Dorilian—"

"Oh, no." Palimia stiffened with rebuke. "You know I cannot. You must understand—"

"Please hear me out. This isn't about him as a person, and I don't want anything from him, except... he won't listen to this, not if he knows it's from me."

"Are you sure? Have you tried?"

Emyli drew a breath and looked to the ceiling to gather her thoughts. Palimia, too, knew that Dorilian would, even if begrudgingly, at least read any message Emyli sent. "I cannot. My son forbids any of his subjects to attempt contact. That includes his mother. I just… oh, how I wish some things had never happened! But they did happen and this thing between them will never end."

"Someday it will." Palimia leaned forward to offer a small tray of tiny cakes. "All things do eventually end."

"Only by death, between those two—and neither of us wishes for that."

Palimia looked at her hands and Emyli realized she was being thoughtless. She was not here to be Stefan's advocate.

"There's no longer any hope things will get better between them," Emyli continued. "All any of us can do is try to prevent things from getting worse." She picked up a little round cake iced with pink flowers. It was too pretty to be eaten, but to not do so would be impolite. Palimia had no reason to poison her. Emyli slipped the cake into her mouth; notes of anise and cardamom dissolved upon her tongue.

"Well, then, I don't understand."

Of course. Emyli had not gotten to her point yet. "Oh! For the love of Leur, I want to keep them from killing each other!"

Startled brown eyes searched hers and softened. "I think we both do. Your father wanted that, too."

"I know. Father tried so hard to bring them together, but at every turn they resorted to hostility. That year at Gustan was all about… everything! But I—" *I made things worse. I took Stefan to Amallar when I should have made him stay at Gustan and face Dorilian, deal with him. Maybe, if I had….* Emyli looked toward the window, with its panoramic view of the High Citadel—and the Rill's powerful structures engaged in a dance which all worshipped and few understood. "I need to warn the Hicrarch."

"Warn him? About Stefan? Please. After all you know about them, after what happened at Stauberg? You think him not warned enough?" Palimia gently coughed into a square of cloth. Emyli could see that even this soon into her visit, conversation tired Palimia.

"Not about this. I hope"—Emyli drew a breath and looked down at her hands, surprised to see them clenched and white—"I hope to salvage what can yet be salvaged. But I cannot have this warning be traced to me." Palimia lifted her head to hear more. "My son would be enraged if he knew I was here. My being in this building is an act of treason. So is speaking with you. My life already is in your hands."

"Is it?" Palimia asked softly.

"Yes."

Emyli watched how Palimia's gaze drifted to different aspects of the room as she gathered her thoughts. How much would she be willing to promise?

"What do you want from me?" Palimia lifted her goblet and took a sip.

"For my warning to reach the Hierarch's ear, only that. If only that happens, and he heeds my warning, this meeting will be worth whatever happens to me. But I beg of you, as a friend, though I have not been much of one, to conceal my part. Give the Hierarch my warning but don't tell him from whom you learned the information."

"He might pull it from my thoughts. He is capable of that."

"And you have been his *lover*, his friend and confidante for years. You know how to direct your thoughts away from discovery and he respects you enough, I think, not to rip them from you unwilling. Dorilian trusts you."

"Yes," Palimia said quietly. A delicate ping accompanied the touch of her crystal goblet being returned to the table. "He does trust me. And his trust is precious, a gift I will not squander on behalf of your son. Stefan took so very much from me—and not me alone but from Dorilian also, and, more than anyone, from Marc. You have no idea—"

"I do, really. More than you know."

"I wonder. I don't know why I so want to believe you. I—I really don't have the strength for this. I am to die any day."

"No—"

Palimia lifted both hands to show how frail and skeletal they were. "See this? I am but a husk. Inside, I am broken beyond healing. Despite the hard work of the Physicians and the dear Sisters"—she cast a thankful glance toward the door—"my organs are failing. They are twisted by scars. Atrophied. Leaking. This body can no longer sustain itself." She managed a weak smile. "I have made the most of my extremely long death."

Oh, Mother. Stefan really had killed Palimia that day, by accident yet through an act of vengeance and hatred launched by cold purpose. It had just taken her poor body this long to perish. Emyli blinked at the cruel horror of such a sentence. What kind of monster was she that she could love Stefan so much, even knowing he had caused something like this? Palimia was not his only victim.

"I am so very sorry. I... I have nothing to give you comfort or aid, except maybe this. My information involves a threat to Dorilian's life." If seeing what little color remained in Palimia's face drain away meant anything, it was that Emyli was being taken seriously. "Promise me you will tell no one but him, and not reveal that I am the source, and I will tell you all that I know about this plot."

Palimia's gaze, from eyes sunk into bony sockets, assessed Emyli anew. "You are terribly conflicted."

Emyli blinked tears. "Dorilian is going to know who originated this plot. I know him, and… whatever happens, whether you tell him or don't and this thing comes to pass… I have to stop the plot from killing anyone. From killing *him*—and his son." She saw Palimia's horror deepen. "Yes, the plot targets them *both*. The man and the child. I cannot even believe I am saying this. I just know that if Dorilian survives, he is going to reach his own conclusions. I cannot prevent him from assigning blame. And yet, whatever comes of it, this is what I must do. The Sordaneons *must* survive, they and the Rill. Do you understand why that matters? I do."

Palimia nodded. "Marc believed this above all else. He spoke of it often. Even his last words."

Emyli gasped. "You know them? What were they?"

"'*Run, damn you!*'" Palimia masked a laugh at Emyli's expression. "He wanted Dorilian to live, don't you see? And all Dor wanted to do was to save *him*. But only Marc succeeded. Dor failed, and he's not used to that. He has never gotten past that Marc would not take his hand." Her next words trembled with feeling. "I even saw and heard. Not in person, of course. More like an image and voices in my head."

"He's a projective empath."

"Yes, and on that day, those memories broke free."

I want you to know I tried to save him. Dorilian had extended his hand and begged Marc Frederick to take it—and Emyli knew why her father had not. She still had Dorilian's note, written by hand, maybe *that* hand, right after. Tears welled hot behind her eyes. "Oh, Mia. Thank you for telling me."

"And I thank you, for letting me know that Marc's heart still beats in this world."

Too overcome to speak, Emyli nodded and wiped at her eyes. When Palimia reached out, Emyli took those chill, thin fingers, bone wrapped in skin, and clasped them.

"For Marc, and for another man I also love, I will give the promise you ask. I will pass along your warning and not unveil who told me. I will protect you too." Palimia's jaw set grimly. "Now, what of this plot?"

42

Heat from the metal framing had been building for some time in the resonator and had reached the melting point. Though his arcanely sheathed fingers screamed to drop the tool, Nammuor inhaled and tensed but did not deviate from his task. A shaving of precious living matrix morphed and clasped the even more precious housing of the immortal blood crystal, grafting it onto the Diadem. The crystal immediately glowed a deep, fulgent red. He dropped the tool, which bounced and scorched a path across the workshop's stone floor. Balathu, recently risen to rival Oarzas as a talented Archmage, pounced upon the tool and scooped it into a deathstone bowl wherein it would do no harm. Nammuor tugged his hand free of the partly melted diffuser net, removing skin as well, and dropped the device to the floor. He frowned at the blisters on his fingers.

More burns that would take weeks to heal. But he had accomplished the needed task. The last of ten Highborn blood crystals blazed alongside its brothers in the Diadem's crown.

Finished. Or at least as far as he could currently take it.

"Beautiful." Balathu stood respectfully behind Nammuor and gazed with wonder upon the device. Something slightly... covetous lurked within his admiration.

"Yes." Nammuor hated that his right hand had begun to ooze. The thought of touching the Diadem with evidence of mortal weakness unsettled him. Such were the demands the crown made of his body that it was conceivable it might someday find him wanting. For now, however, the device enhanced him so well he had become a marvel.

He walked to the Great Mirror and activated the pairing to Aral. The chamber upon which he spied no longer resembled an aristocratic salon but appeared to be completely prepared for his needs. Of particular importance was an immense device that took up half the room and glowed faintly red with the energy of raw, arcanely-contained, volcanic effluvium. Only the most advanced of Aryati arts could have achieved such a masterpiece, and only under the influence of superior direction. Nammuor would test the chamber on a few slaves or captives before using it himself.

But use it he must. The Diadem sapped his body with every use. *Soon.*

With the deaths of the last Malyrdeons, Essera had plunged into even greater disorder. Stefan relied more and more on his Khelds and either did not notice or care about the extent to which he had alienated his kingdom's powerful nobles. Only a deep and abiding loyalty to the memory of the Malyrdeons and their Stauberg-Randolph graft onto the royal dynasty kept the population loyal. The Wall still stood—and the Wall had given them the Stauberg-Randolphs to rule them. Stubborn as that tradition was, Nammuor knew it could be broken.

He signaled an acolyte for healing materials and wrapped his right hand with gauze. The pain was bearable and would soon succumb to the restorative properties of his chamber here. Balathu approached with a slender box.

"Master."

Ah yes. Arcane crystals. Two of the Diadem's sources of energy were not bound to Leur. Those must be replaced if consumed. Nammuor could see the difference as he gazed upon his triumph, but there was nothing to be done about it, not at this moment.

"Give that to the slave and send it ahead," he said. He watched as Balathu placed the box in the hands of a naked, healthy pureblood male. The slave vanished when Balathu lightly touched the crystal at its ear.

Other youths, two of them Nammuor's preferred body servants, had gone ahead with more personal items.

"Send reports, as I have instructed." Nammuor had been extremely clear on that score. "Especially about movement on Othgol's border. I do not want the Sordaneon to take advantage of my divided attention."

"Indeed, Master. Your generals wear your Eyes with pride. You will know all they see and do."

"Zel will be here in a few weeks. Outfit him and his officers for Aral."

Balathu bowed.

With gauzed right hand and naked left, Nammuor lifted the Diadem and placed it upon his head. The weight of the device was now familiar and welcome. The fearsome brow piece with its huge deep-set ruby and space-black points settled above his eyes. In the polished surface of the Mirror he saw the fierce red glow of a crown of high, blood-filled spikes that gave him the look of a menacing god.

Stefan, he was certain, had never met a god.

Dorilian turned over the letter he had just read and, finding nothing on the back of the page, handed it to Tiflan. He had just that morning returned to Sordan from a respite at his estate of Rhondda on the southern end of the island, during which time he had not received petitioners of any kind. He had not intended to do so today. This one, however…

He studied the kneeling man who waited, hands in lap and head bowed. This throne—this room—was one Dorilian used for informal audiences, but that did not make the floor less hard. Sinon Kouranos conveyed not even the slightest discomfort.

"You are offering to serve me?" Dorilian looked to Tiflan, who nodded. That was what the letter said.

"Yes, Your Thrice Royal Grace. In whatever capacity you would find me useful."

Chin on fist, Dorilian considered. There were many uses to which any ruler could put a man of Sinon's skills. The question was rather the veracity of the offer. Sordan—and Sordaneon—diplomacy was one of the Hierarchate's finest weapons. Dorilian achieved far more through diplomacy than he did through military might. It would be a masterstroke if Essera could subvert this advantage by planting someone inside his corps of diplomats.

The best way to prevent this from happening was to assess the man for himself. Sinon had trained under Wall Lords and would have learned skills for concealing motives.

"I could use a trainer of horses."

"I doubt you—or anyone—would find me useful for that."

"But if I assigned you to that task, you would do it."

"Yes, Thrice Royal. To the very best of my ability."

"And if I assign you to taste my wine?"

Sinon smiled ever so slightly. "You are testing me, Thrice Royal.

You would never assign me that task as things now stand. You do not trust me yet."

There it was... the taste of truth. It differed in every person: sharp atop the words in some; subtle within emotion in others. Sinon's truth was bright and clear, embedded in principle and distinct from emotion, a cognitive texture that persuaded Dorilian to move forward.

"What if I wish you to serve as a tutor? To my Heir?"

"I would be honored, Thrice Royal."

Levyathan didn't need a tutor in politics. Dorilian had been more interested in the response. "And should I wish you to advise *me*?" That would be a greater inducement.

"I would be doubly honored. Your Thrice Royal Grace has matured a great deal and has become a discerning man."

And Sinon was being strategic in reminding Dorilian of previous acquaintance. Though from a distance, as administrator for Marc Frederick during Sordan's occupation, this man had known Dorilian as a child. After the events that had landed Dorilian at Gustan, he had conversed with Sinon under Marc Frederick's eye and been party to Sinon's appointment as Governor of Gignastha and Neuberland. Sinon had certainly studied Dorilian since, as Essera's ambassador to the Triemperal Archhalia and also during the crisis that had followed Stefan's botched assassination attempt. Dorilian had no trouble believing Sinon had, as said in his letter, resigned from Stefan's service over insurmountable differences in policy.

"Very well. I need to know more about why."

"A Wall Lord trained me. A great king showed me what it takes to do the hard work of empire. I am a diplomat. Destruction is neither my art nor my goal. I would rather build bridges between enemies, settle disputes, and promote the best qualities of my nation and people. I could no longer serve a man whose policies and actions I consider antithetical to the Triempery I have served all my life." Sinon paused, then continued. "I have noticed that you, Thrice Royal, have not renounced that Triempery."

"Why would I? Sordan is one third of the Triempery." More like one half now.

"Indeed, Thrice Royal, Sordan may be all that remains of it."

Truth emanated from the man's every word and action,

Dorilian turned to his secretary. "Have Sinon Kouranos appointed as an advisor to the Sordan Halia. I wish him to learn our City's issues and laws. The Hierarchate will pay a stipend commensurate with a senior diplomat."

The secretary scribbled.

"Is that satisfactory, Legate?"

Sinon lifted his head now that he had been named, albeit by his new title. If his face was to be believed, he was pleased. "Thank you, my Liege."

This development needed watching. For now, Sinon was well placed to become an asset. Dorilian could always use more of those, especially with the way Essera was crumbling to the foundations.

Legon appeared at the doorway and signaled for his attention. Dorilian allowed Sinon to rise and dismissed him after a few pleasantries. Legon did not even wait until the door had closed to rush to Dorilian's side.

"It's Mia. She has returned without notice and... she had herself brought here. She doesn't look well but she won't go to the Physicians. She insists on seeing you."

Palimia always informed Dorilian of her travels, in part so he could arrange for her security. This...

"Where is she?"

Legon gestured to the door. "Here, right outside. You were in conference."

"I'm not anymore. Bring her in." To Tiflan, who approached with concern, Dorilian said, "This is not like her. She is too ill to travel." He received reports from Permephedon's Physicians.

Men from the Eagle Guard, no doubt conscripted by Legon, bore a litter into the room. Palimia lay upon it, with only a light blanket to cover her and a single pillow beneath her head. Dorilian directed the men to place the litter on the room's large stone table, at which height he could see her without having to kneel. Legon ordered the men away and Tiflan left also, closing the door behind him.

"Mia." Dorilian took her hand in his. That he had not seen her in many weeks was by her choice. She knew perfectly well that if she did not leave Permephedon, he could not travel to be with her. Now he saw why she had stayed away. She was on death's threshold.

Her pale lips opened. "Dor. Don't talk. Listen."

"I—"

"Listen, if you want to live."

Palimia Kastryonis, Basarchessa of Sandalya and Enladris of Toren, patron of gardens and libraries and former mistress of an Esseran king and a Hierarch of Sordan, died on a sunny day while in the presence of a man she loved. Whether the man loved her was subject to speculation, but there was no speculation about the majesty with which he honored her remains. She had requested that the Songbird Palace be her final resting place, and so Dorilian stripped the palace from the Stauberg-Randolph holdings and took possession of it for himself. He ordered a mausoleum of blue marble built where it would be shaded and cooled in years to come by an oak tree she had planted. Marc Frederick's Oak, he thought of it. Palimia's House.

It was the only way he could bring the two of them together.

"The Prism. Just as she said." Legon pointed to the slender bridge beyond which roared the Hidden Falls and, above it, the sky-reaching pinnacles of Sordan's Citadel. The falls and the ravine into which it emptied were located entirely within the Serat and formed a natural boundary between the Hierarchal administration buildings and the private residences. Most people used a series of passages above the falls to traverse the stream and did not even know about this bridge. Only the Hierarchs and their close associates used it to cross between parts of the Serat without using public corridors. Dorilian and Levyathan used the Prism Bridge when they met each week with an eccentric scholar.

From a path below the span, Dorilian listened to Legon lay out the remainder of the plot.

"They used a powerful acid, dissolved the stones. If you look really closely, you can see. Casual observers would never notice. Put in a support—there, see?—but rigged it with a line, thin and fine as silk but stronger. The villains camped out in a cave underneath the bridge. When their targets reached the center of the bridge, they would pull out the support, which would cause all the stones to fall and the bridge would collapse."

Sending the victims to the bottom of the gorge. If the fall did not kill them, they would be finished off by the men lying in wait. Those men had been captured, taken by surprise, but had not yet revealed who had sent them.

Weeks and maybe months of plotting had gone into this.

"How did they do the work in secret?"

Legon frowned. "We don't know yet. Once inside the perimeter, the assassins would have needed to work quietly, but could have avoided patrols. That will not happen again."

No, and neither would Dorilian meet again with Zamenes in the Forecourt Garden. He doubted the scholar had been in on the plot, however. Zamene's entire body of work rested with the godborn. In the meantime, Dorilian would order construction of a new bridge.

Palimia had saved his life. Again. She had lingered a full day, during which he had not left her side. In that time she had not revealed from where or whom she had obtained knowledge of the plot. He had sent men to investigate and then talked with her about those people and projects she most loved. The Songbird Palace. A garden in Essera. Stauberg's great library.

And Marc Frederick. The man through whom they had met was with them both at the end.

Threaded through Palimia's dying thoughts, Dorilian sensed that this—this plot, this disintegration—was related in some way.

"Nammuor didn't plan this." He and Legon ascended stone stairs that would take them to the Hierarch's palace side of the gorge. "That monster wants to slash my throat personally and collect my blood into one of his damned crystals. And Lev is his Heir also. He wants him alive."

"I don't put anything past him." Legon too had been weighing possible perpetrators. "Though my coin is on that thrice-cursed Kheld in Essera."

Legon was better than Tiflan at not speaking Stefan's name. They had reached the landing. Wooden benches blocked access to the Prism. A canopy of rainbows, the reason for the bridge's name, shimmered in the misty space between it and the falls.

"Be sure."

Dorilian could not afford to overlook emergent enemies. Perhaps he had focused on Stefan too much. But this... For how many years had he and Stefan thrown spears at each other from their lofty thrones? People's lives had been lost in their exchanges. In both their lands, power had shifted, then shifted again. Never in his wildest imaginings had Dorilian thought he would live to see Essera cleansed of Highborn blood. Enreddon's sons. Rheger and Elhanan.

And now Stefan had targeted Dorilian again... and Levyathan.

The threat was clear. Whatever the reason, be it madness or terrible purpose, Stefan Stauberg-Randolph was killing off the Highborn race. Not just the men, the children too. He was within a hairsbreadth of succeeding.

Where had it started? Dorilian had not believed Stefan capable of killing Palaistea and her sons. Now he was not sure.

How had this catastrophe happened? And how was he to be rid of Stefan? Dorilian's death gift had promised Marc Frederick that he would treat the Stauberg-Randolphs as if they were his own family.

He had not killed Ermenthalia for her treachery and he would not kill Stefan. Though it might prove Dorilian's downfall, the Highborn never killed their own.

"Your king has become a problem."

Those were not words Erenor had expected to hear from Nammuor Varehos. Of course, neither had he expected to see Nammuor standing in Coram's reception room. Though the room was grand, suited to a prominent ally's ambassador, it felt too ordinary a setting for Nammuor's majesty.

"Your Royal Eminence." Erenor used the proper term for a Nuarch, as Nammuor now styled himself. No longer content to be a regent, Nammuor had assumed the Highborn title. "May I ask why you are here? King Stefan, not I, should receive you. In fact, he is here at Aral."

"We will meet soon enough."

Of course. But what did this mean? Nammuor wore a circlet upon which a host of ruby-red *lr* gems glowed with arcane power. Translocation might be the least of the abilities such a device could bestow.

Coram went to stand beside his sorcerous master. "Meetings between heads of state must, of course, be handled with decorum and delicacy."

Especially when one of the heads of state was uninvited. Erenor disliked being put in this position.

Nammuor smiled. "I am well acquainted with the Stauberg-Randolphs. I met Marc Frederick once. He surprised me. His grandson, I'm sure, will be less impressive."

He might surprise you too. The Stauberg-Randolphs had a way of doing that. Erenor did not want Stefan to surprise him, however, by walking in on this encounter. "Please understand I should not be speaking with you, about anything, without my king's knowledge. He supports our alliance and wants it to continue, but he's had setbacks politically and—"

"Yes. Killing off the Malyrdeons. I would call that a setback." Why did Nammuor's eyes narrow to unpleasant slits? The Malyrdeons had opposed the Mormantaloran alliance at every turn.

"More than that, but… yes, killing them did not help matters. Stefan is beyond fortunate that the Wall did not smite him. Scholars think the only reason it's still standing is that Ergeiron himself is Highborn. Even so, the Eleutheron has become a problem again. And just this morning a representative of the Seven Houses sent a message asking the king about an attempt to kill the Sordaneons and whether he was behind it." Erenor watched Nammuor's expression transform, alarm shunted into anger. Erenor quickly addressed the latter. "The attempt appears to have failed. Still, people aren't going to be happy about it when word gets out, with the Rill involved. The blood bond there has shown itself in the past to be intensely… reactive. If the Sordaneons should perish, no one knows what would happen to *it*."

By their silence, Erenor guessed the Mormantalorans felt similarly. Their country had no experience of the Rill as a political force and did not rely on it to the extent Essera did, but the god-machine nonetheless generated a great deal of commerce for their domains. Not to mention Nammuor's very personal investment in the Sordaneon Heir. Erenor contained a sigh and resolved to reassure them. These were his allies, at least as much as they were Stefan's. In some ways, more so.

"Having Stefan here at Aral, and holding court here, will be a good thing," he explained. "He is away from the corrupting influences of the Seven Houses and further removed from Amallar than he was at Trulo. His main Kheld nobles are here with him, of course, but at least Amallar isn't sitting across the river sending hordes of Highborn-hating sycophants his way."

Coram smirked at his silent master. "Their king is rather too close to that bearded lot."

Erenor shot him a frown. "Don't dismiss all of them."

Nammuor had other concerns. "You are an intelligent man. Surely you can think of someone better suited to rule this degenerate kingdom than that lowborn clod."

"I am not answering that. Now that the Malyrdeon princes are dead, the only legitimate claimants to Essera's crown are Marc Frederick's heirs—or the Sordaneons." Did Nammuor anticipate putting his nephew on Essera's throne as well as Sordan's? Erenor would stand against that ambition as vigilantly as he would against Dorilian himself.

He watched Nammuor walk to a bookcase opposite the marble fireplace. Long fingers, elegantly ringed, passed slowly along the spines of leather-bound tomes arrayed in neat rows. "Dorilian is quite the thorn of the question, don't you think? A vindictive man. He could have created this rumor you mentioned as a diversion, a means by which to harm your king." Nammuor stopped his browsing to look back at Erenor for a response.

"That's possible. Stefan will surely claim as much." Erenor could hear it already. A sigh filled his chest as he realized he would soon be pushing forward just such a defense to Stefan's irate nobles.

"Do you believe Stefan did try to kill him?" Nammuor left the impressive array of books behind. "Of course, you do. You do not even have to say it. And it won't be surprising, not in the least, when Dorilian believes it too... or when he strikes back. Because he will. I hope your king is prepared for that event. I hope you are."

Better than you know. There was no point in apprising Nammuor of Erenor's foresight in securing the Stauberg-Randolph regency. Keeping that prize out of Kheld hands had been a crucial move. That Erenor might also take royal power into his own hands was a tantalizing prospect. He was silently congratulating himself when he saw the glance Nammuor shared with Coram, answered by a slight nod of the latter's head. Only then did Erenor see the trap they had laid and into which he had fallen. His breath thickened in his throat.

One night over drinks, he and Coram had talked about the vagaries of succession, the paucity of heirs and unreliability of politics. He had shared his doubts and entertained the idea that he would be the most qualified to serve as regent. Loyal. Capable. Trusted. Unbeholden to Khelds or the Seven Houses. And ambitious... he had admitted to that, too.

Erenor licked his lips and looked up to see Coram holding out a small goblet of silver.

"The king is going on a hunt in the morning, I hear." Coram insisted Erenor take the drink. "Will you be riding with him?"

Somehow, he wasn't quite sure how, Erenor kept his hand steady. He looked from one man to the other.

Nammuor's black gaze commanded his. "Don't."

43

Stefan patted the neck of his horse and waited for the hunt master's horn. The ancient forest of Aral that abutted the Halasseon Serat loomed before him, drenched with mist. That condensation swelled over land chilled by the domain's guardian mountains. Dawn barely pushed above lofty peaks already crowned with snow. The royal party had reined in at the meadow's edge. Harnesses clanked as horses snorted and stamped.

A good day for a hunt. He had just heard the night before that Essera's Halia had declared him Prince of Stauberg, though his assumption of that title was sure to be challenged. Even so, Stefan had much to celebrate and not just his birthday. After so many years spent with his grandfather's long reign as the only validity to which he might lay claim, he had finally established his own rule and held genuine power in his hands.

"The Aegis of Fortune smile upon you, sire." Lucien wore a pheasant's feather in his red cap. "The huntsman claims some of the great stags of the deep forest have been seen near here. They seek the forest edges for the winter."

"Hear that, Cullen?" Stefan grabbed his bow from the saddle rack. "The Staubauns' munificent god Imenos has finally decided I'm worthy of royal quarry."

"Took him long enough." Cullen turned in the saddle to take in the ghostly veils obscuring the forest. "I don't like the look of this. This murk's so thick we'll see neither the game nor each other."

"The hunt master says the mist will lift with the dawn.

Meanwhile, the beasts feel safe in it and come out from the forest in greater numbers. Erenor planned the hunt with that in mind."

"And just where did he get to?"

"Says there was trouble at the port. He's still Bas of Aral, you know. Things come up." Stefan checked that his hunting knife was well secured to his belt.

A Kheldman bearing a spear rode up. "A fine day for hunting!" Even after several years at Stefan's court, Lowen failed to use proper address. His slips were so numerous Stefan's Staubaun courtiers seldom called him on it anymore. "There'll be feasting tonight!"

"As long as it be venison, and not boar," said Lucien, eyeing the crossbar on the spear.

"Lucien's anticipating his catch," Stefan said to Goff, who guffawed.

"As do all men, or we would catch nothing." Goff's quiver bristled with arrows and the large black horse he rode was one of several gifted by the client king of Merced months ago. "Will we have the grace of Nilla's company this evening?"

"I don't see why not." Stefan inhaled the pungent, autumnal scents of the meadow. "Nilla is feeling quite well these days, and the baby's due next month."

He had high hopes that this child would be the son he so desperately needed. Not only had Faetha Caohme's runes predicted a boy, but so had the flower petals of Aral's Staubaun surgeon. Furthermore, Nilla had been on a diet of sour fruits and honey, and only red meats that had not aged—all known to favor the birthing of boys. At Asphalladra's suggestion, she drank neither wine nor beer, but only clear water.

Stefan wondered if it would be safe for his queen to travel back to Gustan. Having her at his court was a boon that kept the edge off his temper, and sea air was good for any woman's health, but Gustan was safer. His assassination plot against the Sordaneons had failed and now he must guard against retaliation. Even apart from Gustan's reputed magic, Dorilian was unlikely to attack the Manor or do anything malicious on its premises.

His mother was due to arrive any day. Stefan would send Nilla back to Gustan with her. He had been born at Gustan, and his son would be born there also.

The hunt master, dressed in green, shouted aloud the hunt rules, though the party drowned him out with banter and calls to hurry it up. At last the man yielded and sounded the trumpet. In unison, the hunters lifted high their great curved drinking horns, some gilded or jeweled, each used only for the hunt. Stefan's, shaped like a stag's hoof, gleamed as he drained it of mead. He handed it to one of the boys who would stay behind with the horses and gear.

Beaters waited deeper in the forest, along the runs. Stefan heard dogs bawl in the distance as they worked to flush the deer out into the meadow. Hunters staked positions. Some were there only for the easy kill. Other hunters, though, went into the trees, hoping to find better sport. Stefan ran ahead and into the woods with Cullen at his side. Though Cullen's footfalls were steady and determined, his expression was less so. He kept looking behind them.

"I don't like these trees. It's too dark under here. No growth, no nothing."

"Good. We'll see our stag." Stefan clutched at his bow.

"Not in this light, we won't. We're more likely to fall in a pit." Cullen looked to every side where carpets of pine needles muffled every sound and trees towered like black columns wreathed by smoke. "I'm going back."

Though he hated to do it, Stefan turned back with him. As they retraced their steps toward the meadow, the mist thickened and rose up to hide them even from each other. Stefan stopped in his tracks when he heard the hunt master's horn. His pulse quickened with knowledge that game had been spotted. Somewhere in the woods or meadow, the beaters were driving the quarry toward the hunters. He wanted to be there with them. Spotting a shadow on the path ahead where Cullen had gone, he trotted after it. "Cullen! Wait up!"

The forest loomed taller, thick with old giants. What surrounded Stefan was so ancient it remembered the world before humans had returned to reclaim it. Obscured by heavy mists that condensed on branches and dripped rain-heavy onto the sodden pine needle floor, even his footsteps were silent.

Where had Cullen gone to? Bare heartbeats had passed since they had been disagreeing about whether to leave.

Stefan looked around for anything familiar and an eerie disquiet awakened. It was possible to get lost in these old woods. The close air smelled like rotting things. All at once his heart pounded hard against his ribs, beneath his jacket, and he could barely breathe. He reached for his waterskin and lifted it to take a drink of mead, but the heavy brew did not stop his head from aching or lift the hush from the world. On the edges of his vision, the forest thickened with shadows and tilted.

No. This could not be happening. Whatever this was... should not be happening. He fell to hands and knees, down to where the air tasted of mold and spores. Red moisture welled up from the ground he touched, like blood. It was then, as he lifted his head, that he saw the stag. The beast stepped in front of him and stopped. Silver legs with hooves of gold. Stefan looked up to see its golden rack, perfect points free of velvet above a regal head and ruby eyes. Eyes filled with blood.

Stefan jerked back his hands and stumbled to his feet. "Cullen!" With wet hands stained red, he fumbled for his hunting dagger and drew it forth.

All around him the trees glowed crimson. His flesh ran cold as he realized what was happening. *Magic.* Highborn and cold. Dorilian... the bastard had broken his promise and come after him.

"Show yourself, you bastard! Haven't I suffered enough? What more do you want?"

Only laughter answered.

The stag lowered its head and charged, its great silver ruff shining across massive shoulders. Stefan's cry split the forest silence as golden points pierced him yet did not pierce him at all. He felt no pain as the impact threw him backward onto the ground. Something inside him trickled and burned. He struggled to sitting and clutched his dagger. The creature stood over him, hoary gray head inches from Stefan's own. Foul breath billowed from red nostrils, penetrated by the glow of malevolent eyes. Stefan's breath bucked in his throat, a living thing that struggled to break free. His dagger slipped from fingers suddenly numb.

Where the stag had stood, another shape—human and terrifying—stepped forward. Tall. White-haired. Robed with shadow beneath a blood-red crown.

No.

Its voice caressed him.

"You chose the wrong prey, half-man. He's not for you. That prize I want for myself." Eyes black with hate narrowed upon Stefan. "Now die as you have lived."

Pulled by some outside force, Stefan's breath flowed from him, white in the murk as it streamed into a sanguineous dawn. Though he screamed to the edge of forever, he had no voice. Only an animal wail escaped his throat. But he had command of his body. Leaping to his feet, he fled on legs that once again obeyed his will.

Laughter followed him, along with a voice more terrible than any he had ever heard. "Run, fool! Run! You did my work for me. Sordan stands alone!"

Stefan shouted, but only a croak came from his throat. *Cullen!*

He stumbled and fell. His hands plunged to the wrist in pine needles and litter. When he looked down, he saw that his arms were misshapen, furred and brown, and he no longer had hands but hooves. Cloven, golden nubs. *No, no… how?* He groped one with the other and felt hands… fingers, thumbs. So why did he see hooves? He jumped back onto his feet… and saw those too were furred and hooved. But his body moved the same as before, as fast as before, as he dashed away.

He ran on two legs, but some madness had come upon him. With every leap and stride he saw four bestial legs… four hooves cutting into the earth.

Cullen!

Like a dream giving way to a new day, the forest opened before him. Light beckoned between the trees. Stefan broke from the woods into the clear cold morning of the meadow, mist rolling back as the hunt master had said it would. Horns sounded, announcing the shadowy forms of hunters and their dogs. The hounds bayed as they leapt ahead. To a man, the hunters readied their bows.

What did they see? Did they see Stefan at all? But even he didn't see clothing or skin or a man.

Lowen! Goff!

Stefan's kinsmen did not acknowledge him. They laughed to each other, the bloodlust of the hunt upon them. Stefan saw Cullen, then Lucien, run up to join them. Cullen too lifted his bow and reached for an arrow.

Stefan staggered as the first arrows sank deep shafts into his chest and flank. One bolt found his throat. Instinct alone propelled him, and he turned and bounded away across the field toward the lodge. With hounds baying on his heels, he coughed blood but ran his hardest, dragging one leg, to reach that haven. But the hounds were faster. Red pain blinded him as sharp teeth ripped into his shoulder and he struck out in terror. He saw a golden stag hoof strike the hound, one of his favorites. It fell silent. Then another dog was on him, its powerful jaws clamped on his thigh, tearing at it until muscles and tendons ripped free and brought him down. His cries were but brays in the sodden first light.

Within moments, men were upon him.

"Where's Stefan?" Cullen shouted to the others. "He's going to miss the kill!"

Men grabbed hold of Stefan's hair. Someone chortled about a rack of golden horn. Stefan felt his head forced backward toward his shoulders. The move exposed his helpless throat.

He rolled his eye to Cullen, begging. They had been boys together! Fought and laughed and made love to the same woman. He tried to speak but only bleating and bloody froth came from his mouth. He heard laughter and congratulations, tried to struggle but couldn't when he felt the knife put to his throat.

Cullen... please.

The last thing Stefan saw was his childhood friend's face, freckles tan across his nose and the trusted blue eyes grim for the kill, before Cullen plunged the knife and his lifeblood flowed from his throat in gouts of gore.

"The king has gone on a hunt, Your Royal Highness, along with most of his court." Trevor followed a single protective step behind Emyli as they ascended the grand staircase of the Halasseon Serat. Blue stone, a favorite building material of Malyrdeon rulers, surrounded them with soaring arches and vaulted ceilings.

Though it was late morning, most hunts took place at dawn. Stefan had probably spent the night at the Halasseon hunting lodge. Emyli was familiar with the lodge from times her father had used it. She would not be seeing Stefan, then, for hours.

"Why are you not with him?"

"To oversee protection here, Ma'am. His Majesty elected for young Captain Lowenson to head his guard."

"Ah. Then I will take this opportunity to visit the queen."

"Yes, Ma'am. From what I understand, she's been hoping you would soon arrive."

Poor Nilla was probably bored out of her skull. In the name of protecting her pregnancy, Stefan had all but consigned her to bed rest. It didn't help that Nilla's favorite lady in waiting, Asphalladra, had gone back to Wyre to be with her children. Emyli had visited Asphalladra on the way from Dazunor-Rannuli. Upon reaching her suite of rooms, Emyli thanked Trevor and spent some time freshening from travel. She had come as quickly as she could after meeting with Palimia and had learned just this morning that their gamble had succeeded.

And for what, if Dorilian figures out that Stefan was behind it.

She put all her faith on a dead king's hope and a promise written in blood.

Minutes later, as Emyli walked from her rooms in the royal wing to the Queen's apartment, she noted a flurry of activity. Fredda, one of Nilla's ladies, burst through the door, wild-eyed, and ran past the confounded footman.

"Emyli! Emyli! Come now! Something's wrong with Nilla!" Fredda grabbed Emyli's hand and ran with her, again past the footman, into the apartment.

A mad dash took them through the antechamber and reception room, past the wardrobe and into the bedchamber. There she saw Nilla in a sheer white gown upon the bed, unmoving as she gasped for breath and stared with eyes like black pools. Her lips parted, struggling to form words. Faetha Caohme, who was attending this pregnancy, reached out a hand to summon Emyli near.

"It happened just now. She took a potion he gave her. From you, he said."

A potion? "Who said?" Emyli had only just arrived that hour and spoken only to Trevor.

"Your son, King Stefan. He was just here." Caohme picked up a vial from the table beside the bed.

Emyli did not take it from her. She had heard of these symptoms. From Rheger and Palaistea. From Marenthro when she had demanded to know how her father had died. *The poison would have killed him, but he died from the fall.* The others, however... The Highborn had died from fire and blast and murder because of that poison, a poison that did things like this. Dilated pupils. Paralysis. All who had not been Highborn had died from it directly. Emyli fell to her knees beside the bed and gazed into Nilla's pleading eyes.

"Was it Stefan who gave this to you? Blink. Once for yes. Twice for no."

Nilla's lids lowered. Once, then stared. *Stefan.*

Impossible, Emyli thought. But another question needed to be asked. "Did he say it was from me?"

Nilla blinked once, then gulped for air, but did not blink again.

"She lost movement a few minutes after the king left, and speech with it. Oh no... Breathe, child! Breathe!" Caohme slapped Nilla's still face, but the queen did not draw another breath. She did not move at all. Her eyes merely stared, filled with terror, until they faded.

"We must save the child!" Caohme reached to draw up Nilla's gown, but Emyli grasped her wrist.

"It won't matter. The poison is in the baby too. It will never draw breath." *My grandchild. Stefan's heir. Who would do such a thing?* Not Dorilian, surely... or would he, in retaliation for Stefan's attempt to kill him and the boy?

"No, no... there must still be something!" Caohme placed her ear on Nilla's distended abdomen to listen for the baby's heart. At this point a trained ear would be able to hear one. Emyli wept and knew better than to try.

Oh, dear Mother of us all, am I to blame? That monster knows of this drug, saw it used... but would he use it? Will he go after Stefan, too?

After a minute, Caohme pulled her hand away. "No heartbeat. Mother or child." She was Amallar's most renowned practitioner of the healing arts and if anyone could have heard proof of life, it was she. The devastated gaze she turned on Emyli held as many questions as tears. "What poison did this?"

Melsajra. But Emyli was not ready to explain how she knew of such a thing. "It's forbidden. Almost impossible to make."

"Yet you put it in a potion for her to take?"

"What? No, of course not! I only arrived less than an hour ago. And Stefan—" Was not here either. The hunting lodge was a half day ride away. Stefan could not have been here. Cold realization flooded Emyli's body and limbs. "Why do you say he gave her this potion?"

Caohme drew the sheeting up to conceal Nilla's dead form. Her manner remained guarded. "I saw him myself. I was here when he gave it to her."

"Are you sure it was Stefan?"

"As sure as you would have been. I'm surprised you did not pass him in the hallway."

But Emyli had not passed him. Could not have passed him—not if he was at the hunt. Only one explanation explained how *anyone* could have seen her son in this room. A look-alike... or illusion. But a look-alike, she would have seen. And if illusion had been used....

Not Dorilian—at least not directly. One of the great gifts of the Highborn, innate to them, was that any reality to which they were proximate assumed its true form. Even the speaking of lies became so difficult people handed over the truth. A Highborn prince could not create a falsehood even for another to wear. Why had Emyli studied them for so long, if not to be able to differentiate between supernatural threats?

Dorilian would be blamed, of course. How not? Stefan had always blamed him for everything. But Emyli knew the menace that had murdered Nilla came from elsewhere. Now at last she faced her family's real enemy.

"Leave here," she said to Caohme. "Leave at once."

The healer stood with arms crossed. "I will not. Not while the poor child—"

"The poor child is dead, and you soon will be if you do not leave. They will blame it on you." Emyli turned to unmoving Fredda, who still stood nearby and had overheard all. "You too."

"She's dead? And the babe too?" Pale with fear and breathing raggedly, Fredda clearly had yet to believe it.

"Yes." .

"And what about you, Princess?"

Emyli had thought that through. "The footman saw you grab me from the hall while screaming that something was wrong with the Queen. So did the guard at the end of the corridor. Commander Allen was with me the whole time before that. Stefan will know that I could not possibly have done this."

What she needed, and soon—though the news he encountered would break his heart—was for Stefan to return.

44

Word of Stefan's death reached the Halasseon Serat before the body. So did the prisoners, brought in by wagon and taken to the guardhouse under heavy watch. Emyli stood on the landing with the Serat staff and Nilla's remaining ladies. Though Caohme had stayed, Fredda had taken Emyli's advice and fled. Erenor, who had gone to the lodge upon hearing of the disaster, rode in with the remains of his king.

"Princess, I beg you. Do not look."

Erenor looked haggard and marked by what he had seen. Anguish haunted his dark eyes. Emyli had never trusted him before and did not trust him now. She had seen her father's corpse and her brother's. Emyli steeled herself to look upon her son's. What she saw made her close her eyes, though she would never, for the rest of her life, remember him otherwise. Stefan's own hunters had taken trophies and mutilated his body as if he were a beast. His hands and feet had been cut off and lay upon his splayed ribs and his viscera replaced with haste into his gutted abdomen. Blood from his slashed throat soaked his rent and ruined garments.

The prisoners, she was told, swore they had killed a stag. Cullen had been running around waving as his hunt trophy the severed hand of his friend.

"I have seen enough." Emyli listened to the corpse being covered before she opened her eyes again.

"I think we both know treason when we see it, Princess."

"Yes."

"The killers and their accomplices will be executed, of course."

Erenor sounded so sure she would agree. The only treason Emyli was sure about was his. Though Erenor's part was not yet clear to her, she knew he had not been present at the hunt. Why? So he could rid himself not only of his king but of those nobles and kinsmen most likely to stand in his way? If this was the case, she too was in peril.

Being Marc Frederick's daughter would not protect her from this man—but she was not defenseless.

"Please bear with me." Emyli did not need to feign weakness when she laid her hand upon his arm to make her plea. "I—I simply cannot... Nilla and now Stefan."

Erenor moved quickly to provide comfort. "I will see to everything. Send notices, arrange for transportation of the body. Will you travel with him?"

"Yes." There was no question as to where Stefan must go. Every Esseran king, including Marc Frederick, had lain in state where the Highborn were so honored. "We will take him to Permephedon."

As Emyli had been sure he would, Erenor left her to her grief. A woman's grief. A mother's sorrow. He found it easy to believe that her devastation would be so deep, her sadness so extreme, it would blind and cripple her. Once in her rooms, Emyli summoned Trevor.

"Commander Allen. The king, your liege and my son, is dead. Though I do not know what the future holds, I would be deeply grateful if you would return to my service, as Commander of my Guard."

Trevor knelt and bowed his head. "Your Royal Highness, it is my honor to accept. From the days of my great-grands, my family has served the Stauberg-Randolphs, and I have no desire other than to uphold that tradition."

"Thank you. I had hoped you would stay with me."

While he waited in her antechamber, Emyli went to her dressing room to put on a gown of black wool. She always carried one in her wardrobe should need arise. So attired, she covered her head with a long veil of sheer black silk that concealed her well enough. She would draw little notice in a palace filled with women draped in the same manner. Identity obscured, she left her rooms with Trevor at her side.

A short walk brought them to the guardhouse. There she demanded to see one of the prisoners.

"Who is she?" the officer in charge asked Trevor, whom he knew. The Commander had not changed his uniform.

"Someone who gets to visit whomever she pleases."

The cell to which the officer led Emyli, and outside of which Trevor took up a post as guard, was small and stark and cold, a closet built of stone and iron, but it had light and air through a small, high window. The man seated on the cot stood the moment she swept the veil from her face.

"Oh, Lady. No. Oh no... please. I can't—" Cullen collapsed to the floor, head on his hands as he openly wept. He still wore the clothes he had worn on the hunt, with Stefan's blood on them. They had let him wash his hands.

Emyli went to sit on the cot, her skirt a pool of black about her feet. "Cullen, please. Come here, oh don't be afraid. Come." She coaxed him until he knelt before her. She drew his head to her lap, where he lay, dark-curled and sobbing, arms clutched around her legs.

"I didn't know. I didn't know... oh gods... the things I did! I killed him."

"I know."

"Oh Mother's Mercy, how can you even look at me?"

Because she must. She had begged him to return to Stefan's side. "You didn't know, how could you have? None of you did." Cullen. Goff. Lucien. Lowen. Fredda's husband too. Nine men in all were to be executed in the morning. So was *Faetha* Caohme, who had been arrested an hour ago.

"Don't be kind. Please don't be. I—I slit his throat. I cut off... Oh Mother! He watched me do it and I never saw—"

"Hush," she said, though she meant to quiet only his guilt and not his voice. Seeing Cullen grapple with knowing what he had done was as terrible as watching him die. "You loved him. You were like brothers."

"I'd rather have killed myself."

"I know that. He knew it too."

Cullen snuffled back tears and lifted his head to gaze at Emyli with wet, pain-hollowed eyes. "No, Lady. That's not what he knew there at the end. He knew he was fucked." Cullen wiped at his nose. "You should get out of here. Get out while you can. Leave this place and run as far as you can go. Run fast! Whatever did that—" Horror welled to replace grief. "They got him good. The perfect stag, so damn beautiful, the sort men kill to put on their walls. Whoever wanted him dead, that person didn't even *do* it. He had us do it for him! That's how evil it was. And Erenor, that cold bastard, he's finishing the job." He barked a laugh and shook his head as if at something mad.

"Cullen—"

"Listen to me. You leave Hans where he is—wherever he is, this world or the next one, it doesn't matter! Leave him there! 'Cuz you'll lose him too, the minute you bring him back."

Now that he had recovered enough composure to make even that kind of sense, Emyli pressed him. "Do you have any idea who might be behind this?"

Cullen sniffled again but looked her in the eye. "No. I mean, besides the Highborn, who can work that kind of thing?"

Nammuor. But Emyli would not say that name aloud. Not here. She could not save Cullen, but she could still save herself.

Emboldened by her silence, he ventured a question. "Is it true what I hear? That Nilla's dead too?"

"Yes." Truth was what this man needed. "An illusion also. A cruel one that gave her poison. She thought it was Stefan. *Faetha* Caohme saw him also."

"Aw, damn." Cullen's gaze, already haunted, turned sick. "No, no, no. It's killing us all. There's no fighting something like that."

"I'm going to try," she said.

Without warning, Cullen grabbed her hands between his and brought them to his face. Beseeching and warm, his mouth pressed her fingers. "Then you're the only one. No one else even believes me. Please, I'm going to ask, though I got no right at all after what I did. I'll soon be dead myself. I'm so damn lost. Help my wife, I beg you. Phalla and my little ones. I won't be around and—" He choked up again. "The Thegnkeld can't help her much—won't want to, probably, being she's Staubaun—and for sure not against what's coming."

Emyli combed her fingers through his hair and pushed it back from his forehead. All these years she had loved him almost like a son, like Stefan. Like Jonthan. Like so many men she couldn't save. She had been unable to save her own child or grandchildren—but maybe she could save Cullen's. "I will do whatever I can," she promised.

Cullen reached back his hands and pulled a chain out from under his shirt, lifting it over his head to hand it to her. "Would you give this to her, to Phalla? She'll know it was never my choice to leave. I promised to be with her all my life, and I guess I was. But I can't be there for the rest of hers, and I can't protect her."

Gold weighed heavy in her hand. The substantial chain held an amulet both beautiful and striking, a lump of polished ivory ringed by Rill glyphs. Emyli blinked back tears as she tucked it into the small velvet pouch at her belt. Though she did not wish to leave, she could not stay much longer.

"I must go," she said. She would see none of the other men. She kissed Cullen on the forehead. "Mother's Blessings, Cullen Brodheson, and Lud give you strength. May your spirit find its way home to dwell in peace."

Goodbye, Stefan. Emyli whispered her son's name as she walked away from the guardhouse and the condemned men it held. Stefan stood before the Mother now, his deeds to be pinned upon his shade. *I cannot help you anymore.*

She was done with promises and obligations to dead men. It was time to tend to the living.

"Good news." Legon handed over a message. The Gate of Wings that loomed behind his back framed him like a divine being. "You can travel to Essera again."

"What are you saying?" From astride Caillessar, Dorilian reached over to take the piece of paper. He had just returned from the harbor. The *Vata*'s maiden voyage had been a success. Dorilian had spared no expense over the five years it had taken to build the vessel: shipwrights had strapped the hull with Sordaneon silver for greater stability and fashioned the masts from tall silver spruces chosen by master shipbuilders in Gweroyen. Those features, and design innovations inspired by his voyage on the ill-fated *Raudra*, had resulted in a formidable warship. His personal banner now flew above that of the Hierarchate on her stern.

The message was scribbled, probably from one of his informants among the Epoptes who had gotten it off a Rill communique. Upon reading, Dorilian resumed his ride toward the Serat. Legon fell in on his right, mirroring Tiflan's place on Dorilian's left. People lined the way, kept at a distance by the remainder of their guard.

Stefan dead.

That... seemed unlikely. Dorilian could not envision his adversary as other than alive and annoying. "Has anyone verified this?" He looked to Legon, whose face remained expressionless, before he handed the message to Tiflan.

Tiflan's brow furrowed. "If this is true, we will hear more—and soon."

By the time they entered the Serat and walked its wide corridors, the news had been verified. Diplomats and gossip mongers converged on the Sordaneon seat, seeking to learn whether Stefan's best-known enemy was responsible. Every domain wanted to know what Dorilian might do next. The world itself would not believe he intended to do nothing.

Dorilian cancelled all audiences and meetings. Instead, he retired to his private sitting room in the seclusion of the residence and delved into swirls of rumor and conjecture in search of the truth.

"Enough of the lurid details. You know what I find offensive? That people actually believe I would kill him that way." Dorilian took a document from Tiflan, whom he had charged to sort through diplomatic inquiries and Archhalial issues. As a pragmatic—though not official—matter, Sordan was at war with Essera over Gignastha, a situation certain to be part of any blame-casting for the royal demise.

Legon perused several pages of reports on Stefan's death compiled by means of array and Rill from Sordan's network of informants throughout Essera. Dorilian could tell he spent more time on the graphic accounts.

"You would not have wanted him to be gutted, I suppose." Legon flipped to the next page.

"No. Just dead." Dorilian was happy simply to have Stefan removed from the number of problems he dealt with daily. A dead man was unlikely to seek to assassinate him again.

"They think you killed his queen, too." Legon looked up with mock rebuke. "She was pregnant."

As far as he remembered, Nilla had always seemed to be pregnant. Dorilian gave Stefan—and her—credit for trying. Stefan's reasons, however, prompted another thought.

He put aside a communique from the Bas of Leseos, a man he actively disliked. "We may not know who killed Stefan, but we do know the reason. Essera is going to need a new ruler."

"The succession is all but decided. Stefan has a brother—and Emyli too has a claim." Tiflan continued to sort through his pile of correspondence.

Another claim existed as well. Dorilian's. He had left the Sordaneon claim sitting on the shelf for years.

Legon handed over a paper on which he had been writing. "Here is something odd. Nine men are accused of shooting arrows into or striking blows against the king and will be executed. Several more accomplices to the deed, including a Master of Horse and a Kheld woman accused of being a poisoner, will also be executed. These are the names I have gathered. All of them are Stefan's close supporters. There are even some family."

Dorilian took the list and read the names. High ministers. Close friends. The Heir to Serrain. The newly minted Bas of Rannul. His attention fixed on one name. Cullen Brodheson, Archon of Heddros. Dorilian could not even put a name to what he felt. He and Cullen had not been friends—not exactly—but their lives had intersected so often Dorilian felt a connection. An understanding. Nothing about Cullen being on this list was right. Dorilian tapped the paper.

"This man… I know him well enough to be sure he would never do this thing. It makes no sense at all."

Tutto entered the room with a new batch of dispatches and unwelcome news. "You may have to make an appearance or say something soon. The antechamber to the Informal Throne Hall overflows with ambassadors. They're getting testy with each other. A war might break out."

"If one does, let them fight it out. I have more important things to unravel than their concerns."

Legon had gone back to reading. "Gsch. *This* report says the hunters who killed him claimed the king looked like a stag, not a man. Not like himself. A four-legged, antlered stag when they brought him down. That's why they cut off the hands and feet, for trophies." Tiflan too put away the papers he had been reading to hear Legon's information. "What drink or drug would cause men to believe something that bizarre?"

"They also gutted the man," Tiflan said. "That they thought him an animal fits the actions."

But what compulsion could make men do such a thing? Dorilian had studied toxins and knew of none that caused mass hallucinations of this sort. A poison would not know to single out Stefan.

"Illusion." Tutto met the three interested looks that swung his way. "We have seen it before."

Dorilian recalled the enemy ship he had encountered in the Kolpos, missed by his escort ships. "Someone cast upon this king an illusion that made him look like a *stag*?"

"Bear in mind, official accounts don't mention that part," Legon reminded them. "Nothing at all."

Tutto added the papers in his hand to the stack beside Tiflan, who frowned at how tall his reading had just gotten. "I am saying illusion is something anyone discussing the Esseran king's death should consider. It is my business to know all possible means of attack that might be made upon a person, godborn or human, and while in service to your grandfather I saw illusion demonstrated one time, by an Arch Epopte of noble birth using a device and a high-level *lr* cluster. He made himself look like a woman. Nude. Very convincing.

"Your kind"—he said to Dorilian—"cannot create illusion because of your nature, neither can it manifest in your presence. Any not godborn, however, would be susceptible."

As for possible perpetrators of such an attack, there were few to be had. The Seven Houses, who could afford exotic mage work, might want Stefan dead and his queen also, but they did not want Dorilian to be free to enter Essera again. Neither would they want him to exercise his right to claim Essera's throne. So not the Seven Houses. Essera's Purists also might want Stefan dead, and some of them might even be able to wield a *lr* device, but they would not do so in a way certain to ensnare purebloods such as the Heir to Serrain or Bas of Rannul. As for Erenor... although ambitious and certain to benefit from the removal of Stefan's inner circle, Erenor did not have the resources to purchase nor the bloodlines to use *lr* weapons.

Unless.

"Nammuor," Dorilian said. He rose and walked to the window wall overlooking a serene view of the lake. Sarkuan glowed soft silver beneath a canopy of clouds.

"He *is* a sorcerer," affirmed Legon.

Tutto concurred. "Illusion is an Aryati art. Exactly where his talents lie."

"And he has devices." The Undying Crown among them. Dorilian was sure now. "He has been making inroads into Essera for well over a year, maybe longer. Their stupid king invited him in. Against good advice not to, I might add."

"What will you do?" Tiflan asked.

Yes, what?

Dorilian turned to Tutto. "Tell the mob of ambassadors that we are saddened by the death of Essera's king and his queen, and that we share the deep grief of Essera's people during this difficult time. Tell them also that I will not be meeting with any of them until after Essera's king has been properly mourned and laid to rest."

Tutto bowed and left to deliver his news.

To Tiflan, Dorilian said, "Fucking Stefan. He gave away the kingdom. Now I have to do something."

45

"Erenor seeks to be made ward over my children. Are they going to let him do that?"

Wearing a mourning dress of midnight silk with sleeves and hems of purple velvet, tasteful and modest, Asphalladra sobbed in Emyli's arms. Hair the color of spun gold spilled from Asphalladra's pinned back widow's veil.

"Don't mind anything that man says or does," Emyli counseled. They were alone and away from the scrutiny of other eyes. "The children are safe, remember? We hid them where none will look."

Asphalladra nodded, but her gaze remained desperate. "My own father supports turning them over. He is pushing for me to marry Kondros Bragord. You know why. They want to put Wulf aside to make *that* man Archon of Heddros."

Of course. When the powerful fell, so did all that they possessed… and most often into the hands of people far worse.

The reception room to which Emyli had brought Asphalladra was completely secure and private, as only spaces in the High Citadel could be. This chamber was used by the Kings of Essera during their visits to Archhalia sessions. For now, Emyli alone could make use of it. Until the Archhalia decided otherwise, only the Stauberg-Randolphs stood to inherit the kingdom.

"There is still a great deal to be done here today," Emyli assured the distraught young woman. "If I succeed, you will be with your children tonight."

Nearly six weeks had passed since Stefan's death. During that time Emyli had seen her son lie in state at Permephedon and be accorded the honors he was due. She had received the condolences of his kingdom's highest nobles and many rulers of distant lands. Though people had speculated Dorilian might make an appearance, he had not; instead, Sordan had sent a representative from their Halia. Though many Khelds had pleaded with her to do so, Emyli had known better than to petition for Stefan to be interred alongside her father in the Vault of Incorruption. Instead she had accompanied Stefan's body and that of Nilla to Dazunor-Rannuli and downriver to Gustan, where she had seen them laid to rest in the mausoleum with Jon and Moreen. The same vault where someday she, too, would be buried.

Serving as Emyli's lady-in-waiting, Asphalladra had been with her the whole time, assisting with a busy schedule of ceremonies and meetings and arrangements to be made. The Cullenson children also had moved with them, from place to place until, somewhere along the way and through Emyli's connections, they had simply gone missing. Though questioned and threatened with consequences, Asphalladra claimed no knowledge of where they were. She would never tell for as long as they were in danger.

In Asphalladra and her children, Emyli saw reflections of her own plight. Cullen's Archonate, like Essera itself, was too rich a prize to leave unpillaged. Already Erenor and the Archon of Chennor, Asphalladra's father, had determined the man they wanted in Cullen's place. Kondros Bragord was ambitious enough to wed an unwilling woman and it took no imagination to think he might murder half-Kheld heirs to ensure inheritance by one of his own.

Emyli's situation was similar. A son hidden away. An inheritance under siege. And a complicated interregnum.

"When I become Regent for Handurin, I will bring him back. Then we will set them all on their heels." Emyli walked to the room's full-length mirror and adjusted her dress. Cloth of gold beneath a black overskirt and black bodice. On her head she wore the simple but marvelous tiara her father had given her upon making her sons his heirs. *Always my Princess.*

"I will be in the room with you." Asphalladra had dried her tears and looked brave again. She managed a sad smile. "I cannot be at your side, but I will stand in the back and stare so hard at Erenor Tholeros, every hair on his body will stand on end."

Emyli laughed. "Please do. My father always said the best way to diminish anxiety about a person was to imagine them naked—but I like your way much better."

They left the room for the small anteroom that separated it from the main Archhalial Chamber, where her steward, Gareth Morgan, waited with a case of documents and box of writing implements in hand. "High interest in the domains, Your Royal Highness. Many are asking if the young prince will make an appearance."

"Not today. I must secure the regency before I will bring him back."

How she wished Marenthro had followed her wish and brought Hans back when she had first asked! Then all these questions might be already settled.

Or might that instead have been a terrible mistake? *Hans would have been at the hunt. Stefan would have kept his brother—his heir—close at hand, with him always.* Would that have changed things? Or would Erenor have found a way to execute Hans too?

Dear Mother.

Her thoughts these last several weeks—of mistakes made and might-have-beens never to be—gnawed at the last shreds of a once-vibrant hope.

"You cannot blame our people for wondering." Gareth walked at Emyli's side as they exited the room. "The late king's death, attended as it was by so much madness—"

"I know, Gareth."

She hoped that her tone conveyed she didn't want to talk about it.

An unimposing doorway opened onto the Archhalia floor. The chamber itself was grand and storied, its scale suited to statements of power and purpose. It had been the throne hall of the Aryati Hegemons before they and the First Creation had succumbed to an enemy from beyond the stars. Since the Return, it had served as seat of the Triempery. At the rear of the chamber were benches for delegates to the Archhalia from foreign lands or invested parties. Ambassadors or rulers of member domains occupied blocks of chairs and desks in the middle, with room for their advisors. At the front of the hall stood an imposing half circle of a table backed by chairs allotted to the ruling factions of the Triempery: Essera and Sordan. The seats for Mormantalorus, forfeited decades ago, sat empty.

Situated behind those seats, arrayed in power upon a broad dais of blue onyx, stood three splendid high-backed thrones. Identical in size and shape, at once beautiful and mighty, the Thrones of Light proclaimed the Triempery's origin. It was said the Three themselves had fashioned them at the dawn of the Second Creation, and that when the godborn sat upon the thrones the entire

Chamber would fill with light. In generations since, Highborn Kings, Hierarchs, and Nuarchs had graced and illuminated those seats. Marc Frederick and then Stefan, by edict of the Malyrdeons, had been the last to sit there.

Today, as suited the occasion, the Thrones were empty.

Once inside the chamber, with the private door closed behind her and Trevor standing guard, Emyli looked for a friendly face and found one. Attired in mourning colors, Kathanos Niarchos walked toward her, hands extended in greeting. He was certainly here as an advisor to his son, Estevan, who as Bas of Gweroyen was also present.

"Your Royal Highness."

"Kathanos." Emyli put her hands into his palms and squeezed his strong fingers. "I hope I can count on you this day."

He met her hope-filled gaze kindly. "You know I do not hold my domain's vote."

"But you influence he who does."

"Ah, and there is the rub. I hold memory of your father—but Estevan holds memory of your son."

Emyli ducked her head. Truth stung. Had so much of her father's reign faded that Essera would turn its back on his heirs?

With a sigh, she looked around the room. People gathered in small groups, heads together and whispers exchanged. Her sister-in-law Ionais stood with the newly widowed and visibly pregnant Basarchessa of Rannul and a somber Hebron of Lacenedon, none of whom deigned to meet Emyli's gaze. Phellan of Serrain, whose Heir Lucien had been one of the men put to death for Stefan's murder, spoke with Grenant of Dannuth. It saddened Emyli to see the Kheld ambassador, newly installed just that morning, standing alone and trying to look as though he were doing so by choice. Throughout the room, conversations melded to form a kind of anxious hum.

She scanned the room for Erenor but did not see him. It would be just like that man to sequester in one of the side chambers with missing members of the Archhalia. Indeed, Emyli didn't see the Bas of Leseos, or the Governor of the Eleutheron, or any of the Sordan domains. Not even one.

Plots hatched behind closed doors.

Voices lifted and were swallowed by movement. People turned toward the massive bronze doors of the chamber, both of which had been pulled open. That in itself was unusual. One door sufficed to allow people to enter or leave. Guards poured in, a stream of emerald silks and shining armor. Swordless, but enough soldiers to take up strong positions at every entrance and exit.

Emyli could but stand and stare.

It had been nine years since Dorilian had appeared in Essera... reason enough for the Chamber's collective inhalation. Few members of the Archhalia, mostly ruling nobles related to Highborn houses, had ever seen him in person, and those persons remembered a surly adolescent prince, not a Highborn ruler in his prime. Taller and even more forceful than Emyli remembered, Dorilian strode into the room with the intentional boldness of a conqueror. Silk and velvet garments of rich, nonfunereal hues, embroidered with gold eagles and subtly adorned by jewels, announced his royal rank. The crown on his head, ablaze with arcane emeralds, could only be the famed Sordan Coronal.

Dorilian had chosen to wear a crown of state. *Why?* It could not be just to proclaim him Highborn—every damned thing about him marked him as Hierarch and ruler. Even his left hand, upon which the Rill Stone blazed a brilliant, Entity-bound green.

Cold realization seeped into Emyli's bones as she looked upon her family's perpetual nightmare. Dorilian had come bedecked as a monarch in order to press his own irrefutable claim.

Why else meddle in Essera now, after all these years? To put an end, once and for all, to Stefan's memory?

A glance behind the newly arrived Hierarch showed Erenor, storm-faced as he and his supporters hurried into the room last of all. Emyli wondered if he had sought to confer with Dorilian beforehand and been rebuffed. The lords accompanying Erenor looked similarly miffed.

Ionais, resplendent even in mourning colors, stepped into Dorilian's path and spoke to him. He stopped and appeared to be listening to her. Onlookers gawped and strained to hear. Euella, the Basarchessa of Rannul, stood at Ionais's elbow and gazed upon Dorilian with the stunned expression of a dazzled girl. Emyli simply wished she could know what the cousins were saying. A familiar profile among the Sordaneon entourage caught her eye, and she barely stopped a cry. *Sinon?* Sinon was with Dorilian? And wearing an ambassador's colors? That he had left Stefan's service she had known and lamented, but she had not heard where he had gone. When Dorilian moved on, he turned to Sinon and said something that evoked a slight smile.

Numbed, Emyli proceeded to the table for Essera's ruling faction but did not sit. Gareth stood at her side. Erenor and his secretaries, too, found their places at that table but remained standing. The remaining Archhalial representatives filled the center of the chamber, all on their feet. So were the delegates and privileged onlookers at the rear, including Asphalladra, who kept her promise by way of hard stares—but also closely watched the Hierarch who walked with his collection of secretaries and diplomats toward Sordan's chairs. To Emyli's relief, Dorilian did not attempt to seat himself upon one of the Thrones. He did take Sordan's primary seat, however, and as soon as he did so, all others in the Chamber followed. Sinon joined him along with two secretaries.

He had not even once looked at Emyli.

The Archhalia's Chamberlain, who represented the independent and neutral City of Permephedon, called the special session to order. After a statement of this session's business, Emyli stood to address the room. She barely had to raise her voice to be heard throughout the Chamber. The Archhalia's acoustics were famous.

"The death of my son, King Stefan, brings us to this sad occasion. As you know, Stefan Stauberg-Randolph died without legal issue and never formally named an heir. There is, however, a blood relation, his brother by birth. My younger son, Handurin Marc Frederick Stauberg-Randolph, was adopted by my father to be one of his legal heirs, just as Stefan was. Handurin is legal successor to Stefan. Therefore, I propose that Handurin be declared Stefan's Heir and that he shall be invested with his brother's domains and titles. Furthermore, I propose this body declare Handurin as rightful king of Essera."

At those last words, Emyli held her breath and looked directly at Dorilian, who for the first time lifted his gaze to meet hers.

The entire Archhalia seemed to wait for him to say something, at the very least to put forth his claim. Perhaps he wanted them to ask him, after all these years. Acknowledge him and, with that, their folly for having allowed her family to rule them. Perhaps he had other plans, some Highborn scheme too complex to be unraveled. Yet for reasons of his own, Dorilian said nothing. He held her gaze just long enough to gauge her response, then looked away. Emyli released her breath as other people took the floor and the lead, asking questions. Supporting. Opposing. Dorilian listened to them as well and waited, silently, while Sinon, seated beside him, showed him documents or whispered information for which he leaned near.

What was Dorilian doing?

Emyli barely heard others speak or grasped what they said, too intent on watching the man whose indifference and vast power had fostered Stefan's ruin. *You caused this.* Anger welled within her. *You undercut Stefan at every turn. You played with him like a cat with a wounded bird. You never meant to let him fly. For you, Gignastha was just a move on a game board. You gave the Malyrdeons their Wall Stone again, knowing full well that Stefan feared them most of all.*

You drove him to Nammuor. You did. No one else.

She closed her eyes, drew a breath, and reined in those thoughts. She was dealing with a projective empath. Hatred. Fear. Indecision. Dorilian could drive people to feel all those things, but he could also pick up on what others felt.

The Highborn shape our World… but we also shape them.

Emyli had been away from the Highborn too long. She needed to remember these things.

"Your Royal Highness." Erenor rose to speak. He looked apologetic and at the same time smugly defiant. "We understand why you propose your son to us. Handurin is indeed Marc Frederick's adopted son and legal heir. However, no one has seen him in nine years. Even if he were to return tomorrow, and his identity be proved, your son has lived away from this kingdom and its people for most of his life. His education, his associates, his experience, are likely unsuited for someone you say should inherit his late brother's crown."

Emyli had expected that argument. "Handurin's education has been the equal of anyone here. He has studied under the auspices of Marenthro Permephedeon. The Highborn themselves"—here she gave a nod to Dorilian, who frowned for her to get to her point—"can claim no more exalted an educator. Believe me when I say my son has been raised with an eye to his fitness to rule should such become necessary."

Erenor gestured to the Chamber and its host of ruling lords and ladies. "With all respect, Your Royal Highness, most of us here can make the same claim. Don't all sons and daughters of noble blood receive an education at Permephedon? What we additionally acquire through associations and family is the experience of our culture and traditions, as well as in seeing to the welfare and governance of our respective domains. Handurin has not had such responsibilities or experience. Indeed, we might—and should—question putting this kingdom into the hands of a feckless youth. I would further venture," Erenor said with a nod to the group, "that Essera has suffered serious losses and requires a firmer hand than a mere boy can provide us. Surely the Triempery as a whole will agree."

Yes, he appealed to Sordan as well. Sordan—and Triemperal Law. Stefan had been Marc Frederick's Heir, invested by Essera's Halia. Save for war or disaster, every succession was so secured, each by its own domains. She had argued with Stefan to do the same. Instead, because Stefan hoped to force his brother's return before naming him as Heir, Emyli faced having to convince the Archhalia as a whole—with Sordan holding half the votes.

"Sister." Ionais rose to stand before them, her gold-bright hair piled atop her head beneath a crown of pearls. "It was all along the intention of Endurin Malyrdeon that Marc Frederick should rule not only as king, but that he should marry into the Malyrdeon kindred. The intent was that Marc Frederick's heirs—the Stauberg-Randolph heirs—be of our royal blood."

"Which we are, by virtue of *his* mother."

"Yes, but *you* are the daughter of a commoner, and you *married* a commoner. A Kheld. Your sons are no more royal than yon Kheld ambassador."

Said Kheld ambassador, Robdan Aelfricson, simply propped his face on his hand and endured the gazes cast his way. In his own country, he was high clan. That, however, did not count for anything in Essera.

"You draw a sword to crack an egg." Grenant stood to speak for Dannuth. That he did so was something Emyli found hopeful. "Handurin's royalty is not in dispute—at least it should not be! His mother stands before us and who here will state she is not of royal blood? And Marc Frederick *adopted* Handurin. No one at that time said, 'Well, he can adopt him, but he won't be royal.' Shall we vote on whether Handurin is royal?" Grenant waited an uncomfortable period of time before speaking again. "So let us put that to rest." He held his head higher. "The matter before us is whether Handurin Stauberg-Randolph, as full brother to our late King Stefan, should be named his Heir, invested with his properties and titles, and be granted Essera's kingship."

Erenor took a moment to glance at both Emyli and Dorilian. That Erenor feared her was certain, but no one, ever, knew what Dorilian would do. Half the Chamber expected him to jump up and stab someone. "The boy is seventeen years of age—"

"Eighteen... soon," Emyli interjected.

Erenor smirked. "Very well, eighteen—but he has been away from his own country for eight, soon to be nine, of those years. He has been schooled among barbarians, for all we know, and I do not see Marenthro standing before us to testify as to the quality of his education. Furthermore, do we really want *more* years of Kheld rule?"

There it is. Emyli closed another panel in the puzzle box of Essera's shifting loyalties. Had anyone ever truly wanted what her father had tried to give them? When she looked out at the people who filled the Chamber, she glimpsed the answer to Erenor's question.

"We have had our fill of Khelds." Hebron, Lacenedon's formidable Bas, had even during Stefan's reign been a proponent of return to purely Staubaun rule. That Marc Frederick's kingship had been a just and long one, prosperous in the extreme and gifted with lingering Highborn consensus, had bought Stefan some time but little goodwill.

Another person rose to speak. Kathanos. Estevan, who would issue Gweroyen's vote, sat back in his chair, yielding the floor to his father, the elder statesman. "This is not a simple matter of our wants," Kathanos reminded them all. "The Esseran kingship is not electoral, neither is it a meritocracy. It is hereditary, as was the Malyrdeon Dynasty from which it stems. When Marc Frederick was named by Endurin Malyrdeon to be his Heir, when he was so invested with the Stauberg name and affirmed by Essera's Halia, when the Leur's Ring accepted him on the day of his coronation—*that* is when the Stauberg-Randolphs became the rightful rulers of this land. His heirs *must* therefore succeed him."

"Stefan was Marc Frederick's fully invested Heir," Emyli persisted. "And Stefan's rightful successor, by birth and blood, is his brother."

"What sits so foul is that we have so little else to choose from." Ionais's bitterness bled through. She resented that she had not provided Jonthan, and Essera, with an heir. Her resentment was not lessened by what looked back at her from the head of the Triemperal tables.

Now that the matter had been raised, all eyes in the Chamber turned with varying degrees of accusation or discomfort to Dorilian.

He needed to be careful here.

Dorilian understood better than anyone what made his presence at this meeting so unwelcome. He thwarted nearly every agenda. What he hoped to accomplish was very different from what Erenor wanted, or Emyli, or the Denizens of the Seven Houses, seated as delegates in the gallery and terrified of what he might do.

Already Ionais had intercepted him to whisper something vile. *"Did you kill him? Half this chamber wishes to crown you king for having rid us of him."*

And so would begin a civil war.

He did not feel safe among them, not even with delegates of his domains at hand. Not even with his soldiers—unarmed as the High Citadel demanded—guarding every door. He had been in a chamber such as this one before, in this very Citadel... a chamber invaded...

Not now! Dorilian battled back against the ghosts of his dying kinsmen. This time was different. He was *armed*. He wore the Sordan Coronal. Should Nammuor or other enemies make an entrance, Dorilian would not be helpless.

He had chosen to appear at this special session because only he— not an ambassador or surrogate—could achieve the needed result. He needed to put rumors to rest and contain Nammuor, although few paths remained that might accomplish this. He needed to create allies and at the same time neutralize enemies both known and unknown. Marc Frederick's kingdom had disintegrated into factions that held little prospect of uniting against an enemy many already knew to be within their borders but whom few had the will or means to oppose.

Dorilian, however, they *all* saw as a threat. Possibly a murderer. And Ionais wanted to talk about choices.

"Choices, Cousin?" Dorilian responded to her insinuation with the familiar form of address to which he was privileged. He did not bother to rise to his feet. "Essera made its *choice* eighty years ago when it voted with Endurin Malyrdeon to place its ruling power outside of Highborn hands. Essera made its choice again when it invaded Sordan and imprisoned its Hierarch, my grandfather, rather than have my family come to power over you. For the last nine years Essera *chose* to tolerate a king whose ambitions fomented the deaths of the Princes of Stauberg and the Eleutheron, and who *ordered* the slaughter of the last of Ergeiron's line. Essera not only *made* the bed of its current misfortunes, it gilded the posts and laid down silken sheets. Do not complain to me now that you do not like what sleeps in it!"

There. They could chew on those words or move on. As he had expected, none of them—even Ionais—knew what to do with him at all, and after a few feeble protests the discussion moved on to arguments more to Esseran liking. Something about whether to invest the young prince with his brother's domains and titles. Sinon and his secretaries could give Dorilian a report about that later.

His time was better spent studying the players. He was here to ensure Essera did not fly apart. While he listened to the conversation flow from one self-interested speaker to the next, he scribbled on a piece of paper. He wrote a few names, circled some and drew arrows to others, and showed it to Sinon. Sinon added a few arrows. A handful of connections grew clearer.

On one of his scans about the room, Dorilian noted Cullen's unfortunate widow, Asphalladra, standing beside a pillar at the back of the room. The stare she fixed on the front of the Chamber resonated with anxiety and grief—and fear. Emyli, too, radiated an impressive range of emotions, though he expected that from a mother fighting for her child.

Handurin. Dorilian had seen the boy one time, and one time only, being swept up into his happy grandfather's arms.

Marc Frederick's arms and smile… and laugh. That day. Dorilian would give anything to have that day back—though in a way he did have it again.

Emyli *still* thought he was a danger to her child.

Emyli struggled to withhold her disappointment when the Archhalia decided to put aside the question of investing Handurin with Stefan's domains and titles. That could be decided later. Instead it moved to her petition to have Hans declared Stefan's Heir and rightful successor to the Esseran kingship. The Chamberlain issued a call for a vote.

Dear Mother, please. Let them remember my father and what he stood for. Let us have enough on our side.

The call circled the Esseran tables first and each member declared his or her vote. A page chalked the tally on the roster of domains that comprised the Archhalia, moving marker rings upon twin poles. Emyli was not surprised when the vote proceeded along lines of loyalty. The tally delineated allegiances clearly. So clearly. The stalwart Stauberg-Randolph loyalists, Gweroyen and Serrain, voted in favor along with Dannuth. For all her posturing, Ionais voted Merrydn in favor and even Erenor, grimly, voted a yes for Tahlwent and another for Stauberg. The Basarchessa of Rannul, to Emyli's surprise and probably due to influence from the Seven Houses, voted in favor. The Rill cartel, more than any, never wanted the Sordaneon claim to come into play. Amallar, of course, voted in favor. A few more trickled in. Emyli breathed a sigh of relief as eleven of the thirteen votes necessary to install her son were received.

A block of opposition took shape around Hebron, who voted Lacenedon against and carried the vote of his neighbors. Whether the steel-willed Bas voted his own mind or with Sordan, she did not know. Leseos, long antagonistic to the Stauberg-Randolphs, and still unhappy over Stefan's missteps in Gignastha, also voted against.

Emyli gripped the edge of the table but remained standing straight, cold-lipped as she watched the count. She had not thought she would lose Lacenedon. Hebron had appeared to side with Ionais. It was also true his relations with Stefan had been icy since the deaths of the Malyrdeons. With the defection came worry. Sordan's domains owed Essera few favors—and none to her family. To Dorilian they owed many. If he truly wanted to be Essera's king, now was the time to make his move.

Monster. Do you ever think of my father? You tried to give him your hand—for what?

She steeled herself to the sliding of the marble tally rings: eight against. Nine against. Sordan's mighty girdle of domains, using votes in place of swords, aimed to strike down a hated regime. The call continued. Ilmar: ten against. Teremar...

And there it stopped.

All attention turned to the seat where Tiflan, Bas of Teremar, leaned forward, chin on his fist. For twelve years he had sat in that very seat, his massive presence as predictable as the sun. Tiflan *never* voted in opposition to Dorilian, even in small matters. And now his was the vote that would even the tally. So why did he look so thoughtful?

"Yes." He spoke in his great deep voice, then settled back into his chair. "Give the boy his due."

Astonished, Emyli put her hand to her mouth. A small buzz took hold of the room. Even Asphalladra stopped staring daggers at Erenor. This thing was not over. If Suddekar, then Sordan itself—if Dorilian—voted against, as of course he would...

The Archhalia looked as a body to Dorilian, whose glare at Tiflan conveyed something subtle and new. Every soul in the room felt the texture of it, a frisson of warning. The Teremari Bas simply folded his arms across his broad chest. Suddekar came next. That domain's Bas, Deleus, in appearance so like his Sordaneon cousin, voted firmly.

"Yes."

The buzz exploded into hard disbelief and surprised cheers as those in attendance grasped the new total and that the matter was decided.

For.

Heart racing, Emyli breathed again, too stunned to even form a coherent reaction. *The vote is for! Dorilian's vote does not matter!*

She turned to meet Dorilian's gaze. No one else in that chamber merited as much. She remained as she was, confused emotions stopped in her throat. *What did you just do?*

When the call for his vote came, Dorilian did not bother to stand. Without a word, he lifted his black card and voted against. He did not attempt a veto. His statement was naked, uncompromising. He had never acknowledged Stefan as king and now he need not acknowledge Handurin. He also had not put aside his own claim. He had simply, elegantly, seen his claim shelved in a legislature that, to him, did not matter at all.

He did not vote the block. He split it.

She saw the maneuver for what it was. It could have happened no other way. He had not even tried to disguise his strategy and had used men whose loyalty to him was absolute.

Emyli gathered herself to watch others dissolve into the confusion Dorilian had created. Even the Hierarchate domains, loyal to the Sordaneons, chattered with speculation. The move had caught them as off guard as the rest of the Archhalia. Only when she looked to Erenor did she see a look of acknowledgement, a cool and almost congratulatory half smile. A move foreseen, then... but by whom?

No matter. The vote was done. A simple majority sufficed. Handurin was confirmed Stefan's Heir. Her son could be brought back home.

A Stauberg-Randolph king upon Essera's throne as intended. One more chance to stand against what the Wall had created them to battle.

Erenor rose from his seat again with a document in his hand and stepped forward to present a petition of his own. "Lords and Ladies of the Archhalia, we have an Heir to the throne who has yet to be invested with lands or titles, and who is moreover not present at these proceedings. But let us consider this Heir. Are we even certain he still lives? Moreover, as his fitness cannot be ascertained nor presence guaranteed, no coronation can be set nor investiture planned. Until he *does* appear, we are for all purposes kingless. Yet

Essera must be governed and its peoples' needs met. I therefore petition that Handurin's kingship be placed into regency."

Emyli remained standing. "And I remind you I am already his regent by Law."

"Your Royal Highness's devotion to Essera and this Triempery is unquestioned. Your noble father's memory moves us still, as does our... regard for your late son. Already we have confirmed Handurin as Heir to Stefan and his succession is but a matter of time. But a regent does not have to be a blood relation."

The shock of Erenor's petition resounded through her carefully laid plans. Was she the only one who thought his ploy reeked of conspiracy? The need for a temporary regency, she had known. She had assumed that it would fall to her.

Erenor continued to speak before Emyli could regain her composure. "These times have become dangerous, fraught with conflict. Not all in this kingdom were content with Stefan's rule."

"Or with me?" She looked around the room.

Emyli had long known that few among her father's peers loved her. Stefan, whose rule had earned so much censure, had won over some of these lords, even to becoming his friends. She had been less successful. In Emyli, these nobles still saw Marc Frederick's headstrong daughter who had run off with a Kheldish rebel and married him, and who years later for a fortnight had ruled with that man as Lord and Lady of Gignastha. That act had started her family's ruin and brought with it a train of consequences, even Dorilian himself, into their lives. Bloody Gignastha. Bloody Neuberland. Bloody Merath and that bloody horse! A trail of tragedy all stemming from her.

Cathar of Leseos stood. He looked uncomfortable but determined. "It might be best, Princess, if someone besides yourself stood as regent for your son." In his strong face and hard amber stare Emyli saw the shadow of his brother, Ral.

A barely controlled tremor awakened within Emyli at the memory of that man and what haunted the reasons for their suspicion. Their opposition. Her gaze took them all in and saw only marginal support. These people would allow her to bring back her son to sit on their throne, even those who questioned his paternity, but they wanted nothing of *her*. What did they know of all she had gone through? What of her son but that she had given him birth? They knew only that Handurin was, because of her, a grandson of Marc Frederick and continuation of a dynasty their Wall Lords had chosen to rule them.

At the Sordan table Dorilian watched and waited, more royal than any of them and ever the unanswered question. She noticed that while others in the Chamber watched and measured her, he watched Erenor, even when Sinon leaned in to whisper something in his ear.

To her relief, the Kheld ambassador rose to speak. Robdan Aelfricson, at least, would be a friend. "Good Lords and Ladies, Princess Emyli has already demonstrated that she is a suitable regent for her son. These last many weeks, she has ably dealt with the affairs of the royal family and performed every duty laid upon her. She has done nothing deserving of censure." Though in no way a visual match for the Staubaun aristocracy he addressed, Robdan had the voice for doing so. His Stauba was perfect. "The regency for which Bas Erenor is asking would appear to be a short one, but I am not convinced it is *meant* to be a short one. Let us be cautious here. Who better than a mother to look after Handurin's best interests?"

"The regent is not for him," Hebron pointed out. "The regent is for the state."

"With the prince and state to be governed by the regent," Robdan countered. "I think Emyli is more than able."

"And have the boy slip into Kheldish ways, as his brother did? I think not!" Ionais was having none of it.

"Perhaps Marenthro could serve," someone suggested. Emyli thought it was Phellan of Serrain.

Now that he saw her and the Archhalia immobilized, Erenor stood taller. He lifted the petition in a call for attention and waited for silence. "I have in my hand Stefan Stauberg-Randolph's declaration that I serve as Regent should he die before his Heir achieves majority. His Heir, which I believe we have just declared his brother to be. Therefore, at this time I put forth in fulfillment of the late King's wishes that this body name me as Prince Regent until Handurin is crowned as king and takes up the full duties of his office."

Discord exploded through the Chamber, the sudden release of hundreds of voices: some expressing dismay and alarm, just as many others raised in jubilation. That Erenor could garner so much support surprised Emyli. She had hoped for more from her family's factions and only now saw how thoroughly they had been decimated.

"How do we know that document is real?" Phellan raised a key question. He exchanged glances with his seated secretary and surviving son.

"Review it for yourselves. You will see that the writing and signature are authentic."

Erenor passed it first to Emyli, who looked at it from curiosity. She already knew the document was real. Stefan had told her about it. What hurt was to see her son's strong writing, his pen strokes, the words he had chosen. *Trusted. True and loyal.* She handed it to the Chamberlain, who carried it to the next table and placed it there for Dorilian to examine. Dorilian did not look at it, but simply let the paper lie there like an accusation.

He knows it's real, also.

It did not take a mind reader or expert in pen strokes to read a room.

Knowing herself outmaneuvered, Emyli stepped out from behind her table so she could stand on the floor in full view before everyone and face Erenor. "How many have you convinced to support this mockery? Why plan ahead a document such as this? I will not have you placed in power over *my son*! Or do you mean for him, too, to die in the forests of Aral?"

Other members sprang to their feet to express shock at her allegation.

Erenor tensed. "What are you suggesting?"

It was Dorilian who answered: "Only that you have a nasty habit of advancing by way of corpses."

Erenor spun to face Dorilian, enraged but unsure how to confront him. Dorilian was himself famous for leaving corpses. At a loss, Erenor turned again to Emyli.

"The matter stands, Princess. For the good and the honor of Essera, I ask you to respect Stefan's wishes and respect the validity of this document. As soon as I file this, I will be Regent for your son."

She knew his thinking in it, in all of this. Stefan had called Erenor clever and had loved him for that trait against the machinations of his Staubaun nobles. Cullen had told her Erenor was behind Stefan's alliance with Mormantalorus, against the wishes of the Malyrdeons and nobles aligned with them. That alienation had done its work well. She had even done her part by having Stefan's younger brother declared his Heir. And now, with the regency secured, Erenor would hold in his hands the power of the crown. Especially if she chose not to bring her son home.

If that should happen, he might be Regent for years, or maybe for life. Eventually he would persuade this Archhalia that he should be king. And if I do bring Hans back—

She had laid this path. The Mother's Path. Creative, World-binding, paved by her choices. A path that had given the World her two sons to use, to break. But maybe, this time, to *build*...

"Put my regency to a vote." She would not make it easy for Erenor—or them—even though she knew how it would end. But they would remember.

Ionais stood and faced the head tables in front of which Emyli stood, a lonely figure in mourning dress. "I am sorry, Sister." Ionais's expression of regret did not soften the harshness of her words. "For the good of Essera and the Triempery, I believe it best you step aside."

Phellan of Serrain struggled more and Emyli heard his heavy heart within his words. "I want your son to return, Your Royal Highness. Handurin is Essera's rightful king. However, I wish him to return to as little controversy as possible, and to a better start to his reign than Stefan had. Bas Erenor will not govern without oversight and will conduct Handurin's regency under the guidance of this government. I put my faith in that and wish you well."

Her father's old friend. Even he. Emyli lifted her gaze toward the ceiling, feelings thick in her throat.

From his domain's table, Cathar stood again to give Emyli a cold stare. "I'll have your son back if this council wills it. I want as good a look at him as any man. But I want none of you. No."

There were a few moments of respite in that assault. Robdan Aelfricson quietly asserted that perhaps they could vote on this later. And blessed old Kathanos, speaking for Gweroyen with his son's approval, said, "What is taking place here is damnable."

The Archhalia stirred as might a beast upon waking. It shook out its skin to acquaint itself again with its own shape. It had rearranged its parts to become something altogether new—something Emyli wanted never to visit again. Her seat would be filled from this day forward by the traitor who stood regent for her son. Erenor's triumphant smirk told Emyli all she needed to know. He had planned his usurpation well.

Nammuor may have murdered Stefan and those other men—but he did it to put you where you now stand.

"You are no longer regent for your son, Your Royal Highness." Confident of his new power, Erenor was not yet smug, though Emyli could be sure he considered her among his enemies. "You are hereby ordered to produce Handurin before this body, that his fitness for investiture can be determined and his future kingship decided."

She could not tell if he wanted her to do so, or hoped she would refuse.

"Very well. I will tell Marenthro that Handurin is to be returned to us." Erenor could make of that whatever he wished. If she appeared to comply, he might not order her arrest.

A crack like thunder accompanied documents slammed onto a table. All conversation stopped as people looked to where Dorilian stood. The room chilled with emanated rage.

"You waste that boy's life and this body's valuable time, well knowing that I hold the only true claim to your worthless throne. Yes, worthless!" He gathered papers and shoved them at his ambassador. His gaze raked the assembly with contempt. "You know damned well that Handurin will never see his throne. This vile little pig's cock"—he pointed to Erenor—"will see to that. He has filled your damned Halia with minions and pretenders. He's worse than Stefan! You deserve whatever comes of him."

Dorilian signaled his Eagle Guard to prepare an escort. "This is a travesty of a Regency and I will not recognize it."

Cries erupted from the assembly. "Thrice Royal! You cannot—"

"I can!"

To Emyli's astonishment and that of the assembly, Dorilian turned, strode to the dais, and mounted its steps to the Thrones of Light. The Rill Stone blazed green fire upon his hand as, throne by throne, he pressed his left palm to the cartouche on each high back. Veins of light awakened in and poured through each gray, empty chair to carve dull surfaces anew. Blue. Green. Red. All now saw the brilliant ensigns of the Three—filled with radiance, ringed by glyphs and outlined by glory—upon the Thrones' backs. On the featureless gray wall behind the Thrones, another design blazed into incandescent being: the Wall, the Rill, and the Sword. Fixed. Intertwined. Encircled. The Triempery made whole.

When Dorilian faced the assembly again, he stood crowned before a shining testament.

"Here stands my claim. I will return when you have finished murdering the other heirs!"

He descended the dais and walked toward the great doors, which his soldiers had opened wide. To his Commander of the Guard, he snapped, "Let no one follow me!"

No one said a word, not so much as a whisper, when he walked past them all and exited the room. The lords and delegates of his domains hurried to rise but they remained where they were. Dorilian's soldiers had closed the doors. Sinon spoke to the Archhalia.

"His Thrice Royal Grace wishes to speak to no one." He gestured to the doors, which the soldiers then opened again. Dorilian was nowhere to be seen… but all knew what they had just witnessed.

Dorilian had declared himself. Descendent of Entities and born to power, he had thrown down the gauntlet of his birthright.

Emyli looked around the disrupted room and contained an urge to smile. Though the game was not finished, she had played her part. Daughter. Wife. Mother. Neither was she finished. A Mother's work never was. Her father's kingdom was in shambles. Enemies contended for his throne. One of her sons was dead.

And she had just placed her living son's fate in the hands of monsters.

46

One moment Dorilian stood in the center of a vacant guard room off the main Archhalia rotunda, secure in knowing Legon guarded the door. In the next moment he was...

Here.

The floor beneath his boots was no longer a patchwork of functional tiles, but a vast, gold expanse inlaid with glorious images of marvelous Entities and shining immortals. He stood at the center of a towering structure that extended away from him in long galleries defined by columns of stacked white and greenish-black stone. Massive from base to crown, the columns held aloft intricate domes and arches, which supported the weight of mighty Permephedon itself.

Here in the Vault of Incorruption he would find what he sought.

Here among the already murdered and already dead.

On his every other visit, Dorilian had turned to his left, toward the crypts of his ancestors all the way back to the First Deben, son of Derlon the Rill Bringer, interred along a corridor thick with Rill pageantry, lined with silvered sepulchers.

Not this day. Instead, he turned a half step to the right and entered a resplendent corridor of blue and ivory alcoves within which slept the remains of princes. If Dorilian walked far enough, he would reach the golden biers of Essera's first Kings. The deeper into the Vault of Incorruption, the older the corpses. Permephedon's magic was such that the most recently interred were the first encountered. Dorilian walked past the newer bier to the right, to the one in front of him, solitary, bathed in soft tomb light.

Marc Frederick Stauberg-Randolph lay in state beneath a silk canopy supported by four stately pillars topped by a golden crown and silver moon. Upon each midnight panel of the raised platform a silver horse with spread golden wings took flight as though to bear him into the heavens.

Night was fallen; the sun of this man's life had set.

Dorilian approached the bier and his throat clinched.

He had expected a ruin. A body crushed or burst open as Levyathan's had been. Pitiful and broken. The man he looked upon was whole. Dead, yes. No life remained within the bloodless, mortal flesh Dorilian immediately recognized and wished he had never needed to see this way. For nine years he had refused to let this man die. Had kept him alive by every means at his command. Visited him in Palimia's body and bright remembrances. Heard his voice speak again from the pages of books. Had looked for him everywhere but here.

And Dorilian had searched in vain.

Marc Frederick's features were serene: the strong nose and clean-shaven jaw, forehead not furrowed by worry or pain, the noble mouth relaxed. The eyes were closed, eyelashes dark upon skin that was waxen and pale. Dorilian grieved that he would never again know a look of approval from those blue eyes or glimpse the force of personality within them.

Gone. The man was gone... only this corpse remained. Dorilian supposed he had the Leur's Ring to thank for the condition of the body. Marc Frederick's right hand rested upon the sapphire-graced hilt of his great sword. That was a surprise. Dorilian had assumed Stefan to have taken custody of the weapon. Marc Frederick's left hand curled upon his breast. Naked. The Leur's Ring was not on it. Dorilian noted a glow, faintly blue, where Marc Frederick's dead hand yielded to a finger—the third one—that was less pale, more rosy. Not Marc Frederick's finger at all. Endurin's, still filled with immortal blood.

Mismatched, those fingers clasped a relic of bone and gold and hair.

Dorilian's death gift. His bone. His hair. He wondered if his blood-scrawled promise, also immortal, still resided within.

"Damn you." If there was a spirit here that he could yet reach, he wanted it to hear him. Even if he must do so using a voice choked with tears. "Were you really saving me that day? Or did you know?"

When no hint of a response lifted to his senses, Dorilian continued. "I thought I could do it, keep my promises to you. I thought I could support your heirs. I thought I could finish what we started. I thought… if I promised, you would be there with me. I thought you would at least try to take my hand. That we would flee together."

He tipped back his head, blinked away tears. Why was he doing this? He looked at Marc Frederick again. "It should have been you at my side. Keeping those promises, rebuilding the Triempery and making it strong. Instead, I was alone. And I had *him*."

Anger thickened his words. "I let Stefan live. Do you know that? I hope you do, because he didn't. I let him live and I left him free. Because I promised you. Because if I took him to Sordan—" Dorilian wondered how much to say about that. Lying upon golden tombs nearby were the remains of all the Wall Lords that had ever lived. "It was going to repeat. The whole thrice-cursed thing the Wall put between you and Labran, that you thought you broke. Well, you didn't break it. You didn't free your family from its coils. I did! I broke the damned thing, the moment I set Stefan free. I would have hated him, tortured him. I saved Stefan from *me* so I could save both of us from *that*. And look what happened."

Dorilian turned his gaze over his shoulder and looked at the newer bier, so different from the others.

Rheger and Elhanan lay on their backs, father and son side by side upon a single slab. Above their corpses hovered a softly radiant red orb. Dorilian had heard about Marenthro's handiwork but could not bring himself to admire it; if he did, he would also have to admire how neatly Marenthro had placed the dead men's mutilated heads in respect to their severed necks and hacked torsos.

"He killed them." The words escaped as a sob. "He murdered them. Maybe Palaistea's sons too, I don't know. But the Wall Lords are gone."

Rheger. Elhanan. Dorilian's tears spilled freely now, with only dead men to see them. Men he had not treasured enough in life now reduced him to ruin. Was Marc Frederick hearing any of this? Maybe it was enough to be speaking to himself.

He addressed Marc Frederick again, corpse and man. "So you saved me for what? To be the last of my race? What fucking Wall plan didn't you tell me? The same one they didn't tell you? Because I don't think you would have wanted this. I won't believe that." After drawing a deep breath of dry, scentless air, Dorilian shook his head. He had come to make his peace with his promises to this man, not berate him.

"At least Stefan is dead. If you didn't know that already, find peace with it now. He can do no more harm. You still have Emyli and that other son of hers. All manner of usurpers and opportunists are upstairs right now figuring out how to control or kill *him*."

He stepped back from the bier and its burden of uncorrupted flesh and bones that were no longer his friend. Marc Frederick resided in memories now. "If you are going to hold me to my promises, don't expect too much. Emyli believes nothing good of me and I cannot help the boy short of invading and conquering Essera. Nammuor is hunting me. I am risking my life any time I go where he knows I will be. But I had to try. I did try. I can do no more.

"As for the Rill, I will remember my promise to you, if it ever becomes possible again." Dorilian turned his back on the bier and lifted his left hand to touch the rim of the Coronal. "I will never forget you, but I am going to try. Enjoy your eternal sleep."

A flick of space and he stood again upon plain floor tiles and looked upon stark pale walls. The guardroom again. Legon stood, a discernable presence, on the other side of the door. Disruption from the nearby Archhalia Chamber hummed into Dorilian's nerves.

He should feel more unburdened. He had not banished his ghosts; they had followed him out of the Vault.

All things happen in the same moment, Dorilian reminded himself. The First Law of Creation: When a thing is created, so are all its possibilities.

Stefan's boot hitting his face. Austell on whose bier the Wall Stone gleamed. Meeting Marc, knowing Marc, *loving* Marc. And Stefan, happening because of Dorilian. To him, *with* him. Dorilian was all these things. All that followed *and* all that had come before.

Same with Stefan and the same with…. Dorilian bit back a bark of vexation. The Stauberg-Randolphs were still happening.

Handurin. About Handurin, Dorilian knew next to nothing—but he was Leur enough to perceive a temporal construct when he saw one.

He exited the guardroom to the shouts of soldiers clearing the way so he could leave. He had nothing to do here. Whatever it had set in motion, the Wall had yet to reveal.

—— End ——

To be continued in Book III, THE SECOND STONE

PLEASE TURN THE PAGE
FOR A SNEAK PREVIEW
OF BOOK THREE…

THE SECOND STONE

"Handurin."

Dorilian spoke the name to spare himself having to listen to the other men in the room speculate about the identity of his attacker. The *deiknya* sat as a gray lump beneath a waterglobe, its colors obscured and design all but invisible against the table. Tutto, standing cross-armed beside a second, smaller table nearby, frowned at the thing. Legon scowled as Tiflan bent over the device, jaw clenched as he looked for clues.

All three heads turned to their Hierarch upon hearing him speak.

"Handurin *Stauberg-Randolph*?" Legon practically gnawed on the last name before he spoke it. "*Stefan's* brother?"

"That would… make no sense at all," Tiflan said, though he abandoned the *deiknya*. He picked up a small round object embellished with a white horse and rider. "This is interesting."

"I saw Handurin once. A long time ago. I got a good look at him, which is how I know who he is. Look into it. You will find I am right." Now that he had settled the matter, Dorilian pointed to the table where Tutto stood. It held something else he wanted — no, *needed* — to be answered. "But Handurin was not holding *that*."

Three weapons lay upon the red cloth atop the rough-hewn table. One was but a knife such as common folk used for eating. Beside it lay a well-forged but otherwise unremarkable dagger. The third weapon, however… golden *lr* gems of various sizes gleamed within a length of reddened metal warped and fashioned into a deadly blade. A larger *lr* gem glowed orange in the hilt. A mage-weapon. Or something worse.

Legon indicated the knife. "This one was taken off the Kheld. It was still in his belt. He never sought to use it even for defense. And the dagger appears to be the blade your attacker used on Caillessar." He named Dorilian's horse, the wound to whom had been minor. "He deliberately startled the horse. Perhaps to place you in the path of…" He too pointed to the third weapon.

"A translocation device." Tutto named the thing.

Although called a sword master, Tutto had made the study of weapons his life work. *Lr* weapons, while rare, were among the deadliest. Especially so in this case.

"Plant that in you, maybe your leg, maybe your neck—" Tutto

made a jabbing move with his right hand, then twisted. "Make it hard to remove, then—" He clenched his fist. "Activate. The victim either vanishes or the device malfunctions and he dies a gruesome death along with every living soul in the Dekkora."

Dorilian's bet was that Nammuor wanted him alive. For a while. Being Nammuor's captive, anywhere, would be a living hell — and it wouldn't end there. It would end with Dorilian as an immortal lifeforce welded onto the Undying Crown.

"One way or another," said Legon, "it appears Handurin was not trying to kill you. But he may have been enlisted."

Perhaps. Dorilian was dealing still with how near he had come to disaster. Again and again he relived the vibrant energy of the Dekkora, the crowd, his command of them. Save for the years his father had declined to do so, Sordan's Hierarch always appeared before the Rill and beneath the Three Sisters, showing himself to his subjects on the eve of First Day. Doing so last night he had felt nothing out of the ordinary, until... the unexpected violence, the now-obvious diversion with the statue... Caillessar's movement that had caused Dorilian to look down at a hand so near his leg... a move designed to distract?

"...the one named Mallogh swears—" Tutto was speaking now, reading from a paper in his hand, "—that both Khelds are accomplices, recruited in Amallar—"

That last gave Dorilian pause. *Amallar* made no sense. Handurin's interrogation and that of the Kheld had contained talk only of boats. And Handurin was supposed to have been hidden somewhere in the First Creation. How could the boy have possibly been in Amallar to begin with? Or have reached Sordan from there in so short a time? Unless Marenthro...

Dorilian had finally reached a point about which he was certain: even he did not believe that Marenthro wanted him *dead* or that the Stauberg-Randolph's pet immortal would put Handurin into such a plot as this. He shifted his weight and winced as his ankle throbbed. It was not quite true that he had escaped the attack uninjured. His attention renewed, he listened to the rest of Tutto's report.

"—the man who bore the *lr* device claims that the one who distracted you, Handurin, responded correctly when given a code phrase."

"In Kheldic?" Dorilian knew the answer already but wanted to hear it.

"Yes."

There again. Evidence that meant nothing. Handurin had spent enough of his childhood with Khelds that he almost certainly spoke the language. So many things about how this night had happened felt wrong, out of alignment, as if they belonged to… separate events. Still, Dorilian's history with Khelds was murderous enough that Kheldish participation was not impossible.

After speaking to someone at the door, Legon trotted over to Dorilian and drew him aside. "You heard the report of what Mallogh and the other said under torture? The one Tutto just read?" Concern sharpened Legon's already sharp features. "Well, they said it again and again that they and the Kheld prisoners came here solely to attack and kill you. My men are bent on serving up punishment. Now. All of them. I have had to remove two men already for proposing summary execution."

Damn. The last thing Dorilian wanted was for the Eagle Guard to take things into their own hands, especially with passions this high. The City was already on high alert.

"I am not yet satisfied. Handurin looked terrified. And I don't think just of me."

"Maybe he was terrified of having not succeeded. The men may have the right of it, Thrice Royal. These Stauberg-Randolphs have always had it in—"

"Stop."

Legon didn't. "We have to consider every possibility, including that one. Many think you Stefan's murderer. It might be your enemies in Essera have joined Nammuor against you. Do not discount how likely that is to have happened — or do you believe all this is a coincidence?"

Dorilian did not discount a Wall design. "Probably not."

Resolve hardened the set of Legon's jaw and a knowing glint entered his eyes. "We know you were close to the grandfather… and so do your enemies. We know you promised him something… and so do they. Perhaps they are counting on that. Maybe you cannot kill this Handurin, Thrice Royal… but there are others who will do it for you."

———

COMING In 2023 from Forest Path Books

Author's Acknowledgements

This novel owes a debt of thanks to some amazing people.

My mother, Betty, is living proof of the ferocity, tenacity, and fighting spirit of mothers.

My son Ken, who many years ago shared his thoughts on what he considered to be the best and most visual elements of a certain scene involving a stag.

Sarah Stanitis, idea person extraordinaire, who has encouraged this shy, socially awkward author to venture onto new social media platforms and find new readers.

Jeanine Hennig, whose belief in this series has been absolute and a force behind getting the books published.

Artist Larry Rostant, for the book's moody, portent-laden, and utterly perfect cover art.

All the wonderful people who have helped inform and polish this book with their editorial wisdom and insights: Christina Wooden, Susan Curnow, and Carole the Copy Editor.

My gratitude also to the readers and reviewers whose enthusiasm for books they love is essential to every author. Special thanks to Max Amrabure, whose video review of Sordaneon called it a "hidden gem." It feels wonderful to be discovered.

Steve, whose support never falters even at international shipping costs.

And always my family, the people who surround me with laughter, good food, and good times and don't in any way resemble the characters in my books. Except when they do.

–L. L. Stephens

TRIEMPERY APPENDIX

CHARACTERS

MALYRDEONS—Past

ERGEIRON One of The Three, sons of Leur and Amynas. After his brother Derlon gave life to the Rill, Ergeiron founded the Wall, sealing dangerous Time Rifts opened during the Gweroyen War, protecting the Malyrdeon stronghold at Stauberg, and serving as a means by which his descendants could discern past and future events.

CIENORR Son of Ergeiron, founder of the Mormantalorus Nuarchate.

TELARION Son of Ergeiron and founder of the Stauberg Principate, first Esseran king and ancestor of current Malyrdeons.

EMRYSEN Wall Lord and great-grandson of Ergeiron, who bestowed a conditional pardon on the Hen Kyon.

ERYDON Great-great grandson of Emrysen, who granted the Khelds the wilderness of Amallar for their homeland.

ENDURIN Last true Wall Lord and last Malyrdeon King of Essera. Endurin's Heir died unexpectedly, leaving only a natural daughter, who fled to sea and was caught in the Rift. Endurin later brought her son Marc Frederick back to the World.

ARIANDE Granddaughter of Endurin. Mother of Marc Frederick.

MALYRDEONS—Present (and associated characters)

APOLLONIA Queen of Essera (family name Halasseon); daughter of Elegiros, Prince of Tahlwent. Wife of Marc Frederick and mother of Jonthan.

AUSTELL Wall Lord, third cousin of Endurin and distaff cousin to Marc Frederick. Brother of Enreddon II. Died in the Demise.

ELEGIROS Prince of Tahlwent (family name, Halasseon); third cousin to Endurin. Father of Apollonia. Died in the Demise.

ELHANAN Son of Rheger Dannutheon; Wall-gifted; one-time tutor of Stefan and Dorilian at Permephedon.

ENREDDON II Prince of Stauberg; cousin to Endurin and distaff cousin to Marc Frederick. Scholarly, but not Wall-gifted, Enreddon supported Endurin when the aged king named Marc Frederick to be his Heir. Both trif Enreddon's wives died in childbirth, failing to produce living sons. Later wed Palaistea. Died in the Demise.

IONAIS Princess of Merrydn; daughter of Regelon and betrothed of Jonthan Stauberg-Randolph.

OSTEMUN Prince of Dannuth (family name, Dannutheon); distant cousin to the Stauberg Malyrdeons. Sired three daughters. Grandfather to Kerr. Died in the Demise.

Palaistea Princess of Lacenedon; daughter of Lakron. Married Enreddon II. Mother to Eldon II and Enreddon III, Heirs to Stauberg and Lacenedon.

Regelon Prince of Merrydn (family name, Merrydeon); matrilineal cousin to Sebbord Teremareon. Father of Ionais, betrothed of Marc Frederick's son Jonthan. Died in the Demise.

Rheger Prince of Hespera (family name Dannutheon); brother to Ostemun. Father of Elhanan. Possesses strong spatial ability and is one of few Malyrdeons who can use an enhancer for translocation.

Margarid A princess of Gweroyen who weds Elhanan. Daughter of Kathanos. Sister to Estevan IV Niarchos.

SORDANEONS -- Past

Derlon One of The Three; known as the Rill-Giver because he integrated his immortal body and life with Rill's remnants, facilitating its rebirth. Epoptes believe Derlon's integration still directs the Rill's actions, though he has lost the ability to interact with other beings.

Deben I/II/III grandson and great-grandsons of Derlon (collectively known as the Three Debens), ushered in a Golden Age of Rill expansion and Triemperal growth that secured the Sordaneon dynasty. Builder/creators of Leseos, Bynum, Gignastha, and the Vermillion Aqueduct.

Peleor Son of Derlon; slain by the Aryati, who poisoned his blood and spilled it on the mount at Simelon to be absorbed by the Rill. His blood still stains the platform and Rill structures.

Tarlon Hierarch of Sordan during the Second War with Ardaen. The youngest of his three sons wed an Ardaenan princess to secure the truce. Tarlon was the last manifested Rill Lord, able to communicate with and influence the Entity. Opened the Rill node at Randpory Crossing.

SORDANEONS -- Present (and associated characters)

Daimonaeris Princess of Mormantalorus. Daughter of Camas, the Mormantaloran Nuarch; half-sister of Nammuor. Married Dorilian. Mother of Levyathan II.

Deben IV Sordan's Heir and regent. Son of the captive Hierarch, Labran, and Ermenthalia, daughter of Mezentius, Prince of Suddekar. Deeply paranoid, Deben had not set foot outside of Sordan's Serat in thirty-five years. Married Valyane, daughter of Sebbord Teremareon. Father of Dorilian and Levyathan I. Died in the Demise.

Deleus Son of the Heir to Suddekar; great-grandson of Mezentius and grandson of Sebbord. Although a first cousin to Dorilian, Deleus is not Highborn.

Delos Deben IV's twin brother. Son of Labran. Used the Lacenedon Crown to break the Vermillion Aqueduct and end the siege at Gignastha. Died after that deed from plasm shock.

DORILIAN Son of Deben IV and Valyane. Brother of Levyathan I. At the age of seven, witnessed his mother's murder. His precocious physical and empathic gifts allowed him to save his neonate brother. Determined to right wrongs done to his family.

ERMENTHALIA Daughter of Mezentius and a Mormantaloran princess. Wife of Labran, mother of Deben IV. Bears title of Gracious Hierarchessa. Inclined to favor alliance with Mormantalorus, from which her mother hailed.

LABRAN Grandson of Tarlon; his mother was a princess of Ardaen. He wed Ermenthalia, daughter of Mezentius, Bas of Suddekar, and is father of Deben IV and grandfather of Dorilian. He objected to Endurin Malyrdeon naming Marc Frederick as Heir to Essera and at Marc Frederick's coronation refused to acknowledge him as King. Labran fought his way into the Rill node at Permephedon and was able to command the Rill to stop running, creating wide-spread panic. Taken captive by Marc Frederick and considered too dangerous to release, Labran was imprisoned at Stauberg, far from any active Rill nodes.

LEVYATHAN I Son of Deben IV and Valyane. Grandson to Labran and Sebbord. Brother to Dorilian. When enemies poisoned his mother, Levyathan was born months too soon to survive. Although saved by Dorilian, Levyathan's development was affected, and he suffered neurological deficits.

LEVYATHAN II Son of Daimonaeris and Deben, raised by Dorilian as his own son. Heir to Sordan.

MEZENTIUS (family name Suddekeon); Bas of Suddekar. He wed a princess of Mormantalorus. His eldest daughter Ermenthalia wed Labran and gave birth to Deben IV. Died in the Demise.

SEBBORD (family name Teremareon), Prince of Teremar. Possibly Rill-gifted, Sebbord trained as an Epopte and rose to the level of Archmage in service to the Rill. He wed twice and sired three daughters. Grandfather of Dorilian, Levyathan, Deleus and Tiflan.

TIFLAN (family name Morevyen). Bas of Teremar. Grandson of Sebbord but not Highborn. Seven feet tall, he is Dorilian's first cousin and a loyal ally.

VALYANE Princess of Teremar. Sebbord's daughter, wife to Deben IV. Mother of Dorilian and Levyathan I.

ENDELARIN (family name Nemenor) King of Ardaen, brother to the throne queen. Romantic and rumored to have one hundred wives. Cousin to the Sordaneons and fond of reminding them of it.

LEGON (family name Rebiran) Son of Terveryen, Bas of Anit-Rebir. Youngest of six sons. Sent to Sebbord as a boy to enter Sordaneon service. Dorilian's friend. Commander of the Eagle Guard.

TUTTO (family name Rhunnard) An Estol who served as Sebbord's sword master and now serves Dorilian. Later Bas of Kolgya.

BERSYAS (family name Garheleon) One of Dorilian's generals.

PANDAROS (family name Vidyamemnon) One of Dorilian's generals.

NOEMI Wet nurse to the infant Levyathan I, later his governess. Mother of Fahme.

RAXA Levyathan II wet-nurse, trained by Noemi.

HERAN (family name Albos) Mormantaloran agent who wed Noemi. Father of Fahme.

FAHME Princess of Sordan. Noemi's daughter by Heran. Adopted by Dorilian.

HAESKOS (family name Periskleron) Dorilian's Admiral.

TIDUS sailor on Dorilian's ship *Raudra*.

QUIRIN (family name Chrysolemnos) Psilant, or leader, of the Brotherhood of Epoptes.

LARISSA NORSA Speaker of the Sordan Halia.

STAUBERG-RANDOLPH (AND ASSOCIATED CHARACTERS)

MARC FREDERICK King of Essera; great-grandson of Endurin Malyrdeon through his son Estevan II and Brenna Almarresda. Son of Ariande Malyrdeon and William Randolph. Considered a Malyrdeon in recognition of his relation to and support from them, but he is not Highborn. Marc Frederick first married Thora, a Kheld woman. After Thora died of a miscarriage, he wed the Highborn princess Apollonia as a condition to becoming Endurin's Heir. He has two children: Emyli, his daughter by Thora, and Jonthan, his son by Apollonia. Died in the Demise and interred in the Vault of Incorruption.

EMYLI Daughter of Marc Frederick and Thora; was betrothed to Deben IV Sordaneon but ran away at age fourteen with charismatic Kheld rebel Erwan Cedrecson. The pair wed and Emyli gave birth to Erwan's son, Stefan. To free Erwan from prison, Emyli helped Kheld rebels gain access to the stronghold of Gignastha, resulting in three Highborn deaths and the bloody siege of that city. She later gave birth to her second son, Handurin.

JONTHAN Son of Marc Frederick and Apollonia. Prince of Dazunor. Married Ionais, princess of Merrydn. Their union was childless.

STEFAN Son of Emyli and Erwan; grandson of Marc Frederick and adopted by him after Jonthan's death. Succeeds Marc Frederick as King of Essera. Marries Nilla Lowenda.

HANS (full name Handurin) Son of Emyli, reputed son of Erwan. Grandson of Marc Frederick. Brother to Stefan.

GARETH (family name Morgen) Marc Frederick's steward, in charge of his household.

TREVOR (family name Allen) Captain of King's Guard.

CADDO Stefan's Permephedon-based chamberlain.

GORAN (family name Soames) Stefan's valet.

MARENTHRO Wizard of Permephedon; ageless and possibly immortal.

No one knows much about him save that he is apparently benign and possesses both Wall and Rill affinity. Responsible for finding Marc Frederick for Endurin and bringing him back to this World.

MORMANTALORUS (AND ASSOCIATED CHARACTERS)

NAMMUOR (family name Varehos) Ruler of Mormantalorus, half-brother to Daimonaeris. Reputed to have Aryati blood. Has recovered the lost Diadem of the Devaryati. Responsible for the Demise. Is intent on collecting the blood and lifeforces of the remaining Highborn princes.

OARZAS Nammuor's Chief Crystallier.

CORAM (family name Barzanes) Was with Nammuor at the Demise. Nammuor's emissary to Stefan. An adept in mage arts.

BALATHU Archmage.

SALKREN Zel Mormantaloran general. With Nammuor at the Demise.

SEVEN HOUSES (AND ASSOCIATED CHARACTERS)

CHYRALANE (family name Rannuleon) Denizen of Phaer, most prominent of the Seven Houses. Daughter of a Highborn prince of Rannul. Opposed to any action that would lessen the cartel's control over the Rill. Very tall.

RHYNOS (family name Tybenos) Denizen of Koillos.

IPHITHUS (family name Phaeros) Nephew and heir to Chyralane.

PHILEMON LEANDER Wealthy Staubaun merchant, not noble but aspiring to the nobility. His daughter married the Denizen of House Haralambdos.

ESSERAN STAUBAUNS (AND ASSOCIATED CHARACTERS)

ASPHALLADRA (family name Velos) Youngest daughter of the Enlad of Chennor; weds Cullen Brodheson. Sister to Zoranna.

JARON VELOS Enlad of Chennor. Father of Asphalladra and Zoranna. Ambitious nobleman intent on arranging high-ranking mates for his three daughters.

ELDONUS (family name Kastryon) Enlad of Velsitha; late husband to Palimia. Very old friend of Marc Frederick.

PALIMIA (family name Attora) Daughter of a high-ranking Sordani noble killed to facilitate confiscation of his estates. Later married Eldonus Kastryon. Mistress to Marc Frederick, and later Dorilian.

ERENOR THOLEROS Cousin to the Halasseon rulers of Tahlwent; grandson of a natural daughter of Elegiros. Friend of Stefan. Commander of the King's Guards.

KONDROS (family name Bragord) Ally of Erenor.

ESTEVAN IV (family name Niarchos) Bas of Gweroyen. Son of Kathanos. Maternal grandson of Estevan III, last Highborn Prince of Gweroyen.

KATHANOS (family name Niarchos) Archon of Peleddor. Father of Estevan. Friend of Emyli. Son of Smaragda.

SMARAGDA Venerable mother of Kathanos. A princess of Stauberg.

EVLANN Wife of Kathanos. Daughter of Estevan III, Prince of Gweroyen. Mother of Estevan IV and Margarid.

HEBRON (family name Ursenos). Cousin to Lakron, Prince of Lacenedon, and Palaistea. Bas Regent and later Bas of Lacenedon.

MACHON EPIROSI Archon of Penrhu. Breeder of blood horses.

ALBAN ESKEROS Gignasthan lord whose lodge Dorilian used during his rebellion.

PHELLAN ILLARION Bas of Serrain, married to Linne, one of Ostemun Dannutheon's daughters. Father of Lucien and Raphelon.

LUCIEN ILLARION Heir to Serrain. Supporter of Stefan.

RAPHELON ILLARION Younger brother to Lucien.

GRENANT AIGELLEROS Minor lord loyal to Ostemun. Wed Raeva, eldest of Ostemun's daughters. Father of Kerr.

KERR (family name Aigelleros) Son of Grenant and Raeva. Grandson of Ostemun. Nephew of Rheger and cousin of Elhanan and Raphelon.

SINON KOURANOS Marc Frederick's administrator in Sordan during that City's occupation; later governor of Neuberland. Stefan's Archhalial Ambassador.

BURELAN (family name Phaeros) Bas of Rannul. Grandson of the last Prince of Rannul.

EUELLA (family name Phaeros) Burelan's sister.

THEMACRYSA (family name Rannuleon) Daughter of the last Prince of Rannul. Mother of Burelan and Eulla.

ARTON (family name Metagoras) Third son of the Archon of Eddethel (Merrydn). Assistant to Cullen Brodheson. Later weds Euella Phaeros.

KYROS (family name Eulodes) Son of the Enlad of Rhiarren.

ALKRON (family name Eulodes) Enlad of Rhiarren. Kyros' father.

KHELDS (AND ASSOCIATED CHARACTERS)

CULLEN BRODHESON Cousin and best friend to Stefan. Keeper of the King's Trade. Enlad (later Archon) of Heddros and Wyre. Weds Asphalladra.

ERWAN CEDRECSON Son of Cedrec Aelfricson; ran off with young Emyli Stauberg-Randolph. She later bore his sons, Stefan and Hans. Died at Gignastha.

TOBOLD FORBASSON Thegnard (leader) of the Thegnkeld, the foremost clan of Amallar. Died at the Demise.

LOWEN TOBOLDSON Son of Tobold and father of Nilla.

CEDREC AELFRICSON Late Kheld representative to the Triemperal Archhalia. Father to Erwan. Grandfather to Stefan and Hans. Died at the Demise.

ROBDAN AELFRICSON Cedrec's brother; a scribe. Uncle to Stefan and Hans.

GOFF HORVADSON First Minister during Stefan's reign; Enlad of Kelmene.

PERIC GOFFSON Goff's son. Becomes Commander of King's Guard after Erenor. Killed by Dog Men.

NILLA LOWENDA Daughter of Lowen Toboldson and niece of Goff Horvadson. Marries Stefan.

NALF RHYS A Kheld chieftain.

AUBREY AMUNDDA Friend of Nilla and Lark. Niece of Nalf Rhys. Daughter of Amund Rhys and Vallsa Elslethboern. Cousin to Cullen. Inherited a kings grant in Neuberland.

WODD Aubrey's sworn man.

LARK RAPPELEYE Friend of Aubrey and Nilla. Daughter of a powerful matriarchy famed for runes and rune reading.

CAOHME ORMSDA *Faetha* and healer.

TRAHOC CADDENSON Neuberland rebel whose son and brother died at Gignastha. He meets Stefan at the inn in Bellan Toregh.

NEDDIG DARRONSON One of Stefan's friends.

FREDDA OVARRSDA Neddig's wife.

MAHON GORMLADSON Another of Stefan's friends.

REARD ARGLLSON Another of Stefan's friends.

RANWULF FORBASSON Assistant to Cullen.

OTHER CHARACTERS

JOOAR ZETHARNNA A prince of Lahgael, not in the line of succession. Governor of Ben-Aranath.

BARAN REDHARG Hen Kyon leader, Lord of Gloanneach. Looks nearly fully human.

ENTITY-BOUND DEVICES

THE LEUR'S RING Fashioned from the body of The Leur as last living act. Rejects non-Leur flesh and can only be worn by the Highborn. Used at coronations to identify the true king of Essera (Heir of Ergeiron). Manipulates real world/Leur's Creation. Removes barriers. Opens doors. Reveals truth and restores Leur's reality.

THE RILL STONE Device created by Derlon, who encapsulated his immortal blood in Rill matrix. The Rill Stone will identify a Sordaneon who wears it by glowing green. The Rill recognizes Sordaneon wearers and will not arm itself or lock locations against them. Can be used to burn a permanent Eagle mark onto any other substance, including human skin.

THE WALL STONE Shard of the Wall containing Ergeiron's immortal essence. It connects directly to the Wall, regardless of proximity, and must be used carefully by individuals open to its gifts. Allows wielder to peer into discreet temporal flows. The Wall Stone unlocks the Aidion and provides access to the Archive, which it assists in revealing.

OTHER ENTITIES

THE DIADEM Also the Undying Crown, or the Diadem of the Devaryati. Pre-Devastation device created in secret by the Aryati from the immortal core that remained of Vllyr after that god was destroyed by Amynas and the Leur. Generates and commands arcane forces. Vastly powerful when fully tapped into an immortal being. Retains vestige of Vllyr's godhood. Malevolently self-aware and fixated on destroying that which destroyed Vllyr. Succeeded in corrupting the Aryati, destroying Mulsor and the First Creation.

GREATER ENHANCERS

SORDAN CORONAL Also called Derlon's Crown. Most powerful of the Greater Diadems. Now in possession of the Sordaneons.

STAUBERG CORONAL Also called the Star Crown; Ergeiron's Crown. Now in possession of the Malyrdeons.

MORMANTALORUS CORONAL Also called the Crown of Fire; Ciennor's Crown. Now in possession of Mormantalorus and its ruler.

LACENEDON CROWN Also called Ulnossi's Bane. Used by Delos Sordaneon to break the Vermillion Aqueduct.

OTHER DEVICES

DERLON'S ARMOR The fabled Eagle Breastplate, helm, and gauntlets. When activated sheaths the wearer's torso and limbs. Kinetic negation. Any blow to the armor is absorbed. Invincible to nearly all weapons.

SWORD OF AMYNAS Also known as Derlon's Sword or the Gweroyen Sword. Greatest of the *tullun* blades made from Vllyr's skeleton. Most effective when paired with more powerful enhancers.

RINGS OF ORDER Three rings created by Derlon Sordaneon before the Inception. Used in accessing Rill stations and communicating with the Overlay. The Head Epopte (Psilant) keeps one of the rings.

BACKGROUND -- HIGHBORN ORIGINS

ARYATI Human strain engineered to replicate the powers and immortality of Leur. Creators of greater and lesser devices that generate quasi-magical powers. The Aryati rose to extraordinary heights through genetic manipulation and technology but were arrogant and acquisitive; they ultimately destroyed their world. A remnant of the Aryati survived into the new Creation but most were slain following their defeat by the Highborn during the Gweroyen Wars. The survivors scattered. No pureblood Aryati survive but the strain persists in noble Staubaun lineages.

LEUR Immortal beings that created the World. Elusive, mostly hidden from humans until technological advances revealed them. Leur magic built the Five Cities, each in a day, and, combined with Aryati technology, engineered the living matrix of the Rill. During the Devastation brought by the Aryati, the Leur sacrificed itself to create the temporal disjunction that preserved the Creation. The lone Leur survivor mated their immortal bloodline with that of the Aryati clone-prince Amynas, conceiving three immortal sons known as The Three.

MALYRDEON Descendants of Ergeiron, one of the three sons of the gods Amynas and Leur; Ergeiron settled in what is now Stauberg, where he created the Wall as a barricade against the Rift. The Wall exists throughout all Time. Some descendants of Ergeiron are able to "walk the Wall" and by that means divine future events or reveal the truth or import of past events.

SORDANEON Descendants of Derlon, second of the three sons of the gods Amynas and Leur. Derlon settled Sordan, home to one of the surviving Five Cities of Leur, from which he gave life to the Rill by melding his immortal body with that of the vast machine. The descendants of Derlon carry the potential to connect with and communicate with the Rill, which would allow them to alter the god-machine's operation and physical structure.

HUMAN RACES

HIGHBORN Males descended from the immortal sons of Leur and the human Amynas. Leur traits pass only to male offspring, who must mate with human females to reproduce. For this reason, the adage is that the Highborn take the race of their mothers. Almost exclusively, the Highborn have chosen to reproduce using Staubaun lineages.

STAUBAUN A people originally created by (and related to) the Aryati and still manifesting some traits of the parent race. Some can wield lesser devices. Tall, fair-skinned, brown or gold-eyed blondes, beardless (with little body hair), Staubauns are intelligent and long-lived. They also, after generations of success and prosperity, tend to be rich and privileged.

ESTOLAN Amalgamation of races, the general population. Disdained as mongrels by Staubauns, Estols nonetheless rise to positions of influence and become minor nobility. Most are servants, laborers, soldiers and craftsmen. Because they are of mixed blood, Estols can have any human color of eyes, hair, or skin.

KHELDA Barbaric people that entered Essera through the Rift during a period of instability following the First War with Ardaen. Khelds generally have blue or green eyes. They also have dark hair, sturdy builds and are shorter. Adult males are usually bearded. Their language is completely separate, as are their ways of life. Kheld naming differs from the Staubaun, as does their system of inheritance.

NEMENORA Seafaring people that forms the ruling families of Ardaen, Callorn, Lahgael, and the Isles of Maskos. Traditional enemies of the Triempery in the past, a marriage by treaty to a younger son of the Hierarch of Sordan instilled Ardaenan Nemenor blood into the lineage of the Highborn Sordaneons.

NONHUMAN RACES

LEUR Magical race, as explained above, creators of the original World and the tripartite Creation they fashioned to salvage it from destruction. Originally the Leur people inhabited the area now known as the Bogs, a marshy delta where the Dazun River flows into the sea. The last Leur was slain by the Devaryati and the race is now only legend.

HEN **K**YON The Dog Men, created by the Aryati as hunters and servants, specifically to track down and kill the magic-gifted offspring of Amynas and Leur. Intelligent and reclusive, the Hen Kyon are bipedal, often with fur covering parts or all of their bodies. The most true-to-breed have long, wolfish faces with well-developed olfactory organs. They have incredible stamina and strength. They can interbreed with humans, from which race they were originally fashioned. The Hen Kyon nearly eradicated the young Highborn race. Though they later repented their deeds, the Dog Men were abhorred and hunted nearly into extinction until the Malyrdeon King Emrysen cloaked them in obscurity and gave them the haunted wilds of the Kragh in which to live unmolested. They have since become feared and avoided.

PLACES (BACKGROUND)

(MENA**)**TROHJANA The Second Creation. The present World that moves forward in Time.

(MENA**)**TANTAUREUS Archived world/Past world, living remnant of the First Creation. Birthplace of Marc Frederick.

GSCH The World of Fire. The moment of Devastation, forever happening, never completed. A single moment in Time that has both already occurred and will never occur.

FIVE **C**ITIES Eternal cities built in the First Creation by Leur and continuing in the Second Creation. Îs (vanished), Permephedon, Sordan, Mormantalorus, and Mulsor (destroyed).

MULSOR Destroyed in the Devastation. As a Leur creation part of it remains eternal. A ghost city whose appearance portends doom.

DALN **B**ARRIER Created by Leur to separate the World in Time. Past World/Gsch/Current World.

THE **R**IFT Transient instabilities in the Daln Barrier that permit passage between the Past World and the Current World. The appearance of Mulsor is one such occurrence.

TRIEMPERY A confederation comprised of three aligned Highborn empires: Essera, Sordan, and Mormantalorus.

ESSERA

STAUBERG Capital city of Essera. Home of the Malyrdeons. Major seaport. Location of the Wall. Site of a dormant Rill mount.

ASAE **E**RANOS The Malyrdeon Serat or Malyrdeon Tower. Royal palace in Stauberg.

Aidion Heart of the Wall. Located under the shrine at the Gate of Transformation. Where gifted Malyrdeons walk the Wall.

Gate of Transformation Original city gate of Stauberg. Transformed by Ergeiron and now site of a shrine.

Eleutheron Domain also ruled by the Prince of Stauberg. Rich and deep in history.

Bynum Foremost city of the Eleutheron.

Danae Palace Princess Palaistea's seat. Near Bynum.

Gweroyen Domain in Essera, north of Stauberg. Former stronghold of the Aryati.

Ennsa Capital city of Gweroyen.

Iddolea Destroyed city in Gweroyen. Former capital of the Aryati.

Permephedon City-State presided over by Marenthro. One of the three remaining Five Cities. Neutral seat of the Triempery and home of the Triemperal Archhalia. Northernmost Rill city and a major Rill hub.

High Citadel Central redoubt of Permephedon's city core. Also called Marenthro's Tower. The Leur Arcana and Harmonic Hall are here, as are the Archhalia Chambers.

Jewel Tower Malyrdeon tower. Floats above the Mirror in Permephedon's city core.

Sordaneon Tower Sordaneon hold in Permephedon's city core. Congruent with the Rill, which it is near.

Lacenedon Domain in Essera, north and east of Permephedon.

Kenelm Capital city of Lacenedon. Site of a dormant Rill mount.

Serrain Domain in Essera, just west of Permephedon

Simelon Capital city of Serrain. Site of a dormant Rill mount.

Rannul Domain in Essera.

Terna Capital city of Rannul.

Dazunor Principality in Essera, holding of Essera's Heir.

Dazunor-Rannuli Pre-eminent city in Essera due to its position on the Dazun River and presence of a major Rill node. Home of the Seven Houses.

Dazun River Largest river north of the Telarkan Mountains. Major economic resource and highway. Has no navigable egress to the sea.

The Fan Egress of Dazun; fens, marshes and channels that go nowhere. Also called the Bogs. No one knows how or where the Dazun empties into the sea (or even if it does).

Rillhome Sordaneon palace in Dazunor-Rannuli

Customhouse Seven Houses seat in Dazunor-Rannuli.

Illystri Palace Malyrdeon palace in Dazunor-Rannuli, located on island in the Lago.

Lago Lake in heart of Dazunor-Rannuli near the Rill mount.

Emrysen Palace Esseran monarch's residence in Dazunor-Rannuli, on the Upper Canal

Upper Canal Large canal north of the Rill mount and Lago, where the wealthy live.

Lower Canal Main canal of Dazunor-Rannuli. Largely commercial properties along it.

Beard Fen Kheld neighborhood in Dazunor-Rannuli

Merrydn Principality in eastern Essera. On the Dazun River. Home to the Merrydeon Princes. Site of a dormant Rill mount.

Merath Capital city of Merrydn. Famous for its palace and walls of blue stone.

Dannuth Principality in Essera, holding of the Dannutheon Princes.

Kyrbasillon Capital city of Dannuth. Famous for its beauty and public places. Four gateways of Virtue: Arch of Mercy, Arch of Truth, Arch of Courage, Arch of Justice.

Tahlwent Principality in Essera. South of Stauberg and on the sea. Home to the Halasseon Princes.

Aral Capital of Tahlwent. Major sea port.

Halasseon Serat Palace of the Halasseon Princes.

Gustan Town on the Dazun River near the Fan.

Gustan Manor Marc Frederick's personal residence, which he designed and built using materials from his home world.

Trulo Major city on Dazun River. Seat of the Princes of Dazunor.

Golden Palace Highborn palace in Trulo.

Kragh Badlands of high hills and dangerous gorges. Home of the Hen Kyon. Near Trulo. Site of the destroyed Aryati city of Gyges.

The Maw Huge hill in the Kragh

Amallar Semi-autonomous domain of the Khelds. Considered part of Essera.

The Bogs Kheld term for The Fan; endless marshes of terminal Dazun River.

Rhodhur Capital of Amallar. Site of Rhodhur Hall.

Eastmeary Brenna City in Amallar.

Aurdollen Sanctuary near Rhodhur and site of a school for girls.

Bellan Toregh Town on eastern edge of Amallar. Site of a dormant Rill mount.

Flohe River that flows through Bellan Toregh. Tributary of Dazun River.

Orqho Mines in southern Amallar near Leseos.

Neuberland Esseran domain/protectorate. Kheld and Staubaun populations often in dispute over land.

Saemoregh Kheld town in Neuberland.

Amundhal Kings grant holding of Aubrey Amundda. Near Saemoregh.

GOBBA Frontier holding east of Neuberland, loosely affiliated with Essera.

ANNECH Frontier holding allied with Gobba, increasingly at odds with Essera.

LESEOS Former Principality of Essera, now a semi-autonomous Basarchate. Rill city. Located south of Amallar and west of Gignastha.

GIGNASTHA Former Principality in Essera. Made a Crown Protectorate after its Highborn Princes were murdered by Kheld rebels.

SAR'PRYANNIS Poisoned lake in Gignastha. Gignastha is built on cliffs overlooking this lake.

VERMILLION AQUEDUCT Raised by Deben II Sordaneon to provide water to Gignastha and also power the locks securing the impregnable gate of the Watergilt Palace. Broken by Delos Sordaneon during the Gignastha War.

LOWER NEUBERLAND Part of the Principality of Gignastha, south of Gignastha and bordering Randpory, the northernmost territory of Sordan.

HORCROD Fortress in Lower Neuberland.

SORDAN

SORDAN One of the three remaining Five Cities. Called the City of Light, City of Amynas. Site of the Inception, originating point of the Rill, and a major Rill node. Island city surrounded by a large and very deep lake.

SORDANEON SERAT Palace of the Sordaneon Hierarchs, in Sordan, and congruous with the Rill. Portions of the palace are part of the immortal Citadel forming the core of the city.

VIRIDIAN RIVER Man-made river contained within the Serat. Site of numerous features, including a waterfall over the Serat walls.

WELL OF BIRDS Located in a courtyard of the Sordaneon Serat.

THE PRISM Rainbow-laced waterfall and deep gorge on grounds of the Serat.

VA HAIRA First Creation underground passage connecting the Rill, Citadel, Serat and other pre-Return structures in Sordan's city core.

THE INCEPTION Sordan's Rill mount. Largest Rill complex, where Derlon's presence has fully completed its transformation. Multiple levels, platforms, and crown of portals.

KING'S HOUSE Palace near the Serat, connected to the Va Haira. Former residence of the Malyrdeons.

SARKUAN Lake surrounding Sordan.

SORAND'RUIL River that flows from Sarkuan to the sea.

SANSORDAN Domain attached to Hierarchate. Largely desert/wasteland. Western coast poisoned by destruction of Mulsor.

IRIDONOS Fabled treasure city of the Aryati, rumored to lie in poisoned Sansordan.

ILMAR Domain of Sordan. Located at mouth of Sorand'ruil.

IVERNESSE Capital city of Ilmar.

NEREID **P**ALACE Sordaneon palace in Ivernesse.

KOLPOS Gulf between Sansordan and Ardaen. Also known as the Gulf of Mulsor.

LAHGAEL Kingdom of the Gaels, a Nemenor-Estol people allied with Sordan.

BEN **A**RANATH River port of Lahgael on the Sorandruil.

SUDDEKAR Principality located on the southern shore of Sarkuan. Borders Mormantaloran domain of Othgol. Home of the Suddekeon Princes.

BATRAZ Capital city of Suddekar; location of the Palace of Dawn.

ILDURRIA Domain located on northern shore of Sarkuan.

TOLLECH Principality located north of Ildurria.

RANDPORY **C**ROSSING City-State. By agreement a free trade city because of its Rill mount.

RANDPORY **R**IVER Navigable river that forms the border between the Sordan Hierarchate and Trongor.

ANIT-**R**EBIR Domain located north of Teremar. Mountainous.

TEREMAR Principality located on eastern shore of Sarkuan. Rich and powerful, home of the Teremareon Princes.

ASKORRAS Capital of Teremar.

TULAMANTA Palace at Askorras.

HESTYA River port in Teremar. Site of an active Rill mount.

TIRIS Estate on Sordan island given by Dorilian to Daimonaeris.

RHONDDA Sordaneon estate on Sordan island. Personal estate of Dorilian.

TRONGOR Independent nation of sea folk located on Kolpos north of Sansordan, west of Randpory, and south of Amallar. Separated from latter by the Telarkan Mountains.

OGARTH Capital city of Trongor. Site of a dormant Rill mount.

ARDAEN Monarchy located on large peninsula west of Trongor. Seafarers known as the Sea Kings.

AMROSET Capital city of Ardaen.

CALLORN Region of Ardaen.

CAERDON Principality. Former region of Ardaen, ceded to the Sordaneon Hierarchate as part of a treaty and now included among the Hierarch's title domains.

MERCED An independent island kingdom near Ardaen, loosely allied with Ardaen.

MORMANTALORUS

MORMANTALORUS One of the three remaining Five Cities. Sits on an active volcano and is livable only because the City itself creates an environment conducive to human habitation. The environment immediately outside the city's bubble is toxic.

DZALARAD The volcano.

ILGAON Main tower of the Citadel of Mormantalorus, where Nammuor creates his arcane crystals and devices using the energy of the volcano.

NUARCH'S TOWER Residential tower of the Citadel of Mormantalorus.

MAGISTRY Part of Ilgaon tower where mage work is done.

ORM Domain. Borders Suddekar.

OTHGOL Domain. Borders Teremar.

TELEG Southernmost domain of Mormantalorus.

NALAPAR Eastern domain of Mormantalous.

XEBBETH Large island domain west of Mormantalorus.

ULAN-JANA Mountainous domain south of Teremar and northeast of Mormantalorus. Gifted by Nammuor to Dorilian and Daimonaeris on their wedding.

WORDS AND TERMS FOUND IN THE BOOKS

CHARYS Rill conveyance. Created by the Rill at need and uncreated when no longer needed.

DEIKNYA An oval medallion created by Marenthro that displays the royal or noble house to which that person is bound. Given exclusively to Highborn, royal, or high nobility.

FRA'DON Means 'royal brother.' Used by the Highborn for another of their kindred.

GYNEKOS used for a Highborn lineage that has reverted to purely human. This happens when a Highborn sires daughters instead of sons.

ORBUS/ORBI Balls of light Highborn princes generate in their hands. A minor power.

THRICE ROYAL Proper form of address for a Highborn prince regardless of age or rank. Highborn are considered royal three times over: Father. Mother. Entity. Generally, a Highborn prince is born to a royal father and mother, though the latter is not always the case… but it usually is.

TULLUN Material created from the god Vllyr's skeleton. Can be sharpened to an edge that can cut anything but itself. Shaped by the Aryati into blades from daggers to swords. The Sword of Amynas is a *tullun* blade mated with device matrices.

L.L. Stephens

has been writing science fiction and fantasy full-time
for several years. Published works include a debut science
fiction novel in the deep dark past and a medical journal, as
well as lots of short stories, and local brochures, newsletters,
and pamphlets for everything from local politicians to
an international airport.

The Triempery series, which includes *Sordaneon* and *The
Kheld King*, is a six-part series and life's work. For excerpts
from existing or upcoming books, lore, maps, and other
related content, visit the L.L. Stephens website at:

https://triempery.com

Twitter: *@triempery*
Facebook: *L.L. Stephens Author*
Instagram: *1.1.stephens_author*

INDEPENDENT PUBLISHERS ROCK!

We appreciate your purchase of a Forest Path Book. We do our best to cultivate distinctive and compelling stories for our readers.

If you enjoy our authors' efforts, kindly consider that a reader review at your favorite retailer can help spread the word.

To keep track of our latest releases, sales, & happenings, please join

INTO THE FOREST
https://forestpathbooks.com/into-the-forest
(the Forest Path Books reading group and newsletter)

When you sign up for the newsletter, as our "thank you!" you'll receive a code for 25% off your first purchase at our store!

FOREST PATH BOOKS
https://forestpathbooks.com